Sisters of Angst

Simon Wright

Copyright © 2021 Simon Wright

Acknowledgements

As it will always be, my greatest thanks are extended to my wife, Kerry, who remains patient, encouraging and resilient throughout the time-consuming process of crafting these tales! Without her there would be no story, indeed, there would be no writer. She never loses faith in what I can achieve, regardless of my own opinion. Once again, my friend and ally in this endeavour, Neil Doran, provides insights and sub-context while proof-reading that help me develop characters and story in a more rounded fashion. His regular praise, and long discussions between chapters, always reinvigorates me for the next; his constant insistence that this would make an epic movie is always well-received! Finally, a special thanks to my children, who tolerate my laptop being more important than boardgames far too often, and always congratulate me on my success, regardless of whether they are old enough to actually read the book or not!

Prologue

Heletha kept running as fast as her legs would allow but the crumbly dark soil beneath her feet made for slow progress. Her heart hammered in her chest and her breath was coming in ragged lungfuls; she could no longer call out to her brother. Pulling up short and placing her hands on her hips in irritation, she took two long breaths before crying out.

'WARDIN! Wardin, stop and wait!'

He was always so frustrating, having to prove that he was faster despite being younger, and she was annoyed every time Czerna told her to play with him. Being two years her junior, he was just so immature, not refined like she was at ten years old. She sat on the ground and took off one fur boot, shaking out some small stones before replacing her footwear. The soil felt oddly warm underneath her, in contrast to the cold air all around, and she remained there for a moment, looking up at the ominous shape of the ruined citadel. True enough, they could see it from the town, but the closer you got, the more eerie the place became. They had been to the cliff many times, despite the adults insisting that it was too dangerous and that nobody should travel within three miles of the crumbling structure. Of course, that just made it all the more exciting.

'What are you doing, Heletha?' Her brother's voice floated to her, 'You have to come and see this! You won't believe it otherwise!'

She sighed; this was undoubtedly another one of his stupid games. Or perhaps he had found some insects in the soil, which would be quite unbelievable as nothing lived in this dark ground. Climbing to her feet, she brushed off her overskirts and trudged towards the plateau that overlooked the broken fortress, maintaining a dour look to prove she had not fallen for his ruse. Arriving alongside him, she replaced her hands on her hips and began scolding him, 'You know better than running off, Wardin, I've got a mind to tell Czerna...'

He cut her off excitedly, pointing down to the worn cobblestone road that led to the great metal gates, 'No, Heletha, stop whining and look down there!'

She shook her head derisively at him but followed the direction he pointed, her jaw dropping open when she realised he was not tricking her. Between the massive gates, one wedged permanently open and the other collapsed at an angle away from the road, a small girl was crouching down, examining the cobbles. The child had the palest blonde hair hanging down to her shoulders and wore a blue summer dress patterned with yellow flowers, not really fitting with the cold weather. Heletha strained her eyes but could not make out any further detail; she was certain the girl was not from Hercatalana, however.

'Hey, you there! Hello!' Wardin shouted from beside her, waving his arms for attention. Heletha grabbed him and shook her head.

'Stop, Wardin! We do not know who that is or where she is from! Nobody is supposed to be near the ruins.'

'I know that, Heletha, but *we* are near the ruins! And she looks like a little girl to me, we do not need to be afraid of little children!' He shook her off and moved closer to the edge of the cliff.

The girl had heard him and was now standing looking up at them. Her toes turned in slightly and she rocked from side-to-side gently as she waved back at them with one hand. Heletha knew that she should grab Wardin and run back to town, maybe bring Czerna or another grown-up to help; but the girl was all alone and looked very small against the black fortress behind her. Seeing Wardin already scrambling down the makeshift path that navigated the steep slope in front of them, she jogged to catch up and then pushed herself in front of him. 'Stay behind me, Wardin, okay?'

He nodded and they carefully picked their route down to the road. Now they were much closer, she could see the girl was shorter than either of them, and held the roundness of babyhood in her countenance. She hadn't moved from her spot, watching them all the way down, and a broad grin stretched across her face. Heletha returned her smile as they joined her by the gates.

'Hello,' she said, 'My name is Heletha. This is my brother, Wardin. What's your name?'

'Kastani,' she replied, with a slight lisp.

'That's a lovely name,' Heletha continued, mimicking the adults she often overheard, 'how old are you, Kastani? And what are you doing here?'

'I'm five!' she exclaimed excitedly, 'I like finding stones and bits. I have a correcting.'

Heletha held back a laugh at the mistake and couldn't understand how such a cute little girl could be out here alone. 'A collection? That sounds very nice. But I mean, why are you near the ruins? It is not safe and we are not allowed to be here.'

Kastani looked confused and pouted slightly, 'I am allowed! I live here.'

'No, that cannot be right,' Heletha corrected, sudden anxiety running down her spine, 'Nobody lives here. You should come back to town with us and they will be able to find your parents.'

'No!' Kastani shouted back, voice laced with fear, 'You can't take me away! Mother would cry without me! And I won't leave my correcting!'

'It is okay, Kastani, we don't want to take you away. I did not know your mother was with you; where is she?' Heletha tried to be as soothing as possible but could feel herself trembling, Wardin was already backing towards the cliff and she wanted to turn and flee with him.

'She doesn't come out much. But she says I can look for stones anywhere I like.'

'Kastani!' a strangely melodic voice called out from beyond the gates. Heletha looked up and saw a woman approaching from the blackness of the ruin. She wore a flowing white dress which was streaked with terracotta, her hair was short and ill-kempt with similar staining running through it. Her movement was graceful, giving her the appearance of floating towards them, and Heletha found herself transfixed despite the terror washing over her.

'That's my mother,' Kastani's voice rang through the paralysis, 'she might be cross with me for talking to you. You should go.'

Heletha studied Kastani and saw only innocence in her piercing blue eyes. Turning her head back to the rapidly approaching vision, she wondered if this was what a ghost looked like; the woman was close enough that she could now make out markings scarred across the skin of her face.

'Here, take this to remember me. Maybe you can come back, and we can be friends?' Kastani continued, pressing something small and hard into Heletha's palm. The sensation was enough to break the spell of terror upon her and she looked down into her own hand. The gift was a human tooth.

Heletha screamed and bolted, sprinting in the footsteps of her brother, catching up to him at the verge of the cliff and dragging him with her as they fled back across the dark plain towards Hercatalana. She did not look back.

Chapter 1

Sunlight streamed through the large kitchen window, warming the slate floor tiles, and casting dark shadows beneath the central preparation table. Leaning against the edge, Treya let out a heavy sigh and blew a strand of hair out of her eyes. Looking at the three loaves of bread before her, she tried to determine exactly what had gone wrong. The first loaf hadn't risen at all and had a bland, chalky taste to it; the second looked quite presentable but had a crust like bark, and uncooked innards; the third was mostly black. She was sure that each had been made with the same ingredients, same measurements and baked for the same amount of time, so why the drastic differences? Restraining her internal anger, she wondered if the gods had predetermined that she was never to be adequate in a kitchen; for a year now, she had broken from the manual farm labour, bred into her over a lifetime, and turned her hand to food preparation. So far her only successes were fresh fruit platters and sandwiches. Pulling off her apron, she gathered the three bread disasters together and strode to the exterior door, tossing them into the long grass away from the house. As she washed her hands in the back-porch water pail, the sound of children caught her attention.

Rounding the side of the farmhouse, she stopped and leant casually against the limestone wall. Two children ran amongst the grass and buttercups, picking the flowers and chasing one another, trying to hold the petals under their chins. Treya smiled wistfully as the sight reminded her of her sisters all those years ago; Rayne and Catalana had played together so nicely, always having time and patience for one another. As she watched, the little boy tripped over and rolled into a thick patch of the golden flowers, amid hysterical laughter from the little girl; when he sat up, he was also overcome by uncontrollable giggling. The girl flopped down next to him and they began chatting happily but too quietly for Treya to hear.

Strong arms suddenly wrapped around her waist, pulling her close to the man behind her. She laid her own hands atop his and squeezed gently, leaning her head back against his shoulder. Warm tingles ran through her as his lips gently caressed her exposed neck and she pressed her cheek against his affectionately.

'Hello, beautiful lady,' he purred.

'Hello, my love. Where have you been?'

'Just in town. What are they up to?'

She frowned at the quick deflection. She kept no tight leash on him; they had agreed long ago that both would retain whatever freedom they required in their movements. That had resulted in very little time apart but the more hands they had hired for the farm, the less direct input was necessary on their part. She had found other activities to fill her time, like unsuccessful baking, but he had not been so proactive and took daily visits into

Rennicksburg to socialise. However, he was seldom furtive on his return and it raised some concern in her. He must have felt her tension and continued without a reply from her.

'It cannot be denied, we have made some gorgeous babies, Treya.'

She turned in his arms and wrapped hers about his neck. Studying his face to gauge if something was wrong, she detected only a little anxiety. Pushing herself forward into a lingering kiss, she addressed him with a smile, 'Yes, as you tell me every day, the twins are more wonderful than we have any right to be blessed with. Now, what do you need to tell me? You've never hidden your worry well from me.'

He flashed a dashing smile but averted his gaze nervously, 'Aha, Treya, how deeply you know me! It is nothing, really. I was in town…'

'In a tavern from the taste of you!' she japed, keen to lighten any trepidation he had in being honest with her.

'Aye, my sweet blossom, tavern indeed! The Fox Ears, in fact. But that is not the point. I met a scholar in there and we began talking…'

'A scholar? From where? Do you mean a cleric?'

'No, Treya, I know the difference between academia and religion. This was a bard, in fact, and his accent was reminiscent of the Five Kingdoms…'

'The Five Kingdoms? You mean Lustania? That concerns me, we have heard nothing from that region since the last donations sent to the Dussen five years ago.'

'Treya, don't be so suspicious, everybody has to hail from somewhere! And it is natural for fable-spinners from that area to be interested; our story involved them after all.'

'What!?' She snapped sharply, pulling out of his embrace, 'Our story? No, we left it behind; you promised me. All in the past, you said. We would move forward and leave it there. I sent everybody who came calling away and there has been nothing for three years at least. Who was this man? What did he say?'

'Please, my sweet, calm down. I know how you feel, and I was forthright in educating him on your views regarding that tale. But, Treya, it is an epic saga and it became clear that the ballad is already written, using whatever records and rumour he assembled himself. He only wants to clarify some details to capture the whole story in the correct manner. Would it not be better to ensure he tells the tale with truth, rather than relying on whatever nonsense he may already have pieced together incorrectly?'

'You are so infuriating sometimes,' she scolded, realising her children were now watching them with mischievous grins on their faces and lowering her voice accordingly, 'This is the same argument we had all that time ago. Alissa died in that evil place, I nearly joined her there, these are not events I care to recall or want tales and songs spread across the land. What have you told him?'

'Nothing, I swear it. But he was very insistent.'

'Meaning what?'

'Meaning, he is waiting in our front parlour to meet you.'

Treya punched him hard in the shoulder, satisfied by his wince of pain, and then pushed him aside, 'Straker, you are a constant thorn in my side!'

'Yes!' he replied, following quickly behind her, 'But a thorn is just part of the larger rose!'

Running a hand through her shoulder-length, tawny hair, Treya composed herself before entering the parlour. Their visitor rose to greet her, offering his hand; he was dressed in fine travelling clothes and held the air of education in his expression and bearing. She noted his curly hair must have been brown once but was now mostly grey and neatly trimmed; his face was lined with age, but the creases indicated severity rather than gladness, leaving his smile a false mask. She stopped before him and ignored the offered hand.

Rescinding the gesture, he maintained the smile as he spoke, 'Good day, milady, I am Silas Zendar the third, a bard of the Writing Guild. May I express my gratitude for agreeing to meet with me; your husband explained your reservations…'

'We are not married,' she interrupted him, 'and I have agreed to nothing.'

'Of course,' he agreed amiably, retaking his seat, 'then perhaps you would allow me to explain?'

'I have heard it all before. Grand stories or books of fables to make you a pretty penny at the expense of my family and my privacy. I am not interested; you have wasted your time.'

'Please, Lady Fimarr, you misunderstand my presence. The stories you speak of are already written. The tales become legend as we speak. My only concern is to their accuracy. There is much to be said for the exaggerations and expansions of a good bard, ensuring a tale is apt for the enjoyment of an audience, that all elements are suitably exciting and satisfying. But herein lies the biggest flaw; such tales lack any accuracy and fail to respect the truth of events. I have made it my goal to provide an honest re-telling of many of the greatest stories that are recited throughout the lands. I will admit that your own father has featured in several of my efforts. I refer to them as stories of accuracy and I make little profit from them, my altruistic ideal is to have factual historical records of significant events.'

Treya paused to consider the words before taking a seat opposite him, keeping her back straight as she felt the tell-tale twinge of pain through the scar that ran from shoulder-blade to hip. 'Why should I believe you? And what difference does it make after all these years?'

'I admit that there is little to convince you of my ideals, and I am used to reluctance from those I meet. But the saga is poorly told at best, with glaring holes throughout. It also fails to acknowledge the real human losses involved; the entire Gaesin family, for example, or your own sister?'

She felt a comforting hand placed on her shoulder as Straker took up a position behind her. 'Alissa?' a tremor had crept into her voice, 'My sister died under tragic circumstances. It should never have happened, but it did. That story remains true in the memory of those who were there. That is enough for her and that is enough for me. I'm sorry but you're not welcome here, Bard Zendar, I suggest you leave and do not return.'

'Treya…' Straker started as she stood and made for the door, but she turned fierce eyes on him.

'No, Straker!' she cried angrily, 'Make certain he leaves!'

Tears were forming in her eyes, so she stormed back towards the kitchen to avoid breaking down in front of them. Vivid images of her youngest sister had returned to her, days of joy and happiness from years past, and every one of them tainted by the madness that had corrupted her before the end. Reaching the back door, she dropped to her knees and a despairing sob escaped even as she covered her mouth with her hand. Uncontrolled, the agony poured from her freely as years of suppressed grief rose to the surface. Suddenly, tiny arms wrapped around her with unconditional love as her four-year old twins hugged her tightly. She understood that they had no concept of why she was crying but their desire to stop their mother's pain was the strongest consolation she could ever have. She squeezed them close to her and smothered them with kisses.

The slightest ripple of movement in the heavy ornate drapes before her indicated a door opening somewhere in the chambers beyond this one, suggesting that he was, perhaps, on his way. Already delayed much longer than originally anticipated, the wait had pushed her patience to the limit; crouching on the mid-balcony of the resplendent audience chamber, behind the privacy curtain, had generated several cramps and aches, each of which required easing through fingertip massage. She exhaled heavily; her body had never used to struggle like this, only since the long convalescence had her suppleness, endurance and agility been so reduced. Absently, her hand moved to the left side of her face, fingers tracing over the rough scars that covered almost half her visage. There was no sensation in her damaged cheek, but her fingertips could feel every mangled and twisted line, even through her black glove. As with any time she caressed her old wounds, thoughts drifted back to the storehouse, the promise of riches and the unexpected betrayal.

She had followed an offer, a bribe really, allowing a victim to live in return for the location of a great stockpile of wealth. It had taken weeks to locate the promised reward and investigating had triggered a fire trap. There had been no riches for her to claim and seemingly no way out as powder flares ignited the entire building, sealing her in to die. Never one to concede defeat, she had managed to prize up some floorboards, drag herself to the building's edge as it burned above her, and waited while the structure razed around her. She had lain there for hours, struggling with intense heat, screaming when burning timbers had fallen against her exposed flesh, agonising as her skin crackled and burned upon her. But she had lived. Dragging herself free of the smouldering ruin when the flames subsided, she somehow found herself at a river's edge and was saved by passing fishermen. Recovery had taken over a year and she knew her skills would never be as they were, but determination pushed her to return to her trade and re-establish her reputation. Silver Rain rose once more.

Footsteps approaching along the polished-tile corridor outside snapped her attention back to the present and she slowed her breathing in preparation. The main door swung open, rippling the curtain before her violently, before she heard five men enter. The first entrant, wearing soft, cushioned footwear was speaking loudly as the others followed behind; the rearmost two clanked metallically, clearly wearing armour and most likely his security detail.

'I told you already that this is unacceptable! How long can I remain in hiding here and still generate any respect from the community?' the voice was aged but full of arrogant power, 'I must engage directly, I cannot be seen to be cowering in fear!'

'I know your feelings on this, Sir,' this voice confident and laced with military authority, 'but you want to remain alive, then this is how we do that. Your home is secure, but I cannot guarantee your safety beyond these walls; you become an easy target for archers or decent cut-throats the second you leave the residence.'

'And I pay you to prevent that! What am I wasting my money on if you are simply going to hide here in my home with me?'

'The fact you pay me is why I'll let that comment slide. I will stop any killer who comes for you; stopping them before they achieve your death is a different matter and I need the advantage to do that. Being here gives me that advantage.'

A pause dragged out and she heard the scraping of a heavy high-backed chair being dragged back from the large dining table she knew stood in the centre of the chamber. The original speaker slumped down into the cushioned seat, sounding like a sack of flour dumped at the roadside.

'Fine,' he growled with resignation, 'then I will hold a party tomorrow evening. I want my closest associates and fiercest rivals all here together. I want them to know that I run from nothing and I control all; it must be lavish, and it must be extravagant. A spectacle of the Winterfire empire!'

'Of course, Master Winterfire!' a new voice, simpering and ingratiating, 'It will be the finest of events in many a year! We will have performers, dancers, musicians, wine, and a great feast. It will be a night never forgotten!'

'Another risk, but yours to take,' the military voice once more, 'Ensure I am involved in your preparations, I want to know who is coming and going at all times…'

'Yes, yes, deal with this elsewhere!' the first voice again, 'Leave me now and report back when the plans are finalised. I do not wish to be disturbed by anyone other than my children. We will discuss party details this evening after I have taken some rest. Now, leave me.'

Some sounds of ascent accompanied four sets of footsteps exiting and the slam of the heavy door closing once again. Behind the curtain, Rayne rose silently to a standing position and allowed the tingling sensation of blood returning to her legs to abate before straining her ears to ensure only one man remained in the chamber. Her target, Chee Winterfire. Easing the curtain aside silently, she moved to the balcony's edge and peered down into the room; of course, she had memorised the entire setting before taking up her hidden position so her only concern was the position of Winterfire himself. He had moved over to the drink's cabinet and poured himself a brandy, she had already examined the bottles and knew this was a locally fermented spirit, downing one glass before pouring a second with an unsteady hand. As he shuffled back over to the table, she vaulted the balcony rail and landed softly off to his side. He started, stumbling against his chair and spilling brandy onto his velvet outer robe.

'Don't call out,' she stated flatly, flicking her own cloak back over her shoulder to ensure easy access to her throwing knives if required.

The surprise that had consumed him momentarily was quickly replaced by a practised confidence and he smiled broadly. 'Hello, Silver Rain, how ironic that it should be you who has come for me.'

'It is your time. You provided many contracts for me in the past so I will allow you a moment to compose your last words but any attempt to summon your men will end our conversation prematurely. Agreed?'

'Agreed,' he spoke smoothly, and she wondered why he remained so calm; perhaps he believed he could talk his way out of the predicament. 'I would like to start by thanking you. When you removed Albrecht Gauduth from his opposition of me six years ago, there were none left in my way and I reached the pinnacle of my community. You brought me wealth and power beyond my expectations, and I have thrived from that; I assume a new upstart has commissioned this strike on me?'

He had retaken his seat while talking and shifted to a comfortable position whilst sipping his drink politely. She assessed him closely but could detect no threat. 'No. Not a rival. Does it really matter?'

His eyes narrowed for a second but then his nonchalant expression returned. 'It would be nice to know who decided my time was at an end. Would you care to take a seat? Perhaps join me in my final drink?' He motioned to the seat at the opposite end of the long table.

Rayne slowly moved around the table, skirting the chair he indicated, and continuing past it to take a seat on his right side. His smile faltered again, and she saw a thin beading of sweat breaking out on his forehead. The chair he had suggested she take would have placed her in front of the hidden crossbow mechanism on the underside of the table; she had been thorough in her earlier examination of the room. 'I won't drink. It dulls the reactions.'

'Of course,' he replied, desperately trying to retain his composure, 'So, your new employer. An old enemy perhaps? Would it be worth offering a counter-payment?'

'No. My reputation would be nothing if I reneged to the highest bidder. I am an assassin, not a mercenary. As for my employer? Your daughter.'

Genuine shock filled his eyes and he gulped down his remaining drink. Placing the tumbler onto the table with a trembling hand, he turned to face her. 'Seppenia? But why? She has never had an interest in my business or even my fortune? What does she hope to gain?'

Rayne stared hard into his eyes and leaned forward to gain his full attention. 'She wishes to gain nothing. Your death is your punishment for the atrocities you have committed upon her. Your own daughter…' Anger was rising inside her, so she stopped speaking and reclined back into her seat.

'Atrocities? I do not know what you are talking about! I have given her everything she could possibly hope for. Everything she could need!'

'And many things she did not!' she spat back in disgust, 'She is your daughter and your actions have been despicable and perverse! I am pleased she hired me.'

'Please, Silver Rain, whatever she has told you, it is not true! This must be a tale she has spun to ensure your loyalty! Let us discuss a renegotiation, after all, she is paying you with my money!' Finally, his eyes betrayed the panic she had expected from the beginning.

'She was very convincing, Winterfire, but my loyalty was secured with coin, not stories. There will be no negotiations. It is time for you to die.'

'No! Wait, please! I can offer you more than mere money! What about your face? Those scars are horrific, and I can help to relieve them; medicine, religion, even magic, I have the resources to try them all for you, simply for sparing my life!'

Instinctively her hand rose back to her face, but she snapped it away again quickly. Rising to her feet, she replied through clenched teeth. 'My scars? You want to heal them for me? Am I not attractive enough for you? You do not like the fact that my hair does not grow there now? You are a fool, old man! I have no qualms about how I look and the fact you would try to bribe me over it just shows what a small and pathetic man you are! I will delight in your death!'

'No!' he suddenly cried out, clumsily scrambling to his feet and stumbling away from her. 'Help me! Assassin!' he screamed out, heading for the door. Rayne leapt up onto the table, sliding two throwing knives from their hip sheaths in one hand and loosing her thin grapple line with the other. Winterfire staggered as he passed the far edge of the table, dropping to his knees two steps later. As the main door burst open, two heavily armed men entering with weapons drawn, the old man reached out a hand towards them even as a bubbling froth filled his mouth and prevented further sound from escaping. The two warriors paused in surprise as he gargled frantically before dropping face-first to the stone floor. Then they turned their attention to her.

Meeting their stares with a cold fury, she called out an ultimatum, 'Chee Winterfire is dead! He has fallen at the hand of Silver Rain! The contract is complete and neither of you have to die!'

One of the men pushed forward but the other held him back and she recognised his voice from earlier when he spoke. 'You are Silver Rain?'

She nodded, keeping her body poised for combat. He lowered his sword cautiously and continued, 'Then I want no argument with you. Your contract is complete, and I will not attempt to prevent your departure.'

The other man turned on him, 'Are you mad? Or a coward? We have failed in our task and she is the reason! We must kill or capture her! Have you no pride!'

The first man never took his eyes from her as he replied to his partner, 'I choose to live. Our employment is already terminated due to our patron's death, and she would kill us both with little effort. You should listen to me.'

'You are a disgrace!' his comrade retorted before charging forth. Flicking her wrist forward, she released the two narrow blades at her attacker. One sliced directly into his throat, puncturing his windpipe, while the other burst through his eyeball and penetrated his brain; he was dead before his body crashed heavily to the floor. Rayne returned her gaze to the remaining bodyguard.

After a long pause, he gestured towards Winterfire's body with his sword. 'How?' he asked.

She considered killing him for a moment before relaxing her stance and replying, 'Poison. In his brandy. He takes a drink every afternoon.'

'I see. We should have been checking his drinks as well as his food. So, he would have died today without you being here?' She nodded and he continued incredulously, 'So why risk yourself by attending?'

'I like to be sure,' she said distantly, 'and I wanted him to know why he was going to die.'

'So now I know what you look like, will you have to kill me?' The question was laced with fear and resignation.

'No,' she replied, almost surprising herself, 'but if you tell anyone about me, then I will execute everyone you know before taking your life.'

Relief washed over him, and he returned his blade to its scabbard, 'Understood.'

Watching him leave, pulling the heavy doors closed behind himself, she tried to rationalise why she had allowed him to live. It made no sense; he was simply a hired protector with no ties to her at all, yet she had felt strong desire to avoid his death. She could not fathom her own decision and, as she retrieved her deadly knives, her mind drifted back to the black citadel. She had been there with her sisters, attempting to rectify a mistake by their father years beforehand. She had not been hired or paid to do so, there was nothing in the Assassin's code to control her activity during that quest. Yet she had accepted a bribe to abandon her own sister, the sister she had been closest to in childhood, the sister she had promised to protect in their youth. She knew now that Catalana had survived despite Rayne's actions, and the promised payment had been a clever trap. She bore the scars of her betrayal but had felt no emotion about it. And now she allowed a random enemy to live without reason?

As she raced through the streets of Corinth, the cool air whipping through her hair and refreshing the ever-raging facial scars, her mind was filled with confusion. Ever since her narrow escape from fires that should have been fatal, she had been selective in her assignments; each had needed some 'justification' before acceptance, some underlying moral flaw in the victim. That had never been a requirement before. And, regardless of how many warranted the slayings she inflicted, none could dig into the smouldering pain deep inside her; remorse, regret, guilt combining to form an unshakable distress. When she had first left home, she felt loneliness and longing for her sisters, but it had lasted for only a few months; once her training had begun, she had never looked back. But the decision to return to them five years ago, a decision she still struggled to rationalise, after their father's death, had changed her life completely. It was as if Silver Rain and Rayne Fimarr were two different people inside her and the latter had been punishing the former ever since the betrayal of Catalana. Just thinking her once most-beloved sister's name caused a cramp in her stomach, and she pulled up short as she reached the edge of a rooftop. Blinking, she realised that the building opposite was her own accommodation and the entire journey had passed without any consideration for avoiding detection or pursuit. Crouching behind a stone chimney, she scoured the area keenly, knowing it was a futile gesture by this point, and relieved when she could find no sign of any observer. Chiding herself, she made the impressive leap over to her balcony and pushed the wooden window shutters to one side.

Dropping her heavy cloak to the floor, she followed the light from the parlour and found a roaring fire already in the hearth. Sliding onto a large divan, the heat of the flames adding to the exhaustion suddenly flowing into her, she looked across at the other occupant of the room.

Rebecca sat silently, transfixed by the fireplace. The agent was every bit a courtier but not the fawning, sycophantic adulators adorning most festivals and functions of the rich. She oozed confidence, strength and her presence demanded respect. Rayne often wished she could watch her in action when negotiating contracts on behalf of Silver Rain. Her chestnut skin was smooth and unblemished, full lips always painted in a flattering hue and a hint of colour always on her upper eyelids. Lustrous, tight-curled black hair was pulled back into a ponytail with three perfect ringlets hanging to either side of her face. This evening she wore a multi-layered silk dress with folds of green and blue that shone wildly in the flickering light, the neckline sank tantalisingly to a few inches below the collarbone, such was the current fashion in the city. The stoic reaction to her return was not new, Rebecca was every bit the opposite of Rayne's previous agent, Ansaro Le Vitti.

Waiting a few moments, watching the other woman intently, Fimarr finally spoke, 'It's done.'

'Good,' Rebecca answered, unmoving, 'did it help?'

Rayne considered the question before slumping back into her chair and sighing deeply, 'Honestly? No.'

The agent now turned to face her, sitting forward to indicate her full attention, 'It never does, Rayne. We have been going a long time and I cannot ignore how profitable you've been as a client, but it seems to me you are struggling with your chosen career. Far be it from me to dissuade you from continuing, you make me a lot of money, but the level of distraction in you continues to increase and I fear it will get you killed.'

The concern laced into the statement caught Rayne's attention and she felt a slight flutter in her heart. 'You could be right, Rebecca. Nothing has been the same in the last few years, you didn't know me before...'

'As you've told me many times; but I knew of you. Nobody in my field had not heard of you. And since we have been in partnership, you have still been exceptional, rebuilding your reputation since your... injuries.'

She could not prevent a grimace as the words were spoken and she rose to stand closer to the fire, 'Things haven't been the same, I know that. Every contract, regardless of the price, they all feel so empty. I used to cherish being the very best, and now that pride has been stripped away. I just feel so...'

'Alone?' Rebecca finished for her quietly. Rayne turned and imagined unspent tears in the other woman's eyes. Kneeling before her, she clasped the smooth manicured hand tightly and searched the hazel gaze before her for encouragement.

'I don't have to be. You are the closest person to me. You, I consider my friend. You, I could consider more…'

Rebecca recoiled slightly, pulling her hand free and sinking back into her chair. Panic and embarrassment cut into Rayne's heart and she returned to the fire, subconsciously covering the scarred side of her face with one hand, thumb rubbing the ruined nub of her ear. Tugging at the awkward area of her hair above the scar, she tried to obscure the damage with her dark red locks. 'I'm sorry, Rebecca, I shouldn't have done that. I know someone like you cannot be with an ugly monstrosity like me. Please, do not let this impact on our professional relationship.'

A hand squeezed her shoulder and she turned to look back into those beautiful eyes again. 'No Rayne, your scars have nothing to do with this,' to emphasise the point, she traced her fingers gently across the extensive disfigurement, 'I simply do not feel like that for other ladies; my sexual desires lie strictly with men.'

Turmoil felt for years finally erupted within her and Rayne broke into a fit of sobbing tears, emotional release that she had not experienced since she was a child. Immediately Rebecca pulled her into an embrace and the contact eased the tension and pain from her for a moment.

After minutes that felt like hours, she straightened and turned towards the rear of the room. Wiping her tear-streaked face on her long black gloves, she paused before moving beyond the bedroom doorway. 'Why do you continue to tolerate me, Rebecca? Is it just the money?'

The reply sounded more distant than the space between them, 'You were right before. I consider you a friend and my concern for you is personal, not business. I do not believe you will ever feel peace until you face your past. And maybe there is a way I can help with that.'

Intrigued, Rayne remained where she was, hoping her silence would encourage the agent to continue. It did not, so she prompted further, 'How, Rebecca? What magic can you perform to smooth away my past?'

The sound of the other woman shifting uneasily was a new experience, even her voice held the first tremor of uncertainty Rayne had ever heard. 'Another contract. From Lustania. From the Prince of Lustania.'

Wet, salty twine dug deep into the grooves of his powerful hands as he hauled the weight up onto the beach. Years of callouses prevented any pain or damage but the strain on his body was never less, regardless of the number of times he completed the task. He had considered placing less traps per line but the reduction in load would be counteracted by the extra repetition with more lines. Besides, it kept him strong and he had become accustomed to gauging the weight against the number of lobsters or crabs most likely in the haul.

With the last of the cages safely ashore, Mareck took a moment's rest, leaning against the freshly filled saltwater barrels prepared for his catch. Casting his gaze along the beach, he smiled at the site of his fellow fishermen at work; off-shore casters wading out to their midriffs with lines in the deeper waters beyond; netsmen preparing their single-man clippers with wax and fats or hauling nets of fish into storage crates upon their return; and the free-divers on their floating rafts, collecting shellfish from the reef. Dipping his hat into the barrel next to him, he then scooped it back onto his head, allowing the chilly water to cascade over him and ease the heat from the sun. Stretching out his back and shoulders, Mareck opened the first of the cages and began transferring angry crustaceans from there to a barrel. He was onto the third container when panicked cries floated to him.

Instinct drove his hands to a net and harpoon nearby and he leapt into a ready-stance, eyes scanning for the danger. Other men were staggered along the water's edge, yelling and waving frantically out to sea. Beyond them, thrashing wildly in their desperate efforts to reach land, he spotted three free-divers. Rushing towards the cohort on the beach, he saw one of the distant swimmers vanish from view; by the time he reached his destination, a second man had similarly disappeared.

'What has happened?' he cried to his fellows.

'Zere is something out zere!' one man called back in the strong regional accent of the area. 'Three men 'ave been taken!'

Mareck stared back out towards the remaining swimmer, knowing a hundred and fifty yards was too far against underwater predators. 'Have any of you seen it? Shark? Squid? Adax Whale?'

'No!' replied another, in clear distress, 'Zere are no signs! It is attacking wizout breaking ze surface!'

Mareck tried to think of any creature that was so stealthy when poaching from the depths but dismissed the distraction as he waded out into the brine.

'Be careful!' another man called, 'Sharks and squid can strike in ze shallows!'

'Prepare aid!' he shouted back to them against the sound of the crashing waves, 'He may be hurt when he gets here!'

Keeping his eyes fixed on the frenzied diver, he found himself waist-deep before stopping his progress. He could make out the fear-stricken face of the man, the strain in his arms from the frantic race to safety, the swell forming in his wake; he could be no more than forty yards away. And then he was gone. Mareck continued to scan the surface, praying that he would breach again, closer so aid could be provided; edging further out, he could feel the cold water against his ribs and the pressure of the current threatening to drag him under. For a moment the waves continued to crash and even the cries of his compatriots on the shore vanished as he concentrated on any sign of the free-diver.

When it erupted from the water in front of him, Mareck was caught completely by surprise. The creature had created no sign of its approach despite its massive size; the head of a shark on the body of a six-metre eel with twelve crab-like legs sprouting from its sides. The horror's smooth skin seemed to shimmer in the light, perfect camouflage beneath the waves no doubt, and its speed was uncanny. Before he could bring his harpoon to bear, the monster had snapped its jaws upon him, catching him cleanly on the shoulder. As agony ripped into him, the beast thrashed its muscular body, lifting him like a rag doll clear of the water and casting him off to the side. Smashing into the waves, the cold water brought immediate relief to the jagged injury before the accompanying salt brought new lightning pain. Struggling to catch his breath in the tumultuous water, he finally forced his feet underneath him and staggered back towards the sand.

Reaching land and falling to his knees, he looked down to see blood pouring from his injured body, the damage enough to prevent him lifting his left arm. His comrades seemed to have faired worse, however, as the gore-soaked sand was littered with body parts and the breaking tide was bright crimson. The ocean-dweller was not in sight, but the unmistakable tracks indicated it had followed the dune path up towards the village. Mareck's head spun in confusion; he had not encountered such a twisted creature in many years. Not since his travelling days, not since his time with the great Rork Fimarr. They had slain many such beasts back then and celebrated every victory with vigour; but that was when the mightiest of warriors still lived, when his entourage had comprised the greatest fighters in their fields, when Mareck himself had been a young man of twenty-nine. At fifty-four, he was slower, his skills rusty and now sporting a severe injury; but he could not leave that thing to decimate his home.

Hefting the net in his weaker right hand, he set off in pursuit, his left arm swinging excruciatingly with every movement. By the time he reached the edge of the village, drawn ever faster by the sound of chaos and screams, his breathing was ragged, and he felt weak from the loss of blood. Seeing the decimation of buildings and bodies before him renewed him and he threw the net back over his shoulder, prepared to whip it forward as needed. Following the echoes of breaking wood and terrified cries, he found the monstrosity half-obscured by the shell of a hut it had just smashed through in pursuit of a small child. Driving himself forward, he flicked out his corded weapon, covering the thing's head before it could clamp razor teeth down on the tiny girl. Hauling back with all his remaining might, the net pulled tight across the shark-like maw, forcing it shut. The expected result was furious thrashing and the hut exploded around the violently writhing body. Mareck tried to dig his feet into the harder sand of the village pathway but the creature's strength dwarfed his own and he was dragged painfully across the surface, tumbling into a rack of sun-drying fish. Breath forced from him, he gasped as he tried to rise to his feet, seeing a woman in the domicile behind the rack moving to assist him. Waving her away, he reached his knees as the amphibious animal shook the restrictive net free; unwavering eyes of jet fixed upon him and he knew it was preparing to charge. His good hand fixed onto a short piece of splintered wood, an ineffectual weapon but perhaps he could hurt the beast enough to drive it off.

Sunlight glinted off the monster's slick skin majestically as it darted forward like a snake winding through grass, and Mareck prepared for the impact. It never came and he watched in astonishment as a vicious-looking fish hook the size of his hand zipped through the air on the end of a twisted leather cord. Embedding into the corner of the beast's mouth, the line pulled taught and veered its catch off to the right. As it smashed into one of the concrete uprights that formed the skeleton of each house, Mareck rolled clear of its bulk and crawled toward one of the stored coracles alongside the community sheds. FInding a gutting scythe in the trim of the small boat, he looked back along the length of the cord and found it wrapped around two lantern posts, providing increased leverage, before the skilled wielder straining at the other end. A lithe young woman with determination etched across her face, his daughter, Crystal.

Fear for her safety galvanised him again as the stunned beast used three of its crustacean feet to free the biting hook from its mouth and turned on its latest challenger. In a rapid series of turns and body undulations, Crystal recalled her deadly line to her, the cord wrapped across her torso and limbs with the weighted end spinning freely in her right hand. He had witnessed her practising the strange form of rope combat as part of her daily exercises, but never seen it in action. Now was not the time for spectating, however, and he forced his feet forward with new weapon raised. The creature sensed his approach and turned; too late, as he threw himself to the ground, swinging the sharp blade before him. It sliced cleanly through three outstretched legs and the monster released an eerie gargling cry of pain. Attempting to roll clear, lightning lanced through him again as he passed over his ruined shoulder. Sensing weakness in its prey, the beast snapped forward once again. This time Crystal released the spinning hook directly, avoiding the need for extra leverage, and the weapon sunk deep into one of the blank eyes of the animal. Pulling the cord tight across her shoulders, the curved blade retracted slightly, digging into the sensitive flesh within the eye socket. This time the frantic thrashing was reactive and uncontrollable, indescribable agony driving the insane movement. The hook had lodged deep and the cord quickly began to tangle around the monster. The unrestrained fury was unanticipated by the girl and she was dragged from her feet as the rope uncoiled from the wraps she had made around her own body. As the creature found its feet, fleeing in pain and panic, Crystal was thrown free and crashed into the stacked coracles.

Silence gently settled over the village and Mareck allowed his body to succumb to agony and exhaustion. Before he could drift to unconsciousness, Crystal appeared at his side.

'Fazer! Fazer! What was zat zing? Are you, able to stand? Your wound looks grave, we must get you to ze 'ealer!'

'My sweet girl, the danger has passed. You were marvellous, you saved the village and you saved me. I do not know what that was, and I pray it does not return. I will get to the healer, but you must inform the Elders; the capital must be aware of such dangers. They are only thirty miles upstream of this very bay...'

'Shh, Fazer. Zat is not important right now,' she shifted her body under his good arm and dragged him to his feet, 'once you are safe, zen we can look at warning ze rest of ze land.'

'You never cease to amaze me, my sweet girl,'

'Quiet Fazer, you must be delirious.'

He smiled despite his agony; could nothing daunt this young woman?

The large chamber echoed with arguments and recriminations of rising intensity and volume. Lennath, Prince of Lustania, sank back into his plush chair and allowed the sound to blur into a background drone; it was bad enough his brothers seemed to believe that loud meant right, but it seemed to be having a draining effect on their father such as he had never witnessed. At the narrowest end of the tear-shaped meeting table, the King was leaning forward on the polished marble surface, propped up on his elbows but head hung low between his broad shoulders. It could be the long journey he had taken from Mainspring Palace, arriving only minutes prior to this debate beginning, but Lennath felt there was more to it. Could it be that his spoilt, bickering offspring were finally becoming too much to manage? Was the old man feeling the ravages of age?

'Lennath! Lennath! Answer the question, you wretch! Are you so full of yourself that you will not even join us in this discussion?'

Turning nonchalantly towards the incensed speaker, Lennath appraised his brother. Porthus was the embodiment of decadence; fat, red-faced, usually sweating heavily, and clothed in the finest materials that could not hide his enormous bulk.

'What would you have me say, brother?' he replied coldly, 'What can I possibly do to ease your temper so that this verbal assault can return to the discussion you imply it to be?'

Porthus increased to a deeper shade of rouge, spittle flying wildly as he unnecessarily screamed a reply, 'Take some ownership, you whelp! These matters are no doubt a result of your secret misdeeds; there is no other explanation!'

Lennath retained his cool demeanour, 'Well, it would seem you have the matter deduced; perhaps we can call this meeting to an end?'

'Flippancy and disregard! Who do you think you are, runt?' Porthus heaved himself to his feet, toppling his chair and wheezing through the effort, 'You have answers to provide and we will beat them from you if necessary!'

Lennath reacted like lightning, on his feet in seconds, a palmed blow knocking Porthus' flailing arm to one side before catching the ruffle of his shirt and slamming the side of his head onto the table before them. Sudden silence fell and his three remaining brothers rose in surprise, Kendoss even reaching for his sword. The King was suddenly alert once more but said nothing, eyeing his youngest son with curiosity. Lennath smiled easily, watching Porthus in his peripheral vision in case of reprisal, but keeping his posture relaxed. It had been many years since a gathering of this kind and back then Lennath had been an under-developed boy playing at being a Prince. But in the last five years, since the dark affair with the wizard, Ramikain, he had worked himself hard. Physical strength, speed, combat skills and discipline had become his playmates and he never tired of the rigorous training regime. The best instructors and mentors he could find had been used to make him the powerful and intimidating man he now was. He had no doubt that he could defeat any of his brothers on the battlefield; he could likely defeat them all at once.

'I am the runt no more, brothers. You would do well to show some respect whilst sat within my home. You have plotted and planned amongst yourselves for years to gain greater powers and better resources. And now you have generated unfounded accusations against me to undermine me in front of the King? I have been tolerant of your political machinations since we were gifted the Five Kingdoms, I have even hosted you here knowing that your motives towards me were malicious. But I will be your whipping boy no longer. I am stronger than before, Lustania is stronger because of it, and I will have no hesitation in jettisoning you beyond my borders if you cannot keep a civil tongue in your heads.' After allowing those words to sink in, receiving neither challenge nor rebuke, he continued, 'I have not squabbled with any of you for five years, I have maintained all trade agreements and allowed unobstructed flow of goods and peoples. There has been no questionable word spoken about you or your lands among my people or to our father. So, what is it that you have decided I am to be culpable for?'

It was the King who replied, 'My son, remain calm. I have not agreed to this meeting in some misguided witch-hunt to bring blame to your door. Your brothers have worries, some of which may be justified, but you have stated none; that is why I asked you to host the gathering; Lustania may be the most unbiased of the Kingdoms beyond Mainspring itself.'

A smile had filled the eyes of the old man and there was a hint of pride that Lennath had never seen before. As Gregor began a new tirade, the King's hand rose and the Prince of Tunsa knew better than to keep talking. 'My sons, take you seats, and we will try to bring some order to your concerns.'

Lennath lowered himself gently back to his chair and avoided smirking as Porthus made a meal of righting his own seat and hauling his girth back into it. While their father began a series of speeches about the unity and ongoing strength required of the Kingdoms, Lennath considered what the old man had created.

Once there had been only one extensive region ruled over by his father, a land of abundant riches and resource and a prime target for foreign powers, and those closer to home. Having produced five sons mere years apart, the King had found a clever way to circumvent their traditional route of succession; he dissected his realm into five Kingdoms, retaining a small central land for himself, Mainspring. His objective seemed clear, give all of the sons a Kingdom of their own to rule and avoid the temptation of taking the throne by force. Better still, he had placated his people by allowing a democratic vote; each proposed region was permitted to vote for one of the brothers to take leadership of their lands. Some, like Kendoss, had been popular, topping three of the votes; in these cases, the total number of voters cast the decision. So, the more engagement from his people, the better their chance at a desirable leader. However, the Kingdom to the East had been defending a Dussen incursion during the process and ended up with last choice; Lennath. After the rulers were in place, the Kingdoms were named, each after a Queen from their lineage, trade agreements were created to ensure each supported the others and, by virtue of this, each relied upon the others. It was the perfect plan to bring harmony, balance and peace. It worked up to a point; that point being the greed and ego of men. There remained a continuous competition for favour and privilege, but at least there had been no civil wars between the Kingdoms and trade embargoes were usually short-lived. Until recently, Lennath had had little understanding of all this, relying on his ministers and advisors to deal with such matters. They had done so adequately, but always retained Lustania on a yielded footing, placating the stronger regions to maintain relations.

Lennath resumed his focus as it became clear the King had finished with the trivialities and was keen to move onto business. 'So, it has been too long since we have sat together, and this is evident in the lack of unity between you. The Five Kingdoms are not rivals, you are family and you are allies; sadly the lack of an enemy beyond our borders has sewn mistrust rather than amity. But we can rectify that today. Already I have seen your tempers flare and I will not condone it again. You will speak truthfully. You will speak respectfully. You will honour me and each other. Now, who will be first?'

Kendoss stood and levelled his gaze at Lennath. He was the tallest of the brothers with thick black hair cut cleanly at the level of his jaw. Handsome and regal, he was the very image of royalty; his agile mind and confident prose drew his people to him organically. If there was ever a natural choice to replace their father, he was it. 'Tell me, Lennath, why the agreed cereal convoys from Lustania to Beaufessa have become intermittent with no reduction in cost?'

Lennath remained in his seat, answering matter-of-factly, 'The simple answer is risk. There have been higher levels of interdiction between our fair Kingdoms and I will always balance any threat to my people against the relative cost of the goods delivered.'

'My citizens provide no such threat, why should we be made to pay?'

'That is not my concern, dearest Kendoss. Perhaps you could levy a tax from those causing the problem?' he turned his gaze meaningfully towards Gregor. One of the twins, the Prince of Tunsa rose slowly and anger simmered beneath his forced calm. Only four years older than Lennath, he had always been the most headstrong and stubborn of the brothers and his hardiness had proven essential in his rule over the most mountainous and severe of the Kingdoms. That environment had also provided him inordinate influence as his miners produced most of the coal, ores and precious gems that generated the combined wealth of the Five Kingdoms. Emeralds and rubies glittered from the two rings on his left hand as he leaned on the table, as if restraining himself from violence.

'You know well that my increased military activity is in response to your own actions! How dare you suggest otherwise!' already Gregor's voice was rising, and his face had flushed scarlet, 'You have claimed land across our shared border and moved a thousand troops there on so-called training manoeuvres; three envoys have returned to me stating you refuse to discuss the matter!'

'Gregor, this is not the forum for such trifling matters,' Lennath chided but spotted the inquisitive stare from his father, 'however, I will pamper to you on this occasion.'

As the other man appeared to be on the verge of explosion, Lennath continued, 'I have been studying our joint heritage, history and law in some depth. It appears that when the borders were originally mapped, the land to the East of the Omapindi River was bequeathed to Lustania. At some point, due to my early inattention of such geographical boundaries, you moved several ranchers onto that piece of land. Under our own laws, the Right of Domicile came into effect, meaning land settled for more than a half-year became the property of the settlers' Kingdom if connected by land. I believe this to be my mistake and an area in which I have failed my people. At this moment, I am three weeks from rectifying that mistake.'

Gregor could hold back no longer, 'You crazed snake!' he yelled, 'Do you expect me to allow this! My armies will drive your men off this land or kill them where they stand! I will not stand for such slander and abuse of our traditions…'

'ENOUGH!' The King bellowed, again bringing instant silence, 'I demanded civility and you will provide it!' An icy stare drove Gregor back into his chair, but his furious eyes never left Lennath. 'In this matter, Lennath is duly right to make effort to reclaim land rightly given to his people. Gregor, you also have a right to defend your own lands with force if necessary but do not doubt that Mainspring will intercede at any threat of civil war. I expect parlay between you both over this matter no more than seven days from now. In the meantime, no embargo has been enforced so interdiction of goods to Beaufessa will cease and prices will return to normal. Do I hear consent?'

Kendoss, Gregor and Lennath all provided an 'aye' of agreement but there was little conviction in their voices.

'Now,' the venerate continued, 'what other matters of concern must be raised? Porthus, yours was the voice that convinced me to arrange this assembly; share your thoughts with us.'

The most rotund, and eldest, of the brothers stood shakily, a wary glance at Lennath before focussing his statement directly to their father, 'There have been... incidents, along our border. There is no explanation other than Lustania for this.'

Rolling his eyes, Lennath leaned into his brother's field of vision, 'A hard one to answer, that, Porthus. Perhaps some clarity over what you class as an incident?'

The older man turned to face him, some courage returning with his frustration, 'You know to what I refer, ru... brother. Attacks against my people, monsters from the darkness, horrific beasts that harken back to the time of Ramikain!'

Lennath paused and ran his tongue across his suddenly dry lips. He had not heard that name for five years; an undead wizard who had risen in the Dussen lands of the East, who had threatened all lands with his evil sorcery and infectious dark that twisted normal beasts into the horrors of nightmare. Indeed, even his own people had proven susceptible to the taint; but during the whole affair, none of the Kingdoms had shown him support, even the King had scoffed at his claims of the danger. Only a small group of adventurers led by the Fimarr sisters had proven the difference between their current existence and total domination by that heinous power. 'I... was not aware that such beasts had appeared in Zendra, Porthus. That is the truth. But now that you speak of it, I, too, have had encounters within my borders.'

'So, you admit it is your fault they are in my land!?' Porthus exclaimed incredulously.

'That is not what was stated,' the King interceded, 'why have you not informed us of this before, Lennath?'

Lennath could not restrain his disdainful laugh, 'Why have I not told you? Do you forget so quickly the reaction I received when I warned you of Ramikain's return? Why would I expect anything different this time?'

A glimmer of guilt flashed in his father's eyes before he raised placating hands, 'Very well, I understand your actions. But for how long has this been occurring? Have they returned from the Dussen wastes?'

'Nay, father,' Gregor butted in aggressively, 'these creatures are Lennath's doing and he will no doubt be planning a similar incursion into Tunsa. This is a repeat of the threat from five years ago!'

Lennath's temper finally broke and he leapt to his feet, 'And how did you react last time? When Lustania stood between all of you and a dark threat beyond measure? Did you send aid? Troops? No, you cowered in your holes and allowed my people to face the danger, my lands to suffer the devastation!'

'Do not preach at us, Lennath! You took no suffering from that time! Your army never even crossed the border; turned tail at the sight of the enemy forces! It was blind luck that destroyed Ramikain.'

'No Gregor!' Lennath spat fiercely, 'My people proved they would risk their lives to protect the Five Kingdoms! My General may have betrayed my trust and fled, but he was dealt with for such treachery. But I helped the Fimarrs, sheltered them, provisioned them, and ensured the success of their ultimate goal. The threat is no more because I was not afraid to act; can any of you claim the same?'

His brother waved a hand in dismissal but neither he nor any of the others broke the heavy silence that fell. Lennath used the time to compose himself, leaning both fists on the cool marble surface before him and dropping his head as he continued, 'But I use every ounce of my being to forgive and forget the misdeeds of the past. You all need to realise that I am your whipping boy no longer; Lustania is strong, I am strong and the imbalance between us must change.'

'And so it shall,' the King committed quietly, 'but the matter of these creatures must be addressed. What do you know of them?'

He sighed heavily, 'They have been seen within my borders, sporadically, but enough to be brought to my attention. Why in the last few months, after so many years, I do not know. I had prayed it was confined to Lustania; this is the first I have learned of the troubles spreading to Zendra. I do not know where they have re-emerged from, how they have returned, for I believed them to be the direct spawn of Ramikain himself, or if they have some purpose other than carnage.'

'Do you think it is a sign of Ramikain returning once more?' Porthus whimpered, fear etched into his doughy face; Lennath felt only disdain at his weakness.

'As stated, I do not know the cause. I have increased roaming patrols to try and destroy the beasts, but they are not easily found. My people are alert, and I have taken measures to investigate the citadel in the Dussen Wastes where these things came from originally. Already I am expending Lustanian resources to overcome the threat, yet here I face only accusations from my kin.'

'Perhaps if we held such forums more often,' Kendoss offered, 'then we could avoid suspicions growing to such extremes, understand each other's lands more closely and settle disputes more amicably. Lennath, you have my apologies. What assistance can Beaufessa provide?'

Lennath looked up and studied his brother's face, finding nothing but sincerity. Not all were so quick to alter their position, however. 'And we should just believe this because you have said it? Your attempts to inspire guilt do not disguise the fact you are expanding your territory and may be using these creatures to generate terror as a distraction! Provide me proof of your innocence before I will concede to your unsubstantiated claims.'

'Enough, Gregor!' their father growled again, 'I raised you all in the traditions, heritage and beliefs of our ancestors. You rule a Kingdom each to ensure none of you felt disadvantaged beneath the others. Most importantly you are brothers and *together* you represent the future of the Five Kingdoms. This incursion will mark the beginning of a new era of cooperation and understanding. I will provide a portion of the Royal Guard to bolster your patrols in Lustania, each Kingdom will supply one percent of their military strength to provide custodians for villages in both Lustania and Zendra. To avoid bias, Kendoss will determine what strength is provided to each dependent on the threat. To ease Gregor's concern, an envoy will be provided from Tunsa to observe and support Lennath. The decree is spoken; go now and enact my wishes, I will discourse with each of you again in the coming weeks.'

Lennath grimaced at the mention of an envoy but said nothing. His brothers dispersed quickly, Porthus scurrying away like a wounded rat, until only Gallth remained, still seated and silent. Gregor's twin had little to do with Lennath throughout his life, and had seemed disinterested since his arrival. Now he was watching as the King placed a conciliatory hand on the Prince of Lustania's shoulder. No words were spoken but it seemed as though the old man was perhaps more hunched over than usual, more tentative in his footsteps. Dismissing the thoughts, Lennath turned to his waiting brother.

'There is something else I can do for you?'

'You would be warned to tread carefully,' Gallth spoke casually, no level of threat perceptible in his voice, 'Gregor can be more dangerous than you realise.'

'I'll bear that in mind, Gallth. Perhaps you'll pass along a similar warning in the other direction?'

The Prince of Kaydarell finally took his feet and stepped close to his sibling, 'You should not antagonise us, Lennath, remember we are four where you are one. Father will not be around forever, and you are creating a powerful axe that will fall upon his death; you should be sure it does not fall on you.'

Lennath looked into the faded green eyes of his sibling. Gallth was taller but nowhere near as broad, and the strength Lennath knew flowed within himself was not evident in the other man's build or stance. There was a surety in his words, though, that made him wonder if Gallth held more influence over the other brothers than Lennath realised.

'Thank-you for your kind words, Gallth. I will heed your sage advice. I hope all of this can bring our family closer together.' He hoped that his words sounded genuine, the stare held between them suggested otherwise, but was pleased as his final kin left the chamber. Sitting back on the edge of the table, he exhaled deeply; the whole meeting had been unanticipated with little time to prepare. Had he known that creatures were already appearing outside of Lustania, then he probably would have convened the gathering himself. As it was, he felt uncertain of how his family had taken his words. And now he would have to conduct his duties in the presence of an envoy? It was certain to be both a frustration and an obstruction; the fact he had not revealed all his knowledge regarding the monsters would now be a secret much harder to keep. But if his plan worked, if the knowledge proved to be accurate, then the threat would be easily contained, and the Kingdoms really would find the harmony the King dreamed of. Only the arrogance and impatience of his brothers could obstruct this; the plan would have to be accelerated.

General Audack entered the room cautiously, his sword slapping against the plate hip-guard of his armour as he walked. He had gained more weight since his promotion, his hair had greyed completely, and his short stature suggested a bumbling nature; his stewardship of the Lustanian army could not be faulted, however. It helped that all activity had been primarily defensive which was his tactical speciality, but he seemed to have the respect and faith of his men, important after the failures of his predecessor. And above all else, he followed the direction of his ruler without question.

'My Prince, their Royal Highnesses have all opted to depart this day, Princes Kendoss and Gallth were assigned a room for this evening but the option has been declined despite the length of their respective journeys home.' Audack always sounded like he was out of breath.

'Thank-you General. A shame my hospitality is declined, perhaps I could have built some bridges had they remained. No matter, a thought for another day.'

'You seem… pleased, Sire. The discussion was successful?'

'Moreso than I could have imagined. We will be receiving enhancement to our patrols from the Royal Guard themselves. Ensure they work the Dussen border; if we do have any threats to the East, I would appreciate their skill on hand. We will also be providing some militia to a combined Five Kingdom force to provide further protection to the more exposed villages and townships; select sixty of the most vulnerable locations for when this force is made available.'

Audack looked shocked, 'This is excellent news, Milord, but do you feel the danger is that severe? There have only been three attacks in total and no indication of anything even occurring across the Dussen border; not that I would refuse any extra addition in strength to the military, of course.'

'Of course not! You are a loyal servant of Lustania and I never lose sight of that. However, I will take no risks this time, complacency and slovenly response could have cost us our lives or liberties last time these beasts were abroad. Now, go and make the arrangements I have detailed.'

'Yes, Sire, without delay.' Audack spun smartly and headed back for the door.

'And General?' Lennath called after him, smiling at the immediate halt and spin to be formally addressed by his sovereign, 'Be sure to give my family personal Lustanian escorts to the border; it would be unthinkable if some tragedy were to occur to any of them!'

Audack looked momentarily confused before saluting and departing, leaving Lennath alone in the grand chamber, chuckling quietly to himself.

Chapter 2

Moving swiftly along the ornate corridor, Rayne noted the high ceilings, marble pillars and thick azure carpets, realising nothing had changed in the five years since her last visit. She ignored the shocked or horrified looks as she passed members of the household staff and retained an impassive disposition. This was a challenge in itself; crossing the border into Lustania had reinvigorated the contempt she had left the region with; entering the city had regenerated the suspicion and anger she felt towards the traitorous people; crossing the threshold of the palace had restored the vengeful rage towards the Lustanian Prince. His army had not only abandoned her party on the border, facing a vast army from the Black Citadel, but had even attempted to trap them within a ring of fire to allow for bombardment from machines of war. They had survived, and she was not one to judge others for their betrayals nowadays, but the injustice required redress, and Lennath would be the one to answer. Luckily, she had seen no sign of the General who betrayed them directly; she would provide that man no time to plead his case, his death would be instant.

She recognised the large doors of the official audience chamber and was surprised when they turned off beforehand; perhaps the Prince wanted a more intimate space for a single audience, or maybe he hoped their negotiation could be kept secret. Turning her head from side-to-side slightly, she assessed the four, armed escorts; burly but undoubtedly slow, with ambulation indicating mild complacency and less than full interest in keeping their skills sharp. The leading footman was barely more than a child and presented no threat. Even disarmed as she was, it would probably take less than thirteen seconds to incapacitate all five. She smiled to herself; that was if she was truly weaponless, of course. The weight of the needle-thin stiletto was comforting along her forearm, where it was housed in a custom sheath within the long black glove. Having permitted the excessive scrutiny the armourer had shown in checking her for concealed weapons, just how much he had expected to find hidden beneath her bosom or within the crease of her groin she did not know, but his over-familiar use of hands distracted him from noticing the blade she had retained.

Turning into a long corridor with identical doors on both sides spaced evenly every ten yards, she spotted only one other occupant of the passage. As he passed them in the opposite direction, she noted his resplendent travelling clothes, slightly soiled from unknown journeying. Standing two heads taller than her, he was gangly but refined, curly grey hair cut neatly close to his scalp. A face lined with age and grimacing peaked in a sharp nose upon which balanced a pair of delicate spectacles. He had the haughty disposition of a man whose intelligence made him believe he was more entitled than those around him. She felt he belonged as master of some enormous library. His eyes flicked across to appraise her momentarily, left eyebrow rising in surprised recognition although she had no recollection of having ever met the man. Another stride and he was out of sight and beyond her concern.

Abruptly they came to a halt, the footman knocking upon an oak door studded with steel but decorated with gold; a smaller antechamber or private parlour, perhaps? The young man followed a summons to enter and returned moments later, ushering the assassin to enter. Stepping inside alone, the door closed behind her and she spotted Lennath leaning over a large fireplace, goblet of liqueur in his hand. He was more than twice the size he had been at their last meeting, his body bulging with muscle that indicated a physical regimen she would never have believed possible from the whipped youth. The increase in body mass generated a formidable appearance and she supposed he was more attractive with chiselled features and strong jawline. Normally this gave her an advantage; pretty men sported huge egos, and this made them easy to manipulate, or at least it used to before the fire.

The Prince turned to her with an open smile, offering her a seat with one outstretched arm, 'Ahh, Silver Rain! It is truly an honour to have you grace my halls again.'

Suddenly springing into a blur of motion, Rayne leapt forward, vaulting a drinks' table and lavish couch before rolling forward and surging to her feet before him. Her concealed blade flashed in the firelight as she pressed it against his throat, but he held his arms out in submission.

'Obviously, you are upset,' he stated carefully, a trickle of blood forming as his throat moved against the stiletto, 'Perhaps you would allow for explanations and my contract offer before killing me?'

She gritted her teeth, imagining the relief slicing his jugular would bring, but slowly released her grip on him and stepped back. 'I will hear your words. But choose them wisely as they may well be your last.'

'And I would not want to waste them,' he indicated a seat for her again and moved over to the nearest drink's stand, 'Can I get you something?'

'Don't you have servants for that?'

'I live my life somewhat differently than you remember. I'm certain I have learned as much since those days as you have.'

'I strongly doubt it,' she replied, failing to keep the bitterness from her voice.

There was a pause before he answered, the sound of gurgling liquid indicating the two drinks poured from an ornate decanter, 'Ahh, yes. I heard of your period of convalescence but not the extent of the injuries you suffered. Have you found your abilities diminished?'

She bit back too hastily, 'Would you care for a demonstration? I would end you in a heartbeat!'

'Please, be calm. I meant no insult; I am only curious. Does the scarring cover your whole left side or just your face and torso?'

Rayne felt suddenly exposed and regretted wearing the Basque without the thin black undershirt. Of course, he could see where the burns had covered her shoulder and upper arm, spreading across her chest as far as her sternum. His guess was right, the damage had been extensive and little of her left side was not permanently ruined by hard and twisted reminders of the inferno she had survived. And now he could, undoubtedly see the uneasiness his interest was causing. Perhaps killing him immediately had been the better option. 'I am not here to be examined or reminisce about misfortunes of the past. I suggest you get to the point or our time together will be brief.'

The Prince placed a goblet in front of her and then took a seat opposite, 'Very well. I know your feelings towards me are extreme, but I encourage you to heed my words, for they are sincere. You and your kin were betrayed and left for dead five years ago, but I had nothing to do with it. Surely you must have realised that after all this time? Why would I expend the effort and resources of dispatching an entire army only to turn them around at the last moment?'

'To lull us into a false sense of security? To ensure we left your land without causing further disruption or panic?'

He smiled, nodding his head in acceptance, 'Understood; that is conceivable I suppose. But it is incorrect. I admit that I was weak when we last met, physically and mentally, and this left me unaware of the lack of authority I truly held in my own Kingdom. It was Jacob Frost who betrayed you, called a retreat against my orders and was found to be colluding with the enemy. He left you for dead and he was dealt with accordingly. But I never made proper reparations to you all and, by the time my body and heart were powerful enough to do so, it seemed like too much time had passed for any offer of restitution to be seen as genuine. But I have not forgotten or forgiven myself for those failings and that is part of the reason I requested your presence today.'

She watched his eyes closely, looking for signs of deception but his relaxed manner gave little away. 'I do not believe any offer you have could compensate that betrayal. My services demand more than simple monetary value; something a Prince could not conceive.'

'We shall see,' he replied, absently dabbing at the superficial wound in his neck with a silk handkerchief, 'I am currently in a difficult political situation…'

'Electoral rival? I am too expensive for such simple removal.'

Lennath's smile broadened and he showed no irritation at the interruption, 'No, no! I would not insult a professional of your calibre with such mundanity. Perhaps you are not aware of the brewing crisis that links our histories? For several months now, twisted creatures akin to those abroad during the days of Ramikain have returned to the land…'

'I am no trapper. Pest control can be dealt with by even *your* soldiers.'

The smile did not waver but the pause before resuming was longer, 'Correct, and I have patrols scouring Lustania to destroy these monsters. But the evil taint is spreading, not just within my borders but now into the lands of my brothers. Sadly, they blame me for the outbreak, not realising that my own people are likewise suffering and failing to recognise the underlying threat this may be heralding. They have threatened…'

'The rulers of the other Kingdoms? You want me to murder your own brothers? But the King would surely conclude you were responsible; so, him also? That is a request of extreme magnitude; not beyond my ability of course…'

This time he met her interruption with his own, voice filled with aversion as he sprang to his feet and turned his back on her, 'My family? Of course not! How could you even… Has our past really tainted your view of my humanity so much? My brothers, my father, are strictly off limits to you! I want you nowhere near them and no harm to befall them. Even the suggestion makes me believe this was a mistake. Perhaps we should terminate this consultation, your opinion of me is clearly going to make this impossible.'

Almost against her own will, she moved over to him and took hold of his arm, turning him back to face her. A single tear ran down his cheek and he quickly wiped it clear; was it frustration at her, or shame that she would accuse him of such debasement?

'I apologise for insulting you,' she stated flatly, 'My work brings me into contact with all manner of clients willing to justify their requests regardless of family, morality or propriety. I will pre-empt your request no longer. Please continue.'

He moved clear of her grasp and stared at the stocked bookcase to the rear of the room. Returning to her seat, she was satisfied as he quietly recommenced. 'This returning plague has created tension between my family and places all of our peoples, and ourselves, in growing danger. I have spent the past months researching all I can find out about the rise of Ramikain, his power, these creatures, and everything that occurred. I discovered that there is a way to destroy the taint completely, eradicate the monstrosities from existence and I must ensure it is achieved.' He stopped and turned to look at her, clearly appraising her reaction, but she said nothing as she took a sip of the brandy that had been offered.

'There was a sceptre, crafted centuries ago, that held the essence of a vast power. The power was stolen, years later, and the artifact lost. This power was later taken by Ramikain, providing him longevity and necromantic sorcery until his destruction. The sceptre was uncovered by my people and brought here.' He reached forward and pulled one of the books, revealing that ten of them were false and provided a hiding space in the unit. Retrieving an ornately crafted staff approximately half a metre in length, he tossed it to her. Examining it closely, she could tell it was gold, intricately carved symbols adorned the entire surface and it looked like an overtly lavish incense burner. The weight did not match the size, however, and she wondered if it was simple gold-plating over a heavier but cheaper substance within.

'Right now, it is an expensive doorstop,' he explained, 'but there is a pool where the power is trapped, stored until a conduit is provided. Place the sceptre in the pool and it will absorb the magic once again. That magic can end the threat these creatures pose permanently.'

'I can determine no contract that would require my skills here,' she replied, 'if you want to douse this stick in a pool you believe is magical, then send one of your scouts. Unless you do not know the location of said pool.'

'The location? That is one factor I considered when summoning you here. The pool is housed in the Black Citadel on the Dussen Wastes; your familiarity with the fortress will be beneficial.'

'It is a shell. Abandoned since his fall. Anyone can do this for you.'

'Your assumptions in this matter are wrong, I'm afraid. It has never been deserted. A new resident has hidden within those walls since last you were there. And I need them also. For only one who is touched by that dark taint can wield the sceptre. I need her brought here; I need Alissa Fimarr.'

The name hit her like a thunderbolt and ringing filled her ears as her mind reeled from the revelation. She found words but they were forced out as she tried to order her thoughts, 'She died. There is no-one there. Not for this long, alone.'

'I never said she was alone,' Lennath continued, seemingly unaware of her vexation, 'a loyal retinue of guards has remained to protect her. That is why I need you. The sceptre must be immersed in the pool and returned here with Alissa Fimarr, for she now carries the taint of that dark power. All others are expendable, but she must be unharmed. Only you, her own sister, can I trust to do this. So, do you accept?'

Rayne felt breathless and desperately tried to focus against the sudden rush of speculations. Her youngest sister had died in the confrontation with the evil wizard, that was what the stories told. True, she herself had departed beforehand but if Alissa had survived, Treya and Catalana would have returned for her, wouldn't they? And his suggestion that her attachment to kin would ensure her success? Was he unaware of how she had abandoned Catalana to death in that very same fortress? Could this be the chance she was waiting for? Bringing Alissa back from that evil place, ensuring the final destruction of Ramikain's lingering influence and securing the redemption she craved? If this was even all true. The lingering silence became suddenly oppressive, so she straightened and drained her goblet in one swallow before standing abruptly.

'I am intrigued by your offer,' she stated, louder than anticipated, 'I do not believe your tales; my sister is dead, of this I am certain. But, if you pay the required fee, I will travel to the Black Citadel, drown your stick in this supposedly mystic pool and prove that the ruin is deserted. But the fee will be significant.'

Lennath grinned again, 'Excellent! I can ask no more than that. But, if she is there, then I will require her brought here unharmed.'

'And what would you propose to do with her? How exactly could she use this device to stop the beasts?'

The Prince paused and for the first time looked unsure, 'That is less precise,' he offered, 'but you can be certain that without her the device will be useless; her survival and good health are essential in this so you have my word that she will be safe.'

Barking a harsh laugh, she replied derisively, 'And why would I trust your word?'

'Perhaps you have no concept of redemption,' he returned slowly, choosing his words with care, 'but this is my chance at mine. Help me to do this, whether solely for riches or not, and maybe I can overturn the wrong that I allowed to be committed. Let me undo the wrong that I did to your family.'

Bright sunshine warmed his shoulders while he leaned on the shaft of his large timber axe. Beside the chopping stump lay an unruly pile of halved logs and only twelve remained upright waiting to be hewn by his powerful blade. Pulling an old rag from his pocket, Herc Callid wiped the sweat from his brow and the back of his neck, inhaling sweet breaths of the forest air. A sound to his left caught his attention and he couldn't hide the broad grin as he spotted his son scampering towards him. Spreading his arms wide, Jarrod flew into his embrace and he squeezed the boy tightly to his chest. Amid a flurry of kisses, he gently returned him to the ground and held his shoulders as he took a knee before the child.

'Ahh, Jarrod, you are growing into such a strong little man!'

The boy looked at him with a perturbed expression, 'No father, I am not.'

Herc cast his gaze back in the direction his son had come from and saw his wife, Therese, gracefully crossing the bright Spring grass with their daughter, Marielle, in her arms. As she arrived, he wrapped one arm around her hips and rested his head against her abdomen. 'You get more beautiful every day, my sweet lady,' he mumbled.

'No, husband, I do not.' Her voice seemed distant and detached, and he began to feel an uncomfortable heat against his face. Pulling back from the sensation, he saw her skirts beginning to discolour before his eyes. The feel of sand running through his fingers drew his attention back to the boy and he looked down to see Jarrod's arm dissolving under his touch. Withdrawing his hand in panic, he fell back onto his elbows as the limb vanished completely. Jarrod smiled, thick black fluid spilling forth as his lips parted, 'I am not growing at all.'

Scrambling backwards, Herc looked to his wife for help but her clothes had now started to smoulder, and her skin was blistering and charring as she stood holding their burning little girl tightly. 'We are not beautiful,' she told him, voice cracking and harsh against the flames licking from her mouth, 'We are nothing at all.'

Suddenly Marielle began to scream, and Therese pulled her ever tighter as the flames began to engulf them and the foul stench of burning flesh filled his nostrils. Eyes flicking to Jarrod, the stump of his arm was now gushing dark blood and the black ichor was erupting from eyes and nose. 'If only you had saved us, father,' he gargled against the flow.

'Yes, if only you had been the husband and father you promised,' Therese agreed as her right eye popped in the extreme temperature and the socket began to sizzle with thick yellow gore. Herc Callid screamed.

Jolting upright, his eyes snapped open and he stared down the cobbled road of Guilders Street in Rennicksburg. He was sitting alone beside the pretty hand-crafted fountain that stood in the crossroads between Guilders and Raven Streets. His brief confusion passed, and he realised he must have drifted off whilst taking a momentary rest from his journey. Spending several hours that morning in the drying sheds, a brief interlude did not seem too much to ask before delivering the large sacks of herbs to the store. And, despite the unsettling nature of his dream, it warmed his heart that his mind allowed him to see his family again. Almost six years since their loss but their absence cut as deeply as ever. Standing and stretching out his heavily muscled back, he began to gather the large satchels together and noticed a man hurrying towards him. Sighing inwardly, he raised a hand in greeting; this was why he had lived deep in the forest, his social interest in people had always been limited.

'Hail, Herc Callid!' the well-spoken voice floated to him, full of camaraderie.

'Hail, Milius Taytafen!' he responded, trying to mask his indifference.

The younger man arrived in a flurry of tails from his exuberantly bright coat. His smooth skin and coiffured hair instantly marked him as a member of the gentry and, indeed, he had been so by lineage. When he had taken ownership of the town's brothel, however, he dropped somewhat in the levels of social esteem. His wealth still demanded great respect in most circles, just not with Herc. The man had never been unpleasant or generated any reason for Callid to distrust him, however, and he tried to be amiable whenever they crossed paths.

'More wares for the shoppe?' he asked politely, 'Replenishment or a new concoction?'

'Just replenishment,' he replied in his strong deep voice, 'and we make no 'concoctions', just herbal remedies, preservatives and cooking ingredients.'

'Yes, of course,' Milius smiled nervously, he always seemed to smile nervously whenever the pair conversed, 'No offence meant, I sometimes just choose the wrong words.'

'None taken, Milius. You seem flustered, is there something I can help you with?'

'Aha, err, yes. I would not dream of reaching out in normal circumstances but there is an issue. And Vanis has been hurt, so I would usually defer to the Town Watch, but they were called to a poaching incident…'

Vanis was the brothel bouncer, a burly and capable ruffian who kept order well, despite his brutish and loathe personality, 'Calm yourself,' Herc reassured, 'what do you need of me?'

'There is an incident with a client. He is refusing to allow access to the room he is using, Almia is locked inside with him and when Vanis confronted him…'

'Vanis got hurt?'

Milius lowered his head, 'Yes. And that is why I do not wish this request upon you, but I can think of no better man to assist under the circumstances.'

Herc gazed towards the large and ornately decorated frontage of the brothel, 'I can talk to this man for you, convince him to leave. Does he still owe money?'

'Yes, he does, but that is not my concern. I fear he may hurt Almia as he is refusing to let us even talk with her. I am not sure what he even wants.'

'Show me.'

Callid followed the slighter man quickly along the cobbles, through the entrance and up the wide staircase. They passed only employees and Herc assumed Milius must have cleared the place of other clients when the situation arose. Arriving at a closed portal, the owner stepped back and waited nervously. Wrapping his knuckles on the sturdy wooden door, Herc called out evenly, 'Hello in there. My name is Herc Callid, I have come to ask you to leave the premises peacefully. Leave now, without incident, and nothing more will be said.'

The voice beyond sounded manic and full of rage, 'Who are you to demand anything of me! I will leave when I choose, not when you tell me! I am not finished here; when I am you will all know about it!'

'You have had the time allotted to you. Let the girl out and you can remain in the room for the duration you wish,' Milius looked concerned but Herc shook his head, indicating it was merely a ruse.

'I told you I am not finished. That means I am not done with her. Last chance to disappear!'

'Let me know she is well, and we will leave.'

The sounds of movement could be heard, followed by something heavy being dragged. A light whimpering and sobbing carried forth before being suddenly cut off by a solid thump. Milius' eyes went wide with fear and he made for the door but Callid restrained him. 'You asked for my help, let me handle this,' he whispered.

'But that sound! What if he just killed her?'

Herc nodded and gently pushed Milius back. Taking a deep breath, he raised one foot and slammed it against the door. The handle and lock splintered free as the entry smashed open. He had only seconds to absorb the scene before him; the girl on the floor, head streaming blood from the temple; the destroyed furniture and further smears of blood around the chamber; the complete lack of the expected opponent before him. Movement to his left warned him just in time as a knife arced in towards his stomach. Catching the wrist of his attacker before the blade struck, Herc left himself open for a crunching blow to the side of the head. The punch was heavy, and he allowed himself to be driven to his knees by the impact, never releasing his grip on his assailant. Extending his own arm, he dragged the other man over his shoulders before standing and heaving him bodily from the ground. Tightening his grip, he felt the bones in his opponent's hand grind together and the knife was dropped alongside an agonised squeal of pain. Callid threw himself backwards, landing atop his foe and driving all the air from his body. Rolling to his feet, he slammed an elbow into the thug's head on the way up, feeling the nose give way under the force. Face covered in blood, his enemy staggered up and charged with wild eyes full of hate. Herc smartly stepped to one side, catching the man by collar and belt, and used his own momentum to propel him full circle into the door frame. Striking with enough force to shatter the wooden jamb from the mortared wall, the man's bulk crumpled to the corridor floor beyond.

Callid turned back to Almia, relieved to find her breathing, and he pressed a balled-up pillowcase against her bleeding head. 'She will need a healer quickly,' he stated without looking up.

Milius was immediately by his side, taking control of the makeshift compress and placing a hand upon Herc's shoulder. 'Thank-you so very much, my friend. I don't know what I would have done if you had not been here.'

'This is neither a place nor a profession that I condone, but I would not stand by while such violence is perpetrated without just cause. I am sorry for the damage I was too late to prevent.'

'Think nothing of it. Almia is rescued, everything else is a minor inconvenience.'

Callid stood and noticed blood from her wound smeared across his hands. Wiping it idly across his breaches, he made for the door, disgust curling his lip at the fallen cur he had engaged.

'And Herc,' Milius called again, not meeting his eye this time, 'I must confess that I propositioned Catalana again this morning. Please accept my apologies.'

Exiting the building and retrieving his satchels, he felt suddenly unsettled; not by Milius' confession, the man had propositioned Catalana countless times over the last five years and Herc always reassured him that he had no romantic claim over her, but by the wildness in his recent opponent's eyes. He had seen such mania before and that had led to great pain and darkness for Catalana, as it had been within her own sister's eyes.

Conflict over whether to reveal his suspicions to her or not clouded his awareness for the remainder of his journey and the archway leading to 'Wild Goods', the store he ran with her, came upon him almost by surprise. Leaning against the warm stone of the entrance, he shook his head to clear the memory of those eyes, the crazed eyes of a young girl lost to sanity, and the painful decision it had forced Catalana to make. He determined that he would be honest regarding the interlude with Milius.

Trotting hooves clattering on the cobbles drew his attention and he watched as two horses drew up next to him. Upon them rode a man and a woman; the first held strong elegance in her face, tawny, shoulder-length hair bouncing against her shoulders and a green jerkin complimenting the emerald of her eyes; her companion sported bronze skin lined with creeping age, dark hair just starting to drift towards grey at the temples, but the same self-confident smile firmly in place.

'Hail, Treya! Hail, Straker! Have I forgotten your visit?'

'Greetings, Herc,' Straker Forge replied jovially as he swung down from his mount, 'You have forgotten nothing. This visit is unplanned but seeing you is a pleasure as always!'

'Is my sister here?' Treya added, joining them at the doorway, 'I must speak with her.'

'I have just this moment returned myself. Come, we will check inside. Straker, you can secure your steeds at the rear of the store.' The other man nodded and took both sets of reins as Treya followed Callid inside. As they passed through the aromatic sales area of the building, Herc studied the woman's pensive face; there was little similarity between the sisters and the lustrous red of Catalana's hair was stark contrast to the lank tawny tresses of her oldest sister. It was the inner strength and confidence that marked them as kin; he had met no others like them and doubted he ever would. It was that courage which had created the bond between him and Catalana in the first place.

Continuing through to the living area beyond the store, he spotted her instantly and felt the weight in his mind lift instantly. Beautiful beyond comparison, hair held back in a long, simple plait, adorned in a pretty summer dress of pink and white, she was a sight to behold and he had never denied it. She smiled easily as he entered, and the expression widened when she spotted his companion. As he lay the satchels at the back of the room, the sisters rushed to each other and embraced.

'Treya! How wonderful! I did not expect you so soon. What brings such joyous reunion?'

'We must talk, Cat,' the older woman replied, loosing her hold and taking a seat, 'I recently received a visitor at the farm, and it raised fears from the past,'

The smile vanished from Catalana's face and she sat opposite Treya, leaning forward intently. Herc took up a standing posture behind her and placed a comforting hand on her shoulder. As if in response to his offered support, she prompted her sister to continue, 'A visitor? Someone you know?'

'Sadly no; this was some scholar from the West. He was asking about the death of Ramikain, wanted some details about the Citadel and what occurred there.'

He felt Catalana's shoulders shrinking in as the words were spoken and could imagine the guilty expression on her face. 'What did you say to him?' she asked quietly.

'Nothing, of course! I threw him out before...' Treya stopped and stared at her sister, 'Have you seen him?'

Dropping her eyes, Catalana nodded, 'He came here a few days ago. He just wanted to tie up the stories. There are so many versions and I thought bringing some clarity to it all would help. He seemed harmless and he paid for the truth. What difference does it make?'

'How could you!' Treya screamed in fury.

'Enough, Treya!' Herc interjected, moving to Catalana's side, 'This is our home and we have done nothing wrong. Just because you have decided this conversation with Master Zendar should not have taken place, we are not beholden to your desires!'

The side door opened, breaking the tension that had fallen, and Forge entered the room with the perpetual grin still in place. 'Oh, I see you are already down to business! I take it from the colour of everyone's faces that someone here did speak with the scholar?'

Treya turned on him frostily, 'This is no joke, Straker. Catalana has revealed all to that man. Who knows what he is doing with the pieces that were kept secret...'

'Don't be so condescending, Treya!' Catalana snapped back, verve back in her voice, 'I spilled no secrets; just clarified the order of the story, the personalities of those involved and who should have taken the real glory.' The last was spoken meaningfully in Forge's direction.

'Hush now, Embers,' Straker casually dismissed. Herc quite liked the nickname he had for the fiery-haired Fimarr but could not bring himself to use it. 'We have talked about this at home and there may be more to this writer than any of us realise. All we want to know is any specific detail he may have asked for or any indications he may have given of an ulterior motive.'

'He seemed amicable and genuine,' Herc spoke sternly, 'Had it been otherwise, we would not have entertained him.'

'But did you tell him anything new?' Treya pressed.

Catalana placed a hand on Herc's arm to ease him and he stepped back obediently. 'I think maybe he probed most deeply about the geography of the Citadel itself, but I could only give him so much. He knew a lot about the history of Ramikain already, and even more about father's involvement with him. I don't know what else you want?'

Herc felt an uneasiness in his stomach again and blurted out words before he could help himself, 'It's in the eyes!'

Everyone turned to him in surprise and their stares bore into him. 'I... I do not know if it is related,' he stammered, 'This writer, so interested in our encounter at the Black Citadel, and today, at the brothel, a man filled with madness. Madness that I last saw in...' He could not bring himself to finish as he saw the colour drain from Treya's face.

'What man?' she demanded.

'Was Milius there?' Catalana asked.

'What were you doing in the brothel?' Forge added with a wider grin.

Treya slapped her partner across the thigh to silence him and waited for Callid's response. 'He was a stranger; I know not from where. His madness had caused him to hurt Vanis and one of the girls, Almia. I subdued him but his eyes were just as I saw in... her. I fear you may be right; this is not a coincidence.'

He felt Catalana's fingers wrap around his hand and he smiled down at her apologetically. 'If you feel there is danger in this, then I will follow your instincts,' she spoke softly to him. Turning back to her sister, she continued, 'Perhaps I have been hoodwinked by this writer, perhaps not. But if there is more to this matter then we should discover it. Together. What do you propose?'

'We have left the children with Hederna Thriss. She is content to look after them for a few days. I propose we return to the Dussen lands, investigate, and question the people of Hercatalana in case he has been there also, and search the Black Citadel for clues if need be.

A finger of ice ran down his spine. The Dussen lands were where his family had died, and he had never returned since. And the Citadel? That was where they had left Alissa Fimarr for dead. There was no way Catalana would be able to return there.

'That idea is ridiculous,' she told her sister, 'But we are with you.'

Light filtering through the jungle canopy overhead seemed to flicker through his vision as he passed from shadow into the shafts of daylight and out again. He had long ago become accustomed to the sensation, however, and his eyes adjusted rapidly regardless of the ambience around him. The vine and leaf covered earth beneath him was slick with moisture, but his footing remained sure throughout, every step calculated, modified, and placed in the briefest of moments, as taught for many years. As he maintained the sprint, feeling his own perspiration sliding around his pronounced brow and away from his eyes, he vaulted a fallen tree, using both legs to spring off an upright trunk before him into a tucked roll. His momentum carried him immediately back into a full pace run and he glanced to both sides quickly for signs of any danger. Even knowing that this was a practise, an exercise repeated each and every day, he never allowed complacency to filter in. As the trees began to thin, the sporadic tufts of Kennoff Grass began to condense, and the man-high shafts waved in the breeze around him. His speed was enough to make each strand a pencil-thick whip against his body, but he knew from experience that it could not penetrate his tough skin; they were more of an annoyance. Narrowing his eyes to slits, ensuring none of the plant-life accidentally injured those vulnerable organs, he increased pace, pushing himself to the limits of his endurance. Suddenly, a kaleidoscope of green and gold butterflies burst into the air from the grass ahead of him, startled by his approach. Unwilling to barrel into the frightened insects, he darted right, feeling the enormous pressure in his ankles at altering course whilst at such high speed. Driving himself on through decreasingly tall flora, he abruptly pulled up short as an unexpected sight greeted him.

At the edge of the field, the green-brown turf petered away to reveal sand. He stood still, panting and pouring with sweat as he tried to make sense of the scene. This was no new place; he had explored every inch of their land but the Course of Moirai was the area he knew better than any other. The sand should not be there; could not be there. The only similar substance lined the mountain salt-pools in the Alpinit Range, many miles from here. Carefully, he picked his way forward and stopped at the edge of the recognised grass, crouching and reaching out the tip of one finger to touch the sand. Giving way beneath the contact, the grains moved easily about his appendage, feeling warm, light and slightly damp. Recoiling, he realised that this was no dream or vision, the landscape he had always known was inexplicably different. He looked to the Boundary, the shimmering, cloud-like wall that protected them and sustained all things, estimating the distance between him and it to be about three feet. A thought entered his mind, and he shook his head to clear it; there was no way, surely? Only a foolish child could conceive that maybe the Boundary had moved?

'Mazt Kae-Taqar!' a voice called out sternly from behind him.

Turning sharply in surprise, realising he must be very confused by these events to have allowed another to approach undetected, he collapsed to his knees, placing his hands one atop the other on the ground before him, with elbows straight out to the side, before dropping his forehead to his knuckles. 'High Augur,' he replied into the ground, not raising his head, 'forgive my distraction, it is my failing and I will repent upon return to Dawnrise.'

'First you will tell me what you now understand,' the elderly man continued.

Mazt slowly returned to his feet, keeping his head bowed until fully upright as was the proper demonstration of respect. He regarded the newcomer anxiously; it was rare to meet any of the Elders, let alone the High Augur. The old man was shorter by at least two heads, but that was mainly due to his own uncommonly large size, standing at over seven feet. He shared the dark leathery skin common to their people, each ecru panel of skin folding against the others almost like the scales of a lizard, but these were beginning to fade, a sure sign of advanced age. Once broad shoulders had now begun to sag forward slightly but there was no doubt the Augur had once been a capable Guardian; his mere presence would be enough to hold back all but the most dangerous of foes, Mazt was certain. Perhaps his awe had allowed for silence to extend too long, for the venerate gestured towards the Boundary.

'High Augur, I have been to this place many times, studied and learned every inch of the Course of Moirai, but now I have found something new.'

'Indeed. Sand, is it not?'

Mazt was stunned at the matter-of-fact response, could this be some kind of test within his training? 'It is. Between here and the Boundary. The soil beneath the Kennoff Grass is fertile and lush, a dark brown, almost black in colour, so it cannot be crop desolation that has revealed this sand.'

'You are accurate in your understanding. What more?'

'It is a narrow strip of land, only three feet wide, perhaps forty long. It may be that it covers only a thin layer of the surface, obscuring the normal soil beneath.'

'Explain why this may be.'

Mazt wracked his brain for an answer but nothing seemed to make sense, 'This could be the work of my competitors, to trick and confuse me.'

'Consider further.'

'But I was here yesterday, even if they had collected sand from the mountains beforehand, there have been only thirteen hours since I last passed this point; too short a space of time to achieve such a feat.'

'Your understanding is astute. What more? What answer is it that you do not wish to confess to me?'

Mazt began to panic, the High Augur led the choosing of the Guardians, there was no way he could lie to him; but his own thoughts suggested madness and were certain to alter the man's opinion against him. He dropped his gaze but knew that he must be honest, 'I... I fear the Boundary itself has moved and this is new land that was previously beyond our reach.'

The High Augur remained silent for a few moments and then gently raised Mazt's head with gnarled fingers until their eyes met. 'Your understanding serves you well.'

Mazt's mind exploded with thoughts and terrors beyond his ability to comprehend, 'But, High Augur!' he stammered, 'That is impossible! Is this not the catastrophe that we live to prevent? Has something befallen the Rondure?' He realised he was babbling and dropped to one knee, bowing his head again.

The High Augur placed a hand on the top of his head, 'Be soothed, Mazt Kae-Taqar. You are to return to your preceptor and discuss the matter with him. But maintain your convictions; you believed the Boundary had moved and this is true, your insight is powerful and will serve you well.'

Mazt played the words over in his head throughout his journey back to Dawnrise. If the Boundary had moved, then all he had known was being overturned; yet the High Augur, leader and advisor of their people, seemed almost unconcerned. Could the power of the Rondure be failing? What would that mean for them? As part of the next quartet of guardians, what remit would they now follow? And if the Boundary was moving, how far would it go and what threats might it reveal?

Arriving at the garrison house, he pushed the heavy log door open with minimal effort and stepped across the threshold, finding all four preceptors and his three fellow trainee Guardians already present. With each student kneeling before their respective instructor, only one man remained alone.

'Mazt Kae-Taqar, take posture,' his own preceptor called out, waving towards the empty space before him, 'we have been waiting for you.'

Obediently, he pulled the door closed behind him and assumed the kneeling position before his trainer, casting a sideways glance at his peers. Diast, Atae and Keris knelt silently facing their masters, maintaining the discipline educated into them over years of routine. Each was skilled as he was, but with particular strengths aside from his own; this was part of the selection of a cohort, matching complementary skills and abilities to ensure the four were the most powerful whole they could be. Placing his hand on his thighs, Mazt relaxed his shoulders and waited silently for further guidance.

'Disciples, you have spent fourteen years gaining and honing the skills required to become Guardians,' it was Atae's preceptor that spoke, taking lead over the gathering as was customary, 'and I do not fear accusations of bias when I determine that you have the most potential of any current cohort; mayhaps more potential than I have ever seen. The time for your final selection approaches swiftly and I am confident that you will take your places as the new Guardians.'

Mazt felt his heart swell with pride at the words; all the hard work, sacrifice and total commitment would be worth it if he could serve his people in this most essential of duties. He kept an impassive expression, knowing his own preceptor would be studying his reactions for any breach of concentration.

'However, for you, this tradition will not follow the course of previous generations. For you, the preparation and necessity will be more important than ever before. Some of you may already have understanding,' he looked meaningfully at Mazt, 'but all potential Guardians are being given this enlightenment today as guided by the Elders.'

He allowed the preamble to sink in to the four novice warriors, giving them time to absorb the unique situation they found themselves in, to understand the magnitude that such an announcement given in this manner indicated. He took a deep breath, indicating a slight reticence to deliver the next part of his message; even such a tiny sign of uncertainty was more than Mazt had ever seen from any preceptor.

'Today, seven hours ago, the Rondure awakened.' Mazt heard the restrained gasp from Diast and he could not prevent himself turning in shock to look directly at the preceptor, gauging the man to see if these words were just another test. There was no sign of deception, rather the faintest trace of fear. A hand struck the side of his neck and he knew his own mentor had taken umbrage to his movement. Immediately he returned to his neutral posture and awaited more clarity.

'As your scholarly studies have taught you, the Rondure will do this only when a great threat presents itself and the Guardians will be called upon to act. There is all likelihood you will be those Guardians, but I cannot tell you what the requirement of you will be; none can, for such an occurrence has never been known in spoken history. But, when the awakening occurred, the Boundary itself was affected. Movement has been discovered, outward movement, revealing areas of land we have never seen before. Currently trackers are investigating all of these to bring back understanding of what they mean or any indications of the threat to come. All preceptors have been summoned to the Great Shrine at mid-sun, so we will be unavailable to guide you for the remainder of the day. You will undergo training practise led by Mazt and return here for further understanding at sun-fall. Express any misunderstanding.'

Mazt felt greater pride at being assigned the responsibility of training his peers but could barely believe what was being said regarding the Rondure, let alone come up with questions. It seemed his cohort were similarly perplexed as all remained silent and motionless until the four preceptors left the room.

Regaining their feet, the four would-be Guardians regarded each other in silence for a few moments until Diast could resist no longer. 'The Boundary has moved? Can this be true?'

'It is the truth,' Mazt confirmed, 'I have seen it.'

'And what did it reveal to you?' Keris questioned. The only female in their cohort, she was half the bulk of the other three, but her speed and agility compensated for reduced strength.

'Only sand. But not like that in the mountains. Paler, finer; like sugar but a light tan in colour.'

'And what do you think it means?' Atae joined in. He suffered a rare skin condition that made his flesh much paler than most, and Mazt realised it was almost the same hue as the sand he had discovered.

'I do not know. A warning perhaps? Or an attempt to breach the Boundary from beyond? I understand too little to be certain. What I can reveal is that I met the High Augur there.'

'You mock us, Mazt,' Diast countered with a half-smile, 'the High Augur does not leave the Great Shrine! And if he did, it would not be to consort with the likes of us!'

'Forgive me, Diast, but my words hold truth,' Mazt said with sincerity, meeting his ally's gaze, 'the High Augur questioned my understanding when I found the Boundary moved. He did not speak from fear or concern, therefore we must continue to prepare as normal. I believe this is a good omen, that we will be the guardians called upon to protect our people and deliver glory as our ancestors could only have dreamed of.'

Another silence followed as his three companions realised he was neither exaggerating nor jesting with them. Recognising that this was the first time they were all looking to him for leadership, he placed his fists on his hips and smiled. 'Free your minds of concern. We are ready for any challenge presented to us; you heard the preceptor's words. Now, take on refreshment as we will train hard until returning here tonight; for expending the strength of our bodies will allow our minds complete focus. Then we will understand more deeply what this means, and we will use that knowledge to ensure we are the chosen cohort. Are we agreed?'

'We are agreed,' they replied in unison.

The left wheel of the hand-drawn cart jammed in a rut of the cold earth floor for what seemed like the hundredth time. Terex released an exasperated breath as he hauled against the leather harness that distributed the weight evenly across his body, feeling the wheel overcome the obstacle and return to free rotation. He could barely believe they were still resorting to dragging these carts through the hidden passages after all this time, but he would take no chances at discovery. It amazed him to think the tunnels were created organically, by some giant worm creature years before, and had been used by their enemies to access the Black Citadel unnoticed. Now it allowed the remaining loyal to traverse beyond the Dussen border unseen, retrieving supplies from other lands. Despite the necessity, there was no denying it was back-breaking work.

Up ahead he could see dim light and knew he was not far from his chosen exit; the opening was closest to the cobbled entrance road into the fortress, meaning less difficult manoeuvring of his heavy wares. He stopped just prior to leaving the shelter of the tunnel, taking a well-earned break. Unstrapping himself and recovering a canteen from the top of the cart, he sat down to take a few long sips. As he rested, looking out at the dark barren land beyond, he considered the stark comparison between this end of the passage and the one he had travelled from; the Lustanian entrance was thick and often blocked by thriving foliage, opening into a vibrant forest which, in turn, spilled out into lush rolling fields. He wondered if it was some remnant magic that kept the earth around the Citadel devoid of life or if nature was just too afraid to return. At least he and his men got to experience other environments, to take respite from the constant cold and dull light, to feel the sun or bathe in fresh water. The river that still ran near the fortress was oily and slightly viscous, the air of stagnation always upon it. But no matter how often he had debated, how persuasive his arguments, the Lady Fimarr refused to leave the isolation, rarely stepping beyond the walls of the Citadel itself, let alone outside the black land around it.

But his real sympathy fell to Kastani, the little girl was not permitted to stray far from the fortress gates and Terex believed she should experience more of the world. Still sweet, open and innocent, she was a vast contrast to the place in which she lived. He knew she secretly wanted to accompany him on one of his runs, had seen the wonder in her eyes whenever he brought her new gifts. And he had brought her some amazing trinkets; toys of all kinds, costume jewellery, ornate brushes and combs, dresses and shoes, even books. Her mother permitted all of these things but prohibited any positive talk of the outside world. He was certain the time would come when Kastani would sneak away against her wishes and he feared for the outcome when that day came; for now, she was too young to question her lifestyle and had no other to compare it to.

Reaching back into the cart he located the most recent gift he had brought her, a bright bonnet of pink and scarlet, white ribbon forming a chin strap to secure the headwear and several small glass orbs affixed in the shape of a giant raspberry on one side. It had cost him more than it was probably worth, but he could not resist an opportunity to gain her gratitude. He could not quite explain why he felt so strongly about the child; she was not his by birth, although he had helped the Lady Fimarr to deliver her, and he had spent his former years training to be a military leader, not a nursemaid. But when Kastani looked upon him with naïve, beautiful eyes of piercing blue, it brought meaning and purpose to his life. He would do anything to ensure the young girl had some chance of a normal future, of choosing a path rather than being forced along one; he also knew this would one day bring him into opposition with his current mistress. And that would not end well for him.

Returning bonnet and canteen, he re-harnessed himself and made the rest of the journey to the Citadel doors without incident. Releasing the load again, he was surprised when the large portal remained sealed; usually whoever was on watch would open them as soon as they spotted a supply run heading past the outer gates. Banging on the door hard several times, he waited longer, anxiety beginning to gnaw at his stomach. He counted in his head; it would take the guard no longer than eighty seconds to get from the vantage room down to the door, even at a bored meander. Reaching one hundred and twenty, Terex rooted through his cart of goods and withdrew his small Warhammer; light enough to be wielded one-handed, heavy enough to crack the thickest skull. Concern building within him, he raced swiftly to the small side door. This entrance was almost obscured from view by fallen masonry and he scooped up a thin piece of slate as he arrived. They kept this door wedged from the other side should any prying eyes locate it; only his own people knew to push the wedge free from this side first. Clear of the obstruction, he controlled his panic and took care to replace the wedge and re-secure the door behind him; there was every chance the guard could be taking a piss-break, or had fallen asleep, or some other complacency had occurred.

Rushing to the vantage room, he threw open the door and his heart leapt into his mouth at the sight; the guard, Foleck, lay dead with a needle-dart lodged in his left eyeball and his throat cut cleanly from ear-to-ear. His weapon was still sheathed. The old planks that usually kept the sentry window narrow and hidden from external view, lay scattered about the room; somebody had gotten inside. His pace increased as he took off through the maze of corridors, passing three more bodies but taking no time to check if they still lived. As he neared Lady Fimarr's chambers, he discovered his closest comrade, Narem slumped against the wall. The sounds of combat dully echoed from a room ahead, but this time Terex could not ignore the fallen warrior.

'Narem!' he hissed, sliding to a knee before the other man. His clothes were soaked with blood, but any wounds were not obvious.

'T-Terex,' his ally whispered weakly, trails of bloody spittle drooling from his mouth, 'Too fast, d-did not even see it coming… here for the mistress, you must…'

Terex shook the man to keep him conscious, to find out who their adversary was, but it was too late; Narem was dead. For a moment, he remained locked in his own thoughts before bolting back to his feet and sprinting past the door from which the noises were coming. In the chamber beyond, he arrowed to the far wall and lifted the prize he wanted; the uniquely carved, perfectly balanced, two-handed axe. It had once belonged to the mighty warrior Rork Fimarr before being responsible for the death of Terex's previous master, Ramikain. If any weapon could fell whoever had assaulted them, this was it. Returning to his mistress' chamber, he kicked the wooden door free of its hinges and surged forward, diving into a precautionary roll as he entered. The distinctive chink of metal on stone indicated his decision had been a good one, as whatever weapons had been launched in his direction collided with the wall beyond him.

Gracefully gaining his feet, Terex hefted the weapon before him and assessed the scene. Four more of his people lay dead around the room, that meant all the defenders who had stayed loyal following the fall of Ramikain were now slain. Lady Fimarr was slumped in the grip of her attacker, but she looked unharmed and seemed to be breathing, although unconscious. Her aggressor was a woman dressed all in black; knee-high boots, leggings, pouch-filled belt, leather Basque, shoulder-high gloves, hooded cloak and a mask that obscured the lower half of her face. Crimson hair could be seen beneath the hood and the minimal amount of flesh on show bore scars from some long-ago fiery injury. There was no mistaking Silver Rain, and Terex had spent long enough with his mistress to know the assassin was her very own sister.

'What are you doing here? If you have hurt the mistress…'

'You are fortunate that my reflexes are slower now; you should already be dead.'

'It is you who shall perish this day, assassin, by your own father's weapon.'

The remark seemed to catch her off guard and she took more interest in the axe he carried. As realisation and surprise dawned in her eyes, Terex leapt forward, swinging the heavy weapon in a sweeping arc before him. Silver Rain was faster than he, dropping her victim and back-flipping out of reach before loosing a throwing blade from her belt. Finding purchase in his shoulder, the sharp pain threw him off balance and he staggered against the large vanity table. Using the momentum of his fall, he allowed the axe-head to slide underneath him and kicked hard with his foot, spinning the weapon back up behind him. This his foe did not anticipate, and he felt contact before whipping his head around to see the woman skipping back out of reach.

'Well played, warrior!' she remarked with genuine respect, lifting her left arm to reveal the slight nick he had caused. 'There are not many who can claim a successful strike on me.'

'It will not be the last! I give you one chance to leave now and avoid my fury!'

'You are loyal, I will admit that, but you are woefully outmatched. I have already killed your allies. Alissa is drugged and cannot aid you. I am the better fighter and your life ends here.'

'Why tell me? Why not kill me already if you are so confident?' He spat the words in anger but again spotted uncertainty in her eyes. Tensing to drive forth with another attack, he stopped instantly as Kastani rushed out towards him from behind the bed.

'Terex!' she cried, sweet voice laced with terror, 'She hurt ever'body! She is going to hurt me!'

Terex dropped the axe to his side and scooped the girl into his arms, turning as he stooped to shield her with his own body.

'You have a child? Here?' the assassin's voice rang out behind him.

'No,' he replied quietly, resigned now to a fate he could not avoid, 'She is your sister's daughter. But I will die to protect her. Take Lady Fimarr if you must, kill me as you will but leave Kastani unharmed.' The little girl felt tiny and fragile in his arms and her sobbing was more than he could bear.

'Alissa?' the quavering voice of his opponent replied, 'Alissa had a child? I do not believe it. Know this, Terex, I did not know my sister still lived until this very day. I would never have dreamed that she had a child. I feel much of this is a result of the security you have provided them both. For that you should receive gratitude.'

His shoulders sagged slightly as he realised the woman was struggling with inner turmoil. Perhaps he still had a chance to get through to her or distract her long enough to land a killing blow. 'Yes,' he replied without looking up from where he held the trembling girl, 'I love them both in my own way and I would do anything for them.'

'I believe you would,' she whispered in his ear, having somehow closed the gap completely silently. A sharp pain lanced into his neck and his vision began to blur. As he felt the strength drain from his limbs, he could only mumble a few words.

'I am sorry, Kastani…'

Chapter 3

The parlour was warm and pleasant, the small fire providing both heat and light enough to fill the space. Seven chairs were staggered around the room and five were now occupied; the opportunity to relax was most welcome after their long ride and the raucous greeting they had received. The level of excitement their arrival had generated still took her somewhat by surprise; her actions, alongside Herc, had resulted in the liberation of many children now living in Hercatalana, but the success of the community was all down to their own efforts. She had believed the pedestal they had placed her upon back then would have diminished over the years, but apparently not. To her side, Herc sat upright, hands clasped on his knees and arms locked straight; he never seemed to look comfortable in social gatherings, certainly not those indoor anyway. But the joy in him when they went hunting together or gathered roots and fungi in the foothills near Rennicksburg, reminded her of a child. She reached across and squeezed his wrist gently in reassurance and he returned an acknowledging smile through his bushy beard.

'Elderflower tea?' a quiet voice spoke to her. She turned back to see the young girl, Heletha, holding a teapot in cloth-bound hands to protect her from the heat. Catalana nodded and smiled, holding out the small cup she had been provided when entering the house earlier. The hot yellow water steamed gently as it poured, and the sweet earthy aroma was pleasant to the nose. Cautious of dropping the cup, she removed her elbow-length silk gloves and became immediately aware of Heletha staring at her disfigured left hand. Self-consciously, Catalana moved her drink to obscure the stumps of her two missing fingers.

'Heletha?' she coaxed kindly, 'Perhaps the others may also be thirsty?'

The girl appeared instantly flustered and side-stepped towards Herc who held up one hand in refusal. He caught Catalana's eye again and she smiled to assure him she was neither embarrassed nor offended by the natural curiosity. Soon drinks had been served and the five adults were left in privacy. Having spent three days in conversation with Treya and Straker, their personal and trivial matters had been fully discussed; that left the fifth member of the group, Czerna. The young woman was another refugee of the Black Citadel and instrumental in coordinating the construction of this tribute town, a haven for the survivors of that awful nightmare and the returning Dussen people displaced during the crisis. Despite her tender years, she had become part of the council and a spokesperson for most foreign negotiations. The house in which they sat was hers and she had opened it to home several of her fellow orphans, Heletha amongst them.

'Thank-you for the welcome,' Catalana enthused with a genuine smile, 'we never receive such celebration when we return home, I can tell you!'

'It is always such a great joy to see you, all of you,' Czerna replied, 'you are reminders of what we have survived. You are our saviours, and these people will never forget that; our fate without your intervention would have been short and brutal. No modesty can ever hide that; and you bear the scars of those efforts.'

She leaned forward and held Catalana's injured hand in both of hers before raising it to her lips and kissing softly. It continued to amaze her at the level of maturity Czerna displayed, showing insight well beyond her age and finding humility and diplomacy in abundance.

'You owe us nothing, Czerna,' she replied, withdrawing her hand, 'the success of Hercatalana is your own and we are simply thankful to have been able to free you all from that dark place. These are lighter times, and we are so pleased to be here again; it never seems to be often enough.'

'No, and you would be most welcome every day, but I understand that you have lives in Rennicksburg and have told me many times that you want to erase that period from your minds.'

'Though, of course, we regret nothing and would not change our actions,' Treya added quickly, not noticing Catalana looking down in shame, 'but sadly it is because of those very events that we have come.'

'Don't hold back, love,' Straker commented, 'we shouldn't waste any time on social graces, should we?'

Treya slapped his arm and Czerna smiled broadly, 'It is fine, I expected such a surprise visit to have been forced upon you rather than planned. Only something of concern would initiate such a hasty journey. Please, confide in me what you must.'

'We were visited recently by a stranger,' the older Fimarr continued, 'he asked many questions about the fall of Ramikain, the Black Citadel, the events and journey surrounding them. His questions were prying and focussed on details that none had questioned before. He stated it was for an honest retelling of that saga, but I did not believe him; something about his manner was untrustworthy and I think there is more to it than that.'

'Quite; we must always judge a book by its cover...' Another slap followed Straker's latest flippancy.

'Actually, Straker Forge, I think I agree with Treya,' Czerna said slowly, 'A man came here some weeks ago, but we provided little to him and he was soon on his way. I feel it may be the same scholar of whom you speak. He made me uneasy and those of us who have any memory of our time in the Citadel were reluctant to share with him.'

'That is good to hear,' Catalana reassured their host, 'do you recall anything of note that could indicate anything about the man?'

'Not really, he was very false in his bearing, condescending in his manner. Like an aristocrat walking amongst peasants. I suppose that is normal for a Lustanian?'

'What!?' Treya blurted out, 'What made you think he was from Lustania?' She looked meaningfully at Forge who elected to remain silent this time.

'He told me. Apparently, his work is sponsored by the Prince. Maybe he felt this would carry more weight with us because of the aid we received from them in the early days.'

'I knew it!' Treya stood with unheralded triumph on her face, 'I knew Lennath could not keep clear of our affairs. Why would he do this, knowing it will antagonise us when he is still not forgiven for his betrayal?'

'A moment, Treya,' Herc spoke for the first time since entering the domicile, 'Czerna, you look perturbed; is there more to this?'

She took a sip of her tea and mulled over her next words for a few moments before answering, 'I... I am not sure. Maybe this is related or maybe simple coincidence, but it seems the Black Citadel has been occupied since your victory there.'

Catalana's breath caught in her chest and she almost dropped her cup. What was the girl saying? The Citadel occupied? But it had crumbled to ruin when they departed; nobody could have survived there. It was impossible. It had to be impossible. She studied the suddenly ashen face of her sister and watched as she began to sway on her feet until Straker eased her back to sitting. It was he who spoke next, 'Please, Czerna, tell us all you know.'

Smiling apologetically, she explained with the reluctance of a scolded child, 'It was a few weeks ago now; Wardin, Heletha's brother, began having nightmares that would rouse him from sleep. After a few days of asking, he revealed that he had seen a ghost; at least, so he described it. For fear of reprisal, the pair had kept their visit to the Black Citadel a secret; it is out of bounds to all as you know. They spouted a story of another little girl there and then a ghost that attacked them. We just didn't know what to believe, and his terror seemed genuine enough, so I petitioned the rest of the council and they allowed me to travel there with an armed escort.'

Czerna stood and began to pace the room, the retelling generating some restlessness within her, 'When we got there it looked undisturbed until we passed beyond the outer gates; that was when we found a cart loaded with provisions, much of it still fresh. After some searching, we spotted a window that must have been boarded up previously but was now exposed. We managed to get inside, and it was clear the boards had been broken from the outside as they lay within the chamber beyond, along with the body of a soldier.' She paused for a moment, words catching in her throat making Catalana wonder if this was the first time Czerna had witnessed death directly. 'There were more bodies, we found them as we explored that place, but I could tolerate no more than a few hours inside; the memories were too awful.'

Catalana stood and pulled the younger woman into a warm embrace, 'Shh,' she whispered to her, 'You did more than any could have expected of you. Such a trial must have left you very shaken; you do not need to go on, we can investigate further ourselves.'

'No!' she cried unexpectedly, 'You must not go there! I would not wish that experience on anyone, let alone those I cherish so dearly. I tell you now, there was no little girl and no ghost. The bodies we found were fresh and their attire was similar enough for me to believe they were former followers of Ramikain. It looked like they were well-established there, maybe since the very day of the sorcerer's demise, but I found no indication of their purpose. You do not need to go there.'

Herc now stood and took Czerna by the shoulders, holding her gaze evenly, 'And what else? What is it you are avoiding telling us?'

Her eyes shone with unspent tears and her lower lip trembled, 'There may have been one,' she whimpered.

'One what?' Treya asked the question that the others could not bear to.

'Girl.' Czerna released, a weight visibly shifting from her as she did so, 'We found dolls and wooden toys, small clothes and apparel suggesting a young child. But there was more, a whole room decorated as for a princess with adult garments and even a vanity table; it was like a duchess' room had somehow been transported into that foul place.'

Catalana could not speak, her mind reeled with thoughts and memories as she knew what this must mean. Looking at Herc, she was amazed at his cool composure seeing as their worst nightmare was coming true. Alissa, left in the Citadel for dead five years ago had somehow survived and lived on, abandoned by her sisters. How must she have felt? What did she now think of Catalana? She and Herc had been the last to see the youngest Fimarr sister, blood-soaked and driven to pure madness; it seemed impossible that she could have lived on. But now it seemed she was no longer just the victim of abandonment by her sister, Rayne, she was also the perpetrator of the same heinous act to Alissa. She flicked her eyes to Treya, wondering if her eldest sister was about to figure out what had happened.

'Women's clothing?' she clarified with Czerna, receiving a nod of affirmation, 'So these men had a woman living with them and a small child? Well, it seems clear what this means.' Her eyes fixed on Catalana. 'They must have held a woman prisoner against her will, perhaps with the intention of child-bearing for them. Did you find any female bodies?'

'N-no. Just the men. No signs of woman or child.'

'Then they had already fled or may have been saved by some other party. Perhaps the same people who killed the other occupants.'

'Perhaps,' Czerna offered, clearly unconvinced, 'so what will you do?'

'I believe we need to dig out the root of this matter. We must confer with Lennath in Lustania and demand answers.'

Catalana wanted to protest but Herc beat her to it, 'Treya, we cannot ignore what has happened at the Citadel. I do not believe this to be coincidence where the events in Rennicksburg are not. Even if they are, it may be that a woman and child lie in the clutches of some dangerous group of brigands or mercenaries, suffering who-knows-what fate. We must investigate the fortress and attempt to track the raiders.' Catalana dreaded to think who they might find if following her companion's plan, but she would not be able to live with herself if they did not try.

'Three days ago, you said you would follow my ridiculous ideas. I expect you to honour that.' When it was clear she had unsettled the big woodsman, Treya continued, 'Listen, I understand your point and agree, this is unlikely to be a coincidence. Therefore, this is even more reason to go to the Prince; if he knows about the writer, he probably knows if the madness is resurfacing among his people. It indicates he would also know about any purchased raid to save a captive in the Citadel; he may even have raised a contract himself, for Yanis' sake!'

Czerna winced at the blasphemy and Catalana remembered that the girl had developed a much stronger religious belief in the wake of her captivity. Stepping forward, she placed her hands on Herc's powerful forearm where it was folded defiantly across his chest. He instinctively bent forward, and she kissed his cheek.

'I hear both of your arguments, but I must side with my sister in this instance. Lennath is more likely to have all, or at least some, of the answers we seek. If brigands have taken a woman from the Citadel, then she is probably not much longer for this world,' she repressed a shudder at the memory of her own such experience, 'if it were mercenaries then such a contract would be known across the Five Kingdoms. If Lennath does not already know about it, then he may be able to find out for us. It is the very least he can do to make up for his previous indiscretions. This way we can also find out about his suddenly reinvigorated interest in our encounter with Ramikain; it could even be that he wants to have himself painted in a more positive light within that tale.'

'Ha!' Straker laughed aloud, 'The only way that man could appear more positive is if the world went blind!'

Catalana could not hide her smirk at the comment but turned her attention to Czerna, 'But, my dear friend, I cannot allow you to think we are here only to harass you with questions and desert you once again. We will discuss lighter news this evening and maybe you have somewhere we can all rest tonight?'

'Of course,' Czerna smiled, 'you will be my guests here.'

'Agreed,' Treya confirmed, 'But it would be appreciated if some of your people keep watch over the Citadel until you hear from us again? Just in case…'

Shallow movements of the chest indicated that her prisoner was still breathing. Rayne stared down at her sister pensively; could this really be the same young girl who had embraced her so warmly after years of separation? Whose bright determination and positive nature had convinced her to band with her in the pursuit of Ramikain five years ago? She checked herself quickly; the same sister who had displayed possessive rage over a man she had just met, who had murdered an unsuspecting ally, whose gradual plunge into madness had helped them all assume her demise long ago. The blood-stained white robes covered her slender frame from neckline to ankle, like some charnel bride-to-be, and Rayne could not keep her eyes off the thin scars ritualistically carved into the formerly perfect complexion. Each symbol seemed to have been painstakingly carved with an instrument of medical precision, leaving the markings slightly raised and white but completely clear to decipher, if only she had any idea of their meaning. Tracing one of the symbols lightly with her finger, her hand brushed against the matted hair; once beautiful, long and golden, it was now a tangled mess, hacked short and crusted with congealed gore.

A muffled sob attracted her attention to the other occupant of the room. She had kept the child gagged and obscured her awareness with a burlap sack over the head. Oddly, the girl had remained reasonably calm throughout the journey back to Lustania, tolerating the feeding and watering schedule Rayne enforced without attempting to remove the hood and never crying out when the gag was released. Was it possible that this really was Alissa's offspring? A niece Rayne had neither considered nor wanted? She turned her back on the table where her sister lay and assessed the small dim chamber she had been guided to but tactical planning against any potential ambush was unachievable amidst everything else clouding her mind. Reticence had allowed her to believe stories over proven truth, accepting that Alissa had died instead of investigating it herself. No, not reticence; guilt. She had wanted no reason to engage with her kin again; had she found Alissa alive, she would have to inform the others, would have to look Catalana in the eye after abandoning her to almost certain death. And now she found her youngest sibling alive, and with a daughter, but had still not returned to let her family know of this news. Instead, she was fulfilling her assigned contract and was about to abandon her newly found kin in favour of wealth. Again.

Echoing footsteps approached along stone corridors lined with no carpets or finery, this was definitely not the public face of the palace, and she selected a position with her back to a solid wall, one door off to her right within ten paces, the other directly in front of her. As the sounds grew louder, she unclipped the retention strap on the curved dagger at her back and dropped two throwing knives into her left palm, just as a precaution. The larger door swung open and four armoured guards entered, followed closely by Prince Lennath himself who pulled the exit ajar behind himself; she could have sworn there were six sets of feet but perhaps the echoes had confused her.

'Silver Rain!' the Prince gushed, 'You have returned in timelier a fashion than I ever imagined! And it would appear you have proven me correct; Alissa Fimarr still lives.'

'Yes,' she conceded evenly, aware that the soldiers had flanked her, one now blocking her escape route, 'your insights regarding her survival were true. Now, explain to me how she will aid in destroying these beasts you spoke of.'

'First, tell me that she is well. Drugged I assume? What have you used so that we may safely revive her? Then we can complete payment and send you on your way.'

Rayne gauged him closely, recognising his dismissive deflection of her question, 'The drug is made for me. I believe the main ingredients are Nightshade and Dara Root. You did not answer my question.'

'Did I not? How foolish of me. Do you have the sceptre with you? Did you immerse it in the pool? Let us not delay, provide the item and this payment is yours.' He withdrew a large satchel from his waist and tossed it to the floor beside the table on which Alissa lay. The noise must have startled her own prisoner, as the child released a gasp. 'What is this?' Lennath peered into the gloom and spotted the cowering form, 'Why have you brought a second prisoner? I expected everyone at the Citadel killed.'

'She is of no concern to you,' Rayne snapped quickly, moving between him and the girl whilst producing the sceptre he had requested, 'this is what you require. I dipped it in the foul pond you spoke of and it did nothing. Regardless, it is yours as agreed.'

Accepting the device from her, the Prince hefted it aloft and took time marvelling over its appearance, despite the fact it had not changed since he had last seen it. 'So, it is done. You have brought me both artifact and wielder and your payment is before you; but it is you who has now avoided my question. Who is the child?'

Rayne shifted her stance for greater balance and shuffled the hilts of her throwing blades between her fingers, 'Not part of the deal and not your concern. She will leave with me. Now, my question, how do you intend for Alissa to destroy the monsters roaming your land?'

Lennath paused, a crocodile smile on his lips, eyes flicking to the soldiers on his left and back again. 'Destroy? I don't recall saying anything about destroying,' she noticed him backing away slowly as he spoke, 'the sceptre now holds the power responsible for creating those ghastly mutants, your sister is attuned to that power and I will use her to bring them under my control.'

'So, I was right all along? This is just a power-grab to usurp your father?'

'My father? No! The entire Five Kingdoms! With these beasts at my beck and call they would not dare to challenge my right.'

'Still the little man, despite the size you've achieved! Do not concern yourself, I have no interest in your aspirations or how you achieve them. Our contract is done. Take your prizes and I will depart with mine.'

'That sounds ideal!' he exclaimed, nodding to the other two guards who moved towards Alissa, 'But I will need the little girl as well; I fail to believe she is insignificant in all of this.'

The soldiers to her left sprang forward and she swept out her arm, releasing the deadly knives she held. The first sliced the exposed neck of one man, dropping him to the ground with his hand clutched to the wound, desperately trying to contain the arterial bleed. The second passed cleanly into the open mouth of the other soldier, puncturing the soft palette before protruding from the rear of his neck; his death was instant. Spinning around, she slipped the curved dagger from its sheath and cartwheeled into a downwards kick, striking Lennath on the chin. Whilst dazed, she slipped her free arm under his, forcing him into an armbar restraint, and kicked his right knee out from under him. Dropping in front of her, she pressed her blade against his throat and pushed one leg around his, removing any leverage for him to throw her off. Looking up at the remaining guards, she saw a sword tip pressed against Alissa's gently heaving chest and a short blade pushed to her temple.

'Stand-off?' Lennath mumbled through bloodied lips.

'Do you really believe that?' she hissed, 'I could kill you all in seconds.'

'But would you accept the death of your sister?'

'I brought her to you for money, why do you think I would care?'

'Like I told you before,' he spat smugly, 'I know all about seeking redemption.'

'And is this yours?' she asked, pressing the blade closer to his flesh, re-opening the cut she had inflicted during their previous encounter, 'A second betrayal to compound the first? Or are you trying to remove us completely to satiate your guilt?'

'Honestly? I could not care less about the Fimarr sisters! I just want Alissa; I am assuming from our current position that the child is hers, which will provide me the leverage I need. Your only choice is surrender.'

Rayne frantically ran through her options. She could definitely end all three men rapidly, but her own defensive posture meant precious seconds lost disentangling herself from the Lustanian Prince after slitting his throat. Even at her best, she doubted there was enough time to kill the two soldiers before one of them executed Alissa. Until a few days ago, she had believed her to be dead already; what difference did it make if that happened here instead? At least that way she could save the girl.

'Are you actually considering it? After your betrayal of Catalana?' her breath caught at his direct pronouncement of her guilt, 'Yes, Rayne Fimarr, I know all about your choice to sacrifice your own sister, and the retribution you suffered in the fire. It did not cleanse the remorse from you, though, did it? I do not believe you will make that same decision again.'

Blood was flowing freely from his neck and she could feel his pulse quickening. 'You know nothing about me!' she snapped, assessing which of the soldiers was more likely to hesitate in murdering the unconscious woman on the table when Rayne cut their regent's throat.

Suddenly the main door pushed wide, and a figure glided into the room. He was tall and lithe, body seeming completely relaxed amid the swathes of robes he wore. The only breaks in colour were his crimson gloves and the tan flesh around his eyes. Although his lower face was covered with thin black scarves, she knew he sported a long beard and thick moustache; most likely now grey in colour. He was Sergience Mozak; he was the Master Assassin who had trained her. Stabbing fear filled her belly as it never had before, and she felt her grip on her captive loosen.

'I believe you have met my colleague?' Lennath goaded, 'As head of the Veer Assassins, he is even more highly recommended than you.'

'I... I do not,' she began breathlessly, 'What are you doing here, Master Mozak? Why are the Veer this far East?'

'They were already here,' the rolling voice replied, every syllable taking her back to the harshest trials she had ever undergone, 'you are responsible for the spread of our influence into these lands. Did you think we would never investigate your undertakings?'

'Of course. But here, now, with him?'

'Keep disdain from your voice, novice,' the heavily accented voice boomed, 'I follow our creed. It is you who have bastardised our methods to suit your own purpose. Now choose; do you act or surrender?'

Sweat began to bead on her forehead and she felt uncertainty as never before. Her eyes darted between the opponents facing her and she tried to devise any scenario where she could save Alissa, the girl and herself. Or any of the three. There was none, but Silver Rain was nobody's prisoner. Tensing to tighten her grip again, there was a blur of motion from Mozak and she felt fire across the back of her right hand; looking down, her dagger was already falling to the stone slabs beneath her. She withdrew her flaming limb, dousing the burning fluid on Lennath's shoulder, and moved to break the man's neck instead but her former master was already upon them. He caught her wrist with one hand, twisting fiercely and numbing all sensation. Freeing her leg from Lennath, Rayne tried to spin free, but the grip was unyielding, yanking her back and flipping her over the tall form of Mozak. Managing to get her feet beneath her before she hit the ground, she drove a palm-strike towards her opponent's throat, but his free hand parried the blow with ease as his knee crashed into her chest. Air was driven from her instantly and she fell back awkwardly as he maintained his hold on her throbbing left wrist. Grounded, she crossed her legs over his ankle and tried to leverage him to the floor, knowing it would be futile against his great balance and strength. As she struggled, he dropped his knee down hard into the top of her thigh, paralysing the limb. Gasping for breath, she began to drag herself free of her attacker as he released her useless left arm.

'Well, it would appear you have met your match, Silver Rain,' she heard Lennath's gloating voice behind her, 'now you will know complete failure; failure to complete your contract, failure to protect your family and failure to find redemption.'

'I advise a swift death, she was a fine student in her day,' Mozak spoke flatly, no malice detected in his words.

Rayne tried to inch away from them and regain strength or feeling in her injured limbs; she knew thrown weapons were futile against the superior reactions of the Veer Master Assassin and needed time to generate an alternate strategy. She felt no fear of impending death, just disappointment that she had been overcome so easily.

'I think not,' Lennath continued smoothly, 'I think some mental anguish is the appropriate punishment for breach of agreement; time in our dungeons will provide opportunity for me to repay some of the damage she has caused me recently as well.'

'She will escape,' Mozak countered, 'and likely kill you.'

Lennath released an annoyed sigh, 'That is why you will supervise the required restraints in her cell. And I am happy to continue payment for the duration of her stay here. Understand that she lives only until I am certain the other sister will work for me; if I no longer require her as potential leverage then she will be executed. Agreed?'

'I simply follow what you contract,' Mozak replied impassively, 'while I provide you service, you have nothing to fear.'

'I will kill you both,' Rayne mumbled weakly.

A final blow slammed into the base of her skull and the room went black.

Crystal patted her horse gently on the neck as it carried her along the winding track through the dense trees. She adored the constant warmth that emanated from the animal and how the hair was smooth in one direction yet resistant and bristly in the other. And they were so strong; powerful and fast over even the most difficult terrain, yet docile and passive enough to be trained to serve people. They were truly majestic beasts, and she was pleased her travelling companions had convinced her to use one for this journey. She had to defer to their wisdom; the furthest she had strayed from the village on land was under three miles and the capital was over one hundred. But had they gone by water as she had wanted, she would have been completely at ease; rounding the horn and accessing the city by river added another seventy miles to the journey but she had no doubt it would have been faster. Any skiff could cover water at five or six times the pace of the horses. But her father had been concerned about the thing that had attacked the village still patrolling the offshore shallows and refused the idea.

Her father. His injuries had been significant, and she had not wanted to leave him. But others had suffered worse; twelve men dead, two injured and unlikely to recover, a further five severely mauled. She had no place to consider her situation more traumatic than any of theirs; even if she only had her father, he was alive and would heal eventually. Some families would never be the same again and she could empathise with that, especially having never known her own mother. Maybe it was sympathy, for the pain that was coming to all those who had lost, that drove her to join the warning party; their goal was clear, ensure Prince Porthus heard of the attack. The village leaders believed their Lord would send aid, both to slay the monstrosity and aid their resource losses; Crystal was more concerned that the Kingdom learned about the new threat as soon as possible, to prevent further attacks along the coast or, even worse, upstream.

As a breeze drifted across them, she picked up the scent of something unexpected, acrid, and out of place in the woodland they traversed. Pulling her steed to a halt, she clicked her fingers rapidly, attracting the attention of the three men with her. Placing a finger against her lips, she was pleased that the message got through and they all silently dismounted. The youngest of the travellers, Deenys, was handed all four sets of reins and moved off the track with the horses in tow; the two remaining men obediently followed her lead as she moved softly towards the source of the smell. Brambles scratched at her skin and she considered that her father may have been correct about her attire; he had recommended thick woollen breeches and loose cotton shirt. Instead, she had donned her preferred thick pleat leather skirt, a souvenir of her father's travelling days when he had encountered great warrior women, calf-high riding boots, a figure-hugging sleeveless jerkin and fingerless leather gloves. True enough, her outfit was impractical in the current situation but if she needed to fight, feeling the cord of her hooked line against her flesh was essential for calculating the correct angles to achieve maximum momentum. Her hand idly moved to the line coiled at her hip and she noted her companions easing their own weapons free of sheaths; they too could sense something was amiss.

After proceeding downhill for a short duration, Crystal recognised that they were heading towards the larger supply road to the capital; the road they had opted to avoid. Keeping her eyes and ears alert to any signs of danger, she continued to pursue the increasingly pungent aroma until she spotted something out of place ahead. Raising her hand, they all stopped as one and she pointed out the shape of a man crouching behind a tree. He was clearly concealing himself from anyone on the road, which left him exposed to the direction from which they were approaching. In his hand was a crossbow, and Crystal assumed he must be a bandit. He kept glancing off into the trees beyond her line of sight, so she knew he was not alone, the only questions were how many in his party and what was their target? She turned back to her allies.

'It is an ambush, for certain,' she whispered, squatting down to make best use of the flimsy shrubbery as cover, 'but I cannot see 'ow many zere are.'

'What of it?' Eljan replied abruptly, 'Zis is no business of ours. We 'ave ozer concerns. Our message to ze Prince 'as to get zrough!'

'We cannot just stand by and watch zese men rob or murder some unwitting traveller, Eljan! 'Ow can you suggest it?' her other companion countered.

'Garren, you 'ave no idea 'ow many ozer men are out zere. We may just get ourselves killed, and zen no warning to the capital about zat monster or ze bandits.'

'You 'ave a good point,' Crystal agreed, 'but so does Garren. What if I sneak around ze flank, try to see 'ow many zey are in total? If I zink we can prevail, I will send a signal and you can surprise zem from 'ere when I attack. If zey are too many or zere is no sign of any travellers approaching zis trap, I will return, and we will make all 'aste to ze capital with our warnings.'

After a moment's thought, Eljan nodded, 'Very well, Crystal. But be careful in your approach and remember, neizer one of us is as skilled as you in combat so do not bite off more zan we can chew!'

She smiled and nodded before providing both men a farewell pat on the shoulder. As quickly as she dared, she wound her way carefully past the bandit's position, remaining a good forty feet from him as she cut a route parallel to where she suspected his allies would be lying in wait. The smell she had tracked here got stronger and stronger until she located the source; no more than twenty feet ahead of her, with a clear line of sight to the road, stood what she assumed to be a fire cannon. The device sat on struts and several large buckets stood to the rear of it. Each contained a sodden clump of rags, flora and metal scraps. She remembered her father's sketch book and the stories he told of adventures past; armies used such weapons during fortress sieges to cause internal damage and panic beyond protective walls. She had never encountered one herself and she could not fathom how a group of highway brigands had secured one. The device would hurl the 'ammunition' bundles at a target, igniting it as it left the end of the barrel. The flaming mass would impact on its target, dousing the exterior in flame, whilst the metal would shred outer layers, ensuring total fiery devastation from inside and out. It felt like overkill for travelling riders and would leave little to salvage if used against carts or wagons. Three outlaws were huddled around the weapon, presumably the firing crew, and she had passed a total of four whilst scouting; it was safe to assume there would be at least another two or three she had not seen yet. These were not good odds.

Beginning to shuffle back to a safer distance, keen to avoid being spotted in her departure, Crystal stopped at the sound of horses. Straining her ears, she managed to detect multiple hooves and the unmistakable clattering of a carriage being pulled. Estimating that she would not have returned to the others before the approaching procession fell victim to this brutal attack, an unwelcome choice arose; risk the lives of her own party or abandon unsuspecting travellers to a fiery death. Taking several slow breaths to calm herself, she released her hook and line from the retaining strap on her hip and waited motionless for the opportune moment to strike.

She spotted the lead horses through the trees at the same moment as the ambushers and knew that their attention would be fully focussed on their imminent strike. The approaching carriage was their obvious target, so she maintained her position until one man leaned forward to light the muzzle torch. Leaping from hiding, she launched her line forward, hook impacting heavily against her target's wrist, before hauling back on the leather cord. Completely surprised, the bandit yelled aloud and watched as the kindling flew from his grasp and into one of the nearby buckets. Aware of other men bursting from the trees towards her, she began to twist and leap in wild arcs, recoiling her rope and allowing it to wrap around her legs, torso and arms, maintaining the tension and keeping the hooked end in permanent motion. As one man closed the gap quickly, she slammed her foot down on the taught rope and watched the hook fly out from around her wrist into his snarling face. She had no time to enjoy the victory as an explosion erupted from the fire cannon, followed by three others of equal magnitude. The force blasted her from her feet, careening into thick bushes before coming to rest at the foot of a tall elm. Catching her breath, she realised the spare ammunition must have ignited and gave a silent prayer that none of the metallic projectiles had hit her.

Climbing to her feet, legs feeling unsteady and ears ringing from the blasts, Crystal took her bearings. Fire raged in front of her and to the right, one body lay nearby, charred and with several scraps impaling it, but she could not see her previous attacker or any of the other bandits. Thick smoke was beginning to drift across the scene, and she gathered her rope before making her way towards the road. Emerging from the trees, coughing and spluttering from the cloying black mist, she found herself grabbed by the arms and forced into a kneeling position on the ground. A voice cried out as she struggled against her two captors.

'No wait! She is wiz me!'

She recognised the alarmed cry to come from Eljan and blinked away heat-stoked tears as the pressure on her limbs released. Wiping her eyes with the heels of her hands, she stood and noted the men on either side of her were dressed in the bright tunics and silver armour of the Zendran army. Making her way shakily over to her travelling companion, she accepted his offered arm for support.

'Crystal! You are well? I see no injuries; it is a miracle!'

'Ze cannon fuel exploded,' she coughed, 'I could not see if any of ze bandits escaped.'

'Heed no concern on that front,' rolled a thunderous voice she did not recognise. Craning her stiff neck up, she saw the occupant of the ornate carriage standing on the top step of the vehicle, perusing her with interest. Instant recognition hit her; he was not as comely as portraits suggested but there was no mistaking the imposing form of Prince Porthus.

'Sire,' she bowed her head in reverence, 'forgive me, I 'ad no idea I was in your presence.'

'Indeed? And yet you and your friend here attacked these ruffians and risked yourselves anyway? Noble, very noble. Well done! You must be rewarded.'

'We ask for nozing, my Lord,' she replied graciously, still trying to order everything in her mind, 'Save for a moment of your time.'

'Well, I can honour such a trifling request with ease,' Crystal couldn't help but think how amusing his lack of accent was; none of the Princes held the native inflections of the various peoples, which must have presented a significant barrier when trying to rally their 'countrymen', 'what question can I answer?'

'A moment, Sire,' she said, scanning the area but finding only soldiers readying equipment and dragging some bodies from the woods, 'I would prefer if my ozer companion joined us before we begin?'

Eljan moved his hand to her shoulder and shook his head sadly, 'I'm sorry, Crystal, but Garren did not make it. 'E was caught by a crossbow bolt when we charged to attack.'

Guilt formed an icy lump in her stomach. 'I did not realise you 'ad been involved. The explosion 'appened so fast and zen I made my way 'ere; what time was zere for such misfortune?'

'Per'aps you were dazed by the blast?' Eljan offered, 'For it 'as been many minutes since zen. Regardless, we have survived and rescued the Prince of Zendra no less. Garren would feel it a worzy end.'

'I, too, recognise your loss and will ensure the man in question receives a hero's tribute when I reach Giltenberg. But, please, we will soon be underway, what can I do before I depart?'

'Of course, my Lord,' she shook her head to focus on the matter at hand, 'we were travelling to bring you a message and would be grateful if you could 'ear it now?'

'By all means,' the Prince stepped down before resting his large rear on the edge of the topmost stair.

'We are from Shail, a fishing village some twenty miles south of 'ere. Zree days ago, we were attacked by an abomination from ze ocean; a twisted beast like none I 'ave ever seen. It killed men, injured more, and escaped before we could kill it. We fear it will stay near 'abitated shores or, worse, move up-river towards the capital itself!'

The Prince visibly paled, 'Towards Giltenberg? No, we cannot have that. I thank you greatly for this warning, alongside your heroism against these rogues. Have no fear that I will dispatch a platoon of my finest footmen to destroy this beast for you. And they will bring you fresh supplies, food, medicines, and linen, from my own stocks. Would this suffice?'

Crystal bowed to one knee, Eljan joining her immediately, 'Yes, Prince Porthus, this generosity and 'elp is nothing more zan reputation speaks of you. We are grateful and 'umbled by your kindness.'

'It is nothing. The fair people of Shail must be provided aid in their time of need and so it shall be. I am, if nothing else…'

What was undoubtedly about to be a speech of altruism was cut short by an arriving soldier. 'Sire!' he called out, a little too frantically, 'Sire! You must see zis!'

The Prince turned irritably, clearly unhappy at the interruption, 'What is it? What is so important?'

''Umblest apologies, my Lord, but we 'ave recovered some bodies and found ze source of ze explosion.'

'And what?' Porthus' ire was rising, 'I already know that this heroic girl destroyed a cannon, putting her much higher on my patience threshold than you!'

The soldier swallowed before rambling on quickly, 'Of course, my Prince. It was not a normal cannon, 'owever, it was a fire cannon. Zere are only two countries zat 'ave zese weapons in use…'

'Yes, I know! But they can be stolen from anywhere. I'm sure smugglers make a tidy price on such weapons.'

'I am certain you are correct, Sire! But a fire cannon would not 'ave allowed zese men to rob you. It would 'ave destroyed your carriage and killed you.'

Some of the rage petered out of the Prince's voice, 'So you think this was an attempt on my life?'

'Yes, my Lord,' the soldier returned quietly, 'We 'ave found no survivors but two of ze men were carrying short warhammers. The kind issued to soldiers of Lustania…'

Dim light penetrated the gloom as she forced her eyes open despite the deep throbbing pain from the back of her skull. The coppery tang of blood filled her mouth and she spat crimson saliva out onto the damp stone beneath her. Muscles cried out in awkward stiffness and the build-up of lactic acid in her joints felt like pustules ready to explode. It took a few seconds to realise she was bound, more securely than she had ever experienced before; her arms were covered in steel plating from shoulder to wrist, the bracers moulded into a tight bend and joined across her back to ensure her limbs were pulled behind her at perfect right angles. Two large iron rings were secured about her upper thighs with a short chain connecting them to similar ankle restraints. This forced her to remain in the kneeling position and a little testing revealed she was also chained to the ground. There was little freedom to move so she began a sequence of gentle finger and toe movements to try and recover her waning circulation. Adjusting to the particularly severe strain across the back of her shoulders, she realised she was shivering; whoever had bound her had been thorough, removing all her garments except her thin black leggings. Deliberately or not, they had stripped every tool and weapon from her arsenal. Years before, her nudity had been no problem for her, often used as a weapon in her assassinations; looking at her own naked torso now brought remorse, pain, and shame. The scars that covered over forty percent of her body were worst up the left side and she felt involuntary tears well when she compared the smooth pale skin of her right breast with the hard, matted scar tissue of the left. Not until her injuries had she realised the suppressed vanity she had harboured through her youth. Just knowing that at least one other person had now seen her disfigurement generated an uncomfortable anxiety within her.

Her mind drifted involuntarily to a time she had experienced a situation like this; of course, she had been on the other side of it. A team of mercenaries had been dispatched to kill Rayne and her sisters in the days following their father's death. It was because of them that her previous agent, Ansaro Le Vitti, had died and she had taken Umbridge to that at the time. In hindsight, she felt it was beneficial fate, for she may never have met Rebecca if not for his demise. She had tracked the killers through their blatant trail of death and killed them all with little effort; all except their leader, Reevus. Her decision to torture him had been under the guise of discovering his employer but there had been vengeance simmering beneath. Stripped naked and bound with rope, in a position that mimicked her own current predicament, he had not panicked or begged for mercy. Even as her torture had begun, he had given her little other than threats of retaliation and she still admired his resilience to this day. When her patience had reached its end, she had surprised even herself when her frustration drove her to castrate him. Somehow he had broken free of his bonds and fled, a futile effort as she pursued him with minimal effort and finished him on the run. Why was this memory so clear now, though? Was it a reminder that hope should not be lost for escape was always possible, no matter the severity of restraints or injury? Or was it a case that her own sins would be returned upon her tenfold?

Blinking her eyes rapidly, Rayne realised she had been drifting out of consciousness. Leaning as far forward as she could, liquid fire coursed through her back and shoulders, focussing her senses back on the environment about her. She quickly tested the limits of movement and the results were dire. She had no way to raise her feet or knees from the ground and her arms may as well have been paralysed. Her head and neck had full motion but there was no obvious effect she could have with just her teeth. She was utterly constrained and so her only option was survival; if she could last long enough, perhaps they would remove her from this cell, or at least remove some of her shackles, to interrogate or torture her. Those were the times she would need to be ready. Deep breaths slowed her accelerating heartbeat, and she assessed the tiny prison; the heavy stone walls were bone dry, a contrast to the floor, with no powdery residue evident, indicating a slate-type rock that could not be easily eroded or weakened without tools. No mortar present, on this side at least, suggesting that digging blocks free would not be an option. The dryness proved that none of the walls were exterior of the larger building they must be within; the damp floor meant the cell was at ground level. The single door into the room was a dark wood she did not recognise, but it looked solid and well-maintained. A small hatch that could be opened from the outside would undoubtedly be used for visual inspections and to provide rations, should any be forthcoming. Maybe she could devise a way out of this room, from there escaping the larger prison would prove straightforward for certain, but she could enact nothing while bound. Suppressing her fear and desperation, she began to plan until noting the air gap at ceiling level in the wall to her right. A gentle flickering light could just be seen beyond, so she knew the gap led to another room or corridor rather than freedom. It was only a single stone in dimension, and too high for her to realistically climb to, so represented no means for escape. Most likely, due to the fact it was lit, the room beyond was either a simple passage among the cells or a guard post for the wardens. Sagging back into her forced position, an involuntary groan escaped her.

'You are awake?' a voice cracked with age floated to her from beyond the air gap.

For a moment she considered ignoring it, feigning ignorance or sleep, but perhaps there could be some gain in interaction, to further understand her surroundings. 'I am. Who are you?'

'Prisoner, like you, in the next cell. I heard them drag you in; it sounds like you are well bound in there.'

'My restraints are a symptom of their fear. Do you have light in your cell?'

'Aye, indeed! My sentence is a long one and I seem to have earned a lantern to ease the incarceration somewhat. I take it from your question that you do not?'

'No. What else do you have? Are you shackled?'

'I imagine our cells are similar. I have some old straw and the rags of my shirt for a bed. My wrists are shackled and bound to the wall by chain. I have tried to snap the links many times, but it is futile. And you?'

'Yes, the same,' she lied. The speaker could be a prisoner, true enough, or perhaps this was a clever interrogation to catch her off-guard. She would be cautious in what she revealed whilst trying to learn as much as possible. 'How long have you been held here?'

'I...' the pause lasted a considerable time. 'I can't remember,' the voice trembled with emotion, 'Years for certain.'

'For what crime?' she continued, planning out a series of questions that would catch out an unsuspecting interrogator.

Another pause, 'Treason. Against the Prince and against Lustania. But I was falsely accused.'

'Of course you were,' she replied sarcastically, 'Isn't everyone?'

'Were you?'

The question took her by surprise, 'I have been accused of nothing, so I suppose not.'

'So why are you here? If you have no sentence, what is your crime?'

'I am a threat. Used and betrayed by your Prince. Who knows why I am alive; he should have killed me when he had the chance.'

'But he chose not to?'

'Not through some nobility. He wants something from me. I do not know what yet, but something important. Why are you still breathing? I assumed treason was a death sentence in any land.'

'True. But I am allowed to live so that I can suffer, and my former liege may gloat at his leisure. I doubt he will do likewise for you; he will execute you once your sister complies.'

'What!?' she could not mask her intensity; this must be a ruse for how would any prisoner know the details of her arrival or her identity? 'You have revealed yourself, pretender, your scheme has failed. Go and tell your master he will get nothing from me!'

'No, wait, do not disregard me!' genuine panic filled the aged voice, 'I do know of you, but not for the reasons you think! You are Silver Rain, the assassin, you captured your own sister, Alissa Fimarr, and brought her here at Lennath's request. He has repaid you with incarceration and eventually death; you are alive only as a means to coerce your sister, to help him achieve his goal.'

Rayne fell silent and ran the sudden confession through her mind. How could a prisoner of years know so much? What purpose did he have to engage with her at all? Lennath's people would have all the detail just passed to her, but there was fear in the outburst, the kind of fear she heard when her victims were about to meet their end. 'Who are you, old man? How do you come by this information?'

'My name is Jacob,' he offered reluctantly, regret heavy in his tone, 'Jacob Frost. I betrayed you many years ago under the influence of Ramikain's dark power; when he was destroyed, Prince Lennath declared me traitor and put me here to rot.'

Rayne was instantly returned to a night five years ago, when she and her sisters had stood upon a clifftop, facing an army amassed by the villainous necromancer, Ramikain.

They had been allied with the Lustanian army, led by General Jacob Frost, and ready to battle for the freedom of all lands. Until Frost had sprung a trap, surrounding them with raging fire and setting them as target for the ballistae of the enemy forces below. He had abandoned them to their fate and fled with his soldiers in tow. Through skill and ingenuity they had survived and her sisters had been responsible for the wizard's eventual downfall. But no thanks to Frost.

'You are where you deserve to be, vile betrayer. It is fortunate that you are too insignificant for me to have remembered or a far worse fate would have befallen you. What purpose is there for me to listen to you?'

'I hear the rage in your voice and that is justified. I beg no forgiveness but profess that I was not of my own mind during that time. I failed myself as much as any of you and I have felt the guilt gnawing within me ever since; it is unlikely you can understand such a thing.'

Sudden images flooded her mind; Catalana hanging precariously from the edge of a deep pit trap, her own refusal to bend and offer a hand to pull her to safety, the discussion of riches offered to abandon her own kin to death, the despair in Catalana's eyes as Rayne walked away. She could not be certain the crack in her voice remained hidden as she replied, 'Yes, unlikely…'

'Perhaps Lennath feels it ironic to incarcerate you next to me. Perhaps he wants us to speak, so that each of us can be tormented by guilt or anger respectively, but this is his true mistake. I know all that is happening beyond this prison and I know how to escape.'

'If you know how to leave, then why haven't you? Your story is weak.'

'I am old, and this prison has robbed me of much of my desire and prowess; if I left this cell, I would be killed before fleeing the city or hunted to ground easily before making the border. But with your help…'

'Are you insane? If I escaped this cell, my first act would be to kill you where you stood. What possible benefit would there be for me to help you?'

'What he has planned will threaten us all, you, me, your sisters, everyone. If you help me to escape, I can ensure that he never succeeds in his plot, I can gain the redemption I seek, and you will have saved your sisters. If you do not help me, then you will still be free, and I will be dead by your hand; I can see little to lose from your perspective.'

'Perhaps,' she responded icily, 'what is this plan he has concocted?'

'He wishes to use the dark power of Ramikain to twist animals into the horrors that roamed the Dussen Wastes during the necromancer's reign. Years ago, he tracked and captured the surviving mutants, becoming obsessed with the power that created them. He experimented with them, studied the histories surrounding Ramikain and his dark sorcery and pieced together some of the knowledge he required. Now he knows that the sceptre you charged for him at the Black Citadel will both control those beasts, and create more, but only if wielded by one suffering from the taint. He is too much the coward to risk his own sanity by imbibing that foul essence into himself, but your sister is already cursed with it. If he can convince her to fulfil his desires then all is lost.'

Rayne was content that the story matched Lennath's own confession earlier, 'Cursed or not, Alissa will not do his bidding to save my life.'

'No,' Frost's voice was filled with grief, 'not for yours.'

Kastani. Rayne chided herself internally; not only had she brought Lennath his object of power, she had also presented him the wielder and his leverage in one neat package. As soon as he realised this, she would become surplus to requirements. 'What do you know of the bodyguard he has here? The man who bettered me?'

Hesitation from beyond the wall before Frost's response, 'Bettered you? I imagined perhaps you had been manipulated into surrender? I do not know of any new protector.'

'And how is it that you know as much as you do?'

'Traitor I may have been declared, but there are still those loyal to me within these walls. Men who can see the wrong dealt to me and are desperate to help. I have allowed them to keep me updated on events but dissuaded any rescue as futile.'

'Until now?' she inquired.

'Until now,' he confirmed and she could imagine the smile on his face.

Chapter 4

Forge scanned his eyes across the beautiful scene around them, maintaining his nonchalant expression throughout, as he noted escape routes and attack vectors. Their last visit to the palace in Lustania had been variable at best, although the majority of issues had been caused by the influence of Ramikain, but currently all seemed peaceful. He took a seat on one of the exquisitely crafted marble benches in the enclosed gardens and ran his hand softly up Treya's back where she sat beside him. A shudder was followed by her brushing his hand away irritably.

'What is it, my love?' he whispered into her ear, aware that Herc and Catalana were well out of earshot, 'Are you still angry that I brought Zendar to the farm?'

She turned to him and kissed his lips briefly before taking the hand she had just rejected in her own. 'No, Straker, I'm not angry. Being here just feels a little uncomfortable. And my scars ache terribly. I don't know if it is the travelling or…' she trailed off.

Forge pulled her fingers to his lips, kissing them softly whilst meeting her eyes and seeing the anguish within. The scar up her back was significant and he was amazed she didn't suffer more from it; in truth he was still astounded every day that she had survived such a grievous wound. Astounded and grateful, for he had never loved anyone so deeply as he did Treya Fimarr. He slipped an arm about her waist and eased her back to rest against his shoulder, stretching his legs out before them. 'It will ease when we secure answers and have returned home. This has been a longer journey than expected; I even miss the children!'

'You are so flippant about things, Straker. I do not know how I put up with it. You adore the babies, why pretend otherwise?'

He smiled and kissed her hair, 'Aye, love, there is no fooling you. My heart is tortured by our time away from them, a pain that could only be surpassed if I was also torn from you.'

Her hand pressed against his stomach and caressed him affectionately. If not for the surroundings, and their reason for being there, it would be idyllic. The gardens about them sported organised, but not sterile, loose slate paths that wound between lush beds of flowers and shrubs from all the Five Kingdoms and many lands even further afield. There were many even *he* did not recognise, and he considered himself quite well-travelled. As the warm sun licked over them, he watched Catalana and Herc, standing arm-in-arm beside a display that sported a small pond. They had been particularly quiet since departing Czerna's hospitality and even now looked anxious; despite that they were an odd couple, he so big and rough, every bit the woodsman, she so beautiful and perfect, like a lady of means. He supposed it was even more odd because they were not a couple. Or so they claimed. Could they really have lived together for so long, spent so much time together, and be as close as they were without romantic consummation? He left the question where it was; too many times had he been chastised by Treya for remarking on the situation, let alone the times he had tried to pry directly from either of them.

Gently squeezing his lover's hip as she relaxed against him, he recounted the palace guards in the gardens with them. Four stood by marble pillars far to the left, the entrance into the palace proper, two were nearby on the path they had taken from the outer arched gate they had been escorted through to get to the seating area, he had also spotted two more who were patrolling the slate paths but were currently out of sight. He idly wondered if this was normal routine or precaution because of their visit. Despite the warmth, it had not gone unnoticed that they had been kept clear of the palace itself; how often were visitors entertained outside only? He avoided scurrying down rabbit holes of paranoia; perhaps it *was* just because of the fine weather. In fact, since they had been confronted by patrolling outriders soon after crossing the Lustanian border, they had been treated with respect, cordiality and good nature. The offered escort by that patrol, the city watch meeting them at the outer wall and palace guards personally guiding them to the gardens was all excellent hospitality; and meant they had been observed for their entire time on Lustanian soil.

The sound of chinking armour attracted their attention as the guards brought themselves smartly to attention, heralding the arrival of their host. Prince Lennath swept onto the scene, followed by one tall, black-garbed bodyguard, and his demeanour was one of elation. Arms spread wide and a huge grin adorning his face, Forge almost did not recognise him at first. The Lord of Lustania must have at least doubled in size with densely packed muscle and his face had become chiselled and powerful in the process. Even his hair seemed more lustrous and flowing than the last time they had met, and his wardrobe was now simple but elegant, a flowing shirt indicating no real desire to show-off his new physique.

'My honoured guests!' he enthused warmly, 'I had been notified of your approach two days ago but could not bring myself to believe it! I am so pleased that you have finally returned!'

Straker leapt to his feet and moved to embrace the Prince, keen to investigate if the show was genuine or not, but the bodyguard was fast as lightning, moving between the pair and forcing Forge backwards with one hand.

'Mozak, no!' Lennath snapped sharply, 'My guests present no threat! They are my friends and allies; you will not insult them in such a way.'

The tall guardian dropped his arm and stepped out of reach with a courteous bow. 'Apologies, Sire. Apologies, Straker Forge,' his deep voice rolled.

'Accepted,' Straker replied, slightly bemused. Slightly became very as the Prince surged forward and squeezed him in a hearty hug.

'Straker! Legendary warrior in my own home once again. This should be a regular event at least! Why has it been so long?'

He moved to sweep Treya into a similar embrace but her firm stance as he approached stopped him in his tracks.

'Prince Lennath. It has been a long time,' she stated, clearly trying to keep contempt from her voice, 'but we are not here for camaraderie or frivolity. We want to ask you some questions.'

'Well, that sours the mood slightly, but no matter. Please tell me how I can be of help. What answers do you seek? Perhaps you could share how I can best repair any rifts of the past?'

'You could drop the act and remember how things ended between us all,' Catalana jumped in as she approached with Herc, 'why this pretence at friendship?'

Her aggressive approach elicited barely noticeable tension in Mozak, the warrior clearly preparing to intercept if required. Forge assessed him closely as something familiar in his dress and deportment was beginning to nag at him.

'Lady Fimarr,' soothed the Prince, 'so much time has passed, and I hoped that we could start on a fresher foot than we left previously. I have changed greatly in those years, my Kingdom has changed, and I am certain you have, likewise, all changed. I have fine memories of our last meeting,' his eyes lingered on her for just a little too long, 'and hope that we can make even better ones from this day forth. But first, perhaps an introduction of your escort?'

Catalana paused at the word escort but a deep breath allowed her time to compose herself with a smile, 'This is Herc Callid…'

'Oh, of course!' Lennath gushed, 'Instrumental in the destruction of the evil sorcerer Ramikain yet largely unnamed in most of the chronicles of that event. Somehow that doesn't seem quite right to me…'

'I desire no recognition, Prince Lennath. I fear you misunderstand the desires of those involved wholeheartedly.'

Forge watched as the Prince took a step back from them all and placed his hands on his hips. His smile had become slightly distant and disappointment filled his eyes. It was hard to see what was going on in the man's mind but something about his manner, and the conditions of this meeting, was concerning.

'It appears that rekindling a friendship between us may take more than I assumed; you are all filled with anger towards me and I can understand that to some degree. But this is due to misunderstanding on your part, I am certain, and some mismanagement of the reunion on my behalf? Please, ask me your questions and perhaps my responses will help to quash some animosity.'

Before Straker could speak, Treya had voiced her concern directly, 'Why did you send Silas Zendar to us? What was the purpose of his interrogations? What do you hope to take from us?'

Lennath placed has hand to his heart, 'I had hoped he would explain his task to you personally. I suppose I could have handled the matter better, approached you myself with the request but I felt that my presence could make the matter worse. I have suffered bards aplenty in the last five years, spinning their songs and yarns of the downfall of Ramikain and none ever rang true. Most excluded those involved, something not befitting the heroic acts you all performed, missed the beginnings of the tale or twisted some of the events...'

'In whose opinion?' Treya countered with fire, 'I assume you are speaking of your involvement and the shame your own actions bring? Why not just commission a version of the story that you approve of and cast the truth aside?'

'You misjudge me, milady,' Lennath countered sincerely, 'I have discussed those days at length with Master Zendar, and I have hidden none of the shameful actions conducted by Lustania; but I have also included the rationale behind them. My closest General at the time was the true betrayer, manipulating me, luring you into a trap and attempting to usurp me upon his return. He paid for his crimes, but the damage done stretched beyond the borders of my fine Nation. There seemed no clear way to atone for those actions to yourselves so I believe a true telling of the tale could be the right way to lay some demons to rest, for all of us.'

The statement seemed to generate some doubt within Treya and Straker took his opportunity to join in. 'That seems a most noble cause, Sire,' he enthused, 'a good way to ensure people see Lustania as the decent land it is, and eradicate any fears of that evil wizard returning to wreak havoc once more. If we had understood this sooner, maybe we could have avoided this awkward meeting in favour of a more agreeable affair. Perhaps we could discuss the details you don't know of that story over lunch?'

As anticipated, Lennath suddenly looked uncertain and licked his lips nervously before answering, 'I am afraid that will not be possible. There are several renovations and other visitors that make hosting inside complicated today. I would be happy for a small luncheon to be served to us in the gardens if that would suffice?'

'Of course, we have no intention of imposing upon you...' he continued before Catalana interrupted.

'Cease this wordplay, Lennath! You have no intention to rewrite our story; you just want information about the Black Citadel. What do you want from that place? Why did you send men to attack it? Who did you discover there?'

The Prince became suddenly flustered and struggled to regain his former composure, 'I don't... that is I haven't... very well, I concede. I did send a team of scouts to the Citadel recently. I wanted to see if the location was safe, for Master Zendar to gain a feel for the place to assist his writing. I realise now that it was a mistake; my men returned reporting bandits in residence and they were forced to slay them. It is another reason why your own rendition of the story is so important...'

'Liar!' Forge cried, suddenly leaping forward and grabbing Lennath by the front of his shirt. Almost immediately, a curved blade was at his throat and his free arm was twisted up behind his back. He flicked his eyes down to see the silver markings along the honed edge of the black blade, even as Mozak dragged him clear of the Prince.

'No, no, no!' Lennath implored, 'This is not what anyone wants. Mozak, release him!' The lean bodyguard responded immediately without argument and Forge returned to his shocked partner's side.

'My apologies,' Straker pronounced, attempting to sound as genuine as possible, 'my temper got the better of me. The journey has been tiring and your story-gathering has proven stressful for us all. I am certain my curiosity can be satiated by an honest answer; or do you really expect us to believe you expended resources to check the ambience of that foul place? What was your real motive?'

A silence extended for a moment and he could not determine if Lennath was planning on unleashing his guardian upon them or generating another story to placate them. Either way, Straker's diversion had provided the answer he needed; the blade Mozak wielded was a Veer weapon. That meant he was a member of the most proficient assassin clan in the land, or he had killed one of the aforementioned assassins and taken the dagger from them. Either way he was a deadly opponent and could most likely best them all. Unless Forge was alone, of course. No skill or ability could overcome the curse laid upon him; he was undefeatable in battle provided none were there to witness his triumph. He smiled at the thought, a fitting punishment for the arrogance of his youth and difficult to manage amongst others. His natural abilities became less with each pair of eyes viewing his combat, providing he had no intention of killing those watching. Worse still, he could tell no living soul of his affliction without his strength and skill being stripped from him. A conundrum, and one he had left behind for the last few years; Treya had given him the chance to lead a quiet life full of the joy of love and family. But should anyone ever threaten that...

'You are more insightful than you look, Master Forge,' Lennath's thinly hidden insult snapped Straker's attention back to the conversation, 'I did have an ulterior motive for investigating the Black Citadel, one that was of true intention but may just anger you more, I fear. I wanted my men to retrieve the axe of Rork Fimarr, I had hoped this would be a fitting gift to seal a truce between us; and to search for any remains of your sister.'

'What?' Treya managed the word before an involuntary sob escaped her. Instinctively, Forge wrapped her in his arms as she turned sudden tears towards his chest.

'Please, see this as the candid gesture I meant it to be. I felt that providing you with the closure of a burial, of physically acknowledging her passing, it would help you all to place the horrendous loss behind you. I can only imagine what the death of a sibling must feel like.'

It appeared neither sister could find words at the revelation and it was Herc who responded on their party's behalf, 'Your actions are poorly judged, Prince Lennath,' he declared without emotion, 'You are desecrator of a tomb, not benefactor of a family. Perhaps our worlds are too far divided for you to understand what the daughters of Rork Fimarr would want. This is why there will be no resolution or friendship formed between you.'

'Yes,' Straker quickly interjected, 'It appears that this reunion is a futile effort, and we should resolve to avoid each other rather than force an unwelcome alliance for both parties. But, before we depart, would you share what your scouts did find?'

Lennath was glowering at them, a simmering rage beginning to burn through his outward veneer, 'You do little to avoid insulting me. Is it possible that the past can never be forgiven? Can the destroyers of Ramikain be so chaste and perfect that their grudges reflect no guilt back upon them? I believe you are unleashing your anger at yourselves upon me. I can tolerate that no longer. But you will leave here knowing that I proffered the olive branch, that I was the one willing to make amends, that I swallowed my own pride for as long as I could, and you rejected those efforts. My men found nothing beyond the bandits; no axe, no human remains. I wish they had brought back either to prove my intentions were honest.'

The Prince turned back towards the palace and began to walk away with shoulders slumped in defeat, Forge could not determine whether it was an act or not, but Mozak stood his ground, staring at them impassively.

'My men will escort you to the city walls. Safe journey, daughters of Fimarr,' Lennath's disconsolate voice floated back to them.

As Treya composed herself, Straker ushered them all along the path in the wake of the two guards who had led them there in the first place. He was relieved that Mozak did not accompany them. Once beyond the garden boundary, quiet conversation started again.

'That was unexpected. Lennath was acting most peculiarly; did we engage too harshly?' Catalana seemed almost pleased to have been ejected.

'Too harshly?' Treya echoed, 'Are you being serious, Cat? He felt none of the real fury within us and managed to dodge all our questions with his falsehoods and deflections. We have gained nothing from this journey!'

'Unless he was telling the truth, but you did not wish to believe it,' Herc remarked. He seemed to have a way of stating the thoughts that everyone else knew better than to voice.

'Did you believe him? That the ruler of a Kingdom waited five years before deciding to altruistically go in search of a complete stranger's remains to placate a family that mean nothing to him? No, he is devising some scheme that we cannot yet fathom.'

'Yet?' Straker asked in surprise, 'My love, this is no longer our concern! He defiled a place we made an oath not to return to and he is now aware that he will get no information from us, be that for some written tale or other purposes. We should return home and leave this behind us.'

Treya pushed his arm from her shoulders and faced him with fury in her eyes, 'This from the great adventurer, Straker Forge? What are you talking about? Running and hiding because of his status?'

'Running and hiding from what, Treya? Aside from Zendar's visit, Lennath has done nothing to us,' Catalana joined in, placing a calming hand on her sister's shoulder.

'But it is clear he is plotting something, and it is linked to our encounter at the Black Citadel. We cannot just remain idle while he…'

'While he what, love? I know that this has stirred up real pain in your heart and recognise my fault in that. But even if he has some plan or scheme, it is neither our business nor duty to interfere. We have children to think of.'

'What is wrong with you, Straker? Most of your life has been devoted to exactly that kind of interference. If he is defiling Alissa's memory in some way, or using father's axe to commit heinous acts, then I have to prevent it.'

'This is all supposition, Treya, maybe even just paranoia. We are not adventurers. Save for Forge, we never were. Why would you want to jeopardise the peace we have in Rennicksburg by chasing a threat that may not be real?' Herc made his point clearly and some surety left the oldest Fimarr.

'I… I do not know. I just have a feeling that there is far more hidden here than we realise. That our inaction could cause us greater peril than action.'

'I understand, my sweet,' Forge pulled her back into his embrace and started them all walking once more, 'and there is every chance you are correct. But I suspect the bodyguard who accompanied Lennath was a Veer assassin; they are renowned for their skill throughout the lands. They are the only people I have ever seen come close to defeating your father and they cost a small fortune to hire. Expenditure of that kind suggests he is either very frightened or very determined; I don't care to find out which. I think we should leave this matter because I am afraid; afraid for you, afraid for us and afraid for our children.'

His words seemed to hang in the air, and he could feel Treya's pensive stare boring into him all the way to the city walls.

The incoming blow was predictable and thrown with minimal conviction, Mazt batting the arm aside with ease. Following a second probing jab, delivered with no real relish, he stepped back out of reach and held up his hand to pause the sparring match.

'Keris, what are you doing? There is no benefit to this practice if you do not engage fully. Today we are Guardians, defenders of the Rondure and protectors of our people. You must attack as if I am the threat to those things.'

The young woman he had known since birth stared back at him, still retaining her fighting stance and breathing more heavily than her minimal exertions so far should induce. There was something in her eyes he could not read so he waited patiently for her response. It took longer to come than he expected but he remained impassive as a warm breeze passed over them, stirring the grasses around them and tugging at the long stray hairs that had fallen free of her tight topknot. Eventually, she replied.

'I am cautious not to harm you, Mazt,' she answered with complete sincerity, 'you have stated that our responsibilities as Guardians are now realised, my heart swells with the honour, but yours is greater still. You are now our leader and no harm should befall you.'

'So, I should be pampered and protected? No, your theory is flawed; if I am not tested now, then I will be poorly prepared for a real opponent. Your eyes betray you, Keris; this is not the reason you are holding back. Now, as your leader, I order you to spar to your best!' He stepped forward as he spoke the last words, driving a heel strike punch towards her chin.

Her reflexes were sharp, and he noted her breathing relaxed as she slipped back into the combat, head skipping to the right of his strike and both hands wrapping around his wrist. Spinning herself under his arm, she hauled back, attempting to twist him into a restraining hold. Tensing his shoulder as his hand was drawn parallel, he stopped the rearwards motion before dropping to one knee and swinging his free arm around at waist height. Keris avoided the blow but was forced to release her grip as she skipped out of reach. Leaping forward with a jumping knee attack, Mazt was pleased when Keris intercepted with a stinging kick to his shin, retaining the gap between them by pushing off from the contact into a backflip.

'Better!' he called out to her as she landed gracefully, 'Now take me down!'

He noted her adjusting her footing and recognised the indicator that she would charge into a flurry of kicks. As she sprang forward, he counted the steps; she always took five to gain sufficient momentum. From the fifth pace, she leapt into a graceful roundhouse kick; he knew this would be aimed at his head, most likely leading to a strike against his ribs as she landed and a downwards scissor kick into the centre of mass depending on his position. It was a level of complacency in their training he had become keenly aware of in recent months and not one unique to Keris. It was something they had to rectify. As soon as she left the ground to begin her sequence of kicks, Mazt threw himself to the floor, barrel-rolling beneath her and sweeping a leg out as she landed. Completely surprised, Keris' legs flipped out to the side, crashing awkwardly onto her back. Taking the advantage, Mazt regained his full height and swung an arcing blow towards her. She displayed remarkable grit to get back to her knees before his attack arrived, it was clear the fall had winded her, and it took both hands to block his wrist before he could connect with her face. He had not seen surprise in her expression during a fight since they were children. Still, her mind was clearly not focussed as she failed to recognise his pronounced attack as a feint for the follow-up from his left hand. Keris' eyes widened as the unexpected punch rammed into her stomach, lifting her to her feet and causing her to stagger back several paces. Mazt could see that she was unable to catch her breath so aimed an upwards kick towards her chin. He was not fast enough this time, though, and she caught his outstretched leg at the ankle with both of her hands. Spinning around whilst throwing herself to the floor, she managed to drag him into a leg grapple, his foot held up against her shoulder as she exerted pressure into his groin with one leg and tried to force her other foot into his throat. He had seen her submit Diast with just this kind of ground restraint before and wondered briefly if she had lured him into it deliberately. Regardless, she should have known better; he was a lot stronger than Diast. Gripping the foot at his throat in one hand, he pushed up with his free arm, ignoring the intense pain from between his legs, and gaining a seated position. The action caused Keris' leg to angle painfully and she released her hold, rolling quickly out of his reach. Mazt tried to regain a defensive stance but the pain she had inflicted slowed him down noticeably; she was already leaping forward with a high elbow strike. He couldn't help but admire the height she could generate from a standing start, at least seven feet clear of the ground, but refused to be distracted; as she dropped towards him, he reached up, catching her leading arm by the tricep and her other by the wrist. Landing under his restraint, her only option would be to twist out of his grip and land a delaying strike to put distance between them. Before she could do so, Mazt drove his forehead into her nose. Blood erupted as she fell back, eyes failing to focus, and her hand instinctively covered her face as she stumbled several paces. Concerned that she could not continue, Mazt did not take advantage, pausing as she dropped to one knee and her free hand; the other continued to cradle her injury as significant amounts of blood continued to pour between her fingers.

'Keris? You can continue?' he asked with concern.

A muffled howl, of pain or rage he could not determine, erupted from her and she suddenly arced upright, raising her free hand with fingers outstretched, palm facing him. Time seemed to slow about him as he realised what she was about to do. He focussed on the delicate piece of jewellery that adorned her hand; gold rings on each finger attached to slender jointed legs, all converging on an inset gemstone in the middle of her palm. A Guardian Palmstone, crafted long ago and passed down from each successive generation of Guardians for as long as their people had lived. He recalled the Ceremony of Confirmation only three days prior, when his cohort had been announced as the new Guardians, and he had been granted the honour of speaking the declaration of fealty to the Rondure, the Elders and their people; true and just service until death or ten years had passed, whichever was sooner. It had been an elegant and traditional event, ending with the presentation of the Palmstones to each of them in turn as they swore never to remove the tokens until completion of their service. For Mazt, the ceremony had been more solemn than the previous one he had witnessed; he could not be certain if that was a result of his own sense of responsibility or the revelations of the High Council in the week before.

His own voice snapped him from the memory as he instinctively cried a warning, 'No, Keris! You do not have the control…'

Another scream escaped her, sharper and clearer as she pulled her hand away from her blood-soaked face, and the fingers of her outstretched hand curved forward with the tension evident along her arm. He spotted the grass between them suddenly flattening and dirt and small stones inexplicably rising from the ground before flying in his direction. He had no time to react as a raging gale struck against him, hammering like a battering ram, dragging him from his feet and casting him back like a rag doll. Tumbling in the air, he could gain no sense of direction and his impact with the ground moments later came without warning. Rolling and careening across the field for what felt like minutes, he finally came to a stop on his back and lay still as he caught his breath. Blinking several times, he could feel multiple bruises and lacerations across his body, whether from the landing or the debris in the air as he had been thrown he was uncertain, but no breaks. Suddenly, Keris was at his side, blood still running freely from her nose.

'Mazt! Please tell me you are well! I should not have used the Palmstone, forgive me!'

'No,' he replied, struggling to speak through the tightness in his chest, 'you should not. But at least we both have new understanding of their power. Perhaps my attacks were unreserved, but your discipline must be stronger; the weapons of the Guardians must not be used until the preceptors deem us ready.'

'You are correct, Mazt, and I recognise your truth,' she stated humbly, placing a hand upon his chest, 'I allowed embarrassment to cloud my mind. I accept any admonishment you must apply.'

'Embarrassment?' he echoed in confusion, rising to a seated position, 'We have fought more times than I can recall, and both secured victories over one another. What reason is there for such feelings?'

He stared at her intently for several seconds before she suddenly leaned in and pressed her lips to his. Complete shock left him paralysed as she parted his mouth with her tongue and passionately probed for response. For a second he succumbed, feeling the ecstasy of desire race through him as she pressed her body close to his. Then his sense returned, and he pushed her gently away.

'No, Keris,' he spoke flatly, 'union is not our calling. We are now Guardians and that is all that can matter. Intimacy and desire detract from this vocation and cannot be permitted. You risk much in your advances; there have only been three female Guardians in our history, and you should not be the one to generate reason to prevent this in the future. We are neither men nor women; we are only Guardians.'

She met his gaze evenly, 'You speak truth again, Mazt. Perhaps I was imbalanced by the events of recent days or my concern for your wellbeing overcame my senses. Accept my apology for this.'

'Let us consider this matter privately resolved. I have no interest in tarnishing your reputation or unbalancing our quartet,' he stated, rising painfully to his feet and offering his hand to her. Accepting his assistance, she made no attempt to pull away from his grip and he studied her closely; no amorous intention was apparent in her profile and he realised he was holding the hand that had led to his current injuries. He dropped his eyes to the Palmstone she wore; a clear stone with irregular facets across its surface, the golden setting about it polished to a high shine, the joints maintained in flexibility with a mineral-based oil. His own held an oval, red jewel with a perfectly smooth surface and he wondered if the power within it was the same as Keris' or would result in some alternate effect. Running fingers gently across the back of her hand, he felt the callouses formed in combat, marking her as the formidable warrior she was. Only now he could not help but see her as the beautiful woman she also was.

'Keris,' he began before realising she had still not looked back at him. He reached out a hand to wipe some of the blood from her chin and turn her face towards him, but she resisted as irritation spread across her visage.

'Forget my injuries, Mazt, forget your own! Can you not see this?'

Finally, he followed her stare, out across the grassy field towards the shimmering Boundary. Narrowing his eyes, he became aware of what had caught her concern; the barrier had moved again. Releasing Keris' hand, he walked slowly forward across the grass until the tips of his boots met the sand previously revealed by the Boundary's movement. He realised he was not far from the spot where he and the High Auger had discovered the revelation weeks earlier, and suddenly felt the need to scan the area around him. Looking left and right he could detect the presence of no others; behind him he noticed Keris had still not moved, although now she was watching him intently rather than the Boundary. He indicated for her to join him but then returned his focus to the new concern. Before there was perhaps three feet of sand beyond the thick grass of the field, now there was closer to twelve feet; more concerningly there was a further foot of water beyond. Almost without his own control, he stepped forward onto the beach, feeling it give slightly beneath him as millions of grains individually moved and adjusted to the presence of his boots. It felt as though he had entered a completely different world as the warmth beneath him flowed into the soles of his feet, easing some of the aches there. Reaching the edge of the water, he crouched and stared into it; the liquid was clear with a turquoise shading to it, making the white sand beneath it appear a greenish-blue. He stretched out one hand towards the surface and heard the cry of alarm behind him.

'No!' Keris called out and he could see she had advanced to the grass border as he turned his head, 'Do not touch it! It may be a trap! Or cursed! Or a dark magic of some kind! Come back and we will spread this truth to the Elders.'

Mazt could see the fear in her eyes and remembered the week before the Confirmation as he had joined the gathering of the Elders with Keris, Diast and Atae. They had been the last to arrive following his own poor judgement, allowing a training session to continue for too long and not giving enough time to return to their quarters by mid-sun. When they had arrived, a message had been left instructing them to attend the Great Shrine itself; normally only Elders, preceptors and Guardians were permitted, but an exception had been made in this instance to allow all of the potentials entry as well. Atae had been the one worrying throughout the rushed journey that time, insisting that they would be punished for their tardiness and probably lose the chance at guardianship entirely. They were not greeted upon assuming their kneeling posture at the rear of the open auditorium, but the High Auger had begun his address as soon as they were settled. He had spoken of their history and tradition at length, hardly necessary in Mazt's opinion as all present had studied this in great detail, before addressing the key concern that had unsettled their entire population, the Rondure. The artifact had been little more than a relic for generations, despite receiving almost divine reverence from the Elders. On that morning, the day he had discovered the first movement of the Boundary, it had surged with power, an inner glow becoming visible and an ethereal force filling the chamber in which it lay. The High Auger had further revealed that part of their joint history had remained shielded from all save the Elders; originally there had been another artifact, a stave of equal power that had once provided further protection and untold bounties. Hundreds of years ago, this item had been stolen from them and taken beyond their reach; this was the event that had generated both the inception of the Guardians and the creation of the Boundary itself. The Elders had conferred on the awakening of the Rondure at length and believed the recent change to be a forewarning of a coming threat, something the Boundary would not be able to protect them from and so the Guardians must be prepared for combat against an external aggressor for the very first time. One of the assembled preceptors had suggested promoting all trainees into the position, to strengthen the ranks of the Guardians and provide increased protection to the Rondure. The High Auger had dismissed the idea, insisting there were four Guardians for a reason; any unsuccessful potentials would form the leadership of a militia. This was also met with surprise as their people had never had, or required, any standing military capability. There was no further clarity, any attempt to anticipate the threat or the effect on the Boundary was foolish in the eyes of the Elders; better they and the Guardians were simply prepared to react to whatever presented itself.

Mazt turned back to the liquid before him. He was prepared for any danger but before him was only calm, gently lapping azure waters. Ignoring Keris' concerns, he dipped the tips of two fingers, feeling the relative cool on his skin and a mild tingling in the surface scratch on his index digit. Lifting his hand to his face, he could detect the scent of the preserving fluid they used for many of the meats stored in the central larder. Touching the tip of his tongue to his finger, he tasted salt. What was happening to their homeland? Was the Boundary revealing something that had always been there? Some mighty river surrounding them? Or perhaps they sat within a mighty lake? But why was this water saturated with salt? What purpose was there to a river or lake that could not sustain aquatic life or be utilised for drinking? What if he was mistaken in his assumption? What if the Boundary was not revealing existing extensions of their land but creating them? Could it be that the Rondure was reacting to a threat created by the Boundary itself? Could it be creating water around them in which to drown their people entirely? Was this some kind of Divine punishment after all?

A hand on his shoulder made him start and he realised he had devolved into unsubstantiated panic. Calming himself immediately, he looked up at his peer and found concern in her eyes.

'You should not interact with this… place,' she stated through thinly-masked fear, 'we should return to the Great Shrine and report to the Elders. They will provide full understanding.'

Mazt stood and held her upper arm for a moment, preventing her from retreating, 'Keris, you must not be anxious. This is our purpose. Whatever these changes mean, whatever happens with the Boundary, we are destined to confront and defeat it. If a threat appears to take the Rondure as the stave was stolen all those years ago, the thief will regret setting foot here. You are strong; ensure others know it.'

She searched his eyes for any subterfuge, 'This is the truth, Mazt. I will follow where you lead, and the Guardians will stand as one. Come, we must provide our knowledge and dispatch sentries here to monitor the Boundary for any further changes.'

He released her arm, 'Agreed, but we will attend to the worst of our injuries first; our current appearance could generate concern before any word is spoken.'

She let out a small chuckle and he could see the tension vanish from her posture. As they set out towards the quarters that skirted the Great Shrine, he wished he could likewise release the uneasiness their latest discovery had created within him.

Hot, rose-scented bathwater swirled about her gently and she remained transfixed on the flower petals that followed those currents across the surface. Trying to sit up and pluck one on its journey, she found herself firmly but patiently restrained at the edge of the large bathing pool.

'Now, now,' came the matronly voice once again, 'there's a lot to do, getting you presentable; no time for chasing flowers, young mistress.'

Alissa flicked her eyes up to the speaker and studied the stout features of a heavy-set, mature woman, sporting a thick apron over her maid's uniform. Her captor failed to make eye contact despite Alissa maintaining an unblinking stare for several moments. Finally, the youngest Fimarr conceded, relaxing her neck to return her attention to the water before her.

This was the second pool they had submerged her in. The first had become so polluted with dirt, grime and dried blood that the bathing team had opted to move her to fresh water rather than fighting against the suspended filth all about her. As soon as they had eased her from that initial bath, however, she had lashed out with fingernails at one maid and kicked the larger woman in the chest before fleeing across the pool chamber. Of course, she had been soaking wet, so the journey was mostly spent sliding on knees or backside into walls and obstacles before reaching the outer door. Yanking the heavy wooden entrance open, she was struck in the face with the flat of an axe blade. She must have blacked out because when she awoke, she was lying in her second bath; this time four women were carrying out ministrations to her.

'I do say, whatever have you been doing with your hair, lady?' the matron, who had recovered well from their previous scuffle, continued, 'You will have to let this grow a bit so we can tidy up your ends; did you cut this with scissors or shears?!'

A nervous giggle ran amongst the servants, but Alissa barely noticed, 'A sword,' she answered quietly bringing the laughter to an abrupt halt. A smile crossed her lips as a petal floated too close and she snapped it up into her fingers.

'Yes, well, that's as may be,' matron went on, 'for the time being we will give it a proper wash and comb through. It will look odd being short, especially on a pretty little thing like you, but we can try to smarten it up a bit with some headwear; maybe a flower ring or a tiara?'

Alissa looked at the pink petal in her hand, tracing her nail down to the bottom where the colour faded to white. She noticed her own finger, as if for the first time, nail ragged and short with a large section missing all together. She tried to remember when that had happened but couldn't.

'It will make little difference; look at her skin, she's ruined!' The comment was barely audible, coming from one of the younger maids assigned to this task and Alissa failed to acknowledge it at all, such was her interest in the rose segment. Even her attention was caught by the sharp crack as the matron slapped her colleague fiercely across the face, however.

'How dare you!' she thundered, 'This is a guest of the Prince and you will serve her the proper respect! Make another comment like that and being removed from the palace will be the best result you should hope for. Are we clear?'

'Yes, ma'am,' came the tear-strained reply, 'I'm sorry, milady.'

Alissa realised the last comment was aimed at her and looked up to see the tearful maid with the bright red cheek. 'You look like your face is on fire,' she confided conspiratorially, 'but at least you aren't bleeding. The last one did. When I scratched her. She didn't taste very good though.'

The young servant recoiled at the last statement and began busying herself away from the water's edge. Alissa stared at her for a moment until her head was yanked backwards by a comb catching in one of the many matted tangles throughout her butchered hair. She returned her attention to the petal, smooth and perfect yet already beginning to wilt having been torn from the sustaining plant. So it was with her; for five years she had been wilting, waiting to die without that which sustained her, without Kale Stanis. The one living memento of him left behind, Kastani, had given her some reason to continue; her lover was clearly evident in their daughter's face, and Alissa would spend hours just staring at her to rekindle some memory of the man she had lost. But their relationship was tenuous at best, the girl had no understanding of her father at all and seemed incapable of mourning him properly. Terex always claimed this was because the child was too young, but Alissa knew it was more to do with her not being her father. If Kale was still alive, Alissa doubted she would have kept the child around.

'But, ma'am,' another voice, more timid than either of the previous two, 'what are we to do with the marks on her skin?'

The first action to be taken when doused in the initial bath was to scour her skin with coarse leather flannels in an attempt to remove the years of ingrained foulness from her. It had been quite clear that fresh bruising and scars were difficult to distinguish from old blood and muck, leaving several areas raw and sensitive. The result was pink skin adorned with the carefully etched, slender white scars she had inflicted across her body.

'They are not marks,' she stated melodically, seemingly to the petal in her hand, 'they are arcane symbols of dark magic, and they retain my power.'

Silence fell across the chamber, broken only by the gentle sloshing of water at the pool's edges. The comb continued to be worked through her hair, slowly becoming less jagged in its passing as knots and tangles were eased away. Alissa remembered being bathed like this before, but long ago, when she was merely a child. She recalled her hair being longer, the bath being smaller and her bather being far less tolerant than the current ensemble. Back then the duty had fallen to her sister who begrudged the task somewhat and was less than delicate in both scrubbing and combing. Her sister. Treya. The woman who had murdered the only person in the world who mattered.

Alissa suddenly sprang upright in the water, no force applied strong enough to hold her down. She snatched one of the fishbone combs from the basket beside the pool. 'Killed him, bitch!' she shrieked insanely, 'Killed my love, my life, my Kale!' she raved before plunging the comb into the left breast of one of the screaming attendants. As the young woman fell backwards, clutching at the implement in her chest, sudden splashing alerted Alissa and she spun around to see the matron had leapt into the water beside her. Instead of attacking, the large woman swept her into an embrace, pulling her head into the ample bosom.

'Shhh, dear lady,' she soothed, as if to a small child, 'It's all right now, you are safe here, they can't take anything from you anymore. It was not us that took your love away. We just want to care for you. Just be still and let us finish getting you cleaned up; you will be the princess you deserve to be in no time.'

Alissa did not fight the embrace and watched with interest as the maid she had stabbed was gagged by the hand of her peer to keep her silent as the matron spoke. It was an odd contrast; she was unharmed and being coddled while the woman bleeding at the side of the pool was restrained and muffled from crying out. Without warning, Alissa broke into a fit of giggles, returning the embrace before slipping back down into the water and resuming her position at the edge. The matron, still fully clothed, sank down in the water next to her, gently caressing her face with a soft woollen sponge as the two unharmed maids aided the third out of the bathing chamber.

'Doesn't that feel better?' the woman cooed to her, 'We just need to get you feeling right and looking right and then you'll be thinking right. You are very beautiful, milady, you must not neglect that.'

Alissa allowed the gentle massage to continue, gathering more petals into her hands and rubbing them over her throat and collar bones. The sound of footsteps echoing along the corridor beyond the chamber drew the attention of the matron and she suddenly dragged herself from the water, leaving a torrent in her wake as she rushed towards the exit, her drenched clothes slapping wetly against her scurrying legs. Alissa glanced up quickly, to ensure the woman's attention was elsewhere, before stuffing the petals into her mouth. The flavour was disappointing, but she finished her impromptu meal before reaching out to gather more. The sound of arguing reached her as soon as the chamber door was opened, but she remained focussed on her task.

'No, Sire! You must not be here yet!' the matron's voice was forceful but full of distress.

'Nonsense, Tarraget, you have had sufficient time to prepare her; I am eager to discuss her stay,' a well-spoken male, full of self-confidence, replied, 'Why are you soaking wet?'

'Apologies, milord, I entered the water to soothe her following an... incident. You cannot see her yet, she is naked!'

'I have waited too long already to bring her here; I will not be delayed for prudish trivialities! I assume the incident has something to do with the hysterical maid I passed on the way here?'

'Yes, Sire, a stabbing without provocation. This girl is not sane, and I fear she presents a danger to you. Give me time to dress her, and converse with her alongside your own guards. My concern is only for you, my Prince.'

A slight pause followed before the male voice continued, 'My thanks, Tarraget, you are loyal and true. Your concern is noted but my words are private, only for the ears of the Lady Fimarr and myself. I believe she has not lost her sanity, merely her purpose; I will restore this for her. Now, go and clean yourself up and take some rest, I will summon you when she is ready for dressing. Lock the door on your way out, I will knock when I require exit; tell the guards outside that I am not to be disturbed until then.'

'But, milord, if she loses control again…'

'I assume any deadly combs or brushes have now been removed?' he returned mockingly, 'I can deal with so slight a woman should she choose to attack me; if not, then I have wasted five years honing my body to its current state, have I not?'

'No, Sire, you are a great figure of a man, she would pose you no threat. I only fear for you, as I have since your youth.'

'And I appreciate that dearly, Tarraget. Now go and do as I command.'

Footsteps approached through the resonate pool chamber as the heavy exit doors swung closed once more. A loud audible clunk followed announcing the locks dropping into place. Alissa was still chasing petals as the newcomer stopped alongside her bath; forcing another handful of roses into her mouth, she turned to face him. Tall, broad-shouldered and well-manicured, he was nothing compared to Kale Stanis but she felt she recognised him.

'We have met before,' she stated while chewing noisily.

'Indeed we have, Alissa Fimarr. Five years ago, you came here with your sisters and caused much disruption. I would like you to make some repayment for that by helping me.'

'No,' she replied flatly, 'You are Lennath?'

'I am,' he responded, undeterred by her initial refusal.

'I remember you. Pathetic and desperate, like a lost child. Are you taller, now?'

He studied her face closely and she could see the icy coldness in his pale blue eyes. Swallowing the remains still in her mouth, she pushed towards the pool edge, gliding forward like a swan across a river. He offered a hand and aided her in stepping up onto the marble walkway beyond the raised edge of the bathing pool. A thrill of coolness swept across her as she left the warm water, and she delighted in the tickling sensation as droplets formed tiny streams down her naked flesh. Making no attempt to cover herself, she continued to watch his eyes as they explored her body.

'You are the most exquisite thing I have ever seen,' he whispered, more to himself than her, 'This language, what is it?'

'I am darkness. This is my power,' she replied, noting his vulnerable neck as he crouched down, tracing a finger lightly across two of the symbols carved into her left thigh.

'Yes, I believe you are a conduit for dark power. A dark power I want you to use for me. What can I offer you to generate an alliance between us?'

'You are Lennath. You are just a mortal; even your blood provides no draw to me. You have nothing I want; Terex could explain this to you. Return me to the Citadel for more time is needed to prepare,' she answered.

The Prince continued following symbols over her skin, moving around her, over her buttock to her lower back. The sensation was stimulating and generated involuntary goosebumps across her. 'I think not, Alissa, for you have been preparing for today. What if I told you that I would execute your sister, Rayne, if you do not join me?'

'You would have to speak with Terex,' she replied, staring ahead blankly, 'I don't recall a Sister Rain.'

A small chuckle came from behind her and she felt his fingers moving up her spine to the back of her neck. 'Fascinating. I suppose someone must have aided you in scarring yourself like this; the symbols would not be so meticulous across your back otherwise. You must have been supported by most loyal servants. How about the girl? The one with you at the Citadel? What if I promised her safety in return for your fealty?'

'Kastani? You must not say her name for that is blasphemy against his. I think I would be annoyed if you killed her, and your life would then be forfeit. I recommend you confirm with Terex.'

He continued to circle her, fingers now tickling her throat and up to her cheek; they lingered on her lips for an unusually long time considering this was the only place she had no markings. 'You have spoken of your power, but you have displayed none,' he said softly, a flush beginning to fill his cheeks as his fingers moved, 'what if I could offer you a way to realise this potential, to channel Ramikain's magic?'

She felt her fists clench and this time spoke directly to him, making focussed eye contact for the first time, 'Then my preparations would be complete! I could exact my revenge upon the murderous whore and breathe life back into my Stanis! All would bend before my power and weep at the torment I would unfold! Terex would sit at my right hand'

'And what if I told you Terex was dead?' Lennath continued, moving his caresses down over her exposed breast, seemingly no longer interested in the markings themselves. Her nipple hardened under the touch but no excitement accompanied the reaction for this was not Kale Stanis. 'What if I told you that partnership with me was the only way to achieve those goals?'

'I would need to hear that from Terex himself,' she remarked with no hint of humour, 'Perhaps I would consider you as a replacement ally with his consent.'

'I think you are not as unstable as you appear to be, Lady Fimarr,' the Prince spoke with a smile, 'but we would not be allies; you would be mine.' His fingers moved delicately down her stomach, not pausing as they slipped between her legs and inside her. She did not react despite the sudden lust that spread across his face and the unconcealed excitement as his other hand grasped her buttock fiercely. 'You will be my weapon, my concubine, my queen!' he growled huskily, 'You will provide me both power and pleasure and, in return, I will gift you the opportunity at revenge and ensure the safety of Kastani.'

The word had barely left his mouth before she lashed out with terrifying speed. Her first punch slammed into his throat hard, staggering him and releasing his grip and penetration of her, her other hand whipped out with ragged nails bared, tearing four deep scratches across his chest. The shocked cry was knocked from him as a faint gasp when her heel slammed into his solar plexus, toppling him backwards into the pool she had exited. For a moment she watched him thrashing wildly as blood stained the water around him until he found his footing in the chest-deep bath. Licking her fingertips, she stared at him impassively.

'You taste sour,' she told him, 'I want the link to Ramikain. You can use this body if you want but your touch will not be pleasant, and your yearning will not be reciprocated because you are not Kale Stanis. Only he can have or know me. I want to talk to Terex so bring him to me. I am thirsty, so have blood brought to me. I will know your plans and decide if they match my own. And never speak her name again.'

Lennath looked up at her with a peculiar smile on his lips, 'Yes, I think we can manage all of that. Would you help me out?'

She looked at his thin, sodden shirt, plastered to powerful toned muscles, his firm jawline, and absorbing eyes; even his hair had remained shiny, smooth and perfect despite his dousing. 'No,' she replied before skipping lightly around the pool chamber walkways.

Biceps contracted like grapefruits beneath his skin, huge veins distending across the surface as he heaved his massive frame up. Once his chin was level with the thick manacles around his wrists, he slowly lowered himself back down until his knees touched the stone floor. Standing straight, he unhooked the chains from around the wall bracket above and allowed them to clatter noisily before him. Rotating his shoulders to free up some tension, he marvelled at how strong he had become despite the rigours of age. Two hundred continuous pull-ups were beyond his imagining five years ago; it was a shame that his incarceration limited him to such basic training. If he had the opportunity to do more than pull-ups, push-ups, crunches and squats, he would have more extensive definition and vastly superior endurance. Of course, if he had not been incarcerated, he'd have had a completely different focus.

Resuming his pacing around the cell, Jacob Frost thought about his long imprisonment; the first year spent as an amusement for the Prince but his torturous visits had eventually dwindled to nothing. The next four months had consisted of planning an escape but, the closer it got to implementation, the more he had wondered if escape would benefit him. There was nowhere to run, no allies to turn to and no way to exact revenge upon his former liege. Instead, he had turned to training, the regular routine helping his sanity as well as rejuvenating his ageing body. He had discovered that some within the army had remained loyal to him regardless of the propaganda that had been spread surrounding his captivity; thus, his rations and water had remained plentiful. When asked by these few what he had planned, he would remain secretive but confident; in truth, he had stopped looking towards the future to avoid feelings of hopelessness. Revenge had filled his heart in the early days but the cell in which he lived brought him nothing but time to consider such things, and he soon realised that revenge was a hollow and pointless goal. Thus, his ambition had dwindled and with it his desire for freedom. Until now. The arrival of Silver Rain in the dank hole beside his own had provided him an epiphany; he had continued to live for redemption. For now he had the opportunity to balance the terrible betrayal he had enacted upon the Fimarr sisters, by saving the life of one he had tried to end.

For a moment he stopped his movement, slowing his breathing despite his recent exertions, allowing the chains permanently secured about his wrists to settle in silence. Straining his ears, he could detect only the faint crackling of the torch that lit his dismal accommodation. He guessed she was awake; outside of their minimal conversations, he could only ever hear her when she was sleeping and even then, only because of her faint breathing. Despite this predicament, she maintained whatever learned control she had developed to mask her presence whilst conscious. Frost could not determine why.

'Silver Rain?' he called quietly, 'Have you decided, yet? Time is dwindling.'

When no answer came, he returned to stalking up and down the confines of his cell, scratching idly at the scar tissue under the patch that covered the ruin of his right eye. He had avoided clarifying details of the escape, just in case there were unseen observers. That created a problem as his cellmate was unforthcoming in her communication and he could gain no confirmation from her. The fact that he intended to leave this very night added an extra complication to proceedings. What if she refused to join him in his departure? He needed her help if he was to make it beyond the border, let alone bring a halt to Lennath's dark intentions. Worse still, what if she enacted her original threat to kill him where he stood? At least then he may have gained some redemption by freeing her, he decided.

Footsteps approached and he could distinguish three separate sets, not the metallic clanking of the guards' armoured boots, but the muffled sound of sturdy leather. The time was at hand and he could feel his heart pounding rapidly in his chest, a sensation he had not felt since his first charge as a cavalryman some forty-two years hence.

'Silver Rain!' he hissed again, more urgently, 'Now is the time. Are you with me?'

His only reply was the jangling of keys, followed by the heavy click as the lock of his cell was undone. The metal-bound oak door swung inwards and three men were revealed; two remained outside but their leader rushed into the cell and embraced Frost tightly. Unable to return the gesture, Jacob made no attempt to resist, the simple human contact making his legs weak with unexpected emotion.

'General!' the newcomer enthused, 'At last you have agreed to freedom! We must away from here with haste. We will spirit you away beyond the reaches of this corrupt empire and begin the rebellion that will free us all from this shrouded tyranny of the Black Prince!'

'Taltan,' Frost returned, 'it is joyous indeed for us to finally meet again without that door between us. But there is much to do; release my bonds and we can talk of future plans once we are safe.'

Taltan Rydell did as he was ordered, and Frost considered the young man as he worked through the keys to find one that fit the manacles of the former General. He could not be even half of Jacob's age yet carried wisdom and confidence beyond his years, neither yet tainted with the cynicism of failure. And that despite standing at Frost's side during the brief civil uprising that had led to this long sentence. It remained as clear now as the day it had happened; having overcome the dark influence cast upon him by Ramikain, he had tried to reason with the Prince, to explain his own actions and apologise for intimidating his liege whilst under that power. But Lennath had not wanted to listen, despite having agreed to the plan of treachery against the Fimarrs through his own cowardice, and had ordered Frost's surrender. Of course he had fought, out of some lingering remnant of the curse or his own pride, he could not say for certain, and many of his soldiers had flocked to his aid. The conflict had torn through the city, Lustanian soldier against Lustanian soldier, until he could watch the futile deaths no longer. His surrender had ended the civil uprising and the Prince had honoured his word by allowing all those who had fought alongside the 'traitor' to return to their lives unpunished. Somehow, Rydell had maintained his military position and presented enough false loyalty to climb higher in the ranks; he was now a major. A sudden release of weight from his hands reminded him of his ally's actions and his rubbed his manacle-free wrists for the first time in five years.

'Thank-you, my friend,' he sighed, holding back a swell of emotion that threatened to overcome him, 'I can never repay the loyalty you have shown me.'

'Enough, old man, it has been no burden for me to continue my service to Lustania and playact to a fake master. Yours has been the ordeal and the suffering; I regret that you have taken this long to permit your own escape.'

'Aye, I have kept my cards close all these years but now I see it has all been with purpose.'

'I am sorry, General...'

'Jacob, Taltan, I serve the military no longer.'

'As you wish, Jacob, but we cannot remain here; I fear the situation beyond this prison is changing rapidly and we should not linger. You have kept yourself strong in body; I pray our flight will not be too arduous upon you.'

Feeling the younger man straining to urge him from the room, Frost held him back. 'Wait, Taltan, what new situation causes such alarm?'

Rydell could not mask his impatience but stopped to explain as requested, 'I fear the Prince is closer to success than we believed. Since we last spoke, access to the palace has been minimised. He is hiding something there and I have been unable to discover what. And only today there has been an omen too ominous to ignore; Treya and Catalana Fimarr met with him. I do not know what occurred, but they were rapidly dismissed and left the city immediately; this cannot be coincidence. If we do not flee now, begin planning and take action rapidly, then the sorcerous machinations we have feared for many years will come to fruition. If that happens then I do not know if we will be able to defeat him.'

Frost saw fear in his friend's eyes for the first time and was about to provide some reassurance until a soft voice filtered to them.

'Let me out.'

Rydell looked startled but Jacob grabbed his arm and dragged him to the next cell, urging him to find the correct key. After a moment, the door was open and they paused at the awful sight; Silver Rain, half-naked, heavily scarred across the left side of her body and face, hair lank and matted with blood, severe restraints preventing any significant movement of arms or legs, a puddle of urine beneath her indicating she had not been provided even basic facility. She did not look up as they entered but her predicament was enough to generate a gasp of shock from Rydell.

'I don't understand,' he murmured, 'how is she here?'

'It doesn't matter, Taltan,' Frost urged, 'We must free her for she could be an ally of great significance. You are correct in your fears, Lennath now has Alissa Fimarr to wield the weapon on his behalf; Silver Rain may be our only chance of stopping him now. Release her bonds, quickly!'

Rydell once again did as he was commanded, working through the significant bonds holding the woman in place. When he finally released the arm braces, she dropped forward heavily into his arms. Gingerly assisting her to her feet, they approached the door.

'I must protest this course of action, Jacob. She is in no condition for this and her burden jeopardises…'

He did not finish as she suddenly launched herself from his embrace, staggering him back, before wrapping an arm around Frost's neck and levering him to the floor.

Landing heavily, pain shooting through his back, Jacob had no time to react before her thumb was pressed into his throat, just above his sternum.

'Give me a reason not to kill you!' she hissed, disinterested in the three men that rushed forward. Frost held up a hand to stop them.

'Like I told you, Silver Rain, I am content for you to end my life, be it right now or in the future. These men will not impede your escape if you choose to execute me here; likewise, no revenge would be taken if you killed me after we defeated Lennath. I would like to see the latter, but I leave the decision to you.'

For a moment the pressure increased, and he believed his life was forfeit, but then she was off him, rising to her feet before stumbling woozily against the corridor wall. Frost rolled up onto one elbow, coughing to relieve the dull ache now present at the base of his windpipe. His rescuers remained paused only for a moment before Rydell swept forward, unhooking his cavalry cloak, and wrapping it around the woman's shoulders, despite her shrug of derision.

'I don't need your gallantry,' she spat hoarsely.

'Well, you have it anyway,' Taltan replied softly, 'Besides, your body is suffering from exposure as well as exhaustion, the warmth will provide you some strength until we can get you food, water and rest.'

She put up no further resistance as he wrapped an arm about her shoulders and began to lead the group through the passages of the prison.

'How is it so quiet?' Frost asked as they jogged, feeling the exhilaration of really stretching his legs for the first time in years.

'It has taken careful manipulation to achieve,' Taltan replied honestly, 'Weeks to arrange all the shifts and personnel to align so that all within this area are those loyal to our cause. I fear the opportunity would not have arisen again.'

'No, fortune has been on our side,' Jacob agreed, 'for what you have told me about the Fimarr sisters' visit would surely have heralded the execution of our new ally.'

'I am not your ally,' Silver Rain replied, somehow managing to keep pace, 'you are simply a means to my escape.'

Silence fell again, save for the sounds of their breathing, until the soldier leading the way suddenly stopped before a corner, indicating for the others to do likewise. Frost quietly crept to the front of the group and joined him.

'What is it, Creif?' he whispered with concern.

'We have lingered too long, General, the guards at the front have changed shift. I cannot guarantee the loyalty of these new men.'

'I will remove the problem,' Rayne suggested, 'just give me a blade.'

'No,' Frost replied, 'these men are not our enemies. Taltan, can you deal with this peacefully?'

'Probably not,' he replied with a half-smile, 'but we can avoid bloodshed!'

The young officer straightened out his tunic and led the two men he had arrived with around the corner. A muffled conversation was too distant to be distinct but, as Jacob peeked around the corner, he saw the two new guards being choked into unconsciousness by his saviours. Moving to join them, he and his fellow escapee took the men's overshirts to cover themselves, allowing Rayne to hand Rydell's cloak back to him. Frost also claimed a sword and scabbard from one of the fallen guards, noticing the assassin opting for a dagger and a pouch containing manacle bolts from a small store cupboard.

Already standing with more surety, the woman took several deep breaths before joining Rydell at the prison entrance. She peered up towards the palace with a slightly bewildered expression; perhaps she had believed the prison to be linked to the small series of cells located underneath the royal compound. Maybe there was even a time when she would have been correct, but Lennath had banned their use immediately upon assuming the throne; he wanted no dangerous criminals anywhere within his proximity, even if they were incarcerated.

'It makes things easier,' he whispered conspiratorially, 'Once we are beyond the outer prison wall, we can easily pass unnoticed through the streets and exit through a patrol door that Creif would normally be manning. Do not worry.'

She ignored his comforting smile, 'The guest accommodations, they are within the palace grounds?'

'Aye, Lady, they are,' Rydell offered, 'but your sisters did not stay. They left hours ago. I have horses by the patrol gate, however, so we should be able to catch them if we hurry.'

'I was not enquiring about my sisters,' she stated coldly, 'I saw a scholar in the palace when Lennath hired me, I'd never seen him before, but he seemed to recognise me. He was foreign to this region, I know that for certain, and I suspect he may have been the one to provide the Prince with some of the secrets he had been searching for.'

'You mean Master Zendar,' Rydell confirmed, 'he has been in the Prince's employ for three years now. He travels a lot but spends much time in the Royal libraries when he is in the city.'

'And he stays in the palace accommodation when he is here?'

'Yes, but we can discuss this when we are out of the city…'

'No. We must retrieve him and take him with us,' she said with finality.

'But Lennath already has all he needs,' Frost interjected, 'taking Zendar will not hinder his plans.'

'No doubt,' she agreed, 'but he can clarify many of the details we are missing. Moreso, he may even know how to prevent or reverse the power of the sceptre. It is an advantage we should not be without.'

'Your escape will not remain unnoticed for long; we must get to the patrol gate before somebody realises Creif is not manning it. A detour into the palace to kidnap a bard is too great a risk; if either of you is caught again I do not want to consider the consequences.'

'Death is death, it makes no difference if it occurs in a cell or on the run. We will be conspiring in the dark, making plans based on speculation at best, unless we bring him with us.'

'You don't know that he has any real information…' Rydell began but Frost placed a hand on his shoulder to quiet him.

'Silver Rain,' he spoke sincerely, 'explain to me why we should take this man rather than Alissa herself? Surely rescuing her would remove Lennath's ability to use the sceptre?'

She paused for a moment before replying and he noticed a slight trembling in her shoulders; he knew better than to confuse the onset of exhaustion with fear, however. 'My sister is Lennath's ultimate prize and she will therefore be guarded. I believe the odds of escaping with her are slim at best and I have no doubt Mozak has been ordered to prevent her departure. Even at my best…' she trailed off before finding her thoughts once more, 'No, our real chance lies with this Zendar; once we know the extent of Lennath's plan, we can counter it accordingly.'

'Nobody will be filling your purse, assassin,' Rydell retorted unnecessarily, 'why are you so concerned with helping us against the Prince?'

Before she could speak, Frost laid his other hand on her shoulder, becoming a human bridge between the pair. 'Because perhaps I have a kindred spirit in my desire for redemption,' he explained.

Rayne shrugged his hand away, 'Or in revenge,' she countered.

The group made their way through quiet streets, sticking to the shadows where possible and quickly progressing to the outer palace walls. Using their own allies to replace the guards at each gate they came to, access was simple and left a quick escape route if necessary. The guest accommodation consisted of a series of ten luxury cabins spread across the manicured lawn to the left of the main building. It was clear only one of the cabins was occupied and they approached with caution, keeping the structures between themselves and any observers within the well-lit palace. Frost felt anxiety bleeding into him and ran through options for a rallying speech once they had assembled an army to usurp their enemy. It was a futile distraction, but he persisted with it to maintain his focus. Reaching their destination, Rayne signalled for Creif and the other soldier to block the front door while she led the other two to the rear. Vaulting lightly over the wooden rail that skirted the short veranda at the back of the cabin, she was already opening the insecure door as Rydell and Frost were clambering over in pursuit. Rushing to follow her inside, he found a shocked, slender man sitting bolt upright in a wingback chair, stare fixed on Silver Rain, a book spread open at his feet where it had fallen. He looked very slightly younger than Jacob himself, but ashen skin and wide eyes indicated the sheer dread he was now undergoing. Frost realised he recognised the man, from years previously when he had been sent to the prison to interview him; now their roles seemed suddenly reversed.

'S-S-Silver Rain?' he stuttered in a terrified whisper, 'But I thought you were imprisoned, awaiting execution.'

'You are Master Zendar, yes?' she demanded, voice like razors.

He could find no words so nodded as vigorously as possible.

'You have studied at the behest of the Prince, tracked the history and stories surrounding Ramikain and his power and given Lennath all the power he could ever need?'

Another nod and Jacob noticed the man's fingers constricting involuntarily around the arms of his chair.

'As a result, you led me into a trap and have forfeited my sister's life to him?'

A final nod with tears now beginning to weep from the corners of his eyes.

'I should kill you now for what you have done, no protestation can convince me that you are not fully cognisant of the effects your actions have wrought. Luckily, I need the information you have. Do you choose to repent and live?'

'I-I do,' he finally managed, whimpering like a child, 'I will do anything to help you. All I have done for the Prince is wrong, I see that now. Please, show me how to repent and I will do it! In the name of Yanis, I will do it!'

Frost knew this was simple begging, if a chance arose for him to raise the alarm or escape, he would take it. Regardless, if it helped them get him clear of the palace, it was useful.

'You will come with us and you will divulge all that has been happening,' she continued, 'If your words are useful, I will release you. If not, or you make any attempt to escape, one of us will kill you; if it is me, it will not be quick.'

'I will help you, I swear it, please do not harm me!' he sobbed. Frost moved forward and grabbed his arm, hauling him free of the armchair he still clung to. Pushing him through the back door, he pulled alongside and spoke quietly into his ear.

'I will end you if you cry out; unlike Silver Rain, I see no benefit in what you know.' The trembling scholar nodded his understanding, and they began to creep towards the exterior wall, utilising the cabins as cover once again. Suddenly, the sound of hand bells from the city began to float towards them, the ringing growing as more bells joined the chorus.

'The watch alarm!' Creif cried, urging them all into a faster pace.

'Your escape has been detected,' Rydell shouted over the noise, 'I do not know if I can still get you out of the city!'

'Stay calm, my friend,' Jacob called to him, 'all is not lost yet!'

The words felt empty as he cast his gaze towards the palace itself to see several guards running in their direction, whether because they had been detected or just towards the nearest gates to respond to the alarm, he did not know. Immediately, Zendar began waving his arms and shouting for help, forcing Jacob to knock him senseless with the hilt of his sword. Dragging the unconscious body across his shoulder, he thanked the gods that the man was so scrawny before loping into a more tiring canter with the added weight.

'Maybe they didn't hear him?' he panted to any of his allies who may be listening as he ran.

'I fear they did!' Rydell replied, pointing with his own sword as five men broke off and headed more directly for them. Beyond them, a tall man in black robes appeared from one of the exterior doors. As he began to sprint, it looked as though he were running on air, so light were his footfalls. The Major paused, waving at them to continue, 'Keep going, I'll hold them off!'

Without warning, Rayne ducked across towards the last cabin they were passing, placing one foot on the veranda rail and launching herself onto the roof. Rolling forward to the edge nearest the approaching guards, she released one of the small manacle bolts she had collected. The lead-most guard dropped to the floor although the dim light prevented Frost from seeing where he had been struck.

'Come on Rydell!' he cried out, 'She can deal with it! We need you to guide us!'

Continuing the flight across the grounds, the old warrior began to lose pace and knew his burden would be too much. Despite this, he pressed on, aware that three more enemies were now prone but the man in black was fast-approaching. Finally, he made it to the gate and dropped Zendar to the grass. Gasping for breath as his allies worked the portal open, he turned back to find Silver Rain sprinting towards them, a wall of fire climbing towards the sky behind her. Awe filled him as the gate was swung open to the street beyond.

'How…?' he began.

'A barrel of roofing tar in the stable, I toppled it and knocked a lantern free to ignite it. Should delay pursuit but not for long.'

'With a bag of manacle pins?' he asked incredulously.

'Fail to believe it later,' she chided irritably, 'we have no time!'

As if to support her words, the black-clad warrior appeared beyond the flames and leapt up to the vantage point Rayne had previously occupied. Dragging the scholar with him, Frost followed Rydell and Creif through the gate, Rayne close behind him. Their final ally suddenly slumped against the gate, forcing it closed in their wake and Jacob saw the tip of a slender throwing knife protruding from his throat. Gargling bright red blood, the man was unable to speak but his eyes were full of resolve as he slammed his palm down on the key, snapping it in the lock before he collapsed to the ground.

Before the faces of all those who had died in service to him over four decades began to flash through his mind, the sound of hooves distracted him. A rider approached rapidly up the cobbled road and Frost distinguished him as a scout, most likely dispatched to inform the palace of the prison escape.

'Ho there!' Rydell called out amicably, 'What news?'

Despite the unexpected interception, the rider must have recognised the Major's uniform and pulled his horse up short. 'Sir!,' he responded promptly, 'Escape from the prison. Two fugitives on the loose. Both to be killed on site. Treasoners, Sir!'

'Well done, Lancer,' Rydell continued the ruse, 'I'll pass the message presently. First though, I'll need your horse.'

Confusion swept over the younger man's expression, 'No, Sir, I cannot delegate my duty, I must report to General Audack directly,' he glanced at the flickering light beyond the walls, 'Is the palace on fire, Sir?'

'Aye lad, it is,' the Major returned before reaching up, dragging the youngster from his steed and cracking him smartly across the jaw, 'Sorry, Lancer.'

Jacob pulled Zendar forward and heaved him up onto the animal. 'Good work, Taltan. Now get him to the patrol gate and we'll meet you there.'

'No chance, General. You two are exhausted and in no state for a fight, take her and ride! I will meet you at the Daneslight Gate'

'No time for arguments,' Rayne joined in, 'he is correct, now get on.'

Frost only paused for a second before jamming his foot into the stirrup and swinging himself over the saddle. With Zendar prostrate across the beast's lower neck, undoubtedly to awake with some severe bruising from the pommel, Rayne leapt up behind him, wrapping her arms about his waist for security. Kicking his heels, he spurred the horse into a gallop despite the excess weight; the animal would cope for such a short journey. The faintest chick of metal against stone caused him to look back and he saw their pursuer atop the palace outer wall, no mean feat as they stood over fifteen feet high, arm outstretched from where he had released more throwing knives. There was no indication that Rayne had been hit and he could see Rydell sprinting away in another direction, presumably unharmed. Creif was pressed against the wall directly below their attacker and it appeared he remained unseen. With unbelievable grace, the black-garbed man leapt down from the significant height, landing in an elegant crouch. Creif took his opportunity and leapt forward with a downward swing of his sword; his opponent reached back and caught his arm by the wrist without turning to look. Spinning on the balls of his feet, he sprang upright without letting go, driving his free hand up into Creif's outstretched elbow. The snapping of bone and tendon could be heard even over the sound of their retreat, but the battle was not yet done. Creif bravely kicked out with one boot but his persecutor danced aside easily, raising his own foot and dropping it forcefully onto the exposed knee. With two joints shattered, Creif collapsed in agony and his torturer loomed over him as their steed carried them from view.

Frost focussed on steering them into the narrower mud passages between and behind the large structures, hoping to avoid any patrols or ambushes. The escape had already cost them two lives and he had to ensure that was worthwhile; hopefully Zendar would not turn out to be a false necessity.

'Was that the man you feared?' he shouted over the wind rushing past them.

The response was muffled as Rayne remained pressed against his back, but he could make out enough to understand her, 'Mozak, yes. And I do not fear him. His is a Veer assassin and cannot be underestimated. I am sorry about your men.'

There was no emotion in her words, but he was surprised that she had chosen to provide any sentiment, real or not. He continued his wild route towards the Daneslight Gate, he had not forgotten his mental map of the city during his five-year imprisonment, it had been created over too many years to ever be lost to him. It was one of five gates along the wall closest to the Dussen lands and had a foot trail beyond that led down to the Callabine River. They could use the river to evade trackers whilst also having the shortest journey to their goal; Rydell had already told him of the rebel camp they had been forming over the past year and a half, hidden in the depths of the border forest on the edge of Dussen. With no other options until they had interrogated Zendar, it seemed prudent to stick to that original plan.

Soon they drew up beside the single-man, steel-latticed door that marked the exit onto the Daneslight road. Despite leading to one of the most popular recreational towns; Daneslight sporting all manner of hunting, fishing and gaming, alongside a purpose-built theatre for travelling player troupes; this gate remained locked at all times with only the guard stationed here holding the key. That had been Creif's official duty this night and, had he followed orders, he would be very much alive. Frost shook his head and allowed Rayne to dismount behind him before alighting himself. Dragging Zendar down and propping him against the outer wall, he noted the mare was sporting a frothy sweat. Slapping her hard on the rear, he watched the animal gallop away; it was unlikely she could be coaxed through the small door and fresh steeds were waiting on the other side. Or so Rydell had promised.

'What are you doing?' Rayne questioned stretching her back and rubbing distractedly at the scars across her neck.

'The horse is exhausted; she'll do us no good in that condition. We will use other mounts to leave the city.'

'Not what I meant. We have no way out yet; we should have held her here until your man joins us. If he joins us.'

'His name is Taltan Rydell. He is the most loyal man I have ever met, and he will be here,' he silently prayed that his confidence was enough to make the words true.

'And then what? What is your escape plan beyond this gate? Ride wildly across the countryside until you clear the border? It hardly makes you safe.'

'No, indeed. A force has amassed in the Dussen forest, soldiers and militia loyal to me. Once we are united, we can wage war against this oppressor and replace him upon the throne.'

'That's a stupid plan, in fact, I struggle to call it a plan.'

'Perhaps then, Silver Rain, you would enlighten me as to why?'

'It has only been days since you divulged to me all you know of Lennath's strategy, to create and control an army of monsters the like of which cannot be described if you have never encountered them. I have. If he can summon more than ten of these beasts, they would rip through your army as though it were nothing. All resistance and all hope lost in a single skirmish.'

'I assume your naïve dismissal indicates an alternate plan?'

'You wanted to free me, wanted me to come with you, wanted me allied to your cause. That is because you know warfare is not going to work. We need to interrogate Zendar, find a way to neutralise these creatures or the way in which they are controlled; if all else fails, then the controller will need to be destroyed. In any one of those scenarios, I am the best option.'

'You would destroy your own sister?'

She studied him for several moments before answering with far less bravado, 'Only if it was unavoidable. I would prefer to rescue her and return her to my other sisters. Regardless of what happens, Lennath will be usurped and a new power will take the throne. When they do, you will be there to guide them in their new reign; you will ensure I am paid handsomely.'

He smiled and shook his head, 'Of course, I should have guessed. Well, if Lennath is stopped, you will be worth every coin that can be found. So, once we are clear of the city, we can follow the river…'

'No. There is no gain to be had at your camp, only distraction.'

'And what is your counter-proposal?'

'We head north, to Corinth. My agent is there, and she will be able to resource our mission properly. I also have several safehouses where we can hold Zendar while I question him.'

'That seems reckless, once he discovers you are free, he will likely send hunters to Corinth; it is your known base of operations. Likely he will also scour my home village. We should avoid both for safety.'

'No, we go to Corinth and collect my agent; I will not leave her as an unwitting target. Do what you will, but my help comes with conditions.'

'Very well, Silver Rain, although this will prove a hard sell to Taltan! But concede this to me; if Zendar provides us nothing and we are able to deliver your agent to a place of safety, then you will join with my forces in Dussen?'

She stared hard into his one eye. 'Maybe,' she said.

He laughed again, 'You are a tough negotiator. Tough in all respects, I think.'

'Someone is coming,' she whispered, suddenly alert and pressing herself back into what little shadow there was. Frost turned in the direction she indicated and was overjoyed when he saw Rydell jogging towards them.

'Sorry, Jacob, but it takes a little longer without a horse!'

'You have lost all pursuit?' Rayne snapped at him, crouching before Zendar and slapping his face sharply to rouse him. In short order, a low groaning indicated he was coming round.

'Yes, I was unobserved, even the assassin did not follow me; too absorbed in the nightmare he dealt to Creif,' his eyes dropped with his voice at the mention of his lost comrade. Jacob slapped a conciliatory hand onto his shoulder.

'He was very brave, Taltan, and his sacrifice will not be forgotten. Now, get us clear of here so we can put this coup into motion.'

The younger man moved to the gate, unlocking it noisily, penetrating the night air with the loud squealing of hinges, audible even over the distant bells. Aiding the groggy scholar to his feet, Rayne moved through first and this time Frost waited until last before joining the others. Pulling the lattice shut behind them, to an equal measure of noise, he secured the lock before hurling the keys as far into the undergrowth as he could manage. Turning towards the four horses that had been tied to a stanchion, he noticed the woman had taken little time to forcibly mount Zendar atop one of the two chestnut steeds, tying his hands tightly to the saddle. She deftly mounted the other and Frost realised she was still barefoot, bloody soles revealing the pain control she continued to demonstrate. Knowing better than to mention such trivialities to her, he instead settled himself onto the white and grey dappled stallion. Looking across, he noticed Rydell sported a bloodied calf.

'Taltan, you are injured?' he inquired.

'Just a nick, my friend, from one of the assassin's blades. Hasn't even slowed me down.'

'You are exceptionally lucky,' Rayne added, 'not many survive a Veer throwing knife.'

'Then I guess luck is with us!' Rydell smiled, turning his steed and ushering them all towards the river.

'STOP!' came a cry from high above. Jacob looked up and saw two guards peering down at them. Perhaps the squealing gate had attracted their attention, perhaps they were just coincidentally patrolling this section of the wall. It didn't matter; grabbing the reins of Zendar's horse, he spurred his own into a gallop.

'Call the watch!' came the voice, quieter but still too close for comfort, 'Summon the guard commander!'

Jacob jammed his heels in again, generating the increase in speed he desired, much faster outside of the narrow streets he had previously been navigating. Looking back, he saw the terrified scholar holding on desperately despite being tied to his steed, obviously a novice to horseback riding. Beyond him Rayne was lying low over her mount, generating as small a target as possible. Rydell was at the rear, a huge smile on his face as they raced dramatically from the city. Without warning his expression changed to surprise and then pain before his horse slowed and he slumped forward with an arrow protruding from his back.

'NO!' Frost screamed, dragging back on his reins to stop his mount. He had to go back for his ally; he could not lose Rydell as well, not after the loyal support he had provided for five years.

'Keep going!' Rayne yelled at him, striking the rear of his horse hard as she passed, 'We all get caught if you go back, and then this night was for nothing!'

He knew she was right, but tears streamed from his eye regardless as they fled into the darkness.

Chapter 5

Sweat dripped from his thick eyebrows as he trotted rapidly along marble corridors, panting heavily against the exertion. Raising a hand to wipe the salty droplets from his eye, Audack failed to spot a maid who was diligently scrubbing one of the huge white support columns and bowled her over in passing. Almost losing his footing, he shouted at her irritably, 'Look where I am going, woman! Next time will be the last time!'

The sound of terrified sobbing erupted behind him and he knew he was just venting his own frustration. Not only was the forced pace taking its toll on his soft, rotund body, but the anxiety he felt over reporting to the Prince right now was exceptional. The sun had just crept over the horizon and yet the fire on the grounds from the previous night was still smouldering in some areas. There was no sign of the escaped prisoners, one of whom was his own former leader, Jacob Frost; who knew what revenge the man had planned for Audack's decision to remain loyal to Lustania and replace him as General? As if that was not enough, this latest news was not likely to improve his sovereign's mood and he was already dreading having to deliver it.

Arriving at the huge double doors of the audience chamber, he stopped and leaned back against the ornate frame, taking several deep breaths to calm himself. Pulling the corner of his cloak up to his face, he wiped himself dry and flicked his thinning hair away from his forehead. After a moment, he felt composed and hoped he wasn't as beetroot red as exercise usually left him. Adjusting his sword belt, he knocked gently on the door before him, secretly hoping that the sound would not be heard over the muffled voices within; sadly, he was summoned to enter immediately.

Inside, he found the Prince stood at the far end of the room, fists on hips, frowning impatiently towards him. The new bodyguard, who had been ever-present over the past few weeks, had obviously been the target of whatever previous barrage Lennath had been releasing, and now observed Audack by craning his head over his own shoulder. The only other occupant was a distressed-looking footman standing beside an additional drinks table off to the side of the throne usually used for receiving visiting dignitaries.

'What?' Lennath snapped.

'My Liege,' Audack mumbled nervously, 'I have news.'

'Do you command my armies with such declarations of the obvious? Of course you have news, you idiot! Why else would you risk my wrath?' the Prince vented, stalking towards the drinks table, 'I have no desire for further complications this morning; the failures around me are becoming intolerable.'

Audack swallowed hard, uncertain whether his ruler actually wanted him to continue or not. The tall warrior all in black finally stopped staring at him and looked back towards the Prince. It was he who broke the silence in Audack's stead.

'Prince Lennath, you had not allowed me to finish my report. The interrogation of Creif Hayman yielded useful intelligence,' the voice was smooth and controlled, holding none of the trepidation that Audack could hear in himself when he spoke, 'It seems there is a guerrilla force assembling on the Dussen border, intent on usurping you from power.'

Suddenly a decanter of brandy was sailing through the air, flashing past the unmoving bodyguard and crashing to the floor only inches from Audack's feet. Tiny shards of glass and sticky liqueur showered him, but he dared not move in the face of a potential onslaught.

'Is that supposed to improve my mood, Mozak!' the Prince screamed in fury, 'To add to everything else, I now have a civil war on my hands?'

'No, Sire,' Mozak returned coolly, 'Appraise this news without emotion and you see the advantage. If this band of insurgents has remained hidden for so long, then they have been waiting for something. Normally this is an event, a sign, or a breach in defence. In this case it is a person; they have been awaiting Jacob Frost to lead them. Having briefly encountered the man, I assume this is symbolic leadership only; there was nothing exceptional about him in my opinion.'

'You are wrong!' Audack added suddenly, surprising himself, 'Frost is dangerous and holds a vengeful vendetta against those of us who stood against him last time.'

The outburst suddenly drew Lennath's attention back to him and he regretted his words immediately. Luckily, something in Mozak's explanation had soothed some of the fire in the Prince, 'Mozak has a valid point; if Frost has been released by these rebels, then we can prepare our forces to crush any strike against us. Have the trackers reported back?'

Audack licked his lips and tried to keep his voice level, 'The trail ran cold at the edge of the river and we have not located any exit points. One of the escapees was found dead upon his horse, however; Major Taltan Rydell.'

Lennath slumped back against the drinks table, disappointment etched across his face. For a few moments, silence fell until the Prince gestured for the footman to furnish the other men with drinks. Despite no interest in lingering or confusing his own judgement with alcohol, Audack accepted a delicate crystal goblet of Tunsan sherry. After Mozak had likewise been served, the young servant scurried from the room in relief.

'I remember presenting honour colours to Rydell for his courage in vanquishing raiders along the Eastern border. How deeply have we been infected by this treason?'

'I cannot be certain,' Audack replied, acutely aware that he had done no analysis of the problem whatsoever, 'but it is surely limited. You are well-loved within the military.'

Lennath raised an unconvinced eyebrow at his general, 'Really? Well, I think any of those not loyal to me would lose such concerns should I remove their alternative, which is why I find little comfort in your report, Mozak. If Frost is set to lead forces against me, how have we gained anything other than pre-warning from your interrogation?'

'Pardon me should this sound condescending, Sire,' Mozak returned, 'but Creif revealed the location of the encampment, I determine that Frost will join the forces there, allowing you to destroy the entire threat in one strike.'

A smile spread across Lennath's face and Audack felt his own tense fear ease slightly, 'Of course, I was not thinking clearly, a single attack before Frost can rally and prepare this rabble ends the threat before it is realised, and outside of the awareness of impressionable eyes within the population.'

'I can ready a battalion within a day, Sire...' Audack began but was waved to silence.

'Quiet, General, there is more yet to discuss before I decide on a course of action. What of the other prisoner? Were all tracks lost at the river together? Do you believe she has remained with Frost?'

The question flustered him a little, he had not even considered the escape of Silver Rain to be of consequence; surely the threat lay within their old enemy, Frost. 'I am led to believe they are together.'

'She will not join his army,' Mozak stated firmly, 'but she will exact revenge should you not dispose of her. I can...'

'No!' Lennath cut him off sharply, 'You are to remain with me. What course do you believe she will take? And what of their hostage?'

'If she was still devout to our teachings, then we would not see her again until she struck against you,' Mozak stated, 'but this is not the same woman I trained. I believe she will return to her home in Corinth to gather supplies and recover from her injuries. Even if she does this, she cannot hope to defeat me, so a direct attack is unlikely. More feasibly, she hopes to extract information from the scholar, Zendar, to find either a weakness to exploit or a way in which to prevent your plans to overcome the other Kingdoms; preventing your goal could be seen as vengeance enough for her. I would advise you take measures to kill both her and Zendar.'

The Prince rubbed his chin thoughtfully, 'Are you certain that this will be her direction? Do not forget that I hold her sister here at the palace; do you not believe this will alter her strategy?'

Mozak absorbed the question for a moment, 'No. Her bond to family was already limited when we accepted her into the Veer clan, the fact she willingly brought her own kin to you for a simple payment informs me that this will not be her goal.'

'You are wrong,' Audack blurted out, ice suddenly running down his spine as both men turned to stare at him, 'I mean, holding such a high-profile prisoner…'

'Guest,' Lennath corrected.

Audack cleared his throat nervously, 'Guest, of course, Sire. Alissa Fimarr's presence does complicate matters. Silver Rain may not choose to attempt a rescue, but she could warn the other Fimarrs. That is, if they do not know already; was their visit here a coincidence? Or were they assessing the palace, and yourself, for a potential strike?'

The Prince suddenly strode directly towards him and he prepared himself for an attack; he had seen this before from his superior and any attempt to parry a blow was met with increased ferocity. It was better to simply ready yourself for the pain. As soon as he was within reach, Lennath raised his arms and grasped Audack's shoulders warmly.

'Brilliant, General!' he gushed enthusiastically, 'You bring the exact balance to this discussion that I hoped! I had already forgotten the other sisters! Of course their visit was not by chance; you are astute, Audack, do not stop adding such value when our focus becomes too narrow. Well done!'

Relief and surprise sapped all strength from him, and he almost dropped his drink. Luckily, Lennath tuned away and began to pace animatedly around the room, allowing Audack time to compose himself again.

'Yes, I may have piqued the Fimarr sisters' interest through my own actions but having had all four of them on the grounds simultaneously is unlikely to be a coincidence. Mozak, you do not believe Silver Rain holds any feeling for her siblings but what if she was content to use them as a distraction? Send them on a futile rescue attempt while she exacts her revenge upon me?'

'It is feasible,' the assassin conceded, 'but she will still know that an attempt on your life will bring her into conflict with me, a battle she knows she cannot win.'

'My Liege,' Audack added, confidence returning following the praise he had received, 'there is another matter to consider, one of even more pressing concern, I fear.'

The Prince stopped and offered his full attention to the General, 'Of course, you came here with news. What is it that concerns you?'

'Your brother, Sire, Prince Porthus of Zendra. Our scouts have confirmed that he returned home for only a single day before departing once again with an armoured retinue. He has sent no formal notification, but it appears he is returning here.'

Another silence dragged out as the Prince contemplated the news. Eventually he moved back to the drinks table and poured himself a large fortified wine into a hightail glass. Draining half of the contents in one swig, he took a seat on the throne and observed them both closely for a moment before smiling.

'It appears my hand is forced,' he spoke slowly, as if containing an inner excitement, 'now we will see just how reliable Silas Zendar's research has been. General, I want you to activate any agents we have in Corinth and Rennicksburg, if there are none then hire mercenaries. Ensure they act quickly to slay the Fimarr sisters and their allies; hopefully, Silver Rain is not yet recovered enough to survive. Double the size of our border patrols and begin preparations for three battalions who will be used as occupation forces when the time comes. I want the Palace to be at heightened defence for the duration.'

'But, Sire,' Audack protested, 'What of the insurgents? With three battalions prepared for invasion, I will not be able to muster forces to quash them!'

'Fear not, General, follow your orders and ensure everything is ready as directed. I will deal with the treasonous offal in the East and my loathsome brother in the same manner. I brought Alissa Fimarr here for a reason; it is time for her to begin proving worthy of the effort. If both problems can be erased without any link back to me, then I can maintain the status quo with the other Kingdoms for longer.'

'This strategy still proves flawed,' Mozak joined in once again, 'Silver Rain will not die by the hands of poorly-skilled mercenaries, regardless of her injuries or exhaustion. You will only provoke her further.'

Lennath's smile widened, 'Mozak, you are a leader within the most prestigious and deadly clan of assassins to exist, are you not?'

'The Veer have no equal,' Mozak confirmed.

'And how much would it cost to bring all of your available clan here?'

Audack turned and hurried from the room to begin organising the army as ordered. As he scurried back along the corridor, downing the small sherry to settle his nerves, he could not resist the involuntary shudder that ran through his body. It remained unclear as to whether it was the thought of war against the other Kingdoms that caused the knot of fear within him, or the idea of more of the unnerving assassins throughout the palace.

In the distance, the familiar rooftops of Rennicksburg ran parallel to the track they currently followed and Treya felt her mood lighten at the sight. The journey from Lustania had been a tense affair, Straker insistent on remaining clear of any settlements and forcing them all to camp rough; not something she found difficult, but it felt unnecessary. Most of his conversation had fixated on the black-garbed bodyguard allied to the Lustanian Prince and the level of concern it raised in him had left her rattled. She had never heard of Veer assassins and wondered why her partner was so determined that the threat affected them at all; this visit was their first interaction with the man in years. Still, his worry had been palpable, and she could not ignore it. Maybe that was the reason she had been able to get nothing of consequence from Catalana or Herc either, if they were also disturbed by

Straker's warnings, perhaps that explained their avoidance during conversation. Ultimately, she felt isolated from her companions despite their proximity.

Now some of that concern had drained away, and her thoughts drifted to what awaited them at the farm. Joseff and Melody brought such joy into her life and being away from them had been the hardest thing she had ever done; the anticipation of seeing their innocent little faces was almost more than she could bear. She had felt deflated when Straker insisted that Herc and Catalana joined them before returning into the town proper; she would make the best of it, however, and it was always a delight to see the twins interacting with their aunt.

Up ahead, the perimeter gate of their ploughed lands was creeping ever nearer, and she resisted the urge to break into a run. The sentiment was not shared by one of the workers tilling the soil as she spotted the man turn and sprint towards the main house, undoubtedly announcing their return to those within. Sure enough, once they were beyond the gate and heading up the long track towards their home, Hederna Thriss appeared with the joyful twins at her heels. Their excitement could not be contained, and they broke into a carefree gallop towards the approaching party; Treya heard the laughter around her at the sight and knew the soothing effect of her children was already taking effect.

Movement from the right caught her attention and time suddenly seemed to slow to a crawl. A flash of silver in the sunlight revealed the narrow short sword drawn from a belt previously concealed under a heavy cloak; the wielder had been disguised as a worker in the field but was now driving across the turned earth toward her defenceless children. Treya knew she was breaking into a run, but it felt sluggish and detached from her own perception, each step seeming to take an age to fall. To her right, Forge was already striding ahead, determination etched across his face with the tinge of fear in his eyes; there was no way either of them could get to the twins before the charging attacker. The dim awareness that another assailant had stepped from behind one of the orchard trees registered in her mind, but she could not pull her gaze from the scene ahead of her; Hederna screaming and trying to lurch forward in her cumbersome skirts, the children oblivious to the danger and the killer closing in with blade rising for a fatal strike. Trying to scream, the terror filled her throat and prevented the sound escaping; she pushed her legs in the vain hope that she could defy physics and intercept the weapon that was about to end her reason for living.

Suddenly, a mighty double-bladed axe flew end over end across her vision, spinning through the air like a cartwheel. In the slow motion her perception was trapped within, she could make out every detail of the finely crafted weapon; sturdy oak hilt, ornate tree designs on the flat of the head and perfectly honed blades. Every element familiar to her for it was her father's axe. Her own shock was only matched by the sprinting attacker whose eyes widened too late to prevent the heavy weapon burying itself in his chest and stomach, throwing him backwards several feet. Relief swept over her and time reverted to its normal speed, at the same moment the strength drained from her legs and she tumbled awkwardly to the dirt road. The twins were screaming now, but still running towards her, Forge was closing the distance to them rapidly and Hederna must have also tripped as she lay wailing in the dirt. A thud next to her drew her attention to a crossbow bolt that had just appeared in the ground a few inches from her arm. Flicking her head back to the orchard, she saw the culprit reloading his weapon and realised he was not alone either, a second man taking aim with a longbow towards Straker. Rolling herself into one of the ploughed furrows of earth in the field beside the road, her eyes fell to Catalana who had leapt onto the back of a crop cart, avoiding several bolts that now protruded from the raised wooden side of the vehicle.

Flipping herself over to her front, she watched as an arrow struck the ground between Forge's pounding feet, but he failed to react to it at all, all focus on his children. Staying low, she began to crawl forward quickly, closer to her babies and closer to the house where she could retrieve a weapon. Her hand fell upon a large rock and she snatched it up as an alternative for the moment. Scanning back to the warriors in the orchard, she spotted Herc crashing through the saplings towards them; he must have taken an indirect route to avoid attracting their attention but could remain stealthy no longer. The crossbowman turned at the sound and released a bolt that pierced the big woodsman's side but did not slow his momentum. Slamming heavily into his opponent, Herc lifted him from the ground and used him as a battering ram into the archer. All three men toppled to the ground among the larger fruit-bearing trees and beyond her vision. With the long-range threat removed, Treya leapt to her feet and returned to a gallop. As Straker collided with the children, dragging them to the ground in his cradling embrace, elation swept over her and her focus turned to another warrior sprinting towards the small group. Well-maintained leather armour adorned the newcomer, and he wielded a vicious-looking Warhammer in his right hand; he would close the gap before she could. Sliding to a stop, she took a single deep breath before hurling the rock in her hand; the throw was uncannily accurate and caught the sprinting man on the cheek, taking him by surprise and staggering him to one side. It was not enough to stop him, however, and he recommenced his charge with blood streaming from his savaged face.

'Straker!' she screamed out in warning, alerting him to the danger and watching as he shielded the twins under his own body. The warrior reached them but leapt over their prone forms without pausing, continuing his run and smashing his Warhammer into the skull of another man she had not even seen. A second blow to the jaw, the crack of shattering bone echoing through the clear air, ended the combat without reply. The unexpected saviour stopped where he was, wiping blood from his weapon while placing one hand against his facial injury. Treya broke back into a run, forcing herself to ignore the cries of her children as she retrieved her father's axe from the corpse in which it still stood. Hefting the enormous weapon before her, she brandished it towards the stranger as she stalked back towards her family.

'Who are you?' she demanded, 'What are you doing here and why have you helped us?'

The initial answer came from the twins who cried out and whimpered for her until Straker pulled them into his lap and soothed them softly. Treya did not turn her attention from the warrior, though her heart ached to throw her arms about them and kiss them until they could take it no longer, and she kept steely eyes upon him. Having finished a basic clean of the Warhammer, he hooked it back into his belt and turned to her, still dabbing at the wound on his right cheek.

'That was a good throw, Treya Fimarr,' he replied amiably, 'almost enough to prevent me from saving your children. Again.'

Confusion filled her, 'What are you talking about?'

'Your father's axe,' he gestured to the over-sized weapon in her hands, 'I had always planned to return it to you, perhaps not under these circumstances, however.'

'That was an amazing throw,' Catalana joined in, arriving from along the main track, 'or incredibly lucky. But we owe you a debt of gratitude regardless.'

'Yes,' Treya agreed, 'but with that I require answers. I am never a fan of coincidentally good timing, especially when the other party already knows my name. Tell us who you are.'

He smiled, meeting each of their eyes evenly, 'My name is Terex, I have come here for your help. I will admit that my timing is not pure coincidence; I knew of these mercenaries and their plan to ambush you. I had hoped that aiding you during the attack would prove my intentions towards you.'

'What!?' Treya snapped in fury, throwing the axe down and surging towards him, being restrained by Catalana before reaching him, 'Did it not occur to you that warning us might prove your intentions? Without endangering my children?'

'Easy love,' Forge soothed from behind her, 'Remember how we met? Poor judgement may have been shown by, err, Terex was it?' a nodded response allowed him to continue, 'But maybe we should allow him to explain himself?'

Treya halted her struggle and turned her back on Terex, pacing over to the huddled group on the floor where she dropped to her knees, welcoming the enthusiastic hugs thrown upon her by the twins. Closing her eyes and crushing them to her, she mumbled another question, 'Terex? I think I know that name from somewhere; indulge us with your story.'

'It seems our fates have been intertwined for far longer than any of you realise. We were once enemies,' Catalana tensed at the statement and stepped to the side, ensuring she was between Terex and her sister, 'but rest assured that is no longer the case. My tale may be shocking or unbelievable to you, but I implore you to listen and understand that I would not have come here unless I had no other choice.

Five years ago, I was general of Ramikain's armies, I fought many great battles against the Dussen people all in his name; I believed that he was destined to control all lands and I chose to be part of that new empire. But you destroyed him, I returned from my victories to find it so; I will not lie, I plotted revenge against the Fimarr family for many months but, as time passed, my rage ebbed, and I found new direction. For when I searched the ruins of the Black Citadel, I discovered my new loyalty, my new mistress, your sister, Alissa Fimarr.'

'Liar!' Treya suddenly cried out, releasing her infants and leaping to her feet once more. Before she could launch an outraged attack against the man, she was stopped in her tracks by Catalana's words.

'It is true, Treya, Alissa still lives,' emotion filled the words, and she could see the tears streaming from her sister's eyes as she turned to deliver the admission, 'I'm so sorry, but I knew back then that she had lived. I had assumed she died years hence, but recent events have made it clear that she survived. I can now see that Terex had a part to play in that.'

Treya could find no words; her baby sister, the girl she had raised to adulthood and then lost tragically, had not died at all; the sister she had mended bonds with five years ago now stood before her admitting that she had lied about this for years and had been content to abandon Alissa to death; an ally of the villain who had almost killed them all was now here divulging his part in protecting her sister and asking for their help. It was too much to process and she could feel the tears pouring from her own eyes as her voice failed.

Hands fell upon her shoulders and she felt Straker's body behind her, strong and steady as it always was. He pressed lips against her cheek and whispered into her ear, 'I cannot imagine how you feel, my love, I would not pretend to understand the pain in your heart right now. We can talk with Catalana later about this deception. Right now, we are nursing our fears following an attack on our family and this man may have the answers. Please allow him to finish his tale; when we know what danger faces us, then we can decide on what action to take.'

She pressed back against him and nodded.

'Go on, Terex, but be warned that the beginning of your proclamation has not brought you much good will. You are still alive right now as recognition for defending our children,' Forge stated.

Terex opened his palms to them and bowed slightly, 'I understand. It may not help but know that I am a soldier at heart; my enemies are my enemies whilst I am at war. We are no longer at war, in fact I have new reason to consider you allies, reciprocated or not. Know that I, and a small enclave of trusted men, protected and concealed Alissa Fimarr for the past five years. I cannot explain why, exactly, we felt the task was of such importance; perhaps I wanted to redeem my failure in allowing Ramikain to be defeated; perhaps I simply sought a new goal after failing in the one I had been raised to complete; no doubt we all had different reasons. What I can tell you is that your sister became everything to me, and I would allow no ill to befall her; even her imbalance was something I became accustomed to. I cannot be certain if she ever recognised my loyalty, but it did not matter to me; as long as she was safe I was succeeding. She felt great rage towards you all for the murder of her true love…'

'What?' Treya could not comprehend what was being said, 'Do you mean Kale Stanis? He was a servant of Ramikain all along! He corrupted Alissa, turned her mind, and struck me down to defend his Master! Even after all that we did not kill him; he was responsible for his own death!'

At her rising anger, Terex nodded placatingly, 'I do not pretend to know what happened on the day you confronted Ramikain, I can only tell you what I do know and what Alissa believes. The details of her dispassion towards you are not of concern right now. The point is that I cared more for her and Kastani than any I have ever known...'

'Who is Kastani?' Catalana voiced the question with a tremor in her voice, as if she already knew the answer.

'Kastani is her daughter, born several months after your time in the Citadel; I suppose I helped raise her almost as if she were my own. Know truly that I would die for that child. But, it seems I may have also failed in that task.'

Silence filled the air for a moment and Terex took a deep, controlling breath before continuing, 'They were taken, weeks ago, kidnapped and stolen away from me. I was impotent to prevent it and so I have come to you for help. Only you care for Alissa Fimarr as I do; regardless of our pasts, I had hoped that you would help me to save her, save them both.'

Treya swallowed back the heartache, anger and confusion swirling through her, grasping one of Straker's hands for strength as she spoke, 'My sister, my niece, are kidnapped? But even I did not know they lived; who has taken them, and why?'

'Please, take a moment to compose yourself, for the answer will hurt even more than all I have already said,' Terex said genuinely, pausing before revealing the answer, 'They were stolen away by Silver Rain.'

Treya felt her legs weaken again and only Forge's strength kept her upright, 'No,' she sobbed with despair.

'I am sorry to have to tell you this,' Terex continued, 'but she killed all of my men with little effort and I was only the slightest of obstacles despite my desperation to save them.'

'But you live,' Straker added, 'you fought Rayne Fimarr and are still alive?'

'Indeed, that is something I cannot explain. She bested me and I believed my time had come. But I awoke hours after our battle to find the Citadel deserted. Although I decided to track them in the hope that I could enact a rescue, I brought your father's axe with me; perhaps I already knew that I would not succeed alone and this could be the olive branch required to earn your trust; the very weapon that slayed my former Master, previously wielded by your father. A strange item to bind us but a symbol of our potential union, nonetheless.'

'And what did your tracking reveal?' Catalana questioned, power returning to her voice.

'Very little,' he admitted, 'I trailed them to the North for many days only to find the tracks were actually an old supply run by one of my own people. Your sister is not easily followed it seems. I even travelled to Corinth briefly to locate her; I had hoped to offer a ruse contract to her, allowing me to question her at least, but I could not even locate her agent to do so. So it was that I travelled here to seek your aid.'

'And how did you find out about this attack?' Straker pried.

'I believe I was mistaken for a mercenary simply because of my travelling garb and weapons. The first man I killed today approached me and asked if I was for hire; out of interest I played along to discover that a bounty had been placed on your heads. The plan was to await your return and use your children as leverage, allowing us to kill you all without a fight.'

'And then the children?' Treya pressed.

'Aye, the children too. Be assured that even if this plan had gone awry, had one or all of you been killed due to a failure on my part, I would not have allowed any harm to befall the little ones.'

'Who hired them?' Cat' asked.

'That is where things become a little more confusing,' Terex admitted, 'because the contract was raised by envoys from Lustania.'

'Lennath?' Treya couldn't keep the shock from her voice, 'He is involved? He has ordered our deaths? Is this because of the perceived insult during our visit? Or could he be responsible for Alissa's kidnap? By Yanis, could she have been there at the same time as us? We could have...'

Straker turned her to face him and held her tearful gaze as he spoke, 'We do not know that this is all linked; even if she were there when we consorted with him, there was no way we could have known and nothing we could have done. Remember the Veer assassin? We need to take some time to absorb all this and discover what is really happening around us.'

'No, Straker, he has her, I know it! We must return to Lustania and free her, kill Lennath if necessary and bring her back to us!'

'If I may offer an alternative,' a deep but shaky voice spoke from the road; Treya looked beyond Straker to see Herc holding the shaft of a crossbow bolt where it protruded from just above his hip, both hands covered in the blood of his enemies, 'perhaps a little time to rest, recuperate and plan would not go amiss?'

Catalana rushed to him and took some of his weight onto her own shoulders before easing him towards the farmhouse. Treya watched her sister before turning her eyes to the still-hysterical Hederna Thriss, her incredible children who waited patiently for her direction despite their fear and back to the man she loved more than any other. Finally, she turned back towards Terex.

'Terex, I thank you for your actions here today and the confessions you have provided. Know that you have earned forgiveness for all past animosities, whether we physically crossed swords or not. I can never express my gratitude fully for protecting my sister and niece for all those years, but you are welcome here no longer. I provide you my word that Alissa and Kastani will be saved, and their tormentor will be rightly punished. But this is now a family matter and we neither need, nor want, your help.'

Ushering her children before her, she followed her family towards the house without a further look at the man who had saved them.

Rebecca caressed her finger over the rim of her glass, enjoying the light ringing the motion caused. Crossing her legs, she readjusted the heavy silk dress over her petticoats to ensure her modesty was retained; only her ankle high boots were visible below the decorative hems. This party had proven ill-advised; originally she had assumed the organiser, one Lord Barrismund, to be an immigrating noble from one of the Five Kingdoms. Instead, it seemed he was simply a member of the gentry who had come into a windfall. That meant temporary money, superficial functions such as this, and little in the way of significant personalities invited to be worth networking. Of course, as per usual, she had no shortage of interested parties wishing to converse, usually men desperate to demonstrate their own wealth and influence, completely unaware of her profession. None had presented themselves as potential patrons, either directly or indirectly, and it appeared even the least prestigious of her clients would get no work. Still, some of the wine had been palatable, and she had been able to re-use an older dress having not attended this district before.

With little hope of gaining any significant business from the event, she was preparing to make her farewells when an icy chill ran down her spine. Composing herself quickly, so as not to alert any onlookers to her sudden concern, she took a lengthy sip from her drink and slowly scanned the room again. Luckily, the table she sat at was tucked towards a corner, only a few guests were behind her and out of view, so she could assess most of the other attendees and retain a casual posture. Her eyes quickly secured the reason for her unease, but she kept her gaze moving past him and onto a local merchant banker she had conversed with earlier, nodding and tilting her glass as he noticed her. Returning her eyes to the table, she considered what she had noted from her brief observation. Whatever the reason for his attention, the man she had attempted to overlook stood out painfully in this environment; he was tall, heavily built and wearing garments that were clearly not tailored to him. Much as he was placing stress upon the seams of his coat and breaches, he was also unshaven and his shoulder-length hair was unkempt, as if straightened only with hands and goodwill. What she had glimpsed of his weathered face indicated an age upwards of mid-fifties and the worn grey of his locks supported this theory. There was no missing the deep intensity of his one eye as it had stared directly towards her; it was not paranoia unnerving her, the thinly-disguised warrior was here for her.

Rebecca was no novice at being stalked, both potential patrons and suitors had often resorted to such measures when their nerve to approach her directly had escaped them, but she was in no doubt that her current watcher held no such anxieties. Rising elegantly, she sauntered across the main floor, where some couples were performing a local dance, ignoring the intimidating presence to her right and greeting the banker enthusiastically with both hands. Squeezing his fingers tightly, she smiled sweetly and put on her best doe-eyed expression.

'Hello again, Thellus,' she purred, 'I was thinking about our earlier discussion all evening. I really do agree that the changes suggested by the Fulansian Monarchy could really affect the incoming trade routes to Kazgrat as a whole. It is so wise of you to foresee such concerns and raise interest to accommodate for any financial shortfall the banks may face.'

The slightly pudgy man was perhaps ten years her senior and his finery was clearly superficial; she imagined he wore the same outfit to any such event. Her arrival had certainly caught him off-guard, but she was pleased to note his focus had instantly shifted to her and away from his previous conversation.

'Erm, I think, of course! How wonderful of you to remember our discussion!' he enthused, slightly condescendingly, 'Many of the cities in Kazgrat could feel the strain of such significant political change and new trade agreements are inevitable. Corinth must be ahead of that curve and I will ensure the banks lead in that endeavour.'

'I believe you will,' she replied, dropping her voice to a huskier tone and running one hand up the outside of his arm, feigning interest in the deeply hidden muscle there, 'it would be so wonderful to discuss this in depth with you.'

'Of course,' he blurted out too quickly, 'there is so much…'

'I meant in private,' she continued, 'perhaps in your accommodations?'

His eyes widened in surprise and he licked at suddenly dry lips as he tried to find his voice, 'Y-yes, that would be most acceptable,' he stammered, 'but I live several streets away.'

'A cool night's walk is always invigorating. And I have no fears if you are with me.'

Thellus fumbled nervously as he located a flat surface to lay down his half-finished drink before offering her his arm. Hooking it with both of hers, she pressed herself against his side as they started towards the exit. It became clear her ruse had not worked after only ten paces, at which point her observer stepped in front of them. Almost as broad as her current escort and herself combined, the interloper stared at her with his solitary grey eye before speaking in an urgent whisper.

'Rebecca Pallstirrith? You must come with me; you are in danger!'

'Excuse me, sir,' Thellus piped up with the bravery of his surroundings, 'but this young lady is my consort and therefore favours my protection. I assure you she is quite safe.'

The grey eye flicked from her to the man at her side, 'With no disrespect meant, you cannot protect her. Do not force my hand, allow her to come with me.'

'I speak for myself, you brute!' Rebecca countered, 'Now get out of our way before we summon the house guards to eject you!'

Her voice was firm but her confidence less so and she could feel the tremble in the man beside her. For a moment there was silence between them, and she watched, fixated, as their antagonist rubbed idly at the patch over his right eye, mulling over the words they had said. Suddenly, a powerful arm lashed out and planted an open palm into Thellus' chest, staggering him back out of Rebecca's grasp and sending him crashing to a seated position on the floor. Stunned amazement was plastered on his face as the crowd around him backed away amid gasps of surprise. A heavy grip closed on her wrist and she flicked her eyes back to the impassive face of her attacker.

'Please, we don't have time for this. You must come with me; Silver Rain sent me!'

The words were unexpected, and she found herself dragged across the room with little resistance, feet moving of their own accord as she tried to process the admission. Rayne was still away on the Lustanian contract; it had taken far longer than Rebecca had imagined but such was the nature of her work. If that task was complete, then she would have come herself for there was nothing Silver Rain feared. If she could not come herself then there was nobody she would send in her stead; there was nobody in the world that she trusted. Rebecca realised this must be a trap; an angry former patron looking to claim revenge for a contract incomplete perhaps, or maybe the family of a victim using her to get to the assassin. Suddenly she pulled back against her captor, crouching and leaning her weight towards the ground; anything to make this kidnap more difficult.

'No! Let me go! Help me! Somebody, help me!' she cried out, attracting the attention of the whole room, relieved to see two of the door guardians moving towards them.

'This is unhelpful,' her kidnapper growled, 'but I suppose I cannot blame you.'

Phenomenal strength dragged her forward again, spinning her around in front of him and depositing her heavily to the polished wooden floor in a tangle of skirts.

Attempting to find her feet, she watched as the two guards arrived, swords drawn and confronted her assailant.

'I don't think you were invited here, one-eye,' one challenged, 'if you leave now, we won't report you to the Watch. But the lady stays with us.'

'Your offer is generous,' came the reply, 'but wholly unacceptable. Lady Pallstirrith is in great danger as we speak.'

'She is safe right here and right now,' the guard continued, and Rebecca realised he wanted to avoid a conflict. Did he fear the giant before him, or was he concerned for the other guests should a fight break out?

'I'm afraid she is not,' the old man insisted before launching himself forward.

The first guard already had his sword raised but was not expecting an unarmed aggressor to charge straight for him. With no time or space to swing his weapon, he simply thrust it forward. The grey-haired warrior was faster than his age suggested, dodging sideways as he approached and batting the flat of the blade aside with one arm before crashing his other fist against his opponent's nose. An audible crack accompanied the spray of blood that burst from the man's face as he toppled backwards. The second defender now had time to react and stepped into his partner's wake, arcing a backhand swing of his own blade towards the unarmed fighter. The old man leapt out of the way, rolling over one shoulder before slamming heavily against a table. Immediately, he reached up and began tossing plates and goblets at the guard, all easily fended off with a few waves of his sword and free arm. Rebecca realised it was a lure but had no time to cry out a warning before he was in range. With a mighty heave, one-eye dragged the entire table from the floor, swinging it round and slamming the approaching guard sideways. Dropping the massive, improvised weapon, her kidnapper threw himself forward onto his winded opponent and she heard the dull snap as knees crushed ribs.

'I'm sorry!' the old man panted as he dragged the groaning guard up onto his shoulders, 'Please stop and I won't have to kill you!'

No answer came amid bright red blood frothing at the man's lips where he dangled across the bigger man's broad shoulders. His partner was regaining his feet, face awash with blood that continued to pour from his nose, wiping at eyes streaming from the pain. With unbelievable strength, one-eye heaved his burden above his head and launched him like a human trebuchet. Flying several metres through the air, the injured guard smashed thickly into his comrade, an anguished cry erupting from one of them, and both men were sent skidding into the crowd.

On her feet, Rebecca turned to flee amongst the other guests, but a powerful hand yanked her back before dragging her up under one arm. Agony shot through her abdomen as she was carried uncomfortably from the room and down the steps beyond. Bursting from the manor-house main doors, she managed to force out words against the pain, 'Please! Please put me down! I won't try to run; you are hurting me!'

The old man pulled up short and placed her on her feet before him, 'Fair enough,' he replied, still struggling to steady his breathing, 'We will attract far less attention if we are both on foot anyway. I know this will be hard for you to believe, but I really am here to help. Now, get moving, I will direct as we go.'

Placing her hands on her battered midriff, dreading the bruises that would soon appear there, she began forward as quickly as her attire would allow, hearing the heavier footsteps close behind her and feeling the ominous presence of her enforced companion. If this were a trap, she should find out as much from him as possible; better to prepare herself for what awaited her at the end of this journey.

'Who are you?' she spoke quietly, hoping that only he could hear her.

'My name is Jacob Frost. Silver Rain believes she is too well known in Corinth; she didn't want her presence to place you in danger.'

'Jacob Frost? From Lustania?'

'Aye, you know me?'

'Only from tales told to me by Silver Rain herself. About your betrayal of her, your attempts to murder her and her kin, how you left them at the mercy of an entire army. If you are Frost then you have revealed this trap too soon!'

'I am the Frost you speak of,' he replied, and she could hear the shame laced into his words, 'and I shall not shy from the crimes you have stated. But I am remorseful for those actions, I have waited for a chance to make amends and now that chance is realised. I saved Silver Rain from imprisonment in Lustania; her contract there was dishonoured, and the Prince will be hoping to claim retribution for her escape. I want to return and depose him, but she insisted that we come here first. She fears enormously for your safety. You must be a great friend to her.'

Rebecca was filled with confusion at his words and remembered they could be just that, words. She decided to remain uncommitted and see what else her captor may reveal, 'I am simply her agent. We are business partners. It makes little sense for her to come here for me if she is wanted by one of the Kingdom Princes; it is far more likely that Prince Lennath would send his people for me. Far more likely that he sent you.'

'You have a valid point; left here,' he remarked, nudging her right shoulder to steer her, 'and the vengeful nature of Lennath is why I agreed to join her; too many innocent lives have been lost because of that man already. True, I could be one of his agents and I have no time to try and prove otherwise. When you see her in the flesh, you will realise this is all genuine.'

Whilst attempting to concoct a question that could reveal his true intentions, a faint click in the distance caught her attention and she briefly heard a rush of air. A heavy impact slammed into her back as she turned towards the sound and she realised Frost had forced her to the ground, his right hand shooting out parallel to her head. Impacting with the hard cobbles below, she saw the crossbow bolt tear through his outstretched limb, stopping halfway through his palm. She stifled a scream of alarm and felt herself dragged to her feet once again, this time the old man taking the lead at pace, dragging her behind him and almost off her feet as her skirts impeded her stride. Ducking behind a building, another thud indicated a second bolt had narrowly missed them. Frost pushed her back against the wall and knelt before her; grabbing her hems in both hands, he pulled harshly and tore the multiple layers viciously apart. Instinctively, she pushed the folds back down defensively.

'What are you doing?' she hissed in alarm.

'I am sorry, but you need to be able to run. Now your legs can move freely. I do not know how many are out there, but I think we are ahead of them. I want you to run, it is not far, on Millers Street there is a pine door, all the others are oak, and upon it is the sigil of a badger. Go there and enter without knocking; she is waiting for us. I will try and prevent pursuit.'

'But you are unarmed,' she could hear the panic in her words and was disappointed that her nerve was not holding under such circumstances.

Frost grasped the end of the metal arrow protruding from his right hand, grunting at the pain as he tore the quarrel free. Releasing the breath he had been holding, he offered her a genuine smile, 'And now I am armed, Lady. Please go, before this chance is wasted.'

She placed a hand on his arm as he regained his feet, 'I...' she did not know what words were appropriate, 'I believe you,' she finished before sprinting along the short alley in the direction he had indicated. She knew the city well enough to find Millers Street without effort and felt her chest heaving with the effort now that her legs could carry her at top speed. There were few people wandering this district on an evening; as a residential zone, there were no workers conducting their business and there were far richer pickings to be had for the unruly element. She imagined the most alarming thing for any other citizens was the sight of her own headlong flight, ragged skirts flailing about her.

Finally, she reached her destination, leaning back against the wall to catch her breath and wipe the sweat from her face. Reaching for the door handle, thoughts of deceit resurfaced unbidden, and she paused with her fingers wrapped around the black iron handle. If this were all a trick then Frost had gone to extreme measures to achieve it and she could not fathom why he would have allowed her to complete the journey herself if he were not genuine. Taking one more deep breath, she pushed down on the handle and opened the door.

It was dark within and she stepped gingerly inside, heart pounding now from fear rather than her exertions. Stepping just beyond the threshold, she closed the door behind her despite her better judgement; if the pursuers *were* real, then she wanted no obvious sign of her hiding place. In the dim light clawing through the shutters, she could see the building must be a grain store, sacks and smaller containers adorning the floor and shelves and a service counter towards the rear of the room. Behind the counter stood another doorway, this one covered with a simple sackcloth sheet hung from the frame, gentle light flickering from beyond. Cautiously, she tip-toed silently towards the access and slipped through to the storage area behind the storefront. She squinted her eyes against the sudden difference in brightness that a small lantern on the floor provided in the room. Focussing, she spotted a slender, gaunt man, bound at wrists and ankles, tight gag forcing his mouth open but preventing significant sound from being made. Bruises and cuts adorned the skin she could see on his face, hands and bare feet; terror filled his eyes when they met hers, but he did not move or try to call out. Fears of ambush sprang back into her mind and she was about to turn tail and flee when a shape shot from the shadows to her left and gripped her fiercely by the shoulders.

'Rebecca! You are safe! I am so relieved, so pleased Frost did not fail me!' Thick emotion filled the words and tears were welling in the eyes of Rayne Fimarr. Before Rebecca could answer her, the assassin pulled her agent into a powerful embrace, squeezing too hard but clearly impassioned to be reunited.

'I am fine, Rayne, unharmed at least. The fact that we are meeting like this, in this place, under these circumstances, leaves me in little doubt that I am far from safe,' she replied with as much volume as her restricted lungs would allow.

Hearing the strain in her voice, Rayne released her and pulled back slightly before showering her face with kisses. The last one arrived at her lips and lingered. Rebecca pushed her away gently.

'I am happy to see you, Rayne, and so very pleased that you are alive. But nothing else between us has changed, do you understand?' she spoke softly, realising too late how much her final words sounded like an admonishment.

A flash of pain crossed Rayne's eyes before she released her hold and turned back into the room, 'I know that, Rebecca. I am sorry that my joy over your safety overflowed somewhat. It was obvious they would come for you to get to me; you are one of the only links that I have to the rest of the World.'

'I understand,' Rebecca replied gently, 'and I am extremely grateful that you took action to prevent this attack; I would already be dead if not for Jacob's bravery. He is still out there, Rayne, we were ambushed, and he remained behind so that I could escape. You have to help him.'

Despite the ragged outfit she was currently wearing and the exhaustion evident in her voice and posture, Rebecca knew that Rayne could defeat any would-be killers that may be hunting them. Whether she would do so for a man who had left her to die in the past was another question. 'I'm certain he will be fine...' she started.

'No, Rayne, he appears strong, but I think age hounds him. I cannot condone his sacrifice for my benefit. You can aid him. You must aid him!'

'I must do nothing! I am constantly betrayed, used or cast aside by others! I owe nothing and am obliged to no-one!' she spat out in what sounded more like despair than anger.

'Please. Rayne, I am asking you to help the man who saved you and me both.'

The assassin released a heavy sigh and turned resignedly towards the storefront, 'I will do as you ask,' she conceded, 'but because you asked it, nothing more.'

Before she passed the hanging cover of the doorway, heavy footsteps entered via the front door, accompanied by panting and wheezing she thought she recognised. Joining the newly alert Rayne beyond the curtain, relief washed through her at the sight of Jacob Frost trying to catch his breath whilst leaning forward heavily, hands on thighs for support.

'You made it,' Rayne said flatly.

'I was lucky,' he replied through gasps for air, 'only two of them out there.'

'Are you certain?'

'Rayne!' Rebecca scolded, 'Let us attend to his injuries before your interrogation begins!'

Frost released a chuckle, 'Do not fear, Lady Pallstirrith, I am already accustomed to my travelling companion! I would not object to a binding for my hand but let us administer it in the back store; it is less likely we will be detected.'

Returning to the larger room, Rebecca tore a strip from one of her underskirts for Frost to use as a bandage. 'So, what has caused this retaliation against you, Rayne? And who is this stranger you have captive?'

'I was betrayed by Lennath,' Fimarr replied, unable to hide the venom in her words, 'he had no intention of honouring the contract and it seems he plans to use the package I delivered to conquer the Kingdoms.'

'The package?' Rebecca echoed, 'You mean your sister?'

'Aye,' Frost interjected, 'the package poses a significant threat while Lennath can use it towards his own ends. I believe he would not be content with only the Kingdoms.'

'But, I mean, your sister? She is just a girl? What threat can she pose?'

'The threat is real!' Rayne snapped, 'This man,' she indicated their prisoner, 'knows all about it. A power, nay an evil, so strong that it will tip the balance in his favour. It has to be stopped.'

Rebecca moved forward and took her friend by the shoulder, turning her face-to-face, 'Your sister, Rayne, Alissa. She was the package. I am so sorry, but I already knew when I dispatched you to Lustania. I thought it might help provide some closure to find out if she lived. The Prince had told me she could help him cure an emerging plague. I had no idea of his wicked intentions. This is my fault.'

Clarity filled the assassin's face and a smile flickered briefly as she spoke, 'It is nobody's fault. He would have contracted to somebody else if not me, and then we may not have forewarning of his plans. And we would not have the depth of knowledge Zendar can provide, either. Know that there is no blame at your door, but you cannot simply return to life as normal. Lennath's people will continue to hunt you until I am dead, or he is defeated. I cannot risk that you will be harmed; I need you to come with us.'

A wave of fear flowed over her, 'I cannot, Rayne, my life is here. I am a socialite at best, not an adventurer, not even a wanderer, certainly not a warrior. I will be a burden at least, a liability at most. Perhaps I can simply hide in the city until this is over?'

'I will not take that risk; I cannot. There is no discussion here.'

Rebecca didn't know how to respond, and a tense silence fell until she could find words, 'To go where? Attack Lennath? Recover your sister? What?'

'Firstly, I will need to visit one of my safehouses, to gather supplies and fresh clothes; I'm certain something there will fit you too, something more appropriate for travelling.'

'And perhaps somewhere to wash?' Rebecca added attempting to lighten the mood, 'you both smell like the sewer!'

Frost smiled but Rayne continued without reaction, 'There is a way to prevent Lennath's plot from being realised, I mean from *ever* being realised…'

'You cannot mean killing your own sister!' she blurted out before she could stop herself.

For a moment Rayne looked hurt at the suggestion but quickly continued, 'No, to destroy the power they intend to harness. But I may need her to achieve that.'

'You want to kidnap her from Lennath's palace? Just the three of us?'

'I intend to retrieve her from Lennath, yes. But it will not be just the three of us. There are only a few people who can be trusted to help, though. We will need to recruit my sisters…'

The bowl of candied fruits bobbled precariously close to the edge of the plush cushioned seat as the carriage wheels struck another rock in the road. Porthus shot out a chubby hand to rescue the delicious treats before they fell, tugging the dish back towards the rear of the seat alongside him. Sighing heavily, he banged on the roof of his spacious carriage.

'Keep your eyes on the road! I am not a sack of potatoes; let us make the journey comfortable for everyone shall we?' he hollered, hoping the driver could hear him. Idly plucking three of the sweets and popping them into his mouth, he chewed slowly, enjoying the luxurious flavours as they mingled on their way down his throat. His valet had assured him that there was enough food for the entire journey, but boredom soon turned into appetite and he had run out of snacks two days before arriving home on the reverse leg; the last thing he needed was to arrive at Lennath's palace exhausted from hunger. Shifting his bulk forward, he eased the curtain of one window to the side to find that dusk was setting in; another few hours and they would be making camp. As one of the thirty soldiers in his retinue trotted past him towards the front of the caravan, Porthus reclined back again, adding a larger handful of fruits to his palate, and considering the confrontation his journey's end would bring.

It still seemed unfathomable that Lennath could have ordered the attack against him. Even if they had simply been insurgents or highwaymen, all evidence pointed to resourcing from Lustania. Porthus had given the situation much thought and there was still a chance his youngest sibling was innocent, that parties beyond his awareness had provided access to weapons or finance to the perpetrators of that ambush. But his brother had changed so much in recent years, shaping himself into a dominant leader among his people, antagonising the other Kingdoms with new trade deals or aggressive renegotiations, and crafting himself into an intimidating force; Porthus rubbed unconsciously at his face remembering their last encounter. Lennath could not remain unchecked; despite his father's warnings, Porthus had to confront him, reveal the truth and bring him to account for his actions. Of course, there was a risk in arriving unannounced, hence why he had brought thirty of his finest warriors to ensure any further 'surprises' were dealt with efficiently. No amount of bravado or intimidation could alter the direction this discussion would take; it was likely the youngest Prince would buckle as he had for most of his life when discovered to be in the wrong. There had always been squabbles between the brothers through the years, but surely an assassination attempt was a step too far?

Another bump in the road snapped him from his musings and he saved his appetizers once again. Growling in frustration he was about to slam fists against the roof when the carriage lurched to an abrupt halt, throwing him onto the wooden floor with the cushioned seat opposite preventing any injury. Recovering from his surprise quickly, he noted the fruits now scattered around him and his ire rose; forcing his mass up angrily, Porthus swung the carriage door open and peered out.

Bustling activity met him; animated voices crying out to each other, horses galloping forward, weapons chinking in preparation and an unusual sound like the frantic breathing of a large animal. A young officer appeared at the foot of the carriage steps, fear evident in his eyes.

'Sire! You must stay inside! Zere is danger 'ere but we will protect you,' he nodded curtly and turned his attention to the unseen driver atop the vehicle, 'Be prepared to turn back. If ze retreat is sounded, we will form a rear phalanx to ensure your escape!'

With that the soldier was gone. Porthus blinked rapidly as he took the information in; his caravan was under attack again, someone stupid enough to ambush his heavily armed elite guards, but enough of a threat to panic his officers into a potential retreat. Surely another Lustanian attack was impossible? There had not been enough time since his return to Giltenberg for such an ambush to be prepared. Curiosity overcame his natural cowardice and he swung himself out onto the steps, hefting his weight up onto the drivers' ladder to peak over the vehicle roof.

Ten riders had formed an advancing line shoulder to shoulder beyond his transport and he could see the heads of ten more dismounted troops who were readying bows. He could hear the other ten soldiers who must have been reigning their own mounts in around the carriage. Maybe sixty feet beyond his defenders stood a huge, black-skinned beast, hairless and seemingly oozing a viscous fluid across its body. It looked akin to a bull, but with three sets of oversized horns protruding from the sides of its skull and a further set of tusks jutting from its jaw. Standing almost fifteen feet at the shoulder, the massive creature was densely packed with muscle, but the rear of its body narrowed to powerful, feline-looking back legs and a thick cone of a tail, possibly ten feet long itself. His heart began to race, he had never seen one of the mutated monsters before, and his grip tightened on the rungs he clung to. As he watched, the beast tramped its front hoof in warning, not rounded and flat like a normal bovine, but layered with razor sharp ridges. A horrifying bellow, rumbling like an avalanche, rang out from its huge maw and he could see the forward teeth were jagged like a predator. He began to tremble with fear but could not drag his eyes from the monstrosity.

The advancing soldiers began to break into a canter and a cry rang out at the same instant, archers releasing a volley towards the animal. Two shafts stuck into its chest, looking like nothing more than splinters, but the others seemed to slide around it on impact, as if the slimy surface prevented purchase. It was enough to rouse the creature into action and it dropped its head before powering into a charge. His riders spurred their mounts to match its pace, the six outmost levelling spears to harpoon their adversary, the four in the middle, including Captain Mozillier the expedition leader, drew their swords amid the hollering of battle-cries. In seconds, the two forces met, spears sliding harmlessly along the monster's flanks as it trampled through the line, crushing horses and riders alike. It showed no interest in pursuing the survivors as they peeled away from its path of destruction and raised its head to release another bellow of rage. Porthus could see one soldier still flailing wildly where he was harpooned upon one of the outermost horns, blood gushing from the huge cavity now in his stomach. As another volley of arrows flashed harmlessly towards the creature, it dropped into a second charge, depositing the screaming man roughly to the ground as its head dipped.

'Flee!' Porthus screamed at his driver, 'Turn the carriage now! That thing will destroy us all!'

The response was instant as whips lashed out, spurring the team of six stallions into action, beginning the large turn that would be required to set them into a retreat. Porthus bolted back inside the carriage, throwing aside the curtains to watch the battle beyond. His decision to force the vehicle into motion had removed the static base from which the defence had been created; the archers scattered to avoid the turning wheels and panicked horses. The sudden chaos seemed to confuse their attacker, however, and it pulled out of its charge, shaking its head in rage. The reserve riders took the opportunity to attack its flanks, surging in from both sides, weapons swinging wildly; he was certain that he spotted lacerations and blood before his vision was obscured by the angle of his transport. Quickly changing his vantage point to peer through the smaller rear window, he saw the monster spinning around to locate some foes, enormous tail sweeping those behind it into the air. Too late he realised the beast was not about to stop and the heavy appendage slammed into the back of the carriage. They jerked forward and Porthus cracked his head against the corner of the wooden window frame. Rolling backwards, he found himself jammed between the two seats, blood trickling from his forehead. For a moment he sat there dazed before clarity registered that they were not moving. Crawling to the door, he almost fell down the steps as he rounded to the front in search of the driver. The man was down from his position and examining a horse at the opposite side of the team.

'Wh-what are you doing?' Porthus stammered through lingering shock, 'you need to get us out of here!'

'I am sorry, my liege, but zat zing struck us 'ard. It has crippled zis animal; she cannot walk for I fear 'er leg is broken.'

'It is a horse, you idiot! Unharness it and get us moving!'

'But she will surely die 'ere if we leave 'er!'

'You will die here if we do not' Porthus screamed at him, 'I order you to leave the beast and get us away!'

The frightened servant began to do as ordered and Porthus crept to the rear of the vehicle, terrified at what sight may greet him. The monster had moved further from them, and paused to drag a man from the ground, devouring him as an impromptu meal. Several soldiers still moved around the battlefield, at least five still mounted, but it seemed disorganised and lacking command. More arrows flew in towards the enemy and it appeared the hindquarters were more vulnerable than the fore, multiple shafts embedding into the flesh. The attack just enraged the creature further and it spun towards its aggressors, bellowing and charging without pause. The soldiers fled but this time the beast tracked a small group of runners, crushing them into the ground in its passing, the sound of pulverised bones echoing across the scene.

The sudden lurching of the carriage pulled his attention from the ongoing slaughter and he quickly returned to the safety of the interior, wishing the turn to be completed more rapidly. Kneeling upon the floor, in case another unexpected impact occurred, he clasped his hands across his chest and found himself praying to any gods that would listen for his own safety. Finally, the change in direction was complete and the carriage surged forward, now heading for the safety of Giltenberg. The waning sounds of combat began to fade and the frantic cries of his driver urging the horses forward filled his awareness. Closing his eyes, he slumped back against the cushions and released a heavy sigh.

When the thundering sound rose above the sound of the rattling carriage and galloping horses, his heart rose into his throat and he knew what was coming before the impact. The edge of a huge horn tore through the vehicle wall as the pursuing monster rammed them from the side, toppling the transport onto its side and dragging the tethered animals with it. Porthus was thrown around within like a stone in a shoe and he felt something crack in his elbow as he struck the ceiling. For a moment, all was still and he took the opportunity to catch his breath, before terrified whinnying announced his team of horses were now the attacker's next meal. The sickening sounds of the carnage turned his stomach, but he had no time for paralysing terror; he had to escape. Jamming one foot between the central seat cushions, he pushed himself up to the door, currently above him, and used his uninjured arm to try and open the heavy hatch. The effort was too much, and he slipped back down, sending jolts of pain from his damaged elbow. Stifling a cry, he prepared to try again even as a giant sharpened hoof crashed down upon his hiding place. This time his scream could not be contained as the foot missed him by mere inches. As the beast lifted its leg again, he could not believe his luck; the impact had splintered the entire front of the carriage free providing him an escape route. Wasting no time, he stumbled forward and set off into a run, slipping and sliding through the savaged corpses of the butchered horses. Making no attempt to look back, knowing it would just cause him to stop his flight, he pounded as fast as his heavy body would allow, breath rasping in ragged gasps. Another bellow rang out, the sound passing through him in physical waves and joined by his own involuntary screaming.

Suddenly, he felt an impact and his body was soaring through the air, it seemed graceful and contrary to his desperate running until he impacted heavily with the ground. Crashing and tumbling through wiry long grass, he felt agony flashing through him from so many places that he could not determine where he was wounded. Unable to sit up, he craned his neck to view his injuries; his left arm was folded in a right angle against the limit his elbow should have put in place, the limb already turning purple and red through the torn shirt sleeve; further down were the ripped remnants of his right leg and he assumed he must have been caught in the thigh by one of the beast's massive horns. Transfixed by the layers of red meat, white fat and another yellow layer he did not recognise, he barely noticed the splintered bone protruding upwards from the gaping wound. The deafening snorting from his attacker heralded its approach and soon he found himself looking up into its demonic visage. Nudging him with its nose, sending new torment through his damaged bulk, he thought he spotted a flash of pity in the pure black eyes. Then its teeth snapped forward and he felt the salient incisors clamp down on his body, belly splitting like an over-ripe tomato as he was drawn into the air. The pain was so intense, his mind could no longer register it and he stared in horror as flesh and intestines spilled from him towards the ground far below. As the monster tipped its head back, his useless body toppled into the depths of its mouth and the light dimmed alongside the crushing pressure that separated his upper and lower halves. The maw opened in preparation for a second bite and Porthus thought he saw the carriage driver scampering away towards a small, wooded area; that was a relief, he thought as teeth plummeted back down and awareness ceased.

Chapter 6

Mareck felt the strong breeze pushing against him as he perched atop the mooring post, seemingly keen to topple him into the brine below. The poles stood over twenty feet high but only the uppermost few feet protruded from the shallows. Adjusting his footing slightly to compensate, he firmed his grip on the thick line in his hands and kept his focus on the murky water before him. The dull ache from his shoulder was a constant now and he wondered if his wound would fully recover, as such injuries had in his youth, or if he would forever feel crippled by that monster's attack. A tug against the rope had his heart racing until he realised it had simply snagged against something on the seabed. It was an interesting plan; they had noted the destruction of lobster pots along the shore following the retreat of the mutant from the deep, it made sense that this may be a favoured food for the creature and therefore a perfect bait. Now he found himself effectively fishing for the very beast that had almost killed him; he did not consider his fellow fishermen cowards, but none had been willing to volunteer for this role. He hoped those on shore could react quickly enough should their quarry appear.

His mind wandered back to their arrival a few days ago; twelve men in matching warrior's garb, armed with spears, tridents and nets. They had spun a tale of being sent by the Prince to help rid the village of the threat offshore, but Mareck had not believed them. Their accents were not Zendran, of course they could have been mercenaries or specialists hired by their liege, but his minor probing questions revealed they had never been to the capital. Alongside that, they seemed intent on bringing the animal to shore alive; any water-based huntsman knew that drawing an aquatic predator to land against its will was difficult at best. Something about their presence didn't quite make sense, but the offer was too good to refuse; they were going to end the threat and allow the community to return to normal. He risked a glance back at his temporary allies and spotted Crystal amongst them; ordering her to stay at home was a wasted effort and it had been hard enough to convince her to let him run the lure. Her return, mere days before the arrival of the hunting party, had filled his heart with joy and brought the realisation that they had never been separated for such a long period since making their home here. Her story of the attack was concerning, a simple bandit ambush unlikely to be so well-planned and resourced, but he had no time to worry himself with such matters. No, he chided himself, he had no *reason* to worry himself; his life here was what mattered for he was done with adventuring or getting involved in the troubles of others. Once the village was safe, his part was played. He just hoped that recent events had not triggered some wanderlust in Crystal; he could not bear to think of her facing the dangers he had in his life.

Another tug on the rope drew his attention, followed by a second, hard enough to slip the line back through his hands. Again, he felt his heart pumping for something must be biting at the lobster pot, it could be a shark taking an interest in the trapped crustacean within, but his instincts told him otherwise. Gripping the rope, he leaned back and allowed his rear foot to rest upon the mooring post behind him. It was a slightly hyper-extended stance but gave him a better base than teetering atop a single pole. He pulled hard on the rope and felt significant resistance before having to tense his whole body to avoid being pulled from his perch, his shoulder screaming in protest.

'It's here! I can feel it on the line!' he cried back to those on dry land, hearing the sudden activity beyond him. If they were following the plan, four of the men would be taking the slack of the line and would reel the monstrosity beyond the edge of the huge net they had lain in the shallows. The other eight hunters were positioned to retract that net as fast as possible, dragging the mutant to shore, entangled within a double-layered mesh. Sure enough, he felt the line tighten against his ribs as the tension was taken up to the rear and he prepared to release his own grip. The hunters moved too soon, however and he felt them begin to yank the line in, dragging him from his position and sending him tumbling into the brine. His head slapped hard against the post as he entered the water and he flailed momentarily as he tried to gain his bearings in the water. Finally, he oriented himself and took powerful strokes to head for the surface. Gasping in a huge breath, he found it laced with seawater as frothing waves crashed all around him; the sea was calm, so he knew the disturbance must be caused by the creature's thrashing resistance. Sure enough, he felt the huge slick body brush against him, but the predator had matters other than food on its mind and ignored him completely. Despite this, its struggle was frantic, and the end of its tail struck against him, driving the air from him as he was forced beneath the surface again. Spinning and rolling through the water, he could see the monster casting a silhouette between himself and the light of the sky above them. Multiple pressures against his back indicated that the net was being reeled in and he was within its boundary; if he was dragged in with the beast, its frantic bucking would surely kill him. Fighting the rapid movement towards the shore, he twisted himself around, using the grip of the net itself to traverse sideways and slide himself free of the edge before breaking the surface again.

Taking a moment to catch his breath, easier now that the broiling waves were heading towards the beach with the monster creating them, he began treading water and tried to make out the scene at the water's edge. The eight haulers were racing up the sand, as fast at the heavy ropes they were pulling behind them allowed, while the four hunters on the capture line were being yanked wildly back and forth as they tried to prevent it from retreating beyond the limits of the net. He spotted Crystal off to one side, grabbing two spears from those planted further up the shore in preparation; inside he prayed she would hold back and let the others slay their prey. Angling his body forward, he began swimming towards the beach, shoulder feeling like it was full of granite and every stroke bringing new agony.

Dragging himself from the water, it took several moments to steady his breathing before he could clamber to his feet. The sounds of the roaring creature and the men struggling to combat it drew him back along the shore at a run and he squinted to determine what was happening through the dusky light. He could see the massive form of the long beast, writhing and thrashing within the net that became more tangled with every movement, and several of the hunters around it pointing their long weapons towards it. Just pointing, not stabbing. The higher pitch of his daughter's voice caught his attention, and he slowed his pace as he fixed his vision on her. Arguing with two of the men, she had her own spear fixed on them and Mareck felt a rock form in his stomach; what was happening?

'Ho there!' he shouted, 'Calm yourselves! Our enemy is a common one!'

'Fazer! You 'ave survived!' Crystal called back with relief, moving herself sideways to meet him as he arrived, 'Zese idiots will not kill ze monster! And zey would not send anyone to find you!'

'I am fine,' he reassured, moving himself between her and the two tense men she was confronting, 'they undoubtedly knew I was a good swimmer; the beast is the priority.'

'Your girl is lucky,' one of the hunters addressed him, 'if not for the primary mission, she may have found herself on the wrong end of our spears.'

'You would stand no chance against me…' Crystal began to retort angrily before Mareck cut her off.

'There is no need for threats, we want rid of that thing and have done all we can to aid you in capturing it. Why would you now turn on us? Let us be done with this thing and part as allies.'

'The creature will no longer be a danger to you; we will take it, and your community will be safe. If you interfere then we have our orders.'

'Orders? From Prince Porthus? Why would he not want it destroyed immediately?'

'That is not a concern for you, villager. Would you question your own ruler? Now stand aside and let us complete our task.'

Behind them, Mareck could see a large flat wagon being backed down onto the sand by a team of six very nervous horses. The other hunters continued to drag the enraged creature up towards the arriving vehicle and it was clear they planned to transport it.

'Fazer!' Crystal hissed intently, turning him to face her, 'We cannot allow zis! What good is zere in moving our problem elsewhere? What if it breaks loose while zey travel? What if zey plan to release it elsewhere to punish ozer towns or enemies? What if zey 'ave not even been sent by our Prince? We must stop zem, we must kill zat zing!'

Mareck heard her words and felt the responsibility fall onto his shoulders from the truth within them. Studying her eyes, he could see the passion, the belief and the sense of purpose; he could see himself thirty years ago. Taking the spear from her, he squeezed her shoulder and smiled, 'I know you are right, my sweet girl, I know what we must do.'

Surprise took over her as he cast the weapon down into the sand, 'But we cannot do it. We must let these hunters leave with their prize. We must not think of what they may do with it, of what could happen, of who could be hurt. Our priority has to be keeping the village safe, returning to normality, protecting what we have.'

'No,' she whispered in disbelief, 'zis cannot be your decision. Zese are not your words, zese are the words of a coward! You are no coward, why do you say zese zings?'

'Please, Crystal, you are everything to me. Let this danger leave, let us live as we always have; in peace.'

The push was unexpected, and he tripped as he staggered backwards. Reaching out a hand as he slammed into the sand, he was too slow to stop her launching past him and into the two hunters beyond. Their surprise was almost as great as his and they were completely unprepared for the assault. Crystal grabbed hold of the first man, using his height to swing herself into a two-footed kick striking the chest of his ally. Continuing the arc around his neck, she dropped her weight behind him, dragging him onto his back heavily, before turning towards the struggle at the wagon. Mareck regained his feet and saw she was loosing the weighted rope at her hip; he had to stop her before she got to the larger group. Breaking into a run, he realised the first hunter she had floored was on his knees notching an arrow. Altering course, he slammed his knee into the back of the man's head; the face first plummet back to the sand indicating he was stunned at least.

'Wrong choice, old man!' the second warrior was now on his feet, with sword drawn towards him, 'We would have just taken the creature and left; now we have to kill you both!'

'Listen, I want no trouble from you. You can still leave, and nothing will be said. I do not care who you are or where you came from. Just take your prize and go. I will calm my girl, there is no need to harm her.'

'No need, perhaps, but it will be a lot less complicated.'

Mareck sighed and then lashed out with a side-swiping kick against the flat of the blade before him. Continuing the spin full circle, he closed the gap between them, driving a powerful roundhouse punch into his opponent's temple. As the younger man staggered to the left, Mareck noted the focus leave his eyes and did not hesitate to capitalise. An uppercut to the jaw stood him bolt upright before a kick to the stomach drove him uselessly back to the sand. Reaching down, Mareck grabbed the dropped sword and tossed it into the darkness; just in case his blows had less lasting effect than they used to.

Turning back to the beast-loading activity, he spotted Crystal spinning her weapon above her head as she closed on the nearest hunter. Letting fly, the weighted end flew over his shoulder, causing him to spin around in alarm. Crystal dropped and rolled to her right, pulling back on the line and causing it to suddenly wrap back around his neck. Spinning rapidly as the excess rope became shorter and shorter, he reached up to free the constriction before the metal weight slammed into his face. Mareck had seen her do this when trapping deer in the woods but the makeshift lasso had to be manually released, meaning she had sacrificed her weapon. Seemingly undeterred, she rose from the beach with two rocks in her hands. Charging forward, now with the attention of a further three of the trappers, she hurled one of the makeshift weapons at the one sporting a crossbow, but it crashed against his chain-mailed shoulder with little effect. As all three men readied their weapons to meet the oncoming threat, two with spears and the third loading his crossbow, Crystal heedlessly continued her attack. Only twenty feet from them, Mareck slammed into her ribs and dragged her back to the ground as the fired bolt whistled through the air above them.

Struggling beneath him as he tried to hold her down by her wrists, Mareck felt the sting of her anger directed towards him as never before, 'Fazer! Release me you coward! Zey must be stopped and zat monster destroyed! Let me do what is right if you are wizout ze courage!'

'Stop Crystal!' he shouted back at her, tears streaming from his eyes, 'Just let this go! It is not our fight and you cannot win it! Please, do not make me lose you!'

'Nozing will be lost! If I cannot do zis alone, zen do it wiz me! Fight! Be ze man you 'ave told me stories of!'

He pushed back down against her formidable strength, hating himself for doing so, 'I am not that man anymore, Crystal!'

All struggling suddenly ceased and fiery eyes looked into his, 'No,' she agreed, 'you are not. I wonder if you ever really were.'

His response was cut off as she used the distraction to kick both legs up and almost throw him from her. He knew that the resistance would not cease, and their struggle was drawing the attention of the other hunters. Pinning one of her wrists under his knee for a moment, he slammed his fist against the side of her head, feeling her body go instantly limp.

Taking a few deep breaths to steady himself, he slowly stood and turned to face the six hunters who now gathered about him. He raised both hands in supplication. 'I apologise for my daughter,' he said, trying to keep the emotional tremor from his words, 'she is impassioned by the deaths this beast is responsible for. Many men from our community lost to its appetite. There is no malice toward any of you, just a desire to kill that thing. Please, take it and go. I will explain it to her when she wakes. There is no need for further hostility.'

'You think so?' the man was untangling her rope from around his throat and blood streamed from a large gash on his cheek, 'We are trying to rid you of this animal, and she attacks us? No, she deserves far more than an explanation…'

One of his comrades placed a restraining arm across the younger man to hold him back, 'We are not bad men, we are just doing what we have been paid to do. As with my friend here, the desire for revenge can be a powerful one. Stay here and keep her out of our way should she recover. There will be no second chance at leniency and you should tell her how lucky she is to have a smart father and forgiving adversaries.'

'I will, sir, and thank-you for understanding,' Mareck returned, keeping his gaze lowered. For a few more moments, the silent stand-off continued until the men returned to their tasks. Turning back to Crystal, he sank to his knees, pulling her unconscious form into his arms and holding her tightly. He had never struck her in his life, and he felt numb inside. Watching the hunters continue their work, he noticed that their quarry had almost completely stopped fighting, a weak gurgle and slight flap of its tail the only remaining resistance it seemed capable of. The ten men managed to haul the enormous weight up onto the flat bed of their wagon and proceeded to lash bindings over it, ensuring the lines wrapped under the vehicle as well. It did seem unlikely that the creature would be able to escape. And what were the chances that, should it be kept as an indiscriminate weapon of war, it would ever be deployed in Zendra? Let alone anywhere that could affect their home? No, this was the right thing to do, the only thing they could do.

Eventually, the hunters seemed content with their preparations and the man who had accepted his capitulation returned. Mareck gently eased Crystal to the floor and stepped over her to meet him.

'Your task is complete?' he asked, keeping his voice even.

'Aye, it is. And now we will be leaving. I'm sure you realise it will be in the best interests of your village if nothing more is said of the matter.'

'Of course,' Mareck replied, no stranger to underlying threats, 'I hope your onward journey is uneventful.'

The other man smiled, clearly trying to determine if the statement was sarcasm or encouragement to leave, 'I am certain it will be,' he conceded at last. Half-turning to go, the soldier paused before adding another question, 'You are no simple fisherman. I think it may have been a difficult decision for you not to engage us all to protect your girl. That thought alone leads me to ask who you are?'

'I am sorry, sir, but you are mistaken,' Mareck answered without pause, 'I am a fisherman of these waters my entire life. A father's love can drive him to many great achievements, but I think facing you and your men would have proven folly.'

Another smile. 'Your actions, and your accent, betray you, my friend. You are no native of Zendra. Still, that is not my concern this day. We part company here; pray we never meet again.'

'I will,' Mareck responded, relieved that this time the hunter continued back towards the wagon that was already being slowly coaxed up the track beyond the beach. Watching the horses strain against the massive load in the loose sand, Mareck allowed the tension to drain from his body, pain washing over him from the recent efforts. Looking down at his daughter, the dark bruise already forming across the side of her face, he tried to imagine how they would move on from here; her disappointment would be a blade in his heart forevermore. He was unaware of the two men approaching until they were already upon him.

'Hey, fisherman,' one called gruffly, almost making him jump from his deep thoughts, 'that was an interesting fighting style back there.'

'Just lucky, I think,' Mareck replied humbly, realising that the two men he had incapacitated were not ones to antagonise any further, 'I had to protect my kin.'

'Well, you did that all right!' the speaker continued jovially. 'Not sure what hurts most; side of my head, my jaw or my gut! Well struck blows, those, and really hard too; must be some heavy lobsters out there, eh?'

Mareck smiled despite the lack of mirth in the other man's voice, 'Yes, must be. Again, I am truly sorry for causing you harm.'

'Sure you are,' he drawled before drawing back a fist and smashing it against Mareck's chin. He made no effort to block the predictable blow and allowed his knees to buckle for added effect.

'Ha!' shouted the hunter victoriously, 'Now that is a punch!'

Suddenly his comrade jumped forward and planted his heel into Mareck's forehead, snapping his head back and forcing him onto his rear. 'And that is a kick!' he added with relish.

As expected, the two men began to rain down a series of punches and kicks into his head and body, Mareck covering his ears and face with his arms and whimpering loudly to provide the satisfaction they clearly wanted. Then one of them lashed a boot towards Crystal. Mareck shot out one hand, catching the blow despite the weight behind it, and then driving himself rapidly to his feet. The hunter was toppled backwards to the ground as his ally drew a sword once again. Silence stretched out between them and Mareck stared into the eyes of his opponent, knowing the steel within his own gaze was a stark contrast to the sudden fear within the other man.

Finally, he spoke, 'Not her.'

The hunter swallowed hard and then slowly lowered his blade, aiding his partner up and backing away. 'Aye, well, that's you learned your lesson,' he spoke through trembling lips, 'don't make us teach you again!'

Watching them scurry back to the larger party, Mareck stared after them until the entire entourage was out of sight, allowing the fire within him to slowly wash away. The harmony of his life had been ruined in one night, the careful efforts he had made to keep his past from invading his present erased seemingly by chance, his relationship with his daughter possibly altered forever. He wondered if he would still recognise himself should he catch his reflection in the water, wondered if he would make these same choices if Rork Fimarr was by his side.

Running the soft horse-hair brush through the silky golden tresses of her daughter, Treya could feel the tears running down her cheeks unbidden. Wiping them away with the back of her hand, she maintained focus on the gentle, repetitive strokes, unable to clear the memories of having done this very same thing for Alissa.

'Was 'matter, momma?' Joseff asked, lying his head on her thigh having clambered from his bed to join them.

'Nothing, my darling boy,' she replied, presenting him a smile she could not feel, 'I am just tired and thinking of old times.'

'Why does that make you cry?' he persisted, 'Was old times very sad?'

She placed the brush aside and cupped his tiny, smooth cheek in her weathered palm, 'Sometimes. But there were good times as well. People are just funny, I suppose, we cry when we remember the good and we cry when we remember the bad.'

'I don't think it is funny,' Melody added, still playing with the soft toy Hederna Thriss had knitted for her, 'I think crying is not ever funny. Are old times when Grandfather was alive?'

Treya felt her heart skip a beat at the mention of her father, awesome warrior, legendary adventurer, terrible parent and absent husband. She seldom spoke of him around the twins, so the question caught her by surprise. 'Yes, your grandfather was alive in the old times.'

'D'you think he would like us?' Joseff enquired, enjoying the feel of her fingers as she ran them through his hair.

'Oh yes,' she lied, 'you would mean the world to him! I think he would never stop playing games with you and I would have to tell him off so I could put you to your beds.' Of course, she could not believe such things; she would more likely have had to fight him on every front to stop him putting the children through the same vicious lessons that he had 'taught' her and his other daughters.

'I would love to see him,' Melody said wistfully, 'was he really a giant?'

Treya considered the question, 'He was very big. I think you would have thought him to be a giant, but he was just a man.'

'Would he have deaded the bad men for us?' Joseff continued.

'What?' the question was even more unexpected, 'What do you mean, my baby?'

'The bad men who wanted to hurt us all today. The other man deaded them for us and Dada said he used Grandfather's axe. Would he have done it if he was here?'

'These are not nice things to talk about, my little ones,' Treya answered, pulling them both up onto her lap, 'What happened today was scary, but it is over. You must not think about it anymore because you are safe in your home with Dada and me to protect you. Nobody can harm you and that would be the same if your Grandfather were here. But what can harm you is tired eyes and sleepy heads!'

Lifting them both under her arms, she spun them around, regretting it when the strain tugged across the scar in her back, before laying them gently in their own beds. Staying with Joseff, she pulled his covers to his chin and smoothed them down about him.

'Sleep well my wondrous son. My arms enfold you while you dream, I keep you safe and warm, our hearts are always as one,' she cooed the night-time rhyme before kissing him softly on the lips and then forehead.

'Love you, momma,' he replied, obediently closing his eyes.

Moving over to Melody, she repeated the routine and she, too, closed her eyes with a declaration of love. Moving towards the door, her daughter's voice gave her pause.

'Momma?' she ventured quietly.

'Yes, Melody?'

'Did you love Grandfather like we love you?'

Treya couldn't find the words. 'I... We will talk about it tomorrow, sweet one.'

'And Momma?'

'Yes?'

'Don't cry anymore.'

Her heart melted where she stood. 'No, Melody, I will not cry anymore. You both make sure of that for me.' Blowing them each a kiss, she shut the door and headed for her room. The children had never spoken of her father before and, suddenly, after the trauma they experienced that day it suddenly came up? No, Straker was the cause. Once again, his mouth had gotten ahead of his good sense; she would address this before they joined the others downstairs. That said, she could not ignore the irony; her father was one of the most legendary heroes of all time yet never had his deeds followed him home, she wanted nothing of such a life and yet already her children had witnessed horrors from hers. Sometimes it felt as if fate was always contrary to her own desires.

Reaching the master bedroom, she placed her hand against the jamb and took a deep breath; approaching Straker with tact would help to ensure he was supportive when she confronted Catalana over her revealed treachery. Her stomach flipped at the thought; Alissa abandoned five years ago under the pretence of a grisly death in the Black Citadel. Treya simply could not fathom why such a lie had been deemed necessary, let alone a reason for leaving her behind. The girl she had raised from youth was still alive but had made no effort to come home, instead choosing to live in isolation with the foot-soldiers of their former enemy? Banging her head gently off the back of her hand, she counted silently to three and then entered the room.

Her plan of tact vanished when she found Forge stood by the window, stuffing basic provisions into a travelling sack. At the sound of the door, he froze and his shoulders slumped, but he did not turn around. For a moment all was still.

'What are you doing?' she asked finally, voice taut with barely restrained anger.

'Treya, my love, this is how things must be. I have to go. I have to resolve this matter so that we can return to being the family we have cherished for these past years,' she could hear the resignation in his voice and his head dropped as he spoke.

'What do you mean? Why do you have to? What happened to planning a strategy?'

'I… it is something I cannot explain to you. Can you trust me and allow me to travel to Lustania? I will find your sister and remove any future threats to us, to our children.'

'Alone? You intend to face Lennath and whatever soldiers he has at his disposal? On your own? And then somehow bring Alissa back here?'

'Yes,' he sounded so certain it almost quelled her rage. Almost. 'In fact, I must be alone.'

'And what makes you think that you would succeed ahead of us all going together?'

'I have… that is I cannot…' surety was now replaced with fumbling uncertainty, 'I just can, Treya. If I go, then I will succeed, and you will have your sister back; I promise.'

'And what if you do not!' she suddenly screamed at him, rushing forward and turning him to see her tear-stained face, 'What if they kill you? Are you content to leave us all behind? Fatherless children, a widow, our family facing the reprisal of your actions? How can you be this selfish?'

For the first time in years, she witnessed her battle-hardened lover sobbing as he responded, 'Please, my one true love, I cannot tell you how, but I can and will do this. Nothing could stop me returning here to you. Let me do this, for you, for us, for our children.'

As he reached out to embrace her, she pushed him away, 'No! You ask me to trust you in this decision, yet you will give me no justification? There is a lie sitting between us, there always has been, so many times I have given you the opportunity to be honest, to break down that final barrier, but you will not! I am the mother of your children, the woman you claim to love, yet still you will not trust me with your secrets! It is all that is common with everyone around me; you all choose to hide things from me, to lie to me! How can I trust any of you?'

'Treya, calm yourself! This is no lie I hold back. If only you could understand that I have been honest with you in all things. Only one circumstance have I omitted from our life together and you would understand if I could explain it to you, but I cannot! Let me prove myself to you; tell me not to go and I will abide by your decision.'

Treya paused, tears still pouring forth. His words felt like a trap, like he was forcing her to choose whether success or failure was to be achieved. She knew that he was a fine warrior and had held his own when travelling with her father, but no man alone could infiltrate a country, battle a palace full of guards and safely escape with a freed prisoner, could they? Suddenly all her anger vanished, and she felt only fear.

Rushing into his arms, she whispered her response into his chest, 'Don't go.'

She felt him kiss the top of her head tenderly, 'For you, Treya Fimarr, anything. We will do this together if that is your wish.'

'Together,' she repeated, 'in everything we do. Always.'

She had no idea how long they remained in that embrace, but it felt like eternity. When they finally broke away, he kept hold of her hand and led her from the room, towards the stairs. She felt exhausted and reluctant; the last thing she now needed was a confrontation with her sister, but it seemed inevitable. And how could she control her rage sufficiently? There was no option to ostracise Catalana completely, for they would need to work together if Alissa was to be saved. Fate bound her once more in the actions she could take; was there even such a concept as free will?

Their guests were speaking in hushed whispers when Treya followed Straker into the front parlour, but Catalana rose to greet them as they entered.

'Treya,' she almost wept, 'please let me explain what happened.'

She found herself stopping short and her stare must have betrayed her emotions for her sister halted abruptly, leaving them in an awkward stand-off. 'There is no explanation for what you did. You may as well have murdered Alissa yourself.'

Tears erupted and Catalana seemed to fold in on herself as she sank to the floor in fits of sobbing. Treya remained cold; guilt did not repair the damage. She watched Herc come to the aid of her kin before rounding them and seating herself in the high-back chair closest to the window. Catching Straker's eye, she noted his face full of concern and tried to swallow some of the venom forming within her as Herc aided Catalana back onto the sofa. After a few moments, her sister had composed herself.

'We saw her in those last moments, while the Citadel was falling apart. It was not Alissa anymore, Treya, she was crazed, a lunatic, only bloodlust remained within her. She was lost to us before we left her behind.'

Clenching her fists to control her temper, Treya could feel fingernails penetrating her palms. 'In your opinion, Catalana. Our Little Fawn was beyond saving and as good as dead according to you, yet here we are in the knowledge that she is alive!'

'She was taken by the Taint,' Herc added quietly, 'You don't want to believe it, I understand that, but it is true. She was dangerous to us all and to herself; none of us were in a physical condition to restrain her and I believe she would have caused harm. Do not forget what she did to Joseff.'

The words stung her unexpectedly. Joseff Gaesin, the son of one of her father's most notable travelling companions, had joined them in their quest to destroy the wizard Ramikain. He had been loyal and true to them, yet Alissa had killed him without provocation; it was in his memory that she had named her own son so any suggestion that she could forget him was ludicrous. 'Do not condescend to me, Herc Callid, my memory of those days is clear and I, too, carry the scars. But you tell me that our combined weakness is justification for leaving my baby sister to die?'

'She is not dead,' Catalana sobbed.

'But you did not know that!' Treya snapped at her, 'You fully expected her to perish! And you have lied to me for five years ensuring I could not save her! How can you live with yourself?'

'I do not know, sister!' she wailed, 'It gnaws at my heart every day! Since we were reunited, I have cherished our bond, the feeling of family, the happiness we have shared. But I have never lost sight of my crime, never forgiven my failure back then. Even now, though, I cannot see any other way for things to have happened. We were all broken, physically and mentally; what was left of our sister had already perished and I shudder to think of what she is now. But I did not lie; Alissa died five years ago in the Black Citadel.'

'You would play semantics with me? You think that this is true because you say it? You have no clue what has happened to that child since you abandoned her! No idea about what she is thinking or feeling! But I raised her, I know her heart; as long as she lives, she is my kin and I will save her,' Treya could hear the ire and distress mingling in her words but refused to allow emotion to overcome her.

'Listen to me,' Straker softly interrupted, 'this argument is justified, and I cannot condone what has happened in the past. Likewise, I cannot erase the torment those actions have caused for you both. But there is little time for this now; Alissa is alive as far as we know and likely held hostage by a Prince of the Five Kingdoms. Our priority must be to strategize over how we resolve that matter first.'

'Agreed,' Herc chimed in, both men clearly keen to avoid the emotions at play, 'I spoke to Silas before the workers left, he agreed to escort Hederna Thriss home and will inform the Rennicksburg Watch of the attack in the morning. I am certain they will collect the bodies of our attackers in due course. What, if any, investigation into the hiring of such assassins will occur, I cannot say.'

'It is rare for any action to be taken over hired killers, they are legal in most regions and the local watch's powers are limited. We have no choice but to deal with this matter ourselves. Of course, we are few in number; we must be stealthy or find allies.'

'We must work together,' Treya asserted, shooting Forge a meaningful stare, 'gaining entrance to Lennath's palace will be difficult. Escaping with Alissa in hand will be more so.'

'If she is even there,' Catalana added through a throat cracked with her recent crying, 'we do not know for certain that it was Lennath who took her.'

'Really?' Treya asked in disbelief, feeling her anger rising once again, 'He hired killers to come here and wipe out my family! How can he not be responsible for Alissa's kidnapping?'

'Do not cloud your judgement with our personal argument, sister,' Catalana replied evenly, clearly keen to avoid enraging her further, 'the mercenaries sent for us today could be an over-reaction to some implied insult during our visit to his Palace. Maybe he allowed himself to be goaded into the response; he was always easy to manipulate.'

'She is there,' Treya asserted, 'but there may be a way to satisfy any doubt without placing ourselves in the spider's web too soon.'

'I see a plan in your eyes, my sweet,' Straker enthused, 'this is good! Now we are thinking instead of reacting; this is how we will succeed.'

'Perhaps,' she replied, 'but I am still keen to avoid unnecessary delay. You mentioned allies a moment ago; did you have any in mind? Former journeymen who would aid the daughter of Rork Fimarr? You must know of some skilled warriors who could aid us?'

His confidence seemed to diminish somewhat, 'Erm, aye, Treya, maybe a few remain who are young enough to provide assistance. It will depend how rapidly you anticipate moving against our enemy.'

She seemed undeterred by his non-committal response and turned to her sister, 'Did you track Terex as you said you would? I dismissed him too quickly in my confusion earlier. He would be an excellent stooge, an unexpected spy to infiltrate Lennath's fortress on our behalf, to locate Alissa and perhaps even provide us a way into the palace.'

'I am sorry, sister,' she answered, voice returning to the softer tones more common to her, 'I followed his trail for a mile or so past Rennicksburg but then lost it abruptly. I assume he did not want to be followed so took measures to obscure his tracks. He did not take father's axe with him, however.' She gestured over to the fireplace where the enormous weapon leant against the stone mantle.

'We will have to find him,' Treya continued undeterred, 'while we do so and he carries out the espionage required, Forge will gather forces to aid us in the rescue. The only matter left to determine is how we deal with Lennath, how do we prevent continued reprisals once we have succeeded?'

'Treya, slow down,' Forge spoke firmly but his voice was tinged with concern, 'there is much you have stated which is still open to chance, yet you want to discuss how we seal the aftermath? We require a much clearer plan before we revel in success.'

'Yes, I know that! Would you have me plan for failure?' she retorted petulantly, 'We must consider the outcomes of success because there is only one for failure.'

The statement was met with silence and she suddenly felt the reality of their situation; death was the most likely outcome. If they did nothing, more killers would arrive at their door, she was certain. If they assaulted Lennath's palace and failed to rescue Alissa, they would all be slain. If they succeeded, Lennath would undoubtedly come to reclaim his prize if he were still alive; even if they killed him, was there any way to know that his successor would not continue the pursuit? She shook her head to avoid spiralling into a hopeless scenario.

'There is another factor to consider,' Straker said, breaking the tension, 'it means that stealth will be the required solution, it is part of why I was considering doing this alone.'

Treya almost shot out a bitter comeback until she spotted fear in her partner's eyes.

'Go on,' Catalana coaxed.

'The bodyguard that was with him at the palace was a Veer assassin. They have no equal in their skill. If we encounter him during any attempt to breach that fortress, then I fear for our chances of survival, let alone success.'

'I have never heard of the Veer,' Herc challenged, 'but, regardless of skill, he is still a man and all men are fallible.'

'But you must understand…' Straker was about to continue insistently when interrupted by a knock on the front door. The sound startled them all but Catalana was first to react, standing and moving over to the oak entrance. Treya followed but remained a few feet behind, aware she was unconsciously using her sister as a human shield. Grasping the metal ring handle, Cat' swung the door open and gasped

Standing in the dim twilight was Rayne Fimarr; black cloak damp from the night air, dark red hair hanging loose around her face, a face that was mutilated across the left side by ageing burn scars. Before Treya could form words, Catalana had thrown a slap towards the new arrival, the fierce blow easily blocked with a lightning-fast parry.

'Hello, Cat',' Rayne offered as she blocked a second slap from the other side, 'I will assume all is not forgiven?'

'You bitch!' Catalana screamed at her, surging forward even as Rayne dropped into a ready stance. Herc Callid suddenly arrived and swept Catalana into his arms, holding her tightly and dragging her back from the doorway despite her continued struggling and cursing.

'I suppose that is a better welcome than I could have expected,' she said, easing back into a relaxed posture, 'I am sure this is somewhat of a surprise, but I need your help.'

This last was directed at Treya but the sudden appearance of the fourth Fimarr sister had left her stunned. Almost outside her own control, the oldest sister stepped forward and her arm lashed out of its own accord. Even the highly skilled assassin did not expect the attack and the straight punch cracked against her jaw, toppling her backwards to the earth beyond the doorstep. As she had just witnessed with Catalana, Treya suddenly found herself carefully restrained by Straker; contrary to her sister, she sank into the embrace.

Rayne sat where she was, rubbing her jaw with an impressed smile on her lips, 'I deserved that,' she admitted, 'but you only get one. Not many take me by surprise, Treya; you have my respect! But if this is how you greet *me*, I am not looking forward to introducing you to my travelling companions…'

Shuffling her slippered feet quickly along the smooth stone floor of the echoing chamber, Kastani counted thirty-six shuffles between this pillar and the last. She stopped and put one arm out against the cold column beside her, steadying herself as she readjusted her footwear following the awkward gait just used. Putting her hands on her hips, she cocked her head with lower lip jutting forward, deeply considering her next choice. With walking, crawling, running and shuffling all used up, she eventually decided on skipping. Focussing on the next column, she readied herself, pulling the pretty dress she had been gifted up from the ground, and then merrily skipped the short distance to her target. This movement took more effort and left her panting a little when she arrived. Eighteen skips. So that was more than running, but less than the others. Before she could consider her next challenge, an inhuman screeching caught her attention.

Pressing herself against the pillar before her, she peeped out of her hiding spot to see her mother still standing in front of the marble dais. She had been standing there for several hours, Kastani hoping all the while she may get bored and come to play with her, seemingly focussed on nothing but the air before her. Terex would say she was daydreaming when they had been back at home, and she did it a lot then; this was the first time since they had come to Lennath's house. Lennath was nice, always full of smiles, always taking time to ask her what she was doing or telling her stories from the old days; he was a lot like Terex but not as good, and she hoped her best friend would join them soon.

Her mother was wearing one of the thin gowns made from a fine mesh of silk, Kastani had seen several when sneaking through the closets in her parent's room, and she thought it was very pretty. A pale blue in colour and light so it flowed with every movement or hung to every angle of the body when stationary. It was also almost completely see-through which Kastani thought was very funny, as her mother's normally pale white skin was transformed into a shade like the beautiful fountains in the gardens upstairs. Although Kastani was only allowed out of the palace with Lennath or Mozak, she adored the gardens with all their wondrous colours and scents; she could not understand why they didn't get some at their own home, instead of all the black stone and barren soil.

The sound she had heard was not uttered by her mother, indeed no sound had come from her since they had been left in the room, and her right hand had remained tightly closed around the funny wand Lennath had given her. She'd had no idea her parent could do magic tricks but that seemed to be the point of this room; earlier a goat had been led into the deep pit in front of the dais and left there for something to happen. After a few minutes of watching, Kastani had gotten bored and played marbles with some of the gems Lennath had given her. That had led to seeing how far she could flick each gem along the floor which, in turn, had led to the 'fast move between the pillars' analysis. So, something must have now happened. Creeping further forward, she peered over the raised lip of the pit and saw the goat had disappeared. In its place was a horned monstrosity with black scaly skin, four times the size of the previous animal, with what appeared to be little mouths all along its flanks. It reminded her of the tiny lizards that she often found scouring the dry, cracked earth at home but was much uglier.

'Away from the edge,' her mother's voice rang out, 'it will eat you if you fall in and I would be displeased with you.'

Kastani looked up at the words but her parent had not broken from her trance and it would be easy to think she had not spoken at all. But Kastani knew better than to ignore a rule once made. Sullenly she moved back over to the pillar she had come from, wondering when the magic spells would begin. Slumping down with her back to the column, her dress fluffing out around her, she idly raked her nails across the stone beside her, proving that she was old enough to look into the pit if she wanted; the message did not seem to get to her mother, though. As she stared at Alissa, once again convinced that she was the prettiest woman in all the world, and making yet another vain attempt to count all the symbols on her skin, Kastani wondered when they would be returning home. It was really lovely visiting with Lennath, although she hoped that she would be allowed to see on the journey back, and she couldn't complain about how pleasantly different everything was here, but she missed being in her own room with the toys and gifts Terex always brought to her, she missed exploring the tallest spires with him always by her side, she missed playing hide and seek in the courtyards with him; she missed Terex.

The sounds of the creature in the pit began to fade and she imagined it was being led away along whatever passages down below that the goat had originally entered through. After a while, a droning sound like the wings of a large insect began to emanate from the hole and she noticed a furrow of concentration cross her mother's brow for a moment before she returned to impassive. What was the point of all this? Then it dawned on her; they must be here selecting a pet! This would make a wonderful playmate and she wanted to look back into the pit more than ever to see what was on parade now; as long as her mother did not pick the big black creature because that had not looked very good for cuddling, then Kastani was certain this was a move for the better.

Movement from the large double doorway leading into the chamber attracted her attention and she watched with interest as the two guards walked cautiously down the central aisle towards the pit. This was interesting because every other room they had been into since arriving had soldiers who stood by the door no matter what, usually staring at each other with great discipline; Kastani wondered how they managed it, when she tried to stare at someone else, she normally ending up in hysterical laughter. The two men were talking in low voices but they were soon close enough to hear.

'…is completely unaware,' the bearded man was finishing.

'I don't know, I heard about what happened in the baths; this one is dangerous,' his comrade replied.

'No, I heard it is just fast movements that alarm her. Like an animal. I promise you, last time I was here, she didn't even know what was going on.'

'I'm not sure, what if she said something afterwards?'

'She doesn't, she's completely gone. You remember after the Battle of Stiris? The five men who got captured?'

'Yes, I know. They could not even speak of what had happened to them. I heard stories about the horrors that happened to them until the rescue; I do not know if any of them are true but it broke their minds for sure.'

'That is right, could not feed themselves, could not work, totally reliant on others to just keep living.'

'Until they were executed.'

'They were not executed, they were culled. For their own good. But that is not the point anyway. This one is about as aware of things as they were; you can do anything to her.'

'Anything?'

'Look, I will put you at ease. Watch what I do and then tell me I am wrong,' the bearded guard spoke with finality as his partner stepped off to one side, studying Alissa's face for signs of reaction. Kastani watched curiously as the main speaker stood beside her mother and waved a hand in front of her face. Seemingly pleased with himself for having proved something when Alissa did not flinch, he ran a finger down her cheek and then over her lips to a similar lack of reaction. His friend seemed amazed but Kastani was far more used to these trances; it was no real magic trick, just annoying when you wanted to ask a question. As she watched, his hand moved down and into her mother's dress, clasping one of her breasts firmly and squeezing several times, a strangely wild look filling his eyes.

'See, you can do anything and she does not even know. And why would anyone waste an opportunity like this? Be honest with yourself, even with the scars she is a sight more attractive than any of the whores in the city.'

'But if we got caught…'

'Get caught? Our shift is eight hours, and nobody has ever come here between shift changes since I started this duty. Besides, how long do you think it would take?'

A nervous laugh followed and then the beardless man moved around behind Alissa, tentatively running his hand down her spine and onto her buttock. After a moment, he pulled her dress up and shoved his hand between her legs. It was all very confusing and Kastani wondered if they were here to perform the magic trick too. As she craned her neck to see what would happen next, an unexpected sneeze erupted from her and she shook her head to clear a further tickle in her sinuses. Looking up again, she realised the bearded man was now approaching, waving to his friend who had now dropped his breaches and was manoeuvring himself close behind her mother.

'Hey there, little one,' he spoke to her amiably, 'I did not know you were in here. What are you doing?'

'I was just playing,' she replied, spying past him to see the other man had started to rock himself up against Alissa, like he was pretending to ride a horse, still raising no reaction from her, 'What are you doing? 'Because you are supposed to be standing at the door.'

'We were but it gets boring and we thought some games would be fun. Do you like games?'

'I do!' she enthused, 'How about marbles? Or jump-step? Do you know how to play?'

'No, no, I was thinking about a different game. Something like the one my friend is playing? Would you like to try that?'

'It looks boring to me. And mother is not even smiling.'

'No, she is not. But that is because my friend is not very good at the game; I am much better, you would enjoy the game with me.'

'Do you promise?'

'Yes, of course.'

'Can we play marbles after your game?'

'Yes, sweet little thing, we can play anything you like.'

'Okay. What are the rules?'

'Stand up for me,' he said, a strange expression creeping across his face as he licked his lips. Kastani complied and looked up at him as he stepped even closer. Taking her hand in one of his, he pressed it against the front of his breaches.

'Can you feel that?' he asked in a hoarse whisper.

The hard bulge under her palm felt like a thick twig but seemed to throb ever so slightly. She smiled and nodded, 'I can! What is it?'

'It is the important part of the game. You need to rub it and then, when I get it out, you hold it tight. After that we see if there's anywhere you can hide it.'

She pulled away, clapping in excitement, 'This sounds fun!' she giggled, 'But I do not think it is the same game as mother.'

'It will be,' he growled, reaching down to undo his belt. Suddenly he crashed to the side and she saw Lennath appear before her, his attention focussed solely on the guard.

'You sick filth!' he screamed, rage as she had never seen in him before boiling from the surface. The staggered guard looked to try and regain his feet until a boot heel slammed into his nose, crushing it across his face in a fountain of blood. Kastani rushed forward, grabbing Lennath's hand.

'No, Lennath, we were just playing a game!'

'Stay there, Kastani!' he ordered, turning his attention to the second guard who was now desperately trying to pull his undergarments up, terror evident in his eyes. Lennath crossed the distance between them in seconds, smashing his forearm across the rapist's throat and driving them both to the ground. Ensuring his knee landed atop the rapidly shrinking groin of his opponent, Lennath wasted no time, rolling forward over the guard and springing back to his feet. Ignoring the vomit spewing from the man's mouth, he jammed one hand inside, gripping the lower jaw and yanking him to his feet. Blood gushed from the corners of his mouth where the flesh tore apart and tears streamed from his eyes. A futile attempt to resist resulted in a knuckle driven into his inner elbow and the arm went limp immediately. Lennath continued the assault, gripping the front of his uniform and his already mangled groin to hoist him across his powerful shoulders. In one smooth movement, he flipped the guard over to the side, slamming his spine onto the edge of the pit with an audible crack. His whimpers of agony echoed back to them as his crippled body tumbled to the depths.

The guard she had been playing with had clambered to his feet nearby and was trying to clear his vision. She skipped over to him and tugged on the hem of his jerkin.

'Are you okay? Your nose looks sore; do you still want to play?' she reached out towards him, hoping he might carry on if she did, but he slapped her hand away.

'Ged away from me!' he managed through his ravaged face and pushed past her towards the exit. It was too late, as Lennath was already upon him, grabbing the back of his neck and crushing him face-first into the ground.

'You would touch a child in this manner?' he seethed, holding the man down with ease, 'You would conspire to rape the single most important woman to me? In my own palace? Have you no concept of where you are? Of who I am?'

'I am s-sorry, Lord! Please forgive me!' the bearded guard spluttered through a growing puddle of his own blood, 'A madness took me!'

'She is barely even a child,' the Prince growled, 'you are twisted by a sickness too great to be ignored. You must be an example to others for such foulness!'

'Yes, my Prince! I will tell all of my depravity! I will tell them of your stance against it, of your just and righteous treatment of me, of how your lenience has allowed me to spread that message!'

'Not that kind of example,' Lennath replied and his rage had been replaced by a calculated hollowness. Flipping the man over, he jammed his thumbs against his underling's eyeballs and began to press down. Screams filled the chamber and his captive clawed out trying to pull his hands away, but Lennath remained strong and suddenly his thumbs overcame the resistance, disappearing inside the guard's skull amid an overflow of blood and ochre ooze.

'You shall not cast your tainted gaze upon another,' he whispered, pulling his digits free as the victim writhed in agony before him. A futile gesture saw the man pull his sword from its scabbard, but the Prince easily dispossessed the blind soldier of his weapon. Thrashing wildly, he was unprepared for a powerful swing removing his right hand just above the wrist.

'Ahhhhhh!' he screamed piteously, 'Please! My Prince! Please, stop!'

Lennath threw the bloodied blade aside and Kastani watched it spin away across the smooth floor, fascinated by the spray of crimson it left in its wake. The guard had rolled back onto his front, desperately attempting to crawl away but with no concept of where he was. Lennath dropped a knee into his back, driving the air from his lungs and turning his screams into breathless sobs.

'You shall not ever spoil another with your tainted touch,' he continued, reaching out to the remaining hand and snapping the fingers back like twigs.

Turning back to Kastani, she saw his happy smile had returned and he reached out a gore-soaked hand to her. 'May I borrow two of the gems I gave you? Just little ones?'

She returned his smile with a broad one of her own, reaching into her little leather pouch and pulling out the two rubies, each about the size of a grape. They were her least favourite. She skipped forward and placed them in his outstretched palm.

'Thank-you,' he said warmly before turning back to the grisly business before him. Twisting the man's head so that it lay sideways on to the floor, he pressed one gem against the opening of his ear. In a sudden blur of violent motion, he slammed his fist against the stone, driving it forcibly into the aural cavity. Whether this hurt more than everything else was unclear; the gurgling, desperate cries had become background noise. The Prince flipped his victim's head to the other side and repeated his brutal operation.

'You shall not hear the torment your taint has caused,' he finished, rising back to his feet, and only then seeming to remember where he was. He looked back towards the doorway and saw Mozak standing in the entrance, flanked by three more palace guards.

'Ahh, Mozak!' he called out, breathing heavily from his exertions, 'What do you think? Not bad for a member of Royalty, eh?'

'You allow your rage to overcome your awareness,' the assassin replied flatly, 'it would leave you vulnerable in battle. But you were indeed effective, and against two opponents, so you should be pleased.'

'Well, good then,' Lennath replied, seeming a little deflated by the mediocre praise, before addressing the accompanying guards, 'this man is to be taken to Justice Square. He will be restrained there until he dies and for three weeks afterwards. He is a twisted pervert of the lowest order so ensure he is displayed as such.'

The soldiers rushed forward and dragged the weakly moaning individual from the chamber. Watching them leave, Kastani was drawn to the thick smear of blood that marked exactly where his body had travelled; it looked like a scarlet cart track against the grey stone. She was about to place her hand in it, to see if it was warm, when Lennath held her shoulders gently and knelt before her.

'What was happening here, Kastani? Why were you letting them do these things?'

'It was a game, Lennath!' she replied excitedly, 'they were going to show me how to play. They said mother played it too, so I would be good at it! Did you not want us to play?'

'They were not playing, innocent girl, they were going to hurt you. They were hurting your mother. I cannot allow that, so they have been punished. But I need you to know that what they did is wrong. They were tricking you.'

'That is mean,' she agreed, 'Like the princess who got tricked by the goblin? He made her cut off all her hair and give it to him and then the king put her in prison?'

Lennath looked confused for a moment before softness filled his eyes, 'You mean in the fable? The tale for children? Yes, just like that. But I am not like the king, I would not put you in prison for being wronged. If I were in that story, the goblin would be hanging in Justice Square.'

'Oh. I like the story but I do not want to be locked up, so thank-you.'

He squeezed her shoulders before standing and walking over to her mother who had still not broken from her concentration. Smoothing her gown where it was still hoisted up over her waste, he tenderly caressed the back of her shoulders before moving around into her field of view.

'Alissa? Why did you allow this?'

There was no response and her gaze remained blank. 'Alissa?' he tried again, more forcefully.

Nothing.

He reached out his hand and yanked hers away from the sceptre she held. 'Alissa!' he shouted. Sudden focus returned to her and she lashed out with a backhand slap across his cheek, staggering him with the force.

'Do not interrupt me! This is difficult enough without you interfering! It takes time to know the animal first. You should bring me the same animals many times; that would make this easier.'

'Alissa, that is useful to know,' he said, rubbing at his reddened face, 'but you were being violated moments ago. Your own daughter was about to be besmirched! Why did you do nothing?'

'The pathetic desires of men? It is meaningless. These are just shells, what happens to them is of little consequence. You want me to make these new lives, to control them in your name and I am learning to do so. What does it matter if others use me for their wants? How is it different to what you do?'

'Because I am not using you. We are allies. Your power is magnificent, and I know you will see the benefit of using it in this manner soon. You must not be touched by any other than me; I may never be your Kale Stanis, but you are every bit my queen. We will rule together and one day you will see me as the lover I want to be. But it was not just you at risk; what of Kastani?'

'As long as I live, she will not die. She is the last remnant of Kale Stanis and I will not allow death to find her.'

'She is a tiny child!' Lennath retorted in exasperation, 'grown men were going to have their way with her!'

'She would have survived, you may not if you break my contact with the Stave again,' Alissa replied, taking hold of the rod once more, 'why do you care? You will murder her if I do not follow your bidding.'

The words cut into Kastani like a knife. Murder her? She was sure that meant kill her, like in the stories. But Lennath was her friend, he was nice to her and gave her gifts. He had just killed two men for being mean to her. Why would he then kill her? It didn't make any sense but sometimes her mother was confusing to talk to. She looked up and realised Lennath was looking at her anxiously; when their eyes met he smiled again, and she couldn't help but return the expression. No, he would not kill her!

Unexpected laughter erupted from her mother, 'Ha, ha, ha, ha, ha!' she guffawed, 'You should just call it the Four Kingdoms! And then what? The One Kingdom!'

Lennath rushed forward and very gently took Alissa's face in his hands, turning her head towards him, 'What are you saying? Has one of my brother's died? Was it Porthus? Can you see what your beasts are doing when they are at your bidding?'

'Like the sweet treats he enjoys!' she almost sang back at him before leaning forward and sucking some of the ichor from his thumb. Licking her lips with a smile, she pulled free of his touch and returned her attention to the Stave, dropping back into an impassive trance.

The Prince seemed suddenly distracted and strode towards the exit, 'Mozak, put two of your people on guard here. In fact, make sure two stay with her unless she is with me. And one with the girl!'

The tall assassin nodded as his employer passed and then cast her a brief glance before closing the heavy doors behind himself.

Kastani sighed and sat back down on the floor. She idly traced one finger through the congealing blood next to her; it was sticky, slightly warm, and thicker than she expected. The two rubies had been her least favourite, but she still liked them; if she'd known that borrow meant keep, she wouldn't have given them to Lennath at all. She wondered when Terex was going to visit and hoped it would be soon.

Catalana rested her chin in her palm, staring across the kitchen table at her sister with utter disdain. Conscious of the disgusted sneer that kept creeping into the left corner of her mouth, she forced the expression away but had still not found the strength to speak to the woman who had left her to die. Her eyes traced the twisted maze of hard scar tissue that adorned Rayne's left cheek, stretching up along her temple and round towards the back of her head. Although her deep red hair hung loosely down, obscuring the mangled ear on that side, Cat' assumed the damage was complete around to the back of her skull. The burns spread down as well, along the formerly smooth jawline, looking taut and uncomfortable as they disappeared down her neck into the collar of the black jerkin she wore. Her eyes remained unblemished, however, a haunting, exotic green, devoid of any warmth; had they always been so cold? Or was it just her current bias? No matter, Cat' felt no sympathy for her kin as whatever physical damage she had suffered was insufficient punishment for her betrayal.

A hand moved onto her arm and she turned her head to see Herc watching her intently; she shot him a quick smile and slid her own palm into his. Feeling strong and safe while under his touch, she returned her attention to Rayne who was just finishing her tale of coming to be amongst them. Cat' cast her gaze across the other three newcomers; the woman, Rebecca, reminded her of the courtiers she used to associate with but less brash or loud, perhaps contemplative, perhaps afraid; Silas Zendar, the scholar who had claimed to be a simple bard and writer but was now revealed to be an investigator in the employ of Prince Lennath; and the last man, stood furtively glancing out of the rear window between spates of focus on Rayne, another betrayer, another enemy allowed access to them; Jacob Frost. She still could not fathom how Treya had stomached his presence across her threshold.

'Once we had Rebecca, this was the only logical place to turn. We had no choice,' Rayne concluded.

'Just your last resort? Is that how you justify your return here?' Treya demanded immediately, body tense with her bridled rage.

'Who else would even consider helping me rescue a madwoman from one of the most powerful countries in the land? You care for Alissa, so you are invested.'

'And you are not?' the eldest Fimarr screamed, 'You damned her to this fate! You are running scared, hunted by your enemy and you want us to fix it for you?'

'Not *for* me,' Rayne corrected, '*with* me. I have made mistakes throughout my life, who has not? But now I wish to remedy them. My reasoning with Alissa was flawed; by the time I had overcome the surprise of actually finding her alive, it was too late to stop her being taken from me.'

'Taken from you?' Catalana snarled, 'You handed her to Lennath on a platter! You are speaking like these events happened to you, not because of you. You betrayed your youngest sister and left her to whatever dark fate is planned; find a way to betray Treya and you have completed the set!' She felt the squeeze from Herc and left her rant where it was. Rayne displayed no reaction to the tirade, but her eyes were fixed on Cat's own.

'I do not hide from my actions, nor do I try to defend them. What is done, is done. I am here to galvanise what happens next.'

Surprisingly, Treya rounded on Catalana, 'If you must speak, make it constructive. You have no place in chastising Rayne, for your own actions have been no better! The views of a hypocrite have no bearing on this discourse.'

The words stung her, but only because they were true. Catalana had stored so much anger, resentment and pain at being abandoned by the sister she had always been closest to growing up, that she had never taken the time to compare their actions. Were they the same after all? She had left Alissa behind when the girl had been at the height of madness; physically dangerous, disregarding of her own health, wild like an animal and separated from them by a seemingly impassable barrier. But those were the justifications she had built in her mind over time; could she and Herc have rescued the youngest Fimarr then? When they had fled the Citadel, they were both severely wounded, terrified for their lives and desperate to escape that dreadful place; perhaps there *had* been time to find another way to Alissa, to keep her docile and get her to safety. Maybe she had acted selfishly? But what of Rayne? She had abandoned Catalana to almost certain death under the offer of reward. Certainly, the delivery of Alissa to Lennath was likewise under the promise of hefty payment. These decisions were cold and mercenary, completely different to Cat's own, weren't they? The new confusion quelled her anger, and she lowered her gaze to stare at her entwined hand.

Unexpectedly, it was Rebecca who broke the latest silence. Her voice was soft and almost melodic but laced with a deep confidence, 'I realise I am a stranger here, to both your home and this situation, but I have known Rayne for several years now. I do not believe she is the woman you remember, for I have witnessed how her guilt has altered her. She will not thank me for telling you, but I met her when she was nothing but a broken shell, physically and emotionally devastated. In time her body has healed but her spirit has not; I have seen her try so hard to balance all the wrong she has done, to you and many others, but her heart is the least developed part of her. We have talked and I know much of this can be traced back to her upbringing, I would hope both of you can empathise with that, but she was further hardened by her training with the Veer and then the isolation of her chosen profession. None of this excuses the pain she has caused you, but I hope it supports her sincerity in coming here now.'

'I am sure Rayne appreciates your words,' Treya answered curtly, 'but you are correct; you are a stranger here and your opinion carries little weight. As far as I see it, you are simply an inexplicable burden that my sister has collected and dumped at my door. I would suggest you refrain from further input to this family matter.'

'Please, love,' Straker moved forward, sliding a hand around Treya's waist, 'I know this is sudden and happening faster than any of us can keep up with, but we should listen to all that has to be said. When we have the full picture, we will be better prepared to make decisions.'

Catalana expected another rebuke from her sister but none came. Instead Treya sank into the embrace and her face softened slightly, 'Straker is correct,' she conceded, 'Accept my apologies, Rebecca.'

She received a nod in reply before Rayne spoke again, 'If there were time, then I would gladly talk with you at length about all that has happened since we were children. Maybe it would improve our current relationship, maybe it would help us to understand each other or resolve our issues with the man who spawned us. But we do not have that time. We must either act or run and hide from the dark that is coming. I have told you all that has happened to now, but I will let Zendar explain what is coming.'

The statement sent a chill down Catalana's spine and she looked up at the fragile academic. His face held the light discoloration of extensive bruising and she imagined he had not been very loose of tongue when first questioned by Rayne. Those lingering marks undoubtedly explained why he was so immediately forthcoming when prompted in this instance. Straightening in his seat, he cleared his throat before addressing them in an eloquent but paper-thin voice.

'I am Silas Zendar the third,' he proclaimed, 'I have been a researcher and scholar for all of my life and travelled the lands in search of true facts. When the Prince of Lustania approached me to research on his behalf, I could resist neither the offered recompense, nor the lure of the subject itself. The truth behind the power of Ramikain, his longevity, the dark taint that surrounded his existence, the creatures that were present during his reign, all of it. I studied for years, locating and revising ancient texts, securing first-hand accounts of his first rise to power and the subsequent one that affected all of you...'

'I am certain you are both professional and diligent,' Catalana snapped, losing patience with the rambling, 'get to the point.'

Panic flashed across his eyes momentarily and he furtively glanced at Rayne; when no reprisal came from her, he composed himself and continued. 'As far as I was able to determine, Ramikain harnessed an ancient power, left over from the gods, or so the legends claim. This power was balanced between a Stave and Globe, each the equal but counter of the other; the artifacts were lost to time but at some point the Stave was discovered by Ramikain. He learned to utilise its power and even removed the essence from the device, enabling him to use the dark power itself to corrupt all about it. Over time, the presence of this taint in the ground spread out, killing most life and twisting what remained horribly. Having absorbed the power into himself, it made his spirit timeless but burned his body rapidly; this is where his need to feast upon mortal flesh came from. When Lennath heard of the side effects of the taint, he invested a small fortune into seeking out the original Stave so that it could safely contain that power once more. His fear of being corrupted is so great that he will not wield the artifact himself, but it is known that only those touched by darkness will have any chance of using it at all; Alissa Fimarr was the prime candidate. Her corruption is significant, and her mental instability presented an option to be manipulated.'

'But to what end?' Herc asked with a hint of frustration, 'He has already contained that darkness once more, inhibiting its effect significantly I assume? What threat does he truly pose?'

'Alissa Fimarr is more powerful than you realise,' Zendar continued, 'Prince Lennath's original goal was simply to control the creatures mutated during Ramikain's most recent return; Lustanian trappers have been gathering them for more than five years, creating an unwholesome 'zoo' of sorts under the palace. When early forays into training or controlling the beasts failed, he knew that magic would be his only recourse; with the Stave, your sister can directly manipulate these monsters. No mere suggestion or urge, she is able to control even their slightest actions.'

'We have fought these creatures,' Forge offered, 'they are powerful and dangerous in isolation so would present a grave threat if coerced into an army. But they are still only living things, finite in number and killable. Undoubtedly no threat to the entire land. What are you not telling us?'

'Very astute, sir,' Zendar replied, 'Although the coordination she provides to these unfortunate mutants makes them more formidable than you recall, they are too few in number to curb all armies into submission. But the Stave also provides the wielder the ability to taint, that is true of both the minds of those she chooses and their bodies. Given enough time she could create an army of the beasts so huge that none could stand against it; there are no shortage of living creatures to twist. More than this, she is thick with the power of Ramikain himself and the Stave will help her to focus this. Eventually she will be able to control the minds of more evolved animals such as ourselves, and may gain other powers formerly possessed by her predecessor.'

'This is no lecture, Zendar!' the exasperated cry came from Frost, although he kept his attention fixed on the world beyond the window, 'Stop mincing your words and tell them what you fear will come!'

Silas swallowed hard and shifted in his seat, 'Yes, o-of course, but you must understand that much of this is theorised from legends and precursors, there has been no demonstration of such things and her limited mental facility may prevent her...'

'To the point!' Treya now joined in, failing to make any acknowledgement of Frost's previous words, 'What is going to happen?'

'She may be able to move items with only a thought…'

'Ramikain could do that, he still fell,' Forge stated before being gestured to silence by Treya.

'She could gain control of the environment itself,' the scholar continued, 'plants, water, fire, the wind, whole mountains; all could fall under her control. Further than this, she could extend her will over life itself, forcing the very essence of existence out of a living body. If these abilities were achieved, with the imbalanced mind she has demonstrated, then all we know could be forfeit.'

Catalana could not find words; the idea was completely ludicrous, wasn't it? Ramikain had possessed this same power but been unable to demonstrate the feats Zendar suggested. Or had they simply stopped him before he was able to do so? Alissa was her baby sister, even now, not much more than twenty years at most; how could she represent such a threat? And would any of this be happening if she had not been left for dead in the Black Citadel…

'That is what may happen,' Rayne said, causing Catalana to jump at the sudden break in silence, 'it is why we should be determined to prevent the current course of things. The real reason that you are going to help me to stop this is to save Alissa and bring her back here. We may all see things differently, but we are kin and she is in danger, from Lennath and from her devolution into corruption. If we act now, we can prevent both.'

'No, your logic is flawed,' Cat' countered, not through malice or anger, 'if we bring Alissa back here, Lennath could just come for her again. Even if not, he could find someone else touched by that darkness to be his stooge. If we killed him, someone else could use your knowledge and that Stave to recreate the threat. What is the real plan here, Rayne?'

'You are right, Cat', I should have known better than to try and do this in stages,' Rayne seemed to be amused at some inner joke but quickly reverted to her matter-of-fact tone, 'Zendar told you at the beginning, there are two artifacts. The other is a Globe and he knows where we can find it; with that, we can nullify the Stave and end the threat forever.'

'So why do we not get this item first? Have the advantage when we confront Lennath?' Treya asked.

'Therein lies the biggest problem, these items were protected by curses and ancient magic, as if the gods who left them behind wanted only those of commitment to have them,' Zendar joined in again, strangely enthusiastic, 'the Stave could only be taken by the sacrifice of three bloods; three unrelated victims had to die before the fourth could claim the prize. The Globe, perhaps gifted to us by a more benevolent deity, has a different requirement; it must be claimed by a quartet joined by blood. Only then may it be claimed and utilised by any of those four.'

'As you see,' Rayne cut him off, 'The only way to stop the threat permanently is with the Globe. The only way to claim the Globe is with four joined by blood. Four sisters. We need Alissa to stop Alissa. Somewhat ironic, don't you think?'

'So, we have to rescue Alissa and then convince her to join us on some quest for a device to remove the power under her control? Ironic is not the word,' Treya replied, taking a chair at the table as if her legs could no longer hold her.

'But wait,' Rebecca chirped up brightly, 'you have another option do you not? Joined by blood? Meaning family? Your children! If they accompany you, then you can claim the Globe before facing your sister!'

'No!' Treya snapped, 'My children will have no part in this! They are just babies and I will neither endanger them nor fate them to a life of constant threat as any part in such quests seems to bind us to. I would rather risk Rayne's plan than have them involved in any way.'

'Aye, I agree,' Frost rumbled once more, 'there is no place in this for children. In fact, we should leave one of our number behind to ensure their safety as more killers may yet target them seeking the bounty laid down by Lennath for the Fimarr family.'

'We?' Forge asked mockingly, 'Who said anything about you being involved? My good lady rejected the last man trying to force his aid upon us, what leverage do you think you hold to force your way into our party? You may have assisted Rayne in getting here but that earns you little good will from this household!'

'I ask for no good will,' Frost continued, 'I have recognised my mistakes and I pay for them every day. Whether you choose to believe it or not, my only goal is to rectify the damage I caused through my betrayal of you. I am old and dare say less useful in either battle or adventure than any of you, but you have my sword and my loyalty nonetheless.'

'A lovely gesture from one who is facing judgement from the gods on his deathbed!' Forge continued sarcastically, 'but as you say, you provide little of use to us! Perhaps your part is played out, old man?'

'You are no less arrogant than last time we met, Straker Forge,' Frost replied without resentment, 'but I do have more to offer. We need to attack the heart of Lustania to free Alissa Fimarr, and I can give you an army to do so…'

Chapter 7

Lennath leaned forward on the wide window ledge, peering out beyond the latticed window over the city. The lamplighters must have been about their business as he could see snake-like trails of light through the streets, sprading as he watched. Releasing a satisfied sigh, he contemplated how perfectly everything was falling into place. His enemies were scattered and hunted, soon he would receive word of their deaths; admittedly it would be preferable if Silver Rain had been executed in her cell, but her escape had actually given him fine excuse to order both her and Frost's deaths without losing any favour among his people. Blaming them for Captain Rydell's murder actually seemed to generate more support for the former General's demise. Mozak had proven true to his word, with more than thirty Veer assassins arriving within days of his request; the palace was surely now impregnable, and he even had surplus to finish off any of the Fimarrs or their allies who might evade the current contracts on their lives. Then there was Alissa. Not only had she proven far more adept with the Stave than Lennath could have hoped, but she was unexpectedly compliant to his demands. She had controlled his captured beasts with ease and, although clear confirmation was hard to achieve with her, it seemed she had already removed one of his brothers from the playing field. And her power to mutate was growing daily; three new creatures generated on the first day, now she was capable of more than ten. Soon whole armies could be produced in mere weeks, following his commands through her; all of this while avoiding contact with the dark magic himself. Unexpected benefits had also been realised; he would not deny how strongly attracted he was to the sorceress and she seemed content for him to treat her as his lover, despite failing to reciprocate his attentions. Kastani was also an unanticipated boon, a sweetly naïve child who accepted him as he was; her innocence, charm and joy became infectious and he had grown far more attached to her than he would ever have planned. Thinking of her made him grow wistful over his own neglect of family, he had made no attempt to wed and wasted no time considering offspring of his own, yet this little girl had completely enchanted him; he wondered if he would be able to kill her as previously threatened, not that such leverage seemed necessary with Alissa.

'You will visit your father?' the voice startled him, although he knew Mozak was always nearby.

'Yes, I must retain the pretence for a while longer. If the other kingdoms realise the threat I pose, let alone decide to unite against me, they may have the opportunity to prevent my coup. It is something that must be avoided if possible; at least until the Lady Fimarr is strong enough to defend our borders.'

'So that is still your goal? To claim the Five Kingdoms as your own?' Mozak pressed.

Lennath paused, there was something in the assassin's tone that he did not feel comfortable with. Was the other man concerned for the safety of his own island? Did he sense that Lennath's plan could expand beyond the Kingdoms, perhaps to the whole world? Having the deadly warrior on edge was an unacceptable risk so he opted to play down his ambitions. 'Yes, the Five Kingdoms will be mine. I will unify these nations under my banner and become a great political power across the land once more. My family will be justly punished but my people will reap the benefits. You and yours will have riches beyond measure when I am successful.'

'Indeed,' Mozak gave nothing away, 'will you require me to escort you to Mainspring?'

'Of course.' Lennath was curious about the question, what other purpose would he have for his bodyguard?

'Very well. In this case I will assign one of my people to stay with Alissa and another with Kastani. That way you will be assured of their safety in your absence.'

'That will be adequate,' Lennath agreed, suspicion abating slightly, 'I am certain the Veer are more than capable of protecting my interests.'

Mozak nodded but Lennath still felt uncomfortable, why had he not already considered the risk his departure could generate? Perturbed, he stalked along the corridor towards the suite he had allocated to Alissa; by this time, she was usually finished in the creation chamber, although her mental endurance using the Stave had been increasing with each session.

'I would be alone with her,' he stated as he turned the handle to her quarters.

'As you wish, Sire,' Mozak replied, taking up a position to the side of the double door, 'I will be ready as you require.'

Lennath nodded and entered the room, closing the door behind him before releasing a breath he hadn't realised he was holding. Days ago, he had felt completely secure around his hireling and trepidation would fill him when interacting with Alissa; now those roles seemed reversed. Making his way through the outer rooms of the accommodation assigned to her, he admired all the finery in place, the most expensive materials available woven together to make a beautiful domicile fit for any princess. Not that it seemed to make any difference to her; he was not certain if she even noticed the décor or recognised anything provided to her. Even at her most lucid she rarely discussed matters beyond the power at her disposal; her detachment was both frustrating and uncontrollably alluring. But he had noticed that her more severe mania seemed to be reducing, perhaps the structured environment around her was improving her disposition.

Flickering candlelight filtered through the last doorway indicating that she was returned from the day's activities, and he quickly made his way into her bedchamber. She was sitting on the edge of the huge four-poster bed with her back to him, and he felt both his heart and his loins stir at the sight of her naked back; the delicate creamy flesh contrasted by the runes etched across it. He insisted she dress when out of her private area and the sheer robes most commonly chosen had now been removed from her wardrobe; temptation for those in his employ had to be reduced and this could only be achieved if her exquisite body was not on show. However, she seldom remained clothed here, complaining that she felt too hot and restricted, and her gown from today was cast upon the floor. Crawling over the bed behind her, he lay on his side and gently traced some of the scars with his fingertips. As he found his hand moving down the curve of her spine and to the top of her buttocks, he stopped himself, despite the arousal he felt, and rolled into a seated position beside her. She gave no indication that she was even aware of his presence as her eyes stared forward at nothing and her hands were clasped around a goblet held in her lap. For a moment, he just sat there, absorbing her strange beauty and admiring the complete lack of self-consciousness she felt about her body. But why should she have any? She was an attractive woman in her own right and with the meticulously crafted body-scarring, she was a unique work of art. Beyond that, she was proving capable of magical feats that most could never imagine, let alone achieve; it was almost as if this were what she had been designed for.

'You want my body?' she asked amicably, not altering her focus.

Lennath felt a surge of desire at the question, she had permitted him to lie with her several times and he had thrilled at each opportunity, but she remained distant from him. He wanted her to want him, or least physically engage with him when he loved her; he could not even be certain she recognised his attentions when applied. He hoped the fact that she permitted him sexually at all was an indication that she was warming towards him; as she always reminded him, however, he was not Kale Stanis.

'Always,' he whispered and kissed her neck gently, reaching out a hand to cup her breast. He stopped before making contact and instead placed it comfortingly on her thigh. 'Do you want me?'

She took a sip from the drink in her hand, 'The eyes were dull, and my heart ached.'

So often his questions were met with ramblings and he wondered if she did it deliberately at times. He took the goblet from her, feeling no resistance, and then raised her arms. Slipping his shirt off, he pulled it gently over her head and slipped it down to cover her body; the act drew her attention and he found her looking into his face when he finished his ministrations. He smiled at her and reached out to tuck stray hair back behind her ear; he would love to see her golden locks grow in fully as they had been when they first met years before.

'It is cooler tonight, I don't want you to feel uncomfortable, Alissa. What eyes are you talking about?'

'When I spread myself amongst my children, I could not see clearly.'

He had realised days ago that she referred to the mutants she was creating as her children; did this mean she was reaching capacity with how many she could control at once? He handed the goblet back to her. 'Did you lose control of them?'

Her face contorted into an expression of insult, 'My children love me! They will always try to please their mother!'

'Of course they will,' he soothed, kneeling behind her on the bed and massaging her shoulders slowly, 'did you take any time to examine tactics with Audack's military advisors?'

'Soldiers bore me,' she replied sharply but he could feel her muscles relaxing under his touch, 'My children need no such guidance, they will defeat any foe because it is what I wish.'

'As you say, my queen,' he continued, 'but what is it that you want? You have helped me no end already, creating scores of new beasts and commanding them towards my goals. Yet you ask for nothing. I would like to believe this is because of the leverage I hold over you, but you make no mention of this. Why do you aid me?'

'I have power. I am power. You brought this to me. Terex has been gone so long and you are the next best thing to provide what I need.'

'Yes, but I could be so much more,' she failed to respond to his hint, so he continued, 'but you have not told what it is you need?'

'Sustenance,' she replied before taking another sip from the goblet. Peering into the vessel, he could see the thick crimson fluid swirling within. Fresh human blood that she had demanded from the first day. She ate whatever food was provided but seemed to crave her gory beverage; he wondered if it was required to satiate the darkness within her.

'Blood. The stories say that Ramikain used to eat whole bodies. Is it necessary? To use the Stave, I mean?' he had taken to using the formal title of the sceptre as any other name seemed to anger her.

She turned towards him suddenly and pushed the cup forth, 'It is to be a god,' she whispered excitedly, 'feel it!'

Such direct engagement was so thrilling that he did not hesitate, swigging a deep mouthful. The coppery tang filled his senses immediately, but the congealing consistency was alien to him, and he could not swallow. Without warning, Alissa kissed him passionately, the ichor in his mouth flowing freely between them and out over their faces. She had never initiated such intimacy and he felt giddy with desire. Then it was over, she broke the kiss and turned back to face the wall, licking her lips but ignoring the gore that now covered her face and neck, staining his borrowed shirt red. Unconsciously, he swallowed, almost gagging as the remaining blood in his mouth found its way to his stomach.

'That was... you are, do you see me now?' he fumbled for words.

'You should bring me more birds tomorrow. Not enough of my children take to the skies.'

He deflated slightly, disappointed that her focus had shifted again. 'I will see to it. Speaking of your children, I spent some time with Kastani today.'

'You speak that name? I told you not to do that,' she said, seemingly returned to an almost daze.

'I do say her name, and yet I still live. Perhaps it is not such an insult to you after all. She told me how much she enjoys being here, the food, the toys, the beautiful clothes; we played croquet in the gardens. She misses you. I would be happy for you to spend some time together under chaperone if you like?'

'Crackling bones and popping flesh, that's what you wanted!' she asserted, suddenly standing.

'What does that mean, Alissa?' he queried in frustration.

'You want to talk family? I am complying with you, Prince Lennath.'

'What? You cannot mean that is what you want for Kastani? She is your true daughter!'

'Your family, foolish man!'

'Do you mean Porthus?' he pressed, suddenly realising that she may be about to confirm his brother's death at last.

'Popping in my teeth, draining on my tongue, sliding down my throat. Family can be so delicious!'

That was it, clarity that the massive monster she had dispatched to attack Porthus' caravan had been successful. Of course it had, that was the only reason for his father to summon him so suddenly. At least now it was highly unlikely that the death, or the cause behind it, was anything more than an assumption on their part; that knowledge would aid him greatly during that meeting.

'Red and green and purple,' Alissa continued, voice beginning to become shrill, 'lights shining beyond so blinding. My head cannot see, my hands cannot feel; my future will not continue, my past does not exist. Bodies are coming towards me, filling me with ice; she will not leave me be until my life has joined his. I have to run and hide, keep away from the eyes and the hands of the killer. Why will you not stop her? Why must I be the one to die?'

By the end of her rant, Alissa was screaming at the top of her lungs before suddenly crumpling to the carpeted floor. Lennath was quick to react, leaping forward and catching hold of her across the chest and shoulders before her head could hit the ground. Cradling her in his arms, he saw her eyelids fluttering, barely on the edge of consciousness. Nothing of this sort had happened since she had been brought here and he wondered again if she had reached her capacity with the creatures; or was the dark power itself too much for her fragile form? He lifted her delicately and laid her upon the soft bed, staring down into her face. She looked so soft and child-like when the rage and madness were absent from her expression. He took a cloth from the gold basin that had been left in the room for washing and softly cleaned the drying blood from her skin. After doing the same for himself, he climbed onto the bed beside her, placing a single kiss upon her lips before curling himself about her and closing his eyes to sleep.

Racing through the undergrowth, perkitins scattered before him, their fluffy tails whipping out behind them as they fled. The vermin were the least of Mazt's concerns as he dropped a shoulder and rolled under a fallen tree blocking his path. Regaining his feet, he saw Diast somersaulting forward where he had taken the high line over the obstruction; the other warrior hit the ground still in parallel and they continued forward at the frantic pace. Atae was off to the right, following the rocky border of the cliffside on the terrain he preferred and Keris was further to the left than Diast, leading them all by several yards. She was so much faster than all of them and he realised she was holding back so that they could arrive in unison, unity before pride.

Before them, the trees opened out onto a mossy plain and two members of the newly established boundary patrols stood waiting, clearly anxious from their body-language. The Guardians slowed to a stop before the relieved men and Mazt addressed them.

'You raised the alert? You understand what it means to summon the Guardians directly?'

One of the pair nodded vigorously, 'We know, Guardian Kae-Taqar, and our revelation is worthy of your presence! Runners have been dispatched to bring the Elders, for this truth will affect us all!'

'Be calm, patrolman. What revelation merits such extreme notification?' Mazt tried to keep irritation from his voice but could not bring himself to believe that the skittish man before him had made the correct choice in alerting both the Guardians and the Elders.

'The Boundary is breached!' came the frantic reply and he felt a boulder forming in the pit of his stomach, 'Invaders have come!'

'Lower your voice, fool!' Atae responded, unexpectedly calm despite the proposed situation, 'Even if your truth is not simply clouded, as it must be, if there were aggressors in our lands, you would draw them straight to us!'

The patrolman silenced himself, but the terror remained in his eyes. Mazt placed a strong hand on his trembling shoulder. 'Take refuge, my countryman, remain safe and obscured until the Elders arrive. If your truth is clear then you have fulfilled your duty; the Guardians are here, and we will defend our home from any threat.'

Whether his words brought comfort or not, Mazt turned to his allies and raised a fist, prompting them back into action and the quartet set off at a more cautious pace towards the beach beyond the edge of the cliffside they had been following. As Atae took to the higher ground, the remaining three took refuge behind a clump of thorny bushes to investigate.

Looking out over the pale sand, Mazt felt a surge of disbelief; the Boundary was now over fifteen hundred yards from the edge of the shore, with azure waters stretching as far as the barrier would allow him to see. Just within the limit of their former protection was a dark shape floating on the still surface; it looked like an enormous canoe but much deeper, with high poles reaching towards the sky, each adorned with a creamy-white sheet. He had never seen anything like it, but it was of least concern to him at that moment. Sitting on the sand at water's edge were several long rowboats, twelve sets of oars secured upright, and the centre of each craft packed full of crates, barrels and tightly wrapped bundles. The cargo was being unloaded onto the beach by scores of strangers; the invaders his kinsmen had spoken of. They were similar in appearance to Mazt's own people, but smaller in height and stature, with a variety of skin colours and that outer layer appearing smooth and soft. They covered themselves almost completely in fabrics and metals, which suggested his assessment of fragile skin to be correct, and all were armed. Their current focus seemed to be preparing a temporary camp and there were no tracks suggesting they had dispatched any scouts beyond the beach.

Mazt took a deep breath, the omens were realised at last; this was what the Guardians existed for. He reached out his hands to the shoulders of his companions, attracting their attention silently. Through a series of hand gestures, he commanded Diast to the furthest edge of their cover and indicated Keris should hold her position; she would commence her attack once the confusion of their initial foray was at its height. Turning towards the cliff, he signed a series of orders to Atae, who was concealed from their enemies by several large boulders, before moving to the opposite edge of the shrubbery. Counting down in his head, he ran through a series of minute muscle exercises, loosening tendons and preparing his body for the upcoming activity. Then the countdown was complete.

Atae heaved with all his might against his cover, shifting the mighty rock only slightly, but enough to begin a small avalanche of shale and debris. As stones and boulders crashed down towards the trespassers, Atae slid down expertly among the landslide, obscured from all save the most diligent observers. As Mazt watched those on the beach, he saw only confusion and panicked fleeing from the danger. As one, he and Diast sprinted forward from their hiding places, targeting the clusters of men nearest to them. He was amongst them before they were even aware, slamming one foe into two others, stunning all three. Spinning around on the spot, his massive arms struck two more men, smashing them easily to the sand, before he ended the movement with a driven punch into the metal chest-plate of his primary target. The armour buckled under the force of his blow and he both heard and felt bones beneath splinter like firewood. Whoever these attackers were, they were flimsy under their protective garb as he had suspected. Casting a quick glance towards Diast, he saw his ally was similarly embedded in the heart of his opposition, whirling like a dervish, using the lightning-fast reflexes he was renowned for to land multiple blows without reply.

Now the initial surprise was over, the invaders began to rally. Cries rang out across the battlefield and weapons began to be drawn. Mazt rose to his full height as those around him sported expressions of dread; he stood head and shoulders above the tallest of them. The man in front of him still fumbled at his scabbard for his sword and Mazt slammed both fists down upon his shoulders, forcing him to his knees with an agonised cry. Spotting an aggressor to his side lunging forward, Mazt shot out a hand, grasping his enemy's wrist like a vice and redirecting the attack. The sword blade sliced easily into the face of his kneeling foe before popping cleanly through the rear of the skull. The weapon was dragged away as the dead man collapsed and Mazt squeezed hard, feeling his opponent's bones slide together before pulverising under his phenomenal strength. Screams of pain were mingling with cries of defiance and he knew there was a threat of being overrun should the forces rallied against them begin to work coherently. Retaining his grip on his injured foe, he pushed hard with powerful legs, propelling himself into a second spin and dragging his human weapon with him; the man's flailing body disarmed some of those around him, swiping others from their feet.

He noted Atae in the distance, now at the foot of the cliff amid the rubble his distraction had generated, hurling rocks before him as he closed the gap to a trio of intruders; despite his efforts, they held weapons ready when he arrived. As the central man stabbed forward with a spear, Atae raised one foot high, stamping down on the tip. The weapon snapped a foot from the end, staggering the attacker forward, at the same moment Atae launched himself into a high flip over the three. Two stood dumbfounded by the incredible agility but the third spun around quickly, swinging his hatchet before him. Atae blocked the attack with his forearm, the wooden shaft of the weapon striking him harmlessly, before driving a straight kick into his foe's groin. With one man down, the broken spear-wielder stabbed forward again with his neutered weapon. Atae stepped left, the wooden staff narrowly missing his hip, before clamping his arm down and spinning a hundred and eighty degrees. The spear was freed from its owner's grasp but not before dragging him forward at pace; Atae had planned for this and drove his elbow up sharply, shattering his nose and driving the bone backwards into the soft tissue beyond. His enemy was dead before he hit the ground.

Mazt had little concern that his fellow Guardian could deal with the remaining two opponents he was currently facing, at the same moment he realised he was not paying his own situation enough attention. A scratching sensation against his shoulder drew his focus back and he noted a slight scrape across his leathery flesh. Looking up he spotted an archer twenty feet from him, already notching a second arrow. He realised he was still holding the screaming man in one hand and tossed him towards the bowman before assessing his original adversaries. Recovering from their surprise, all now had weapons drawn and were closing in about him, but he could sense the fear within them. Releasing a roar of anger, he coaxed the desired result as two of the men whipped their weapons forward in terror. Mazt dropped to the sand on his back, watching both sword and halberd sail harmlessly over him, the latter striking the shoulder of a warrior opposite. Smiling to himself, Mazt reached out and grabbed the ankle of an opponent in each hand, flipping both men to the ground with a single movement. As they crashed against their own fellows, it left only one man still on the attack and his mace arced down towards Mazt's head. Catching the heavy spiked head of the weapon in his palm, surprised that one of the skewers actually pierced his skin, he pushed up with all of his strength, regaining his feet and throwing his attacker backwards several feet. Watching the dead body crash to the ground, blood spurting from the punctures in jaw, neck and chest where his own weapon was now lodged, Mazt slammed a foot down onto the hip of one floored fighter, feeling the pelvis pulverise under his weight.

He noticed men beginning to flee back down the beach, the efforts of the Guardians clearly intimidating enough for such cowards as these. Despite his previous distraction, he allowed himself a moment to ensure the plan was being implemented as he expected. Sure enough, as the invaders reached the first of their boats, Keris appeared from within, wielding one of the massive oars as a makeshift quarterstaff, decimating the first men to arrive. Content that there was no escape, Mazt returned his focus to those about him. Lashing out a foot into the knee of the halberd-wielder, he marvelled at how easily the limb snapped in the wrong direction. Another sword attack deflected harmlessly from his side and he grappled the perpetrator in a headlock. Flipping the discarded halberd up into the air with one foot, he pulled up sharply on his hostage, breaking his neck before catching his claimed weapon. Twirling it in one hand, he swept the weapon around in a semicircle, cleanly removing one man's lower arm, with short sword still in hand, and tearing open the stomach of a second. His only able-bodied foe turned and fled; Mazt let him go, knowing that there was no escape beyond Keris. Silencing the broken-kneed man with a bootheel to the throat, he surged across the short gap to his one-armed enemy, jamming his hand into the screaming man's mouth. As involuntary bile surged forth, Mazt yanked hard, bracing himself against his enemy's chest; the jaw tore free and the shocked man dropped to the sand twitching involuntarily in his death throes.

Feeling the thrill of real combat surging through him, Mazt snapped his attention to the archer again. It seemed the bowman had still been attempting to shoot him throughout the recent combat, arrows in the bodies of the fallen and sand about him testament to the effort, and was now rapidly retreating. The broken-wristed warrior was vainly trying to crawl after his comrade, several splinters of bone now protruding from his arm where he had mistakenly tried to put weight on the limb. Mazt covered the distance between them in five powerful bounds, punching down onto the base of his spine and feeling the vertebrae separate under the force. Holding his prone enemy's face down into the sand, he waited for the futile struggle to end, ducking his head to one side as a more accurate arrow whistled his way. Satisfied that his current foe was dead, Mazt charged forward, batting yet another arrow aside with the back of his hand before leaping into the archer's chest with both knees. More bones gave way under his weight as they landed, and he wrapped his hands around the man's throat. Squeezing hard and straining with all of the power in his back and shoulders, he watched the face before him turn purple, eyes bulging and strangled gasps escaping desperately. When the head tore free, spraying a torrent of blood amongst the shards of spine and wiry tangle of ligaments, it took Mazt completely by surprise; these people were truly fragile.

Tossing the severed head to one side, he looked up to see Keris annihilating those still attempting to flee; with her makeshift weapon, she had slain more than double the number of foes than any of her peers. Shaking his hands to clear the worst of the ichor, he saw Diast was already examining the fallen for signs of life, Atae had moved to the edge of the water, looking out at the giant canoe where frantic activity appeared to be underway. He raised his arm and Mazt realised it was the one adorned by his Palmstone.

'Atae! Wait…!' he called in warning, but it was too late. A ripple of disruption over the surface of the water indicated the direction of the unleashed attack, seconds later a plume of water almost half the length of the boat shot skywards mere yards from the vessel. Almost like a living thing, it reached a height of forty feet before angling down and smashing into the deck of the craft below. The massive boat split in two with explosive force, timber, supplies and men thrown in all directions even as the intense downward force of the spout dragged the remaining sections instantly beneath the waves.

Atae's look of amazement must have mirrored his own and he had to physically lower his friend's arm for him.

'That was more than I knew possible,' he whispered in awe and Mazt patted his shoulder in support.

'Indeed, the Palmstones are formidable weapons. That is why they are blessed only to us as Guardians; it is also why we are forbidden to utilise them without permission of the Elders.'

'I hear your truth, Mazt,' Atae replied honestly, 'The affront these invaders have caused took control of my better judgement. Accept my apology.'

'Of course, Atae, I understand.'

'But I beg you, share your understanding of what has happened here. The Boundary has retreated once more, further than ever before in a shorter time of passing. It has presented us with enemies such as we have never encountered. To what purpose? Are we being tested?'

'Those truths Mazt cannot provide,' Keris announced, joining them whilst still toying with her newfound weapon, 'none of us can. Perhaps this is a test, or we are fortunate enough to have earned Guardianship at the very time that such danger was prophesised. No matter which, these attackers were feeble and presented little threat in the end.'

'Guardians!' the voice resonated out from the high end of the sands, where the pale yellow blended into the lush mosses and grass beyond; the flora that had been all they had known until recent days. Approaching was the High Auger, flanked in procession by the other Elders. Never had they all been beyond the Great Shrine together, let alone this far out; Mazt joined his fellow combatants as they rushed to form a kneeling line, heads bowed in respect to their leaders.

'What have you done here?' the High Auger asked when he was before Mazt and there seemed to be an edge of fear in his voice, although it may have been his imagination.

'We have fulfilled our destiny, High Auger. Invaders have come, to destroy or plunder we do not know, and the Guardians have destroyed them!' he could not quite keep the excitement from his tone.

'Foolish children,' the High Auger continued, 'did you leave none alive?'

'No, grand one,' Mazt replied, losing certainty with every word spoken, 'the threat is eradicated in total, safety is assured.'

'Is that your truth, Mazt Kae-Taqar? Is that all of your truths?' the High Auger pressed. This time they all remained silent as it was becoming clear they had done something wrong. 'Do you believe this handful of trespassers were an entire species? Or the entirety of the threat passed down from generations hence? If that were so, what purpose would there be to have Guardians at all? Such meagre opponents would pose little threat to our people, would they not?'

Like a hammer the realisation hit him; their victory was a paper one. Of course, these flimsy warriors, in their limited number, were not the danger spoken about throughout the ages. More likely they were a symptom of the real menace; the movement of the Boundary itself.

'High Auger, we have acted rashly. What advice can you provide to improve our truth?'

'When we fish the lake, we send coracles out to different areas, to test the density of the population within the water. When one secures the highest mass, the rest join them for maximum yield. Yet never do we send all our people to fish at once. When a predator within the water, a barracuda, crocodile or serath perhaps, becomes too large or aggressive towards our fishermen, we dispatch our warriors to destroy it. At best, these people have located us by chance, at worst they are scouts for a larger force. Regardless of their reason for arrival, their failure to return will draw others. Have no doubt that these were just the fishermen.'

The words spoke such obvious logic that he felt like a scolded child for his naivety. He was pleased that the Elders had come alone, for such reprimand in front of the wider population could generate dissent for their rapid progression into the roles of Guardians. He was the leader, however, and needed to represent his comrades.

'I hear your truth, High Auger, and it is one that I am ashamed to have so easily missed. Guide me for the future so that we may better serve the people.'

The venerate before him placed a hand atop Mazt's head and the contact was instantly soothing. 'Do not misunderstand me, Guardians, for you have proven yourselves every bit the defenders we need. But should such intrusion occur once more, we must learn from our enemies; captives are essential, for only if you know your opponent completely can you ever truly defeat them.'

'We will do as commanded,' Mazt asserted, 'we will show the restraint necessary to leave survivors should any be foolish enough to breach the Boundary again.'

'I believe your truth, Mazt Kae-Taqar,' the High Auger continued, 'and you must believe mine; the Boundary will most assuredly be breached again…'

A kick to the flanks spurred her horse into a canter and Rayne found herself breaking away from the rest of the group. The last four days had been difficult to say the least; her sisters wanted little to do with her, other than the occasional verbal outburst regarding her conduct; they wanted even less to do with Frost. To his credit, the old man had maintained his patience throughout the journey and made every effort to improve the situation; his options to do so had been limited, however. Now they were approaching the edge of the forest that bordered Lustania, it felt like a relief to the tension, but her other anxiety was worse than ever; having expended the effort to collect Rebecca so she could protect the other woman, it felt inherently wrong to have left her behind. Pulling her steed up at the edge of the golden meadow they had been riding through, she assessed the dark treeline before her.

'What concerns you, Rayne? Is this not our goal?' Forge had followed her, but she had paid no heed to him.

'It is,' she replied flatly.

'Oh, good,' he continued amicably, 'I feel much better with your expansive confirmation. Why then are we staring at some trees with such trepidation?'

'Are you sure you should be consorting with me? I doubt Treya would approve.'

'You feel we are consorting? I think you need to spend more time around people! At least you are showing some positive signs; lashing out sarcastically indicates some level of emotion. Consider yourself one step up from a rock, which is real progress since last time we were together.'

'What is your objective, Straker Forge? There is no connection between us, what do you care of my emotional state? Why do you feel the need to speak with me at all?'

'I've always had a charitable nature, Rayne Fimarr, and I have travelled with worse cases than you! But back to the relevant question; what troubles you?'

She stared at him for a moment, usually the person throwing such insults her way would already be dead, but this situation created strange bedfellows. 'I would have thought you noticed already; it is so peaceful.'

'Of course,' he continued with no reduction in his brashness, 'the greatest of dangers! Peace and serenity are sure to overcome us all!'

'How have you survived this long?' she retorted coldly, 'The forest is undisturbed, sounds of life are calm. We are here to track a whole army yet there are no signs of human activity within or without.'

Their three companions had caught up by this point and must have overheard her concern.

'They will be here,' Frost spoke with certainty, 'Taltan said it was so, and I have no reason to doubt his word. The forest is expansive, perhaps we are simply not in the correct area.'

'Not that I care to question your word,' Catalana chimed in, 'but if there is no sign of them, then how do you propose we locate them.'

'Do not lose faith so quickly; there will be signs, I know it!' Rayne had not witnessed such excitement from the old man before. She cast her gaze back towards the trees; he could be right, maybe his people were experts at concealment. They had gone unnoticed by Lennath's patrols for long enough, after all.

'Let us press on,' she urged, 'once within we are better obscured from enemies and may detect Frost's people more easily.'

'You don't give the orders, Rayne,' Catalana snapped petulantly, 'we all agreed that Treya would be in charge.'

Rayne raised an eyebrow towards her sister. Catalana had been intolerable at best, although some of that could be considered justified, but her mood had become increasingly negative and hostile throughout the journey. Rayne wondered how much of that was the animosity she had because of the betrayal years ago, and how much was the enforced separation from Herc Callid. As the big woodsman had been sporting a fresh injury, the decision had been made to leave him behind to recover; he was also charged with caring for Rebecca, Zendar and Treya's twins. It was not the ideal choice but made sense; those involved in the rescue were better to be in a fit state to do so, and the threat to those back on the farm was considerably less now that the local mercenaries had been dispatched.

'I can speak for myself, Catalana,' Treya scolded, 'I agree with Rayne, let us make haste.'

The five riders pushed on and remained mounted for as long as the density of trees allowed. When it became too restrictive, they climbed down and led their steeds on, Rayne keeping her attention focussed for any sign of the errant army. The difficulty they were having with their own animals did not build much confidence in finding any force of consequence nearby. They had driven the horses stolen during their prison escape hard for many days, less so the two they had 'procured' in Corinth for Rebecca and Zendar. These had been passed to Treya and Forge while Catalana had called in a favour from a man in Rennicksburg for her mount. It suddenly struck her as amusing that the first two horses they had taken were soon to be returned home and she smiled involuntarily.

'You find this amusing?' Catalana hissed at her.

'Do you spend all of your time watching my face for something you don't like?' she responded without turning.

'There is nothing *to* like about your face!' came the curt reply, 'And I monitor you for signs of deception!'

'Enough of this!' Treya commanded, 'I thought I had left your bickering behind years ago! We are here to find aid in rescuing Alissa, that should be your only focus.'

'Here!' Frost cried out, bursting through the escalating argument and rushing towards one tree in particular. Rayne followed him and found an intricate carving located just below the lower branches. It was neither a picture nor symbol she recognised, but it was deliberate in its creation.

'What is it?' she asked.

'A crest,' Frost returned enthusiastically, 'from my homeland. I have only ever shared it with a few of my most trusted allies. Taltan must have used it as an indicator for the rebellion, this will assuredly lead the way!'

Forge had moved in close, running his finger over the carving. 'This is reasonably fresh, no more than a few days in my reckoning, what if this is a trap set by Lennath's people? Would any of them have known this symbol?'

'Of course not! My allies remained loyal to me, any who know of this would be part of Rydell's army.'

'What of the man who fell before Mozak?' Rayne challenged, 'Could he have betrayed this code? Under duress?'

The confidence slipped a little, but Frost remained fixed to his assertion, 'No, no, I don't believe this would come up under any level of questioning, and courage would prevent disclosure under torture. I am sure this is genuine and meant for those loyal to the resistance.'

Catalana had replaced Forge at the tree and released a snort of derision, 'When did you last do any actual tracking, Straker?' she asked, 'this mark is well over two weeks old, there isn't a trace of moisture in these cuts.'

'Perhaps my real skills are yet to be demonstrated, Embers,' he countered, 'or perhaps I was simply helping you to look useful!'

'We should not dither here,' Treya interjected, 'Look for more of these symbols and we will follow them to source.'

With a specific marker to follow, their pace increased; the carved symbols providing a clear path South and becoming more frequent the further they went, undoubtedly an indicator of how much closer they were getting. But closer to what? Rayne did not believe that any person was resistant to the extreme torture methods she had been taught so there was every chance this was a trap set by Lennath's men. Or was this just paranoia? It was a lot of effort to lure in one ageing soldier and any allies he may have gathered. Finally, she received her answer. Ahead of them, the trees began to thin, and a large clearing could be made out.

'This is it!' cried Frost in triumph, 'We've found them!'

He sprinted forward before any could restrain him and both Catalana and Forge rushed after him. Rayne looked beyond the treeline, a huge open space, initially natural but it had been extended artificially by the felling of trees and trampled undergrowth. It would be a huge, obvious blemish upon the forest from the skies above but perfectly concealed from onlookers at ground level; one would have to be within four hundred yards to spot it, unless those using it were making too much noise. And therein lay the problem, for she could hear no sounds at all; no sounds of weapons in use, no sounds of construction underway, no sounds of standard camp living. And the smell in the air, like a smouldering fire mixed with over-cooked meat.

'Treya!' she whispered urgently, 'Something is wrong here, we must be prepared.'

Her sister turned towards her, 'You mean we must warn the others,' she replied tautly before running towards them.

Rayne rolled her eyes and sighed; she had not missed trying to overcome the stupidity generated within any group of travellers. Most people quoted that there was strength in numbers, but she knew the larger the group, the more weak links were present.

Cautiously she pressed on, ensuring she remained concealed for as long as possible. When she was forced to break the edge of the trees, she kept her senses alert for danger. Frost had fallen to his knees beside the remains of a ballista, the large weapon of war had been half-crushed and the huge spears it fired lay shattered around it.

'I do not understand,' he spoke quietly, 'I am certain this is the right place. But where are they? And what could have caused this damage?'

Forge was scanning the whole open area where other siege weapons were in a similar state of disrepair and many personal armaments were also strewn around, 'I fear you are correct, Jacob, your army was most assuredly here and strong in their numbers. But they have been routed, perhaps Lennath found them after all and drove them off; we will search for tracks, perhaps we can rally them?'

'But they have been hiding here for many years,' the old man continued, seemingly in a daze, 'how could they have been discovered just as I needed them?'

'We cannot confirm that they have been,' Catalana added, crouching several yards away, examining the ground, 'I see the signs of battle, sure enough, but only tracks of the defenders, there seems to be nothing coming in at them.'

'Sorcery of some kind?' Treya asked.

'No,' Rayne answered bluntly, 'you are all missing the obvious. Look all around us, the puckered holes everywhere? Those are no rabbit warrens or natural phenomenon, they are the puncture wounds of large chitinous legs. Your army was attacked, Frost, but not by men; I would wager this to be the outcome of a confrontation with the twisted mutants Lennath now has the power to create. Alissa must be proving her worth.'

'Don't say that!' Treya snapped defensively, 'You don't know what is happening with her or Lennath. But I fear you may be right as to the culprits of this attack.'

Rayne nodded at the concession but then the slightest noise and a flash of movement in her peripheral vision alerted her to the presence of another. Instincts drove her into motion and she dropped to one knee, launching two throwing knives towards the danger. A cry from her target signalled the others that they had been discovered and weapons were drawn immediately.

'Wait!' Frost called out, 'Those are my people!'

Rayne remained poised but assessed the two men who had emerged from bushes at the far side of the clearing. The first stood beside the tree she had pinned him to, one blade having sliced through his tunic and into the trunk beyond, the other now protruding from his left shoulder. He was whimpering in pain as he clutched his arm below the blade. The second man was stood slightly ahead of his ally with hands raised in surrender and a look of distress plastered on his face.

'We are!' the fearful newcomer shouted back, 'We are your people, General! Please hold off your attacks, we revealed ourselves only because we recognised you!'

'Do not fear, my friends!' Frost began moving towards them, voice filled with unexpected levels of joy, 'This is a simple mistake; you startled my companions, is all. Let us help with the injury we have caused you.'

Rayne moved over to Treya, 'Do you feel he is too willing to believe these men? They could be scouts sent by Lennath, or worse, assassins. We should be cautious.'

'Noted, Rayne,' Treya replied without scorn, 'but you have indicated the attack was likely by beasts, not men. This pair seem too meek to be agents of the enemy; if they are attempting to trick us then Frost is the one in immediate harm's way. And he has just had five years of certainty pulled out from under him, I expect he will be looking for hope in any guise.'

Rayne considered the words; they were insightful and most likely obvious, at least for anyone with a decent understanding of people. As a killer, these were not the attributes she had ever looked to improve. Without dropping her guard, she joined the others in gathering around the two men. Catalana instantly went about removing the knife, tossing it back to her sister with a glare, before tending to the slender but deep wound it had left behind. Her patient slumped to a seated position and tried to stem the flow of tears, whether because of the injury or exhaustion, she could not tell. The other man clasped Frost's hands tightly as he spoke.

'Thank the gods, General, we thought you may have been killed as well. When Taltan failed to return to the camp, all had become concerned. We heard tell of your escape, but it has been weeks since then; when you did not arrive here in those first few days, we feared the worst.'

'There was much for me to attend to,' Frost replied gently, 'but I am here now, with allies who can help us defeat the corrupt Prince!'

The speaker now began to sob, anguish evident in his speech, 'But we are fallen! Your army is no more! When those monsters attacked, we stood and fought at first, but they were powerful and fast. They tore through us like knights against children, it was almost as if they understood where best to strike, targeting our war machines and corralling us for ease of destruction. When many tried to flee, another creature dropped from the sky; bigger than any bird and striking with deadly accuracy. Magin and I managed to hide nearby and avoided detection, for the beasts remained for some time to ensure all were dead. We worked ourselves half to death for a few days, trying to bury our comrades. Finally, we have resorted to burning the bodies. We would not have lingered here much longer but we had no idea where to go.'

'But there must have been a rally point,' Frost insisted, 'somewhere for any survivors to congregate and prepare for a counterstrike?'

'Sure enough, General, but we feared it may also have been compromised and…' he seemed unable to finish the sentence.

'And what, soldier? You can tell me.'

'And he doesn't think anyone else survived,' Rayne offered bluntly.

Frost turned to her with pain in his eyes but the man before him nodded slowly. 'I am so sorry, General…' he bawled.

'It is Jacob, soldier,' Frost replied disconsolately, 'A General has an army to command and mine is now lost. I am sorry, our plan is nullified.'

The last comment was directed at Treya, and Rayne could see how shaken her sister was. She reached out a hand onto her shoulder and it was neither shrugged away nor resisted.

'How many were you?' Forge asked of the distraught soldier, but it was Magin who replied through gritted teeth.

'Almost fifteen hundred strong.'

'Fifteen hundred down to five?' Catalana asked incredulously, 'What do we do now?'

'Seven,' Magin added, 'we will still stand with any who defy Lennath.'

Rayne was impressed by his courage but realised it was futile; without the army to provide a distraction, the palace would surely be too well-defended to breach. Even if she could infiltrate alone, it seemed Lennath already had creatures powerful enough to destroy armies at his beck and call, making escape an impossibility. And there was Mozak, if Lennath had any sense at all, he would have placed the grand assassin to protect Alissa, dooming any rescue attempt to failure. As she began to question why she was on such a fool's errand, Forge spoke reluctantly.

'I can go. I will find Alissa, free her, and return her here. If you are all ready to assist in our flight beyond the border then I am certain we can secure the required artifacts afterwards.'

His overconfidence was impressive, as Rayne was certain his skills did not match her own, and she had calculated her own chance of success at less than five percent. However, the icy daggers from Treya towards her partner indicated some deeper argument between the two.

'No, Straker,' she commanded, 'we have spoken of this already and my position has not altered. Going alone is suicide, only together can we possibly free Alissa and escape.'

'Really, Treya?' Catalana interrupted, 'That is your standpoint? Look, I agree that Straker would probably not make it to the city walls, let alone the palace, alone. I doubt Rayne could, either. But we must face facts, we planned for an all-out attack, a siege to draw all attention away from our infiltration; there is no way to do that now, no way to get to the palace and Alissa without detection. The plan is shattered and this quest futile!'

'Excuse my impertinence,' Magin interrupted from his seat beside the tree, flexing his shoulder to test the security of the dressing Catalana had applied, 'but perhaps all is not lost?'

'What are you saying, Magin?' Frost pressed, despair shifting to cautious hope as he spoke, 'What alternative is there?'

'The rebellion has been planning to overthrow Lennath for many years and very few ideas were based on a frontal assault; the city is sturdy and well supplied so siege-craft becomes almost totally pointless. Other ideas included assassinating the Prince and his closest advisors or capturing the Palace and shutting the city down from within.'

'Are you telling us there is a secret way into the Palace?' Rayne pressed feeling the strange twist in her chest as hope sparked afresh.

'No, milady, I'm telling you there are several…'

Clear liquid gurgled from the bottle to the mug in her hand but only until it was half full; any deeper and she was certain her shaking would cause it to spill. It had been happening every night at around the same time, inexplicable tremors lasting between several minutes and two hours, ever since the others had left on their journey. She had confided in no-one; who was there to discuss it with? Callid was a stoic man and she was not certain where his opinions lay regarding her, Zendar was little more than a captive despite being given run of the farm and Hederna Thriss was a wonderful carer for the children but a simple woman aside from that. Rebecca was sure it was a normal reaction to the anxiety and fear she was currently living under, but that made it no less concerning. She lifted the mug to her lips and quaffed a large mouthful. The alcohol tasted metallic and unpleasant, burning her throat when she swallowed and leaving her instantly light-headed. It was enough to force her to stumble to a seat at the kitchen table.

'You should be careful with that,' Herc spoke from the door to the stairwell, 'it is a local spirit, and they serve it sparingly.'

'I can see why,' she had not noticed his arrival and hoped the tightness in her throat from the fiery drink concealed her surprise, 'I will go lightly in future. The children are asleep?'

'Aye, they are down finally. I think their discomfort over being without their parents is making sleep difficult, but they are exhausted.'

Taking a much more conservative sip, noting that her hand was already trembling less, she observed the big woodsman closely. It was easy to assume he was all brawn, built heavily as he was and standing at a considerable height to most men, but his regular silence was not born of low intelligence; he was a watcher. She had encountered many men like that, those that held their tongue or reserved judgement, silently waiting to gather enough information to make a well-reasoned decision. Of all those associated with the Fimarrs, he had proven to be the most balanced, easily able to cast aside passion from his considerations to find a logical and viable resolution to arguments or problems. That said, it was also clear that he was not lacking in emotion; whatever undefined relationship he shared with Catalana Fimarr was powerful on a level she had never seen. She imagined that he was a formidable combatant, terrifying to his opponents, fiercely loyal to his allies, but she had only experienced his unexpectedly homely side. He had spent hours each day seeing to mundane and menial chores around the farm and its outbuildings; when Thriss was not present, he devoted all of his attention to the twins with a patience and love she could not have imagined had she not witnessed it herself. But none of this made her feel safe. Not simply because his protective manner was undoubtedly not extended to a stranger such as her, but his injuries made him vulnerable and the threat they had all discussed days earlier seemed too much for one man to hold back.

Her thoughts moved to Zendar. The old scholar was neither intimidating nor physical, his lean wiry frame coming naturally, with no exercise or endeavour involved. He was academically clever, though socially weak, and had quickly learned that haughtiness or intellectual rebuttal would not be tolerated from him. He had been released from his bindings the morning after Rayne's group had departed, Callid warning him that there was no option for escape; the woodsman's tracking skills would make pursuit short and the punishment for any attempt would be brutal. The underlying fear was enough to keep him good to his word but failed to generate any sense of community in him. He lifted no hand to help anyone, avoided any location where the twins were, and waited piteously for food to be served to him; if it wasn't for Hederna Thriss, the man would probably have starved to death. Yet this was the one man they were relying on for answers, for direction in how the danger could be overcome, to set them on the path to returning to their previous lives. It seemed a big ask for someone so fragile.

As Herc set about cutting some bread from a loaf they had started at lunch, she considered herself. She was little more than a socialite, admittedly the facilitator of life and death contracts through the Assassin's Guild, but negotiation was where her skills ended. She possessed no combat skills, no deep insight into the problems they faced and no familial connection to any of the participants. She, like Zendar, was a target for execution but had nothing to offer those who were protecting her; if a sacrifice were required then it would be an easy choice. She shuddered briefly and steeled herself with another sip of the potent spirit. At least they seemed safe for now, the expected re-attempts on their lives had never materialised and she hoped this was an indication that the Lustanian Prince's attention was now elsewhere.

She jumped at the sound of knocking from the front door and tried to ignore the sudden return of her trembling hands. Following Herc as he trotted into the sitting room, she paused in the doorway rather than entering entirely. Zendar had risen from the chair where he had been reading a book brought back from Rennicksburg the previous day and was inches away from the outer door when Herc cautioned him.

'Stop, Silas. We do not know who it is; caution is yet required.'

'Surely, Master Callid, you don't believe hired killers would be knocking upon your door? Do you expect them to ask permission to fulfil their ghastly work?'

'Do not be so contemptuous, Zendar,' Rebecca hissed at him, feeling fear gnawing at her stomach, 'Herc is trying to protect us!'

'Very well!' the scholar conceded elaborately, waving his hands dismissively in the air whilst taking a step back and to the side of the oak barrier before him. Directing his next question to those beyond, he called loudly, 'Who is calling here at this hour? Identify yourself!'

She rolled her eyes at his dramatic sarcasm but was relieved by the reply that returned, muffled by the thick wood. 'It is I, Hederna Thriss. I left my shawl here earlier; may I retrieve it?'

Feeling her whole body relax, Rebecca cast her gaze around the room for the item. The woman was clearly not always so reliable as the Fimarrs had suggested, it had been three hours since she left, a long period to fail to notice you were cold! Zendar leaned forward and swung the door open for the sometime matron but it was Herc's reaction that froze her to the spot.

'NO!' he cried out, leaping forth too late to stop the other man.

Rebecca looked out into the darkness beyond and saw only who she expected, the kindly Hederna Thriss, standing in the light provided by the flickering porch lantern, shawl pulled around her shoulders for warmth. It took another second to understand what was wrong. As she watched, something flashed brightly as it moved before the older woman with lightning speed; it must have been a blade of some description, as her throat erupted in a crimson fountain before she collapsed lifelessly to the side. Zendar failed to move, paralysed with fear, even as a black-garbed shape appeared from its concealment and moved to strike. At the same instant, Herc crashed against the open door, swinging it back against the intruder with enough force to drive him out.

'Move, Silas!' he shouted at the terrified man, 'This killer is here for you!' The big woodsman shoved Zendar who stumbled back but was still failing to comprehend what was happening. Rebecca realised that she too was failing to do anything constructive and was about to ask Herc for instruction when the window crashed inwards and a black shape impacted the centre of the room before rolling to his feet. Dressed all in black, loose-fitting garb allowed total freedom of movement while a padded hat and mask provided protection and obscured all except their attacker's eyes; a thin curved sword was held in a rearwards grip as he assessed those before him.

Herc rose quickly but the assassin was already in motion, lashing out one arm and releasing something in Rebecca's direction before rolling forward with his blade outstretched, forcing Callid to dive sideways to avoid being cut. Their assailant leapt into the air, mounting the double bench that faced the fire and gaining the perfect vantage to stab down at Zendar. An impact on her forehead reminded her that she hadn't even had time to move and she toppled backwards under the force. Slamming to the ground hard, she clutched at her head but found only a quickly rising bruise; whatever had hit her must have been blunt and she fumbled around to see if she could locate it. The sound of splintering wood drew her focus back to the sitting room and she sat up for a better view, regretting it instantly as blood gushed from her nose. Through watery eyes, she saw that Zendar had not been impaled. Instead, Herc must have kicked out and toppled the furniture the assassin stood upon. The bench was overturned and a second chair broken, possibly where the killer had landed, while Zendar had staggered back against the other window. The assassin remained silent as he set his feet and hurled the sword out before him; Callid matched his speed, tossing a small side-table to intercept the deadly projectile.

'He is Veer!' Silas suddenly screamed, curling himself into a ball beneath the windowsill, 'Our lives are forfeit!'

Rebecca felt the desire only to run, to escape the nightmare happening around her, but she knew that escape would be impossible. Holding her hand against her face to try and stem the bleeding, she clambered to her feet even as Herc propelled himself towards his foe. A simple side-step avoided the committed charge and Callid slammed into the wall behind his target, leaving a significant indentation in the mortar. The assassin slipped towards Zendar, but not fast enough as Herc caught hold of his trailing wrist; a lithe twist and spin under Callid's arm placed the shorter man directly in front of him, perfectly positioned to bend forward and flip Herc over his shoulder. Crashing back-first through the central table, vase of flowers sent shooting across the room to shatter against the far wall, their protector released a grunt of pain through gritted teeth.

The Veer moved like a living shadow, silently sliding past his downed opponent and over to the whimpering Zendar. The scholar held up an outstretched hand defensively, begging some inaudible pleas of leniency, the assassin seizing the proffered limb and snapping the hand back against the arm with a sickening snap. A squeal of agony escaped Silas, but he could not pull away from the vicelike grip.

'Leave him be!' she cried out almost against her own will.

'You next, woman,' came the hissed reply as the killer flicked his eyes to her. The distraction was enough as Herc slammed shoulder-first into his enemy's midriff, carrying him across the room as his hold on Zendar slipped. Clearly intending to slam the villain against the wall, Herc was unprepared when the Veer lifted his feet rearward and absorbed the force of the charge by bracing his legs against the intended target. Pushing forward, the assassin caught Callid off-balance, flipping over him whilst still grappled and dragging him awkwardly to the floor. Like a writhing eel, the Veer twisted his body around, wrapping his legs around Herc's waist and securing an armlock about his throat. She knew it would take only a few moments for the air to be completely restricted to her ally's lungs and she raced into the kitchen.

She returned mere moments later with the huge axe of Rork Fimarr hefted across her right shoulder. The weight was enormous, and she could barely shuffle forward as the head of the weapon threatened to drag her backwards with each step. The assassin looked up with amusement in his eyes; what threat could she possibly pose with the axe?

'Run, Zendar!' she cried out, 'Get away now!'

Silas looked at her dumbly from his seated position where he was cradling his crippled wrist. As her words sank in, he began to crawl feebly towards the door. Getting close enough to the struggling men on the floor, she employed her gambit; tilting her body forward, she pushed as hard as she could with her shoulder, flipping the massive weapon forward and allowing the deadly head to drop under its own weight towards them. Surprise filled both pairs of eyes as the Veer released his grip and rolled to safety, Callid only just avoiding the crashing blade as it chewed into the floorboards he had occupied seconds before. While he lay coughing and spluttering in an attempt to open his crushed airway, the assassin leapt forward with fury. He had underestimated her though, and she swung the metal skillet she had been hiding behind her back upwards into his face. The blow connected heavily with his jaw and rocked him backwards on his heels, but the victory was short-lived. Moving forward to strike him again, her wide swing was easily blocked, the Veer pulling her arm out to full extension and twisting it painfully until she released her makeshift weapon. Dragging her forward, he laid a sharp blow into her stomach, doubling her over, before spinning her back towards the kitchen. Amazed to be released, she looked up to see a second metal ball hurtling into her face. Cracking against her cheek, she felt something shift in unison with the sudden flare of pain and realised the bone underneath must have shattered. Falling back to a sitting position, her head swam but she retained enough focus to see the Veer snatch Zendar up by his collar, driving him round in a tight circle before smashing him headfirst through the window he had been sheltering underneath. Before the old man could attempt to pull himself free, the assassin launched himself into the air and landed with both feet on the scholar's back. The sudden weight drove Zendar down onto the broken panes still held in the frame and he released a gurgling cry before his body went limp.

'No!' she sobbed, not sure if she had actually made a sound or not. The Veer moved towards his sword, where it still lay tangled in the side table, but suddenly dropped into a crouch as Herc swung Fimarr's axe towards him. Failing to bisect his enemy, Herc did not resist the weight, allowing it to spin him all the way round before angling the weapon to the spot his enemy occupied. The blade crashed into the floor once again, the assassin having anticipated the attack and sprung back out of reach, opening Herc up to another strike. The Veer threw himself forward with a flying kick but Callid was prepared, leaning into the attack as he freed the axe from its ensnarement. When the woodsman did not fall back under the strike, the killer had to absorb his own impact and spring back, this time crashing to the ground instead of achieving a graceful landing. Herc followed up quickly, charging forward with axe raised to strike; the Veer showed no panic as he stretched his body up, landing a powerful kick against the shaft of the axe, forcing the weapon even higher than it was already raised and causing the blade to bite hard into a ceiling beam. Callid staggered as the weapon he wielded stopped dead above him. Before he could tug it free, his opponent had regained his footing, landing a heavy kick to the side of Herc's knee and causing it to buckle. A series of five rabbit punches to his chest followed, with a sixth to the throat causing him to choke and sway where he knelt. Finally, the assassin spun into a roundhouse kick, landing the tip of his boot into her defender's temple and dropping him to the floor, senseless.

Rebecca tried to stand but her legs would not obey her, and her body felt unnaturally heavy. Slumping back against the kitchen doorframe, she noted the Veer taking a moment to catch his breath as he finally recovered his sword.

'One chance, woman,' he hissed, moving towards her menacingly, 'tell me where the Fimarrs have gone and I will not kill you.'

'I will tell you nothing,' she whimpered, less defiantly than she had hoped amid the pain from her cheek.

The corners or the assassin's eyes creased and she thought he was probably smiling under his mask, 'Very well, you will die with these men and the children upstairs.' He raised his sword above her, but her eyes fixed on movement from the outer doorway; a leather-armoured warrior sprinted towards them, feet resounding heavily on the wooden flooring. The sound alerted the assassin who spun to face the newcomer, a reactive swing of his blade intended to cut the man down. The warrior met the blow with his Warhammer, the metal shaft slamming hard against the assassin's wrist and forcing his arm back the way it had come. Continuing the sideways momentum of the landed blow, she saw the flash of silver as the knife in his other hand sliced cleanly through the Veer's wrist. Finally releasing a cry of pain, the killer staggered backwards in shock, tripping over her outstretched legs, and toppling into the kitchen beyond. Rebecca looked down at where the hand had fallen, marvelling at the way it still tightly gripped the hilt of the slender sword.

Her saviour did not pause to celebrate his success, leaping over her to pursue his fallen opponent. Skidding to a sudden halt, he ducked his body down as two kitchen knives flashed across the room towards him. One scuffed the side of his leather jerkin while the other stabbed into the wall behind him. Rising back into a run, the newcomer swung his Warhammer out towards the Veer's head; Rebecca felt her stomach turn over as the assassin used his fresh stump to block the attack. Spinning himself inside his enemy's reach, preventing the secondary knife from being used effectively, the Veer slammed an elbow up into the warrior's face, snapping his head backwards. Having created space between them, the Veer grabbed a tenderising hammer from the worktop and swung forward. Blocking counterattacks with his injured arm and impossibly agile kicks, the killer began landing blows with the small hammer, several to the face and head, two against the back of his foe's knife-hand, dispossessing him of that weapon, and one against the elbow, seemingly catching a nerve and blocking the usefulness of that limb. With both men now fighting one-armed, the Veer clearly held the advantage.

Rebecca turned and used the door jamb to try and rise to her feet. Everything swam as she held on to her vital support, but she had to do something to help her unexpected rescuer. Suddenly she was knocked backwards, dropping heavily to the tiled floor in the kitchen and unable to find the strength to get up again. Turning her head, she saw the Veer dropping his opponent to his knees and preparing to slam the jagged hammer into his face once more. The assassin stopped as he realised the danger to his left; Herc Callid, having knocked her flying in his charge, now flipped the kitchen table up before him and slammed into the side of their attacker. The cacophony of splintering wood and broken glass filled the room as the table shattered from the force applied to drive the Veer over the worktop and through the window beyond.

Herc stood panting amid the broken wood, staring out of the gaping window to the night beyond. After several tense moments, his body relaxed.

'I think he has fled,' he stated.

'He would not have lasted much longer with the amount of blood he was losing. Escape was his only option,' the stranger agreed.

'I think, perhaps, you would not have lasted much longer, Terex,' Herc replied sincerely, 'you have my thanks.'

'This is becoming a treacherous habit for me!' Terex said jovially, 'Can I assume the lady of the house is not present to dismiss me for my assistance!'

'Treya is not here. It is just me and the children,' Herc affirmed, holding his side gingerly where it appeared his previous wound had begun to bleed freely once more.

'And your other guests?' Terex pressed.

'Silas Zendar, an academic employed formerly by Lennath, but I fear he is dead. The lady upon the floor is Rebecca Pallstirrith. Their lives are also out to contract as with the rest of us. Zendar held all the knowledge we required to stop Lennath's plot,' the realisation seemed to hit Herc as he spoke the words.

'And save Alissa and Kastani?' Terex enquired, climbing to his feet and rubbing the various divots the hammer had caused across his visage.

'Aye, their rescue is part of the plan,' Callid confirmed leaning back heavily against the large dry goods cupboard.

'Then let me stay here and help keep the rest of you safe until they return. Better still, tell me the plan so I may go to help them!'

'You are welcome to stay, Terex, and I truly appreciate all you have done. But it is not my place to accept you into this quest they have embarked upon. I can tell you only that I expect them to return when they have secured Alissa and there will be more to do afterwards; I feel your help may well be accepted at that point,' the woodsman offered.

Rebecca realised she was beginning to lose sensation in her body and tried to speak but only an incoherent groan escaped her.

Terex turned towards her and concern filled his battered face, 'I think your companion is more the worse for wear, Herc Callid, perhaps we should...'

But whatever suggestion he was about to make was lost as she drifted out of consciousness.

Chapter 8

Lennath strode along the beautiful corridors of the palace in Mainspring, every inch of the huge complex always looked as if it had just been polished to a high shine and indoor potted plants were in every available space; it sometimes felt like navigating an indoor jungle. The home of his childhood never failed to impress him, and he wondered what it would be like to live there. There was, of course, an elite military presence in the central region, what else could you expect for the King? But the country's defences were poor in comparison to any of the Five Kingdoms; protected on all sides by lands ruled by his sons allowed their patron some level of complacency in this respect. He wondered briefly how effective a response would be mounted if a mutant found its way across that border; of course, that was not part of his plan.

Mozak glided silently alongside him, the taller and older man never seeming pushed to maintain his gait and always offering a calm demeanour in any circumstance. The tension that had risen between them before this journey seemed to have abated and Lennath had put it down to his own paranoia; perhaps the knowledge that he would not be able to foot the payments to the Veer should he fail to claim his family's lands weighed upon his mind. With the increased control Alissa was demonstrating, however, there was less to fear even from those skilled killers. He had convinced the bodyguard to spar with him at every rest-stop along their route to Mainspring. Three days had allowed him to experience formidable techniques he had never imagined and Mozak was infinitely patient with him. But the assassin did not go lightly regardless of his royal status or position as employer; he sported cuts, scrapes and bruises to prove it. Although, he thought again, perhaps that was going lightly; he had no doubt that Mozak expending effort would result in Lennath's death.

Ahead he saw the large, intricately patterned double doors of the greeting room, two of the burly Royal Guards flanked the entrance with their customary halberds held outwards. This indicated that access was permitted and Lennath had been pleased to discover they would be conversing in the smaller less formal setting; being addressed in the grander audience hall was an intimidating event at the best of times, let alone under the circumstances he was expecting during this visit. Arriving before the two men, Lennath smiled casually.

'Greetings from Lustania, noble warriors!' he said with vigour, 'I assume my father awaits?'

'The King resides within,' one of the guards replied gruffly, 'but your man waits here.'

Lennath feigned shock, 'For what purpose? Surely my aide is not unwelcomed in my father's home?'

The guard's expression did not change, 'Only those invited enter. And certainly, no bodyguards may enter; why would you need one?'

Lennath smiled easily, 'Of course, only the King and I will be present, it is a private audience, after all. Let us hope there will be no need for me to summon Mozak, for your sake.'

The guard's eyes narrowed but his tone remained even, 'As you say, milord,' he replied.

As Mozak took a position against the corridor wall, Lennath turned the golden handle and pushed the heavy door open. Beyond lay the greeting room he had been to many times before but not in the last seven years; it hadn't changed at all. Allowing the door to swing closed behind him, he noticed that the King was not seated at the large writing desk, as he had expected, but stood pensively staring into the roaring fire under the marble mantle.

'Father? You summoned me and I am here. What justifies such unprecedented engagement between us?'

The King did not look up, seemingly transfixed by the flames, 'Lennath, good, I'm glad you did not delay journeying here. Matters are escalating and we must find a way to unify the Kingdoms in a time of seeming crisis.'

'Of course, whatever I…' he cut his sentence short when he spotted Gallth lounging in one of the plush wingback chairs in the communal area, 'I was not aware that this would be a conference. Was ambushing me completely necessary?'

The old man turned towards him at last and there was a deep sadness in his eyes, 'Ambush, my son? Having your brother present is some kind of trap? Such paranoia is one of the dangers that must be quashed. Gallth arrived here a week ago, he has brought vital information to my attention; I summoned you as a result of that. There is no plot in place here.'

Lennath composed himself and walked over to the drinks cabinet, pouring himself a glass of Mainspring brandy before casually taking a seat near to his brother.

'Greetings, Gallth, can I assume you are honing the axe we discussed previously?'

Gallth smiled smugly at him, 'So defensive, brother, we haven't even discussed the latest events; unless you somehow know about these already?'

The loaded question was obvious and Lennath took a moment to respond, cautious to give nothing untoward away. 'I expect I am a little defensive, the last gathering at my home felt like a unified attack against me. And now some of the decisions made have not come to fruition so I assume that is why I am here?'

'And what are the issues you feel we are keen to discuss, Lennath? Perhaps you already have some alleviation to our concerns?' his father sounded strained, as if the line of questioning were not one he wished to follow. The strong hero he had always looked up to as a child seemed suddenly very old and very tired.

'Well, the trade problems that were occurring have not exactly been eradicated. I dropped my prices as demanded but the tradespeople within Lustania have little confidence in safety. As a result, they opted to convoy less often. I have to say that I feel the interdiction raids whilst transiting Tunsa seem to have lessened, but that will not bring any reassurance to Kendoss who is not receiving the quantities required. Speaking of whom, I must express my respect to him with regard to the military support that he coordinated; Lustania is far better defended from beast attacks than ever before.'

'You know that is not why you are here,' Gallth snapped impatiently, 'stop playing games.'

'Gallth!' the King barked, some of his old authority returning, 'This is no trial, we are here to find answers together. And I will steer the discussion, not you.'

Lennath was pleased to see there was no real unity between them and his nerve settled somewhat; hopefully, they did not know as much about his activities as he feared.

'I am sorry, Gallth, you will be more concerned with factors affecting Gregor, no doubt,' he added with fake sincerity, 'I have been likewise concerned; when his proposed envoy did not arrive within a week of our gathering, I sent a letter to enquire as to an expected date but received no reply.'

'Really? That is the yarn you wish to spin?' Gallth retorted, receiving only an open look of confusion from Lennath in return, 'Gregor has sent three envoys! None have returned! His investigators discovered the third was last seen in Gerisville, that is only sixteen leagues from your doorstep and well within your border! And there was no letter!'

'That we are aware of,' the King interjected firmly.

Lennath plastered shock on his face, 'Three? And none returned to him? This is worrying indeed, for none have arrived at my home. And my correspondence likewise failing to arrive? Perhaps it is all linked, parties unknown attempting to sew distrust amongst the Kingdoms. There has been talk of terrorist groups lurking along the Dussen border of Lustania, what if that movement is somehow trying to generate animosity between us, or worse still, actual conflict?'

'I cannot believe how easily lies spill from you…'

'Gallth!' the King roared this time, generating a jump of surprise from his son, 'I will not tell you again, one more wrong word and I will eject you from this discussion, am I clear?'

'Yes, father, of course,' Gallth replied, quietly cowed.

'Accept our apologies, Lennath, the suggestion you have made is a fair one and could be the case; just because no disruptive element has tried to play us against each other before, does not mean they are not attempting it now,' the King went on placatingly, 'but these are not the issues that were of prime concern for us. That lies with your brother, Porthus.'

Lennath kept his false veneer in place, 'Porthus? Is he here also? That would be advantageous as I wanted to discuss the beast attacks in Zendra; there have been increased numbers within Lustania and I fear he may be experiencing similar rises.'

'That is what you believe we have brought you here to discuss?' his father pressed.

'I'm sorry, father, but what else is there? Or is this about the residency rights dispute with Gregor? I don't see what concern Porthus would have regarding…'

'He is missing, Lennath!' the King cut him off in a voice thick with emotion, 'Porthus has not been seen for many days.'

'What?' he tried to throw as much fake concern into his voice as possible, ignoring the snort of disbelief from Gallth, 'He was supposed to visit me ten days ago but failed to arrive! I thought he had changed his mind or been waylaid by matters of State. Now you are saying he has vanished?'

'Not vanished, Lennath, murdered; as if you did not already know!' Gallth sneered.

'No more, Gallth!' their father pleaded, a tear rolling down his cheek, 'We have no Proof that Porthus is dead, let alone that Lennath is involved! These accusations go beyond the petty arguments you have all shared in the past!.

'They do indeed, father,' Gallth continued, no longer deterred by his father's threats, 'and with good reason. You saw how he treated Porthus when we last met, he obviously holds great animosity towards him. He played that last gathering well, putting us all off the scent of these beasts and his involvement with them. Are you really going to stand there and suggest the attack was not staged?'

'Attack?' Lennath jumped in, keen to maintain his air of innocence, 'What attack are you referring to?'

'You belong on the stage, brother,' Gallth continued, finding his feet as he ranted, 'Porthus had a heavily armed convoy escorting him to Lustania, conversations he had with his advisors indicate that he had been attacked by raiders using Lustanian fire cannons on his way home. That was why he was on his way back to you, to confront you for your heinous crimes!'

'An attack? With fire cannons? I do not understand, I thought you said he was missing, not incinerated. Are you saying I have paid bandits to attack using my own weapons? Does that not sound particularly stupid? Why would I so obviously incriminate myself?'

'It could be simple manipulation, reverse psychology to confuse us all. Or maybe you are stupid! But that is not why we are here now. Porthus' caravan was attacked and destroyed by some monstrous creature such as we have never heard tell of before. Its tracks indicate mammoth size and the devastation…'

The King moved over to Gallth and placed a hand on his shoulder, forcing him back down into his seat, 'The devastation was complete. No survivors found, horses, carriages and men torn asunder and several of the party vanished with no trace, Porthus amongst them. They are all presumed killed. The attack was precise and total, unlike any previously recorded encounter with these beasts; it has led to suspicions that there are men manipulating the monsters.'

'Me?' Lennath asked incredulously, 'You believe I am to blame for this? Father, please, there was no love lost between Porthus and I, but to kill my own brother? We are family, how can you think such evils of me?'

'Bravo, Lennath!' Gallth joined in again, clapping sardonically, 'Another golden performance! This is your one opportunity to admit your machinations, to stop the current course you are on and receive some level of leniency. Can you not utter a single truthful word?'

'Every word I have spoken is true, Gallth. But, tell me, how am I to believe that this is not a ploy by you to incriminate me? What if it is you who wishes me out of the way? Porthus' death would have no benefit to me, I am last in line and the issues in Lustania leave me unsuited to rulership of an expanded region absorbing Zendra. You, however, may have far more to gain and you are most determined to paint me as the aggressor in all that has happened. How do we know that you have not intercepted communication between Gregor and I? Or staged the attacks in Zendra to implicate me? Or come here now to turn our own father against me?'

'Enough of this!' the King wheezed, falling to his knees against a long divan and clutching at his chest.

'Father!' the princes cried out in unison, leaping to their father's aid, and easing him up onto the soft cushions behind him.

'What is it, father? Should I summon your physician?' Lennath asked with concern.

'No, no, my sons. I am well, just a tightness in my breathing. I think it is the distress of recent days; I will be fine.'

'I… I am sorry, father. Perchance my tongue has run away with me,' Gallth added, 'I too am driven by distress. We can reconvene when you are in better health.'

Lennath looked at the ashen grey face of the old man and felt a great swell of sadness within him. Of all the things he could ever have imagined of his father, weakness was not amongst them. Almost unconsciously, he reached out and grasped the King's hand in his own, squeezing it gently.

'I am so sorry, father, I never meant for this argument to end like this. You should rest now and be assured that Gallth and I will resolve our differences with all due haste. Agreed?' he directed the final question at his brother.

For the first time, the disdain wavered in Gallth's eyes to be replaced by uncertainty, 'Yes, of course, this matter need not concern you any longer. We will get to the bottom of this together, I guarantee it.'

The King reached out and embraced his sons, bringing them uncomfortably close for Lennath's liking. When released, he moved back over to his seat and took a long swig of brandy to settle himself. He had not even realised how much he longed for physical affection from his father, but he could not allow himself to be deterred from the plan.

'So, what do you propose, brother?' Gallth asked, having silently sidled up to him, his voice below earshot of the King.

'I will receive a replacement envoy, chosen from your own people. Hopefully, that will enable you to vouch for me with the others. I understand how black these circumstance paint me but place your personal dislike to one side and assess things logically; you will soon see the truth in my words.'

'Very well, Lennath, an envoy from Kaydarell. But they must be given access to all that is happening in Lustania.'

'Agreed, brother, let me know when you have selected a suitable candidate and I will make arrangements to receive them.'

'No need, it is already decided. I will be the envoy; we will leave within the hour.'

Gallth returned to the King, raised his proffered hand and kissed the knuckles before heading to the exit. Lennath downed the rest of his drink, exhaling sharply against the fiery sensation. Returning to his father's side, he took his hand once more and mimicked Gallth's sign of respect. The King did not release his grip immediately.

'Please, Lennath, make this right again.'

The Prince of Lustania had never heard such a sincere request from the old man before and it made him suddenly angry, but he retained the softness in his reply.

'Worry no longer, father, this matter will be resolved promptly, I guarantee it…'

Sitting against a large rock with his knees up, Mareck used the tip of the long spear he held to idly scrape lines into the sand before him. A cool breeze floated in off the ocean, washing over him but failing to drag his dour mood with it. Staring out over the midnight blue waters before him, he remembered the days when sailing had been in his blood, first as a merchant sailor and later as an adventurer. The roll of waves and salty tang in the air had thrilled him and he had felt more at home on the water than the land. It felt like someone else's life now and he wondered if his younger self could have imagined settling down as a fisherman.

He sighed heavily. These thoughts were just a distraction from what he knew he should be doing; things between Crystal and him could not remain as they were. He had no memory of ever arguing with her, let alone the heinous act he had committed; what kind of man struck their own daughter? He looked down at the carving in the loose sand before him and realised he had sketched an image from the past, a sigil of the Montanai Kingdom in the far North. Transfixed by the image he had created, his mind swept back to the only time he had ever travelled to the frozen realm and the last time he had fought side-by-side with Rork Fimarr.

Twenty-five years had passed since that adventure, but it suddenly seemed vivid once more and he could almost hear the rumbling voice of the mighty warrior. Of course this memory would come to him now; it was the only time Fimarr had ever spoken of a life outside of questing and war. The Montanai people had sent an envoy to find the renowned Fimarr specifically, certain that he was the only man capable of helping them. Mareck had been a regular companion to him for several years and often provided fast transport to many of the strange and exotic lands they visited. When the envoy had found them, Rogan the Barbarian and Vessa the Thief had also been part of his entourage and they relished the opportunity to quest in a new land. A three-day voyage had been required, the last of which was spent traversing ice floes and frozen fjords, putting his seafaring to significant test. He had navigated them safely through, vowing never to tackle such waters again; the land of Annickdor lay further North and reportedly had a port of its own but he could not imagine any vessel being able to reach it. The Montanai were ruled by a young queen; her father had been victim to the very evil they had requested help in vanquishing, forcing her to take succession far earlier than any could have imagined. She was very beautiful, with the fragile and somewhat aquiline features common to her people, and exceptionally grateful to them for coming. It was no surprise that she knew nothing about Rork's companions, he seemed to gain a new retinue every few years as other adventurers could not sustain his permanent drive and constant peril; only Rogan kept returning after breaks of varying lengths. Her gratitude was global regardless of their identities and even Vessa's lack of tact, instantly asking what level of reward would be received, did not dampen the young monarch's enthusiasm.

The accounts from the Montanai people about the danger they faced had been hard to believe, suggesting a giant ice wyrm inhabiting the glacial mountains several leagues away. They called it a Drakiam and recounted how it had attacked many settlements, eating the inhabitants and leaving icy devastation in its wake. The king had led a militia to destroy the beast and never returned, only one young soldier reappearing to tell the tale of doom. Rork had been undeterred and his brash confidence was infectious, as always. He vowed destruction of whatever the beast was, and they had departed the next day. Travelling in that desolate place was an unenviable task as the elements took their toll on strength and will alike; any sign of weakness was quickly met with jovial disdain from the two huge warriors while Vessa failed to speak throughout the journey. Even now he believed she had suffered most from the cold, despite the thick furs the Montanai had provided them; the fact Rork and Rogan had declined such protection amazed him to this day. Eventually they had arrived at the nominated mountains, failing to find any sign of the creature, and being forced to set up camp for days to ensure their search was comprehensive. Just as he had been on the verge of deciding the whole matter was some sort of ruse, they had found signs of their quarry. They had been discounting tracks from the Drakiam as natural channels and gorges; the descriptions they had received did not give credit to the creature's enormous size.

Tracking it back to its lair, they had waited in hiding to assess what they would be facing. When the Drakiam emerged from the cavernous burrow in which it dwelled, Mareck had felt fear such as he never had before, nor ever would again, for it was the epitome of the term monster. Over two hundred and seventy feet long, it looked like a giant snake with four pairs of short legs equidistant along its body. A gnashing beak, akin to an elongated parrot's, sported two tusks and a long tongue that flicked in and out rapidly, two tapered horns swept back from comparatively small eyes with identical appendages tipping its long tail. It appeared scaled like a reptile but was also covered in frost, obscuring whether these were organic or made of the very ice about it. The slightest of blue hues could be distinguished through that white outer covering, allowing the beast to be well camouflaged despite its huge size. Sharp silvery claws sprouted from the toes of its feet, each larger than Rork Fimarr himself. So many times since encountering the Drakiam had he spent wondering if it was some mystical abomination or part of an entire species; though the latter idea gave him cause for nightmares. It was the only time he had seen Rork Fimarr's confidence waver. When they had gathered to discuss strategy, Mareck had agreed with Vessa and Rogan; the quest was folly, and no victory could be achieved. Perhaps it was their determination that the feat was impossible, or maybe the unrelenting danger the monster presented to the Montanai, but something led Rork to disagree. He offered them the chance to leave but he was staying to destroy the Drakiam; at that point, none of them could abandon him.

That night they camped on either side of its lair, hidden amongst icy passages with the intention of ambushing the creature when it returned from its night-time foray. Mareck had ended up with Rork and the potentially fatal encounter that awaited them drove the legend to open up in ways he never had before. Asking the younger man if he had ever hoped for a family, Mareck could only answer honestly that he had never considered the matter. That led to Fimarr revealing that he had a family of his own; a wife he clearly adored from his description of her, and three daughters. His love and devotion for them laced every word but there was also pain in his voice; he explained that his way of life did not blend well with family; that the enemies arrayed against him forced him to prepare his children for danger at every turn; his fear that they would never understand why he taught them the lessons he did; and how every severity laid upon them drove a wedge between him and his adored wife. Mareck remembered going to sleep that night, certain that the morning would bring death, such was the price of hearing such vulnerability from Rork Fimarr.

Strangely he could remember little of the battle against the Drakiam; it was definitely an epic encounter, but he could not recall how long it lasted. There was a plan of some sort, using trickery and the environment to their advantage, cornering the creature somehow. At some point he had hurled his spear, striking true despite the enormous distance, blinding it in one eye amid howls of rage and agony. He retained a clear image of Rogan and Rork landing mighty blows against enormous icicles hanging from the mouth of its lair, the frozen spikes falling upon, and piercing, their foe. Was that how they had finally killed the Drakiam? He still couldn't be certain. He did remember Vessa attempting to claim higher reward than was offered by breaking into the Montanai vaults, how she had been threatened with execution for her treachery and Rork once again stepping in to resolve the matter.

Mareck stood and hefted the spear to his shoulder. Turning towards the cluster of trees that edged onto the beach line, he took four running steps and launched his weapon, feeling agonising fire rip through his tender shoulder. Dropping to his knees in pain and surprise, he had almost forgotten he was injured, he watched the spear flying true along the course he had chosen. It arced down and stabbed deep into the earth some forty yards short of the target. As with everything else, his ability with the weapon had deteriorated over the years but it was not his lack of fighting prowess that had brought that memory to the surface. No more than two and a half years later he had been blessed with Crystal and never raised a hand to her until twelve nights ago. He knew he'd had no choice, but she was of a different opinion. If the greatest warrior of all had struggled with the harsh life lessons his children had to learn, then maybe that was mitigation against his one slip in over twenty-three years? He did not feel convinced, however.

Crossing the sand to retrieve the spear, he knew he had to try and mend the bridge between them again, the matter would not remedy itself. Crystal had taken up residence with Garren Verdieu's parents; since his death they had craved time with any of his former friends, particularly those present when he had died. It made the arrangement ideal; they had space, and she could provide them some comfort. It also left his own home barren and empty as it had never been; without her it was an alien and unwelcome place, leading him to spend much time wandering the land beyond the village when not working. He spent the journey to her current residence attempting to craft a convincing argument for his actions but every word that ran through his mind felt hollow. He found himself staring at the Verdieu front door for several minutes before finally finding the courage to knock.

Myska Verdieu answered the door, glaring at him with disdain, 'She does not want to speak wiz you, Mareck.'

'I understand, Myska, but she is my daughter, and I must make things right with her.'

'You must go. I do not wish for unpleasantness between us, but your conduct is unforgiveable. Now leave.'

'Would you walk away if the rift were between you and Garren?' he knew it was a low tactic but had little desire to argue his point with an intermediary. He regretted his approach when tears began to roll down Myska's face but stood his ground regardless.

'You are a cold man, Mareck. I loved my son wiz all ze fire in my 'eart. Zere is nozing I would not 'ave done for 'im. Most certainly I would not have beaten 'im!'

Mareck felt a spike of rage but swallowed it immediately, 'Then perhaps you are a better man than me, but would you deny me the chance to fix my mistake?'

He could see the other man gritting his teeth against a fresh wave of emotion before his eyes softened, 'No, zat is not my place. But be sure zat I will remove you from my 'ome if she requests it.'

'And I will not resist,' Mareck confirmed, relieved that his emotional blackmail had succeeded, 'thank-you for giving me this chance.'

As Myska stepped aside, Mareck followed the direction of his outstretched hand, traversing a short, closed corridor that led to a ground floor bedroom. Rapping gently on the door, he heard his daughter's voice and felt suddenly nervous.

'Yes? 'oo is it?'

Knowing she would refuse him entry, he took the question as an invitation and pushed the door open. 'Hello, Crystal, we must talk.'

She sat bolt upright on the bed where she had been lying and her eyes were filled with fury, but he was pleased that the swelling on the side of her head had almost completely vanished. 'We 'ave nozing to talk about! You were my fazer, and zen you fought me in favour of complete strangers. Now you are nozing to me.'

'Crystal, please, place your anger aside and let us talk. I understand that you want to hurt me as I have hurt you but, rest assured, those hunters have already done so in your place. It is time for us to resolve this and return to our lives.'

'But zat is the problem, is it not? You 'ide 'ere pretending zat all is right wiz ze world, but it is not! Monsters stalk our land, 'ave attacked our very 'ome, yet you allow one to be taken from 'ere alive. Instead of killing it ourselves, you insisted we ask for 'elp and zose scum came from 'oo knows where, commanding you like a slave and turning on us when we demanded justice against ze beast. Our very own Regent even suffered an attack by parties unknown, an attack I 'ad an 'and in preventing, yet you remain wiz your 'ead buried in the sand like a coward. Our lives are not like zey were and zey cannot be again. Events are overtaking your desire to avoid zem!'

'You are right, my daughter, and if I stand idly by then those events will overwhelm us! I settled here to avoid such things, to put my violent past behind me.'

'So you 'ave told me, many times! You spent your youz adventuring zroughout the land, visiting strange places, experiencing wonders zat most can only imagine, and protecting zose 'oo could not protect zemselves from evil. Now evil is on your doorstep and you wish to 'ide? And you would even 'urt your own family to cower in the shadows? 'Ow can I believe you are ze same man 'oo travelled wiz Rork ze legend?'

He could not restrain a chuckle, funny how she would refer to the very man he had been thinking about, but quickly wiped the smile from his face as he responded, 'It is because I was that man that I wish to avoid being drawn in. Don't you see? For every great deed there was an almighty price to pay, for each evil vanquished, a litany of new enemies wishing revenge; the price of sustaining that life was to push this one indefinitely into the future. I want no part of that for you.'

'And why do you assume zis is your choice? I am a grown woman and I will decide my own future, not live in ze one you 'ave selected for me.'

'Why can't you understand this, Crystal? I have been through all of that, I have made those mistakes and suffered the consequences of them. I love you; why would I allow such struggles to become part of your life? Why is it so hard to accept my experiences as the truth and learn from them? I only want what is best for you.'

She stood and walked over to him, grasping his upper arms in her hands and staring intently into his eyes, 'Can you not 'ear yourself? Your experiences are in ze past, maybe zey were great and maybe not, but zey were yours, not mine. We are different people, we zink differently, we act differently and our paths will evolve differently. Zis is not ze same world in which you travelled long ago; still dangerous, true, but not ze same. 'Ow can you stand zere and tell me zat you are protecting me from somezing you know nozing about?'

He could feel his emotion bubbling up inside him and bit back against a sob. Why was she being so stubborn? Could she really be so naïve? 'I hear your words, my daughter, and I understand how you must feel. But look at what has happened; you saw those men, those very dangerous, well-armed hunters, doing something you believed to be wrong. You wanted to stop them despite their superior numbers and strength. If I had not taken action to prevent you, we would both be dead instead of just bruised in body and pride. This does not feel like a different world to me at all.'

'All it takes for evil to zrive, is for good men to sit back and do nozing.'

He felt the emotional sucker punch deep in his gut; every time she had asked him as a child why he had done all of the heroic deeds in his life, that was his answer. Over the years, he had grown to understand that the words were true enough but came with inevitable sacrifice; for every man who stood and faced down evil, ten more were hewn in its path. 'You use my own words against me, Crystal, but you speak them from a place of innocence. Life is not so black and white; it is no romantic fable. Why would I not want to protect you from that?'

'But you are ze one 'oo told me all ze stories about courage, integrity and 'onour. You 'ave inspired me like most parents can only dream of! Zere is no reason to fear for me, I would take action to protect the weak, to stand where ozers could not. I am capable, strong and intelligent; if you 'ave concern over my ability zen travel wiz me. Come as a fellow warrior or come as an advisor if you zink your body is not up to it any more, but do not try to stand in my way.'

'Crystal, you have always amazed me. You are so strong yet filled with compassion, unwaveringly brave but blessed with humility, patient as the gods but quick to act when called upon. There is no better person that I would choose to travel with if it was required. But it is not. The hunters are gone, I have doubts they were sent by the Prince and too much time has passed to track them. The village has taken a heavy toll over the recent weeks and who is to say that creature was the only one of its kind? There could be another, there could be hundreds! Have you not considered that maybe it is our responsibility to protect this village? To keep safe the people who have done so for us for over twenty years?'

'Because it is like fighting a symptom!' she shouted in frustration, ''You must see zat? Everyzing zat 'as 'appened are the visible effects of some underlying disease! Somezing made zat monster, somezing led to 'unters coming 'ere instead of killers, somezing 'as stirred up all the wrong in zese lands. If we keep fighting ze overflowing output of zat somezing, eventually it will become too much, and we will fail. But if we root out ze cause, destroy zat disease at the core zen we protect zis village and every ozer one as well!'

She was right, he knew it, and she sounded just like Rork Fimarr. Only he had ever seen through danger as the veil it was, a thin cloak to disguise the petty needs of men and the bleak nature of predators. Only when you burned through that veil with courage could you strike at the heart of your foe. Mareck felt strength draining from him and she must have sensed it as well, guiding him down to the hard, wooden seat near the window.

'I cannot argue with you any longer, Crystal, for there is no denying the truth in your words. You sound like the heroes of old and I know you would do all in your power to live up to them. It does not change the fact that you are my child, the one person left in all this world who I love, and I cannot permit you to give your life, even for such a noble cause. You will not leave this village, I forbid it.'

She looked like he had just punched her again, 'You forbid it?' she repeated in stunned surprise.

'Yes. Even if you never speak to me again. The fact that you will live long enough to punish me with your silence will be testament to this being the right decision.'

'So be it, fazer,' she stated quietly, 'Know zat I believe this to be a coward's decision, zat you are everyzing I 'ave grown to despise in ze world and zese will be the last words we speak to each ozer. You are a disappointment to me, and I wonder now 'ow many of your stories are true and 'ow many are the tales of ozers' deeds. Now get out.'

Her calm was almost unnatural, and her words bit deeply into him. Perhaps she would never understand but his own statement was true; whatever pain he would now suffer because of her ill-feeling towards him, it was nothing compared to losing her completely. As he slowly rose and shuffled from the room, he kept telling himself he was doing the right thing.

Treya inched further forward along the narrow drainage tunnel, attempting to prevent her feet from slipping into the few inches of wastewater that channelled along the bottom. The tunnel was almost perfectly cylindrical and not built for passage, but the main network was at least large enough to navigate. As her scabbard scraped against the damp wall for what seemed like the hundredth time, she cursed silently and applied downwards pressure to the hilt, angling the weapon up slightly. The sound of running water and echoes of splashing had become background noise to her by this point, but who knew how far the contrast of scraping metal would carry through the tunnels. Taking a deep breath to compose herself, and regretting it immediately, she looked back for confirmation.

Magin was still behind her, frightened eyes searching the dim light frantically. It was only because of him that they had learned the location of Alissa within the palace; his wife worked as a maid and regularly cleaned one of the large chambers throughout the complex, insisting that the youngest Fimarr was present there every day. It was a lot of faith to go on, but Treya had resolved there was no other choice; at least this way they could simply flee in secrecy if the information proved to be unreliable. She could still not tell if his extreme agitation was generated by knowingly deceiving them or because of the incredible danger they faced.

'A T-junction ahead; which way?' she asked in a hushed whisper.

Still looking like a frightened rabbit, but with nowhere to run as the considerable bulk of Jacob Frost was behind him, Magin's face filled with strain as he tried to recall the directions, 'Right,' he said eventually, 'and then I think only a few hundred yards until we are underneath the room we seek. There are large run off drains in every room that has a skylight, in case it is left open during storms, and that one is no exception. We should have unrestricted access as long as the drain covers have not been secured, Frayjel assured me your sister is always in there alone; any guards are stationed outside the door.'

Another wave of trepidation washed over her; it was still hard to comprehend that Alissa was alive, let alone that she was about to see her again. It should have been a time to rejoice, a union filled with love and hope; instead, it was to be a desperate rescue attempt with danger rallied against them at every turn. Still, she had to trust that the fortunes smiling upon them were omens of success; meeting Magin and Bentram in the forest, their awareness of the secret accessways into the palace, Frayjel's fortuitous position on the palace staff. All factors that had led to their current plan and the potential to save her sister despite the loss of Frost's army.

Frost. She watched the old warrior, he looked particularly uncomfortable in the close confines due to his size, and wondered if he was genuine after all. Everything he'd said and done since landing back in their lives indicated a real desire to make amends for the betrayal he had cast upon them all those years ago. But she had believed such tales of remorse before and tasted the bitter sting of falsehood; the huge scar in her back suddenly ached as if to emphasise her point. However, here he was, five years of incarceration and the loss of his loyal followers behind him, ready to join them in a daring raid against his former liege. Or was he herding them into a trap? She shook her head to clear the thoughts; caution was necessary, paranoia could be deadly. Frost caught her eye and nodded solemnly, waiting for her to command their next move; if they did not arrive at one of the drains and raise the blue ribbon into view, the plan would be abolished. It had been the best way to avoid an ambush and coordinate the attack; now all she had to hope was that they all made it.

Slowly working her way towards the junction again, her heart twinged at the thought of Straker; the decision to send him with Catalana had been a difficult one. It made sense to her, of course, but the heart and mind were seldom bedfellows of late; Straker could protect her sister if any dangers were present along their route and it meant the only unknown factor in that group was Bentram, who presented little threat. She would not have been able to concentrate if Frost and one of his men had been Cat's only escorts; she wondered if Straker was feeling the same way as that was the position she had placed herself in. She cast the thoughts away again; negativity achieved nothing for her, and they had almost reached their destination without incident. She had to hope that the three Lustanians proved true to their word.

Catalana fiddled nervously with the feathers of her arrows, nestled snugly in the thigh-bound quiver she had opted for. The short bow was not to her choosing but made sense under the circumstances; the weapon was easy to bring to bear in tight confines and quick to fire, it simply lacked the power and range she preferred from her own longbow. At her belt were her hunting knife and the small Warhammer Bentram had given her; she had accepted the latter graciously, but knew she lacked the strength to make the weapon particularly effective. In front of her Bentram had led the way through the drainage tunnels;

the network they had described indicated this would provide access to the opposite side of the chamber they wished to get to. In fact, this was the larger primary drain and Treya's group would be approaching through the smaller secondary overflow. It was also comforting that the journey had been uneventful, save for the occasional rat which seemed to bother Bentram more than her. The ease of getting to their destination was a happy contrast to what she expected from the rescue attempt; even if Alissa were in the chamber alone as predicted, it was unlikely guards would be too far from her or short in number. There was a fight on the horizon, she could almost feel it, and victory would be escaping with all their number intact.

She considered the Lustanian soldier guiding them; he had been quiet but held a surety in himself that suggested he was more than competent in battle. Twin swords hung at his hips, shorter than many but also thicker than was common, and she wondered if he was able to wield both simultaneously; if he could then he was skilled indeed. He wore leather armour that was completely piecemeal, each element strapped separately to him; this provided lower protection but increased flexibility and she read this to mean he was fast and agile. She would soon discover if her assumptions were correct, as the likelihood of absconding with Alissa without conflict was minimal.

Following her was Forge and his presence brought her great confidence. She had barely ever seen him in battle, but knew he was a fine warrior; she recalled many years before when he had faced an entire army alone to allow them to evade capture. Days later he had returned to them, leaving no doubt as to his combat prowess. But it was more his conduct and manner that inspired confidence, every word and action displayed courage and self-belief, lifting those around him without effort. Even when he was quiet, as he had been in the echoing tunnels, he felt like a beacon of assured success. There was even greater comfort drawn from the fact he had once travelled with her father, that in itself was testament to the level of skill he must possess. He had brought his trademark scimitar with him but also carried the back-sling with several of his short throwing javelins within; she could not remember the last time he had used them in anger. Perhaps, like her, he hoped to conduct any required conflict from a distance.

A sudden sound startled her, and she felt her heart leap into her mouth. It was an echoing growl that floated from a side passage, but it was filled with pain rather than aggression. Both of her companions had frozen in place and looked towards the smaller tunnel from which the noise carried. Fear suddenly vanished in place of curiosity and she stepped towards the smaller tunnel, crouching to gain access. A restraining hand fell on her shoulder and she turned to see Forge's concerned face as he shook his head vehemently. She offered what she hoped was a confident smile before gently removing his hand with her own. He did not resist, and she cautiously followed the sound along the pitch-black passage. She was aware of her companions following reluctantly behind her and continued her progress until light began to filter to them from ahead.

By the time she reached the source of light, a heavily barred outlet, she was only just able to crawl, having left her companions further back when they could no longer continue in the confines. Pressing her face to the steel obstruction before her, she could see a deep cylindrical pit beyond that reached up to an unseen chamber above, from which natural light streamed down, and the dank circle below; her vantage point was almost equidistant between top and bottom. Writhing in that deep prison was one of the horrific mutant creatures in the throes of its painful transformation. She could see the monster must have been a cat but had already quadrupled in size, muscles and skin seeming to bubble and swim as it grew unnaturally. Once-soft fur was extending and melding together into vicious spines of black that adorned its outer surface, a lustrous and delicate tail thickening and sprouting segmented chitin with a spiked ball at the end. Slender, precision claws now sprouted forward like grappling hooks while its maw stretched forward like that of a crocodile. The sight before her generated no fear, just enormous pity, and she felt emotion threatening to overflow within her. Closing her eyes against the sight, she backed slowly along the tunnel and joined the others as they returned to the main passage. She must have looked shaken as Straker broke his silence.

'Cat', are you all right?' he asked in a whisper, 'What was it?'

She took a breath before replying, feeling the tremor in her chest, 'One of those things. A mutant. The change seems to be extremely painful; they are just animals being twisted by that corruption. For a person…'

He quickly grabbed her arm in support, 'We have no idea about people,' he affirmed, 'we have seen some imbalance to the mind but nothing more than that. I am certain no such fate has afflicted Alissa. And we must believe that the mind can be repaired; it has in Frost.'

She noticed the sudden interest from Bentram at the mention of his leader but had no interest in sparing the General's reputation, 'Yes, but look what he did to us, and we have no certainty that this is not all some ruse in support of that darkness.'

Forge's eyes scanned Bentram briefly but returned to her when there was no retaliation evident, 'I trust him, Cat', he is good to his word and his repentance genuine. So will it be for your sister, I promise.'

She smiled but knew it was unconvincing. Motioning for Bentram to return to their journey, she ushered them on urgently, 'We must make haste, I think the chamber we seek is some way above us.'

'Aye,' Bentram replied flatly, 'we have a climb ahead of us. Follow me.'

They continued only sixty yards beyond the diversion she had led them along before he held up a hand to stop them. A shaft of light shone on the tunnel floor in a perfect circle and she realised he had meant an actual climb. Vertically. She peered up into the ascent and saw no grate above, a small blessing as it meant once that had made the top, there was likely another tunnel in which they could await the signal to strike.

'Do you have a rope?' she asked.

'I am afraid not,' he replied before jumping up into the gap, bracing arms and legs against either side of the shaft, 'let us hope it is shorter than it looks.'

As he began to carefully shuffle his body upwards, she pulled the piece of blue ribbon from within her jerkin; if they did not make it, then the others would not even attempt the rescue.

Rayne kicked hard against the metal plate beneath her. As with all the others, it gave way easily and she muffled the squeal of twisting copper by holding her outstretched foot against it while it bent. Sliding through the gap she had made, she dropped down onto a brick surface. She had finally made it to the ceiling vents constructed between each floor of the palace. There was no way to ignore the marvel of architecture that had been used, ventilation gaps built as part of the original design criss-crossed through ceilings and up supporting walls until eventually reaching egress chimneys on the very top of the palace roof. The copper sheets equally spaced up every vertical run were mounted on rotating joints which allowed them to be easily pushed upwards by enough warm air. It was an intricate, if extremely expensive, cooling system, the like of which she had never seen before. It was also a foolish entry to a heavily defended fortress. The copper plates were one-way valves and so not built to allow anything back down but, because of the design requirement making them as light as possible, easy to bend as she had all the way down. She idly wondered if anyone would ever notice the damage she had caused throughout that system.

Carefully angling and twisting her body, she managed to contort herself onto her stomach within the vent. There was only just enough room for her arms to bend up towards her shoulders and she could feel the brickwork pressed against her on all four sides. Progress to the ceiling vent of the chamber below would be slow but she had traversed more difficult environments in the past and this was why she had opted to enter alone. She had also insisted on being the signal to put their plan in motion; she was sure all her allies would be enthusiastic in their efforts, but she needed everything to go precisely; something she could only guarantee by being there herself. Rocking her shoulders and finding a rhythm, she worked her way along the narrow vent and tried to stay focussed on the task. As usual of late, her mind wandered to thoughts she had never contemplated in the past.

The image of Alissa lying upon the bench in the depths of this very palace drifted to her, the perfectly clear memory of her own confused decision to hand her to Lennath. Why had she not just brought her sister to Treya and the others when she discovered her alive? If she, had, then they would not be forced into a rash rescue attempt in the heart of their enemy's home. Any of her allies who were injured or died as a result would lay their blood on her hands; despite all the lives she had taken, the guilt of being the inception, rather than the device, of another's death was a heavy weight to her. And how far back could she trace such blame? If she had not abandoned Catalana in the bowels of the Black Citadel, would they have found a way to save Alissa back then? Could her actions have avoided the five-year isolation, the fall into madness, the quest by Lennath to find her? Dragging her knuckles across the wall to her right, she drew blood and eradicated the thoughts lingering in her mind.

Ahead she could see the light from the grate and slowed down to ensure the silence of her approach. Another sensation began to fill her, one that was almost completely alien to her; as a lead weight seemed to form in her stomach, she realised it was fear. Every contract she had ever taken, every battle she had ever entered, whether expected or not, she had always known that she had the ability to succeed. Now her foes counted Sergience Mozak amongst their number and she knew she could not beat him. Throughout her years of Veer training, she had never overcome him during any sparring or practise in which she had faced him. In fact, she could not recall any having faced him and emerged victorious. He was the ultimate assassin, the ultimate fighter, the master of combat; how could she hope to defeat him? Another scrape pushed the anxiety down and she manipulated the thoughts in her head; she did not have to defeat him, did not even have to face him, all they required was enough distance to avoid him.

Arriving above the vent, she eased the copper plate upwards slowly so as not to attract any attention from below. When it was high enough to allow her some view of the area below, she peered through the gap. The centre of the chamber sported a circular opening to a deep pit, a foot-high stone lip encircling the edge, with an ornate plinth stood near to it. Fixed into a purpose-built stand atop the plinth was the Stave she had gifted to their enemies, a purple glow emanating from the bulbous end. Seemingly in a trance-like state next to the artifact was Alissa, her gaze completely vacant while her lips mumbled incantations that Rayne could not make out. She was adorned in blood red silks which contrasted against her porcelain skin, and her hair had begun to grow in since Rayne had last seen her, now well-maintained and reminiscent of her childhood golden locks. She did not deserve what had happened to her, none of it, and today was the chance Silver Rain had to make things right.

Straining to see as much of the remaining space as she could, she estimated maybe a third remained obscured to her which increased the risk of the attack greatly. From what she could see, there was only one other occupant of the room, an older, fat man dressed in military attire. From her memory of Frost's uniform, this man was a General and probably the successor to her current ally. He was sat on a marble bench, idly clearing the dirt from under his nails with the tip of a small dagger. Although he appeared neither alert nor particularly threatening, his presence raised hairs on the back of her neck. Magin's wife had insisted Alissa spent her days alone in this chamber, now, on the day they had planned this rescue, a guard was present with her instead of beyond the doors? And a General to boot? She had never been one to believe in coincidence, but she doubted they would gain another chance at getting so close to her. It was her decision, and hers alone, whether to strike or not; the moment she rolled free of the vent and dropped into the chamber, the others would spring from the two nominated drains and usher Alissa to safety. Scanning her eyes down to the two floor-grates in question, she saw only one blue ribbon poking through on Treya's side. Catalana's group were not yet in position so she had just a little more time to assess and consider. She bit her lower lip; did she really have a choice? Could she truly leave Alissa behind again?

'Slow down brother!' Gallth's whinging voice carried to him from further along the corridor, 'What is so urgent? We have had no chance of refreshment and the journey was a long one!'

Lennath stopped and waited for his kin to catch up, 'My apologies, Gallth, but you caused us to dally several times along the way from Mainspring. As a result, many matters of State have gone unattended and I am keen to address them.'

'Really? Do you not have advisors and viziers to deal with such issues in your absence?'

'Well, of course I do,' Lennath continued, making every effort to hide his impatience, 'but these are unprecedented times. With Porthus' disappearance and the strange creatures roaming my land, I try to leave as little to others as I can.'

'Ahhh, struggling to trust your subordinates? That can lead to inflexibility in stewardship of country affairs. I have no such concerns whilst I am away.'

'Always an experienced leader, brother, I appreciate your advice. However, I think your presence is steered towards confirming no underhanded activity rather than improving the style of leadership I employ, is it not?'

'Quite so,' Gallth's tone had dropped a degree colder at the last statement, 'a shame this is even necessary. I will admit that I had enjoyed our conversations over the last few days and you almost felt like family again. Shall I assume that is to be forgotten now that we are back on your home soil?'

'Please, Gallth, do not generate an argument from nothing. You are most welcome here and I want nothing more than for us to rebuild our brotherhood during your stay. But first I have someone of great importance that I want you to meet.'

Suspicion filled his brother's face, 'Really? You made no mention of this before. Who is this new figure of note?'

'It is supposed to be a surprise, brother, but maybe circumstances of late have created too much uneasiness for me to keep such secrets from you,' he glanced past his sibling to where their respective bodyguards stood. Gallth's burly man was watching them closely but Mozak had edged just behind the other warrior and placed a hand on the hilt of his long, curved knife. Lennath gave him an imperceptible shake of the head; this situation was far from being tense enough to merit execution of the two visitors. If all went well, he would be able to alleviate any of Gallth's fears while he was here; if he returned to their father with tales of trust in Lustania then it would make the eventual attack even more surprising and resistance would be minimal. Or so he hoped. Mozak received the signal and relaxed his posture again while Lennath returned to his conversation. 'I would like to introduce you to a lady of significance.'

Gallth's suspicion changed immediately to surprise, 'A woman? You have been courting in secret? Is she from a family of stature or is this why you have kept her hidden?'

'Does everything have to be tinged with distaste, for you?' Lennath feigned distress, 'I think you will agree she is from a family line of superb heritage. I have all intentions to wed her and provide Lustania with a queen.'

'And heirs, perhaps?' Gallth added raucously, all trace of suspicion suddenly vanishing from him, catching Lennath off guard, 'You should have told me sooner, brother, this explains much of your erratic behaviour! The mind rarely sees clearly when the heart is overloaded. Do you realise this would make you the first of us to marry? You must, indeed, let me meet this lady with all due haste!'

The Prince of Lustania was completely dumbfounded by the energetic enthusiasm and support being elicited by his kin. Only three days ago they had been arguing like trapped foxes, now, at the mention of a woman, it was like they had always been the best of friends. He hadn't even considered the significance that none of his brothers had wed, he assumed a fear of sharing their power with another spawned their reticence. If his family had ever engaged with him in the manner Gallth was now displaying, he imagined they never would have reached the levels of animosity currently in place between them. He sighed, too little, too late.

'Thank-you for your support, Gallth, now we must hasten. I promised her I would return no later than an hour past noon on this very day; there is little time remaining.'

'Already under the cosh, eh?' Gallth japed, picking his pace up to match Lennath's, 'She must be a prize indeed to have you so keen to please!'

'You have no idea, brother,' he replied, leading them at increased speed towards the mutation chamber; he could not afford to be late.

Alissa allowed the power to course through her, filling her completely and whirling about her freely. At her whim, it moved and flowed beyond her physical borders and down to the beast far below her. Feeling the energy penetrate every pore of the creature, her will overcame the organic resistance within the cells. Forcing them to multiply and shift beyond their natural ability to do so, she felt the thrill of power released into the newly forming creation and the associated rage that all such new-borns seemed to inherit. As the transformation ran to completion, she pushed her essence forward and found herself pacing around the circular pit impatiently, long spines rattling together along her muscular body and claws grinding thin furrows in the damp earth beneath her. Swinging her tail back and forth, she enjoyed the weight as it slammed against the slick stone walls. The iron grate rolled up to her left and she padded obediently along it to a waiting cell. As the door closed behind her, she withdrew her essence and felt the slender fragility of her human form. Unlike many times previously, she felt no fatigue from the effort at all. Knowing that the next animal would not be herded into the pit for several minutes, she allowed herself to enjoy the power being inside her for a moment. A sound to her left attracted her attention and she allowed sight to return to her eyes.

Glancing across she saw the fat soldier, she tried to remember his name but could not, that Lennath had insisted stay with her. He had nicked a finger with his own knife and was now sucking the wound like a child. Alissa's mouth went suddenly dry and she wondered how his blood would taste; she swallowed hard against the temptation and tried to keep her thoughts in order. Such distractions were usually beyond her, but this was the day the Prince had promised her, and she was acutely aware of her surroundings. Turning back to the beautiful Stave before her, she raised a hand and reached out her fingers towards the glowing end. Immediately, her other hand flashed across and slapped the fingers away. She knew the fat man was now watching her uneasily, but she kept her attention on the magical item. Placing the fingers of one hand in her mouth, she clamped her teeth down hard, tasting blood but maintaining her grip; she would not let that hand get in her way again. Reaching out with the other fingers, she felt the tug against her teeth but did not release her captive appendage. For the first time, her skin contacted the artifact and an electric jolt of pleasure shot through her. All at once, every creature that had been transformed by the power of the Stave were in her mind, she could see all that they could, and her intentions were theirs. She was distantly aware that her body was beginning to convulse and her breathing had become erratic, but these were minor concerns as her perception stretched out to the air around her and beyond. She could feel her thoughts, her will, entering everything around her, stone pillars and the sediment of which they were formed, the smooth marble benches, the metal drain covers, the people beyond…

Suddenly her connection was broken as her companion dragged her from the Stave, her expanded self crashing back into the limited physical shell left twitching in his arms. A choked cry escaped her lips as she tried to process the unexpected return to limitation, and she looked up into the terrified eyes of the fat man. Audack, she remembered. She reached up with one hand and touched his forehead; she felt a brief pressure behind her eyes and his head snapped back, lifting him from the ground and dumping him several yards away.

'You must not touch the Prince's things,' she mumbled as her breathing began to steady. From his position on the ground, Audack was moaning loudly and she knew he must be relatively unharmed.

Sitting upright, she looked at her robes and saw they were singed along the hems, but her body felt undamaged, just tingling all over in the aftermath of her brief foray into real power. Raising her hands, she saw that her nails were all black and red blood rims edged them; the fingers she had bitten seemed to have cauterized themselves, but she licked them anyway. They tasted like rusted steel.

Suddenly, the panting Audack dropped to his knees beside her, this time refraining from touching her at all, 'Are you well, milady?'

'I feel hollow,' she offered, 'are you bleeding?'

'No, thank the gods,' he babbled, 'just bruised and…'

She cut him off short, 'That is a shame, I am very thirsty,' he shuffled back nervously, 'did you feel the everything?'

'The everything?' he repeated, 'I saw you in distress, your body shaking like a leaf in the wind. Then you could not breathe, and I had to do something. Please accept my apologies if I have insulted you in some way.'

Springing to her feet like a child, she hopped over to the plinth and stared intently at the still-glowing Stave. Feeling warmth filling her head through her eyes, she waved him to join her. Stepping forward with trepidation, he remained out of arms reach. 'I am not insulted, just disappointed. I will have to decide whether to have Lennath execute you or not. Isn't she beautiful?'

Audack gulped loudly and smacked his lips several times as he tried to select the right words with which to answer, 'Isn't who beautiful, milady?'

'The power. She fills me with desire, don't you agree?'

'I feel no desire!' he blurted out hastily, 'I am loyal to my Prince!'

She turned to him and smiled, 'Stupid man, missing the point as all men do. Have you heard them? In the floors?'

Colour drained from his face and he inched away from her slowly, 'I have heard nothing, milady, I'm certain his Highness will return soon to deal with such problems. Perhaps it was rats?'

'No, not rats. Sisters…'

Kastani kept watching her mother as she spoke with Audack. It all seemed peaceful again after the frightening events moment ago; the purple waves that had swept out from Alissa minutes before had now all faded back into her but the sweetness that had accompanied them lingered. She had thought her mother would eat Audack, or at the very least bite him, but she had not. Kastani was glad, Audack was very funny, always looking nervous and red-faced but never saying no when she asked anything of him. She briefly considered asking him to play a game of gem toss with her, but he appeared busy looking after her mother. She sighed, it was often very boring and lonely being in this room, but she tried to do it at least five days out of seven in case her mother needed her. No, she told herself, no point lying about it, this was the first place Terex would come if he were to visit and she did not want to miss that.

She returned to her concealed corner of the room; a blanket lay on the floor between her and the wall, she had placed it to stop any noise from her game. She had placed a big emerald two thirds of the way along the sheet and was now trying to throw each of her remaining gems as close to it as possible. Any that hit the main stone or the wall beyond were discounted. She thought it was a brilliant game for two but, since inventing it, she had not seen Lennath at all, Audack had seemed very distressed most of the time and she had not raised a single word from her mother since they had arrived at the palace. Terex would have played with her straight away, she knew. Looking down at her palm, she had only three stones remaining, one amber and two blue. Carefully she launched each forward, one getting very close but the other two disappointingly short. Counting her points, she gathered the gems back into the pouch gifted to her by Lennath before moving the emerald to a slightly different location.

She suddenly felt a buzzing in the back of her head and instinctively rubbed at the spot with her hand. The sensation did not stop, and she looked up to see a small orb of the purple glow seemingly trapped in a large stone of the wall. She stretched out a hand and the light leapt forwards into her palm. Falling onto her bottom in surprise, she turned her hand over to see the light contently sitting there; her head told her it should hurt but instead it just felt warm. She felt the heat spread through her and, when it reached her eyes, she found herself drawn to look up. There, somehow inside the ceiling, she could make out the shape of someone lying beside the ventilation plate; that was silly, of course, so she knew her imagination was playing tricks on her. The orb had vanished when she looked back at the cup of her palm and she rolled onto her belly, just able to see her mother and Audack; this was also strange as a large stone pillar stood between them. She pointed her open palm at the rotund General and felt suddenly uneasy, filled with a fear of the unexpected. She remembered soothing words from Terex about the dangers of the world, that they would always exist and all that could be done was to face them if they appeared, moreso he would always be there to support her if they did. The uneasiness abated and was replaced with a deep sense of calm; beyond the pillar, Audack's posture released all tension and he stood taller than before. Without thinking, Kastani tossed the gem pouch into the air and flicked her hand towards it. The little sack tore apart instantly, scattering gems against the walls and across the floor at the same moment that the comforting warmth drained from her.

Breathlessly, she tried to comprehend what had happened as she shivered against cold that had not bothered her moments before. This was all vey confusing so she decided that she must reveal herself to Audack and ask for his advice. Before she could do so, the main doors to the room swept open, banging back against the walls with the force in which they had been pushed. Lennath strode into the room, bringing a smile to her face, and he was accompanied by another man she did not recognise. Following close behind was a broad-shouldered brute, another guard no doubt, and Mozak. The tall man was always with Lennath and had never been mean or threatening to her but always left her feeling a little scared; he closed the doors in their wake. Kastani considered running to Lennath for a hug, she had missed him more than she realised, but was too unsure with the newcomers present. She watched as Audack brought himself to attention and began to talk formally to the Prince, though she could not hear his words. Lennath quickly dismissed him to the side of the room and moved over to her mother. He lifted her hand to his lips, receiving no resistance, before turning and seemingly introducing her to the other elegantly dressed man. It appeared to be a very friendly affair, so joining in was probably not a bad idea.

Before she could step out from the corner, her imagined person in the ceiling suddenly appeared, forcing the copper vent cover out of her way before somersaulting against one of the stone pillars and then pushing off for a second somersault carrying her to the ground. It was a long way down, and Kastani was amazed she didn't twist her ankles. Seconds later, two drain covers popped up from the floor and three people streamed out into the room from each one, weapons drawn and seemingly prepared for a fight. Fear flashed through her at the sight, she wanted to help somehow but her body was frozen in place; she had to remain hidden because she recognised one of the intruders as the woman who had taken her from the Citadel, and she did not want to be taken again.

'Lennath!' she heard the older of the women call out, 'Hand Alissa to us and you will live!'

Kastani could not see the intruders very clearly as their backs were to her, but they numbered four men and three women. She knew that made seven. Lennath had four other men with him and her mother; that only made six. It wasn't fair, so she hoped this was some game rather than a real attack; if she ran to join Lennath, the sides would be fair, but she didn't want to fight anyone in case she got hurt.

'Treya!' the Prince replied, loudly and in fair spirit, 'So good to see you! Pray tell, why have you come here in such a manner? My doors have always been open to you in friendship; why do you crawl from the sewers in such a fashion? I cannot hand you anyone, for your sister is not mine to give; she is here of her own free will.'

Sister? Kastani struggled to understand what that meant. She recalled a time when Terex had sat with her in a sunbathed chamber of the Citadel, idly talking about the bonds of family. He had mentioned something about her mother having sisters and this made them her family too. Had he called them alps? Or maybe ants? There was definitely a proper name for them. But could this really be the case? And if this woman with sword drawn was her family, why had she chosen to attack her friend, Lennath? There was too much to understand and she felt a sudden lump of fear in her stomach; she didn't want all these people to fight but what could she do to stop it? How could she let them know that they should all be friends?

'Save your breath, Lennath,' this was from the scarred woman who had taken her in the first place, 'we have no time for your games. Let her leave with us or we will take her from you.'

Lennath looked shocked and confused, 'Please, let us all remain calm. Put away your weapons and we can discuss this matter with civility; there is no need for conflict.'

Kastani watched Mozak and the broad-shouldered guard moving slightly to the side and forward, as if trying to make sure they could see all the warriors before them without obstruction. It all looked very tense and she jumped when the third woman, pretty with thick red hair tied away from her face, suddenly cried out in rage.

'He is stalling! Take them!'

Then chaos erupted and Kastani began to cry.

Catalana called her fellows to strike and loosed the arrow already notched in her bow. It flew straight and true towards its target but the Prince of Lustania ducked to the side with an impressed smile on his lips. The shaft flew harmlessly by him and she silently cursed herself for attempting a head shot; her father had always taught her to target the centre of mass. Taking several steps to the side and dropping to one knee while she reloaded her weapon, she was aware of her comrades surging forward about her. Treya made straight for Alissa, with Frost trying to keep up in support; the other man with them seemed slightly lost and jogged non-committedly in their wake. The threat the tall Veer assassin posed had been heavily emphasised by Straker and Rayne before they had put this plan into action, and she noted them both sprinting in his direction. Bentram had his swords held in a rearwards grip, allowing him full freedom of movement as he headed towards Lennath and the unknown visitor with him. She vowed that at least one of those men would fall before her ally got there.

Firing an arrow forwards and this time retaining her position and posture, she was able to loose a second rapidly; there was no way he could dodge both. Lennath sprang back the other way, grabbing the other man, who looked completely stunned by events around him, and pulling him out of the trajectory of the first arrow. As it sailed past, Catalana could see the second now on course for the broad target of the Prince's back. Unbelievably, a flash of silver heralded a tiny throwing blade slicing through the air, impacting with her shot, and diverting it harmlessly into a stone column. The gentlest of whistling sounds then preceded her bow springing from her hand. Falling back in surprise, she looked down at her weapon and saw that the string had been sliced neatly in two, transforming the bow into nothing more than a useless stick. A second throwing blade protruded from her jerkin but had, thankfully, not penetrated the armour. Looking up she spotted Mozak and knew he was responsible despite his attention being focussed on the attackers heading towards him. Feeling both awe and fear at his skill, she pulled the blade free before drawing her own knife and Warhammer, the latter in her weaker hand. It appeared dealing with Lennath would have to be a more personal affair.

Audack settled his nerves as the attack commenced; he had not been forced into direct combat for many years, but it seemed this confrontation was inevitable. It had felt all too convenient that he had been ordered to keep watch in this chamber, where none had been previously allowed, on the very day that his nemesis chose to attack. As the blonde woman charged towards Alissa, oddly sheathing her sword in the process, he watched Frost approaching beyond her; the warrior was old but looked strong despite the extra years. The other man with them, clearly filled with fear rather than will, looked to be little threat and Audack realised that this was the work of the gods. Clearly it was their Divine whim that he should face his one true enemy here and now; it was time to put their five-year rivalry to an end.

Drawing his trademark war pick, Audack pressed forward, panting after only a few steps, but making no effort to intercept the woman; her attention was completely on the Prince's consort. Instead, he fixed his eyes on Frost and placed himself in the path of the oncoming warrior. As the gap between them closed, he remembered how much taller the other man was.

'Come then, Jacob Frost!' he cried out in defiance, 'Let us settle things once and for all! For all the years of hate and plans of revenge, our time is at hand. Let this epic rivalry end here today!'

Frost seemed to slow slightly, narrowing his eye to take in Audack's presence. Sliding to a stop before him, the white-haired veteran held his weapons before him.

'Do I know you?' he rumbled, 'Is there some quarrel between us?'

Audack felt suddenly unsure of himself. Was this some clever ploy to place him off-balance? 'I am Delegar Audack, General of Lustania's armies and your successor! It was I who ensured your coup failed, I who replaced you, I who have been the sole target of your revenge. This confrontation has been years in the making!' He was disappointed at the tremor in his own words and the way his voice cracked at the end of his statement.

Frost's shoulders relaxed slightly, 'I am sorry, but I have no recollection of you. Whatever revenge you think I seek is non-existent. However, you have placed yourself in harm's way and I will not be stopped this day. Defend yourself!'

Audack knew it must be a trick, he had feared this day, this battle, from the moment Frost had been imprisoned. It was a mind-game, used to gain the advantage in combat, no doubt. But it would not work; Frost was a villain, an enemy of the throne, and Audack was the figurehead of Justice in this land. The outcome was already decided.

'Your words will not win this day, Jacob!' he cried in defiance and launched himself forward, war-pick swinging towards his enemy's heart. Frost angled his blade to intercept and then flourished it in a smooth circle, catching the end of the pick and disarming Audack with ease. All confidence drained from him and he stared dumbly after the weapon as it skittered across the stone floor away from him. Flicking his eyes back to the giant before him, he was just in time to register the powerful fist as it crashed against his nose. Blinded by the sudden swell of tears, he felt a pressure against his chest as he was swept easily aside, staggering backwards before tripping over the raised lip of the mutation pit. He was suddenly filled with the feeling of weightlessness as he tumbled from the room.

Forge bore down on Mozak and considered his options rapidly. The assassin was far superior to he and, with so many onlookers, his chances of success may as well have been zero. The only option they had was to distract the Veer long enough for the others to escape with Alissa; and hopefully not die in the process. He realised he was making more headway than Rayne, odd as she had always been faster, and realised that she had the body language of reluctance. Already the tall enemy had managed to save his employer using the trademark throwing blades of his people and it seemed odd that he had not utilised the same weapons against them. Perhaps he only carried three, or maybe he was looking to practise his close combat skills.

Closing within twenty yards, Forge suddenly released one of his javelins, noting three of Rayne's blades joining it in quick succession, making dodging seemingly impossible. Unexpectedly, Mozak dropped flat on his back, avoiding any impacts but leaving himself incredibly exposed and vulnerable. Straker arrived above him, scimitar flashing down for the kill, but the Veer had already lifted his knees to his shoulders, flipping into the air with incredible agility. His feet impacted heavily with Forge's chest, driving the air from his lungs, and launching him back the way he had come. Crashing heavily to the ground and rolling several times, he realised he was almost twenty yards back again.

Gasping to regain his breath, he watched as Rayne reached her target, leaping deftly over Mozak's low spinning kick only to be caught in the ribs by his trailing raised arm. Knocked to the side awkwardly, she cartwheeled out of reach as a scissor kick slashed down to where she should have landed. Like lightning, Mozak was upon her with a flurry of straight punches absorbing all her capacity to block. The last broke through her defences and landed against her jaw, the impact snapping her head to the side. With no movement wasted, the Veer assassin wrapped his arm about her neck, dragging her before him as he attempted to secure a stranglehold. Luckily, their struggle had brought them next to one of the pillars and Rayne stretched out her legs, running them up the support and allowing her to flip over her adversary and break the hold. Kicking out, failing to stagger Mozak at all, she used the leverage to backflip away from him and gain some breathing space.

Forge regained his feet and withdrew another javelin; things were not going well so far. Launching the weapon forward, he knew he was being observed by someone as the throw lacked his preferred accuracy despite still heading for the target. The Veer assassin glanced up briefly, catching the steel bolt with ease before spinning it in his hand and shooting it forward towards Rayne. She barely managed to palm the weapon aide as it lanced towards her and Straker saw the line of red it left across the side of her neck.

Sprinting back towards Mozak, he hoped Treya would achieve their goal sooner rather than later.

Bentram closed in on the Prince and his brother, as a Lustanian citizen all his life, the faces of the King and his sons were etched into his mind. He had no quarrel with Gallth or any other Kaydarellian but he could not allow that to stand in his way. This was the one chance that they had built an army to achieve, the chance that he assumed was lost when the Prince's monsters wiped out all his comrades, and now, unbelievably, had come to pass thanks to the Fimarr sisters. Here and now, he could kill Lennath and overthrow the evils he was committing in their lands, perhaps even securing the King himself as their ruler. He secured his grip on the twin blades that had served him so well throughout his military and rebellion days; the Prince was unarmed so victory was assured.

'Hear me false-liege!' he called out, releasing rage stored throughout years of hardship, 'today I bring your villainy to an end! Happenstance has brought you within my reach, but it will not save you from my wrath!'

He leapt into the air with blades raised, eager to drive as much force into the killing blow as possible. Lennath moved with remarkable speed, dodging to the side as the blow was struck, sparks flying from the edges of the blades where they crashed against the stone floor.

'Happenstance my man?' the Prince replied, landing a kick to the side of Bentram's head and toppling him over. Turning the fall into a roll, he quickly regained his feet as Lennath continued, 'This is no chance encounter! Much as you are an irrelevant extra here, I am the sole reason the Fimarrs made it this far!'

Uncertainty filled Bentram as he prepared for another attack, observing his foe who was tugging his short cloak free with his right hand. 'What do you mean? Our plan was unknown, our access in secret. How could you have been responsible for these things?'

The Prince adopted a low fighting stance, allowing the cloak to hang loosely in his grip, 'You are all fools to think that any entry to my home could be achieved without my knowledge. I knew of your plot from the start and removed all defences from your chosen ingress. I knew the time you wished to strike and ensured I was here to meet you; it is fitting that all resistance to my reign fall before me personally.'

'Impossible!' Bentram cried, charging forward with both feint and follow-up strike. Lennath allowed the feint to pass him, although the blade tore through his billowing shirt, before whipping his cloak around the second sword, entangling it and allowing him to use his superior strength to tug it from Bentram's grasp. Off-balance, the kick to the small of his back staggered him several yards before he fell to his knees. Shifting his remaining weapon into his stronger right hand, he clambered to his feet as the Prince continued to gloat.

'Not at all, my good man! I received all the details from a very reliable source, a member of my own staff, in fact. A simple maid here in my home who was most forthcoming when layers of flesh began to be sheared from her. She divulged everything I needed to know and more, all in the futile hope that she would live. I do hope she was not a friend of yours, that would be most tragic. She did mention her husband was part of the rebel army out in the woods; it was not you, was it? That would be just awful! Frayjel I think she said, although it was hard to determine amongst the screaming…'

The mocking sarcasm in his voice was almost more than Bentram could bear but the scream of anguish from nearby cut him to the bone. He realised that Magin had overheard the Prince's words and was now racing forward in blind rage, weapon raised but thought gone. Leaping forward, he tried to close the distance first but knew he would not make it as the Prince suddenly took off to intercept the incoming assailant. Wild-eyed, screaming vows of revenge, Magin hurtled towards his enemy, swinging his blade with fury as he came within range. Lennath easily ducked under the uncontrolled attack, slamming his shoulder into the other man's stomach, and tackling him heavily to the floor. Magin writhed like an eel, desperate to punish his wife's killer, even as the Prince pried his own weapon away from him.

Bentram changed direction and made for Gallth, calling out to Lennath in the hope of distracting him, 'Here, Prince of deception, as you have slain my friend's family, so shall I slay yours!'

Lennath turned his head and smiled knowingly, not even looking back as he drove the captured sword down into Magin's chest.

'Good luck, outlaw!' he called back.

Bentram turned just in time as an axe swept upwards before him. Slowing enough to avoid being hewn apart by the attack, the heavy weapon crashed against his own sword with enough force to send him teetering back. Falling to the floor again, he watched Gallth's bodyguard readjust his grip for less power but more control before heading in to finish him off. Bentram looked to the side and found he had fortuitously landed next to his previously lost blade. Rolling to his feet and snatching the sword up, he clashed the two weapons together before him.

'Very well, if I must cut through both of them to get to you, then so will it be!'

Treya did not look back as she passed the fat soldier, confident that Frost would deal with him. Before her was her baby sister, thought lost to her for five years, looking vacant and almost unaware of the battle raging around her. The closer she got, the more detail she could make out; beautifully clothed and manicured, golden hair shorter than Treya could remember it had ever been but, coincidentally, about the same length as her own. But it was the scars that caught her attention, strange arcane symbols etched intricately into her skin, each permanently recorded as slender raised lines in her once perfect flesh. Who could have done such a thing to someone so pure? Such was Treya's deep love and relief at finally seeing her sister alive, that rage at the insult barely even registered. Then she was with her.

Throwing her arms about the slender frame, she pulled Alissa into a tight embrace, sinking to her knees without resistance from the other woman.

'Oh, my darling girl!' she breathed thickly against her hair, 'I cannot believe you are really here. I love you so much, Little Fawn, let us be away from here!'

Although the embrace had not be returned, she could feel Alissa's body trembling against her, the emotion undoubtedly overcoming her, 'Treya?' she whispered in return, 'It is like a dream that you are really here. Lennath said you would come but I did not believe it.'

'He was right,' Treya soothed, kissing all over the side of Alissa's head and face, unwilling to break her hold lest it all be a dream she may awaken from, 'I could not abandon you here. Now let us be away from his evil.'

'But you abandoned me before,' Alissa stated.

The question caught Treya off-balance slightly and she would have preferred to discuss these matters in safety, but her own immense guilt prompted her to engage immediately, 'No, no, Little Fawn. You were not abandoned. I did not know you had survived! It was kept from me for all these years but now I have come for you; we will never be apart again, I promise!'

'Why?'

The imagined scenario of reunion and rescue was descending into a confused conversation that Treya was struggling to understand. She pulled away slightly, holding Alissa by the shoulders and looking into her beautiful blue eyes but seeing little recognition within them.

'To keep you safe. To make us a family again. There is so much lost time to make up for, and Lennath must be stopped!'

'Lennath is my friend. He cares for me.'

'No, no, Alissa! This is not true!' Treya felt control slipping away, like she was talking to a stranger, 'Whatever lies he has told you are false! He is holding you here against your will, he is a danger to all the lands! I have to get you to safety and then we must stop him!'

Sudden darkness filled her sister's eyes, 'Do you mean like you stopped Kale?'

Treya felt like she had been punched in the gut, words would not form, and she shook her head dumbly instead.

'Did you think Kale was a threat, too? Did you think he would take me away? Is that why you ran a sword through his head?'

Treya's arms fell back to her sides as she sagged against the accusation. Kale Stanis had betrayed them in the face of the wizard Ramikain. He had cut Treya down with her own father's axe whilst under the influence of that evil necromancer. He had then found the strength to take his own life rather than hers. How had Alissa come to the conclusion that Treya had murdered him?

'Alissa, I did not… I mean, that is not the truth…'

'Would *you* now spin some lies? How your sword accidentally slipped into his skull? How you mistakenly executed my true love? And now you plot against one of the few people to have shown me kindness since that tragedy?'

'Please, my darling, I can explain all when we are away from here. You know I would never bring you harm. We have to go…'

'Stupid, murderous, Treya!' Alissa hissed, all softness vanishing from her voice, 'I am no little girl for you to covet any longer! I am all that I was destined to be! I wield power you could not imagine! You think you have come to save me? I brought you here! It was the payment I requested to help my real friend, Lennath. He did everything I asked to ensure you would be here before me now.'

'Alissa,' Treya sobbed as unbidden tears erupted at the words that felt so alien coming from the girl she had raised, 'please, I do not understand…'

'I wanted you here, all of you, because there is no pleasure in your deaths unless they are by my hand!'

Her arm suddenly whipped forward from under her robes and Treya felt the blade slice across her cheek, just below her eye and over the bridge of her nose. Hot blood mixed with tears down the left side of her face, but her shock was so deep she barely flinched. She could see delight filling Alissa's expression as she pulled back her arm and plunged the small knife into her eldest sister's stomach. Suddenly, Frost appeared, landing a powerful boot on Alissa's chest and throwing her back across the room, knife still in hand.

'Treya, we are undone! It is folly to remain here!' he bent to scoop her up, but she pushed him away, pressing her free hand over the narrow wound in her abdomen.

'No, Frost, she must come with us! I cannot leave her again. Take her by force if you must!'

'Aye, Treya,' he replied heavily, 'if that is your will. But first let me get you to our escape path. We will follow you once she is in hand.'

Ignoring any further resistance, he lifted her with one mighty arm and aided her back towards the drain.

As she darted across the chamber, Catalana picked out Bentram, his blades swept skilfully across each other in an effort to deflect or distract the axe-wielding warrior he faced, the unknown companion backing towards the main chamber doors with fear plastered on his face, and Lennath staring off to her left. Having seen Forge and Rayne struggling to compete with their single foe, she knew time was not their ally but could not resist following his gaze. She spotted Frost just as he kicked Alissa away from Treya and for a brief moment imagined he had betrayed them once again. Then she saw the blood and the way he delicately raised Treya from the floor and realised that it was not he but Alissa who was allied against them. She had no time to process the revelation, however, as she moved within striking distance of the Prince, her foe having now noticed her advance.

Dropping down to her knees and sliding in towards him at the last moment, she lashed out with her hunting knife, the blade pressed along her own forearm to ensure power and precision in the strike. Lennath nimbly hopped out of reach, bending forward to push his midriff out of range of her swing. She had hoped for this and bounced to her feet, cracking the top of her head into his chin and staggering him. Swinging with the unwieldy Warhammer, she found the clumsy strike parried aside by his blade before he swung a punch with his free hand. Cat' ducked her head back and slashed her knife against his outstretched arm, drawing blood and causing him to pull back. He smiled and she saw crimson on his teeth from her first strike.

'Very good, Catalana!' he praised, taking a moment to spit the excess blood from his mouth, 'You are just as agile and athletic as I remember! Although I must say, I preferred your use of such skills in the bedchamber rather than the battlefield.'

Rage filled her, generated by guilt or shame at her own actions in the past, she was unsure, but her focus was washed aside by the reminder that she had given herself to him to levy his support against Ramikain.

'Bastard!' she cried, 'You will never hope for such intimacy again!'

Leaping forward, she swung with the knife, feeling the bruising impact in her arm as he intercepted with his sword. With his weapon otherwise engaged, she tried to swing the heavy Warhammer up towards his head, but he caught the shaft and dragged the tool easily from her grip. Spinning away from him, she shifted the knife into a forward grip to provide more reach but was disappointed to achieve no contact. His smile remained fixed in place and drove her into another reckless attack. Rushing in to stab at his throat, she watched as he leaned out of reach and kicked out with one leg, connecting with her knee and pushing the limb back as she was running. Unable to place the foot in front of her, she collapsed forward into his arms. Gripping both of her wrists tightly, he dragged her into a tight embrace, with her own arms crossed in front of her while his belly pressed against her back. Leaning his head down like a lover to her ear, he took a long sniff of her.

'I can't deny you smell good,' he leered, 'but I think I'm done with you. Your sister is far superior to you in every respect, and so much more adventurous to lie with! Perhaps she will let me bed your other sisters before she kills you all; I could be the only living man to count all of the Fimarr sisters among his conquests!'

'You would have to live first!' she retorted, jamming her head back against him. She imagined the impact was only against his collar bones but was enough to relax his hold somewhat. She flicked her foot up to the rear as high as she could and heard the satisfying groan as she connected with his genitals. His grip released but he threw a wild punch as she tried to break away, the dull thud against the base of her skull leaving her light-headed and dizzy as she crashed to the ground.

'You little whore!' he gasped through the pain, 'I'll kill you myself for that.'

Bentram found himself backing further and further from his original target as the unrelenting salvo from his enemy continued. The power of the bodyguard's blows was phenomenal, and his own arms were beginning to labour under the onslaught. He could see that his allies were struggling, some already fallen or on the verge of defeat and he could not fathom how they could fail so badly. For years he had simply waited for General Frost to return, to lead the revolution and usurp Lennath; now that time had come, and they had fallen into a trap. There seemed little hope of escape, even less of victory and he wondered why his body didn't simply give up in the face of such futility. The axe swung around towards him again and he barely blocked it with both of his swords, pushing back with all his strength but to no avail.

Realising he had to gain some distance, he feinted forward with one blade, watching his opponent pull the heavy axe up to block and using the brief reprieve to dance himself several steps out of range. He watched as Catalana freed herself from Lennath's grip, but his eyes were drawn beyond them. Magin's body lay still, eyes wide open, clothing soaked with blood even as the pool around him continued to grow. They had been friends for years, had joined and trained together in the rebel army, had fought skirmishes with the Prince's men and even survived the attack in the forest when others fell about them, but now he was dead. Maybe that, too, was an omen, that they were destined to die together. An overhead strike arced down towards him and he side-stepped the deadly axe, only to be shoulder-barged to the ground as the bodyguard released his own weapon to land the secondary strike. Thrown to the ground, he had no chance to run as his enemy ripped the axe-head from where it had lodged in the stone floor nearby and raised it above his head to strike.

Bentram crossed his swords above his chest, praying he would have the strength to stop the blow and watching as the axe swung down towards him. It stopped before striking his blades and he looked up in amazement to see General Jacob Frost stood above him, muscles straining where he had caught the shaft in mid-blow. The bodyguard looked at the old man in utter surprise and tried to pull the weapon free, but Frost held tightly rivalling the younger man's strength. Bentram realised he was transfixed by the awesome sight and drove himself back into action. Sitting up, he stabbed forward with one blade, watching it plunge into his enemy's thigh. Grunting in pain, the warrior released his hold on the big axe and dropped back, pulling a hand-axe from his belt. Frost hefted his stolen weapon over one shoulder.

'Do you really want to face us both? With that?' the General asked gruffly, motioning toward the smaller weapon.

'I serve my lord with loyalty. You will not harm him while I live.'

Bentram found his feet and stood alongside Frost, 'We don't want your lord. Only Lennath matters.'

'He is royalty, and rebellious scum like you do not deserve to speak of such things, let alone bring them to be.'

He yelled an unintelligible war cry and charged forward, swinging his axe toward Frost as the perceived greater threat. The General dodged back out of range and dropped the large axe to the floor, headfirst. The handle stood upright and then fell towards the charging bodyguard who could not avoid it, winded where it jabbed into his gut. Bentram did not miss the opportunity, dragging one blade across the big man's throat before slicing down against the back of his neck with the other. The damage was enough to drop him instantly, his body twitching atop the fallen axe as his head lolled unnaturally off to the side with minimal tissue of the neck remaining to hold it in place.

Frost gripped his shoulder firmly, 'Bentram, get over to Treya. I need you to get her away from here now.'

'What about you, General?'

'I must capture Alissa, all of this is for nothing if she does not come with us.'

Bentram felt sudden courage and hope return to his heart. Nodding confirmation, he spotted where Treya was slumped near the drain she and Frost had arrived from and set off to help her.

Striking with all the grace and skill his years of experience had generated, Forge attempted a variety of attacks from his arsenal, finding each parried or dodged with minimal effort. Even when Rayne joined the conflict, as she had four times already, the Veer before him was able to hold his stance and counter every assault. Straker tried to take it as a compliment that Mozak had finally resorted to using his own thin, curved sword to deflect and parry every blow, but it felt every bit as though his opponent was simply toying with him. Of course, he remembered as sweat poured from his brow, that was not the Veer way. More likely he was simply gauging what Forge was capable of and maybe investigating any fighting style he may not already know himself. Such was the skill of the Veer, that Straker had not risked diverting his attention to see any of the others and felt he was probably lucky that most of the offence had been reserved for Rayne so far.

While another strike was swept easily aside, Mozak landing a light kick up into Forge's armpit and sending needles of fire along his arm, Rayne appeared once again, thin grappling rope held in one hand. Blood smeared her from several cuts across her face and he imagined there were far more hidden amongst her black clothing from the intensity of her private war with the Veer. Interestingly, he seemed to be neither bleeding nor sweating. Straker spotted him shifting weight onto his forward foot and knew he must be intending on intercepting Rayne's leap with a kick. Instinctively, he dropped to the floor in front of Mozak's rearmost leg and wrapped himself about it. Finally, something seemed to surprise the assassin and he was forced to throw up a hand to block instead. Rayne sprang off his planted front leg, somersaulting over him and looping the rope over his raised arm and head. Finishing her leap several feet beyond her foe, she dropped into a crouch and pulled hard against her makeshift noose, snapping Mozak's hand in against his throat. Still the Veer demonstrated no panic, sweeping his blade hand downwards blindly to remove the obstruction Forge was creating; Straker rolled away from the strike but felt the tip bite into his shoulder before he was clear.

Forcing himself upright again, ignoring the screaming resistance from his muscles, he watched as Rayne spun in place, pulling the rope tighter as it wrapped around her own body, desperately trying to strangle her opponent. Mozak looked to be out of options and Straker raised his scimitar to rush in for a killing blow but then the assassin amazed him again. Leaping backwards towards Rayne, he created slack in the line, causing her to widen her stance to avoid falling over, At the same time he pushed forward with his ensnared hand and whipped the noose over his head, allowing it to snap tight again on his forearm. Flipping over the rope so he was facing Rayne, he began to haul her in with her own line, the fact she had been wrapping it around her body now preventing her from breaking free. There seemed no hope of escape and Forge knew there were a hundred ways Mozak could kill her if she was within reach. He cried out in defiance and charged forward, maybe the distraction would be enough to allow his ally to escape, but the Veer did not even look round as he launched his deadly sword through the air. Only just able to bring his own weapon up in time, the curved blade clashed against the scimitar, slashing the front of his chest before its momentum was quelled and forcing him to the ground in his attempt to avoid the deadly missile.

Mozak was almost upon Rayne and Straker saw the flash of fear in her eyes. He glanced over to Lennath, seeing the Prince towering over Catalana, preparing to cut her down as she crawled away from him. Whistling loudly, attracting the attention of all those nearby, Forge hurled his last javelin directly at the Lustanian ruler. The Veer assassin was like lightning, releasing his hold of the rope, rolling clear of any counterstrike from Rayne and launching two blades across the room. Even as the two small knives clashed against his javelin with metallic twangs, the double impact just enough to knock the weapon away from the Prince, Mozak was moving at full tilt towards his employer. Arriving next to the surprised man, he swept him into an effortless shoulder carry and began to run towards the double doors. Forge knew he would return to finish them all once Lennath was safe, and they could not afford to waste the opportunity.

'Rayne! Cat'! No more! This is over!'

Kastani was crying. Everyone in the chamber was fighting. Some people were dying but everyone was getting hurt. This group were all her family or friends, even if she had never met them before. She knew if they all just came and played a game with her, then they would know that it was okay not to fight. She didn't know what to do; her mother was hurt, the aunts she had never met before were hurt and she just wanted it all to stop. When the second man died, she had burst into tears, not because of the traumatic and gory nature of his death but because she would never have a chance to get to know who he was. Maybe she could calm everyone down like she had for Audack earlier. As she tried to concentrate on that, she saw Mozak rushing over to snatch up Lennath and she panicked that he must have been hurt. Her emotions bubbled over her own ability to understand or restrain them, and she screamed out loud, just wishing that someone could stop it all.

Without warning the skylight suddenly crashed inwards, sending shards of red, green and purple stained glass raining down into the chamber, followed by an enormous mutated flying beast. Very insect-like, it sported six legs, each ending with vicious curved hooks. Instead of a standard proboscis, it sported several retractable mouths that seemed to snap back and forth of their own will. Huge translucent wings vibrated rapidly, generating an oppressive downwash and twin lashing tails snaked out behind it like the writhing tentacles of an octopus. Buzzing and screeching like a million wasps trapped in one place, the horrific sight landed in the chamber, throwing the white-haired warrior across the room in its wake, and creating a barrier between the two opposing forces with its body.

'Alissa, what are you doing?' she heard Lennath shouting, he must have thought her mother had called the thing. Despite the monster standing where it was, Kastani believed she could edge past it without being seen; if she could then she would be able to join Lennath, her mother and their new friend. Before she could move, the woman in black appeared before her.

'Listen to me, I never should have brought you here. You or your mother. It was a mistake, and I must make it right. Will you come with me?'

Kastani looked into her eyes. There was no deceit there, no treachery, and her words sounded genuine. But even if she hadn't meant to bring them to the palace, it had worked out very well, providing them better food and beds than they'd had in the Citadel and a new best friend in Lennath.

'No, thank-you,' she replied politely.

'In which case, I am very sorry for this,' the woman spoke sadly before whipping a black robe over Kastani's head and lifting her from the ground. Screaming, she could tell the sound was being muffled by her coverings but continued anyway.

Lennath stayed shielded behind Mozak as the huge flying terror stood intimidatingly before them.

'Should I destroy it?' Mozak offered.

'And remove one of our few flying beasts? I think not! Can you get past it, take out the Fimarrs on the other side?' Lennath whispered back, keen that Gallth should not overhear.

'Certainly, but if it turned on you then I would not be able to protect you.'

The Prince considered his own plan. He had known that the small party who were planning on attacking could not defeat Mozak. He had wanted to witness their defeat first-hand and Alissa had insisted on killing her own kin. He was certain, had this beast not decided to intervene, that his machinations would have proven successful. He was not sure if the monster had even been called by Alissa for some reason, after all, it was remaining reasonably calm and those not under her control were usually filled with bestial rage. Looking over at the young woman, he noticed she was on her feet and heading towards the creature. Reaching out her hand, she stroked one of its chitinous legs and it suddenly spread its wings and fled the chamber once more. The powerful gust of air its departure created spat Alissa back across the room, and Mozak moved like lightning to intercept her slide and ease her back over to them. Lennath scoured the room but saw no sign of his foes.

'Why did you bring that thing here, Alissa?' he hissed, frustration boiling over at her.

'Wasn't it beautiful?' she replied, 'soaring above the trees and buildings, free of all restraints.'

'No! Enough of this! Answer my question; you have allowed our enemies to escape, the sisters you wanted dead still live. Why have you done this!'

She smiled up at him and pushed herself into his arms, forcing a passionate kiss upon him.

'Fear not, Sire,' Mozak spoke in hushed tones, 'they are soundly beaten. Their options are limited, and the defences removed to allow their access will be restored. As an added boon they killed Gallth's man, leaving him alone and vulnerable. There is no loss here.'

Lennath broke from the kiss. Looking round at his brother, face still a mask of fear where he cowered by the sealed doors, he realised that Mozak was right. Kissing Alissa again and finding her fiercely reciprocal, he motioned towards the exit. 'You are right, Mozak,' he said, 'unlock the doors and get some people here to clean up this mess.

'My Lord?' a voice floated to them, weak and full of strained effort, 'My Lord, please can somebody help me? I don't know how much longer I can hold on.'

Lennath tried to determine where the sound was coming from and his eyes finally settled on the mutation pit.

'Oh,' he added, 'and get Audack out of there...'

Chapter 9

Cold damp mud smothered her cheek, soothing the raging fire that emanated from the open wound. Lying on her side, Treya could see the round opening of the drainage tunnel they had just exited, realising that she had no memory of her journey here. Before her, Bentram knelt in the sodden filth on the bank of the river, one side of his clothes covered in blood, and she wondered if he had been injured badly during the fight. His mouth was moving, and concern was plastered on his face, but the only sound she could hear was the drumming of her own heartbeat; it seemed oddly slow, considering.

Rolling onto her back to relieve an uncomfortable pressure below her ribs, agony ripped through her and she remembered the knife wound. A distraught sob escaped her, but it had nothing to do with the pain; Alissa had stabbed her, tried to kill her, and the vivid image of that tore her heart. Bentram appeared above her again but she could still not make out his words; new weight against her stomach indicated he was trying to tend to the damage there. It suddenly occurred to her that the blood covering her companion was probably hers; perhaps she was dying. With his ministrations complete, she felt him hook his hands under her armpits and drag her away from the flowing water beside them and over against the grassy bank where it rose to the wild field above. More silent words flowed from him as he planted a comforting hand, now also plastered in her blood, on her shoulder and drew one of his twin blades. She watched him make his way back towards the drainage tunnel, only to leap backwards as someone else emerged.

Catalana burst forward and dropped to her knees where Treya had been lying moments before, panting from her efforts, tears streaming from her eyes. Behind her came Forge, bloodied but strong, and the pain in her chest eased at the sight of him. The second he spotted her, he rushed forward, pulling her into a tight embrace. At her pained groans, he eased away and examined her injuries with great concern. All at once her hearing returned, but only on the side not caked in mud.

'My love! These wounds are grave, we must get you to help as soon as possible.'

She reached up weakly and touched his face, 'She did this, Straker. Alissa did this. Why would she do this?'

'Shhh, Treya, there is time for such questions later. Now we must look after you; this filth has staunched the bleeding but runs the risk of generating infection. Stay here a moment.'

'Don't leave me,' she pleaded, trying to hold onto his arm but finding her grip too weak to restrain him, 'I need you…'

He smiled back at her as he moved over to the river, but the expression was full of fear. She coughed and tasted more blood in her mouth, leaning to one side, she spat a glob of bright red out onto the grass at her side. Returning, Forge used a sodden rag to clean the mud from her face and she could see the glaze in his eyes, threatening tears, causing her to wonder how bad the cuts must look.

'Did you kill the Veer? Did Lennath fall? Where are the others?' she forced out the questions amid sharp breaths as he tended to the raw flesh on her face.

'Kill the Veer?' he replied incredulously, 'No my sweet lady, it is only by sheer fortune that I am here with you now. As I warned, we must avoid the Veer in future; we were fortunate that he was not trying to kill us.'

'Lennath still lives!' Catalana added mournfully from where she knelt, 'He set all this in motion! We were duped into walking straight into his lair; if not for that monster's arrival, he would have…' she stopped short.

'Monster?' Treya murmured.

'Later, my darling,' Forge soothed, emotion thick in his voice as he tried to clean and cover the savage cuts on her face, 'we can make sense of everything later.'

'There may not be a later lest we away from here now!' cried Frost as he barrelled from the tunnel, 'The enemy will undoubtedly soon be upon us and we have no way to tell from where. There is precious little time to waste!'

'Not until these wounds are bound!' Forge snapped sharply, an edge in his voice that was rarely heard, 'If any happen upon us before then, they will die.'

She reached up and squeezed his arm as tightly as she could, but her gaze rested on the latest arrival. Frost, taking deep breaths, hands on his hips, scanning the area intently for signs of ambush. She remembered he had intervened, saved her from a fatal blow, ensured she got to safety and promised to go back for Alissa.

'Where is she, Frost?' she stammered as new pain lanced through her while Forge began work on her side wound, 'Where is Alissa?'

The old warrior failed to meet her gaze, 'The beast, it arrived before I could get to her. I was only just able to leap clear or I would have been crushed. She was not harmed, I am certain.'

'But she is not here with us, either? So, this was all for nothing?' she wanted to keep the tremor from her voice but failed.

'No, Treya, this is not for nothing! Let me finish here and I will go back for her; I will bring her back, I promise you!' Straker vowed, intensity bleeding into concern as he spoke.

'No level of self-confidence would make that statement come true, Straker Forge,' Frost countered sadly, 'I know much of your renown but remember we were permitted entry this time and the enemy's intent was to ensnare us, not kill us. There is no way you could succeed; there is no way all of us combined could succeed.'

'I think perhaps you underestimate me, old man,' Forge replied, the usual underlying mirth absent, 'I will…'

'No, Straker,' Treya conceded, 'he is right. It is over.'

'So, what do we do now?' Catalana asked desperately, staggering over to sit beside her injured sister, 'How can we hope to stop all this?'

'I don't know, Cat', maybe it really is over,' she replied, reaching out and stroking her sister's face gently, 'perhaps all is truly lost.'

'That does not sound like a very Fimarr thing to say,' Rayne stated as she joined them from the tunnel, captured bundle under her arm, 'and it does not fit well with my reputation.'

'Rayne, you survived!' Forge exclaimed, 'In the confusion I thought you were left behind; with that assassin's skill, I assumed the worst…'

'You are correct, I cannot defeat Mozak, he is my superior in every way. Fortunately, he had no intention of killing me. The unexpected interruption also allowed me to claim a prize of our own.'

She placed the package carefully on the ground and pulled the covering free, revealing a very frightened Kastani.

'We may have failed to capture Alissa, but all hope is not lost.'

Treya regarded the little girl before her, trembling lip pre-empting a screaming fit to come if her own children were anything to go by, and felt an incredible pang of loss at having never met her niece before.

'Hello, little one,' she managed, hiding her pain to bring warmth into her voice, 'are you unharmed?'

'Of course she is, do you think I…' Rayne began to retort but a gesture from Frost encouraged her to silence.

Kastani darted terrified eyes between those around her, 'I'm Kastani,' she said quietly, 'I didn't mean to be spying on you. I am very sorry and I will not do it again. Can you take me back to mother and Lennath now?'

'No, we cannot, Kastani,' Treya answered, keeping her tone gentle, 'your mother is very confused right now, and has been doing bad things. We wanted to bring her with us, to help her understand how to make things right, but we failed. They would not let us return now, even to bring you back to them. You will need to come with us, so that we can keep you safe. Now it is my turn to say sorry to you; this is not what I wanted to happen, no child should be forced away from their parent.'

'I think it will be okay,' Kastani suggested, 'I can tell them that you are all very nice, and then you can be friends. If we go right now, I promise I will show you how to play gems, too!'

'Enough of this!' the strained cry came from Bentram, who had silently watched events unfolding, 'I recognise that there are family affairs in play here and we have met with defeat at the hands of the enemy. But this was one battle and, while we draw breath, the war is not over! We must follow the General's advice, flee from here and regroup; we cannot know what options are available until we assess them in an environment of calm. Right now, we leave ourselves exposed and at risk and I will not die so easily without the chance to claim vengeance for my friends.'

All had turned to him in surprise, but his words held validity. Treya nodded acknowledgement to him and tried to stand, only achieving her goal through the help of Catalana and Straker.

'You are right, Bentram, soldiers could be pursuing us through that tunnel as we speak, and we must not let them find us here.'

'From the drain?' Rayne asked, 'No fear there; I noticed a weakened support on my way out and collapsed it. It will take many hours to clear, any pursuit must surely be above ground but there will be no uncertainty over where to find us; there were few side-tunnels along the way so this is probably the outlet where they expect us to be.'

'Rayne, find us a route that will keep us concealed, we must get back to the forest and find our steeds, or new ones to ride. Returning to Rennicksburg is our best option; we will reunite with the others and make new plans. Maybe Zendar has more to offer us…'

'Forgive me, Treya, but what are you talking about?' Frost commented gruffly, 'Returning to your home is tactically naïve and generates an unnecessary delay! We have been given the directions to find this mystical Rondure, we need four Fimarrs to claim it and defeat our enemies. Well, we have four Fimarrs right here! The enemy has been ahead of us from the start but maybe now we have the chance to turn those tables!'

She had already begun to hobble away with support but squeezed Catalana's shoulder to pause and turn back to the one-eyed veteran, 'I hope you are not suggesting that Kastani be used as a substitute for Alissa?'

'Please, Treya, do not be foolish, here!' he insisted, gesturing to the shivering child on the ground, 'I know she is your blood, but she was also unknown to you until mere days ago! I am not suggesting using your own children, or placing this one in danger if it can be avoided. But you must see sense, the fate of the entire land could be resting on this choice; do not let sentimentality destroy us all!'

She eased her companions away, feeling the agony of carrying her own weight but knowing the importance of demonstrating strength in that moment, 'I am grateful to you, Jacob Frost, for you saved my life this day. For that I release you from any debt you may feel towards me or my family. This little girl, Kastani, is not only innocent in all of this, but she is kin, no different to Joseff and Melody; I will not risk their lives and I will not risk hers. Any suggestion of doing so will not end well for you, do you understand?'

'I do not seek hostility between us, Treya,' he responded, placatingly, 'but you must hear the insanity of your own words. We know what must be done, we have lost lives in trying to make it possible, and the very opportunity now lies in our laps! There is no other way, I know you see that. Do not make a decision now that you will regret.'

'I am not,' she replied with certainty, 'and if you cannot see that then you have no need to remain with us. Neither you nor Bentram are beholden to this situation and have given so much of yourselves to this cause; I release you both.'

'I will not leave,' Bentram blurted out, 'Overthrowing Lennath has been my goal for many years; the threat he now poses makes his destruction ever more pressing. You have my fealty, and I will adhere to whatever plan you determine.'

The outburst was surprising but welcome and she was pleased at the grimace of annoyance that flashed across Frost's face.

'I do not wish to leave, I merely want you to see sense. If there was another option then I would take it, but there is not!'

'Your choice is made then. Farewell, Jacob Frost,' she managed just before staggering under a wave of light-headedness. Straker was instantly with her again, Catalana taking the weight on the other side.

'Frost, bring the girl, make sure no harm befalls her,' Straker barked at him, countermanding Treya's decree.

'This is not settled, Forge, she must be made to see sense!' Frost grunted, following the instructions despite his assertions, and helping the little girl to her feet.

'Straker!' Treya chided, hearing her words as a pained whisper, 'What are you doing? I gave him a choice and he took it.'

'No, you gave him an ultimatum based on the need to use Kastani. But there is another option.'

'What are you talking about? We have no way to know that without consulting Zendar.'

'This should wait until Rennicksburg, when we are all together, when you have proper medical care.'

'No, Straker!' she snapped, pushing him away and hearing a grunt of strain as her sister took her full weight, 'What is it you know? Is this yet another secret you have withheld from me?'

He sighed, looking sadly into her eyes before forcing himself under her arm again, 'Aye, my love, yet another secret that I vowed never to reveal. It weighs heavy on my heart to have held it from you.'

'Enough of this avoidance, spit it out!'

'It is just… that is, there may… there is a chance that there is another who can help us.'

'What other? And how?' she asked, suspicion rising.

'I believe there is another child of Fimarr.'

The words echoed through her mind and she heard the gasp of shock from Catalana mirroring her own astoundment.

A fresh breeze brought a welcome contrast to the sun beating down upon him as he picked his way through the trees towards the beach. The fishing coracle over his shoulder had made progress slow with all the natural obstacles in his way, but better slow than seen he had decided. Using the large paddle held in his other hand, he eased some low-hanging branches aside and saw the light sands open out before him. He had made the entire journey from the fishing lakes to this cove undetected which made him question his own motives; if his plan was for the benefit of his people, then why was he so keen to keep it hidden from the Elders?

Stepping out onto the beach, he felt the increased temperature beneath him and marvelled at how the sand retained so much more heat than grass or earth. As he neared the water's edge, he dropped the coracle unceremoniously and wedged the paddle down into the ground. With so many unknowns ahead of him, he wanted to be as prepared as possible which meant ensuring both mental and physical regimes be completed. Turning to begin a series of slow and controlled stretches, he looked out over the scene about him. Large areas of the beach were still stained with the blood of their opponents, now a ruddy brown in colour as opposed to the scarlets and crimsons of the battle itself. The bodies had been cleared and burned in the Passaging Pits, a decision made by the High Auger amid some dissent; why should these invaders be privileged to such death-rites? The attitude of the

Elders towards recent events left him puzzled, but he had to have faith that their truth was the correct one. Even now they, and the shrine servitors, spent whole days examining and studying the weapons and provisions of their enemies, trying to glean something of their nature or motivations. Mazt fully understood the direction of the High Auger, and the justification behind his disappointment following the attack, but he could not comprehend how such a weak race represented a realistic threat to them. Not unless they were millions in number. Which was what he wanted to find out.

Feeling all hints of stiffness removed from his muscles, he noticed sunlight glinting off metal further along the beach. Allowing himself this one distraction, he jogged over towards the mystery object and retrieved it from its partial burial. It was a small book with a copper plaque adorning the front and he ruffled the pages to find them water-damaged, the writing obscured. The plate on the front could still be read where it had been engraved.

Gambit Glider. Merchant Trading Vessel. Conduct and Business Log.

Trading vessel. So perhaps the men they had fought were not warriors at all, just travelling barterers; although the likelihood that they had no intentions to steal or pillage was slim. The Boundary had kept them safe from such incursions all this time, their history and laws were built around protecting them from an unknown threat beyond, how else were they expected to interpret these strangers' arrival? He took a deep breath and released it slowly; he needed body and mind at ease, yet he had never had so many unanswered questions within him.

'Mazt Kae-Taqar!' a familiar voice rang out towards him and he dropped the book as he jumped at the sudden sound. He turned to see Keris running in his direction.

'Well met, Keris!' he called out warmly, 'What are you doing here?'

'I would ask the same of you, Mazt,' she replied with a hint of disgruntlement, 'what is your truth?'

'Nought that concerns you,' he answered, more sharply than intended, 'I thought we had agreed on separate patrols this day. This is my allocated zone.'

'Perhaps such strange decisions are what led me to you. You have been distant since the battle here and I believe I startled you just now. What has happened to your awareness?'

He smiled but knew the expression must look awkward, 'Indeed you did catch me by surprise; my focus has been on the future and not the present. But you are not a threat to me, so no harm is done.'

'No threat?' she raised an eyebrow questioningly but allowed the unintentional sleight to pass, 'What have you there?'

'Nothing,' he blurted before wondering why he would try and hide his discovery, 'I mean, it is of no use, a book, but all entries are destroyed by that salty water, I intend to pass it to the Elders at the earliest convenience.'

As if to prove the point, he retrieved the journal and proffered it to her.

Keris planted her hands on her hips, 'Not that trifling artifact,' she stated, pointing back along the beach, 'what is that doing here?'

'Oh, the coracle,' he had hoped the small craft had gone unnoticed, 'I intend to use it, to paddle out to the Boundary and beyond.'

Horror filled her eyes and she punched him hard in the chest, 'You fool, Mazt! You cannot do such a thing! None may pass the Boundary; none have ever tried! It keeps us safe from the dangers beyond. Why would you contemplate such a thing?'

'Keris, open your eyes to my truth; the Boundary is not fulfilling the prophecy, it recedes from us every day and has already allowed a threat to arrive among us. If that giant canoe can reach through in this direction then I can do so in the other. We cannot simply hide here and wait for something else to come for us; I need to see our enemies for myself, to know their strength and number. This is our truth.'

His words brought her pause, and he could see her processing what had been said against all that she had known.

'The Boundary is our security, blessed to us by the gods; questioning the truth of generations is tantamount to blasphemy. Why would you say such things before me? I must report your wavering truth and you will be removed as a Guardian!'

He could hear restrained emotion in her voice and noted the watery look to her eyes. He reached out and placed a hand on her shoulder, 'Yes, you must do this, but I believe you will not. I do not challenge the gods, nor the sacred texts, nor the words of the Elders! All those things have been right and true for as long as any have known. But these events are a defiance to all of that; not history nor prophecy has made mention of the Boundary's movement. Dangers and threats from beyond are suggested at length but no clarity has ever been secured; were these men the sum total of that, or merely an advanced warning as the High Auger suggests? I am a Guardian, I am you leader but most importantly I am your friend. Can you not find confidence in my truth?'

A long silence dragged out between them and she wiped a single tear from the corner of her eye before it spilled of its own accord, 'I will share my truth with you, Mazt Kae-Taqar. You are the greatest of us and I would accompany you into certain death if that is what you asked. I have often dreamed of a different path, where we were simple citizens rather than defenders of our people, and in those thoughts we are partnered in all things. But more than all this, my truth is one of fear; I see, as you do, that there must be more to our ancient writings than this simple incursion, sometimes I wish we could read them ourselves instead of having them orated by servitors or Elders. Such thoughts bring anger at myself, what reason have I to believe there is more than I am being told? It makes me wonder that the changes to the Boundary are more than physical, that they are affecting my mind; if that is so, then does that effect spread to all others as well? Are any of us in our right minds? Thus, making a choice, any choice, has become a decision of great magnitude.'

'I value your truth, Keris San-Zukat, and your dreams are mere reflections of my own. But there is no place here for what may have been. Think on my truth from your position as a Guardian. We have no knowledge of our foes, no clues as to their time or mode of invasion, no way to effectively plan or prepare for the predicted attack. I am negligent if I do not seek these things out; perhaps there is even a way for me to avert any assault before it occurs. While we hide here, we will never know.'

'I do see your truth, but the Elders will not. If you go out there, you may be killed, or lost to us in some other way; this would be a tragedy to me and a disruption to the Guardians such as has never been seen before. I will not inform any of your actions, not unless I must. I will remain here until you return but have two caveats for my silence.'

Mazt set his jaw, he doubted he would have even listened to such demands from any other person, 'Continue, Keris, on what does your support depend?'

'I will remain here for three days; you must return and report what you have learned by then and we will beg forgiveness from the Elders for our actions. And I must insist that you leave your Palmstone behind.'

'What?' he bellowed before he could control himself, noticing that Keris did not even flinch, 'The Palmstones are blessed to us in the most sacred of manners, we are beholden to never remove them! You speak of my decision to be blasphemous, then how is your request any different?'

'The truths we are understanding now are all blasphemy, I am only trying to protect our people as you are. If you transit beyond the Boundary and do not return, the Palmstone would be lost to us, or worse, turned against us by the enemy…'

'These pitiful wretches have neither the strength nor will to wield the Palmstones!' he interrupted in outrage.

'Nevertheless,' she continued, 'I must insist. You have already asserted that you do not know what is out there, we must not make assumptions and underestimate the enemy.'

He gritted his teeth, but his voice was calm when he continued, 'Your truth is pure. I have no place to argue your words.'

They returned to his small boat in silence and Mazt delicately unfastened each of the rings that held the Palmstone in place upon his hand. Fighting back a panic welling within him, he gingerly passed the device to his closest companion.

'All I am, I now entrust to you,' he said reverently.

'I will protect this as I would protect you,' she replied.

A lump had formed in his throat, so he turned away and gathered up coracle and paddle once more, traversing the remaining distance to the water and beyond, until the cool brine was up to his thighs. Placing his craft down to bobble gently on the surface, he carefully hopped in and allowed himself to achieve balance before beginning to paddle. His back and arms were powerfully muscled and he quickly generated startling momentum with long strokes, alternating from side-to-side to maintain a straight path to his goal. Without looking back, he knew Keris was watching him intently and wondered if her heart was filled with pride or fear. He considered himself to be courageous but remembered the teachings of his preceptor; courage was not a lack of fear, just the ability to act in the face of fear.

As the shimmering Boundary drew closer, he studied the water around him; it was far clearer than it appeared from the shore and he could see the sands many yards beneath the surface, fish scattering this way and that as his coracle passed above. Everything shone with an aqua-green hue and there was no way to ignore the beautiful majesty of the sight. It was a huge contrast to the fishing lakes inland, where blue and brown water was so murky and opaque that you could only see mere inches into it. He recalled diving in once, to free a net caught upon spiny weed at the silty bottom, and had been required to operate solely by touch, such was the lack of vision when submerged. He idly wondered how far he could see if he swam within these crystal waters, but the thoughts dispersed as he passed over the wreck.

The vessel of their enemies must have been more than a hundred yards beneath the surface, but its shattered frame was clearly visible, wisps of the white sheets waving off to the side as if blown by an underwater breeze. He recognised that this expanse of water, just like the lakes, must have its own currents and marvelled at the fish and creatures already casually utilising the sunken vehicle as their home. There were no signs of the former inhabitants and he wondered if they had been eaten by predators, floated beyond sight, or somehow survived to gain access to his lands. There had been nothing to suggest the latter were true, but he decided that a thorough search for signs of any survivors would be conducted upon his return.

Finally, he closed on the Boundary and allowed the coracle to slow. He could not decide if approaching at high speed would be more beneficial, or even necessary, but it seemed to make sense, just in case there were some resistance. Craning his head to look back, he could see Keris watching from the shore, little more than a tiny silhouette at this distance. He threw one confident wave to her, but it was not returned. Taking a deep breath, he began to paddle faster and harder than before, building up speed as he approached the shimmering wall before him. As the tip of the coracle reached the translucent edge of the Boundary, he unconsciously held his breath and closed his eyes. A sudden wave of cold washed over him as he penetrated the edge and then pressure struck him, like the hardest blow ever laid upon him, and he was thrown backwards with great force. Flying through the air in an uncontrolled arc, he felt his arms and legs flailing in surprise and opened his eyes just in time to see the water's surface racing towards him. Crashing beneath the waves, he held his breath and then frantically began to swim back to the surface. Opening his eyes, he saw he had plummeted almost thirty yards down. Bursting back into the air, he drew in a noisy lungful of air and allowed himself a few moments of treading water to recover.

Looking towards the Boundary, he could see it almost forty yards from his current position; he had been thrown a significant distance it seemed. The coracle was gone, he assumed the craft had continued through the Boundary without him, and there was likewise no sign of the paddle. As his breathing calmed again, he thought he could hear Keris' voice carrying to him and hoisted an arm into the air to indicate he was well. After a few more moments, he shifted his limbs into action and ploughed back through the water to the distant beach.

Keris was to him instantly as he clambered from the salty water, offering assistance that he brushed aside; the swim had been little more than a good daily training regime.

'What happened, Mazt?' she asked urgently.

'The Boundary would not allow me passage,' he stated, 'I could not progress beyond its limit.'

'That makes no sense,' she argued, 'Our enemies have penetrated without ill effect, how could you not achieve this same feat?'

'You ask for a truth I cannot answer,' he snapped, immediately offering some suppositions to make up for his irritability, 'Perhaps my vessel was too small, or maybe the invaders know of some spell or ritual required to pass. It is even possible that the Boundary is a one-way door of some sort.'

'But Mazt, that makes no sense. Why would the Boundary prevent us from passing but not our enemies from entering? How does that protect us?'

'It does not,' he said soberly, sudden concern filling his chest, 'but it does contain us.'

'But that would suggest…' she could not finish the thought.

'That it was created not by a benefactor but by a jailor.'

A sharp intake of breath was her only response and they stood side-by-side looking out at the Boundary for several minutes in silence. He wondered if his anxieties had affected his perception, but the shimmering and warm glow always associated with the mystical safeguard seemed to have dulled. Keris' fingers brushed against his own and he turned to admonish her for such a display of affection until he realised she was placing the Palmstone back in his hand.

'What do we do, now?' she asked aloud, eyes remaining fixed out over the water.

Mazt slipped his blessed artifact back into place and spoke his truth, 'I do not know.'

Gallth tapped his fingers nervously against the side of the silver and crystal goblet in his hands. It was still full as he had failed to take a sip since having it served to him, and he watched the light from the roaring fire dance across the surface, creating a mosaic of plum and fuchsia. Lustanian wine was the best in the Five Kingdoms, something he never admitted to Lennath, and he would not normally be so reticent to drink his fill but right now he had no appetite for such things. Even the heat from the fireplace beside him seemed to be ethereal; despite his proximity, no warmth was spreading through him. The battle he had witnessed played over in his mind and he could not erase the knowledge that he had come so close to death; if the intruders had been victorious, he would no longer exist. Another shiver ran through him and he finally tipped the goblet to his lips, taking only the smallest of sips, but finding some comfort in the rich flavour. His eyes wandered to the serving girl standing beside the drinks cabinet, young, buxom and with a fresh-faced beauty; normally he would demand her attendance in his bedchambers, but even that felt beyond him right now.

The main door crashed open and he jumped bodily from the chair, dropping his goblet and staring dumbly as it shattered on the smooth stone of the greeting room floor. Immediately, the girl was rushing towards him to attend to the mess, but his attention was fixed on the new arrivals. Lennath had entered with a disposition of agitation with his henchman, Mozak he recalled, following serenely behind him. The tall protector had demonstrated fantastic levels of skill during the combat and, if Gallth's own man, Garby, had survived, he would easily be the superior. He wondered where Lennath had found such a skilled defender and if there were more to be had. His sibling had also surprised him with his own skill and willingness to enter the fray; there had been little more than skirmishes fought anywhere in the Five Kingdoms since the brothers had taken their thrones and he could recall none of them ever being involved directly. He had never personally been in combat, nor even attended a battle, and he could not help but feel a grudging respect for how well Lennath had handled things. But he had to put all that aside for the time being; his suspicions had been proven correct and there was something afoot in Lustania. He had to find out what it was but with caution; he was now all alone in his brother's palace and, despite the fact he could not simply be killed without rousing his father's retribution, he did not wish to force Lennath's hand into making that very sacrifice.

'…how completely useless my army appears to be! They were injured and in disarray, trapped in the very tunnels of my own home and yet they have vanished? It is unacceptable! What of your men, Mozak, why are they not bringing me the heads of my enemies?' Lennath was ranting.

'My people have been stationed as guardians of this fortress and hunters beyond your borders. I can set the palace-bound Veer in pursuit if you wish, but it would leave you vulnerable here. Likewise, I can recall those tracking the families and associates of the Fimarrs, but this could lead to more avenues of help for your foes. I would recommend calm, they will need to seek out more help and when they do, my people will execute them. I receive reports by kestrel every five days. I am certain that I will receive notification of their deaths within fifteen.' Mozak's reply was devoid of emotion.

Lennath seemed to calm a little as he heard the facts provided to him, 'No, no, Mozak, you are correct in your thinking. I do not doubt the capability of the Veer, I am simply irritated at the good fortune our enemies have been granted. Of course, the current plan is more than adequate and I do not wish to disrupt the direction your people are following, we were just so close!'

'This is true, but your enemies would be dead if you had not ordered my restraint. I would caution pampering to the wishes of your consort in future; it is she who has allowed their threat to perpetuate.'

'Too far, Mozak; do not cast sleights at Alissa. Her wishes are driven from pain and emotional injury, things I have no doubt you do not understand. However, should we face the Fimarr sisters in person again, you have my leave to slay them all; I will beg her forgiveness afterwards.'

Mozak did not rise to Lennath's implied threat and simply nodded his understanding before taking up a relaxed stance next to a large bookcase. Gallth noticed it was equidistant between both entrances to the room. Lennath turned to face him, almost as if he had not realised his brother was present despite having sent him there immediately after the battle had ended, and a concerned smile spread across his face.

'Gallth, brother, how are you feeling? It seems you have regained some colour; you were white as a sheet when I last saw you! You have had an accident there? No matter, Jasta will clean it up and get you a fresh drink; Altisberg Red, the best I have in the cellar!'

'Don't play concern for me, Lennath, I know it is not sincere. Have you forgotten that I have been sent to report back on you? These events have occurred upon my arrival, speaking ill of your intentions and painting you as a liar for all you have said before!'

Lennath delivered a pained expression, which Gallth assumed to be fake, as he took the seat closest to him, 'Come now, Gallth, do not make this a personal matter. We have both just been through a traumatic event and some irrational thoughts are bound to result from that. Perhaps we should just discuss this matter so I can clarify things for you?'

'Clarify?' Gallth asked incredulously, watching the young maid scurrying away with a small pail filled with broken crystal, 'Are you really suggesting that there is some way you can talk your way out of this? I have seen the monsters in your own home! I have seen renowned heroes attempting to kill you! How do you propose to explain that away!'

Lennath sighed and slumped back in his seat, 'Yes, Gallth, I suppose it does look bad from an outside perspective. Can I beg of you to listen, if only for the next few moments, before you cast judgement upon me?'

Gallth studied his brother closely and it was hard to see deceit in his face; could there be some genuine explanation for all he had seen? What was the alternative? He would report back to the King and Lennath would be removed from his throne, maybe even executed for treason. And then what? Lustania thrown into disarray? Or devolved amongst the brothers? And if Porthus was found to be dead as well, would it become the Three Kingdoms amid civil disarray and political uproar? He shook his head to clear the concerns. No, a few moments was not much to ask if it could divert such chaos.

'Very well, brother,' he said magnanimously, 'I will hear your words, but I cannot see how you can absolve what I have witnessed.'

Lennath smiled warmly, 'Thank-you, Gallth, I appreciate the show of faith. So, where do I begin? Maybe the creatures, or how about the Fimarrs? How will this make most sense to you?'

Gallth snorted irritably, 'I would suggest start at the beginning, but time is finite! Address the most incriminating elements first, if your explanations hold water then maybe we can examine things further.'

'Very well,' Lennath agreed, a twinkle of excitement suddenly in his eye, 'let me begin with the Fimarrs. You know them as heroes; indeed, they were nothing less than that when I last encountered them. They saved this land, all lands, when they defeated the wizard Ramikain, but I must confide that they were nothing less than dragged into that situation and their true morals may well be questionable. One of them is a notorious assassin, another a prostitute; have no doubt that the stories have moulded them into something more than reality…'

'But they did destroy that necromancer at great personal cost. Why do you now suggest they are villains?'

'This is something I do not fully understand myself, so be open to my interpretation. When they faced the evil wizard in his Black Citadel, something happened to them, an influence, perhaps, or a trace of his evil invading them. Only one remained pure and safe; the youngest sister Alissa Fimarr.'

'The Alissa in that chamber? Your new consort?'

'Indeed, consort and the woman I love. She alone remained untainted and this resulted in her own family turning on her, imprisoning her in the ruins of the Black Citadel for years. It was only by chance that I happened upon information leading me to this revelation; with what the Kingdoms owed that family, I could not allow such a travesty to continue so I enacted a rescue and brought her here. She was whole-heartedly grateful to me and it was not long before we had realised our depth of feeling for one another; I vowed then to keep her safe from that day forward. Sure enough, it was not long before the other sisters discovered my actions and have plotted against me ever since; they even recruited a small army with my treacherous former General at its head.'

'The Fimarrs have vowed a vengeance against you? To get to their sister? And what of her actions; I am not blind, Lennath, I saw her stab her kin, and she wants to execute them herself? You expect me to believe she is the injured party?'

'Put yourself in her position, Gallth, if we had locked you away with no hope of freedom for years and then started a campaign of violence against the only person who had offered you freedom and hope, where would your mind be? Perhaps I am wrong to allow her to exact a righteous justice against her sisters, but I can see no way to end the threat other than through their deaths.'

Gallth took a deep breath. The story sounded far-fetched but was certainly not an impossibility; who knew what power to corrupt the wizard Ramikain had wielded? As Jasta returned with a fresh drink, and a brandy for Lennath, he took a larger swig before replying, 'Very well, Lennath, your story may be plausible, if unlikely, but fails to address the original concerns that brought us to your door. What is your explanation for these monstrosities that terrorise the lands?'

'Yes, I see now that my conduct in those matters has allowed suspicion to spiral out of control. Let me explain as best I can. The creatures are also part of Ramikain's legacy, and many strayed into Lustania after his downfall. At first I had them slain on sight, a feat in itself, but there always seemed to be more. I had the idea to capture and restrain them here under the palace for two reasons, I believed studying them may reveal a way to undo the mutation afflicting them or, if they could be trained, I could use them to defend the people from the other monsters still out there; like against like. Sadly, both proved unachievable. And there was a further effect I had not anticipated; those creatures still wild seemed to understand they were being hunted and moved further afield, crossing the borders to the other Kingdoms.'

'If this were true, why did you not declare it so? Why did you lie instead of asking us for support?' Gallth demanded.

'Really, Gallth? You really feel this would have been forthcoming? Hindsight is wonderful but remember how our interactions have always gone in the past. All I would have received, as I did with the story I felt was required, would be anger and recrimination. My lie was a mistake, I see that now, but I believed I could resolve the situation myself. Regardless, I cannot change the past and right now I am simply trying to provide the answers you seek.'

'But you are not providing answers, just raising more questions! Why have you not destroyed these things if they cannot be cured or trained? How has one come to assault the heart of your palace?'

Lennath seemed suddenly very pleased with himself and leapt to his feet, pacing before the fire as he spoke, 'This is the most wonderful of coincidences, brother. I brought Alissa here for her safety, but she has demonstrated to me a fine way to repay that kindness. She is attuned to these things, magically perhaps, or as a result of her time in the Citadel, I do not know for sure. But she has been able to curb their rage, direct their aggression towards others of their kind and, I believe, summon them to defend her in times of crisis. These abilities are only in their infancy but, if she can grow stronger, then perhaps we can eradicate the wild beasts completely, defeat the Fimarrs and, further still, provide a defence to the Five Kingdoms that no aggressor would dare face!'

Gallth felt a deep anxiety spreading through him but tried to keep his voice level as he spoke, 'So she is a witch? And you can control these beasts after all? Why would you tell me this when it seems Porthus was slain by one of these things?'

'Because I am placing my faith in you, brother! I also see how badly this could be interpreted, how easy it would be to condemn me for actions beyond my control. Alissa is no witch, simply gifted with a valuable power. Her control is still erratic and very recent; Porthus' disappearance predates her current ability, and I would have to assume a wild creature was responsible. I have feared revealing the truth because of my own deep-seated resentment towards all of you, but I am willing to put that all aside now and offer the first olive branch to you, Gallth. If you report back to the rest of the family in support of what I have been doing, then that will lay the foundation for unifying us properly as it always should have been. Do you think you might be able to do this for me?'

'I want to believe you, Lennath,' Gallth offered cautiously, 'but right now these are just words. Would you be open to showing me the truth behind them? To allow me to corroborate your claims with others here? I would be content to support you among our brothers but only when I have confirmed all that you have said; it would be a significant reputational risk for our family to be recorded as the ones who destroyed the daughters of Rork Fimarr. Are you compliant towards this?'

Something flickered across Lennath's expression before the smile returned and he extended his hand, 'Agreed, Gallth. Conduct whatever investigation you deem appropriate and, when you are ready to divulge the truth to our family, I will be sure to accompany you. This could be the beginning of a new era for the Kingdoms and we will be remembered as the brothers who initiated it!'

Gallth shook the proffered hand and returned the smile but felt none of the suggested unity from his brother.

'As we sadly lost your man today,' Lennath continued, walking towards the other exit from the room, 'can I offer you one of my personal retinue to replace him while you are here? And are there any burial rites that should be observed?'

Gallth weighed the offer in his mind; was their more risk in wandering the palace alone or with a man loyal to his brother? He felt a strange desire to believe Lennath's words, maybe driven by fear or a reluctance to believe the level of treachery the alternative indicated, but he would not do so without evidence. No, having an observer of his own could easily tarnish any discoveries he made.

'Thank-you for your gracious offer, brother, but I shall decline. I am certain I will be safe enough within your walls without further security. As for Garby, he was a simple mercenary and will require only the standard burial or cremation of any of your own people. Hopefully, I will be able to substantiate what you have told me within a couple of days.'

'I know you will!' Lennath confirmed lightly, nodding back to him as he left the room, Mozak flowing silently out behind him.

Gallth relaxed back into his chair and downed the delicious wine. He felt more certain of himself and confident in his actions. Whether he found Lennath to be true or false was irrelevant, there was no way his little brother was going to risk harming him now, no way he would summon the wrath of the other Kingdoms. He flicked his eyes over to the young serving wench.

'Jasta, wasn't it?' he leered, 'Perhaps you could escort me to my bedchambers; there is much tension I wish to relieve…'

The streets of Rennicksburg felt strangely quiet, with only a few pedestrians wandering between the stores of the main trading area. As they reached the town centre, the ancient standing stone marking the spot from which the settlement grew, Herc cast a glance along Drove's Way towards his own shop as if it may have vanished in his absence. He could see the familiar sign above the door gently swaying in the breeze and felt reassured. Moving on, he followed Straker Forge towards the Traveller's Reprieve, knowing they would be there in mere moments. He had still not fully followed all that Forge had told him; apparently the plan had failed, Alissa was still lost to them but there was another solution to the question of finding the orb. They had been forced to leave the farm immediately, despite no incident following the assassin's failed attempt on their lives, for there was much concern over reprisal from Lustania. Most importantly, he had been told that Catalana was safe and well, waiting to be reunited with him. Turning back, he could see Melody riding happily, held up in the arms of Rebecca, and singing some nursery rhyme to herself. He knew that Joseff was co-mounted with his father which left just Terex bringing up the rear, the warrior alert to his surroundings but physically relaxed. Suddenly they had arrived at their destination and he dropped down, securing his and Rebecca's horses' reins before taking Melody in his arms and carrying her towards the brothel entrance. He still found it an odd choice to gather at Milius' establishment rather than their own but perhaps it was an attempt to confuse any observers.

Following Forge though the main doors, he found the bar area free of patrons; it seemed that Milius had closed for their benefit. Melody struggled out of his hold to rush into her mother's embrace, which gave him time to assess those before him. Treya had clearly been badly injured, favouring her right side as she squeezed her tiny children tightly. An angry cut ran across the bridge of her nose and back over her left cheek, almost as far as her ear; hasty stitches ran along the soft flesh, but the rest had been left to scab. More worryingly, her eyes seemed hollow and distant, something he had never seen before. Forge followed his children to her but sat on a round table just behind them; Herc knew this meant they had been arguing.

Milius himself stood behind the bar, a bottle of light rum in one hand and several wooden shot-sized cups on the surface before him; he had stocked the tableware in wood to reduce the number of breakages from drunken customers. He offered a smile, but the underlying confusion still broke the surface, it could be assumed he had offered the room without question. Herc couldn't suppress some amusement; it suggested Catalana must have asked. Sat upon stools on this side of the bar were Frost and a newcomer Callid had never seen before; both looked dour and failed to raise their gaze from the drinks they were nursing.

Rayne was standing near to the stairs, her clothes torn from combat and multiple dressings clearly visible through the rips and holes. It must have been some battle indeed to leave the masterful assassin in such a state and the urgency of Forge's request to join them now became clear. Alongside the black-garbed Fimarr sat another child and Herc assumed this to be Alissa's daughter, Kastani, or, as Forge had put it, the unexpected consolation prize.

Finally, his eyes found the one he was looking for, Catalana, sat at a table alone near the back of the room. She looked bruised and battered, her expression filled with anguish and pain. It made no difference, however, as his heart soared at the sight of her and he raised his hand as a broad grin spread across his face.

'Cat…' he began to call before a lighter, more shrill voice overpowered him.

'Terex!' Kastani squealed in delight, sprinting across the room quicker than Rayne could restrain her and into the outstretched arms of his latest companion. Herc watched in envy as the tearful reunion played out before those assembled, and he felt himself holding back elated tears at the display.

'Terex?' Treya echoed, looking up from her own children. Callid could not read the tone of her voice and prepared to defend the other man should she break into another tirade, 'I thought you had gone for good when I dismissed you back at the farm.'

'He had, Treya,' Herc interjected, 'but he came back to us just at the right moment. We had been attacked by a killer of great skill, I was beaten, we were lost, but Terex saved our lives. Without him we, and the twins, would be dead.'

'Please, it was fortuitous only,' Terex added amid a flurry of kisses from the little girl, 'I told you I would do anything to protect this child and her mother. I simply wanted to offer my aid to you again.'

'I am so very grateful to you,' Treya responded taking everyone by surprise, 'I should not have questioned your intentions, I was just afraid. Now there are far greater things to fear, and you have prevented them from harming my children twice. Know that I will do likewise for Kastani if ever it is required. But we have no time for proper greeting, who knows when those very enemies I fear will be upon us, we have actions to take and must decide who and how we will proceed.'

Herc took the opportunity to stride over to Catalana and she rose as he approached, allowing him to wrap his massive arms about her. She sagged into him completely and he took her weight with ease, her head buried against his chest and her body shaking as she sobbed silently against him. Concern washed over him as he recognised their encounter in Lustania had taken a heavy toll upon them all. Holding her tightly, he did not let go until she had manged to compose herself. In the meantime, he listened to the discussion behind him.

'Is there really a decision, Treya?' Rayne asked, 'This artifact we need will require four of us that share a kinship. That means you, Catalana and I have to go. Forge's latest revelation means we will have to detour before venturing for the object itself. Everyone else must stay alive until we return.'

'Don't be so callous, sister,' Treya snapped, 'we are companions in this, all of us just as important as the others. Hard as it is for you to understand, we must plan to ensure we all survive this, including Alissa. You may be certain that your skills are adequate to deal with any danger as it arises, but that is not so for the rest of us...'

'Speak for yourself!' Forge quipped, receiving a dark look for his efforts.

'Not the time, Straker,' she warned.

'What revelation?' Rebecca asked the question hanging in the air, making her way over to Rayne and hugging her in greeting; Herc couldn't help but note the awkwardness of the embrace, 'What have you learned?'

Treya struggled to answer but eventually forced out the words, 'It seems that my father may have had another child...'

'An illegitimate bastard, you mean!' Catalana added, her emotional distress forming into venom as she spat the words, 'We are supposed to engage with the result of infidelity, a rancid hole in our mother's memory, and beg them to help us? It is more than I can stand!'

'Curb your temper, Catalana,' Treya cautioned, 'None of us here is so pure to judge others, and whoever this person is, if they are even aware of their heritage, have not chosen the manner of their conception. We must pray to the gods that they are willing to provide their aid, if the man Straker has directed us to even knows of their whereabouts.'

Silence followed for a moment and Herc turned Cat's face towards him, seeing the fury simmering in her eyes instantly fade as they met his. Laying his palms on her cheeks, he kissed her forehead and then her lips. 'Rest your worries, we will face this confusion together. I will not leave your side again, I promise.'

She studied his face closely, slowing each time they spotted a new mark or injury on his visage. Gritting her teeth, she nodded resolutely and turned back to the conversation.

'Very well, this stranger must be found, if the story proves to be true,' she remarked, eyeing Forge with disdain, 'and then we will seek out the object we require. Once this is in our possession, we can wield it to defeat Lennath and free Alissa. Perhaps Zendar will be able to enlighten us as to how?' Her eyes scanned the room before she turned back to Herc enquiringly.

He smoothed a hand through her hair, 'I'm sorry, but Silas Zendar was slain in the attack on us.'

'He is no loss!' Rayne retorted, 'We delay too often with matters that cannot be changed. He already provided us the directions we require, and he can now provide us nothing else! We should depart immediately to claim the orb, either we will find out how to use it or we will not. Worrying about that now simply prevents us from acquiring it at all.'

'I agree,' Frost grunted from the bar, 'dallying here creates much risk. They have already launched a strike on your home, Rennicksburg is no stretch of the imagination to search next. Our injuries are tended, now we must act!'

'I assume this quest is into the unknown? Fraught with peril?' Terex asked, playing a clapping game with Kastani where he knelt on the floor.

'We have no clues as to what it may bring or how long it will take. I would ask none to accompany us outside of their own will,' Treya said softly.

'And I would not hesitate under other circumstances,' he continued, 'but none of you have highlighted the danger of remaining behind. These children should be no part of such a dangerous journey, yet remain targets for execution. We need as much strength to protect them as we do to claim the orb you speak of.'

'Your statement is valid, and I agree,' Treya replied, 'We sisters have no choice but to leave, though it tears my heart again to do so. But my children will not suffer the loss of both parents this time; Straker will remain here with them.'

'Treya! We have not...' Forge blurted out indignantly before she placed a gentle caress upon his leg.

'This has nothing to do with our disagreements, Straker, I must be sure that they are safe or I cannot do what must be done. Please protect them for us.'

'I... You can't...' Straker was uncharacteristically lost for words and any anger within him evaporated at the tears rimming her eyes, 'I will,' he said, finally.

'And I,' Terex volunteered without looking up, 'For only with my own hands can I be confident that she is truly safe. Together we will shield these children from all threats, though we should consider moving away from Rennicksburg as soon as is practical.'

'Rebecca will stay with you,' Rayne stated, 'protect her as you do the children.'

'What? Rayne, no! I may be of help on this journey. I am no helpless child in need of a nursemaid!'

'Rebecca, please, you have no idea what we are about to embark upon. Your place is high society, your skills are negotiation and charm. I would not see you dragged into the wilderness. Stay here and be safe; for me?'

Tension rose between the two until finally the agent conceded, 'Very well. But I will not remain idle. If I am to stay then I will assist as I can. Perhaps there is a way for me to contact my other clients, bolster the guardians who remain behind?'

'However you like it, Lady Pallstirrith,' Frost concluded for her, 'which means the die is now cast; the rest of us accompany the Fimarrs on this journey. Our swords and our bodies now dedicated to retrieving the orb, but there is another consideration that must be addressed. At this point we are all expendable, save for you three. At all costs you must be the ones to reach our goal, if Zendar's research is to be believed. To that end, you will place your lives above ours if the need arises.'

'You have my word,' Rayne spoke for them, too sharply and too quickly for Callid's liking.

'I would like to hear a little more of this other child, how old do we believe them to be?' he asked, hoping to break any unease the previous discourse had generated.

'No, we should leave Forge and Terex to plan their movements, and depart now. At this moment, we are providing an easy and choice target for the enemy to...' Bentram's voice was full of frustration and urgency but trailed off as a rumbling sound began from outside. It grew louder quickly, like a distant earthquake or an approaching storm. As fittings and furnishings began to shake and fall, bottles tumbling from shelves to shatter behind the bar, Herc joined the others as they rushed for the door. They did not make it before the front of the building suddenly exploded inwards, forcing them to dive for cover. Rubble and dust fell about them and Herc felt Rebecca and Catalana beneath him, shielded by his large frame. Feeling enormous weight on his back, he heaved upwards and shifted the beam that had fallen upon him, clambering free with the two women in tow. Escaping the collapsed debris, he staggered out into the cobbled street and tried to gather his bearings. Behind him was the ruin of the Traveller's Reprieve, a huge section of the frontage gouged out completely, leaving the remaining wall teetering precariously. His other companions were beginning to join them outside of the collapsed structure, but his attention was drawn to the deafening sound of hooves.

Beyond them, turning awkwardly in a street that appeared narrow compared to its enormous bulk, was a mutated creature of terrifying size. Having a bovine appearance, it towered above the two-storey buildings about it, crushing walls and roofs alike with its muscular mass. A set of three horns on one side of its head had caused the damage to Milius Taytafen's business, and now the creature was rounding to finish the task of destroying them. As viscous black oil dripped from its skin to the road below and it lashed its thick, cone-like tail, shattering windows and doors alike where it struck.

'Scatter!' came Forge's cry from behind him, 'Confuse it so it won't know who to pursue!'

The entire party sprang into action, Treya, Straker and Terex sweeping up a child each as the others all began to run in different directions. Herc found himself paced by Catalana and Milius as they sprinted towards Cog Street. The sound of the creature was so loud he could not be certain if it was following them or not and risked a glance back. Sure enough, the beast had eyes like coal fixed upon them and charged forward, mouth full of jagged teeth open to snap them up. Herc side-stepped into Cat', sending her barrelling into Milius and both of them sprawling into a side alley, before jumping as high as he could. The monster's nose struck him, and he was thrown forward at ridiculous speed, impacting heavily on the cobbles many yards further along the street. Rolling several times, he scrambled to his feet, relieved to see the beast crashing forward into a bakery and several houses. It was strong and fast but lacked agility.

'Herc! Take cover while you can!' he heard a voice shouting to him and looked up to see Rayne on a nearby roof, 'The others have found refuge, if you can evade this thing now, we can flee undetected.'

'And leave Rennicksburg to be destroyed as cover for our retreat?' he cried incredulously.

'For the good of everyone!' she called back, 'Remember what Frost said, if we stay here and fight then we lose before we begin!'

'No Rayne; if we leave we have lost!'

Without another word she was gone and Herc turned back to the beast as it disentangled itself from the buildings. A bellowing roar escaped it as it searched for its prey and he spotted Forge, no longer carrying Joseff, hiding behind an overturned cart. Without warning, he leapt up onto his cover, releasing one of his deadly javelins towards the creature's head. For a moment Callid held his breath, sure that the missile would strike the eyeball of the giant but, instead, it deflected harmlessly from its eyebrow. Forge had not remained still, however, and was scaling the building next to him; it was clear he would not make it in time.

Herc drew his axe and slammed the head against the cobbles, the metallic ring echoing along the street towards the monster.

'No, vile beast, come for me! Come for Herc Callid, for I have culled every one of your brethren I have met!' he called aloud, ending with a bestial roar of his own. The distraction worked and the nightmare turned to bear down on him once more. Standing his ground, Herc tracked the approach, raising his axe above and behind his head in both hands. Steadying his breathing, he counted down from three and then launched his weapon forward. It spun through the air, straight and true, lodging into the nose of the beast but failing to bring the slightest of flinches. It tipped its head, angling the fearsome trio of horns on its left directly towards him and he realised there was no time to dodge.

Time seemed to slow as he felt a heavy impact in his waist and began to topple sideways. Sparks flew up from the horns approaching him as they scraped along the cobbled road and he could see a dark shape dropping towards the creature's head. Angled as it was to harpoon him, its right eye was now exposed, and Silver Rain slammed against the soft vulnerable organ with both feet. Herc crashed into the ground, rolling out of reach of the deadly horns just as they passed him, and saw that Catalana had tackled him out of danger. Another enraged howl echoed about them as the monster skidded to a halt, leaping and thrashing about amongst buildings as it tried to shake the pain from its eye.

'Done with being heroic yet?' Rayne cried to him from where she had landed.

'Not yet!' he called back, squeezing Catalana hard before helping her up, 'I need you to draw the beast to the town centre, where the standing stone lies.'

'For what?' she questioned irritably.

'We must destroy this thing and I have a plan. Bring it there in five minutes!'

'I didn't bring a sundial with me, Callid!' she retorted angrily but raced along the street towards the crazed animal.

'What are you doing, Herc?' Cat' asked breathlessly.

'You mean what are we doing,' he replied, 'and we are saving the people of Rennicksburg.'

Grasping her hand tightly, he led her rapidly through the narrower streets until they arrived at their own shop. Bursting through the locked door, there was no time to find keys, he moved directly to the trappings section and snapped up a 30-yard length of Bannarick-soaked rope. The rare oil enhanced the quality of the rope, making it exceptionally durable and strong, perfect for climbing or non-lethal bear trapping. He doubted it could restrain the monstrous creature they faced, but if it held for a few moments, that could be long enough for his plan.

'Grab a bow, Cat', we need your best shot.'

'These arrows will not even pierce the flesh of such a creature! Rayne's entire bodyweight did not even puncture its eye. What hope is there with such a weapon?'

'Trust me, sweet lady,' he replied with a calm he did not feel.

'Always,' she replied, claiming a bow and quiver of arrows.

Racing back through the streets, they emerged into the town centre, the circular clearing around the standing stone completely deserted. The ancient monument had been there for as long as records existed and was rumoured to extend down to the very heart of the land. None had ever dug down to corroborate this, but the stone was unlike any other in the region which suggested it could be the tip of some singularly occurring mineral from beneath the surface. Unslinging the rope from his shoulder, he wrapped it quickly to create a looped noose a third of the way down its length.

'An arrow,' he urged from Catalana, tying one end of the rope to it as she passed one to him, 'now fire it into the overhang of Grover's Tavern.'

'Herc, even if I hit that from here, it will not hold to ensnare the beast. This plan is folly!'

He rested a hand on her shoulder, 'Make the shot, Catalana,' he urged.

Obediently, she stepped forward and took a knee. After a moment's aim, she released the bowstring and sent the tethered arrow whistling into the top of the third storey, beneath the thatched overhang.

'Now take cover,' he advised, pushing her back towards the buildings. Grasping the other end of the rope, he made his way over to the standing stone, already aware of the rumbling approach of the beast growing louder. Wrapping the reinforced cord twice around the monolith, he pulled the slack taut and was pleased to see the loop he had made hanging about fifteen yards above the street. Keeping the remaining rope in his hands, he scrambled back across the road and took cover behind some barrels.

All at once, Rayne appeared from a side passage, diving and rolling to avoid some crates that must have been kicked forward by the pursuing monster. Waving to signal his presence, she turned towards him, obviously unaware of his intended plan.

'No!' he called out, 'Not towards me, the other side of the stone!'

Irritation crossed her face as she changed direction with the giant horror gnashing down towards her. Her awareness was exceptional, however, and she leapt forward into a handspring as its teeth closed on the spot she had been occupying, the action allowing her to land upon its mouth tusk and vault forward from there. She landed on a store canopy and continued her sprint, despite the imbalanced surface beneath her, but could not maintain her pace. Herc watched as the creature angled in for a second bite and allowed himself a silent cheer as one horn slipped through the loop he had made. It was enough to pull the massive head away from Rayne so that teeth clashed together on empty air once again.

Catalana had been correct, of course, the arrow gave way instantly, but the loop tightened on the horn as planned. Wrapping the rope around the standing stone provided increased leverage, as long as the monument held of course, which meant all he had to do was hold the loose end. As the powerful beast continued its charge, forced to turn against its will as the rope refused to give, vast strain ripped through him as he gripped the rope and pulled back with all his strength. Muscles and sinew screamed at him as he was dragged from behind the barrels and dug his heels in between the cobbles. The rope slipped in his hands, pulling away from him once, twice and a third time before he overcame the burning pain in his palms and secured his grip again.

The beast roared its defiance and Herc roared back. It had great strength and aggression but lacked the intelligence to simply stop. Following the wide circle around the stone that the rope on its side allowed, the thing continued its headlong charge straight into the spire of the Temple of Yanis. The huge spike slammed into its soft throat before punching up through its skull, bringing the monstrosity to a crashing end amid the ruin of the holy building.

Releasing the rope at last, Herc fell backwards in exhaustion, cradling his blood-soaked hands in his lap. In seconds Catalana was beside him, laying kisses across his face and producing rags to bind his injured palms. Rayne joined them, looking out at the behemoth carcass.

'All right,' she announced, 'that was impressive.'

Chapter 10

Releasing the string that held this side of the tented covering in place, Rebecca flipped the thick linen back to allow a full view of the scenery at this side of the wagon. Everything looked oddly new, small trees and infant shrubs dotted amongst green grasses and tilled earth. It was as if these lands had only just come into being in the last few years and, from Rayne's description of her time in the Dussen Wastes, perhaps it was true. Leaning back against the bedrolls stacked against the other side of the cart, she looked at the twins where they knelt together, playing with some hastily constructed straw dolls. She had felt something was needed as the initial fear and anxiety of their flight from Rennicksburg had faded into boredom for the children. Kastani still slept, head snuggled into Rebecca's lap, her pure, unblemished face belying the nightmare she had already lived through in her very young life. She idly stroked the little girl's thick blonde hair and wondered what it would be like to have a child of her own. An unbidden smile crossed her lips; time-consuming was probably the reality!

'Are you all right back there?' Forge called to her from the driver's seat. He and Terex had taken turns to steer the four-horse team, allowing them to have minimal breaks in the journey; only relief stops, and the occasional leg-stretch, had been permitted. This usually meant one of them was sleeping in the main wagon with them, but right now they were sat together in front.

'Yes, fine, just taking some air and sun,' she replied, 'when do you anticipate the next stop being?'

'Soon, and it will be the last one!' he said mirthfully, 'Hercatalana is already in view!'

She tried to crane her head towards the front, but the cart lip was too high at that side, and she did not want to disturb Kastani by standing up, so decided to take her companion's word for it, 'That is good news indeed! It will be most welcome to feel comforts beyond this cart!'

'Aye, lady,' he responded amiably, 'for us all.'

So, the trek was finally coming to an end; she could not recall if it had been nine or ten days, progress slow initially as Terex insisted on obscuring their tracks for the first twenty miles out of Rennicksburg. She could not help but admire his diligence and caution; he did not seem the kind of man who could have led the dark armies of Ramikain years ago. His manner was one of honesty, patience and calm; there was no request from Kastani that was too much effort for him, and he always had time for her. He reminded Rebecca of her own father, except more doting and focussed than even her own parent had been. It seemed very strange for a man with no blood ties to the child but also incredibly heart-warming, a stark contrast to the situation they found themselves in. The strangest thing was how well he and Forge seemed to get along, kindred spirit perhaps, originally separated through their motivations, now brought together in a common cause. With their joint desire to keep their respective wards safe, it seemed she was the only odd member in the party, with no ties to any of them.

Kastani suddenly shifted and sat up, stretching and yawning loudly. Idly scratching her head, she looked around drowsily.

'Where is Terex?' she asked.

'He is up front, driving the team. Do not worry, little one, we are almost at our destination,' Rebecca soothed, rubbing the little girl's back gently.

'Oh, that will be nice,' Kastani replied, staring over at her cousins, 'what are they playing?'

'I don't know. I think they are pretending the dolls are their mother and father, on some adventure somewhere probably,' Rebecca suggested.

'No, they are at home,' Melody sang back, not looking up from the game, 'Dada is tidying up while momma makes breakfast.'

'But the baddies could attack at any moment!' Joseff added excitedly.

'Can I play?' Kastani enquired hopefully.

Melody pushed one of the other dolls towards her, Rebecca had made six in total, though they all looked the same, being so basic, 'Here you are, this can be your momma.'

There was no negative reaction to the reminder of being separated from her own parent, instead Kastani crawled eagerly across the cart and snatched up the doll to join in. Rebecca took the opportunity to kneel up and look out towards Hercatalana. The settlement was far larger than she imagined with hundreds of wooden and mortar buildings sprawling in seemingly random distribution. There was none of the ordered street pattern that most towns or cities adhered to, as if any who wished to build just picked a spot and did so. There was something inherently organic and serene about that, which made her feel hopeful to arrive, but in the back of her mind were darker thoughts; if the creature that attacked Rennicksburg had done so much damage to a well-built town, what chance would a place like this have?

Her mind drifted to the rapid departure from their previous refuge. There had been panic and confusion all around, with the citizens of Rennicksburg suffering the collateral damage of an attack against their small party. Many had immediately begun frantic searches for family and friends in the rubble of the numerous collapsed buildings, priests of Yanis were delivering both prayers and curses at the devastation of their temple, other townsfolk set about loading wagons and carts to flee the town in case of further attack. Milius Taytafen had tried to explain but few took time to heed his words, only the Watch seemed interested in what he had to say. Treya and Catalana had leant their perspective to his assurances that no further assault would befall Rennicksburg once they departed; something the arriving Mayor had insisted they do with great haste. She recalled staring at the monstrous corpse where it lay, silhouetted by an orange glow from a nearby fire, many had sprung up from shattered oil lanterns broken during the conflict. From her hidden vantage point, shielding Kastani but with Bentram and Frost overseeing them, she had witnessed the incredible feat from Rayne and Herc Callid; she had never seen such strength or courage before. Despite the terror the situation had brought, such efforts gave hope that they could succeed in their overall plan. It also reminded her that Rayne was correct; she had no place on such adventures.

And that was another conundrum. Rayne had professed her romantic desire for Rebecca on several occasions now, and there was real pain in her eyes at every rejection, but she could only reciprocate with friendship. Admittedly, it was a stronger friendship than she felt with any other, but even that filled her with guilt; for all that Rayne seemed willing to do for her, was it right that she could not love her in that way? Even their most recent parting had been filled with that same emotional confusion; a tight embrace had been followed by a gentle kiss, Rebecca allowing it until more passion was driven into it. She had been forced to push Rayne away again, but this time maintaining contact through a hand on her cheek. Once more she had reinforced that she cared deeply for the other woman but could not love her in that way; once more she had been the cause of distress to a person who continued to be her saviour.

The children's game got louder, distracting her from her reverie and she turned to look at them, all three contentedly playing together; perhaps this was how it should have been for the Fimarrs, the traumas the family had suffered seemed vastly unfair. Kastani was brandishing her doll excitedly, making odd whooshing and whirring noises.

'What are you doing, Kastani?' she asked with a smile.

'My mother is making magic, but I don't have any creature dolls so we are pretending,' she answered innocently, 'do not worry, though, I will not make aunt Treya and uncle Straker dead. In this game they are all best friends!'

The twins cheered at the announcement, but a cold shiver ran down Rebecca's spine.

'We are here!' Forge called, breaking the sudden uneasiness, and she realised she had not noticed the buildings appearing around them.

'Wait here for a moment,' she told the three children before hiking her skirts and jumping down out of the cart. Already a throng of people were rushing out to the vehicle, all hailing Forge and greeting him warmly. She eased her way up to the horses to join them, holding back with Terex as the strangers to this town. Looking back, she saw that the little ones had followed her instruction but were spying curiously out from their concealment. Some of the residents of Hercatalana had now moved beyond Forge and were greeting her out of association, such hospitality without demand seemed all the more amazing considering how the town had been born. She had heard the story many times from Rayne; how the survivors of the Black Citadel, those who had been imprisoned but saved thanks to the Fimarrs, had constructed the settlement within leagues of that dreadful place as a symbol of hope against despair. She had always noted a touch of remorse when Rayne spoke of the place, as if she wished it had been built because, instead of in spite, of her. Usually this was followed by cynicism at the support provided by Lustania to help rapid construction; guilt payments she always inferred.

Without warning the crowd began to part from the back, making way for someone of great importance she assumed. Soon the newcomers came into view, three older men and a woman, led by a pretty youngster with silky-smooth brown hair falling to her shoulders. She assumed the venerates must be town leaders or elders of some description with the young maiden their attendant, perhaps? Welcoming smiles adorned their faces, until they laid eyes upon Terex.

'No!' the girl at the front cried out sharply, 'He cannot be here! He cannot live!'

'Czerna, please!' Straker interjected quickly, 'This is not what you think! He is not your enemy, we come here only to seek refuge.'

'Straker Forge,' she replied coldly, 'why do you believe your words would carry weight in this matter? I only hope you do not realise what you have brought into our midst!'

Rebecca noticed many of those around her shifting nervously, some hands moving to the hilts of weapons. Her heart began to race but she could not determine what was happening, very slowly, she began to back towards the children.

'Hail, citizens of Hercatalana!' Terex called, standing tall with no sign of fear, 'Know that I am Terex. I have come here in peace, in the companionship of Straker Forge. We ask nothing save for the safety of our charges; this woman and three children,' he waved a hand in her direction.

'You ask for nothing?' Czerna repeated incredulously, 'Not even leniency for your crimes?'

'Czerna, calm yourself,' Forge soothed, moving forward with his arms raised placatingly, pausing when she drew a dagger, 'please do not act rashly. Whatever your concerns, I wager they are from a long time hence; our situation now is changed. And I mean all of our situations.'

'Changed enough to permit a mass-murderer among us? To forgive all the lives taken because of him?' her eyes were wild, and Rebecca was astounded that Forge held his ground between her and her obvious target.

'I am a soldier,' Terex stated, without apology, 'I have killed only in war, which is far less of a crime than those you herald as heroes. How many unarmed opponents has Straker Forge killed in his time? A fair many, I would wager.'

Straker turned to look at him with a raised eyebrow, 'I am not certain you are helping this situation…'

'Do not compare yourself to him. Killing as a saviour to protect others is not the same as killing because it is commanded. You have no justification for your actions, and you are not welcome here.'

'I have not come here to distress you or your people. Maybe I served the wrong side years ago, maybe I did not. For the last five years I have served Alissa Fimarr and her daughter Kastani. It is them and their safety we should be concerned about right now.'

The resolve in Czerna's eyes seemed to waver and her voice held less certainty when she spoke, 'No, this cannot be true… I spent months locked in a dungeon in the Black Citadel, remembering every face that came to leer or taunt me, committing the face of every guard who dragged someone from our cells to be fed to your master! You were there, in the Citadel, alongside those most evil of men. You came to view the 'livestock' once and there was no compassion in you, just concern that there were not enough of us to last. The other guards feared you, so you were in a position of power then, yet you did nothing to provide us safety; why should we do so for you?'

Terex stepped forward, those closest to him backing away as if his very proximity were toxic, 'Know this, I was the General of Ramikain's armies. I waged war through the Dussen Lands and made orphans and widows aplenty as I did so. I was loyal to that necromancer, as I had been raised to be, and fulfilled the duties expected of me. I lifted no finger to aid those captives within the Citadel and showed no quarter to the enemies I faced. I also saw no quarter given and bore witness to many who had served Ramikain slaughtered when he was destroyed. I wish none of you harm, by my hand or any other, and I ask that you look beyond times past, beyond events that I cannot change, and look only at the infants we have with us. We have come here to hide them in safety; no matter what fighters you possess amongst your number, you will be stronger with us at your side. But I will not force this matter; if you cannot accept me then I will leave.'

Straker turned back to Czerna and laid a hand upon hers, gently forcing the knife down to her side, 'We have no right to ask for this help, no right to put your new home at risk, but I had hoped that this might be our haven, at least for now.'

Tears had sprouted from her eyes and it seemed that all were waiting for her response. Rebecca marvelled that one so young held so much sway.

'Very well, Straker Forge, I will allow this. Bring the children to my house, your lady companion also. He can stay in the blacksmith's loft. I must know what threat has driven you to us, what danger it poses to you and now us before the council can decide on the most prudent course of action.'

With that, the council turned away and Forge joined her and Terex by the wagon.

'That was tense,' Terex remarked as he lifted Kastani gently from the cart, 'I thought Treya's greeting at the farm was cold!'

'Do not be flippant about this,' Straker warned, 'Czerna is the most level-headed person I have ever met, and her restraint was barely held. You may be directly responsible for the worst pain and loss to many of those living here. I urge your caution while you are here, there may be many who would seek vengeance against you.'

'Should we not make other arrangements then?' Rebecca suggested, lifting Joseff down onto her hip and holding him there, 'why not head for Corinth? I know people there, I can summon allies, great warriors who could help us…'

'Rayne already had to rescue you from that city,' Forge reminded her, 'there are too many unknowns in such a place. Here the people all know one another, making infiltration difficult. They have also banded together through hardship and strife, making them tough and resolute. There is no better place for us to take respite.'

'She is right, though,' Terex added, rubbing his nose playfully against Kastani's, 'we should plan to move on. Whether the people here grow to tolerate me or not, the longer we are here, the more likely we will be discovered.'

'We cannot run forever,' Forge countered.

'No, just until your good lady returns to save the day!' Terex finished with a grin. He gave Kastani a big hug and reassurances that he would not be far away before retrieving his travelling gear and heading towards the smithy. The residents parted in his wake.

Rebecca took her bag, keeping Joseff in her other arm, and Straker gathered the rest before leading them towards Czerna's house, the two girls skipping happily behind them.

'Does this place have a messenger bureau?' Rebecca asked.

'Aye, a runner service, but fast ponies as I recall, courtesy of Lustania! A message would be risky in the current circumstances, traceable back to us. What did you want to send?'

'As I said to you, I know people in Corinth who may be able to help us. More precisely, my clients. I represent some of the most dangerous mercenaries and assassins in Kazgrat, remember; Silver Rain was on *my* books! I don't know if they could overcome these creatures, or the Veer, but they may give us a fighting chance.'

'And how would you pay them?'

'They trust me, I would offer future payment, and this would be enough. If not, they simply will not come. Is it not worth taking the chance? Do you really think the two of you and these simple people could fend off another beast like in Rennicksburg? Or a Veer assassin? I shudder to think if the Veer came in number.'

A flash of amusement appeared on his face before he turned back in the direction they were heading, 'I concede to your wisdom,' he said, 'come and observe formal introductions with the council. Once this is done, the messenger station is at the East end of town. If you can, leave your message unclear to the casual reader, assume it will be intercepted.'

'Yes, of course, I can use an identity known only to my clients and codes we have generated for different jobs. Thank-you Straker.'

'Thank-you? For what?' he asked in surprise.

'For giving me the opportunity to help.'

Rain pattered gently against the lead-grilled window of the bedchamber she shared with Lennath, and she watched the world beyond changing shape and colour as each individual droplet struck the glass. It reminded her of the way it had felt to hold the Stave, everything malleable and penetrable through her will alone, a sensation both exhilarating and terrifying at once. She wished she could simply concede to that feeling, to let go of the bond of flesh and become all that she had experienced; the mutated creatures, the crackling power in the air itself, the people far away that had filled her mind with their thoughts. She slapped herself in the face, feeling blood pump to the site immediately in response; no, she had spent too much time carefully crafting her physical body with the runes that made her a conduit for the gods, it would be a waste to lose her mortal form so soon. Of course, she had no idea which of the gods had gifted her with the power she wielded so had found every arcane and religious symbol she could, having each carved meticulously into her skin. Terex had insisted on doing each himself, occasionally allowing Narem the honour if he was not available, after her first attempt. She had tried to carve the sigil of Collanis onto her inner thigh, cutting too deep and too wide; there had been a lot of blood and Terex had been furious with her. It was still the only poorly crafted scar upon her, pink, raised and angry despite the years that had passed. The rest of her body was pure art, however. She wondered where Terex was, it seemed to be taking him a long time to find them, and promised herself that she would have him carve a new symbol when he arrived; there could be some space on the small of her back or he could always shave her head to use her scalp.

She sighed; loneliness was an unexpected side-effect of recent events. Terex had always been around to listen to her, provide for her or simply be company. Lennath had been an adequate replacement since bringing her here and any time she was not in the mutation chamber, he had almost always been with her. But not since the confrontation with her sisters. Alissa pondered if she had done something wrong that day; ever since, Lennath had seemed distracted at best and angry at worst, spending less and less time with her. He had only shared a bed with her once during that period, failing to even touch her tenderly then. The fact that she was unsettled by his lack of desire was also surprising to her; she had not wanted such attention from anyone since Kale's death. Maybe this was a sign, in fact, it must be! It all made perfect sense to her now, Kale had died, his spirit had travelled to Lustania and inhabited Lennath. That was how he had improved his physical appearance and become so much more forceful, and that was why she had not killed him for touching her. If only she had seen it sooner, they would have wasted far less time in bonding. So now she had to find a way to make him content again, discover what it was that perturbed him.

It could be only one of three things. The first possibility was that the spirit of Kale Stanis was struggling to accept its new boundary and the alternate form it was forced to take, there was very little she could do to help with that, other than telling him she knew the truth. The second was that he was still angry about Kastani; when they had discovered her missing, he had gone berserk, cursing her and everyone else for allowing the girl to be taken. His desire to find her was palpable, making more sense now that she realised he was actually her father, but ultimately misguided. The girl was with her sisters who would not harm her, Treya's reaction during the battle was proof enough of that; if Frost had not interfered, she would have exacted her righteous revenge upon her oldest sibling. Missing out on killing Treya should have entitled *Alissa* to be furious, not Lennath, but he had not stopped ranting about finding Kastani and bringing her back, as if it was Alissa's fault. Even when she had sent a creature to retrieve the girl he had not been content, telling her that such an action put the girl in more danger, that an attack like that was reckless. It had been one of her favourites as well, until her quarries had somehow killed it. Since then, even her flying scouts had been unable to track them. If this was the problem, then she could always try again, maybe with smaller beasts who could differentiate better between those they were attacking. Of course, there was the third option, it could all be connected to his brother. She had been introduced to Gallth briefly after the encounter with her family, but that had been fleeting with Lennath ushering her away quickly. Since then, she had been kept away from him, the Stave now stored in these chambers so there was no requirement to leave but making it far more difficult to alter animals at such a distance. Servants had come to move her through hidden passages whenever Gallth had threatened to speak with her and she had complied to placate Lennath. It was unclear why they were being kept separate unless the Prince still wanted his plan to kill his own family kept secret? She felt a little put out that he did not trust her to keep his confidence but vowed not to let him down should the inevitable contact be made.

She idly traced a finger over several of the thin scars covering her face and felt far better than she had for days; finally, she had realised the hidden secrets around her, and things would be better. If Lennath, or should she now be calling him Kale? If he were provided the successes he desired, then maybe he would return to doting on her and she could help to bring his true self to the surface. Yes, everything was beginning to make sense again. Leaning forward she licked the window, finding only the taste of worn lead rather than the sweet rainwater beyond. It was a little disappointing, so she snatched up a heavy candlestick and swung it against the offending barrier. The glass within shattered but the lead frame only bent slightly. She bashed it several more times to no avail and then screamed at it with no further success. Feeling the sudden cold wash over her, easily overcoming the thin gown she wore, Alissa shivered before moving over to the small desk beside the far wall. Inside one of the drawers was the Stave but she resisted the urge to pull it free and release the full power within. Instead, she focussed on the artifact and allowed her awareness to channel towards the nearest of her flying creatures; perhaps finding the missing Kastani was the best first step.

Hasty footsteps in the corridor heralded a visitor long before the doors swung open and her concentration was broken. She looked around irritably to find Tarraget stood in the doorway, the matron panting heavily and looking flustered.

'Quickly, milady,' she puffed with sweat running down her round, red face, 'Prince Gallth is heading here once again, we must away immediately!'

'No, it is quite fine this time,' Alissa corrected her, trying to curb the irritation the interruption had caused, 'I would like to speak with him.'

'But you cannot,' Tarraget responded in a fluster, 'The Prince's rules... you must not be interrogated... I mean, he does not want you talking to his brother unless he is present!'

'I know,' Alissa replied patiently, and offered a conspiratorial wink, 'but everything is all right now. I know just what to say.'

'Yes, milady, of course,' Tarraget continued with a hint of panic entering her voice. She moved over to Alissa and took her arm, attempting to ease her up off the stool she sat upon, 'why do we not find milord, Lennath, and confirm that with him?'

'Because we do not need to, Tarraget,' Alissa stated, anger spiking as she pulled her arm free, 'leave me be and show Prince Gallth to me directly.'

'I am sorry, milady, but I have my instructions. Now come to the passage,' she gripped Alissa's arm again, tighter this time, and pulled with more force.

Alissa snapped out her free arm, grabbing a letter opened from the desk, and swung it at Tarraget's bosom. The veteran maid was faster than she looked, releasing her grip, and managing to catch the attack with both of her hands, eyes wide with fear. Alissa smiled sweetly and launched a straight punch into Tarraget's throat with her newly free arm. The older woman fell back, coughing and choking from the blow, and Alissa was upon her in seconds. She placed the opener firmly against Tarraget's cheek, point within a hair's breadth of her eyeball, and saw blood appear on the plump flesh.

'I said you should welcome the Prince to my quarters,' she hissed. After a moment of pure stillness, she pulled the blade away and slapped Tarraget across the face. Tears and a trembling lip indicated the servant understood and Alissa stroked a finger carefully across the light wound she had caused before climbing off the maid and allowing her to scurry towards the door. Licking the captured blood from her fingertip, Alissa grimaced; ironically, Tarraget tasted sour.

Tossing the opener to one side, Alissa paced impatiently in a circle until the housekeeper returned with Prince Gallth in tow. His eyes lit up with satisfaction when he saw she was present.

'Lady Fimarr,' he drawled, closing the gap between them, and raising her hand to his lips, 'I am so very pleased to finally cross paths with you; it is almost as if you have been avoiding me.'

'Not at all, Prince Gallth,' she replied courteously, 'I have always been in a different passage, is all. Today I decided to change that. I want nothing more than to meet Lennath's family while I have the chance.'

His eyes narrowed at her words but then his attention fell to the hand he held, 'Remarkable,' he whispered, 'such craftsmanship on show, but these must have caused you great pain. What is their purpose?'

'They are beautiful, are they not?' she agreed, 'And there is no real beauty without pain. They are the roots of my power.'

'Really?' he asked, intrigued, 'You are most readily open with your words, unlike many here in the palace. I think this may be a very enlightening conversation.'

'I hope so,' she enthused, ushering him towards the comfortable reading chair near the bed, 'it is one of the ways I hope to please your brother.'

'Indeed,' he continued suspiciously, eyeing her closely, 'and why are you so eager to please him? Is it gratitude for saving your life?'

Alissa knew she must look puzzled as the question was confusing, 'No, he has never saved my life as far as I am aware. He had me kidnapped once but brought me here so that worked out well. And he killed the men who decided to use my body for their own pleasures; I think he felt jealous that another should touch me, so I do not permit that anymore.'

Gallth seemed taken aback and she wondered if he had not asked the question she thought he had. She perched on the end of the bed and awaited any further queries. 'So, you were kidnapped?' he offered eventually, 'held here against your will?'

'No, no,' she assured him, 'I could not be held against my will, I want to stay here with Lennath.'

'I see. Why is that, exactly? Wealth? Power? A Title?'

'None of those things!' she laughed, 'I stay because he has inherited the spirit of my one true love!'

Another pause stretched out and he was staring hard into her face for signs of deceit. She felt herself blush and placed a bashful hand to her chest, 'Prince Gallth, you are embarrassing me! Why do you stare so?'

'My apologies, Lady Fimarr, you are not quite what I expected. Tell me, do you control these monsters for my brother?'

His eyes did not leave her, and she traced her fingers lightly over her breast and down to her lap, delighting that his gaze followed every movement; men were so predictable, 'Oh yes,' she continued, 'I can influence them, at least, and they seem compliant to my thoughts. They are not monsters, you know, just animals with complete uniqueness; it makes them rare and they should be treasured.'

His eyes flicked back to her face, and he shifted uncomfortably for a moment, 'As you say, lady, but you can make them do your bidding?'

'In a fashion, yes.'

'And what have you made them do?'

'I have done many things, scouted the reaches of Lustania, provided beasts of burden, destroyed an army of insurgents, created defences for this very city. They are loyal to me.'

'And you to my brother? This does not set me at ease. Has he told you what he plans for the future? Why he wants these things under your thrall?'

'Thrall? I like that word, it sounds like something a god has, does it not? Thrall, as in to enthral?' she stood as she excitedly played with the word, knowing that his eyes would be drawn to the curves of her body while she moved, wondering if he would maintain focus on his questions.

'Yes, I think you know much about being enthralling, but you have not answered my question.'

'No, I have not!' she agreed, 'But I do know what the future will bring. I would tell you if you answer my question first!' She had twirled her way to the desk and leant forward upon on it, pretending to admire herself in the mirror but knowing that she was presenting her rear perfectly to Gallth. She could see his hungry stare reflected before her and smiled.

'Fair enough, Lady Fimarr, what would you ask of me?'

She turned to him and sat on the edge of the desk, pulling her gown up and bunching it before her, exposing her legs and drawing his eyes there, 'Have you been satisfied during your stay?'

'What?' he asked, perplexed enough to return his gaze to her face, 'What do you mean?'

'I have passed your room several evenings, and even one afternoon, to hear the throes of passion from within. You are quite noisy! Have our serving girls provided well for you in the bedchamber?'

Caught completely off guard, Gallth squirmed in his chair again, losing much of the gusto he had begun the conversation with, 'I had not... that is I am... I apologise if my fornications have upset or insulted you, Lady Fimarr, but I am a man and Royalty in addition; these girls cannot keep their hands from me!'

'I am certain,' she cooed, allowing her dress to drop back over her legs and sauntering forward. Kneeling before him, she placed her head in his lap, feeling the swelling there. 'But have you been satisfied?'

'I... I think we are getting away from the subject I wish to discuss...'

'But you promised to answer my question,' she insisted, caressing his thigh with one hand.

'Then ask it, lady,' he begged with strain evident in his voice.

'Untie my gown,' she demanded, feeling him fumbling to comply as his eagerness throbbed against her face. When she felt the lace go slack, she rose and allowed her gown to slide from her body to the floor.

'My question is this; were any of these girls as exquisite as I?'

'What are you doing?' he rasped through dry lips, words reluctant despite his eyes capturing every inch of her nakedness, 'You are my brother's consort, he would be most displeased...'

'But why should one such as I be reserved only for him?' she countered, taking his hand and placing in on her breast, feeling him squeezing it with barely restrained desire.

He pulled away suddenly but could not stop his eyes leering at her, 'No, temptress! I will not be deterred from my goal here. Perhaps you wish to force my brother's hand, giving him reason to kill me. Maybe you are just insatiable yourself. You are a beauty to behold, no doubt, but you will answer my questions and distract me no longer!'

Pushing herself forward, she straddled him, pressing herself against the bulge in his trousers and pulling his face towards hers. He did not restrain her from kissing him, but his eyes went wide as she clamped her teeth on his lower lip. Leaping up, he threw her back, sending her sprawling across the carpeted floor and following up with a kick to the ribs that drove the air from her lungs.

'You insane bitch!' he roared at her, blood pouring from the holes in his lip, 'I will have you executed for this!'

'I just wanted to see if you tasted like your brother,' she coughed, holding her injured side.

'Sick animal! Are you telling me you have done this to Lennath as well?'

'No, silly man, your other brother! I could taste it when he got eaten.'

Gallth staggered back at her words, unspoken shock clear on his face. Pressing the back of his hand to his face in a futile attempt to staunch the bleeding, he turned towards the doors, just as Lennath burst in.

The Prince of Lustania stood appraising the scene for a moment before speaking with barely contained rage.

'What is going on here?'

'Do not feign innocence, brother! Your witch has revealed all to me! She controls these monsters, as a weapon of war for you and Porthus was murdered by her own admission! It is over for you Lennath! The King knows I am here and why! You cannot have me killed without bringing an unwinnable war down upon yourself! You, and your lunatic, are finished!'

Lennath held his hands up placatingly, 'Please, brother, just wait. Allow me to explain! Yes, Alissa Fimarr is disturbed as a result of her sisters' treatment, which is why I tried to avoid your meeting with her! Despite everything, I love her and so tolerate these unfounded outbursts! She can be fanciful at times, delirious in others but she is everything I have dreamed of when she is lucid. You cannot believe any of her ravings, who in their right mind would? Let us discuss this matter with civility and I will ignore the fact you were alone in my private chambers with her and she has somehow lost her clothing…'

'You cannot talk your way out of this brother! The situation you find here is of her doing and you know it! She is more aware than you suggest. Your only hope is to admit the truth, appeal to father's mercy and hope it is forthcoming. You lose Lennath!'

'This is no game, Gallth, this is real life and things are more complicated than that. Do not condemn me on a bad encounter with the woman I have chosen. We can assuage your fears, I am certain!'

'No, you cannot. I expect a carriage to be waiting…'

Alissa wrapped Gallth in an embrace from behind, pressing herself tightly against him as she slid the letter opener into his side, beneath the ribs. A small grunt escaped him which changed to a wail as she dragged the dull blade across to the other side, opening his midriff. She skipped aside as he fell backwards, innards spilling from him and a look of complete terror on his face.

'Nooo!' Lennath cried at her, in frustration rather than distress, but she ignored him. Leaping astride Gallth as he tried to grip his slippery organs and push them back into his body, she felt the excitement in his groin region had vanished. Stroking her hands over his, feeling them becoming slick with the gore and delighting as blood gushed down over her legs and abdomen, she squealed happily.

'I told you, I want to see if you taste like your brother!' she exclaimed, jamming her hand inside him and pulling a strip of his intestines free. Dragging it to her lips, she bit down hard, finding the meat tough and resistant; grinding her teeth together, she felt flesh give way and swallowed the large mouthful whole. Looking back down, she saw that Gallth was still alive. Leaning forward, she kissed him deeply with her ichor-soaked mouth before rising again with his lower lip between her teeth. Chewing it thoughtfully, feeling the last spasms of life filtering through the body beneath her, she turned to Lennath.

'He was quite annoying. Are all of your brothers like this?'

'What have you done?' Lennath whispered to her, face ashen and grey, 'How am I supposed to explain this to my father?'

'You do not have to. We are strong enough, my love. It is time to take what you want, so you can be happy. So we can be happy.'

'Did you just call me love?' he asked, focussing on her eyes, a slight smile curving the corners of his mouth.

'I did!' she replied enthusiastically, 'Or would you prefer Kale?'

Sitting on the wooden steps that led up to the loft space above the cordwainer's shop, she played the conversation over in her head again. It was logical, well-reasoned and factual, every word received with patience and understanding; but that was in her head. Her father was no more likely to listen to her now than he had been two weeks ago, the very fact that he had not sought her out in that time indicated his resolve. Crystal sighed and leant back against the higher steps, idly scratching a mark from her leather skirt; she knew she should just go, prove her point by succeeding beyond his expectations, return triumphantly on the winning side of this argument. But to do so would break a lifelong bond between them, an honour they had both upheld for as long as she had lived, and she wanted his blessing in her actions. No, she would resolve to listen and counter his concerns calmly until they arrived at the right conclusion, her conclusion.

Climbing from the steps, she allowed herself a moment of preparation before turning the corner towards the home she shared with her father. She stopped immediately at the sight that greeted her. Six horses stood in the middle of the street, reins held by a large, rough-looking woodsman, shaggy beard matched by the heavy furs he wore. Off to the side, another younger man sat on the edge of a water trough, twin swords hanging from his hips, a pensive look upon his face. An old but broad man with an eyepatch stood behind him, one foot up on the trough, arms crossed over the raised knee as he talked quietly to a woman dressed all in black, features almost completely obscured by a hooded cloak and face mask pulled up over her nose. Strangers would be worrying enough, most of the village had been in uproar when the previous hunters had shown up, but these four seemed fixated on the front door of her home. Stood there casually, two women waited as if for a response; perhaps they had knocked but had received no reply from within. The taller of the two women was dressed in fighter's attire, a mixture of light plate joints and leather armour, with a sword slung across her back, dirty blonde hair cascading just below her shoulders; she glowered darkly, suggesting little in the way of mirth ever touching her face. The other woman was more attractive, wearing practical but fashionable travelling clothes, a bow and quiver clearly visible. Her thick auburn hair was tied up and fixed in place, she had only seen such a style during one brief visit to Giltenberg with her father many years ago. They were stark contrast to each other, but she could see a familiarity in the structure of their faces.

As the attention of the strangers slowly began to be drawn to her, she realised she had frozen in place, undoubtedly looking suspicious. She could not decide whether to carry on past the house or change direction completely. Either way, she needed to discover their intentions quickly; what if they were retaliation following her confrontation with the hunters? The choice of action was stripped from her as her father emerged from the house, hurriedly donning his riding coat, and speaking words she could not hear to the waiting party. Immediately, he spotted her and gave a half wave, but his face showed neither the usual joy nor predicted anger at the sight of her; instead, he seemed full of sorrow.

'Hail, daughter!' he called to her, 'It is fortuitous that you are here. I was about to bring these good people to see you.'

Still feeling uncertain, Crystal approached and returned his greeting, ''Ail, Fazer, oo are zese strangers and what would zey want from me?'

'These are the daughters of Rork Fimarr,' he exclaimed with unhidden respect, 'they have been sent here for our help. I hoped you could set aside our recent disagreement and join us? We should discuss matters inside.'

The trace of resignation in expression and voice did not go unnoticed, and she realised this was a matter of great importance. Nodding and making a display of hugging him in front of the assembled travellers, she followed him inside. Eventually they were settled, eight being a tight squeeze in the small front parlour, but none seeming to mind. Mareck had furnished all with a hot drink of the local Furdant Root tea and offered food which had been declined, now he sat in his rocking chair nearest to the fireplace. The other three wooden chairs had been taken by the Fimarr sisters, while their male companions stood in the remaining gaps behind; Crystal leant against the windowsill, looking into the room, having closed the shutters at her father's request. None had spoken since entering the house and even now Mareck stared distractedly into the cold ash of the previous night's fire.

'I am sorry to press you, Mareck,' the stern-faced Treya suddenly spoke, laying her tea to one side, 'but my… that is, Straker Forge insisted you could help us in our search. It is of utmost importance that we find the one we are looking for, and we do not have time to waste.'

Mareck nodded slowly, 'Yes, daughter of Rork, it must be most urgent for that man to send you here. I remember him, from years ago, when he was seeking redemption from your father; he found me by mistake and there was little I could do to aid him, for I had parted company with Rork Fimarr many moons before that meeting.'

'But at some point the two of you shared your knowledge of a bastard child, sprung from our father, yes?' the black-garbed sister asked sarcastically.

Mareck regarded her sadly, 'Yes, Silver Rain, I know of all the Fimarr children, I have listened intently whenever word of your exploits spread. You have my condolences for your youngest sister, as well as your father.'

'We don't have time for these pleasantries,' Catalana spoke sharply, 'The illegitimate child is essential in our quest, if you can tell us or show us where they are then I must impress upon you to do so.'

'I can do both,' he replied, 'but allow me to explain how this came about and why it has been kept a secret, I owe your father that much, at least.'

'There is no mystery about why he kept his infidelity a secret,' Treya said, 'he must have known that none of us, least of all our mother, would ever have graced his presence again if he had told the truth.'

'I can tell from your faces and see in your eyes that you hold great disdain for him, which is heart-breaking for me; he was the greatest man I ever met, and no other has come close to matching him.'

'Fazer, you are not on trial 'ere, you 'ave no need to defend Rork Fimarr even if 'e was still alive. Tell zese women what zey need to know.'

'Defend him?' Mareck asked looking at her, 'No, I have no need to do that. I feel it is just a pity that of all the people to judge him so harshly, it should be his own kin who see the worst.'

Crystal looked away, realising the underlying message meant for her; perhaps she had allowed her anger to tarnish her own view of a parent as well.

'I would prefer simple directions, old man, but if you insist on tales of the past then get it over with,' Rayne demanded.

Mareck finished the last of his drink and leaned back in his chair, 'I do insist, Silver Rain, and there is no doubt you are his daughter; I think his fire runs in each of his children, no? I will tell you of the last days I spent with Rork Fimarr, we were in the Montanai Kingdom and had slain a Drakiam that had been terrorising their people for many years…'

'I know of that story,' Frost interrupted, 'it is legendary! A beast of unimaginable strength and size, impossibly slain by Rork Fimarr. It was always believed to be a fictional myth, or at least an exaggeration. Are you telling us it happened, and you were there?'

'I would question if any tale of Fimarr is false,' Mareck countered, 'I have never heard one that seemed unlikely having met the man. Likewise, the more recent tales of his offspring.'

'Flattery is unnecessary,' Treya replied, 'continue with your story.'

He smiled at her before casting his gaze around the room, 'Very well. Contrary to the widely told story, Fimarr did not face the Drakiam alone but had a travelling party; myself, Rogan the barbarian and Vessa the thief…'

'Rogan? As in Illafrey Gaesin?' Treya blurted out again.

'I believe that was his real name, yes, though it is not relevant to my tale. I heard that he died some years ago, likewise Vessa; I had not thought about being the last surviving member of that group before. Strange to think one such as I would outlive such heroes.'

'I met Illafrey once, he was a good man, and kindly in his final days. I often wish I had not met him as he died because of the help he provided to me and my sister.'

'Then let us hope such history does not repeat itself,' Mareck commented, trying to lighten the mood somewhat, 'We returned to the Montanai to be treated as Royalty, with every wish granted upon us amid a week of feasting and celebrating. The new queen of those lands, Udesny, crowned as the Drakiam had slain her own father, was enamoured with Rork, making every attempt to lure and woo him. Renowned as he was for being stoic, he rejected her bluntly, so bluntly that I feared he would bring her rage down upon us. What transpired instead was, perhaps, worse. On the day of our departure, soldiers arrested Vessa and took her before the queen; Rork insisted we refrain from rescuing her as he did not want our adventure sullied by unnecessary killing. Vessa was accused of stealing from the Royal treasury, her skills and reputation more than enough to incriminate her without evidence, though investigators claimed her bags had been crammed with riches. The queen told us she had no choice, that Vessa would be executed and the rest of us imprisoned until death; her only offer of leniency came at a steep price. She would allow us all to leave, reputations untarnished, if Rork would sire her an heir. She wanted his bloodline to ensure that the

Montanai would remain strong through her progeny; if Rork gave her a child, we would be allowed to live.'

The room had fallen silent. 'You mean she blackmailed 'im into loving 'er?' Crystal asked incredulously.

'Yes, he conceded to her wishes to save the three of us. He never spoke of it, but I know he would not have done so to save only himself. We spent two months in the Montanai prisons, Vessa proclaiming her innocence throughout and I think I believe she was true to her word. We were released when the queen was declared pregnant by her physicians, travelled back to more familiar lands and then went our separate ways. It was enough for me to place my adventuring days behind me and I eventually settled here.'

'So, the child does exist? In the Montanai Kingdom? Can you tell us how to get there?'

'Better!' Crystal suddenly joined in excitedly, 'I can take you zere. I 'ave studied maps for years and am an expert in wilderness travel, I would be 'onoured to help ze daughters of Rork Fimarr in zis way.'

'Crystal, please,' Mareck chided her kindly, 'the tale is not yet done.'

'What, then?' Treya persisted, 'Will you now tell us the child did not survive?'

'No, no, the child survived,' he reassured them all, 'and was born 25 years ago, so a child no longer! The queen proved to be a poor leader for the Montanai people, selfish and disinterested in matters of politics and commerce. Sadly, she was also very trusting and naïve, allowing her own cousin to coerce his way into her trust and murder her, taking the throne for himself. The baby could only have been four or five months old at the time and, to avoid any contention to his rule later, he ordered the infant executed. The queen's handmaid could not allow such a travesty, so she fled with the child, leaving the Montanai Kingdom forever.'

'And let me hazard a guess,' Catalana added, 'they have never been heard from again? So this other child of Fimarr could be anywhere?'

'You ladies are impatient,' Mareck smiled but there was little mirth in his voice, 'no, the child was not lost. The handmaiden sought out your father, to tell him all that had happened and to seek sanctuary for the babe. I don't know the details of that encounter, but I do know that he sought out a dear friend to care for that child and raise them as his own.'

'You cannot mean...' Treya's voice was lost in an unrestrained sob, 'You cannot be telling us that Illafrey raised that child? That the one hope we are seeking was Joseff Gaesin? The very man who died aiding us in defeating Ramikain five years ago!'

Tears began to stream forth and Catalana leant in to comfort her older sister. Crystal felt a rock form in the pit of her stomach; if the boy was already dead, then why had her father dragged out the story? Unless he had not known.

'Joseff Gaesin is dead?' Mareck repeated hollowly, 'That is tragic news indeed, I had no idea, I'm afraid, I have heard no tell of that in the stories of your victory. It appears more condolences are in order, and apologies for rousing that pain back to your heart.'

'Wait, old man,' Rayne cut him off, eyes narrowed, 'You weren't referring to Gaesin, were you?'

He dropped his eyes to the floor, 'Alas, no. Rork did not seek out Rogan, he sought me. Crystal is the errant child you seek; she is the fifth daughter of Fimarr.'

Errabith Chaucer chewed thoughtfully on the mutton sandwich he had purchased, watching the large wooden doors of the disused barn closely. The last man had entered more than ten minutes ago and must have surely been the final member of the gang. He thought back to the discussion with the Watch Lieutenant; the skittish man had insisted it was a gang of seven men, with bounties scaled down from the notorious leader, Grazic Mann. Obviously, the authorities' information was as up to date as usual, he had now counted nine men entering the hideout. Taking another bite of his snack, he flicked several small signals with his free hand and peered to the roof of the structure to see the crouched figure of Fazam Black. Interpreting the returned gestures, Chaucer sighed and tossed the remainder of his sandwich aside; his partner seemed content that the entire gang was now assembled.

Standing from the bench and stretching out his back, Errabith checked that the belts and straps across his body were all in place. Once he was content, he strolled across the dimly lit street, noting that the lamp immediately outside the barn had been vandalised; no doubt an attempt by those within to maintain their secrecy. With a flourish, he flicked his waist-length cloak back over one shoulder and slammed his boot against the large doors. Splintering wood announced the destruction of the flimsy latch on the other side and the portal swung inwards, bathing the dark building with silver evening light. The nine men inside had been casually chatting and moving ill-gotten goods into different piles, but they all spun to face him as he entered.

'Good evening, gentlemen,' he called theatrically, 'may I assume I am addressing Grazic Mann's collegiate of brigands and footpads?'

'What?' an unshaven, rough-looking man answered in confusion. He was taller than Chaucer and broader as well, the big jaw, scarred cheek and curly hair indicated it must be Mann himself.

'I am looking for a renowned group of criminals, specialising in street-robbery and violent burglary, who have been operating within the confines of Corinth for some time now. Would you oblige me by confirming your identities?'

'I do not fink so, dung-sniffer!' Mann spat at him, 'Who do you fink you are, anyways? Some kind of Watchman?'

'Heavens, no, my good man!' Errabith offered with a chuckle, 'I am no law enforcer! I am simply a law profiteer!'

'A bounty hunter, then?' Grazic concluded, 'You cannot be so good if you are coming after the price on us; certainly not good enough to take us all on…' A wicked smile had formed on the thug's face and his allies began to shift their weapons forth.

'I can see where the confusion would come from,' Errabith continued, leaning against a thick wooden support, 'I am, indeed, 'slumming it' with this task. But I happen to be in town, have some time between formal engagements and one of your victims has a most attractive, and soon to be grateful, daughter. So, the contract does state dead or alive, with no reduction in price for dead, which is unusual.'

'You are either very brave or very stupid,' Mann drawled, raising a long-handled meat cleaver, 'Who do you fink you are?'

'You asked me that already, and I do not think, I know!' Errabith exclaimed, 'You may call me Mr. Chaucer, of Chaucer and Black? I am certain you have heard of me.'

The sudden pallidness of their faces indicated they had, indeed, heard of him. Grazic shifted uneasily, glancing among the members of his gang, 'But you do not take any bounties alive,' he stammered.

'No, I do not,' he agreed, idly checking his well-manicured nails, 'which is why the even price makes a nice change…'

The words were barely from his lips when his opponents sprang into action. Mann cried out to fight or die but at least two of the gang immediately turned tail and headed for the rear of the barn. The rest launched their respective attacks as a disorganised rabble. A small throwing axe flew in towards him and he dropped into a crouch as it lodged in the beam above. Performing an elegant forward roll, he drew two black-powder pistols from their armpit holsters firing both simultaneously into two charging attackers with practised expertise; one round steel ball punched through a man's chest before shattering the nearest side of a crate behind him, the other ripped the side of the second target's face off, from eye down to jaw.

Wasting no time, he dropped the ornate firearms and continued his momentum into a run, moving sideways to the remaining adversaries. Drawing his gold-plated machete from the rear of his waist belt, he leapt up onto a barrel before leaping back off it the way he had come. With both hands, he drove his blade down upon the nearest thug, the extra force from his leap cleaving the skull in two, but finding his weapon lodged in the sternum. Abandoning the machete, he twisted sideways as a throwing knife whistled past him and adopted a low stance with arms out, prepared for the next attack despite the loss of his prized short sword. Two men were almost upon him, one with a large bludgeon and the other a rusted sword, when a crossbow quarrel appeared through the throat of each in turn. As they crashed to the ground, bodies almost sliding into him, he looked up to see Black swinging his repeater crossbow back over his shoulder and leaping from the loft beams out of sight. His partner had designed the revolving retainer on the front of his weapon to allow for four bolts to be loaded, a mere flick of the wrist allowing for a new chamber to be brought to bear; they had toyed with the idea of selling the design to armourers or fletchers, but always conceded that the advantage the weapon brought was valuable enough.

Chaucer returned his attention to the two remaining men, one of whom was Grazic Mann; like any ruffian leader, he had held back in the hope his men would do the job for him.

'What you gunna do now?' he taunted, his words lacking conviction, 'no weapons, no partner and no chance!'

'Who said I was out of weapons?' Chaucer smiled confidently, whipping out a miniature beartrap from a pouch strapped to his lower leg and launching it forward. Mann tried to step aside but the device struck him on the chest, clamping down onto his left pectoral and driving a scream of pain from him. His ally used the distraction to leap forward, swinging his sword wildly. Chaucer backpedalled quickly, dipping his hand into the breast pocket of his shirt. Spotting a gap, he darted forward and slapped his fingers across his attacker's eyes. The ground peppers were carried from his hand like a fine mist, instantly entering the man's exposed pupils and burning like fire. Stumbling, the thug cried out in agony, dropping his weapon and rubbing manically at his face. Chaucer allowed him to pass and then kicked him hard in the rear, watching him career headfirst into the barn wall and rebound to writhe on the floor. Looking up, Errabith spotted a heavy-looking crate and dragged it free of the pile it topped; it crashed down upon the thug's skull, ending his writhing instantly.

'Grazic!' he called out with delight, 'It appears it is just the two of us. What say we end this like men?'

'Listen,' Grazic grunted, both hands working to prize the device from his flesh, the act made infinitely more difficult due to its position, 'you have proved a point here. I know I am beaten. I can just leave, Corinth, Kazgrat, as far as you want! You have already killed Lafik and he looks a lot like me; cut up his face a bit and they will never ask a question. It is a win for both of us!'

'Well, you have really thought that out, have you not?' Chaucer replied, 'I get all the bounties on offer plus one extra, they think your gang is only seven strong, you see, you get to walk away with your life, forever indebted to the mercy of Chaucer and Black.'

He walked over to his discarded pistols and recovered them, wiping each with an oiled cloth from his pocket before delicately reloading them, 'Although, the last bit seems a bit weak to bother risking any stories of a survivor.'

'Yeah, okay,' Mann grunted, almost freeing the trap, and then feeling the fresh bite as the jaws tightened again, 'You can take whatever you want from this haul, there are plenty of coins in the back that probably will not make it back to their owners anyway; more than the bounty you will be claiming for my men!'

'Now that is tempting,' Errabith admitted, 'all that extra money, a life debt owed, and the bounty claimed on eight pieces of scum. Very tempting.'

'Yeah, it is,' Mann added hopefully, now on his knees against the pain.

Chaucer stood on the corpse where his machete was trapped and hauled back with all his might, the blade finally pulling free with a wet slurp. Wiping the weapon off on the dead man's shirt, he returned to Grazic.

'Let me get that for you,' he offered, leaning forward and pressing a spring-loaded switch on the rear, forcing the jaws open wide and pinning them in place again, 'funny how much pain such a little device causes, is it not?'

Mann fell back to a seated position, gasping at the sudden relief and holding a hand over his injured chest, 'Yeah, yeah it hurts, all right!' he replied with a forced laugh, 'but we are good now, you and I, right?'

'I am nothing if not a man of my word!' Errabith confirmed, helping Grazic up and pushing him towards the rear of the barn. From behind a stack of crates, Black suddenly appeared, his trademark spiked knuckledusters driven up into Mann's soft pallet with enough force to jam the four-inch spikes into his brain. The thug collapsed in a twitching heap.

'Oh, but I do not speak for my partner, of course!' Chaucer added, barely restraining his laughter, 'Mr. Black, you just cut me up!'

'No, Mr. Chaucer, I cut him up!' Black replied with a snigger.

'What of the two that fled before the combat began?'

'Word of Ballanis,' Black confirmed.

Errabith regarded him with amazement. Word of Ballanis was a favoured trap of his partner, it involved a metal grid adorned with numerous spikes, spikes were Fazam Black's favourite instrument of death, that would swing into or onto a victim when they triggered it. This was usually achieved through a trip-line or pressure plate that would release a spring-mounted bracket, activating the deadly device. How and when he had enough time to set one of the intricate ambushes up, Chaucer just did not know.

Together, the bounty hunters began to gather up their victims and load them onto the flat cart Black had prepared outside. Chaucer used rags to cover the worst of their foes' injuries, not out of respect but to save his fine clothes from bloodstains. As they worked, Black suddenly tapped the side of his arm and he turned to see a young man stood in the doorway, panting slightly. He wore the armband that signified he was a runner from the Assassin's Guild; pity the man who attempted to intercept such a messenger, for the recompense would be fatal.

'Greetings, herald, what news have you?' Errabith called openly.

'You are Chaucer and Black? In the acquaintance of Lady Pallstirrith?'

Chaucer paused at that. Rebecca Pallstirrith was an agent working within the city, seemingly skilled in securing some of the most lucrative and interesting of contracts; because she was freelance, this brought no end of irritation to the Guild. Funny then that a message was being delivered in her name by them rather than from her directly. He liked the woman, and over the last few years more than fifty percent of their work had been presented by her.

'We are the men you seek,' he confirmed, 'enter here so that we are not overheard.'

The messenger complied and joined them by the cart, 'Lady Pallstirrith has passed a personal message via the Guild for she is away from Corinth and has no sure way to contact her sometime clients.'

'Intriguing,' Black said from the other side of the cart, continuing to load the bodies.

'Relay the message,' Chaucer urged.

'She has asked for any who will answer her call to join her in the Dussen Lands. She is taking refuge in a town called Hercatalana, with three small children under her care. It is requested that any who are willing travel immediately, for she is hunted by Veer Assassins and fears for her life.'

Errabith sucked air in between his teeth, 'Veer? How has she gotten on the wrong side of them? That is a dire situation indeed. What is the pay?'

'Sorry, milord, there is no fixed price. The message stated it was negotiable upon completion.'

'Thank-you, young man, you may report your message delivered,' Chaucer slapped him on the shoulder before turning back to his partner, 'What do you make of that, Mr. Black?'

'You do not cross swords with the Veer,' Fazam stated.

'No, you do not!' Chaucer agreed, 'And no mention of a fixed fee? It is a preposterous proposition!'

'It is,' Black affirmed again, 'but a shame, for she is a cordial and pleasant lady to work with.'

'That is a good point, but not worth such risk against unknown levels of reward.'

'Exactly.'

Errabith watched his friend closely, looking for any flicker of emotion or doubt but there were none. 'Although…' he dragged out the word, noticing Fazam stop still in anticipation of the next words, 'rescuing a damsel in distress from the deadliest of killers would do our reputation no damage.'

'Which only matters if we are alive to benefit from it,' Black retorted.

Errabith turned back to the doors, just catching the runner before he departed, 'Hail, messenger. My apologies for impacting on your return but do you know who else has been in receipt of this message?'

The youngster stopped and looked to the ceiling, recalling information that had been set aside, 'Erm, I believe Hondrack, Tueurich, Dinish Fiveblades, Zark Hared and Carmine Fire were all sent word, but those were the ones that I remember. I do not know if they were found, have responded, or if more were contacted as well, Sir.'

'Thank-you, I will send a tip to you through the Guild for sure!' he called amicably, watching the young man set off at a trot into the evening streets. Chaucer turned back to Black who was now leaning on the edge of the cart, studying him with one eyebrow raised, 'That is quite the list of our competitors.'

'It is,' Fazam agreed carefully, 'let us hope that they answer and are slain. That will leave work aplenty for us.'

'But, Mr. Black, what would it say of us? If we are the only hunters who failed to rise to this challenge? Because we are too feeble to hold our own? Or too frightened to face other assassins?'

'Or too smart to put ourselves at risk unnecessarily?' Black countered.

'If you are willing to sell us as second fiddle to Zark Hared and Dinish Fiveblades, then I will defer to your judgement,' Errabith goaded, 'but I feel this unknown reward will be significant, Pallstirrith knows exactly what kind of people she is asking for help and that none of us would answer for a pittance. I guess we are doing well enough financially to throw that aside…'

Fazam Black sighed resignedly, 'Fine, Mr. Chaucer, we will collect this bounty and then we can investigate the situation in the Dussen Lands. But if all is not as it seems, I reserve the right to withdraw at any time!'

Errabith felt a thrill of excitement run through him, 'I bow to your wisdom as always, Mr Black!' he proclaimed.

Chapter 11

Treya rode quietly in the middle of the convoy, her grey mare feeling reinvigorated after the brief stop in Mareck's village. The wound in her side still throbbed constantly but it had become a sensation she was now accustomed to, and she wondered if she would even notice if it stopped. There was so much to think about, so much to try and section off in her mind, and all of it overshadowed by the threat of danger at every turn; again. She shook her head. Why was it that her misfortune at being born in the line of Fimarr continued to punish her despite her every effort to avoid it? Why could she not have lived the life she saw in others, families working the land together, or a craft passed down generation to generation; kin living in close proximity all their lives with no journeys through the wilderness or quests where the only outcomes were victory or death. Another shake of the head; she had no power to change the past or the present, only the future could be moulded, and she wished she had more control of that. It would be a terrible legacy to pass on to her own children, already they suffered because of her actions which, by default, had been generated through her father's.

She cast a glance back down the line. Frost was riding at the very rear, a position he insisted on maintaining, remaining constantly alert to any threat or pursuit. The old man had been ever quieter since the revelation of his army's destruction and their subsequent failure at Lennath's palace, she wondered if he was regretting his oath to aid them. Ahead of him rode Bentram, the younger man still mostly a mystery and she had taken no time to discover more about him. He had been vocal in most conversations when they made camp and seemed keenly devoted to this mission; having spent so many of his recent years as part of a doomed revolution, it was more that he favoured their company rather than being the sole remnant of lost hope. Between her and the two Lustanians were Herc and Catalana; the couple had spent much of the journey discussing the flora about them, plans for their shop and outlandish dreams of extravagance beyond their means. Admittedly, Cat' seemed to do most of the talking but Herc was permanently receptive and provided input when required; it would be easy to believe the pair were simply on a frivolous holiday together. She wondered if this irritated her because of their seeming lack of focus or because she felt jealous they were together; not for the first time, she regretted sending Straker away with the children and hoped they would all be together again soon.

Turning back to the path they were following, she watched Rayne riding a black stallion, she had insisted on the black horse offered in Rennicksburg being gifted to her, and smiled. Over the past weeks, her sister had started to show flickers of personality, not necessarily pleasant ones, but personality nonetheless. She was vain, attempting to cover the scars she bore at every opportunity; when Treya had asked about them, the response was one of remorse, Rayne believing she had received just punishment for her actions. Beyond this, the assassin was prone to selfishness, possessiveness, petulance and bickering with Catalana. All traits that showed some humanity seeping through the outer veneer; when they had been reunited five years ago, her sister had been little more than a shadow of a person. Rayne glanced back at her and Treya offered a smile, imagining that it was returned beneath the face mask her sister insisted on wearing, even among this small group.

Ahead of the whole party, riding a palomino from her own village, Crystal guided them through the pleasant vales of her homeland, leading them to the larger port of Fildenmaw. Mareck had assured them they would be able to secure a vessel to transport them to the destination Silas Zendar had indicated, a fool's errand in his opinion as there were no charted islands in that expanse of ocean. Treya regarded the young woman intently, not just a woman, but another sister, another previously unknown family member thrust upon her as Kastani had been. She had felt none of the resentment she had expected towards Crystal, instead a deep sympathy filled her heart. How difficult it must have been to live so long under one knowledge to then have it torn asunder in moments. Not only had she discovered her lineage was not what she believed, but her whole life had been lived under a pretence, her known father simply a guardian without any bond of blood. Given no time to absorb that world-shattering news, she was then expected to decide on whether to join a quest to save the land from darkness within minutes. She had agreed with startling speed, talking of fate and destiny, as if their arrival had always been anticipated. It was a boon that she had needed little coercion to undertake this quest but also concerning as to why she would risk everything at the word of relative strangers.

There was more to her half-sister than met the eye, that was certain, and she remembered the departure from her village mere days beforehand. Crystal had been tearful then, her surrogate father likewise filled with bitter emotion, but insisted that recent events suggested something coming on the horizon for her. Mareck had been far more resigned, clearly unhappy to see his daughter leaving but the loss seemed far deeper than that; perhaps explaining the truth reminded him that he had no familial claim to the girl, that he was losing her both physically and emotionally. There had been some kind of previous argument around such an event, Treya was certain, for the old man had talked at length about hoping this day would never come and wishing Straker had kept his secret. Ironic as Treya wished her lover would stop keeping them. Crystal had insisted it was meant to be this way, that the world itself had proven she was ready through the arrival of the Fimarrs. She had even asked him to come with them, that his experience and skill would be invaluable upon their adventure, but he had declined. He stated that he had vowed to give up those ways, no matter the cost, and had hoped to steer her away from them as well; in this he had failed but he would await her return with faith. Since then, Crystal had been as stoic as Frost, detached from the group when they stopped, not through any animosity on her part but natural isolation that came from being forced into the entourage.

Treya spurred her horse forward, passing Rayne, joining Crystal at the head of the company. She half-turned and nodded a greeting but the stony expression remained fixed in place.

'It will not be long,' she declared in her thick Zendran accent, 'Fildenmaw lies just beyond zis rise before us.'

Treya admired the smooth bronze skin blessed to the other woman, that, along with the thick mahogany hair that spilled down her back, echoed their father's appearance. Of course, his hair had never been so long or well-cared for. Not for the first time, her eyes flicked to the length of rope hanging from Crystal's belt, vicious fishhook glinting in the afternoon sun. She had watched her practise with the weapon the previous evening, a strangely graceful dance exerting untold pressures on the strong line, allowing the hook to be fired out at incredible velocity. The accuracy she seemed capable of was also astounding, more evidence that she was born of the great warrior Rork Fimarr.

'That is good news, for time has been against us from the start,' Treya offered, keen to try and engage her new sister in conversation.

'As you say,' Crystal returned, 'but it 'as not seemed so 'ere. Incidents we 'ave 'ad. And ze monster zat attacked our village, but nozing since it was captured. You are certain zat Prince Lennaz plots against ze ozer Kingdoms.'

'The Kingdoms and beyond,' Treya asserted, 'the worst thing we could do is show complacency and allow him to build enough power to do so. I believe our plan is sound, and enough of a threat to merit the attempts on our lives.'

'It is unknown to me,' Crystal mused, 'to be 'unted as you 'ave. Per'aps I 'ave lived too sheltered a life, but I 'ave always dreamed of adventuring across zis world, 'elping zose in need where I find zem. Could zis be my true fazer coming out in me?'

'You remind me of Alissa. The way she was before, I mean. She always dreamed of travelling and looked upon our father as a great hero, a great man.'

'And you did not? I cannot zink of anyzing more wonderful zan being raised by such a skilled warrior and renowned 'ero. I wish I 'ad been graced wiz ze 'onour of meeting 'im before 'e died.'

Treya found herself nonplussed by the words but realised they couldn't be more true for Crystal; how romantic a daydream for those who had not experienced his harsh parenting and soul-destroying trials.

'It is funny to hear you say that,' she confided, 'you, who have not known the hardship of being a daughter of Fimarr would take any chance to do so. I, who lived it, would take any chance to erase it. I hate to tell you that his legend is far superior to the reality.'

'It 'urts my 'eart to 'ear such a zing from you. I would not dare to question your life, for I 'ave no basis of comparison. My upbringing was gentle, caring and filled wiz as much freedom as my fazer, I mean Mareck, dared to allow me. Yet I 'ave always looked to ze 'orizon, 'oping for some chance at proving myself; ze very chance you 'ave brought to me. From your words, it sounds as zough you were brought up to survive such an ordeal, to be strong in ze face of danger and prepared for any zreats zat would come for you. Despite zis, you 'ave done all you can to avoid quests, adventures or being drawn from ze simple life you desire. Would it be too much to consider zat it is a natural instinct to rebel against our upbringing?'

The idea caused her to pause; Crystal seemed to be suggesting that the horrific childhood Treya had suffered due to her father's brutal training regimes had been for the best. That she would not be the woman she was without it. A lifetime of believing herself strong in spite of her father now turned on its head to suggest it was *because* of him? No, Crystal lacked the perspective of the daughters who had known the man himself. She decided to lighten the conversation somewhat.

'I hope not, as I am trying to raise my own children as it seems Mareck did for you. It would be awful to believe they would want to seek adventures and danger rather than quiet comfort!'

'I do not travel wiz you to spite my... Mareck. You need my 'elp, to save ze land from terrible danger; I believe zis is my true purpose. When I look at your group, it makes me feel zat zis may be ze calling of all children of Rork Fimarr.'

'I did not mean to insult you, or your love for Mare.. your father,' Treya apologised quickly, realising her words had been received in a manner unintended, 'I am grateful for your aid, given so freely, and for the chance to know you as a sister. I only wish...'

'We are 'ere,' Crystal cut her off, raising her voice so the others could hear as well, 'Zere is a shipwright known to my fazer 'ere. Zey will be able to 'elp us.'

Their company gathered on the road, looking down into the busy fishing town below, Treya feeling the frustration of the poorly finished dialogue between herself and Crystal. The bustling port was a contrast to Rennicksburg where the residency seemed calm and peaceful in their business, from up here, Fildenmaw appeared more like the few cities she had seen, a frantic chaos of distressed masses trying to get by.

Passing through the streets, she was amazed that their conspicuous party seemed to draw no attention from those hurrying about their business. She determined that this was both blessing and curse; their movements were unrestricted, but such a place generated the perfect environment for secret observation or ambush. The idea cast her mind back to her first arrival in Rennicksburg. She had been accompanied by Alissa and Joseff Gaesin then, and the three of them were ambushed; it had been obvious, looking back, as the street had been deserted before the attack. They had survived thanks to the arrival of Straker Forge and from there her love for the man had developed and grown; her one true love, discovered only because of an adventure generated by her father's legacy. Gritting her teeth, she determined that Crystal's suggestions were not going to change her lifelong opinion of her father.

'Up 'ere,' their guide called above the background noise, 'ze shipwright we seek 'as a shop on ze dock.'

Following her, remaining in single file to navigate the throng of people, the seven riders finally reached their goal, an inauspicious building with a large stone runoff to one side. Although there was nothing there now, the ramp to the water looked large enough to manage a small schooner at least. A sudden worry crossed her mind as they dismounted, what if Crystal had misinterpreted the need? What if she believed they had the time, or resource, to commission the construction of their own vessel?

There was no time to raise the issue with her as she opened the shop door to the sound of the small bell above it tinkling gently. Joining the others in following her inside, Treya was impressed with the sailing paraphernalia within; counters filled with all sort of navigational instruments, rigging and equipment adorning every shelf and wall space, some even hanging from the ceiling. The place smelled of salt and damp.

''Ello!' Crystal called as no staff were visible, 'Is anyone serving?'

A door to the rear of the shop opened and a young man in a flamboyant shirt and leather waistcoat appeared. 'Welcome,' he said with little enthusiasm, 'how can I help?'

'You!' Rayne suddenly cried from the rear of the group, knives appearing in her hands as if from nowhere, 'This is a trap!'

The young man looked as shocked as the rest of them and had gone ghostly white at the sight of the black-clad assassin.

'Rayne, what is it?' Treya urged, suddenly alert to any sudden attacks.

Frost had moved to block the door they had entered through, Bentram sliding his twin swords free and preparing for battle. Herc was less panicked, simply moving his own body in front of Catalana's in case something did occur. Crystal was left in total confusion over what was happening.

'What are you doing?' she gasped, 'Zere is no danger 'ere! Zis man did not even know we were coming!'

'I have met him before,' Rayne asserted, poised like a cat ready to pounce, 'a few months ago when I took the life of Chee Winterfire in Corinth. Do you expect me to believe his presence here is a coincidence?'

'She is speaking truly,' the man behind the counter stated, 'I was a soldier for hire then, had been for a few years at that point. The fact you spared my life allowed me an opportunity to rethink it and change my direction. I came back here to work for my father.'

Tension filled the air for a moment before Rayne slowly relaxed, 'I do not believe in chance, but I will provide you an opportunity to prove me wrong.'

'Then I am indebted to you for the second time,' he said, releasing the breath he had been holding, 'my name is Makinson, what is it I can help you with?'

Most seemed reluctant to engage as Rayne's expression did not suggest she believed this man's story. Treya moved over to the counter and found herself joined by Crystal. Pulling out the map they had brought with them, she rolled it out before him and pointed to the spot marked with a set of co-ordinates.

'We need to get here, as quickly as possible. Can you help us?'

He studied the diagram for a few moments, leaning forward on the counter for a closer look, before raising his head to regard them both, 'Why do you want to get there, if you don't mind me asking?'

'We do mind!' Frost rumbled from the doorway.

Treya ignored him and searched Makinson's eyes, 'Our business is not yours,' she confirmed, 'but why do you ask in that manner? Do you know this place?'

'Aye, by reputation alone. All the trade ships and fishers avoid that whole area, a lot of treacherous sand banks and maybe even a reef. Nothing worth travelling there for, unless you enjoy swimming!'

'Regardless, 'ave you any ships zat can make ze journey?' Crystal pressed.

'No doubt, for the right price. Bartering such deals is not our usual business but I know enough of the captains to arrange something. It would maybe take two weeks to align such a charter, and there would be a pretty cost involved.'

'Two weeks?' Treya groaned, dismay filling her, 'We cannot wait that long! Is there no faster course of action?

'We could look into current traders, anyone passing nearby, willing to alter their itinerary slightly to drop you there, but you may have a long wait for collection. As there is no land in that area, it would be some feat to last long enough in a rowboat together for that duration.'

'That would be our concern,' Treya insisted, 'all we need is passage to the location on the map.'

'And we would be happy to oblige,' a gruff voice affirmed as another, older, man hobbled through the staff door.

'REEVUS!' Rayne spat at the top of her voice, flicking her arm out like lightning.

The old man ducked his head to the side, two deadly blades impaling the door jamb behind him. 'At your service,' he replied.

Mainspring was a truly beautiful place, comprising only the single city with a radius of six miles of land around the isolated hill upon which it sat. The incline to reach the glorious home of the King was severe, making effective siege an almost impossibility, but the wide trade road had been constructed to wind its way around that protective mound, allowing official access and providing significant forewarning of any approach. A natural fountain adorned the city itself, man-made channels carrying the fresh water through the streets in elegant streams before being allowed to cascade down all four sides of the hill, forming white waterfalls that pooled far below and travelled from the base in natural rivers. The water spouting within Mainspring's boundary was reputed to be the most pure anywhere in all the lands; Lennath had to admit that was probably true and found it ironic that drinking from the channels within the city was forbidden. Aquafiers were employed to bottle and barrel from the fountain itself, allowing the King to sell the water at whatever price he deemed necessary; a questionable practice when the leftovers simply ran unchecked beyond their border at zero cost. Lennath knew that many travelled to the bottom of the natural motte to gather or drink for free, but none broke the law within the city walls. Which is why it had been so embarrassing for Alissa to plunge her head into one of the channels and gulp her fill. Due to his Royal status, the attending guards had given only a warning, insisting that his guest be informed of all Mainspring rules. Lennath had been cordial rather than unleashing Mozak upon them, his attention firmly focussed on the approaching confrontation with his family.

Having undergone the formalities of arrival, being provided refreshment and escort to the conference chamber, they were now relinquishing weapons to a steward seated at a desk outside. Placing his sword and dagger on the table as requested, Lennath cast a glance over to the six heavily armed men sat or leaning on benches outside the grand golden doors; they were obviously his brothers' bodyguards, as with the less formal greeting room he had attended during his last visit, guardians were not permitted within. Flanking the doors themselves stood two of the King's elite guard, dressed in full plate armour with swords and halberds held at ease.

'I have nothing,' Alissa chirped at the steward, twirling theatrically before him to allow her light robes to billow out around her, 'Do you need to search me?'

The servant flushed scarlet, 'No, milady, of course not!' he blurted out, 'This weapon check is merely a formality for the Royal Family and their guests.'

'Oh,' she replied, slightly deflated, 'I do have some weapons, though. My teeth and nails are as deadly as any knife, but I am not sure I could really deposit them with you…'

The steward looked shocked and confused, 'I do… that is, there are…'

'I apologise, my good man,' Lennath interceded coolly, 'my consort is a fine one for mischievous antics! Pay her no mind, she simply seeks a rise from you! I assure you she is no threat to my kin!'

The steward forced an uneasy laugh alongside Lennath's loud chortle, 'As you say, Sire. You recognise that your protector will be required to remain out here?'

'Yes, as is customary. I pity any man who attempts to gain unpermitted access here!' Lennath smiled broadly but the expression was not returned. He nodded to Mozak who moved over to the other bodyguards, acknowledging none of them but taking up a rigid stance that placed all of them between him and the conference chamber doors.

Taking Alissa's arm in his, he moved toward the golden portal, stroking her hand as he chided her lightly, 'Try to stay with me, my love, I would prefer to conduct this engagement in my way rather than yours.'

He could see her pouting from the corner of his eye, 'Your way is boring, you let mouths flap too much!'

'You may be right, my queen-to-be, but if you kill anyone here, we will not return to Lustania. We will not leave the palace alive, I fear, and then all I have worked for will be lost.'

'You should have let me bring the Stave; I could have seen into their heads, or better ripped them open! Or why not just let my pretty pets eat them before they got here?'

'You are exquisitely untameable, Alissa, but there are ways and means to everything. I cannot simply have my family killed, it raises too many questions and I think there is a law that would prevent me taking the throne as a result. Placing Porthus and Gallth aside for a moment, it would be difficult to pass all my brothers' deaths off as accidents outwith my control! No, there is only one way to do this now, which was inevitable from the start, and we will simply have to do it earlier than planned.'

'Maybe just one of them? It would be magnificent to have tasted all of your kin before Kale takes full control of your body and makes it all irrelevant.'

She had mentioned his supposed spiritual passenger many times over the past several days and he wanted nothing more than to stamp out this belief she had. However, it made her compliant and engaging in a way he had not experienced before; she worked hard to remain lucid when they talked and had even started to understand his plans to a greater level. Once the Kingdoms were his, he could then start the work of correcting her beliefs.

'I have given you total freedom to deal with your family as you see fit, with my full resource behind you; please allow me the same courtesy?'

'You are no fun when we travel,' she sulked, 'what is the point of going anywhere if I can't explore the insides of someone important…'

He leaned over and kissed her temple before pushing open the heavy doors, 'Thank-you, my sweet,' he whispered.

Inside was the large oak table he recalled from every formal gathering they had undertaken since the generation of the Five Kingdoms. Shaped as a hollow square, the King sat on the closed side, facing the doors, with an empty seat beside him, which had once belonged to the Queen until she passed. Along one leg, were three seats, two occupied by Kendoss and Gregor and the other reserved for Gallth. Opposite that leg was the side usually shared by Porthus and Lennath. Ignoring the frosty stares of his brothers, Lennath escorted Alissa to Porthus' chair and seated her, before taking his own.

'What do you think you are doing?' Gregor snarled.

'Sitting, brother,' Lennath replied calmly, 'I assumed you were aware of the custom due to your own position?'

'Do not be pedantic, my son,' the King scolded, 'he is clearly referring to your guest's presence here.'

'Of course, father,' Lennath replied warmly, feeling oddly lifted at his apparently improved health, 'this is the Lady Alissa Fimarr, and she is soon to be my bride. As with our mother, there is nothing spoken here that she cannot be privy to.'

'Then I believe congratulations are in order, to you both,' the King continued, lacking surety in his words.

'Father!' Gregor snapped, 'No matter what efforts he wishes to employ to distract us from the reasons for this assembly, I demand we remain focussed and take the actions discussed!'

'Actions discussed?' Lennath echoed, 'I did not know it was customary to decide conference matters prior to the conference itself?'

'Do not come to my home and quote rules at me!' his father bellowed, silencing them all, 'I built this room, I built the Kingdoms; my word is law, and you will abide by it!'

'You are very loud!' Alissa added, applauding excitedly, 'I love the way your words echo!'

'I will thank you to hold your tongue, woman. There are serious matters to discuss and I will accept no interruptions.'

'I have come here freely, father,' Lennath stated, holding his hands up placatingly, 'do not take your anger out on my beloved.'

'Very well,' the old man returned his attention to Lennath, 'then I will take it out on you! I have been tolerant and patient with you, favouring you when I should not and permitting you exceptions that have done nothing to improve your manner. You are here very much accused of treachery such as I can barely bring myself to conceive! When last we consulted, you were to prove yourself innocent of treason by allowing your brother into the heart of your Kingdom, to let him discover if your protestations of innocence were true of false. Tell me, Lennath, where is Gallth now?'

'He is dead,' Lennath replied without pause, 'a shocking tragedy has befallen…'

'You lying, wicked filth!' Gregor screamed at him, 'I knew it! I felt his death days ago, an undesirable side-effect of twinhood I suppose. Now you openly admit that he has been murdered in your care? It is time that you be dealt with…'

Lennath placed a restraining hand on Alissa's leg, certain that she was about to say something foolish, 'Gregor, control yourself, Gallth was not murdered! He suffered a terrible accident! He spent many an evening defiling my serving girls and on one such occasion, he fell from the bed due to his efforts and cracked his skull on the uncarpeted floor. I interrogated the maid at length, but her trauma was genuine, she had done nothing untoward; simply a poorly timed accident.'

'A poorly timed accident?' Kendoss asked with disgust, 'You suggest there would be a better time?'

'No, brother, simply that his death has not aided the perception you have of me. I cannot undo what has been done, but will not tolerate false accusation.'

'Porthus' convenient death…' Gregor began before the King interrupted.

'Disappearance.'

'If you must, father, but we need to accept the obvious! He is not with us because of an attack on the way to confront you, Lennath. Gallth now dead whilst investigating you! This is no unfortunate coincidence! It is only a matter of time before you find some way to kill us off as well!'

'That would be very messy,' Alissa offered, 'your face is like a beetroot, you must be just full of blood!'

'What did she just say to me?' Gregor raged, fire in his eyes.

'No, Gregor, what did you just say to me?' Lennath attempted to distract him, 'Have you accused me of murder? Of fraternal Regicide? I demand you evidence those claims!'

'There is more than enough evidence, brother!' Gregor assured him before turning to the King, 'Father, I demand he be stripped of title and position, imprisoned here prior to a formal trial; I will script the accusations myself!'

'Gregor, what you ask is unprecedented! To place my own offspring in chains and try them for such crimes; what will it do to our people?'

'It will save them from his evil. Can you not see that he has become obsessed with power? If we fail to take action he could destroy us all!'

'I am mad with power?' Lennath asked slowly, 'What is your proposition for Lustanian rule while I am incarcerated, I wonder? And what of Zendra? Or Kaydarell? I suppose it is simply logical that they are split between the two of you? You accuse me of atrocities that I can barely fathom yet you will be the main profiteer. If Kendoss is not with you then perhaps some similar death or imprisonment awaits him? I have simply become the scapegoat in this matter.'

'No, Lennath,' the King replied sadly, 'I have given you the benefit of the doubt for too long, it is time for something to be done.'

'I do not think I like any of you,' Alissa said flatly, 'you cannot see beyond your own faces. There is far more to existing than your fragile frames alone, it is like insects moaning at the birds who will eat them. I think it would be better if you were all dead.'

'An admission of guilt from your bitch, Lennath? She has sealed your fate, brother!'

'Say that again, Gregor,' Lennath replied, his voice a dangerous whisper.

'You think I fear you because you have packed on the pounds? I do not! Your woman is naught but a bitch and should suffer your fate!'

The Prince of Lustania vaulted the table before him with ease, crossing the gap between himself and Gregor in two bounds before leaping over his table to tackle his brother to the ground. Punching him in the face twice as he lay pinned beneath him, Lennath felt his rage boiling over. His third strike was restrained as Kendoss wrapped his arms about Lennath's shoulders and hauled him clear.

'Stop this madness!' the King cried out before collapsing forward unheeded.

Twisting in his brother's grasp, Lennath turned to face him, kicking out fiercely into the side of his knee and driving an elbow into his jaw when he staggered at the loss of support. Lurching to stay upright, Kendoss did not see the boot aimed for his chest and was sent flying back over the table by the impact. There was no time to revel in victory as Gregor leapt upon his back immediately, his older brother heavier than he looked. Lennath stumbled under the weight but angled himself away from the table's edge; heaving with all his might, he threw Gregor forward, over his head, to slam onto Kendoss' chair, shattering the furniture under the impact. A satisfying grunt of pain was released but the chair's owner was already leaping back across the table whence Lennath had sent him. His tall, chiselled frame warned of great strength and skill, but it was naught but a façade; swinging blows were thrown in from either side, Lennath able to duck his head out of range for the first before blocking the second with a raised arm. Kendoss was left exposed and felt the sting of a sharp uppercut before a solid palm-strike to the solar plexus drove the air painfully from him. Doubling over to try and regain his breath, a roundhouse kick struck his temple, sending him sprawling once again.

'G-g-guards!' coughed Gregor, scrambling to his feet with broken chair legs gripped tightly for defence, 'Enter here, we are betrayed!'

Lennath turned as the doors swung inwards. A clatter of metal followed as the King's elite troops were tossed lifelessly before the imposing figure of Mozak. Casting his gaze beyond the deadly Veer, he saw the corridor beyond awash with blood, bodies, and broken weapons.

'What is this?' Gregor stammered in fear, 'you would assassinate us all?'

'No,' Lennath said coldly, walking past his prostrate brother towards the centre of the table, 'I did not instigate this violence, you did. I warn you now that I will not be imprisoned or deposed, and I will settle this matter as it should be done. But see here, what your antagonism has caused!'

The King was lying across the table, clutching his chest and struggling to breathe. His skin was pale, and tears were flowing freely, Alissa had rushed to his side already, gently caressing his hair. Lennath crouched at the other side of the table from him, reaching out a hand to gently wipe a tear from the old man's cheek.

'It pains me greatly to see you like this, Father, and I am sorry that this conference has devolved so. I can take the recriminations no longer and feel the matter must be resolved; I declare Gregor's slander of me to be an act of war and the battlefield will decide who is the righteous party.

'Son, please, do not drag the Kingdoms into Civil War, it will benefit no-one and weakens us in the eyes of external Nations. Please give diplomacy another chance,' his father pleaded with tremoring voice.

'It is too late, father, but I offer you the chance to refrain; I do not wish to meet you in combat, nor do I want Mainspring tainted by this darkness. Resolve to play no part, and stand at the side of the victor.'

'But you will lose,' the King said incredulously, 'Kendoss and Gregor will stand together and, as the harbinger of war, you will have no right to the forces of Zendra or Kaydarell. You will stand alone against the other four Kingdoms.'

'He is correct,' Gregor agreed, still hiding behind his captured chair legs, 'You would have stood more chance of claiming the crown through this cowardly attack than in the field of war! We will defeat your pitiful army with ease, no matter the skill of your henchman! Father, I deny you the option to abstain, choose a side or be damned by your people!'

The King squeezed Lennath's hand weakly, 'I am sorry, my son. I will stand with the Four Kingdoms.'

Lennath stroked his father's hair gently before rising and offering his hand to Alissa. Strolling casually towards the doors, feeling satisfied that Kendoss crawled out of his path, Lennath did not look back as he spoke, 'So it will be, brothers, I will meet you on the field of battle and the victor will be deemed righteous in this dispute, the defeated will abdicate their thrones!'

Alissa wriggled free of his grasp and pulled open the face plate of one of the elite guards. Digging her fingers sharply into the dead man's eye socket, she plucked his eyeball free and pulled until the optic nerve snapped with a wet slap. Swinging it happily before her like a conker, she laughed at them. 'You are all going to die, and I'll get to watch! It is a shame you are not my family!' she called to them before skipping from the room.

The fiery local alcohol burned all the way down and carried a pungent aftertaste that Forge cared little for, but he smiled and released a satisfied sigh.

'Delicious as always, Folt,' he stated, 'Have you improved the recipe since my last visit?'

The leathery-faced barman returned his smile, showing black and yellow teeth, 'Aye your taste is keen as ever, Straker Forge, we have harvested a new berry of late. Never seen it before but it adds a smoother texture on the way down, do you not think?'

'Sure enough!' he agreed politely but covered the glass with his hand when Folt moved to pour a second shot, 'But I need to stay sharp of wits right now, with the children and Rebecca to protect.'

'Right you are!' Folt grinned broadly, 'She is a fine filly that 'Becca! Would it happen that she is single?'

Forge restrained a laugh before whispering conspiratorially, 'She is unspoken for, my friend, and it may be that she is on the prowl for a worthy suitor!'

Folt looked genuinely interested and Straker felt guilty for a moment, but only a moment, as he imagined the scene should the dishevelled barkeep decide to express his intentions to the gentrified lady! Placing a coin upon the counter, he raised a hand in farewell before departing the bar into the crisp evening air. It always seemed that the Dussen Lands were just a little colder than the surrounding Nations and he wondered if the lack of significant hills or forests made a difference in that respect. Meandering down the road towards Czerna's house, he considered the time they had been in Hercatalana so far; his young hostess had slowly cooled over the presence of Terex, but she refused him access to her home. As a result, Kastani had taken to visiting him above the blacksmith's shop at every opportunity, often spending whole days there at a time. The girl was a bit of an enigma, seemingly able to enrapture anyone with her innocent charm, and it was easy to forget the difficult upbringing she had endured so far. The twins simply loved being with her, clearly looking to her to direct many of the games they played, but she seemed equally at home with either adults or children, having received much praise for her conduct from Czerna. She was separated from her mother, had witnessed some horrific events, and been displaced from her home but no word of complaint passed her lips. Was she unique in her resilience, or was it common to all small children he wondered; hopefully the latter, as he would hate all they had been through of late to scar Joseff and Melody in the long term.

The walk was refreshing but seemed somehow unfair, who knew what difficulties and dangers Treya was facing while he was relatively pampered as a guest in the town. He toyed with the idea of journeying to Lustania alone, of removing their antagonist and his hired assassins in one swift strike against Treya's wishes. He knew he could do it, the curse laid upon him guaranteed such victory, but three things stood in his way. Most importantly, he had promised his lady love that he would not do so; could he beg forgiveness afterwards? Perhaps, but he had done so too often during their time together. The second issue was Alissa; if she was a valid target then it would be no problem at all, she would be killed along with the rest. But she was not, and he doubted he could bring himself to execute her with the fond memories he still cherished of the girl she had once been, meaning he would have to face Lennath and the Veer whilst hoping she was not present to watch. Any failure in that regard would nullify the magic protecting him. Finally, the immediate blocker to such a heroic attempt were his children; he liked Terex and felt they could have been friends under different circumstances but did not trust him to protect the twins in the same manner as Kastani. If something happened to them in Straker's absence, he would never forgive himself. Sighing, he opened the door to his current residence.

Czerna was sat in a high-backed chair, all three children gathered before her on the parlour rug, reading a story aloud. They waved to him as he entered but did not rush to greet him, enraptured as they were by the tale. He listened for a few moments, quickly recognising it as the Ballad of Prince Tokarian, a legend that suggested the Dussen was once a lush, green land until he had broken the heart of the goddess Sattaranis who removed fertility from the soil as recompense. They hadn't gotten that far yet, but Forge smiled as he crossed through the room to the kitchen; it was a good story and Czerna seemed to be telling it with enthusiasm. He found Rebecca sat at the kitchen table, a half-eaten bowl of soup before her.

'Not hungry?' he enquired, moving across to the stove to help himself to a bowl of the thick broth.

'I should be, but I have no appetite. This waiting is worse than anything else I have been through. It feels inevitable that we will be discovered and forced to fight or flee again.'

'Aye, that is probably the case. But we may get lucky, perhaps Hercatalana is too remote a place for them to search.'

'This place was built in honour of Catalana Fimarr and Herc Callid, it was one of the first places Silas Zendar came to for information about the Fimarrs; I am amazed they were not here waiting for us!'

'You are in a dark mood this evening, Lady Pallstirrith, does something prey upon your mind?'

'It has been almost four days now, and all we seem to be doing is pretending everything is fine. How am I supposed to continue in this way? I am frightened all of the time, I have sent for aid, but none has come; I cannot determine what kind of life I will even have to go back to and...' she turned her face away as emotion threatened to overflow.

Forge crouched down beside her, taking one soft hand in his own, 'I know this is all new to you and not something you ever desired,' he comforted, 'but you are sitting here, very much alive and that is an achievement in itself! Stress comes naturally when our foes are upon us or dangers are imminent, that is why we must go about our normal business in between or that stress will break us. The letter you sent to Corinth was a fine idea and would have brought useful aid, no doubt, but it was sent to mercenaries without a confirmed offer of pay. I would have been more surprised if they had come! Terex and I are sufficient protection, you can be certain of that; I would not leave my own children less than completely safe. There will be little difficulty in restoring the life and work you previously conducted when this is over, your experience may even make you better at it, having seen some of the practicalities your clients have to deal with.'

'Do you truly love Treya?' she suddenly blurted out. Straker released her hand and stood again, hoping he had not just given the woman an unintended signal.

'I do. More than anything in my life. More even than those darling children out there. There is nothing I would not do for her.'

'How did you know?'

'What? That I loved her? I am not sure how to answer that. Why do you ask?'

'I... that is, I just... there is much confusion for me right now. I have been told that I am loved in the way you speak of but do not know if I reciprocate those feelings.'

'I do not know that I am the best advisor in such matters!' he laughed before attempting to answer her question honestly, 'I loved Treya almost from the second I saw her; she had great confidence and inner strength in abundance, but I could sense her vulnerability from the start. Her heart was in need and, when I first spoke to her, I realised mine was too. I felt nervous excitement at every touch, no matter how inconsequential the contact, and I still do. I carry a deep pain in my chest for every second we are apart, and it vanishes at the sight of her face. No matter what the sacrifice required of me, I want nothing more than to bring her happiness in all things; I no longer dream of what my future might be, only what hers should be. Forgive me, I am not so assured in questions of the heart; why do you ask this?'

'I am aware of one who professes to love me, but I do not know if I can, or will, return such devotions. I feel much of what you have described but it is marred by other confusions.'

Straker was feeling awkward at the depth of conversation and defaulted to his standard defence mechanism, 'You are not talking about Folt, are you?' he asked mirthfully, 'Because I will not have you trifling with that man's affections!'

Confusion was quickly replaced with an unimpressed smile, 'You are difficult to talk to sometimes, Straker, but he could never be my paramour; I insist on all teeth being present and an odour that does not drive me away!'

Forge allowed himself a casual laugh at her words and was pleased when she dipped her spoon back into the meal before her. The sound of the front door slamming open startled her and she knocked the bowl to the floor as she jumped up from her chair. Darting back to the parlour, Straker found Terex filling the outer door.

'Get out!' Czerna shouted at him fiercely, casting the book aside as she stood.

'We have no time for your hate, girl!' Terex snapped, a shadow of his former self flashing through his normally calm exterior, 'Prepare the children to leave, now!'

'Terex!' Kastani called excitedly, 'We have not finished the story yet; Prince Tokarian is building a big statue to get the god-lady to like him. I think they will be in love!'

'I'm sure they will,' the warrior replied in a voice soft and calm, a complete contrast to his body language, 'I can finish the story for you when we have departed. It is not safe here little princess.'

'I do not want to go away again,' Melody sniffed, tears beginning to form.

'Do not cry, my darling girl,' Straker soothed, rushing over and embracing her alongside her brother, 'it will just be another adventure! Come along here, Rebecca will take you upstairs and help you gather your things.'

He ushered the three children over to her and Rebecca nodded, fear evident in her face but nerve held as she was given the task to complete. Once the four had disappeared up the staircase, he turned back to Terex, ignorant to Czerna's defiant posture.

'What has happened, Terex? Why the urgent flight?'

'Something is here, Forge, I saw it with my own eyes,' Terex replied before addressing Czerna as well, 'one of the patrols I have established came to me, took me out to the Southern watchtower and I saw it in the scrub wastes, not more than nine hundred yards from the town's edge. One of the beasts, I am certain, black and not because of the dim light; it was pacing back and forth, as if awaiting an instruction to attack.'

'We have encountered many of the remnant creatures over the years, though none recently. We should kill it, not flee,' Czerna stated.

'No, its movements indicated it was being restrained, either physically or by external commands. This is no random encounter; it is an attack as we suffered in Rennicksburg. Come, Forge, we must deter whatever strike comes while Rebecca readies the children.'

'Wait!' Czerna cried irritably at him, 'We are not helpless here! The Dussen have survived much and we are fine warriors, this beast is as much a threat to us as you. Stand and fight with us and there may be no need to flee!'

'I appreciate the support,' Terex allowed gracefully. 'and killing this thing is definitely the plan. We will have to leave, regardless of the outcome as more will follow eventually; the courage of your people may provide the breathing space we need, however.'

'Good, I will rouse our defenders and meet you at the Southern Tower,' she replied, grabbing a thick leather jerkin before dashing from the building and towards the centre of the town. Forge joined Terex in sprinting to the stated rendezvous.

'I am impressed by her courage!' Terex yelled as they ran.

'She is hardened indeed and a leader belying her years! It is a shame she hates you so much!'

Terex's laughter echoed from the walls of the nearby buildings as they ran and soon their destination loomed ahead. Bounding immediately up the stairs, they ascended at pace to the observation platform where a sentry stood peering into the dusk. He extended his arm and pointed out to the short scrub bushland beyond.

'Fifty yards from dead centre,' he mumbled, 'Move forward of the torches and you'll see better.'

Forge did as he suggested and easily caught sight of the animal in question; even at this distance, it was clearly visible amongst the low, thorny bushes, prowling in a feline manner, hard quills all along its body audibly rattling together. Every so often it raised its long, crocodile-like snout to sniff the air before continuing its pacing, spiked mace of a tail dragging behind it.

'Why does it not attack?' he wondered aloud.

'Maybe it fears the light, most predators avoid the town because of the torch perimeter,' the sentry offered.

'No,' Terex corrected, 'it wants to attack; there is nothing here for it to fear. Something is stopping it, like I said, or it is waiting for something.'

'For what?' Forge asked absently.

'That knowledge would guarantee us victory,' Terex answered before turning to the Dussen man, 'Have you tried to fire the ballista at it?'

He was referring to the huge crossbow mounted on the raised edge of the platform, a deterrent to any raiders who happened upon the exposed settlement.

'No, it remains out of range.'

Terex exchanged a look with Forge, 'How fortunate that this dumb animal has stopped beyond maximum firing range of your main defence; it is as I feared, Alissa controls the beast.'

'You cannot be certain of that,' Straker countered with a shudder, 'surely such finite control was beyond even Ramikain himself?'

'I do not know the expanse of his true power; he was weak from years of dormancy when you… before his downfall.'

Noise below attracted their attention and Forge peered over the side to see a dozen armed men approaching, four of them hefting a large, rolled net, led by Czerna.

'Stay here, arm the weapon in case the creature comes into range,' Terex ordered, 'I will assist below; they will need my help if they are planning what I think they are!'

Straker nodded with a wry smile on his face; Terex was completely in his element when battle was upon them, he would have been a challenging adversary in time of war. He hoped that natural leadership did not ruffle Czerna's feathers, they could do with such dynamic command in this situation. Ensuring the ballista was primed and safety catch released, Forge watched as the Dussen men formed a line, net stretched out over forty yards. Each forced a weapon through gaps in the giant snare that should protect them if their section was unlucky enough to receive the monster's attention. Terex followed the line out, shouting commands to keep them even, maintaining their target at the centre of the large restraint. The beast did nothing other than continue to pace, rattling its spines together more rapidly, as if in warning to them. Straker's mouth had gone dry and sweat formed on his brow as he maintained the aim of the powerful crossbow at the furthest feasible firing distance.

When the Dussen got within one hundred yards of their prey, the mutant stopped pacing and lowered itself under tension, poised to leap forward at them. Terex was still shouting, his words almost drowned out by the clattering of long black quills; no, not just the rattling, there was another noise. A low, droning hum that reminded him of…

'Get out of there!' he suddenly shouted, waving over the top of his current weapon to try and attract their attention, 'Retreat to the tower!'

They could not hear him but the sentry at his side understood and leapt across the platform to start ringing the alarm bell. Without warning, Czerna appeared from the stairwell, face a mask of concern.

'What is it? We have seen the threat already, why raise the alarm now?'

'Because we have not seen the threat!' Forge cried to her, pointing into the purple sky.

Beyond them, several of the men were turning as they detected the peeling bell over the cacophony about them. Terex began gesticulating fiercely, clearly trying to maintain the discipline of the trap and not realising the threat. Without warning, the flying insectoid beast Forge had last seen in Lennath's palace dropped from the air, landing on the central two men holding the net, its tentacled tails lashing out at a third, pulping bones as he was tossed aside like a rag doll. Terex had managed to dive clear and rolled to his feet, warhammer in hand, sprinting forward to try and free one of the trapped warriors but being bowled over by the powerful downwash of the monster's wings.

Panic was erupting as several Dussen turned to flee, leaving the net and their allies behind such was their terror. Czerna was desperately calling for them to stick to the plan, to curb their terror, but they either could not, or would not, hear her. Forge took aim at the newly arrived monster and fired, giant bolt springing forth towards the thorax. Like trying to swat a fly, the attack struck the planned target, but the creature had already lifted off once again, dragging the two unfortunates still hooked to its feet along.

'Reload this thing and go for the other one!' he shouted, already vaulting down the steps. He knew his warning was valid as he burst clear of the tower to see the cat-beast springing forward toward one of the Dussen that had remained at his post. A half-reptilian roar erupted from it as the man facing it levelled his spear to impale it; the weapon shattered against the solid quills. Despite the net wrapping around its forelimb, one swing was enough to tear its victim open, sending the front half of his ribcage sailing through the air as he collapsed backwards.

'Rally! Rally!' he heard Terex commanding, looking over to see him physically pushing one Dussen man back into the fray. Leading by example, he grabbed one of the fallen stretches of net and charged towards his foe, many of those around him following his lead and closing the trap before the quilled monster could free itself.

Forge looked to the sky and saw the shadow pass across the moon, indicating the flying beast was preparing for a second strike. Moving around to the back of the tower, checking to ensure he was obscured from those above and on the battlefield, he took a steadying breath and removed two javelins from the slings across his body. Hearing the drone increasing, he knew the creature was diving and he narrowed his eyes to make out the dark patch blocking the stars. Loosing one javelin, he heard an unearthly screech and knew he had struck the large, segmented eye he had been aiming for. The shadowy form changed from a precision dive into an erratic spin as pain overcame its ability to fight. The bodies it had still been carrying were thrown free as its legs flicked wildly about in pain and Straker released his second javelin. This time there was no sound at all, but its sudden and immediate plummet told him he had struck true again, this time through the thin membranes of its wing.

Rounding the tower to see the battle near the brushland, he felt encouraged as the remaining Dussen and Terex seemed to have restrained their foe. Moving in to try and land a killing blow, however, it suddenly forced its quills out to all sides, tearing the thick net to shreds. Swiping left and right with claws and tail alike, it scattered its enemies, decapitating one man in the process. Forge began to sprint to their aid, hearing the tell-tale click of the ballista safety catch being released. There was nothing he could do to stop the poorly judged action and he called out to any who could hear him.

'Get out of the way! Shot incoming!' he hollered but the monster was still creating too much overwhelming noise. He saw the massive bolt fly out over his head towards the beast, saw the monster leap aside with feline agility and watched as two men were impaled by the deadly missile.

Terex used the distraction caused to roll in under the beast's reach, continuing his momentum to smash his warhammer across the side of its snout. It reared up in outrage and caught its persecutor accidentally with its jaw, bowling him from his feet to crash to the ground within easy striking distance. Forge tried to release his final javelin, but it snagged on his shirt as he ran.

Just as it seemed Terex had met his end an explosive crack rang out across the battlefield and something impacted on the side of the monster's neck, shattering spines and spurting blood from a gaping wound. Howling in pain, it forgot its attack on the fallen warrior and limped off to one side, gnashing at the wound as if to stop the pain. A second shot resounded and this time Straker saw the flash from a muzzle as he slowed his run to a jog. Another grunt left the beast's mouth as the top of its head exploded and it collapsed lifelessly to the ground. Forge watched as the sharpshooter approached his kill, gingerly kicking the long snout with one well-maintained boot. He had the attire and bearing of nobility.

'I do not believe I will be reclaiming my shots from this foul beast!' he declared in a haughty tone, ensuring his voice was loud enough for all to hear.

'Who are you?' Straker called to him.

'I do not care who you are,' Terex added, climbing slowly to his feet, 'you saved my life, and you have my thanks.'

'You are most welcome, but only happenstance has spared your life. My name is Mr. Chaucer, would either of you be able to direct me to Lady Pallstirrith?'

'Sir! Many thanks for your assistance! May we offer our hospitality to you?' Czerna called out, rushing over from the watch tower to join them.

'No need for Sir, beauteous lady, Mr. Chaucer will suffice. And this is Mr. Black,' he waved a hand back across the field to where his partner was approaching, the insect-mutant's head under one arm, javelin still protruding from its punctured eye. 'As I said, we have business with Lady Pallstirrith?'

The sound of bells ringing in the distance interrupted their discourse and Czerna's warmth was replaced by fear. 'The East Tower! We are undone, we will never make it to my home in time!'

Forge was already sprinting before her sentence was finished, Terex hot on his heels. He wasted no time wondering where their two benefactors had come from, only the safety of his children was foremost in his mind. Maintaining his gait, despite the burning in his chest, Forge told himself he was going to make it, that his children would be safe. His heart sank as he spotted a freshly prepared wagon, completely overturned, outside of Czerna's house, one wheel spinning freely. Rounding the corner of the larger home obstructing the rest of his view, he skidded to a halt, mind reeling with confusion. Another large carcass lay in the street, blood and black ichor pooling about it, wounds inflicted across its leathery body. About it stood four figures; one was Rebecca, who was enthusiastically talking to the other three; the only one listening was a short man wearing an armoured chest plate and helmet, a round shield almost the size of his entire body was strapped to one arm and a steel-shafted halberd was held in the other. A tall man, wearing fur boots and loincloth, leather strapping criss-crossing up between the two, was leaning over the slain beast, one foot resting on its head as he retrieved a set of spiked bolas from around its neck; a glorious trident was strapped across his naked torso. The final attendee was a woman, lithe and strong in appearance, silks and veils creating a mosaic of colours across her. Her eyes and skin tone revealed she was from the far East as Straker himself was, the unique triple-bladed and double-bladed swords that hung loosely in her grasp immediately revealed her identity.

'Straker! Terex! Thank the gods you are all right! This beast made short work of the defenders on the East Tower and would have killed us all if not for the timely arrival of my allies!' Rebecca cried excitedly.

'We saw the monster approaching and pursued with all haste. Chaucer and Black said they would assist to the South. I assume they did so?' the short man added.

'Aye,' Forge panted, regaining his breath, 'the danger is averted on all fronts it seems.'

'And not by coincidence!' Rebecca continued, looking far too pleased for the gravity of the situation, 'They all responded to my call for aid. It is through my actions that we have been saved! May I introduce Zark Hared, Dinish Fiveblades and Hondrak, renowned assassins from Corinth.'

'Of course,' Chaucer added, appearing from the Southern road with Czerna and Black, 'most of us are not from Corinth, per se, simply employed there. Now we have all come here together to save you from these disgusting things. And just as well, it would appear, for you were not doing that well from my perspective!'

Forge bristled but held back a retort, 'You have my thanks,' he said instead.

'Who or what else needs to be slain, I have other business to attend to,' Dinish Fiveblades asked in her thickly accented voice.

Czerna suddenly took over as hostess once more, ignoring the flippancy and arrogance of their new guests, 'Please, come inside and we will explain everything.'

Tapping his fingers nervously on the hilt of one sword, Bentram finally plucked up the courage to speak to Rayne. She was sat atop a pile of ropes and nets, the morning breeze brushing salty dockside air through her long, dark red hair; it was rare she dropped her hood in public but now both hood and mask were absent as she cut mango slices from the fruit in her hand for breakfast. He studied the hard scar tissue that covered the left side of her face, the mangled ear exposed as the hair usually stroked down over her disfigured side was pushed clear by the wind. It was hard to imagine experiencing such pain, let alone surviving it and adapting to life after such crippling injuries; he checked himself at that thought, she was far from an invalid, despite the damage. Realising she had noticed his attention, he moved over before her ire grew, pleased that she did not seem as angry as was common when someone observed her damaged visage.

'Excuse the interruption to your thoughts, Lady Fimarr,' he offered to strike up the conversation.

'Ha, ha!' she laughed immediately, a rare sound at the best, 'Lady Fimarr? You can reserve that for my sisters! I have fought alongside you now, Bentram, you may call me Rayne.'

He returned her smile, 'Many thanks, Rayne, I am pleased to find you in such good spirits this morning. I must admit the opportunity for an actual bed last night was well received, I feel much refreshed this morning.'

'Comfort has nothing to do with my current humour,' she replied but her tone remained light, 'what can I do for you? Mango?' She offered a slice of the fruit and he accepted gratefully. They had eaten a meal of bread and eggs upon leaving the lodging secured overnight, but now the wait for Makinson and Reevus had stretched into hours and hunger was creeping in once more. He hoped the pair had not duped them following the tense meeting the previous day, which brought Bentram back to his original question for Rayne.

'This man on which we have pinned our hopes for travel, you know him?'

'Makinson?' she asked with a raised eyebrow, 'I met him once, during a contract, he withdrew when he recognised me, and I let him live. I think it leaves us even.'

Bentram smiled and nodded, 'Yes, that seems fair enough. But I was talking about the other man, his father. I do not know if you discussed this with the others last night, but you seemed ready to kill him on first sight yesterday.'

It was Rayne's turn to smile, 'Noticed that did you? Maybe you misread the situation slightly, if I had wanted him dead he would have been so. My attack was simply a warning to ensure no deception from him. I met him several years ago and we did not part on good terms.'

'Forgive me prying, but what happened between you?'

'He had been hired by agents of Ramikain to hunt down my sisters and kill them. When I found him, it was necessary to educate him on the validity of his task.'

'You fought him, and he lives? He must have been very good.'

'I will take that as a compliment,' she replied sarcastically, 'he was just lucky. I needed information and was questioning him when fortune allowed him the opportunity to escape. I believed him dead until now, not many could have survived such injuries.'

'Is that why he walks with a stick?' Bentram asked idly, joining her on her makeshift seat.

'Undoubtedly. I put that hole in his cheek, knives in his lungs, blades in his back and neutered him before dropping him in a river. He should most certainly be dead.'

'Neutered him?' Bentram whispered, eyes wide with shock.

'I'm afraid so,' she replied thoughtfully, 'but that was then. Today I have spared his life, as I spared his son's; it is possible for any of us to change our path if we desire it enough.'

He realised she had spoken the last words as much for herself as for him and he wanted to press the conversation, find out more about the intriguing woman, until Treya whistled to attract their attention. Looking up the road leading to the dock, he spotted Reevus hobbling along the dirt street with Makinson at his side, discussing matters they were too far away to hear. Retrieving his pack from where it rested against an unused bollard, Bentram joined the others in a huddle next to the fishing hut Treya had been leaning against.

'Good morning, travellers!' Reevus greeted cheerfully, the whistling from his open cheek ever more noticeable now that the cause of the damage was revealed. The puckered hole was ugly and not much larger than a keyhole, but it got him wondering how one ate or drank effectively with such an injury.

'Hail, Reevus,' Treya replied formally, 'were your enquiries successful last night?'

'Indeed,' he continued with gusto, 'I would hardly come to face the Fimarr sisters if I had failed!'

He saw Treya bristle, but it was Crystal who answered, 'Zat is very good news. Can we assume zere is a vessel waiting for us zen?'

'Oh yes, my dear, we have secured you passage on a small trader heading the right way. They will detour and leave you a longboat for whatever exploring you intend. The Captain also confirmed he is happy to stop by on his return journey eight days later; if you are still there, he will bring you back to Fildenmaw. You cannot say fairer than that!'

'The price? Was it as expected?' Treya queried.

'Seven gold for the passage, plus five for the use of the longboat. All meals on board included!' Reevus grinned.

They had sold the horses the previous evening, stabling them was an unnecessary cost as there was no guarantees they would be returning to Fildenmaw; there may be a more advantageous port to use once they secured their goal. This price absorbed most of what they had made on their steeds and Bentram had no doubt there was a sizeable cut heading into Reevus' own pocket. He said nothing as Treya handed over the requested payment.

'You have our gratitude, Reevus,' Herc Callid said, offering a hand which was cordially accepted.

'This was business, my friend,' he said, his accent masking any undertones in his voice, 'but I hope it also concludes the history between us? Both indirect and direct?' He cast a meaningful gaze towards Rayne.

She shrugged, 'The past remains where it is. I have no more reason to want you dead.'

Reevus smiled broadly, twisting his scarred face unnaturally, 'Very good! Then I consider our dispute settled, my actions here bring a fitting end to our association.'

The last comment felt odd and a short silence fell over the group until Makinson broke the uneasiness, 'I will show you to the ship and make introductions to the Captain. Due to the size of the vessel, there may not be separate cabins for you all, but they have assured me the ladies amongst you will be catered for away from the crew.'

The younger man rambled as he led them along the docks towards one of the many stone jetties thrusting out into the grey waters of the ocean. Bentram looked back and saw Reevus still smiling as he watched them leave; noticing his observer, he offered him a parting wave before turning and hobbling back along the street with the aid of his cane. Something seemed a little odd with Reevus but maybe he had also been restraining his own rage at the damage caused him by Rayne Fimarr. Turning back to follow the rest of the group, Bentram thought he saw a shadow move suddenly from the edge of a fishmonger's behind some salt barrels. Fixing his gaze there for a few moments, he saw nothing unusual so jogged to catch up with the rest of the party.

'Is everything all right, Bentram?' Frost asked when he drew level.

'Yes, General. I did not care much for Reevus, I am afraid, and our interaction has left me a little anxious,' he replied quietly, keen to avoid Makinson overhearing.

'Your instinct is good, but I think Reevus would have taken any action against us while we slept last night, if he intended us harm. Taking our money without providing a ship would be foolhardy indeed!' the old man rumbled, laughing at his own comment.

'How are you, General? We have talked little since Lustania, but I have been concerned for you.'

'I am grateful for that Bentram, and I apologise if I have been distant; it is not fair to you when you share all of my suffering. I cannot deny the weight I have carried upon discovering the loss of our allies, all slaughtered before raising a sword in anger against the Prince. More so, I lost my dear friend during my escape from imprisonment; you, likewise, lost Magin at the hands of that cowardly snake, Lennath. It seems that all we had dreamed of for Lustania has been snatched away in a matter of days. We are part of this quest, to find the orb which can stop our enemy for good, but it feels like I am here by happenstance. Like there are no other roads to follow, no future to fight for. If we claim victory, what will it mean now that those most passionate about overthrowing that villain are all gone?' he rubbed the socket beneath his eyepatch absently, realising he had been ranting, and sighed heavily, 'My apologies, these are probably not the words you want to hear from the man who was supposed to lead the revolution!'

'Please, General, you are still a man like me. Your candor is appreciated and I would not have followed anyone who could not speak the truth. I understand what you have said, and maybe the Fimarrs are a lifeline right now, their quest a distraction from facing the heavy losses we have suffered. But while one man still breathes who would stand against the tyranny Lennath represents, then all is worthwhile and Lustania has hope.'

'You are an insightful man, Bentram, I wish I had known you sooner!'

'With all the stories told of you, General, I feel I have known you for years,' he assured.

'And when the Prince is deposed, there will be much for us to do; it is good to know that I will have at least one righteous man to depend upon.'

Bentram nodded and smiled, feeling elated at the compliment. Another shadow flicked across the periphery of his vison and instinct took over as he dived forward against Catalana, taking everyone by surprise. A shuriken hurtled through their midst, cutting the air in which she had been walking seconds previously, before finding purchase in the hull of a fishing schooner.

'What are you…?' Catalana began to scold, being helped to her feet by Herc.

'Run!' he cried back, scrambling to his feet and into a sprint.

'He's right, the Veer are upon us!' Rayne confirmed as she flung out two of her throwing knives across the water gap between them and the main dock. The blades failed to strike but caused one black-bound assassin to dive and roll behind a stack of crates.

Everyone was running now, Treya urging Makinson to get them to the ship as quickly as possible, the others causing havoc as they forced their way through fishermen, merchants and sailors at high speed. Bentram risked a look back across at their pursuers; he thought he could make out three, each maintaining separation from the others but following a parallel course to them. Ahead of him, Catalana vaulted a thick mooring line thrown onto the jetty by an arriving brigantine, but Herc was slower, tripping and falling onto the wooden planks beneath them. As Bentram followed Catalana's course, leaping over the line and the man crouching to entwine it about a large cleat, Frost slowed to aid Callid, the two larger men falling behind the rest of the group as a result. Suddenly, one of the Veer sprang across from the dock onto a sailing boat, scaling the rigging in seconds and then somersaulting from the mast-yard onto the jetty. Frost was quickest to react, grabbing the hilt of his sword but failing to pull it from the scabbard as the assassin kicked hard against his hand before spinning into a second strike to the chest. Driven backwards, the old warrior stumbled to his knee, clutching his injured hand. Herc dispensed with the requirement for a weapon, throwing a punch towards his foe; the blow was caught with two hands before his arm was twisted awkwardly into an extended armbar hold. The assassin landed a kick to the back of his knee, forcing him to a lower base whilst keeping him restrained, a dagger appearing in his free hand.

Frost charged forward, dropping his shoulder to ram the killer in the midriff. The Veer crouched to one side, extending a leg and tripping the General as he passed, sending him crashing to the wooden jetty. Callid had been released as his captor had dodged and began to regain his feet, reaching for his axe; the Veer was unbelievably fast, handspringing back in front of the big woodsman and landing several rabbit-punches into his sternum. The force pushed him back to slump against some fishing crates.

Bentram had skidded to a halt, torn between the desire to go back and help and the salvation of the ship up ahead that Makinson was pointing to. Suddenly Rayne brushed past him, pushing his shoulder in the direction of their escape.

'Get to the ship, get everyone on board and cut the front mooring lines,' she commanded, 'I will help Herc and Frost.'

Bentram obeyed immediately but his progress was slower as he could not pull his eyes away from the scene behind him. Rayne sprinting towards the combat, releasing a throwing blade which skipped harmlessly past the assassin's head as he dipped to one side. A second knife hurtled towards his face, but a swiped movement of his arm slapped the knife off course before it struck home. Her third attack was targeted at his heart and he clapped his hands together before his chest, stopping the blade in mid-flight. He smiled at her failed efforts, just as a large crate was smashed against him from behind, knocking him off the jetty and into the cold harbour waters. Herc waved his thanks for the distraction as he and Frost made best speed towards the ship; the Veer already dragging himself back to the jetty.

Picking up his pace, Bentram raced past the gangplank towards the foremost mooring line, drawing his blades and scissoring them together to cleanly cut the thick rope.

'What are you doing!' a voice from on deck called and he looked up to see a crew member waving frantically at him, 'untie ze lines, do not cut zem!'

'No time! We are pursued!' he called back, moving back to the next line and repeating the cut before mounting the gangplank. With the front two lines severed, the ship had already begun to drift at the fore and the plank was becoming unsteady. Bentram found Treya, Crystal and Catalana already on the deck, looking back anxiously to the jetty, the latter notching an arrow into her bow. He also made out Makinson, remonstrating with the Captain, hearing the urgency of departure being enforced amid complaints that an extra passenger had not been agreed; of course, the likelihood of Makinson making it back off the vessel with the Veer at their heels was minimal.

Catalana loosed her arrow and Bentram watched its flight as it arced towards an approaching assassin. Almost as if he could sense the danger, the Veer stopped his onward run and the attack splashed harmlessly into the water beyond him. All three killers were now on the jetty, closing the distance to the ship quickly. Herc Callid was running up the gangplank already, the board beginning to bounce as it was dragged clear of the jetty's edge. As it slipped clear, secured by ropes to the ship but not the dock, Callid threw himself forward, rolling onto the safety of the deck. Bentram rushed to help him as Catalana fired another arrow towards the enemy. On the wharf, Rayne had cut the third of the four mooring lines and turned towards the fourth, seeing Frost further along the jetty, sword drawn as the three Veer closed in.

'Frost! Come on! Grab the free line and climb aboard!'

'It will not work, Silver Rain!' he shouted back to her without looking round, 'They will cut us down in the water. They have to be stopped here. You can run up that last line and clear it from the ship side. I will give you the time you need!'

'No, I am the better fighter. Let me hold them back, I can still make it once you are on board!'

'You are wasting time, Rayne, all four sisters are required to claim the orb, remember? Now go!'

'We will not abandon you Jacob! When I call, make a run and dive for the loose rope, do you hear me?'

'Aye, Rayne, I hear you!'

Bentram watched as Rayne leapt onto the mooring rope with cat-like grace and began to dash along the narrow surface. A third arrow was flying towards the Veer but this time a somersault evaded the attack, a shuriken flying from his hand. Frost reacted quickly, dodging to the left, but the thin metal sliced cleanly into his shoulder. Staggering slightly, he bellowed his defiance as the assassins closed in. One drew a blowpipe and dropped to a knee, firing almost immediately; a tiny dart zipped through the air, catching Rayne in the thigh as she made the top of the rope. She cried out and fell from the line, managing to grab the ship's rail with one outstretched hand. Treya and Crystal immediately hauled her aboard.

On the jetty, Frost swung his sword in an overhead arc towards the blowpipe-wielding Veer, but his foe easily stepped out of reach as a second assassin hurled a razor-edged disc forward, lodging into his hip. Crying out and falling to his knee on the injured side, Frost grabbed the end of a rope coiled nearby and swung it before him, forcing the enemy to leap back out of range. Putting aside his blowpipe, the third Veer drew a short sword and skipped forward to land a killing strike to the old man's neck but was forced to alter course when another arrow slammed into the planks before him. Frost was quick, slashing out with his sword and skimming the calf of the retreating man.

'Cut the line, damn you!' he screamed at the onlookers.

'Jump for the fore-line! We will drag you aboard!' Herc yelled back, desperation edging his voice.

'Cut the line or we all die!' Frost demanded. The first Veer he had faced suddenly sprang forward, using a crate for increased height and leaping into the air to vault the old man blocking their path. Jacob drove up with a growl of pain and caught the man's ankle, dragging him unceremoniously to the deck. The Veer wasted no time in kicking with his free foot, landing a heavy blow to Frost's brow but failing to break his grip. The second Veer rushed forward, ducking under another shot from Catalana, brandishing a small sickle and swinging it down into the old warrior's thigh; the sound of splintering wood indicated it had gone clean through. Swinging his sword round wildly, the old warrior forced his persecutor back, abandoning the vicious weapon where it was lodged.

'We have to do something!' Catalana cried out, tears preventing her from taking further aim.

Frost dragged the assassin he held towards him, at the same time reaching down to pull the sickle free from his leg. Crying out in pain, he loosed the weapon amid a sudden torrent of blood. Before he could bring it to bear, his opponent bent double, stabbing a small dagger into his armpit. An audible gasp was released as his lung collapsed on that side and his grip failed. Frost swung the sickle round weakly, but the assassin was already out of reach.

Bentram felt his heart in his mouth and Catalana's screams had become a dull sound, as if he were underwater. He could see one of the Veer following Rayne's path up the mooring line as another raised the blowpipe towards them once again. With one swift motion, he sliced the rope clear, sending the approaching killer tumbling into the water, and then tackled Catalana to the deck again. She made no complaint this time as two darts jammed into the cabin wall behind the railing she had been stood against. Peering back over the edge as the ship pulled away, he could see Frost clearly on the jetty, having somehow forced himself to his knees.

'Take back Lustania for the good,' the old man wheezed, bright red blood spilling from his lips, 'and keep the Fimarrs safe...'

His last words were cut off as the remaining Veer swept round with his short sword, beheading the General.

Chapter 12

The thunderous rumbling shook through the ground like an angry giant stamping his feet nearby. Mazt tumbled from the short plinth he had been perched upon in meditation, rolling across the mossy flagstones of the old temple. It was told that this had been the original resting place of the Stave before its loss and was an exact, if unmaintained, replica of the Temple of the Rondure. Springing back to his feet, he staggered sideways as the earth lurched again, loose stone and masonry tumbling from the walls and ceiling above him. He had only experienced such tremors once in his life, as a small child, recalling his father sheltering him with his own body as furniture tumbled about them and walls creaked with the threat of collapse. That had been the result of the usually dormant volcano threatening to erupt; fortunately for their entire society, it had not, the Elders explaining that the Rondure had been used to soothe the fire within the mountain. Rushing beyond the ancient walls, he cast his gaze over to Mount Darkfire but saw no ruby glow around its lip or acrid black smoke rising from its fissure. A third shockwave dropped him to his knees and this time he could even see the ripple in the earth as it spread past him as a moving arc of land. Like a huge circle emanating from a central point, not the volcano as he had feared but behind him, from Dawnrise.

Covering the distance back to his home with frantic speed, he could see the damage from hundreds of yards away. Some buildings were semi-collapsed, not a single fire-pole was still standing, and the sounds of fear and panic carried to him on the wind. He thanked the small blessing that it was still daylight so the fire-poles were not lit, if they had been then the whole settlement would probably be ablaze. Pounding into the village boundary, he was forced to stop as a screaming woman begged for his help. She was clearly in shock and could barely form words, but he deciphered enough of her hysterical cries to realise someone was trapped under the collapsed roof of her small hut. Pushing her gently to the side, he spotted the end of the main crossbeam jammed into the mud where it had given way. Hoping that it was still intact inside the structure, Mazt wrapped his hands under the beam, pulling it from the ground, up to his waist, then to his shoulder, legs shaking with the enormous strain. Above the confusion all about him, he listened closely and heard a soft coughing in the darkened interior.

'Out!' he shouted at the top of his voice, 'Now! I do not know how long I can hold this!'

To his relief, the children who emerged were old enough to understand, scampering clear and rushing to their mother. Praying that there had only been three, feeling the weight of the beam pressing down upon him, Mazt released the huge support and dropped back against the remaining wall. The woman was suddenly upon him, squeezing him tightly, praising his name and showering him with grateful kisses.

'You are welcome,' he soothed, easing her back and smiling warmly, 'but I must go to discover the cause of this devastation. Have no fear, the Guardians will protect you from this danger.'

Leaving her sobbing with relief in the arms of her children, Mazt continued through the carnage, desperate to find the cause but also hoping that no further tremors occurred to guide him to it. Up ahead he spotted Diast, his fellow Guardian helping to shore up a wobbling roof temporarily with three doused fire-poles.

'Hail, Diast!' he called out, receiving a nod of recognition before his ally moved over to join him.

'Hail, Mazt,' he replied, face full of concern, 'this destruction is most terrible. What has happened?'

'My truth here is dulled. I know that this was not caused by Mount Darkfire; it felt like the quake started from here.'

'I fear the same. I was exercising in the field beyond the village when the tremors struck, they felt just like the backlash of using a Palmstone, but a hundred times stronger.'

'Do you think Atae, or Keris…?' Mazt enquired in confusion.

'No,' Diast stated firmly, 'this was not the work of any Guardian, I am certain.'

Mazt nodded and patted his comrade firmly on the shoulder, 'Then let us discover the cause together.'

The pair ran between the crumbling buildings, feeling the pang of guilt for not stopping to help their kinsmen but knowing that preventing further damage was the priority. Without consciously directing themselves, they found themselves at the gates to the Temple of the Rondure. Keris and Atae were already there, pensively discussing the situation.

'Hail Mazt, Diast,' Atae greeted them distractedly, 'it seems our instincts must all be aligned, you also believe the disruption to have emanated from the Temple?'

'I am not certain of that,' Mazt replied, 'but we cannot all have come here by chance. What could have caused such force to be released from here and why?'

'Could it be an accident?' Keris offered, 'Or a reaction to the changes in the Boundary? It is linked to the power of the Palmstones, that much is truth, feel how it tingles against your flesh?'

Mazt raised his hand before him and focussed on the metal against his skin; sure enough, the sensation she had suggested was present, strongest under the gem itself but noticeable wherever the handpiece touched him.

'Could we have been responsible without awareness?' Atae asked, mortification heavy in his tone.

'I do not know,' Mazt replied, looking intently at the closed gates before them, the gates that only the Elders were permitted to pass through, 'there is no clear truth here…'

'Guardians!' an aged but strong voice rang out and they turned as one to see the High Auger and several Elders approaching from their own shrine; located beside the Temple for convenience. The four warriors dropped to one knee, heads bowed in reverence.

'There is much distress throughout the community from this tragedy! You must disperse amongst the people and assist where you can, we will channel the Rondure for answers,' the High Auger stated.

'What if the Rondure is the cause?' Mazt blurted out without thinking; he had managed to keep his subversive thoughts hidden for the last few weeks, but this event had shaken him enough to speak up.

'Explain your truth, Mazt Ka-Taqar,' the High Auger demanded.

'The devastation seems to have be borne of the Temple, which would suggest something of great power unleashed within. You have always taught us that only the Rondure is stored here and that its power sustains us all. Could it be that, like the Boundary, something unexpected is occurring with the artifact? Have your extended examinations of the invaders' articles not revealed any clues as to the extensive changes impacting on our way of life?' he attempted to keep confrontation from his tone but knew that he was failing.

Silence pervaded for a few moments until the High Auger placed a hand atop his head, 'I see the confusion and fear in you now. Do not be ashamed of such feelings, even our greatest cannot know everything and without fear there can be no courage. It is essential that the Elders and the Guardians are united in all matters, without this, chaos will reign. I will help you find the answers you seek, inside the Temple, but this act flaunts our traditions. As such, it will be only you, Mazt Kae-Taqar, who will enter; the other Guardians will do as I commanded.'

Mazt reached out to either side, gently tapping the wrists of Keris and Diast to encourage their agreement. Without words, his three fellow Guardians rose, presented the symbol of fealty to the Elders with their hands and dispersed in different directions to aid in the aftermath of the earth tremors. When the High Auger removed his hand from Mazt's head, he likewise presented the expected sign of loyalty before following the old man beyond the forbidden gates.

The other Elders broke away as they travelled through the majestic sanctuary, disappearing to conduct whatever ritual duties were required of them. Mazt could not help but feel humbled with awe, he was the only member of their community to be allowed access here outside of the Elders. Finally, they arrived at the chamber housing the Rondure and it was not as he expected; the artifact was caged within a circle of metal bars which was likewise encapsulated within three further circles of bars beyond it. As far as he could see, it was an object of gold, ornately carved across its surface, no larger than a grapefruit. A warm yellow light seemed to pulse from within it.

'Here it is,' the High Auger whispered, 'the Rondure that is centre to all things. You are privileged to gaze upon its beauty but your words of late have been radical, almost perfidious. What is it that disquiets you so?'

Mazt was transfixed by the Rondure and his words came out in a mumble, 'I love this land, my people, our heritage and community. My whole life has been devoted to becoming a Guardian so that I can protect all that we are and ensure justice in all matters. Since I achieved that goal, everything we have known since my birth has changed; was it always fated that my time as Guardian would be marred by such upheavals? Has any of this been prophesised in detail or have words simply been interpreted? Why is so much not as I have been taught?'

He realised his last statement was careless, even blasphemous, but he had restrained himself for too long. A hand was placed on his shoulder, but the pressure applied was not meant for comfort and he responded by returning to his knees.

'You ask questions that have not been raised by any other before,' the High Auger spoke softly, walking around the perimeter of the outermost cage as he spoke, 'but perhaps this should be expected as we have never been so close to doom before. All prophecy is an interpretation of words, pictures or feelings; there is no way to truly see the future. But we are guided in our efforts by the stories of old and the power of the Rondure. I will share with you a truth that I know but would never tell our kinsmen; this artifact is unstable and has been for many months. It could have been for far longer, but the intensity of its *disruptions* has only just become palpable. There is only one explanation for this; the Stave is active elsewhere.'

'The Stave?' Mazt echoed, 'but that device was lost hundreds of years ago, believed destroyed! How can it now be in use, why? And who could wield such an item of power?'

The High Auger had completed his circuit and stopped as he reached Mazt's side, 'The truth is that I do not know the answers to your questions. The Stave was once retained in our land, before either of our lives began, and was taken from us, so wielding it is not so unbelievable a concept. Who and why are more relevant queries which I also crave an answer to, but it is not likely we will ever know. Even the real power of the Rondure is a truth lost to antiquity.'

His head swam in confusion, 'But, High Auger, you guide our people with total surety, provide an answer to every question; how can you tell me there is so little known about our situation?'

'Your perspective is skewed, Mazt Kae-Taqar. There is a great deal we know, and we have always guided our people in a manner which brings prosperity and safety. Only the divine may hold knowledge of all things, to believe otherwise is mortal arrogance.'

Frustration roiled within him at what felt like deflection, 'Are there any truths you can tell me?'

A calming hand was placed atop his head once more and the High Auger's voice was full of sympathy for his distress, 'Ask and I will answer what I can. But know that this conversation is for we two alone, others may require a different truth, one which provides confidence and stability.'

Mazt wondered how many truths he thought he knew were actually just impressions generated by the Elders, but he could not argue the point; if the people widely knew what he was learning, panic and anarchy could potentially destroy them all. He started with his most recent question, 'Why is our most holy symbol imprisoned in such a manner?'

'Our predecessors wanted to keep it safe from thieves, they could not risk losing it in the same manner as the Stave. There are also some texts which suggest prolonged contact with its surface can be fatal. We have made no attempts to discover if those warnings are true.'

'If the Stave remains active, will the power of the Rondure continue to grow? Is more devastation to come?'

'This remains unknown. We cannot be certain that the Stave is to blame for the Rondure's recent surges, it is simply the most logical explanation. We had hoped that the smaller previous incidents were each the last but instead they continue to escalate. Should another event occur, the Elders are considering moving either the Temple or the people.'

'But if the events grow worse each time, can it not be concluded that eventually it will destroy our lands entirely? Are we facing extinction!'

'Find calm in your heart, Mazt Kae-Taqar, we will not be expunged by the object of our protection! Know that the Stave is not a device that can be used for benefit or for an extended time. Whoever wields it now must be missing one fundamental truth; their time in this life is already ending as the artifact will consume them.'

'Consume them before the Rondure destroys us?'

'On that point you must have faith,' came the unsatisfactory reply.

'Why has the Boundary expanded?'

'There is nothing to explain this, only our combined thinking on it. The Elders have concluded that the Boundary is either an extension of the Rondure's power and, as the artifact has become more active, that sphere of influence has also expanded, or it is linked to the Stave and the use of that device is drawing the Boundary out.'

There was logic applied to the answer, but it was troubling to learn that the men looked to for the essential answers to all things seemed to rely heavily on guesswork and hope. He decided the High Auger was being open in a manner he had not expected and elected to share his own hidden truth.

'The Boundary does not let us pass where the intruders from the outside were able to. Why is this?'

'How do you come by this knowledge?' there was an edge to the question that knocked some of Mazt's confidence.

'I tried to pass through myself, to scout our enemies and report back; I had hoped it would enable us to properly prepare for an invasion.'

'That was reckless,' the High Auger stated, 'but I believe your intentions were good. The Boundary has never allowed our people to pass, I am aware of none who have tried thanks to the teachings we have provided. In such confusing times, this containment may seem imposing or fallacious, but it is written in the oldest of our texts; safety comes from isolation and this can only be achieved through a lack of contact. The Boundary has prevented the young or inquisitive allowing our presence to be known to anyone beyond.'

'But they have come anyway, passing our protective border without incident. What answer is there for this?'

'It is possible the Boundary has weakened as it has expanded, or perhaps it worked in a way we do not understand for those outside and this is compromised because of the expansion or the use of the Stave. What we do know is that an incoming breach has been foretold since writings began, and this has been the reason for Guardians throughout the years.'

'But if the danger is so great, then why only four Guardians?'

'The Rondure was once decorated with four jewels, each possessing just the smallest fraction of its power. These were removed and fashioned into the Palmstones you wear; four stones so four Guardians.'

'An extract of the Rondure itself?' Mazt asked rhetorically, voice filled with awe, 'So does this mean our use of the stones in recent times may have caused the instability?'

The High Auger sighed heavily, 'It is possible,' he confirmed, 'but not definite. We have not discussed this with you and the other Guardians as the risk of avoiding their use when needed may be greater than any effect they are having on the Rondure.'

'Thank-you for expanding my truth, High Auger, I have much to ponder.'

'I have shared much with you that is unknown beyond the ranks of the Elders. I now place my faith in you, Mazt Kae-Taqar, it rests solely in your hands how far you spread these words. I would only urge that you think on the impact some truths could have on the less worldly members of our community; we have spent many years easing worry and soothing concern, but these are singular times. The choice lies with you. Now I must ask you to leave, there will be much damage here in the Temple that will need attending to and I cannot leave it all to my fellows.'

Mazt stood and presented the sign of fealty once again. Striding from the Temple, still feeling enormous pride at having been permitted access, he considered his course of action carefully. It was not right that the people knew so little about their own existence, that they were given only the required information to be kept docile and content. He saw the fearful eyes of the mother whose children he had saved, recalled the enormous relief in them through the simple acting of being reunited, remembered the mortification in Atae's words when he suggested they could be responsible for the devastation in the village. Before he passed the outer gates to the Temple, he had already decided that the knowledge was a burden he should carry alone.

The gentle rocking motion of the ship provided little comfort as she stared out over the vast expanse of blue water, speckled with white where the sunlight reflected from tiny wave peaks. Great despair filled her at the death of Jacob Frost, so often the driving force behind them as they had embarked on this quest together, and she was racked with guilt over the relief his sacrifice had brought. They were on their way to the orb, had evaded the Veer, and Herc Callid had been spared; it still felt wrong to be pleased at his survival when such a noble man had died to achieve it. Even the fact that he had once betrayed them, left them to die at the hands of Ramikain's army, did not seem to ease the sense of loss. Catalana wiped the tears from her cheeks with both gloved hands, drying them on the front of her jerkin before turning back onto the deck. She noticed two sailors leering at her and adopted a defiant pose.

'Something I can help you gentlemen with?' she asked.

'Jus' wondering if we can 'ave a turn!' one of the grubby men answered, mimicking the motion she had used to dry her hands.

She rolled her eyes and stalked away; how was it that so many men had such limited thought patterns? Eat, rut, fight and sleep; how were they the dominant gender at all? Still, she had spent a good portion of her earlier years profiting from those predictable weaknesses, although it often felt like someone else's life when she looked back. Moving into the cabin area, she could hear raised voices all the way along this passageway, the bulkheads left little option for privacy. Entering the cabin she shared with Herc, she found the rest of the party already present; they had formed a semicircle of sorts around Makinson who was holding his hands up defensively.

'…had nothing to do with those killers,' she caught the end of his sentence, 'they would just as likely have killed me!'

'Easy to say from ze safety of zis ship,' Crystal countered, 'it is a little too much of a coincidence zat Veer assassins stumbled upon us in ze one place we stayed for longer zan a few 'ours.'

'I agree, but it is exactly that, a coincidence!' Makinson pleaded, 'My father has not been a good man at any point in his life, but I refuse to believe he would sacrifice his own son to get to you.'

'I wouldn't be so sure,' Rayne added from her position on the bed, her leg bandaged and stretched out before her; Catalana could not remember ever seeing her so weak. Dark circles had formed under her eyes and the lids seemed very heavy; her pale skin was even more pallid than usual, and she had been suffering a clammy sweat since the dart had struck her. Catalana remembered her crying out to them all that it was poisoned, quickly whipping her belt free and wrapping it above the injury as a tourniquet. It had been Makinson who acted first, slicing open her trouser leg and immediately sucking at the small puncture wound, regularly spitting out and repeating for several minutes. It seemed his quick-thinking had saved her sister's life, but some trace of the toxin had managed to lay her low.

'And if you had been part of a plot to take revenge on me, I doubt you'd have risked your own life to extract the poison from my leg.'

Makinson nodded his thanks to her, 'You are more than welcome, and I would do it again for any of you. Do you not see, until this journey is returned to Fildenmaw, we are stuck with each other.'

'I am not a fan of forced bedfellows,' Treya said, 'but I think both your actions and protestations are genuine. You are bound to us by circumstance, but I ask nothing of you; should you wish to travel to onward ports with this vessel, then so be it. I will not prevent you joining us when we disembark either but warn you that our path is fraught with peril. As you have seen, there are no guarantees of survival.'

'Thank-you for your trust,' Makinson replied, calming a little from the state of agitation he had been in when Catalana arrived, 'I remain undecided on my course of action at this point, but it is good to know that I have options. Although you ask nothing of me, I will assist you during this voyage in whatever way I can; I am indebted to you, Silver Rain, for sparing my life in Corinth, and to the rest of you for allowing me to escape those killers with you. If you need anything, do not hesitate to ask.'

'I assume it is too much to ask that the motion of this ship ceases?' Herc asked from a stool in the corner of the room. Catalana looked at his pale face and noted the green tinge that accompanied it; she would never have guessed that her burly partner would be prone to seasickness.

'Alas, I do not control the ocean,' Makinson answered sincerely, ignoring the poorly masked grins of those around him, 'although many say that remaining in the open helps when feeling unwell?'

Catalana considered scolding her travelling companions for the humour they found in the big man's situation but perhaps they needed something to distract them from the grief hanging in the air.

'I will give that a try,' Herc answered, climbing unsteadily to his feet and making for the cabin door.

'Let us 'ope we do not encounter stormy waters!' Crystal said with a smirk, 'It will be up and down, and back and forth, rolling zis way and zat…'

Herc seemed to become even more sickly green and rushed out of the door amid a sudden fit of giggling from those left behind. Even Catalana laughed, the sound suddenly infectious, despite feeling great sympathy for him.

'That is funny,' Makinson added, 'Cruel, but funny! However, I agree that avoiding bad weather would be ideal, especially closer to our destination; it would take little drift to push us into a sandbank unexpectedly in that area. The last thing we want is to be run aground. But, please, we should all take rest while we can, it is several days journey yet, according to the Captain, so adequate time to recover from recent exertions.'

Murmurs of agreement followed and Catalana considered checking on Herc but decided he would be outside for a while, plenty of time for her to engage with some other matters. Rayne pushed herself over to the edge of the bed and made to stand, swooning sideways before being caught by Makinson.

'Are you all right, Silver Rain? Do you think I have not removed enough of the poison?' he questioned anxiously.

'You may call me Rayne,' she answered in a weak whisper, and you did all that you could. I have suffered worse than this and lived, my body simply needs sleep to overcome the worst of the symptoms.'

'Then allow me to help,' he continued, scooping her up into his arms.

She was clearly too fatigued to resist and her head slumped against his shoulder as she wrapped her arms about his neck for support.

'Worry not, I will ensure she gets to her cabin,' he asserted, heading towards the door, her small frame no effort for him to carry.

'Stay near her door,' Treya told him, 'just in case. I want to be certain she is not disturbed, but have someone close enough should her condition worsen.'

'On my honour,' Makinson nodded to her as he departed.

Catalana took Rayne's place on the bed and felt a wave of relaxation wash over her at the comfort of the cot. She suddenly realised her body was desperate to lie down and sleep, but she resisted the urge for the moment. Treya had turned to Bentram, the Lustanian had said almost nothing since the dock.

'Can you check on them both intermittently? I do not want to distrust him, but my sister's life currently rests in his hands. Be tactful so that he is not insulted?'

Bentram nodded to her, stony expression not changing, and left the three of them alone.

'Well, we have time to plan for the next stage tomorrow, what say we follow Makinson's advice and get some rest? I think that cot is making the decision for you, Cat',' Treya said, and she realised she had sunk down into the pillow behind her. Sitting back up, she reached out and grabbed her sister's hand.

'Treya, please, while there is time for such matters, can I ask if we are resolved? There has not been much time to discuss all that has gone before, but we have not formally dealt with the mistakes I made in the past. Jacob's death has brought this to the forefront of my mind; he died without ever being forgiven, without ever knowing that he had completely redeemed himself. I do not want to risk one of us being lost without knowing...'

Tears had started to roll free again and Treya squeezed her fingers tightly, 'We are resolved, little sister, I forgive your decision back in the Citadel, I think I even understand what drove you to it now,' she said soothingly, unconsciously touching the raw stitches on her face, 'but neither of us are due to die, there will be no more sacrifices save for Lennath himself. Be certain of that. I always have and always will love you.'

'Should zis be a more private moment? I am 'appy to leave you alone...' Crystal said uncomfortably.

'No, Crystal, I had hoped to speak with you also,' Catalana insisted, reaching out her free hand to the other woman, 'I think I have done you a disservice since we met.'

Tentatively, Crystal took her hand and met her eyes uncertainly, 'If you 'ave, it is not one zat I 'ave noticed.'

'I have taken time to consider the situation between us all. None of us have known you, known of you or even considered you may exist; I expect that to be the same for you,' she explained, receiving a nod of agreement, 'and initially we were disheartened and shocked to learn the truth of our family bond. But you are our sister, by birth and now by action as well; how can I ignore the selflessness you have shown in casting aside the life you know to place it in danger alongside ours?'

'It is less of an ask zan you realise, I zink,' Crystal stated with embarrassment, 'I was looking for an excuse to travel away and find some independence. I do not seek ze quiet life zat seems to have evaded all of you, zis feels like my true calling.'

'Either way,' Catalana continued, 'I see now that you are nothing less than a blessing to us. I have lost a sister to madness who may never recover, one who has betrayed me beyond forgiveness and another who I almost drove away with lies; what a fool I would be to miss the chance to gain another due to misgivings about her conception. We all share our father's blood and I want you to know that in my heart you are now, and always, a Fimarr.'

'Zank you, your words are kind and heartfelt. I accept your sisterhood also, and 'ope zat zere are many chances for us to learn more about one anozer. Please 'ave patience, zough, for zis is all very new to me. I love my fazer, and by zat I mean Mareck, very much and will 'ave much to resolve wiz 'im upon my return 'ome. But I would love to learn about you all, and my birz fazer, and I regret zat we are so far into our lives before 'aving met. It would be wonderful to be able to call you all my sisters; you 'ave experience in what zat means where I 'ave been raised alone so I apologise if I get it wrong.'

'There is no right and wrong,' Treya reassured her, 'just family. All I ask is that you do not hesitate to talk with us about anything that concerns you and have faith that we will value you as we do each other.'

'Zank you,' she answered with a tremoring voice and pulled them both into a tight embrace, 'I will do everyzing I can to bring our ozer sister back from ze evil zat has taken 'er.'

Lingering in the embrace for a few moments, feeling an emotional warmth that had been missing since her revelation to Treya weeks earlier, Catalana eventually released her sisters, new and old, and reclined back on the bed.

Crystal rose and left with an awkward wave, clearly not sure of how to depart from such an emotional exchange, but Treya lingered by the door.

'That was a beautiful thing to do, Cat', thank-you. It must be very difficult for her to absorb all of this. Even finding out about her only days ago, it feels like we have been cheated out of a sister for all these years.'

'Yes, I think that is what steered my hand in this matter. Saying that, can you imagine if she had grown up alongside us? With that luscious tan she has, which of us would not have been permanently jealous!' Catalana laughed.

Treya smiled genuinely, 'Yes! I suppose we can blame mother for our fragile colour! She will definitely not have need to avoid the sun as we often do!'

'I wonder what her mother looked like, she is very pretty, don't you think?'

It was Treya's turn to laugh, 'I am certainly grateful that none of us have taken our appearance from father! Can I ask you something?'

'Of course, I only intend to rest for a short time and then go and see to Herc. Is there something you need me to do?'

'More something to consider,' her sister replied earnestly, 'you told Crystal that Rayne's betrayal was unforgiveable, you told me that Frost's death has made you fear leaving resolution of our issues to linger, and our sister could be far more seriously ill than she allows us to see. Can you not find it in your heart to offer the same dispensation to her that I have given to you?'

'Rayne left me to die, Treya, not because of danger to herself or someone else, not as a kindness due to some affliction I was suffering and not because her hand was forced. As far as she knew, my death was certain, and she walked away at the offer of money! I know things did not turn out as expected, Herc miraculously came to my rescue and Rayne found her payment to be a falsehood, suffering her burns as a direct result of her greed. Are those scars penance enough? I don't know, anymore.'

Treya leant her head against the edge of the door, defeatedly, 'I understand, Cat', your feelings are yours alone. We will talk again once we are all rested.'

Catalana was surprised at Treya's reaction, no condescending or demanding comments, just disappointed acceptance. Before she left the room completely, Cat' called to her again, 'Treya? I will think upon your words, I promise.'

'Thank-you Cat', I love you.'

'I love you, too,' she replied before closing her eyes and falling instantly asleep.

The gentle vibrations underneath him were relaxing as he lay stretched out on the folded blankets in the back of the wagon. It was his turn to rest again but there was little hope of sleeping as he estimated it to be not far past noon, though you would not recognise it in the gloomy confines of the tunnel. They had left the cover off whilst underground, allowing the cool, still air at them but removing much of the claustrophobia that came from being doubly enclosed. Looking above him, he watched the light from the cart-mounted torches dancing on the cavern ceiling, the irregular surface creating a million unique shadows; it looked like some mighty battle being played out for his entertainment. A thumping pressure on his stomach reminded him that he was not alone.

'What about this one?' Kastani giggled, sitting astride him and jumping up and down whenever she felt his attention was lacking. She had thrust one of the straw dolls forward into his face.

'Well, I think this one is very pretty, how about we call her Kastani?' he replied with a smile.

She giggled and slapped his chest gently, 'You can't call her after me, we would get all confused during the game! If you think she is pretty, you could call her Rebecca.'

He did not miss the coyness in her voice, and he glanced sideways to where Rebecca was sat watching them, a wistful smile on her lips. 'Well,' he said, squeezing the little girl's thighs to get her wriggling with laughter, 'I don't think any doll could be quite as pretty as Rebecca! What about Genevieve?'

Kastani stopped squirming when he ceased his tickling and took the doll back contentedly, beginning some imagined game between it and the other doll she held upon his chest. Rebecca had flushed slightly at his previous comment and he regarded her with interest; she was a very attractive woman and he had been impressed by her nerve and composure. He had noticed some interest from her, he was certain, and if their situation was different, he may have even pursued her. As it stood, his only focus was protecting Kastani and rescuing Alissa; the latter was going to prove difficult. He had thought about it for a long time and arrived at the conclusion that the Fimarrs' plan was utter folly. If they could even survive long enough to reach the coordinates Zendar had directed them to, there was no guarantee the mythical artifact they sought was even there. The man could have lied, his information sources could be inaccurate or, more likely, simple stories invented to answer some question now lost to antiquity. He had seen magic first-hand, having witnessed the horrors Ramikain had been capable of, but stories of magical objects that perfectly cancelled each other out seemed outlandish.

He had another fear, of course, that the whole thing could be genuine, that the orb, if discovered, would give the other group the ability to overcome Lennath and Alissa. In that case, who knew what would happen during a confrontation? Perhaps the sisters would want Alissa captured, but what of Frost and his lackey? What if Silver Rain decided there was too much risk in her sister remaining alive? What if Alissa was victorious, how could he hope to pry her free of Lennath's clutches with only Straker Forge for help? He tried to push the thoughts aside by vowing to be present should that possible meeting occur; right now, he had to keep Kastani out of harm's way. He realised he was still looking over at Rebecca and she seemed to be holding his gaze.

'Is there something you wanted to say to me?' she asked.

He blinked a couple of times, 'No, sorry, I was lost in my own thoughts for a moment. Now that you mention it, though, I have wondered how you feel about this new plan? You seemed against it back in Hercatalana.'

She looked a little deflated by his response but readily answered him, 'I am not enamoured by the idea, but I think that the logic is sound. Whenever we have encountered one of those creatures, it seems to alert our enemies. As you stated back there, remaining in Hercatalana would result in more attacks, by monsters or Lennath's human soldiers; every such attack would put the little ones at increased risk. And that is not even considering the impact on the Dussen living there; punishing them in such a manner was not fair, whether Czerna protested otherwise or not. But I do wonder if making a stand, with the Dussen and the hunters who came at my request, could have ended our need to run permanently.'

'I do not know your hunters, though I have heard of Dinish Fiveblades, but I have fought the Dussen personally and witnessed what Lennath's mutants are capable of. Remaining there was suicide, but I pray for all those left behind; there is every chance they will still suffer until our destination is revealed.'

'Czerna's people are brave, do you think the plan will work?' Rebecca pressed.

Another jump on his stomach brought him back to the grinning face of Kastani, 'What about this one?' she asked with the second doll in her hand.

'I think you are tricking me!' Terex said with pretend annoyance, 'I named that one already! He was Albrecht!'

'No, no!' she giggled at him, 'That was when he was a different person! Albrecht is gone, he got eaten. This is another man; he loves Genevieve but has not told her yet. He thinks she will not like him because he is not strong.'

'Well, that seems very sad,' Terex continued, 'what redeeming features does he have? Is he handsome?'

'No.'

'Is he clever?'

'No.'

'Is he funny?'

'No.'

'It doesn't sound like he is going to have much luck with the beautiful Genevieve then, does it?'

'I think he will,' Kastani countered, 'he is kind, faithful and honest. Who could not love him?'

'If only that were true in the world,' Terex mused, before thrusting more enthusiasm into his voice, 'he will have to prove himself to her; I hope he succeeds!'

Kastani looked delighted and returned to her game as Rebecca spoke softly to him again, 'You know that she was describing you, yes?'

'What? You mean I am ugly, stupid and serious?' he replied with a grin.

'I was thinking more along the lines of kind, honest and faithful,' she clarified, still smiling.

'Stop, or you will make me blush!' he joked before returning to her previous question, 'I think the distraction will confuse all but the best trackers. We chose carts of similar dimensions and loaded them with the same number of passengers before sending them along five different routes from Hercatalana. Those riding within are brave as I cannot imagine any course of action from the enemy other than to hunt each cart to ground in their search for us; I don't expect any survivors.'

'And how can we be sure we will not likewise be pursued?'

'I do not know of anyone outside our party who has awareness of these tunnels. I used them for years to provide safe passage to and from the Black Citadel and only my men were made aware. They are all now dead. Even Alissa does not know of their existence as she never left the citadel grounds during the five years I cared for her.'

'That is amazing commitment, Terex,' she stated, looking down at her manicured hands, 'do you love her?'

The question caught him by surprise, and he took a moment to answer, 'I do. But not in the way most mean it. I love her as I do Kastani, there is no lust in the emotion, but I care more about them both than I do myself. Maybe that does not really make sense to you.'

'No, it does,' she assured him, seeming to brighten a little, 'but just makes you ever more the enigma.'

'Ha!' he laughed aloud, 'I do not know what that means but I think I like it!'

His mirth proved contagious and even Kastani noticed them and joined in despite her lack of context. Finally, they all calmed, and he wiped tears from his eyes.

'What are you laughing at?' Melody asked from the other corner of the cart where she sat with her brother.

'I do not know!' Kastani called back, a hint of giggle still in her voice, 'But it is very funny!'

'Worry not, children,' Rebecca soothed them, 'we were just discussing Terex and how he is such a mystery.'

'He is not a misery,' Joseff added, not looking up from where he was drawing on the wooden boards beneath him, 'he is just a hero like Dada.'

The statement took him by surprise, especially from the mouth of one so innocent. Hero was not a word he, or any other, had ever used to describe himself. True enough, he had never considered himself a villain either; in war you chose a side, whichever one you sided with were the heroes and your opponents the villains, it was a simple matter of perspective. Joining Ramikain had been his fate since birth, replacing his father at the right hand of the necromancer when he returned from dormancy. He had been more spiteful then, and arrogant, but the months spent fighting battles and skirmishes at the wizard's behest, losing comrades to the rigours of combat, and making every effort to keep his men safe despite the violence about them had altered his understanding of life. Despite all the victories, the territory taken and the success of his tactics, he had lost. When he had returned to the Black Citadel after Ramikain's destruction, he felt worthless and helpless, as if his life of devotion had been for nothing. Finding Alissa there, out of her mind with despair, having lost everything she held dear and being abandoned by those who should have cared; she was every bit his kindred spirit and his path became clear. A stab of fear struck his heart as he realised he was failing again.

'We will need to go back to Lustania soon,' he blurted out.

'Oh yes!' Kastani cooed, 'Back to mother and Lennath! They will be so happy to see us and I think Lennath would be happy to give me some new jewels so we could all play gems!'

'I am sorry, sweet girl,' Terex said softly, placing his hands over hers, 'that is not what I meant. We must take your mother from there and disappear for good. Lennath is not the good man you see.'

'That is not fair!' she shouted, the first cross word he could remember her ever directing at him, 'Lennath is my friend and you all want to keep me away from him! It is mean and nasty, he would make up with you if I asked, you just wait and see!'

'Okay, Kastani, we can see about that later. Why not go back to your dolls for now? Maybe one of them can be Lennath?'

'I do not want to,' she pouted, throwing the dolls down on his chest and clambering over to the twins. She picked up a charcoal and began fiercely scrawling alongside them. Terex raised himself onto his elbows and watched her for a moment.

'She is correct,' he said to Rebecca, 'it is not fair on her. Not fair that people keep selling her lies so convincingly and not fair that we have forced her to be separated from her mother.'

'Nothing about this is fair,' Rebeca responded sadly, 'but what can we do? You cannot be serious about returning to Lustania; surely that is more certain suicide than remaining in Hercatalana?'

'I am not so sure. I think I can get through to Alissa, get her to recognise her predicament with Lennath and draw her away from him. If we were to target her when beyond the palace walls, perhaps Straker or I could even kill the Prince alongside taking her.'

'That plan has many holes, Terex. What reason would she have to leave the palace? How would we discover such plans? A party of seven faced the two of them and their Veer henchman and barely escaped with their lives, why would the two of you be more successful?'

He felt irritation at her logic and failed to keep it from his reply, 'It is only an aspiration right now, not a plan. I have conquered a whole country before, do not underestimate my capabilities.'

She clearly felt stung by his retort and turned to watch the children. Dropping flat again, he returned his attention to the tunnel ceiling. Annoyingly, he knew she had a point and he had not determined how to make any such strike whilst keeping Kastani safe. It was harder being part of this group than he had imagined, the weeks spent fending only for himself had been so straightforward. He hated to admit it, but Rebecca and the twins were dead weight and could easily be the ruin of their current, or any future, plan. The Citadel would provide them better security than Hercatalana but even then, defending it with two would prove challenging; how would he then be able to launch an assault into Lustania and leave only Rebecca to protect the youngsters?

Of course, she had been of some use, he recognised. Bringing five bounty hunters to their aid was a feat beyond his means and there could be significant gain from that. Her allies had agreed to follow behind on foot, obscuring all traces of their passage and wait in the tunnel nearer the Hercatalana end. Should there be no signs of pursuit over the next few days, they would travel along the route Terex had given them and join them at the Black Citadel. There were many unknowns in that plan as well but, when the mercenaries arrived at the Black Citadel, he could offer them a new contract; either they could be placed in charge of Rebecca and the children, hopefully continuing the loyalty they had displayed to her so far, or they could accompany him to Lustania if he included a raid on Lennath's coffers in the job, allowing Forge to remain with the vulnerable. Both options had their merits and he concluded that he would ponder them at length for the remainder of the journey.

For the first time since offering his services to the Fimarrs, Terex felt like he had the option to take some control back. He wished them no ill will now, he believed he never had even when they had been on opposing sides, but if it came down to a choice between any of them and Alissa or Kastani, there would be only one result.

The flickering lights above him appeared to intensify the battle of shadows and he wondered if it was a simple illusion or a portent of things to come.

Darkness blurred into colour and she squinted her eyes as harsh light invaded her brain. Rolling onto her side, she rubbed her face with both hands and blinked to acclimatise to the waking invasion of her vision. Pushing herself into a seated position made her light-headed but she fought the sensation until it passed, looking around the cabin and feeling completely disoriented. She had no memory of getting here so assumed the poison had made her delirious long before she made it to the bed. Dressed only in her underwear and a thin white shirt was also not a tradition she ever kept so she must have been placed there by others; looking over at a wooden seat in the corner, her black attire was folded neatly waiting for her, her trademark Basque hanging from the back.

Looking down at her leg, discoloured suppuration marked where the dart had struck her thigh and she was briefly disheartened; the smooth creamy flesh on that side shouldn't suffer damage when the extensive scars on the other side would not look any different if joined by new wounds. Indeed, some of those suffered at the hands of Mozak had already blended in amongst the old burns. Rayne shook her head; she never considered such vanities normally so concluded that her judgement was probably still impaired by the toxin. More positively, she felt much better physically; Makinson had drawn enough of the poison from her rapidly to prevent the dose being fatal.

Standing and stretching, she moved over to a water pitcher that had been left for her, tipping it to her lips to ease her parched throat before allowing some to flow down over her and cool her skin. Stopping before too much water puddled around her, she stretched more while walking over to the small round mirror decorating one wall. Looking at herself, she noted the dark circles under her eyes and the drawn look to her skin, but colour had returned to her cheeks and she could now see recovery where before there had only been deterioration. The Veer poison would not be one that came in waves; now she was through the worst, she could be confident of survival. Brushing her hair back from her face, she stared at herself closely. She turned so that only her right profile was visible, unmarred, smooth and pretty, she could admit. Turning in the other direction showed the horrific scarring across her flesh, tight, dry and uneven like cooled lava. She touched her ear where the lobe had been completely eaten by the flames and the rest ruined into an ugly shell of an organ. Tracing her fingers up, she found the remaining edge of where her hair grew in, an inch or so above the level of her temple. An uncontrolled tear rolled free and she wiped it away angrily, turning back to face the mirror and staring furiously into it. Self-pity was not something she tolerated in anyone, let alone herself, and why were such worries assailing her now? She had suffered the injuries five years ago and lived with the damage ever since.

But that was all when she had tried to convince herself that there was nothing else to her life other than her chosen profession. That killing and contracts were enough to satisfy and justify her existence and that reputation was all there was worthy of note. She had come to realise that she was lying to herself, maybe she always had been, pretending that she had no need of love. She felt the familiar swell of anger in her chest when she thought of her father, how he had been unable to show her anything but disappointment, always pushing her to train harder and be better, never once offering encouragement or congratulations. His memory obscured her mother's, she knew that the woman had loved her and shown her kindness and care but no specific memories of that remained; this was how she had hardened her own heart and she realised she had simply followed her father's example.

She had tricked her own heart and mind into believing that she had no need of family love, that her sisters were just people who happened to have been born around her. The lie had become so strong that it allowed her to detach from them completely, to spend years absent from them; each day that passed reinforcing the false message she sold herself. When she had reunited with her sisters to face Ramikain, it was the long-trained defences that came to the fore, to protect her heart as they always had but forcing her family to remain at arm's length. Those same learned instincts had allowed her to abandon Catalana at the offer of reward, not a reward she needed either, just an excuse to end the emotional turmoil that had filled her. Every day since, she had awoken with the memory of her sister's pleading eyes and the horror that followed when she had walked away. So how could she justify doing almost the same thing again with Alissa? Why had she allowed Silver Rain to take over and act so cold and calculating once more? Why was her assassin persona so much more powerful than Rayne Fimarr? She gritted her teeth and scowled at herself.

Maybe there was still time, though, she was only thirty years old and many lived to double that age. She had seen more of herself, more of Rayne, rising to the surface, overcoming the cold hard-heartedness of Silver Rain in recent times. She had spared Makinson and Terex during contracts with no real reason to do so, other than compassion. When the shock of finding Alissa had finally cleared, admittedly too late, she had attempted to rectify her mistake in handing her to Lennath, at the risk of her own life. Most importantly, she had admitted her feelings for Rebecca and now felt the pain of her rejection every second. In her heart, she knew that her love for the other woman was real, not borne from regularity of contact, or desperation to connect with normal society as Rebecca had suggested. Their last meeting had been much more tense, but Rayne saw the feeling within the other woman whenever their eyes met. Her emotional naivety made it so difficult to know if the emotion she saw there was platonic or romantic; having never loved anybody in the latter sense, she was unable to tell the difference. Thinking of the other woman created a twisting pain in her stomach and she released an involuntary sob.

Suddenly her cabin door flew open and she dropped into a ready stance facing the intruder. Seeing it was Makinson, wearing a concerned expression, she returned to a relaxed posture.

'What is it?' she asked, a little too sharply.

'I heard you cry out,' he replied quickly, 'I thought the poison may have… or that you were worsening, in need of help. I am sorry for the intrusion.'

As he made to leave, she stopped him, 'No, Makinson, I am sorry. My head is not quite clear yet. You saved my life and now are sitting vigil outside my door? There is nothing for you to apologise for.'

He smiled with relief and remained in the doorway for a moment, 'How are you feeling?' he asked eventually.

'Better, thank-you. The worst is past now, I just need a little time to recover my strength. Did you bring me here?'

'I did,' he replied a little sheepishly, 'you were in a bad way, feverish and not making much sense by the time I placed you in bed. You have been sleeping for many hours.'

'So, was it you that dressed me like this?' she asked, indicating the ill-fitting shirt.

He blushed fiercely and looked to the floor, 'Your other clothes seemed… uncomfortable. I did not mean to take liberties, I just wanted you to have the best chance of recovery; unhindered sleep seemed to be a way towards that.'

She felt suddenly self-conscious, not because of her nudity but because he had now seen the extent of the injury down her entire left side; Rebecca was the only other person to have seen her so exposed, 'So, you have seen…' she tried, losing the words without finishing her sentence.

'I have,' he replied in a half-whisper, 'and it fills me with sadness.'

'Why? Because now you feel pity for me?' she snapped too quickly.

'No, no,' he answered placatingly, 'just because one with the already legendary status you hold should not have been forced to suffer such pain. You deserve reward, not punishment in such a manner.'

'Ha!' she barked, 'You think so? I am not sure you know much of me if you hold that opinion!'

'But I do,' he insisted, 'I have heard stories of you for years, no doubt some exaggerated, or attributed to you incorrectly, but the picture they have painted of you is exceptional. To actually have the chance to meet you was more than I could have hoped back in Corinth, then I could add to that when you spared my life. Now I find myself a travelling companion to you and able to help you in this most recent difficulty; I am humbled, Silver Rain.'

'No, don't call me that anymore. Rayne, just Rayne. I think that perhaps your fiction is very different to the truth of who I am. You know that it was I who crippled your father? That I wanted him dead?'

'I do. He has spoken of it many times and even in his anger he could not hide his respect for your abilities. I hold no animosity towards you for what you did to him; my father was never a good man and even now is far less than that. Whatever the detail of what occurred between you two, I fully believe he deserved all he got.'

The statement surprised her, and she realised that Makinson was a kindred spirit regarding disappointing fathers, 'It is unexpected to hear you say that. It must be disheartening to see the reality behind whatever stories you have heard, physically marred as I am and demonstrating weakness and failure before you,'

He closed the door to give them some privacy and moved over to her, taking her burned hand in both of his, 'I am far from disheartened. Everything I have witnessed since meeting you has not only enhanced the stories but amazed me further. You are skilled beyond any level I could hope to achieve, have displayed heroism and sacrifice that I thought only existed in children's fables and yet you are very much human. It is that last part that is never told in the stories about you; the injuries you have, the symptoms of poisoning you displayed and the tears falling from your eyes now make you real. And, I think, you are more beautiful because of them.'

She had not realised she was crying, and his words swam in her head. His sudden revelation was touching and unexpected, she had never taken time to consider how many of her exploits were known or how that was seen by others. There was honesty in his words, and more importantly his eyes, when he dismissed her scars and spoke of her beauty. She felt overwhelmed and confused and a knife of loneliness stabbed into her heart; she wished that Rebecca were here now, saying those same words.

'Make love to me,' she told him in a hoarse whisper.

'What? That is not what I meant; you have no obligation…'

'Do you want me or not?'

'I do,' he conceded, 'but…'

'No more words, have me now, I am asking you,' she said breathlessly, turning around and pulling off her underwear before leaning forward over the edge of the bed. She could hear him fumbling with his own garments for a few moments and then felt him behind her. She closed her eyes as he entered her and relaxed into the rhythm of his thrusting; she felt no real enjoyment from the sex, but the closeness of his body and the desire in him eased the loneliness a little. As he became more vigorous, she realised he was talking to her, mostly assurances of his enjoyment and her beauty, and she tried to focus on his words. His hands were on her hips but had now begun searching further afield, up her back and around to her breasts…

'Stop!' she suddenly cried out.

'But I am almost there,' he panted, 'this is amazing, you are amazing!'

'I said stop!' she growled, pulling up one leg and kicking out against his upper thigh, staggering him back against the cabin wall. She stood upright and spun around to face him with fire in her eyes.

'Please,' he stammered, trying to pull up his breeches, 'I didn't… that is we… you wanted me to! You asked me to!'

As his words reached her, the fury inside abated, 'I did, you are right. I am sorry for my reaction, but this is not what I wanted. I am still overcome by the poison and struggling with my own problems. It was wrong of me to try and use you like this. Your touch, I mean where you were touching… Nobody has been with me since my injuries, despite your words, I see no beauty in these scars and feeling your hands upon them… I am not angry at you; I am even flattered that you still wanted me in that way despite… can we pretend this did not occur?'

'I meant no offence to you, Rayne Fimarr, I will not speak of what has happened, but I will not pretend to myself, for this is the greatest moment of my life! The words I have spoken are true and will remain so; if you can ever find a place in your heart for a man such as me, I would be honoured. And I do not speak of the physical intimacy, even if that never came again, I would gladly be with you without it.'

She realised she was crying again and wiped the tears away irritably, 'Do not speak further, I am not accustomed to such conversations and there are more pressing matters upon us right now. You have created an attraction for me through an image created in stories; you do not know me, and so cannot have such strong feelings for me.'

'You are everything in those stories and more, Rayne, one day I hope you will let me prove that to you.'

'Makinson, I…' she trailed off as she heard footsteps approaching the cabin, footsteps that were slow and precise, trying not to be heard, 'Beware, we are in danger!' she said, springing silently over to the door. Pressing her ear against it, she could now hear the sound more clearly; two individuals creeping up to her cabin, the slight clinking of metal indicating weapons were drawn.

She looked back towards her ally, seeing he was trying to adjust his clothing in preparation for whatever was coming but notably missing a weapon of his own, and raised a finger to her lips for silence. When she could hear those beyond the cabin had stopped, she gently pushed the handle down and slammed her shoulder against the door. It smashed hard into the man beyond, staggering him and pushing him further down the passage. The other man, one of the sailors she recognised, overcame his surprise quickly, raising the cutlass he wielded above his head. Rayne lashed out with a foot to his groin, doubling him over and causing him to drop his weapon. Driving her knee up into his face, she felt teeth slice her skin as they erupted from his mouth and he flipped backwards in a shower of blood. Dipping low, she claimed the cutlass and tossed it over to Makinson, spotting their other opponent arriving back at the open cabin door. Leaping into a handspring, she launched herself at the door two-footed, the wood splintering as it crashed into her enemy's face, dropping him instantly to the floor. Beckoning Makinson to follow, she jammed a heel into the unconscious man's throat as she passed.

Racing along the narrow passage, she turned the corner towards Cat's room, seeing the door already open. In moments she was in the cabin, finding her sister struggling with a large man who was trying to drive a dagger down upon her. Bounding across the small space, Rayne spun to arrive back-to-back with the sailor, reaching one hand up to grab his chin. Before he had time to react, she dropped to her knees, dragging him unnaturally backwards as she fell and feeling his neck snap when she reached her lowest point.

'Rayne!' Catalana cried in surprise and confusion, 'What is happening? Why are these…'

'No time, Cat', arm yourself and find the others; we are betrayed!'

Not waiting for a response, she hurtled along towards Treya and Crystal's cabin, finding the door open but no-one present. To his credit, Makinson was keeping pace with her but he also seemed dulled by the events going on; sensibly he was reserving his questions for later. The sounds of combat echoed to them from on deck and she followed them at pace, bursting into the salty night air to find the scene lit by the bright moon and few lanterns in place. Her arrival attracted a man carrying a fishing net and he roared incoherently at her as he ran in with his restraint before him. She dived to one side, catching the trailing end of the net in one hand as she rolled back to her feet, and pulled it towards her. The charging sailor found himself dragged awkwardly to one side, hitting the rail of the ship, and tumbling overboard. His departure drew three more attackers in their direction, and she pointed to the single man off to the left, Makinson obediently engaging with his stolen cutlass.

Her two remaining opponents leered menacingly, and she realised that the simple shirt she was wearing was generating significant underestimation within them. Which was ideal. The first man wielded a harpoon and stabbed it towards her like a spear; she shifted her hips to one side, allowing it to pass harmlessly to her right, but hearing it rip fabric as it snagged in her billowing garment. Spinning in towards him like a dancer, the entangled weapon pulled free of his hands and she slammed her forehead into his surprised face. As he staggered backwards, she heard the sound of the harpoon falling free from her clothing and dropped into a crouch as the second man swung a large fishhook towards her head, the attack sweeping harmlessly over her. A backwards roll avoided the following downwards strike and took her within reaching distance of the harpoon. Snatching the weapon up, she regained her feet and spun in a full circle, gaining momentum, before launching the hooked spear at her enemy, puncturing his throat. He released a gargling cry and fumbled impotently at the shaft sticking from his neck, the large barb at the other end preventing him from pulling it free. Rayne skipped lightly over to him, snatching his own weapon from his hand as he dropped to his knees, still clutching at the harpoon. Roundhouse kicking him in the back of the shoulders, she drove him face first to the deck, harpoon shooting up and out of the back of his neck with a wet popping sound.

Turning on the recovering sailor, she began to spin the fishhook on the end of its line and her enemy cautiously circled her, a knife drawn from his belt. Rayne waited patiently until his adrenaline pushed him to action, lunging in with an ill-balanced strike. Ducking underneath his outstretched arm, she swung the hook into his gut and pulled hard, so it lodged there amid his grunts of distress. As he tried to swing back around with his own blade, she jabbed her fingers into the back of his hand, causing his fingers extend involuntarily and his knife skittered away across the deck. Swinging the excess rope up and over a guide rail for the stored longboat, she pulled it tight before leaning all her weight into it. The sailor was initially lifted from his feet by the rusty hook in his belly, sending a gush of blood spilling out beneath him, but she could not hold his weight and he dropped down to his tiptoes.

She spotted Makinson having defeated his opponent and whistled sharply to draw his attention, 'Hold this!' she shouted, not certain if the statement was funny but not having intended it to be so. Makinson was laughing regardless as he ran over to take the end of the rope from her.

'What for?' he panted, 'Just kill him and be done.'

'We need at least one alive,' she confirmed and moved further along the deck, beyond the obscuring bulkheads.

She arrived just as Herc Callid was hefting a man from his feet, hauling him up over his head and hurling him into the ocean. It appeared several other sailors had already fallen before him, Treya and Crystal who were also present.

'Are you unharmed?' she called out to them, 'Do you know what this is about?'

'No, Rayne, do you?' Treya responded.

'Have you seen Catalana? She was still in our cabin!' Herc called with worry laced into his words, already running towards the nearest door to the interior.

'She is fine,' Rayne called back, 'I saw her moments ago. I have no idea what is happening.'

'You are covered wiz much blood, Rayne, are you 'urt?'

'No, it isn't mine. Come, I have a captive to question.'

They all returned to her prisoner, but he was hanging limply from his makeshift restraint. Makinson greeted them with regret, 'I am sorry, he just died. Maybe the hook ruptured something vital?'

'Damn this!' Rayne cursed, 'We needed answers!'

'I got something from him before he passed,' Makinson continued, just as Catalana arrived from the same door that Rayne had used to access the deck. She was accompanied by Bentram who showed signs of having been in battle as well.

'Are you both all right?' Treya called out to them, 'Are there any more enemies below decks?'

'I do not think so,' Catalana called back, 'Rayne killed the man coming after me and I found Bentram afterwards.'

'I killed two men in the passageways, and we have seen no others since,' Bentram confirmed, sheathing his swords as the danger appeared to be past.

Rayne nodded to them and returned her attention to Makinson, 'What did he reveal to you?'

'This attack was only by part of the crew, at least half had no idea it was planned; they have been restrained in the hold. I think there should be enough to still man the vessel, as long as we are willing to assist.'

'What else?' she pressed, 'Why did they attack at all?'

He shifted nervously and looked pleadingly into her eyes before answering, 'They were… that is I… he said my father paid them to kill you all en route. Please believe that I had no knowledge of this! I am ashamed that he is even my kin! I would never…'

'Calm yourself,' Rayne replied, surprising everybody, 'I believe you. This is my fault, I am the real target of this attack, your father was just naïve to think these ruffians would have stood any chance against me. I mean us.'

'We can settle things with Reevus if we return to Fildenmaw,' Treya added, 'for now we need to release the crew and get to our destination. If we cannot locate the orb we seek, then his mercenaries may as well have succeeded.'

Chapter 13

The sound of wooden cartwheels echoed along the stone corridor as Kastani ran with all her effort, pulling the toy trailer behind her. High-pitched giggling followed her as Joseff held on tightly through the ride, his sister running just behind, trying to keep up. The slight decline in this passage was helpful but Kastani was soon out of breath; it was very different being the one pulling the cart Terex had made for her, rather than riding inside, and she couldn't do it for anywhere near as long as her guardian usually could.

'Keep going, Kasti!' Joseff thrilled behind her, shifting his whole body to try and get the little trailer to roll forward on its own.

'I cannot!' she whinged, taking some huge breaths to emphasise her point, 'I am too tired out! You are heavy, Joseff.'

'No, I am not,' he sulked.

'Yes you are!' Melody corrected enthusiastically, 'Dada says you like cakes too much!'

'You like cakes, too,' he countered, slowly climbing from the cart.

'Is it my turn now?' Melody continued, ignoring him, 'Do I have to have Joseff pulling me if you are too tired?'

'Just a moment,' Kastani stopped her with a smile, 'I know where we are! Come on, maybe we will be lucky!'

She received confused stares from the twins and threw up her hands in frustration; they didn't know anything! Skipping over to another door, knowing it was outside of the zone Terex had permitted her to play in, she stretched up to grip the large iron ring handle and turned, hearing the latch shift on the other side. Smiling, she pushed the door open, feeling the rush of cold air from beyond.

'What is that, Kasti?' Joseff asked, cautiously joining her while holding his sister's hand. 'It is very dark in there.'

'Give it a moment and your eyes will see better; that always happens when you move from a light room to a dark one, Terex taught me that ages ago!'

'We never go in a dark place unless Momma or Dada are with us,' Melody pointed out.

'Well, you are with me, so it is okay,' Kastani reassured them, 'and I live here. There is nothing to be scared of when you are with me.'

'I am not scared,' Joseff retorted, unconvincingly.

Kastanı smiled at him. She had never had so much fun and played so many games for consecutive days as she had since meeting her cousins. It turned out that games with other children were often a lot more fun and could be maintained for much longer than with grown-ups. Terex would always try to play whatever she wanted, and she adored him for it, but he was not always around when he had jobs to do and the others had not been very good at games, or making time for them, least of all her mother. Not only did Melody and Joseff always want to play games with her, but they also often showed her new ones and never felt a need to add to the rules and make it more complicated. Grown-ups always seemed to do that, as if it made a game better!

'Look along this corridor,' she instructed, 'can you see any better yet?'

'Yes, it is just a bit dull now. You do not want to go in the cart down there, do you?' Melody questioned fearfully.

'No, of course not! We are not allowed down there, Terex said so. He is not being mean, of course, just keeping us safe. He always keeps us safe.'

'I cannot see very much,' Joseff complained.

'Can you see the door that is three down on this side?' Kastani asked, holding up her left hand to demonstrate.

'Yes, the bigger door with the lighter bit at the bottom?' Melody confirmed for them.

'That is it!' Kastani enthused, 'That is the larder door where they put all the food. Terex told me that the cold helps to make it last longer. The door is lighter round the bottom because of scratches.'

'Scratches from what?' Joseff queried.

'Rats and other pests,' she provided, 'they can smell food from miles away. But that is not what I wanted to show you. Watch this and we can see if we get lucky.'

She reached into her dress front pocket and broke off a crumb from the oat biscuit Rebecca had given to each of them before they went to play. Tossing it as far forward as she could, it bounced to a stop a few yards from the larder door.

'What did you do that for?' Joseff asked, crossly, 'I would have had it if you did not want it!'

'Shhh!' she chided him, 'We have to wait and be quiet.'

After several minutes had passed, Kastani now crouching, Melody kneeling playing with her skirt hem distractedly and Joseff sitting cross-legged with his chin in his hands, making a huge show of how bored he was, she heard what she had been waiting for. Tiny skittering feet were approaching from the shadows, so she patted her cousins' arms for attention. Staying quiet as she had indicated, the twins peered beyond the doorway and soon spotted the black shape of a rat. Tentatively sniffing the air, it was cautious in its approach, but clearly keen to retrieve the offered crumb. After a short pause pressed up against the corridor wall, it darted towards the food. A sudden metallic click made them all jump as small, spiked jaws sprang from the floor, snapping shut fatally on the rodent.

Melody let out a shriek but Joseff seemed impressed.

'Wow, Kasti! That was amazing! How did you know it would happen?'

'There are traps like that all along the corridor,' she explained happily, watching as the metal teeth retracted back into the floor, leaving the mangled corpse behind, 'if you pull the big lever at either end it turns them off, so people's feet do not get caught.'

'That is horrible, Kasti,' Melody told her, with a tremor in her voice and glassy eyes, 'why would you do that? The rat was not hurting anybody!'

'No, Mel,' she reassured, 'rats are very dirty animals and they carry disulls… dismees… erm, I cannot remember the word but it makes you sick! And they get into the food. If they eat any of it, then the rest must be thrown away. If we do not kill them then there would be lots wasted!'

'We should just share,' Melody replied sullenly, 'killing things is not nice and we should not do it.'

Kastani was quite confused by the statement, Melody's own father killed lots of things, people too. What was the difference between that and trapping rats? Or did she mean that Uncle Straker was not nice because he killed things? Thinking really hard, she was not sure she knew anybody, apart from her cousins, who hadn't killed something or someone. It was all too confusing for her, so she decided to just try and make Melody feel better instead.

'I am very sorry, Mel, I thought you would like it. I did not want you to be all sad,' she said, pulling the door closed again, 'we can keep playing with the cart instead, if you like?'

'No, I think I am done playing now,' Melody sulked, 'I am going to go and practise my letters.'

'Please do not go,' Kastani begged, 'I will not stop the game again, I promise, I will even pull two times in a row, so you get more rides!'

'No,' Melody insisted, starting the long walk back to the room she was sharing with her father and brother, 'I do not want to anymore.'

Kastani pouted and put her hands on her hips in irritation, noticing Joseff turning to follow his sister.

'We can still play?' she offered hopefully.

'I always stay with Melody,' he explained, 'just like mother tells us, sorry. I thought it was 'citing with the rat!'

She smiled but did not feel happy. She had spent so many days wandering the corridors alone while growing up here, that doing so now, when it was emptier than ever, was not very appealing.

'Kasti?' She looked up to find Joseff had paused for a moment and wondered if he had decided to stay.

'Yes, Joe?'

'Do you think I might take the cart back with me? I like sitting in it even when it is not being pulled.'

She sighed, disheartened, 'Yes, Joe, you can take it.'

She moped along the cold stone corridors for about an hour, but what felt like forever, after the twins had left, eventually finding herself in the main entrance to the citadel. The room was enormous with four staircases and twelve separate doors leading from it. When you stood in the middle, you could look up and the ceiling was more than thirty men high; sometimes she would lie there and pretend she was tiny like an insect, staring up into a giant's room. The massive double doors that led to the outer courtyard were a black wood, banded multiple times with layered steel and a huge locking bar held them closed; they had never been opened in her lifetime, all egress and exit usually conducted via the side entrances. When there were more people living in the Citadel, they sometimes used this hall for meals or celebrations; which left her wondering once again where everyone had gone.

Over by the doors, Terex was heaving on a rope and pulley system, raising a large, sturdy log to wedge against one of the black doors. He was shirtless and his body had become shiny with the sweat dripping from him. She spotted Rebecca nearby, doing something with oil and small containers by the look of it, and noticed that the woman was watching Terex intently. Kastani felt a blossom of jealousy in her chest, the same way she felt whenever Lennath dismissed her to spend time with her mother; it seemed as though Rebecca liked Terex a little too much. Still, maybe it would help things along, she thought; if Terex had a lady friend, like Lennath and mother were friends, he might be more willing to like the Prince so they could all live together. The hard thing to decide was whether that would be here or in Lustania; here was very much home but they had better food and nicer clothes at the palace.

She shuffled over to Terex, making certain that he could see she was bored. He smiled as she approached but did not stop what he was doing; from the look of his straining muscles, it was very hard work.

'What are you doing, Terex?' she asked.

'I am wedging these poles against the doors, to make them more secure,' he puffed as he worked, hair made lank and untidy from the sweat.

'Why?' she continued.

'Because we may not be safe from more attacks yet,' he struggled to get out, odd stresses evident in his voice where he heaved or strained, 'I want to make sure these doors do not give way.'

'Will people not just use the other doors instead?' she suggested.

The huge support shifted into place and Terex released the rope tentatively until certain it was secure. Wiping a hand back through his hair, he admired his work, 'Yes, little lady, they might do that so I will be working on those next. But what I can be sure of is that no monsters can get through this big entrance. Grab me some water would you?'

Obediently, she skipped over to his water flask, a leather sack that could be slung over his back, and returned, dragging it along the floor due to the weight. He scooped it up gratefully and downed two large mouthfuls.

'Better?' she asked.

'Better,' he confirmed, tousling her hair with his free hand.

'When Aunt Rayne took me and mother away, she did not use the doors, did she?'

Terex laughed, 'Are you trying to invalidate my efforts here, Kastani?'

She laughed with him, having no real idea what was funny, 'I do not think I evalmulate your efforts. What does that mean?'

'Nothing, sweet girl. Where are the twins? I hope you let them know where they are allowed to go?'

'I did. But they have gone back to their room. Mel got angry with me and stopped playing so Joe went with her. I have just been doing nothing since then. Can you play?'

'I am sorry you are bored; this work is very important to keep us safe, and I should try to finish it. Why did Melody get angry with you? You did not do anything to her, did you?'

She had not heard such suspicion or concern in his voice over her games before and felt instantly defensive, 'I did not do anything! She just got sad when we found a dead rat is all!' she lied.

'Okay, okay,' he knelt before her and took her hands, making sure she looked up at his smile before continuing, 'I was only asking, not blaming. I think these preparations are going to take a little longer yet; I know what you can do while you wait. We have been away from here for a long time and I bet your collections are still in your hiding spots. Why do you not get one out, check all the pieces are there, and then see if there is anything you can add to it?'

'Well,' she answered, a little put out that he wanted her to play alone in preference of his current job, 'I can do that, but none of my correctings here are as nice as the gem correcting I had from Lennath.'

Terex paused and gritted his teeth for a moment before squeezing her shoulder lovingly, 'I know, Kastani, but why do you not see which of yours is the best and, when this is all over, I will get you a new gem collection?'

She beamed and gave him a big hug, the front of her dress getting damp from the sweat, 'Thank-you, Terex!' she cried excitedly, 'I will go and find my correctings, right now!'

She turned and ran off happily, even throwing Rebecca a wave on the way past, the woman returning the gesture with a broad smile of her own.

Racing up the stairs and through the narrow passages to the cluster of rooms she used to share with her mother, Kastani felt full of her normal exuberance once again. She knew that the grown-ups were all worried about more creatures or people coming to get them, part of her almost wishing that they did, that way there would be no choice but for everyone to get back together and make friends, but soon Terex would be finished his work and could play again. When he did, she would have one of her favourite correctings ready as she had just come up with an ingenious idea; she would invent a new game just like gems but using items other than jewels! She was incredibly proud at her ingenuity and wanted to practice in case there were any issues that needed to be worked out before Terex joined her.

Speeding into the small storeroom across from her bedroom, she almost ran straight into her uncle.

'Woah there, Kastani, what is the hurry?' he asked distractedly, with a mouth full of nails. He still wore his flamboyant undershirt and was not sweating like Terex but still seemed busy.

'Hello, Uncle Straker!' she bubbled, 'I am just getting a correcting so I can play a new game with it.'

'Well, okay,' he answered, now retrieving a short wooden board that had nails, blades and other sharps attached to it. He moved over to the window and began to affix the board into the stone frame, 'just be careful because this stuff is dangerous.'

She knelt over by the wall where a cracked flagstone marked one of her hiding spots. Lifting the broken corner free, she reached her hand inside, through the cobwebs that had formed and found the little wooden box she was looking for. Pulling it free, she blew a layer of dust from the top. 'Is that for Aunt Rayne?' she asked, not looking up.

Hammering nails into place to secure the vicious deterrent, Forge was unable to retain the final three in his mouth as he responded, the metal tinkling as it bounced on the hard floor. 'What?' he asked in confusion, 'Rayne is not here, why would this be for her?'

'Terex said you are making this place safe, so people and monsters cannot get in. But last time Aunt Rayne came, she got in the window and took us away. Are you putting that up to stop her?'

He chuckled, 'I do not expect she will be making an appearance any time soon, but I am trying to make these portals more difficult to gain access. You see, anyone trying to climb in will get very badly cut if they can get through at all. That is why you need to stay away once I have it in place.'

'That is a very clever idea and Terex should help you with that instead of the doors because there will not be any monsters.'

'Well, we have already had our share of them, remember that is why we had to leave Hercatalana?' he reminded her kindly, 'And why Rebecca's friends are guarding the route we took?'

'I know that,' she replied impatiently, 'I just meant that none of the beasts are coming after us. It would only be people.'

'I hope that too, Kastani, but we have no real way to know.'

'I just told you I do know,' she replied more angrily, frustrated that he was not listening.

He paused and looked at her intently, smile gone from his face, 'How? How do you know that?' he pressed.

'I saw them,' she replied, 'they were on their way, not through the tunnels we used, and then they turned around.'

'Where did you see them? From here? Which side of the Citadel?'

'No, silly, in my head! When I am sleeping, and sometimes when I am not. They were on the way and then turned back.'

'Why?' he asked cautiously.

'Mother called them. I think they will be gone a long time so we can stop worrying about them coming here, okay?'

'Okay,' he mumbled but it was clear he was not listening anymore, thinking about something she could not fathom. Pulling the box open she smiled; it was her favourite collection as she had hoped. Now, what could she call her new game?

'Uncle Straker?'

'Hmmm?' he grunted, still deep in thought.

'Should I call this game Ivories or Pearlies? Because Narem used to call them Ivories and Crutt used to call them Pearly Whites. What do you think?'

'About what?' he asked, coming to her but retaining his perturbed expression.

'About my new game like Gems, what should I call it?' she repeated holding out a handful of human teeth.

Forge shuddered and his perturbation changed to discomfort, 'I think you should put those away and play a different game…'

Standards and pennants fluttered in the gentle breeze as it flowed across the idyllic fields of Telinor Fallow before him. The majestic sight of an assembled army, rank and file of multiple infantry units, ordered with channels to allow cavalry to filter through as required, the main line of which ran the length of the deployed forces, was nothing less than breath-taking. Two raised hilltops on this side of the arena now played host to ballistae and trebuchets while fire cannons waited out of sight as a surprise deployment when required. Each had a team of four horses to ensure it could be rushed to the field of battle as ordered. The land beyond the front line was a beautiful collage of yellow, blue and green, as flowers of unknown name awaited their inevitable destruction.

Audack sighed; he had been a soldier all his life so was no stranger to war but, as he had aged, he could not help but lament the torturous effect such mass combat had on nature. The usual aftermath was a burnt vista of churned earth, littered with the bodies of the fallen; it seemed an unfair collateral price. He consoled himself that this initial battlefield was located in Tunsa so *they* would suffer the costs, although that would matter little should they taste victory. He shifted on his horse and tried to adjust the leather straps holding his plate armour in place; somehow the whole suit had gotten smaller and was now uncomfortable and ill-fitting. At first he had thought it was because he had not worn such heavy armour for many years but now he believed one of his subordinates must have been playing a prank. He noticed the Prince in splendid war attire, not practical but very impressive, watching him with a wry smile on his lips. He nodded over to his Commander-In-Chief and tried to stop squirming.

Another swell of pride filled him as he cast his eye over the pristine troops, discipline shining through as they maintained readiness and patience in equal measure; nothing would occur until the enemy herald had approached and offered terms. He had no recollection of Lustania ever presenting an army of this size and he had his reservations about doing so; if they were defeated wholesale today, there would be meagre defence to fall back on. And this was the initial combat between the Nations, the first skirmish in effect. He had advised the Prince at length of the huge risk, it was a strong show of force but if he had gambled incorrectly, it could end any hope of a successful campaign in just one encounter. As a military strategist, Audack could see the folly of this ploy but the Prince seemed more willing to follow the ideas of his consort; the crazy slip of a girl wielded far too much power and influence for his liking. But the greater concern lay in the construct of the army; there were few veterans amongst those deployed, shiny and new was impressive to look upon but normally indicated fresh-faced and inexperienced. Admittedly, their opposition were most likely fielding a similar cohort, but it left him uncomfortable worrying whether tactical commanders had the required initiative when embroiled in the heat of battle. And that did not begin to address the confusion over the last few weeks as soldiers from all Kingdoms scattered back to their homelands as the original loaned troops to Lustania were recalled.

Movement attracted his attention, and he watched the three platoons of archers forming up behind the cavalry. He smiled as he thought of his latest ingenuity; instead of six squads of bowmen and three of crossbowmen, as was common in the Five Kingdoms, he had combined them into three large platoons mixing both types of fire. This meant every volley fired would strike multiple ranges simultaneously, being more difficult to react to and provided higher defence for traditional archers if assaulted by cavalry charge, crossbows being highly effective against riders. He felt it was a clever and notable change to standard procedure and looked forward to the impact it would have on the conflict. As the beating of drums and a growing cloud of dust announced the approach of their enemy, he thought back to the stirring speech he had given before joining the command chariot on this rise.

He had ridden out before the men, hoping they could all hear him and memories of similar speeches he had received in the past swirling in his mind. He had talked of legacy and legend, about shaping a future worthy of their people, about honouring themselves, their families and their heritage. He hoped he had not stammered too much or interspersed his lines with the 'errrm' that often plagued him during public speaking. Finally, he had encouraged them all to be brave and hopeful for every Lustanian man was worth two of any other Nation. As the opposing army marched into view, he prayed he was right as they appeared to be significantly outnumbered. The gentle murmur of concern began to ripple through the ranks laid before them and he turned to Lennath.

'My Liege, this is a sizeable and unanticipated display of power…'

'Stay calm, General, this is not unexpected.'

'Of course not, Sire, but we are not prepared to engage such a large force. Perhaps diplomacy in the first instance…'

'He said stay calm, not shrivel up into a worm and disappear!' Alissa laughed at him from her position beside the Prince. She wore a long blood red dress completely unsuitable for a conflict, protected only by the heavy leather battle-vest she had eventually consented to wear; it was unlikely the conflict would reach her, but he did not rate her chances if it did.

'Be nice, Alissa, Audack just needs to reassert his faith in me,' Lennath chided, casting a sidelong glare at him, 'Just manage the battle as you planned, and I will interject when needed.'

Audack swallowed hard and wondered if the girl's madness was finally rubbing off on the Prince. Even a novice could see that these odds were almost impossible, what exactly Lennath felt he could do to change that was unclear; they had planned for equal forces as a worst-case scenario, not that the Four Kingdoms would be willing to take a similar risk regarding a loss. Of course, with an army the size of theirs, it was not really a risk at all. Turning back to the field, he saw a herald riding ahead of the arriving column, despite their forces not even being in position yet; it seemed they were relying on intimidation to do the job for them. If Audack were here alone, it would definitely have worked.

Allowed free passage through the formations, the herald continued his journey unimpeded and without jeering or heckling; it was a strange phenomenon of such internal conflicts within the Kingdoms that, despite the impending bloodshed, there always seemed to be great civility during the preamble. Pulling his horse to a halt a few yards from the chariot, the messenger addressed only the Prince.

'Your Highness!' he announced with great gusto, 'The King has little desire for this conflict and asks you once again to reconsider and return to diplomatic routes for your dispute. If you concede, no punitive action will be taken against you or your people and you will be permitted to leave here with no dishonour. If you do not concede, Prince Gregor will destroy your forces to the last man and you, alongside any surviving members of your Command Council will be brought to trial in Mainspring. Do you wish ceasefire to consider this proposal or can you provide an answer now?'

'Is my father here? Or is it just Gregor?' Lennath asked with a dashing smile, slightly unnerving the herald.

'This force is led by Prince Gregor; His Royal Highness, the King, did not wish to witness your destruction first-hand.'

'He has always been a bit partial to me,' Lennath continued as if talking to a close friend, 'it fills my heart with joy to hear such a thing; did not wish to see my destruction? Such a heart-warming olive branch to lay my hat upon.'

'Indeed, Sire,' the messenger agreed uncomfortably, 'a respite then? I can return for your answer in an hour…'

'No need, no need,' Lennath reassured him, 'you will have my answer now. I am no fool, I can see the forces laid before me and there can be only one victor. Tell Gregor that any man that surrenders willingly to me now will be given a place in my Kingdom when I have crushed my kin. Any who do not will be allowed to flee but, if they choose to stand and fight, will be cut down horrifically…'

'And I will bathe in their blood!' Alissa added excitedly.

'Yes, I almost forgot,' Lennath agreed, 'the Lady Fimarr will bathe in their blood. Did you get all of that?'

'I… I did indeed, Sire,' the herald managed before turning his horse away.

'Wait a moment!' Lennath called, causing him to pause and crane his neck around, 'You can provide your own answer now, too. Will you surrender or face me in battle?'

The messenger went pale and swallowed audibly, 'I am honour-bound to refuse surrender and fight for my liege,' he replied.

'Good man,' Lennath encouraged, 'I expected nothing less. Please relay the message to my brother.'

'I look forward to bathing in you!' Alissa shouted after him, giggling like a four-year-old.

Audack felt more nervous than he ever had before; those committing to a battle he was expected to win, had just demonstrated that they were completely insane. He wondered if he would be able to make a break for it when the main combat started, disappear beyond the rise and into the forests beyond amid the confusion. He cast an eye at Mozak who was stood stoic and still, as always, beside the chariot; he doubted he would get more than fifty yards before the assassin had ended his life. As there were no options open to him, his fate was in the hands of the gods; he would manage the battle as it played out and pray for a miracle to bring them victory.

As the combined army arrayed against them moved into battle formations, Audack took a last ride among the men, providing smiles, nods and words of confidence wherever they were required, and reminding all that courage was not something men are born with, it is something they manifest themselves. He was gone just under an hour and returned to find Alissa sitting on the back of the chariot, picking some of the flowers and lacing them into a bouquet; every bit the bored child. Lennath was stood beside his vehicle, practising some moves with the golden sword he had brought.

'Sire, I must insist you replace that weapon. Gold is soft and dull; it will not fare you well in conflict. I have time to return to the armourer in our rear-guard camp and find one more suitable…'

'I am not a dullard, General,' the Prince replied without breaking focus from his routine of thrusts and parries, 'This is the finest tempered steel with a simple gold lacquer. Should I be required to defend myself with it, it will more than suffice but that is a moot point; this battle will not last long.'

'I wish I could share your confidence, my Liege.'

'As I told you before, Audack, have faith!'

'They are ready,' Mozak announced suddenly.

Turning back to the battlefield, Audack watched as the enemy's frontline began to advance, taking up half as much space again as his own troops. There was a very real risk of his forces being surrounded organically just through weight of numbers.

'Archers, salvo when in range! Priority flanks!' he cried out, hearing the message passed down the chain to the three platoons. As the enemy infantry came twenty yards within maximum range, bows and crossbows released a cloud of deadly missiles into the air. Calls from the enemy paused the advance as shields were raised in a classic tortoise shell defence and a clattering cacophony echoed back to them from arrows harmlessly connecting with shields. The crossbow bolts went fifty yards further, just as he had planned, peppering the squads behind and felling several men. It felt like a hollow victory, his tactic had been successful, but the number killed was barely noticeable against the force they faced.

'Infantry, crescent moon with channels for cavalry!' he bellowed.

The foot-soldiers lining the front of their formation shifted position so that the rectangle they created smoothed off to a semi-circle, making flanking more difficult at the risk of being completely surrounded. The only way to prevent that was with accurate suppressing fire and well-timed cavalry charges. He held his breath as the two forces collided and the familiar sound of war and death began to crescendo before him.

'Sire, permission to launch ballistae and trebuchet fire into their cavalry; we can scatter them and delay a charge in support of their infantry,' he asked urgently, preparing the command before receiving a response.

'No, I think we can save those for another time.'

He spun around in outrage, 'But Sire, your people are down their fighting for you! If we do not provide them support, they are doomed! We are all doomed!'

'I said no,' Lennath repeated with frustration, taking his place back in the chariot to reinforce his place in the command chain, 'and withdraw the cavalry to the rear camp.'

Alissa clapped happily and jumped up onto the chariot beside him, standing on tiptoes to get a better view of the carnage.

'You cannot do this, Prince Lennath! You are condemning your entire army to death! I insist that command be passed entirely to me before we are lost completely!'

'Control your anger,' Mozak warned impassively.

'I told you to have faith,' Lennath said, a deadly edge to his tone, 'now relay my orders or you will be unable to do so due to your untimely death.'

Audack's head spun, why had he been brought here to sacrifice their people? What had been the point of everything to simply hand victory to the enemy? How could the Prince be so cavalier with the lives of those brave enough to fight for him? Barely able to force the words out, Audack did as he was commanded.

'Cavalry, retreat to staging!' he called, knowing his voice was weak but hearing the order driven forward with disbelief from all who uttered it.

'And now the archers, they can join us up here. A little defensive line before us, just in case.

Almost feeling like he was living a waking nightmare, Audack obeyed, 'Archers withdraw to Command line.'

Despite the insanity of the orders being given, those at the receiving end were responding rapidly and with discipline. On the front line, their people were heavily outnumbered, and casualties were sure to be high; with all supporting elements removed from play, there was nothing he could do to save those men.

'Now, General, sound the retreat.'

'Gladly,' he mumbled disconsolately. They had all been betrayed by whatever scheme or deal the Prince and his concubine had made with the other Kingdoms. 'Retreat!' he managed with much more volume, 'Retreat and rally to the rear!'

The fighting before them broke into a rout and the enemy did as he would have done himself; the infantry stood their ground, and the cavalry started the charge to run the fleeing soldiers to ground. With an uphill gradient against them, it would be mere minutes before the withdrawing soldiers were mown down.

'Now, my love?' Alissa asked playfully.

'Now,' Lennath confirmed, kissing her cheek. The woman leaned forward and drew the Stave from a compartment at the front of the chariot. Instantly breaking into a trance, with purple energy erupting around her, Alissa's body began to vibrate uncontrollably. Lennath had leapt clear, crouching to avoid the expulsion of energy, a delighted expression upon his face. Audack looked back to the rout below, his men now mounting the slope up towards them, and noticed that the enemy soldiers were beginning to break their own ranks in a confused panic. With the cavalry almost upon them, expecting to be able to pass, a chaotic collision ensued. A deep trembling finally reached him, and he realised that those down below were experiencing some kind of earth tremor; was this the work of Alissa Fimarr, he wondered.

Small relief buoyed him as the gap between his retreating men and the confusion behind them started to grow; this was quickly erased as he watched preparations at the rear lines being made. Archers were pushing forward to bring the fleeing infantry into range and large weapons of war were being brought to bear, both cannons and ballistae, all of which had the potential to reach their current position. He raised his hand to order his own ballistae to fire, hoping to take out some of the arsenal being prepared against them but a hand on his shoulder prevented him. He turned to see the maniacally smiling Prince who was pointing a finger to the sky.

Looking up, Audack was amazed and horrified to see a small swarm of mutated creatures pass overhead. Sporting similarities to birds and insects, one even reminding him of a bat, the flying monstrosities swooped down onto the artillery and archers alike, sending the enemy into terrified anarchy. Even with some brave individuals firing their bows futilely at the creatures they faced, most were now running randomly in blind panic. Almost at the same instant, on the lower battlefield, four enormous burrowing beasts erupted from the earth, smashing into the surprised forces still struggling to make sense of their situation. It appeared the Prince had left nothing to chance as the four massive diggers were followed by hordes of black, twisted mutants of every description, somehow having been herded through the burrowed tunnels, waiting for this moment to strike. They flowed over the scene like a river of pure death, not a single one pursuing the rallying Lustanians. Face white with shock and mind struggling to comprehend what he was seeing, Audack turned to look at the convulsing form of Alissa and wondered just how powerful she must be to coordinate the monsters in such a manner.

'Would you be so kind as to order a ballista strike against their Command group, General?' Lennath asked merrily.

Audack focussed on him for a moment but then everything that had happened crashed in on him at once and he dropped to his knees before emptying his stomach before him. Even after the initial nausea passed, he found himself retching and crying for several moments afterwards. He could hear the Prince regardless.

'Fine, I will do it myself,' Lennath said, clearly a little annoyed, 'Ballistae! Target opposition Command Group and fire at will! Be careful to avoid our pets!'

The message was translated into actual fire orders before being relayed to the relevant teams, and Audack could hear the familiar sounds of the heavy machinery launching the huge spears as directed.

Finally in control of his body again, the General knelt upright and took in some deep gasps of air.

'You see, General, you just need to have faith,' the Prince repeated conspiratorially, crouching next to him.

'But why sacrifice any men if you could just do that?'

'Theatrics! And if they had suspected anything, they may not have sent such a large force. This defeat will not only be crushing for them but will sow the seeds of doubt over any army being able to stand in my way. I may have won the war already...'

Audack watched as the slaughter below continued and his fears began to melt away. Lennath was right and had shown excellent strategy to manipulate the conflict in this manner; it just felt a little unnecessary to have kept the plan secret from his own people. As the ravenous beasts continued to annihilate the enemy to the last man, a new chill ran down his spine; they were going to take the Five Kingdoms, but would they stop there? After all, who or what could possibly stand in their way?

Cries calling him to stop rang out behind him as he sprinted up the path carved into the jagged rocks surrounding the mouth of the volcano. The air was acrid and thick with the rotten smell of sulphur, though only heat vapour rose from the gaping maw ahead. Glancing to his left, he could see one of their opponents, Diast he believed, suddenly reacting and breaking into a run along one of the other similar paths before him. Despite the physical superiority of the islanders, Bentram knew he was going to win this race; he had the advantage of a head start and he could not afford to fail. Focussing only on his target, the four-foot lip at the end of this trail, he reminded himself that the fate of Lustania, maybe even all lands, rested on his success and that thought maintained the strength in his legs. The last three days seemed like a blur and maybe they had been nothing more than a delay to this inevitable outcome. Unbidden, those events returned, swirling through his mind in seconds that felt like hours.

Following the failed mutiny and assassination attempt, they had continued the voyage as planned, moving from the role of passengers to crew. With those who had remained loyal to the Captain and themselves, it proved to be just enough to crew the vessel adequately, particularly as Makinson and Crystal demonstrated exceptional skill and experience in nautical matters. They had arrived at the navigational coordinates within a few days to find only open ocean as far as the eye could see. Despite this, Treya had insisted they utilise the longboat to investigate the area renowned for shallow sandbanks; the orb could very well be a sunken treasure, she had theorised. Makinson had remained behind, vowing to wait for them as long as it took, Rayne continuing to vouch for him despite his familial connection to Reevus. The Captain had no real reservations either, stating that he could not sail onwards with such a reduced crew and returning to Fildenmaw would be likewise just as difficult without their support.

Rowing the shallow-keeled longboat into the lighter blue waters that defined the treacherous zone, he had expected little, so the tingling sensation that came over him was a surprise, but nothing compared to the appearance of an entire island from nowhere. After the initial wonder had abated, they determined magic was at hand. Rowing in large circles revealed some kind of invisible screen obscuring the island from view; they could see through it in neither direction, but passed completely unhindered. Bentram had never been party to such sorcery before but, having seen the dark powers on display of late, it came as no real shock that such feats were possible. They had brought the boat to shore, Herc assisting him in hauling the small craft up onto the beach to avoid the tide absconding with it; they had no desire to be stranded on the hidden island.

Confronted almost as soon as the boat had been secured, Treya had managed to avoid unnecessary conflict with the natives. They looked similar to normal people, only much broader and taller, packed with muscled and bearing a dry, almost scaly quality to their skin. They wore minimal clothing and no armour, suggesting a tropical or less developed lifestyle than that of Lustania, but their weapons and natural posture indicated they were likely formidable warriors. The biggest shock was that they spoke the common tongue of Primedia. In hindsight, he knew that the forward group had consisted of the four Guardians and six Elders, including the High Auger, but at the time he had seen only a war party. Luckily, Treya's own diplomacy had been matched by the High Auger, the pair discussing that the island was forbidden to outsiders, confirming the existence of an orb, or Rondure as the natives referred to it, clarifying that the Fimarrs were four joined by blood as written in lore and therefore had a right to seek the artifact. To his huge relief, the histories that they had come armed with mirrored the legends and prophecies of these people, granting them temporary guest-status. It was fortunate that the Elders were the commanding presence, as the Guardians looked ready to slay them at any moment, that impression never changing even now.

They had been provided guest accommodations just outside the main village and he had noted that many of the buildings were under repair, as if significant damage had occurred recently; he remembered wondering if that was linked to the shipwreck they had passed over when landing, and the animosity the Guardians seemed to have towards them. Although not restrained in any way, they were kept under constant observation for the entire stay.

Unexpectedly, the first evening had seen a grand feast organised in recognition of their arrival, during which the High Auger announced them to the wider population. He claimed that their presence had been prophesised for many years and that they were unwelcome intruders, intent on stealing the sacred artifact that had protected the civilisation for generations. Instead of the attack such a proclamation should have generated, the festivities remained civil and the Elders went on to explain that any quartet wishing to claim the Rondure simply had to succeed in the preordained trials. Although details remained unclear, the High Auger emphasised that each would be a competition against one of the Guardians; this knowledge seemed to settle any unease among the locals but left their party full of trepidation. They had argued the best course of action for hours when released back to their temporary housing, he and Rayne both on the side of striking quickly, locating the orb and escaping without detection. Good sense had won them over, however, as Treya reminded them they had no idea where the item was, how it was protected, what prowess the Guardians possessed and that remaining undetected would not last long whilst under constant guard. Until they discovered more, they were completely beholden to their hosts.

The next day had seen the commencement of the trials. The High Auger had come to them that morning alone, explaining that he would do everything in his power to make the trials fair to them as outsiders; only that way could he ensure the Guardians' victory was not a hollow one. He assured them that any member of their party could represent them for the trials, although only once; it would not have to be one of the sisters. This was echoed during his decree to the People, which was how the natives referred to themselves, and met with generous cheering. As the trials had never been enacted before, they were to be the object of great interest and entertainment; it had filled Bentram with anger that no heed had been paid to any of their protestations, that failing to simply allow them to take the Rondure placed their own people in as much danger as the rest of the lands. He had later tempered this with some logic; any intruders wishing to steal the artifact from the People would undoubtedly invent a similar tale of woe.

The first trial was of strength, all feeling delighted at the High Auger's generous decision to allow them to elect their own contender and Herc Callid being the obvious choice. Escorted to a large clearing, the perimeter lined with excited spectators, they had watched as he was taken towards the centre, his right arm strapped to the end of a thick rope which was, in turn, tied to the top of a fifteen-foot caber lying on the ground. A second identical strapping was taken up by the largest of the Guardians, who he learned was known as Mazt. As a means of intimidation, Mazt had pulled the pole upright with one arm, amid cheers from the crowd. Callid had taken the slack on the other side, balancing the heavy pole on its end. The premise was very simple, the winner was the one to pull the caber down towards himself until the top touched the grass. Mazt looked extremely confident and had a considerable size advantage, even over the well-built woodsman, his disadvantage was overconfidence. When the High Auger declared the trial commenced, the local was still only holding the rope with his strapped arm and talking casually with the other Guardians. Herc took up the strain with his whole body, turning away from the pole to ensure he could pull against it like a plough. It shifted quickly as he pumped his legs, feet digging troughs into the earth beneath him and the pole swinging down to almost forty-five degrees in his favour. Mazt had been dragged sideways off balance, a satisfying look of shock on his face, until regaining his composure and digging his heels in. Callid continued to pump his legs, face red with strain and veins bulging from his muscles as he hauled with all his might, but his forward momentum stopped completely. Mazt had wrapped his other hand around the rope and started walking backwards, strain evident but nothing compared to that being exhausted by Herc. In moments it was over as the big Guardian gained traction and dragged his opponent back, Callid being dragged from his feet and through the grass as the pole returned through the vertical and slammed down heavily on the side of the Guardians. A huge cheer had erupted and Mazt had watched them intently as they rushed to help their friend; there was no smile of victory from him, only aggressive intensity.

The rest of that morning had been spent aiding Herc in recovering from his exertions and assuring him that there had been nothing more he could give. Treya had been allowed to consult with the High Auger, still desperate to make him understand the plight that they would soon face if they did not provide aid now, better to face a threat together than in isolation. Her return revealed failure to convince him, but she had explained that they were a fiercely devout race and pressed them all to think of ways that they could exploit such fanaticism. They were provided a midday meal alone and he concluded the previous evening's events had simply been for show.

Summoned as the sun was in its downwards arc, they assembled at an odd double pathway, separated for a hundred yards by an irregular stone wall. Two distinct routes ran in parallel off into the trees in one direction, appearing from a natural cave mouth in the other. The High Auger declared it was the Course of Moirai, one of the many disciplines learned by initiates as they vied for the honour of Guardianship. The trial of speed was to run the course twice through in competition, simply being the first to return to claim victory. It was clear the Guardians not only knew the route, but had practised on it for years; how it could be considered a fair test was unclear, but no more so than the previous trial. As both Crystal and Rayne volunteered to attempt the race, he remained silent, a chauvinistic argument would gain nothing, he had seen both women at pace already and they put him to shame. Rayne eventually over-ruled her half-sister and stripped off her cloak, several weapons, and gloves. The female Guardian, Keris, passed them, recommending she keep her handwear on but was ignored, it seemed unlikely she would be giving valuable advice to the opposition and Rayne insisted she would be better with firm grip in such unknown terrain; it was unlikely to be a pure foot race in her opinion.

Called to the starting point, the competitors were separated by the wall but Bentram had already seen the Guardian selected for this trial, the one called Atae. Again, the natives had gathered to watch, lining both sides of the track where possible. When the High Auger chimed a small bell to start the race, Rayne reacted instantly, getting up to speed within eight paces, every stride long and controlled, head and shoulders high to allow maximum rotation through the hips, her technique was flawless. As she passed the end of the separating wall, Atae was already fifty paces beyond her and stretching the lead with every step. They were given no freedom to inspect the rest of the course past this point so had to endure the frustrating wait with no idea of what was happening. Roughly twenty minutes had passed when Atae appeared from the tunnel exit, gait strong and smooth, looking relaxed and barely breathing hard. He shared an encouraging nod with his fellow Guardians as he passed them and was soon back out of sight on the second lap. Two minutes later, Rayne appeared, still pushing hard, panting for breath, eyes focussed only on the path ahead. Her face and arms were criss-crossed with slashes and cuts as if she had been running through thorn bushes and her pace had slowed a little. He remembered feeling like he had been punched in the stomach at the sight; he knew this was everything she had, and it was not going to be enough. Treya had been calling encouragement, trying to motivate her sister into achieving the impossible. Another twenty-five minutes passed, confirming that she could not. Completely exhausted and bleeding more profusely than after the first lap, Rayne had collapsed across the finish line, barely able to speak while drawing in desperate recovery breaths. Atae had come to them then and offered a hand to help her from the ground, which she took. He explained that he had not felt the trial was fair, but her efforts put many of their own people to shame; he could never have thrown the race but wished there had been more of a competitive chance. The words did little to console her.

After that first day of competition, they had been in a depressed fugue; there seemed little chance that the next day's challenges would prove easier than these and their opponents had both home and ability advantage. So many questions remained about them, who were they? How had they gotten to the island? Why were they so much stronger and faster than normal people? Why and how was their home shielded from sight? Despite Treya's boon to speak with the High Auger after each trial, few of these questions were being resolved. Rayne had slipped away that night, none of the party able to convince her otherwise, determined that she would find and steal the Rondure, enabling them to flee before the second day of trials brought the expected failure. She had been gone for most of the night and her return brought little positive news; she believed she knew where the orb was being held but had no way to get to it. She also confirmed that she had returned to their ship to find it still moored offshore, beyond the vision-obscuring barrier, however she had needed to swim to it as their longboat had been removed from the beach. He had spotted something hinting at embarrassment or secrecy when she had talked about the ship, but it had been too trifling a matter to discuss under the current circumstances.

The next day had seen them rise with low morale and he had not been able to stand seeing the futility within the others that he had felt since the Lustanian palace. He recalled giving some kind of rousing speech to them all, about their lineage and the insurmountable odds they had overcome in the past; he could not recall the actual words he used, but believed they had some impact on the group. Following a breakfast of dry cereal and flatbreads, they had assembled on a new field of long grasses that edged onto a slim sandy beach, but not the one they had arrived on. The third trial was of skill, a simple matter of hunting one of the local gamebirds in as quick and efficient a manner as possible. It seemed pre-determined that Catalana would take the challenge, and the others immediately crowded about her with ideas on trapping; Bentram had said nothing, seeing the sparkle in her eye that indicated she already knew exactly what she would do. This trial was conducted separately, to avoid one hunter impacting upon the other, and the High Auger indicated that their party would be first.

Catalana had awaited the signal to start, already carrying her bow with arrow notched to save time. She had no clue as to the birds' habits or location, simply assuming they must nest within the grasses before them. As the bell chimed, she sprinted forward into the grass, not heeding the blade-like tips that clawed at her clothing, shouting and hollering like she was insane. After a few moments, a startled trio of birds erupted from the grass twenty yards from her, wings beating frantically to escape the terrifying noise. She dropped to a knee, drew back the bowstring and released in a single motion, her arrow slicing cleanly into one of the birds. Retrieving the animal and returning it to the High Auger for inspection, Bentram's heart had lifted, certainly it was unlikely that her opponent could match such a quick and accurate strike. They had been forced to wait an hour, to ensure the hunting ground had settled fully from Catalana's disruption, before Diast stepped up for his attempt, an odd half-smile on his lips. As the bell chimed, he raised one hand and a column of destruction shot out before him, carving a deep furrow into the ground and annihilating everything in its path for fifty yards in front of him. They had been forced to shelter their faces from the side-waves of the devastating blast and, when they looked back, the Guardian had victoriously scooped up six corpses from the ruined ground. The event had demonstrated why they needed to avoid battle with these people and seemingly ended their attempt to claim the Rondure. That was until the High Auger disqualified Diast for use of something they called a Palmstone; whatever the device was, it should not have been used as part of the Trials.

And so, it had come to the final trial, this one of agility. It felt like he should be the one to volunteer but he had once again remained silent, with Crystal bringing herself to the fore prior to the detail being announced. She had looked nervous and concerned, it was a significant weight to take on her shoulders and she was even more recent to the group than he was, despite her family link. Brought before two large circular pits, it was explained that the competitors simply had to strike every papaya fruit that was thrown into their circle before it hit the ground. The challenge would end, and be lost, when a single untouched fruit struck the stone base of one arena or the other. To her credit, Crystal had been undeterred, leaping down into one of the pits and walking from one side to the other several times. The remaining Guardian, Keris, had taken a position in the centre of the other, looking intently at them while she stretched. When Crystal called up that she was ready, Diast had called out to them, perhaps in frustration at his earlier disqualification, to let them know that Keris never missed during this training regime. Ignoring the attempt to rattle her confidence, Crystal had unslung her roped hook and begun to spin it quickly, wrapping the excess around herself in a complex web across her arms and body. The spinning hook at the end remained constantly in motion as she moved with a dance-like quality, it was a weapon style Bentram had never seen before and found hypnotic to watch.

When the trial began, papayas were launched into the air from small catapults, providing both competitors the time to assess and engage, Crystal deftly shooting the hook forwards, backwards or even in circular swinging motions to intercept each fruit as it dropped to her head height. In the other pit, Keris leapt freely around the space, spinning, jabbing and kicking with expert grace, looking like little more than martial arts practise for her. When ten fruits had been launched, the next wave began with two targets fired simultaneously into each arena. Crystal's movements sped up and a sweat began to glisten across her exposed flesh as she meticulously fired the hook to strike the first fruit whilst losing as little time as possible to hit the second. Keris began to leap higher, engaging her first target sooner and allowing her time to dispatch the second whilst at ground level; each time she rose above the lip of the arena, Bentram noticed her taking sideways glances into Crystal's zone. With continued success, the number of fruits was increased to three and finally he spotted concern in Crystal's eyes. She only just managed the initial salvo by firing her hook high before dealing with the other two targets in the method she had established but lost valuable recovery time in doing so. As another three dropped towards her, she swung her weapon around in a wide circle, desperate to strike the trio of papayas and succeeding, but having lost all of the coils of rope about her body and any tension between herself and the hooked end. Scrabbling to pull the loose excess back to her, clearly hoping to have enough time to reset, another three targets were launched even as a gong was sounded. Crystal sprinted forward, leaping against the arena wall for increased spring, punching out against one hard fruit and launching her hook towards a second as she fell back to the ground. Rolling into a crouch on impact, she twisted around to see the final target split open on the ground; she had failed.

Her dismay was short lived as Bentram called to her that she had won; Keris had missed one of the previous three fruit through a slip and fall on her side. His message got through clearly as the natives were completely silent at their Guardian's failure and there was a long period of waiting as no preparation had been made for the event ending in a draw. Eventually they had been returned to their huts to await the High Auger's decision; he would spend the night with the other Elders, consulting the ancient texts for guidance. The draw had felt every bit like a victory, and they had eaten that evening with buoyed spirits until Rayne brought them crashing back to reality; the People were not about to lose the artifact that they had treasured here for who knew how many generations, whatever 'decision' was settled upon, it would not be in their favour. Of course, they realised she was probably right, but Bentram made a point of further congratulating both Catalana and Crystal for their individual successes; it had given them a glimmer of hope at least.

Later that evening one of their observers, he had found the term less intimidating than guards, had summoned him specifically. His own fear at being separated from the rest of the group was equally mirrored by their expressions, Treya's assertions that any torture or execution could have happened when they arrived feeling like hollow comfort. Escorted to another hut nearby, one with a semi-collapsed roof, he found himself alone with Keris. Once the guard had left them, she had spoken to him with sincerity. She was unhappy with their presence on the island and did not want the status quo she had lived with all her life destroyed by such upheaval. But that was too late to stop now, the threats they had spoken of at the arrival festival felt very real to her and she knew much of her countrymen's arrogance was preventing them providing the support they should be. The Elders and the Guardians cared only for their own land and survival, as they had learned for generations to do so, but recent questions in her faith had led her to think that some of those teachings may be wrong. She did not believe that the Rondure was integral to their existence and felt that the prophecies of an external threat coming for them could even mean the very danger the

Fimarrs were trying to prevent. That was why she threw the Trial to bring it to a tie. She had no idea how the High Auger planned to resolve the matter but wanted him to assure the others that she would assist them in claiming victory if she could. Bentram had asked for some proof of her integrity which she had found amusing, asking if he really believed she would have slipped doing an activity she had practised thousands of times. He then asked why she had confided in him and she had placed a rough palm against his cheek, telling him that his face spoke only the truth. Returning to the group, he had quietly revealed what had been said, leaving out the part about Keris deliberately losing, and receiving mixed reactions. Whether she was honest in her intentions or not, it made more sense to face the next day relying on themselves rather than an unreliable half-promise.

Those events had led them to be brought to the edge of the volcano that morning, notably missing the crowds of the previous two days. The Elders had stood sombrely before them addressing both their party and the Guardians when they spoke. They had reinforced the importance of the Rondure to their own survival and safety, comparing it as no less important than fealty to the ancient texts that had helped them create their current society. Many hours of deliberation had allowed them to interpret that a fifth Trial could be conceived and must be of relevance to the time and the reason for wanting to claim the artifact. Four was a number of great importance to them in their religion and their lives, and the High Auger would not dismiss the omen of the four Fimarr sisters being the ones to have come in search of the Rondure. The final Trial had to be of greater weight and greater importance than the others, to ensure the worthiest claimants could be determined. The fifth trial was of sacrifice and consisted of one simple task, throw yourself into Mount Darkfire for the benefit of your comrades. Both groups had swallowed the shock quickly and broken into urgent discussion to determine how they could overcome the challenge.

Bentram had concluded his actions in seconds; the Rondure could only be claimed by four joined in blood, which meant none of the sisters could die. Callid had already undergone a trial and would be disqualified for attempting this one he assumed, although one of the four Guardians would be required to do so; Bentram could not have lived with himself for allowing the relationship between Herc and Catalana to be eclipsed so fruitlessly anyway. No, he was not only the single valid competitor, but he had already lost everything; dying a hero's death for a noble cause may just earn him back some honour in the eyes of the gods.

Now the edge of the volcano approached, and he knew he was too far ahead of Diast to be caught. He remembered his sister, Amaresia, and prayed that she and his mother were well and untouched by the horrors occurring in Lustania; he remembered his unrequited love, Fendra, killed for insurrection when she had spoken out against the Prince's levy on trade; he remembered the heroes who had assembled to start a revolution, slaughtered by monsters of nightmare; he remembered his best friend, Magin, slain at the hands of the Prince himself; he remembered his hero, General Jacob Frost, who had known this was a worthy quest that would redeem all wrongs. Closing his eyes, he leapt forward, clearing the raised lip.

Massive heat struck him instantly and he plummeted down, eyes squeezed shut, until he slammed painfully into a solid surface. His shoulder jarred and he felt lightning explode from that area as his body fell flat against rock. Opening his eyes, he found himself on a small natural plateau that skirted the entire interior of the volcano; above him he could see the edge only twenty yards out of reach. Within moments, faces appeared above and he began to cry tears of relief and pain, still not certain if he was now expected to roll from his perch to the lava below.

'Congratulations,' the High Auger's morose voice floated down to him, 'you have completed the Trial of Sacrifice. We never wished for your death but needed to know that your cause was real and urgent enough to merit such actions. You have won the right for these four women to try and claim the Rondure.'

'Are you okay?' Crystal's concerned voice echoed, 'You look 'urt!'

'I am!' he called back, trying to mask his sobs, 'And it is very hot down here, can you get a rope?'

A few seconds later and a hastily fashioned sling was lowered to him, enabling him to be lifted from his perilous position without the need to climb; ideal considering he believed his shoulder to be dislocated. As he was hoisted painfully upwards, he couldn't help but fixate on the High Auger's terminology; '...*try* and claim the Rondure'.

Fareesh Nawabi paused for a moment, crouching to touch the tips of his fingers to the rough surface of the tunnel floor. The slightest sensation of warmth briefly caressing his cheeks indicated that the dark passageway ahead was disturbed in some way, most likely by a person or animal. It could be a predator, though he had seen no prints, faeces or territorial markings to suggest so, or it could be an ambush. The latter would be impressive as he had seen no tracks other than those of the cart he had been following; unless they had decided to stop their flight and confront him. Which was both unlikely and insanely foolish on their part of course.

He considered who he may be tracking once again, the overall group having separated at Rennicksburg with a trio of novices sent after the individual riders and he dispatched to find those travelling in a wagon of some sort. He felt this was a punishment for his previous failure; the riders were no doubt the main threat with those fleeing by cart probably non-combatants. For Grandmaster Mozak to deem inexperienced Veer more appropriate for the high priority targets ahead of Fareesh himself, spoke volumes. He scratched idly at the straps securing the prosthetic to his severed wrist; the pain had become a constant that he could now filter out, but the indignity of being maimed by a simple brigand burned him every day. He thought back to those he had fought at the farmhouse, the woodsman, scholar, woman and brigand, lamenting his arrogance at assuming the building had been unprotected and failing to clear the surrounding area properly. How the late arrival had managed to surprise him still played through his head over and over again, but he could find no answers. Nawabi had to ensure that man died so he could not spread tales of how he defeated a Veer in personal combat; if he was a member of the group currently being tracked, all the better.

Rising to his full height again, he peered at the tunnel walls to either side; the strange, ribbed effect suggested organic construction, as if an enormous earthworm or millipede had created it in passing. Which could be true, considering all he had seen and heard during his brief stint in the Lustanian capital. Whatever was responsible, it was long since gone and definitely not what waited ahead for him. He realised he was absently working the straps of his prosthetic again and chided himself for it; his personal failure had impacted his focus and the thirst for revenge driven him to impatience. Looking once again at the replacement device where his hand used to be, Fareesh felt pride at the success of his design, the smith building it for him had proven a fine craftsman and wholly accurate in following both written and verbal direction. Such a shame to lose such skill, but he could not simply allow knowledge of the unique creation to be retained or duplicated and had opted to execute its creator. It consisted of a metallic guard around his uneven and still raw wrist, with a multitude of strong leather straps securing it firmly along his forearm and beyond his elbow making removal impossible during combat. The fighting end sported four blades, each twisted like the bit of a drill with blood channels engraved down the centre. The twisting allowed each blade to puncture a target at a different angle for maximum damage to an area almost five inches in diameter, the blood channels ensured no wound suction would cause the prosthetic to become trapped and, if he was given time to turn his arm through ninety degrees after a successful stab, it would rend a significant chunk of flesh from a victim. Proud as he was of the deadly addition to his arsenal, it was not an improvement to his original hand, and he was forced to consciously remind himself that he had no manipulative ability on that side; he had damaged a variety of items and even himself due to reactive catching or attempting to utilise thrown weapons. It would be sufficient to slay those he pursued and regain some respect from his peers, however.

Continuing along the passage, alert for further signs of a potential ambush, he mused on how long the tunnel system may prove to be. It had been three and a half days since releasing his return message to Mozak by kestrel, and he doubted even those exceptional birds could find him underground; of course, he would be granted the second five-day period to make contact before being declared dead. Another faint flutter in the air, warmer and stronger than before, revealed whoever or whatever was ahead had not changed their position; an ambush then. Silently progressing, keeping his silhouette minimised through close proximity to the tunnel wall, Fareesh found it interesting that he could detect no additional illumination ahead beyond the natural gloom of the environment; only exceptionally skilled or foolish warriors would utilise no additional light for their own benefit and suggested they had anticipated that any pursuer would also not be using a lantern or torch of their own. So perhaps he was on course to meet more challenging foes than originally presumed, but one thing was for certain; he would not be underestimating anyone this time.

The tunnel followed around a curve to the right and he hugged the wall even tighter; this would be a perfect place to spring an ambush. He could feel the air density beyond the turning was less than his current position; a cavern lay beyond. No doubt a cavern with sufficient hiding spots for a number of attackers. The slightest pressure against his toe notified him of the trip wire stretching across the tunnel floor. Crouching to examine it, Fareesh smiled at the complexity of the trap; the first line was almost a ruse, expected to be found, and easily spotted had he been using a lantern, with a second line approximately sixteen inches beyond it. If one stepped over the first wire, they would most likely trigger the second. Beyond the two lines, he could see disturbed earth which he assumed covered some kind of pressure plate; a third trigger for those who opted to leap the first two lines. Finally, a fourth, much thinner and less noticeable, line hung loosely from the ceiling, ready to hook anyone over five feet in height. Just beyond his line of sight, around the corner, he could make out the tips of several spikes; any of the four triggers probably activated a spring-loaded device that would drive those deadly tips round to impale him.

Deftly stepping between the tripwires and skirting the pressure plate, ensuring he kept a crouched posture to avoid the hanging line, Fareesh made his way beyond the trap. He had been correct that the spikes were attached to a metal mesh plate, large enough to strike him from head to toe. Beyond the danger, he stopped and listened, easing one of the heavy lead-iron balls from the thigh belt into his left hand. With the enhanced echo from the wider cavern before him, he could now detect his enemies, five distinct breathing patterns. Three were most definitely men with larger builds, the other two were faster and lighter; slender men, women or even children. Any confrontation could prove to be an unnecessary delay and the trap suggested at least some of them were professional hunters or killers of some description.

'I am Fareesh Nawabi,' he spoke into the apparent emptiness, 'I am Veer. I give you this chance to leave without conflict. I will pass this cavern and any attempt to stop me will be met with your demise.'

'You are confident with good reason, my friend,' an amiable voice floated back from the darkness, he could tell the man was hidden beside one of three exits from the wider cavern, he could imagine that was where the cart tracks would lead him, 'but you do not know us, so I offer you the same bargain; return along those tunnels and do not pass this way again.'

'Very well,' Fareesh replied, determining that drawing them out quickly would be his best option, 'you have made your choice.'

Stepping forward one pace, a shape appeared from the direction of the speaker, still shrouded in gloom but clearly holding one arm raised towards him. Nawabi was already moving as the deafening bang resounded about the enclosed space and a fiery flash announced a pistol shot. Even with his incredible speed, Fareesh felt the hot bullet whistle past his head as he ducked down and to the right. His foes had not underestimated him, however, the shot merely being a distraction as two more warriors charged at him from either side. The closest wore plate armour and helmet across his torso, a large round shield held up before him with a halberd thrust over and beyond the protection, as if he were jousting. The posture maximised defence but removed all dexterity The Veer angled his body backwards as his opponent arrived, catching the shaft of the halberd with one hand and slipping out a foot to trip the onrushing warrior. Spinning his own body in a tight circle, Fareesh dragged the off-balance enemy around and launched him, staggering, into the tunnel beyond, hearing the satisfying metallic crash as the trap activated.

'Hared!' the other attacker cried out, now behind Fareesh. Glancing over his shoulder, he saw the trident being driven down towards his legs; a good tactic to remove his fighting base. With little time to react, he slid his legs wider and the trident tips failed to connect with his calf; however, the weapon was driven hard into the ground, the prongs on either side pinning his left leg down. His bare chested opponent wasted no time on celebration, releasing the trident and swinging an elbow towards the back of Nawabi's head. The blow was easy to duck but caused an awkward twist in the knee of his restrained leg.

'As we planned, Hondrak!' the pistoleer called out. Fareesh had heard the name before, Hondrak was a well-known wilderness tracker and manhunter. Jabbing his prosthetic upwards, to glance a blow on his fast-moving enemy, the Veer was impressed when Hondrak caught the weapon safely at the wrist-guard, pulling his arm outstretched and wide. With exceptional strength, the hunter pulled Nawabi as upright as the trident would allow, grabbing a handful of his hair through his cowl to force his head up. It was an obvious setup to place him in the line of fire for a second pistol shot. Even as the echoing crack of the weapon sounded again, Nawabi let his whole body drop forward, becoming a dead weight despite the agonising tearing at his scalp and the wrenching pain in his restrained shoulder. It was enough to shift his enemy forward, a guttural cry announcing the bullet had found the wrong target and Hondrak instantly dropping away from him.

Released, Fareesh twisted around on the floor, wedging his prosthetic under the trident and levering it out of the ground. He was already aware of the rapid footsteps approaching and their sudden absence indicated that another enemy had leapt from one of the nearby rocks to land a killing blow. Rolling forward and spinning round on his knees to face the latest challenger, he released the lead ball he was carrying out to the side with deadly accuracy. A dull thud and grunt accompanied its impact with the gunman's face. With that foe incapacitated for the moment, he assessed the one landing in the spot he had been mere moments before. She was fast and dressed in a multitude of coloured veils and loose silks which obscured exactly where her body was within; another clever tactic that would force most enemies to target her centre of mass, allowing her to anticipate every strike. She wielded a double-bladed sword, the handle placed between the two, and a triple-bladed weapon with a similar design to his hand-replacement. He recognised her from stories as well; Dinish Fiveblades. She paused following her failed strike, brandishing the triple blade before her, while spinning the other in one hand to her side.

'Concede, assassin, you cannot find victory here,' she threatened.

Drawing a knife from its sheath on the back of his belt, Fareesh feinted forward, allowing her to block and noting the expected counter with her double-blade; it was high, aiming for the immediate kill. Spinning himself low, he glided under the strike before launching himself into a dive past her exposed side, landing an opportunistic knee into her ribs in passing. Fiveblades staggered slightly, giving him the time to roll over the discarded trident, snatching it up in place of his own knife. The longer weapon provided him more parity against the reach of her arsenal, and he spun it overhead to gain a feel for the weight and balance. The woman had turned to face him and now smiled.

'Good, I was hoping you would not surrender,' she sneered.

Leaping forward, the pair traded blows, lightning-fast strikes from her weapons countered with trident or false hand in a cacophony of metallic clangs. She was an excellent combatant but Nawabi was merely assessing her ability and allowing her confidence to build. The triple-bladed sword was far heavier than her other weapon and left her off-balance when employed. As she lunged forward with it, he snared the blades with the prongs of his trident and pushed forwards to full extension. The move left him exposed but she was fully committed by that point with her own weight across her leading foot; she flailed backwards onto her heels and he swung a kick into her stomach. As she doubled over whilst collapsing back, he snapped out his prosthetic across her other hand, slicing fingers and casting her double-blade free. Crumpling to the ground, she instinctively drew her blood-soaked hand in to her torso, becoming an easy kill. Raising the trident over his shoulder, he heard the whistling sound too late. The bolas whipped in around his waist, wrapping around him with painful impact as the three heavy weights struck against his body, and dragging him sideways. Stumbling, he looked to the side to see Hondrak back on his feet, blood pouring from a large wound in his shoulder.

'That weapon belongs to me,' he managed, despite the clear pain from his injury.

Throwing himself into a staggering charge, Hondrak bellowed a cry of rage. Fareesh compensated for the entangling weight of the bolas and set the trident to impale its owner. As the hunter came almost into range, he unexpectedly threw himself off to one side, rolling painfully across the cavern floor. Another distraction. From behind him, the chain swept around his body, the links interspersed with small spikes that bit into his flesh. Turning to face the new attacker, he found it was a shorter, slender man dressed mostly in black, a short sword in the hand not holding the other end of the chain. Nawabi twirled the trident around to strike his enemy, finding the blow deflected and the shorter man skidding past him to create another loop of chain about his waist. Feeling new punctures as the restraint was pulled tight, the Veer could not disentangle himself as Fiveblades leapt back up into the attack and the assailant who had used the pistols had now drawn a golden machete to join the fray. Knowing that the man in black would need to hold back to keep the chain taut, Fareesh quickly assessed Hondrak, seeing that the hunter could barely stand, let alone fight. Focussing solely on the other two combatants, he swept the trident round with expert grace, deflecting each blade strike, despite the complimentary attack pattern they demonstrated. Every so often, another tug of the chain sent electric fire through him and options for victory seemed to be fading. Parrying another attack from the triple-bladed sword, he felt the slack form in the binding around him. Hurling the trident towards the male warrior, he smiled at the elegant dodge performed, knowing it had gained him the precious moments he required. Fiveblades was keen to maintain the pressure and leapt in at him rashly; he caught her weapon on his prosthetic and grabbed her other wrist, forcing it behind her and pulling her into a tight embrace. Twirling around in a circle as she struggled, he wrapped the slack of the chain around them both, hearing her exhale sharply as the spines stabbed into her lithe figure. Twisting his right arm through ninety degrees, he saw the surprise in her eyes as her trademark sword was wrenched from her grasp and tossed out of reach. Seeing her predicament, the man in black dropped his end of the chain, relieving the pain somewhat, and leapt forwards with his short sword. Fareesh smiled at the struggling woman in his arms and jerked her to the side at the very last minute. The upswinging strike was too committed to withdraw and slammed into her back; Nawabi noted with interest as the tip of the blade appeared through her sternum. Shock filled her face and she looked down at the blood-soaked blade protruding between them from her own body, matching red dribbling from her parted lips.

'Uhh, you will… they will kill you…' she stuttered weakly.

The Veer winked at her as the sword was rapidly pulled free from her body and he instantly spun her free of his embrace towards her inadvertent murderer. The man in black caught her in his arms, quickly but gently lowering her to the floor. Unwrapping the remainder of the painful chain from about himself, Nawabi whipped it around towards the remaining armed attacker. Having dodged the trident successfully, this time he was not so lucky, feeling the harsh lash of the spiked metal against his face, driving him sideways. Releasing the chain towards the man's legs, Fareesh was pleased to see it become instantly ensnared about his limbs. Turning towards Hondrak again, he could hear the struggling pistoleer trying to load one of his firearms despite the bindings now hacking at him; it gave the Veer at least one free minute before being ready to fire.

Hondrak was clearly groggy from loss of blood and his injured arm hung limply by his side, but he swung a powerful roundhouse punch with the other anyway. Fareesh dodged his head back out of reach as the blow passed harmlessly in front of his chin, before stabbing his quad-bladed prosthetic into the bare chest of his foe. A cry of pain erupted from him and he grabbed the wrist guard with his working hand, trying to pull the blades free. Nawabi did not resist, dropping his right arm but punching forward with his left, driving the lead-iron ball in his palm into Hondrak's mouth and shattering several teeth. Bewilderment flashed in his eyes and the Veer smiled at him before springing into the air and smashing a knee into the hunter's chin. The crunching of bone accompanied the impact and Hondrak fell back stiff and lifelessly.

Spinning back towards his remaining opponents, Fareesh was surprised that the man in black was charging forward rather than waiting for another shot from his ally. With less attackers, his freedom of movement was increasing and, despite the injuries suffered, his confidence was returning. His enemy arrived and they exchanged blows, Nawabi using his prosthetic, the Veer clearly having the skill advantage and soon turning the enraged attack into a panicked defence. Hearing the loading click of a pistol, he rolled under a thrust from the short sword and released the last of the throwing spheres. It arrived exactly as timed, striking the end of the barrel exactly as the shot was released; the resulting explosion splintered the weapon in a blinding flash, throwing the pistoleer backwards with a cry of alarm. Deflecting another few blows, whilst still crouched beneath his opponent, Fareesh timed an incoming downwards swing and caught his enemy's wrist in a vice like grip. Pulling his arm out straight, Nawabi drove upwards with his prosthetic into his enemy's armpit; even as the agonised cry echoed around the cavern, the Veer twisted his arm, tearing flesh and tendons in a fountain of blood. Driving up to his feet, he delighted as the entire arm tore free and the smaller man staggered backwards in gasping shock before tripping over a rock.

'Fazam!' the pistoleer screamed in genuine aguish, launching himself into a furious attack, blade brandished in his left hand, his right crippled from the recent explosion. His anger gave him vigour, but he was using his weaker hand and the rage clouded his judgement. After absorbing the initial flurry of blows, Nawabi forced his opponent back steadily before disarming him with a spin of his arm and catching the golden blade as if fell back towards them, at the same time flooring the man with a kick to the chest.

'Now you see whose bargain was the more generous, eh?' Fareesh mocked, raising the sword high to slay his opponent.

'Kill me now or I will hunt you until time ceases, so swears Errabith Chaucer!' the other man spat, clearly emotional over his ally's death. The Veer nodded and drove the blade down, even as a pair of thick arms wrapped around him from behind, preventing the blow and heaving him bodily from the ground.

'Forget about me, dung-feeder?' a deep voice growled as the powerful arms crushed the air from him. He could see the shattered remnants of a shield hanging from the straps of one arm and felt the steel chest plate at his back; somehow his first attacker had survived being thrown into the spike trap they had set for the Veer. Limbs soaked in crimson continued to constrict and he could see pools of blood on the floor of the cavern as he was carried backwards by his captor.

'You were wrong to assume you could so easily defeat Zark Hared!'

Fareesh could feel the fire in his lungs as his body screamed out for air, his blurring vision showed Chaucer slowly clambering to his feet. Strong as Hared was, his injuries had sapped him somewhat, and he was forced to lower the Veer to the ground as he dragged him. It was the opportunity Fareesh needed, pushing off with all his might as his feet touched the ground, his head smashed into Hared's nose and the embrace about him loosened. Pushing his own arms outwards, Nawabi created enough space to slip free and hurled the sword towards the recovering pistoleer, harpooning him through the chest. Not waiting to see him fall, he twisted around even as Hared drove down with a two-handed hammer blow. Slowing due to his own exertions, Nawabi tried to dodge clear but the fists connected with his chest, pummelling him to the floor. A follow-up punch was not far behind but rolling to the side was far easier and Hared's knuckles cracked audibly as he struck the earth. He barely seemed to notice, however, allowing himself to immediately fall sideways into an elbow drop; the blow landed on the Veer's left bicep, instantly numbing his limb. The heavy warrior turned the attack into a roll, trying to use his own body to pin the assassin down. Fareesh jabbed his prosthetic into the other man's side just above his hip and heard a grunt as his enemy rolled off again.

Getting back to his feet far slower than usual, swaying unsteadily, Nawabi tried to focus even as Hared charged headfirst into him, the iron helmet he wore crashing into his jaw and causing his teeth to involuntarily gnash together. He felt as though he had bitten off the tip of his tongue and the wash of blood down his throat supported this theory. Allowing himself to stagger backwards several paces created the breathing space he needed but Hared was already closing in for a second similar headbutt. This time, the Veer side-stepped and stabbed upwards with his quad-blade attachment, puncturing both his opponent's eyes and cheeks, and driving the deadly steel into his brain. The dead weight dragged Fareesh to the ground with him, prosthetic still protruding from the ichor-soaked mangle of his face. Despite his foe being dead, Nawabi twisted his arm once again, completely eradicating any semblance of the man he had fought and tearing the front of his head away to expose shredded brain matter beneath.

Stepping away from his final foe, the Veer took a seat on the cold cavern floor, breathing heavily. The battle had taken more out of him than he had imagined, although the majority of his wounds were superficial, and he wondered if he was not truly recovered from losing his hand. Regardless, it was the second time he had struggled to defeat his enemies and he knew his pride was not more important than the reputation of the Veer. As soon as he was clear of these tunnels, and had recovered the cart trail he was tracking, he would send a messenger kestrel to Grandmaster Mozak; regardless of the personal shame it could bring, it would detail the need to send him some reinforcements.

Chapter 14

Sound echoed eerily through the still, dry air, as though they stood within an ancient tomb. Treya steeled herself against the fear that threatened to overwhelm her, somehow the clarity that had brought them here, the certainty of their quest, had dissolved upon entering the chamber. Her head swam, memories, thoughts and regrets all vying for supremacy in her mind, and she struggled to bring it all into order. There was no immediate threat, no perceived danger, yet she had never felt so close to the precipice of death. She tried to dismiss the thought as simple paranoia, but something resisted her logic and continued to gnaw away at her as she slowly followed the curved wall around the room

Images of her children brought a moment's calm, and she recalled a warm Spring afternoon in the garden where they had spent hours picking every daisy and insisting she craft necklaces and crowns from the tiny flowers for them. Straker had built them a tepee to play in that day, providing entertainment and some necessary shade as required. It had been idyllic, perfect, all she had wanted from her life and more; fate seemed to be against her happiness, however. She tried to keep the twins in her mind's eye, but they soon drifted away, leaving only the image of Straker's devoted smile, full of love and care, all for her. She should have felt lifted by that, she knew, but instead she mourned the distance between them, the parting with unresolved anger between them, and the chance they would never see each other again. Something inside her kept reinforcing that idea; maybe the natives of this island would turn on them, rather than see the Rondure removed; or Veer assassins could finally catch up to them; or they made it back to Lustania and fell to their own sister's hand. She felt a twinge in her scarred cheek and knew she had no strength to fight Alissa.

She thought back to her childhood, how she had spent so much time resenting her father and his harsh teachings, the anger inside her closing her off to the outside world, and felt regret. For now, looking back, she realised that there had been love all around her, from her mother and her sisters, and their need to rely on each other, had created a unique bond between them. Of course, her father had shattered all of that, forcing their mother to constantly defend his actions and protest to them that he was cruel against his own wishes, that the hardships he placed upon them were done out of love. She had always denied that to herself, but the years provided opportunity to reconsider; Rayne, Catalana and she had been put through unimaginable trials by him and here they all stood, survivors trying to prevent an evil from swallowing the world. Again. Alissa had been lucky, or so it had seemed, growing up with only love and adoration from Rork Fimarr, none of the lessons he felt necessary to inflict upon his older daughters applied to her. And now she was insane, corrupted and evil. Would she have been so naïvely led by Kale Stanis all those years ago, or so quickly tainted by Ramikain's power, or so easily swayed by Lennath's influence, if she had suffered the same hardships as Treya when she was a child? Treya shook her head, even now it was too much to consider that her father may have done everything out of good intention.

All her life she had tried to order chaos, bring sense to the inexplicable and arrange everything into clear categories of black and white, but now it was impossible. Lennath, a prince who had aided them and looked upon them with awe, a man who should have been a clear ally, was now their greatest threat. Jacob Frost had sentenced them to certain doom five years ago but had now sacrificed his own life for theirs. Her newly discovered half-sister, an illegitimate secret that should bring them naught but shame, was now instrumental in their quest to stop evil sweeping across the land. Terex, the former henchman of Ramikain, was now charged with protecting her own children. Even Bentram, just a faceless revolutionary soldier, had performed a heroic deed to ensure their success. Her whole fundamental belief in black and white had been shattered into shards of grey.

Skirting the perimeter of the large circular cage that almost filled the room, she was reminded of the last cage she had seen. That had been in the Black Citadel, a trap that had been sprung upon her, seemingly confining her with no hope of escape and bringing victory to her enemy. An involuntary shudder ran through her at the unbidden memory and she cast her eyes to the floor as she walked. But it had not been the end, she told herself, for even at the edge of despair, a light shone through. Straker Forge, the man she loved, had appeared from the jaws of death and rescued her. When she had later been betrayed by Kale Stanis, Straker had rescued her once again. From her lifelong fears of being isolated and lonely, with no family of her own, Straker had rescued her. He was not here now, but the hope he represented was a fire in her heart, the punishments of her father had created strength in her body and the sacrifices made by others for the sake of this quest brought resolve to her mind.

Lifting her head, she found she had arrived at the arched door cut into the outer wall of the cage. It was the one furthest from the entrance to this chamber, Rayne having remained at the one now opposite her, with Catalana to her left and Crystal to her right. The doors were spaced evenly around the cage, like points on a compass. Peering through the multiple layers of bars, she was pleased that Rayne had opted to remain at the first door with the High Auger; if the native tried anything to sabotage them, she was the most likely to be able to deal with him. It was still unsettling that he seemed so compliant, despite some reticence in his voice when he spoke, he had honoured everything in his own proclamations. She had no doubt he had expected his Guardians to win the Trials, and their power was certainly great enough to destroy her small party with ease, but their failure had not prompted a renege nor further Trials to ensure a result in their favour. She knew that betrayal was still a possibility, but there was greater evidence with every passing minute that the faith of the islanders was stronger than any fear they may have of losing their precious artifact.

'Now what?' she asked aloud, her voice resounding through the chamber, 'How do we take it?'

Her question was directed at the High Auger, but her eyes were fixed on the prize, a small, golden sphere with delicate carvings across its surface, pulsing gently with a warm yellow glow.

'If you are the chosen, the four joined by blood that the prophecy has decreed, then the Rondure will offer itself to you. Take the handles and know your fate,' the venerate native replied, a mixture of fear and trepidation heavy in his voice.

Examining the door, she spotted what he was referring to, a circular break in the bars was positioned just above waist height and beyond it was a thin metal handle, similar to that of a corkscrew. Taking a deep breath, she slipped her wrist through the opening and took the handle in her left hand. Nothing happened until Crystal took hold of the final handle and a spring-loaded manacle snapped shut on her arm. Panicking, but unable to free herself, she looked at the others frantically.

'It is a trap! We have been betrayed!' she cried out, realising that her sisters were likewise ensnared. Oddly, Rayne was not straining to pull her arm free and Treya met her eyes, feeling a sudden calm wash over her.

'This is no trap,' she stated assuredly, 'stop struggling.'

'No, no trap,' the High Auger agreed flatly, 'just a test of your faith.'

Treya forced herself to relax, resecuring her grip on the handle and bringing her breathing back under control. 'A test?' she replied, 'Then we will pass it. Crystal, Catalana, no matter what happens now, just remember our objective.'

Receiving nods of agreement, she licked dry lips and waited. After few moments, a clockwork whirring sound could be detected. Pressing her face to the bars, she looked down and realised the handle was inside a box, obscuring her view of what was happening. The whirring was soon joined by a swishing sound, like the pendulum of a clock and anxiety threatened to overwhelm her again. Taking deep breaths, she gritted her teeth and retained her grip on the handle. Without warning, she felt a sharp scratch across the back of her wrist. It was followed by another and a third, accompanied by the sticky warmth of blood flowing freely, but she did not release the handle.

'Zis is a trap!' Crystal called out again, voice high-pitched with fear, 'Zey are going to take our 'ands!'

'Stay calm!' Rayne commanded, 'the blades have stopped falling. A test, remember?'

'Yes, yes,' the High Auger agreed, enthusiasm and wonder creeping into his tone, 'your blood is the key, not your deaths…'

Below the handle she still gripped, Treya could see a small pool of blood forming on the flagstone just beyond the gate. The stone must have been angled as the puddle began to trickle away from her and into a groove beyond. Without warning, there was a loud clang and the manacle released her, but she retained her grip on the handle just in case. Crystal and Catalana had snapped their arms back, nursing the narrow wounds now evident on the back of their wrists, but Rayne still stood calmly watching her through the layers of bars.

'What do we do?' she called out to the High Auger.

He seemed to be overcome with awe and took several moments to respond, 'It… the Rondure has offered itself to you. Now is your time to decide if you will take it from us. You may still walk away.'

The last was spoken with clearly futile hope; he knew they had worked too hard to change their decision now. She felt a swell of empathy for him, a kindred being whose choices were already made for him regardless of his own desires.

'No, we cannot. But I swear we will return the Rondure to you once our quest is complete.'

The old native nodded and smiled, but there was no belief in his eyes. Treya turned the handle and found it rotated easily and the door swung inwards. Before Rayne could move, the oldest Fimarr held up a hand to stop her, 'No. Stay beyond the edge of this cage. I need the rest of you safe, just in case.'

Her sister nodded and she stepped forward gingerly. The sudden sound of shifting metal made her jump and she watched in amazement as the three inner boundaries retracted into the floor, giving her free access to the glowing orb.

''Urry!' Crystal urged, watching her intently, 'Take ze zing quickly, before somezing else 'appens!'

Torn between caution and concern, Treya forced her legs into action, striding forward and grasping the Rondure in both hands. Immediately, a staggering heat swept through her, snatching her breath away in shock, and everything went white. She felt like she was falling but in all directions at once, losing awareness of up or down and unable to feel the floor beneath her or even the cool air about her. She could not even feel her own body and wondered if she had just died, if the Rondure had somehow destroyed her body and only her thoughts remained. The falling sensation intensified, and she thought she was screaming although there was no sound.

Suddenly, it felt like she slammed into something solid, there was no pain, just a disorientation at being grounded again.

Grounded.

Blinking her eyes rapidly, she realised that colour was returning but she was not in the Shrine any longer, she was back on the beach. Attempting to raise her hand to rub her confused head, she realised she had no control of her body, in fact, it was not even her body. Like a dream, she was somehow seeing through someone else's eyes, someone in a different place; no, she corrected herself, someone in a different time. She had no idea how she came to such certainty, but she knew that she was viewing shadows from hundreds of years ago.

Standing on the beach of this very island, she felt the hunger and excitement of her host body; it had been a long hard journey to find this place, but she was certain that she would find what she sought there. Images flashed forward and she found herself deep within Mount Darkfire, a cave system having led them to a cavern heated by the lava within the volcano, two natural plinths sporting the mystical Rondure and its complimentary Stave. Her host body took both items and knew their power. Dragged forward in time again, she found herself sitting upon a throne, the power of the artifacts had allowed her to enslave the crew and expeditionary team that had accompanied her, forcing them to build her a fortress and supporting her experiments with the mutation ability she now possessed. However, the use of the artifacts had taken its toll, ageing her prematurely.

Flashing forward again, she felt hollow inside as she looked out from the shrine built in her honour, over the sea towards the land of her origin. Already she had lived an unnatural lifetime, finding the energy she could manipulate withering her physical form rapidly but able to reverse the effects by eating the flesh of other mortals, the younger the meal, the longer her body remained restored. To ensure her longevity, she had forced her slaves to breed rapidly but it would not be sufficient for much longer; she needed to return to the world and take it for her own. The powerful creatures she could create and control would be useful in this endeavour but not enough; she needed an army.

Ten years later and her experiments with mutating humans had proven successful; her new 'People' were stronger, faster and tougher than any other mortals, their intelligence making them far superior to her simple beasts. Too superior, in fact. They had used their intellect and semblance of free will to try and usurp her from the throne, to cast her out and take control of their own lives once more. They had failed, but her inability to control them made her aspirations for a thinking army a thing of the past; maybe someday she would know how to harness their strength and maintain their fealty, but it was not this day. Using the Rondure, she created a Boundary that would keep the island hidden from trespassers whilst also keeping her experiment trapped within. To ensure their existence as a potential army in the future, she created fake texts for them to follow and erased their simple minds of all she had done to them. To ensure they did not escape, she trapped the Rondure in a cage within the shrine. It could only be opened by four joined in blood. As their 'religious' texts told them to limit their offspring to one per family, they would never believe they could release the artifact themselves. If she ever returned to use them, she would reveal the ironic truth; all of the islanders were joined by blood, her blood, for that was what she had used to transform them. Putting her failure behind her, she set sail with only the Stave at her disposal; it held the power of transformation and control, and was all she would need to conquer everything…

Sudden white filled her awareness again and she felt herself being dragged forwards through time and space while still falling through a void of nothing. Eyes flicking open again, she drew in a huge gasp of air as if she had been suffocating. Her body was shaking uncontrollably and she felt icy cold, her vision swam into focus and she found herself looking up into the frightened eyes of Catalana.

'Treya! Treya!' her sister was shouting, 'Can you hear me? Come back to us, Treya, we need you!' Tears were flowing readily, and she could feel warm droplets striking her forehead. She could not form words and panted erratically as the feel of her own body and the constraint of being tied to a single point in time returned. She lifted her hands before her and saw that they were red and cracked, as if she had been working the farm plough for too long. And they were empty.

'Where,' she croaked in a hoarse voice she didn't recognise, 'where is the Rondure?'

'She is recovered!' Crystal's voice came from the left and she turned her head painfully to see a bright smile from her half-sister, 'we must get 'er away from 'ere!'

'The Rondure!' she snapped again, 'where is it?!'

'It is here,' Rayne stated, holding up a leather satchel from where she knelt beyond Treya's feet, 'we must keep it contained. I do not think it can be safely touched.'

Relief swept over her as she realised they had succeeded, the artifact they sought was now theirs, all that remained was to save Alissa. 'What happened?' she finally asked, being helped into a sitting position supported by Cat's knees.

'You picked up ze orb and went into some sort of fit,' Crystal explained, 'your 'ole body was shaking furiously but your grip on zat zing was firm. Even when you collapsed, your 'ands would not let go. We dragged you out of ze cage but zat did not 'elp. Rayne 'ad 'er 'ands covered wiz gloves and was able to pry it from you after a few moments. We feared ze worst as you skin was like fire to touch and your eyes were open but saw nozing.'

'Do you remember what happened?' Catalana asked, stroking Treya's hair gently.

'I… yes, I think I do,' she replied, keeping her voice low so that the High Auger could not overhear, 'it let me see images of the past; no, that's not quite right. It took me back into the past, like I was inside someone else. I saw the discovery of this island; the Rondure and Stave were here from the start. I saw the creation of these People and what their true purpose was, or is, I am not certain. What I do know for sure is that we must return the Rondure once Alissa is safe, the Stave too; return them to this cage and never allow them to be released again. We cannot risk them being taken by someone like him again.'

'Like who Treya? Who was it that you saw?' Rayne urged.

'Ramikain. These people were his…'

Pressing the small lock of hair to his upper lip, Straker breathed deeply, comforted by the familiar smell of her. He lamented the arguments they had been through of late and vowed to make it up to her in whatever way he could; being with her was everything to him and he would not let anyone stand in the way of that, not even himself. He considered the root cause of her animosity and it came down to the same thing every time, secrets. There were so many he had kept over the years but most he had dispensed with when he committed himself to her. Lately, the remainder had come to light which brought both relief, that the weight was lifted, and pain, that Treya continued to discover he had hidden things from her. But with all revealed, they could finally move on without any further secrets to disrupt their love. That was not true, though, he reminded himself, for he held one more secret that he could never reveal; his curse, allowing him to always secure victory in battle provided none remained to witness his success. If he told her about that, then the ancient magic would strip him of his supernatural combat prowess; without it, how would he ensure the safety of his family in the future?

Picking salted meat from between his teeth with his boot-knife, Forge peered out into the late afternoon. They had chosen to eat in the Southern watchtower again, as they had most evenings since they arrived at the Citadel, for it sported one of the view windows they had not sealed or trapped. It also looked out over the narrow road leading to the courtyard gates, the most likely avenue of approach for any enemies. He knew that this structure was scalable, he had done it himself five years previously, as had Rayne, Kale Stanis and Treya. But many of the walls and towers they had used for the ascent were crumbling ruins now. Not so treacherous that Veer would not tackle them, but he hoped the assassins' arrogance would prevent them from trying; why bother when they could easily kill any defenders who confronted them at the gates? Any mercenaries or soldiers dispatched by Lennath would have only the front entrance, however, and that would give the defenders a massive advantage.

Turning towards his companions, he raised an eyebrow in annoyance; Rebecca was utilising her non-too subtle flirtations on Terex again. She was currently removing a large splinter from his palm, pressing her lips to his hand before claiming the shard of wood with her teeth. As she straightened to spit the sliver aside, he kept his hand pressed against her face. Although Straker was not against any union between the two, the timing was inappropriate, he needed the other warrior sharp and focussed.

'Your skin is so soft,' Terex remarked, 'like fine silk.'

'Thank-you,' Rebecca replied, 'I bathe in fine oils and use rose butter to moisturise when I am in more civil surrounds. I can show you one day, perhaps?'

'It would be wasted on him!' Straker butted in rudely, 'Or me! We are fighting men and our skin was ruined years hence! Should any of us survive this whole debacle, we would do well to concern ourselves with living fruitful lives rather than skin care!'

'There is nothing wrong with a lady caring for her appearance,' Terex countered, not looking at him, 'or have you been so long with yours that such things have been forgotten?'

Straker felt a sting on annoyance at the words; was Terex suggesting that Treya was anything less than exquisite? He calmed himself, the other man was simply mirroring his own sarcasm.

'Never forgotten, for she needs no oils or butters to remain as beautiful as the day I met her. Come here, for I am still concerned with the approach.'

Terex sighed, smiling at Rebecca before standing and joining the other man by the window. 'What worries you, Straker? I already plan to build a slalom of fortifications along that road.'

'They will do us no good,' Forge assessed, 'we have no weapons that could hit such a range from here and hoping to lie in wait for opponents in the courtyard, when we have no idea if or when they would appear, is fruitless.'

'I agree,' Terex said, 'but that would not be the point, unless we were attacked by only two or three people, the fortifications would slow them down and provide us extra preparation time.'

Forge nodded; it was a good point. 'I wish we could seal the courtyard gates properly, that would create more problems for them.'

'Wishing does not help us, my friend, those gates are beyond use. Regardless, all the entrances from the courtyard to inside are sealed and blocked. Any attackers will be herded to the single entrance we have left untouched. Once inside, the width of the corridors will prevent more than two men standing abreast at once; their numbers will not matter.'

It sounded logical and simple, Terex speaking the words with such confidence that it seemed any outcome other than victory was an impossibility. Forge prayed he was correct, because failure meant the death of them all, including his beloved children.

'Thank-you, Terex, for standing with me and protecting my children,' he said quietly, sincerity thick in his voice.

'Ha!' the other warrior laughed aloud, clapping him on the shoulder, 'Do not paint me as some altruist! I am no hero, Straker Forge, I am here to protect Kastani, the rest of you are simply benefitting from that!'

'If protecting that little girl is your definition of selfishness,' Rebecca chimed in, 'then you are every bit a hero!'

Terex turned away, perhaps in embarrassment at the compliments, moving over to his pack to absently rifle within. Forge was about to follow up his previous comment with something trivial and light-hearted when the inner door burst open and a tear stained Kastani sprinted into the room.

'Terex! Terex!' she screamed rushing into his arms to be held tightly, 'They are coming here now! I did not know they was such bad men at the palace, I promise! But they are coming, and they want to hurt us all!'

'Shhh, calm yourself, little princess,' Terex soothed, 'Who is coming and how do you know?'

'The black robes!' she sobbed breathlessly, 'First it was just Mozak but then lots of others came. Lennath said it was to keep us safe...'

'Veer!' Forge cursed, 'Of course it would be Veer!'

'All right, darling girl,' Terex continued, rocking her gently, 'you think the Veer are coming for us? How do you know this?'

'I seen them!' she assured him, 'In my head! They are coming and they will be here when the sun is half in the land, you have to believe me, I am telling the truth!'

'I do believe you, Kastani, of course I do. Where will they come from and how many?'

'I saw lots,' she cried, 'more than six! They are coming through the tunnels and then onto the road!'

'Okay, Kastani, you are a good girl for telling me. Remember what we talked about, the hiding I will need you to do with Rebecca and the twins?'

She nodded at him, wiping more tears away on her sleeve.

'Wait, if they are coming through the tunnels, then Fiveblades and the others will deal with them! We have nothing to fear!' Rebecca stated with certainty.

'I am really sorry, Rebecca,' Kastani said mournfully, looking the woman in the eyes, 'but your friends are all dead. One of the black-robes killed them.'

'One of the...' Rebecca's voice trailed off. Forge understood her sudden fear; five of the best warriors she knew falling before a single Veer, and at least six more coming for them. The odds were stacked against them, or at least that was how it would seem to everyone else.

'I believe you as well, Kastani, we will prepare based on what you have said,' he told her, placing a gentle hand upon her shoulder, 'you may have saved all our lives by telling us and, even if you made a mistake, it will be good practise for us to use our plan. Go with Rebecca now and get ready with Joseff and Melody.'

He watched the pair leave and turned to Terex, 'She really has seen them, you know. She mentioned how she had seen the movements of some of those creatures a few days ago.'

'I know she is telling the truth. I do not think she has ever lied to me,' Terex revealed, 'I know how special that girl is, but she has changed even more since her time in the palace, I fear what they may have done to her. That is a matter for later, for now we must ready ourselves for an attack.'

'Yes, at dusk which leaves us little time,' he paused, running his next gambit through his head before putting it into words, 'I need to alter the plan.'

'That is foolhardy, Forge, we all know how the plan is to work. Veer or not, we must put faith in the tactics. We are undone against their skill otherwise.'

'Listen to me, forcing them into a corridor, if they choose not to enter via the few remaining windows, is destined for failure. You and I against two of them in single combat? They will cut us down in moments and then the children will be lost.'

'What other plan is there? We are too few in number to safeguard every entrance or attempt to pick them off as they search this place. Maybe we have time to flee, but we have the children who will slow us down, and the enemy will catch us in short order. I will fight to my last breath to protect the little ones and that will bring us victory, believe me.'

'I do not. The Veer are too skilled in their art. I have heard tell that a single assassin killed thirty warriors in open battle, we cannot defeat them with our current plan.'

'So, what do you propose?' Terex asked in exasperation.

'Station yourself in the room where Rebecca will be hiding with the children, set whatever traps you can to distract any that make it as far as you. I will face the assassins in the courtyard.'

'That is suicide. You will barely delay them, let alone defeat them. And what will that gain? An easier approach for them to face us individually rather than together?'

'I'm asking you to trust me, Terex, can you do that? I will stop them, I promise, but it has to be me alone.'

'How am I supposed to trust that? You are asking me to let you die! Let us stand as one, side-by-side, and vanquish these foes. Alone we will be defeated.'

Forge took a deep breath and clasped Terex's forearm, staring him in the eye and speaking with conviction, 'I will kill the Veer if I face them. Think this through, why would I send myself out to the slaughter knowing that it will result in the deaths of my own two children? I cannot explain this to you, I can only ask you to heed my words. Please, stay with the children and protect them with your life, if all goes well you will not see combat this day.'

Terex did not look convinced, but his shoulders slumped in resignation, 'Fine! Have it your way! But I will be very disappointed if you die!' he spoke the last with a smile, resigned to following Forge's orders, 'But let it be known that I will officially report you as a lunatic when I retell this tale!'

Straker returned his smile easily, 'Thank-you, my friend, I will not disappoint you.'

Leaving his ally to prepare, Forge raced along the narrow corridors, gathering his scimitar and javelins in passing but stopping at the children's room. He watched for a moment as Rebecca calmly helped them prepare some provisions and toys, before calling Melody and Joseff to him. Pulling them into a tight embrace, he kissed the top of their heads.

'Okay my little darlings, it is time to play the hiding game like we talked about. You do not have to be afraid, though, because Rebecca and Terex will stay with you.'

'What about you, Dada? Can you stay with us, too?' Joseff asked hopefully.

'I cannot, Joseff, I have some other errands to run but I will come back as soon as I can.'

'You are going to fight the bad men, aren't you?' Melody added, bottom lip starting to quiver.

'I am going to stop the bad men from coming here,' he admitted, wanting to maintain honesty with them, 'maybe I will have to fight but hopefully not. When they are gone, I will come back to you because then we are all safe again.'

'What if they kill you?' Joseff asked with tears beginning to flow.

He kissed them both again. 'They will not, I promise.'

Unwilling to let emotion overwhelm him, he turned away and headed for the exit to the courtyard. The sun was already low when he emerged, and he cast an eye down the road to ensure his foes were not already there. Looking about him, he said a silent prayer that Terex would stay true to his word and remain within the inner rooms of the fortress. He knew he could defeat the Veer provided no-one witnessed the victory, the curse that had hounded him for all these years would ensure it. Just so long as those he was protecting remained hidden. He expected the assassins to be professional about their business, but he could still try and lull them somewhat, and it had been a long time since he had allowed himself a little showmanship. Arranging two old barrels and a crate into position, he created himself a seat and footstool, lounging back on the makeshift furniture with a disinterested posture.

He did not wait long, seeing the black shadows moving quickly along the road towards the Citadel soon after setting the scene. Silently they approached and filtered into the courtyard without fear, eyes skirting all around for any sign of ambush or trap. The foremost man, brandishing a lethal-looking attachment in place of one hand, pulled down his face covering and addressed Forge directly.

'You are a member of the party who fled Hercatalana?'

'I am!' Straker replied cheerily, keeping the assassins within his gaze but retaining the nonchalant appearance, 'And you are the deadly assassins pursuing us I presume?'

'Whatever clever trap you think you have in store for us will not work,' his enemy continued, 'we are Veer, and we cannot be defeated.'

'Then we have something in common!' Forge went one, 'I am Straker Forge, and I cannot be defeated either. What a coincidence!'

The man in black paused, seemingly assessing the statement and the situation, 'Very well, Straker Forge, I will not pretend that your name is unknown to me. I am certain you are a great warrior but so were the five I executed in the tunnels leading here. You cannot win. If you leave, we will honour your surrender and allow you to live.'

'Well then,' Straker replied, pleased that the seven men tensed when he stood, 'I could consider that a fair offer, if only it was not my children you were intending to murder in there. With that being the case, I will have to decline and kill all of you.'

The words were barely out of his mouth as multiple projectiles arrowed in towards him. Like so many times before, he allowed his supernaturally heightened reactions to take over, body twisting and rolling almost outside his own control, the inexplicable speed of his dodging proof that he had no observers other than those about to die. Given a moment to pause, he realised that the Veer were actually surprised, obviously expecting him to be dead.

'Invigorating!' he said, controlling his breathing to mask the effort he had just exerted, 'My thanks for providing a warm-up. However, I am afraid I can extend no return courtesy, nor an offer of surrender. You will all have to die.' He emphasised his point by drawing his sword.

'Impressive, Straker Forge, but you are not invincible. Already you bleed from our blades.'

He looked down and saw three superficial cuts to his arm and body. Cursed to victory he was, but not invulnerable to harm. This could get messy. Breaking into a sprint, the courtyard erupted into battle as the agile Veer leapt from his path, swinging weapons of their own that found no purchase. Having travelled beyond them, he slid to a halt, scimitar flashing back across his own body and deflecting two more thrown blades. Drawing a javelin, he engaged the closest assassin using the metal spear as a foil to his longer blade, Uncertainty flashed in the eyes of his opponent as Forge's strikes and thrusts met none of the expected patterns of combat. Dropping low into a leg sweep, Forge launched the javelin away from himself, watching as it ricocheted from the cobbled floor and up into a charging enemy who had discounted the attack completely when it had been thrown too low. Slamming into his lower abdomen, the blow toppled him, and the fall pushed the weapon right through him. The man he was engaged with had leapt over the sweep and then landed awkwardly to avoid an overhead blind thrust. Cartwheeling around him, he struck the side of Straker's jaw with his trailing leg, spinning him into the path of another assassin. Ducking below the incoming swing of a bladed nunchuk, he punched out, striking the man in the shoulder joint and watching the arm on that side go limp.

As that opponent withdrew, two more took his place and Forge lost track of his own movements, the odd sensation of serenity filling his senses as it always did when he fell into the heat of battle. His movements were lightning, his blows unpredictable and his accuracy superb. Within moments his blade had stuck home, slicing one man in the jugular whilst he was performing a somersault out of range. Crumpling instead of completing a graceful landing, the assassin clutched his throat tightly to try and stem the gushing arterial flow. His initial opponent had also drawn back, allowing the remaining man to distract the deadly fighter. There was no real awareness of the knife being thrown towards him, but the curse performed its role once more, driving him to deflect a sword strike whilst spinning once again, the action allowing him to strike the incoming knife with the flat of his own weapon and firing it off on a different course. The blade struck the Veer carrying the nunchuks in the forehead, dropping him instantly. His two remaining foes closed in, trying to trap him between them so that one would get an open attack at his back. But such tactics were impossible to employ against him at that moment. Deflecting and parrying blow after blow, from front, side or behind, he could hear the grunts of exertion as the Veer found fatal attacks harmlessly defended. As they intensified the onslaught as much as possible, Straker wriggled a second javelin free into his left hand. Sensing a frustratedly reckless attack launched from the man to his rear, Forge dropped to one knee, forcing his other opponent to parry the swing. As their blades clashed above him, he stabbed out to front and rear with scimitar and javelin, running both men through. Tugging his weapons free, the shocked Veer crumpled to the cobbles.

Taking a deep breath, he walked towards the man still trying to prevent his life's blood slipping through his fingers, casually throwing his javelin towards the nearby courtyard wall, not looking to see it deflect and slam into the skull of the assassin he had struck in the abdomen. Crouching before the gasping Veer, pleased at the desperate defeat in his eyes, Forge prodded him in the chest with his scimitar.

'That is only five of you,' he stated with relish, 'have the others fled to report back to your masters?'

The slightest shake of his head was all the man found achievable, 'No,' he gasped in a whisper, 'you have lost…'

Straker looked around frantically, the unprotected door to the fortress stood wide open and there was nobody there to stop the Veer from gaining access. Heart leaping into his mouth, he kicked the Veer's hand away from his neck before sprinting in pursuit.

Terex knocked lightly on the cupboard door, three short taps followed by a longer one; the same pattern Kastani had just done on the other side. A giggle erupted from beyond the heavy oak and he smiled, listening for the next sequence she would use. In the corridor beyond this room, he detected swift but cautious footsteps, muffled by soft-soled boots; Forge had failed, and their enemies were here. As his ward began to knock again, he hushed her sharply and then whispered against the wood

'Stay silent. Do not come out regardless of what you hear. If this door opens, be ready to defend yourselves.'

He could make out the sound of Rebecca shifting the children in the cramped space, probably putting herself to the front of the cupboard and echoing his warning to stay silent. As quietly as possible, he edged over to the wall opposite the only entrance to this room, lifting the two pre-loaded crossbows onto his knees. Heart racing, he tried to focus on the sound from the corridor, taking long controlled breaths to ease the tension. The footsteps paused outside the door and he wrapped his fingers about the crossbow triggers, silently cursing the sweat trickling down his brow, threatening to drip into his eyes.

Suddenly the portal burst open and two dark clad figures leapt through. Terex fired, releasing two metal quarrels at incredibly short range but watching both slam into the corridor wall beyond the doorway. Knowing retaliations were already on the way, he dived to his left, feeling the impact of a dull metal sphere on the side of his neck. The blow was painful but not debilitating as it would have been had it struck his temple. Rolling forward, he kicked over the barrel next to him, washing half of the room with lantern-oil. Seeing that one of the Veer was standing within the pool, he threw his warhammer at the man, who swatted it aside easily with one hand, releasing a mocking laugh. At the same time, Terex flicked the candle next to him into the oil. Flames engulfed the assassin and he leapt out into the corridor, screaming as he raced away to douse the inferno upon him.

A thin throwing star struck him in the thigh before he could recognise his success, and he instinctively dodged again. The natural movement away from the fire sent him backwards into another shuriken, this one slicing across his left forearm. Pulling the other projectile from his leg, he cast it towards his remaining enemy who barely had to flinch to avoid the off-balance attack. Scrambling to his feet, Terex brought his sword up before him and his eyes fixed on the bladed prosthetic attached to the Veer's wrist; could this be the same man he had faced at the Fimarr's farm?

'We have met before?' he panted, more to buy himself thinking time than anything else, there must be a way he could utilise the oil fire against this opponent as well.

'Oh yes,' the assassin snarled back, 'You took my hand from me and now I will take everything from you. I will allow you to watch those you protect die, of course, before I kill you.'

Terex charged forward, hoping that his enemy would dodge sideways, that way he would be backed against the fire and he could drive him into the flames. He did not dodge, however, neatly slipping low under the presented sword and slashing upwards with the knife held in his remaining hand. Terex was forced to curb his own run as the blade sliced up the front of his leather jerkin before clipping the cleft of his chin. Leaping back, twirling his blade to discourage a follow-up strike, he dabbed his free hand to his face. It was a superficial wound only and the strike had not penetrated the armoured jacket. Edging back in front of the cupboard door, he was pleased that the Veer compliantly circled with him, opening himself up to being pushed into the fire.

'So, they are in there?' the assassin mocked, 'Not the most imaginative of hiding places.'

'You will not touch them,' Terex vowed, swinging a few tentative strikes forward and amazed that they were so easily parried with only a knife. He knew his enemy was only biding his time and he needed to do something fast. Dropping suddenly into a crouch, Terex hurled his sword straight at the Veer, springing forward whilst pulling a small knife from his belt. As his enemy used his own blade to flip the sword up and over his head, his attention was drawn away for a split second. Terex slammed into the assassin, hoping to throw him backwards, but found him incredibly strong and perfectly balanced, absorbing most of the momentum of his charge. Locked together in a wrestling embrace, a sudden pain exploded in his stomach; dropping his chin to his chest he saw the horrific quad blade had been driven into him. He felt his throat and mouth fill with blood and spat a mouthful out onto his enemy with a grunt. A further twist sent new agony flashing through him and he could feel a sudden loss of integrity in his own body, as if his whole stomach had just been cleaved away. With a smile, the Veer began to withdraw his weapon, but Terex gripped his elbow and held the prosthetic in place.

'You may have killed me, but I can take you with me,' he stammered through blood-soaked lips.

With all the strength he could muster, Terex began to push his foe towards the flames behind him, the other man continuing to frantically try and drag his arm free. He felt several sharp twinges in his other side and realised the Veer was stabbing him in the ribs with his other knife to try and break free. The fire was only a yard away. Without warning, a boot flashed up to strike him in the groin, before a second kick to the abdomen drove him to the floor. The Veer leapt away from him and the fire, panting heavily at the close call and taking a moment to compose himself.

'Drop something?' Terex managed.

His enemy looked down and saw his prosthetic still jammed into the warrior's middle. He had not noticed Terex hacking at the retention straps whilst they had been locked together.

'I will claim that from your corpse when I am done,' he spat, turning towards the cupboard.

Despite the pain, Terex rolled over and reached out with one hand, catching hold of the assassin's trouser leg.

'You do not get to them while I am alive,' he coughed weakly.

'Really?' the Veer snarled, 'I seem to remember you owe me a hand...'

His knife flashed downwards and Terex watched as his hand dropped to the floor amid a river of blood that erupted from his stump. He did not have the strength to cry out and watched dumbly as the assassin tucked the knife into his belt to free up his hand for the cupboard door.

'Try and stay conscious for a bit longer, will you?' he taunted, swinging the entrance wide.

Rebecca leapt forward, thrusting one of Forge's javelin's upwards with both hands. The Veer raised his arm to block but the prosthetic was gone, allowing the attack free passage through his soft palate and into his brain. For a moment he stood twitching until his body collapsed to one side, the weapon still impaled in his head.

'Terex!' Kastani screamed, pushing Rebecca aside and rushing over to him, barely able to speak through her tears, 'Terex, get up. Do not be hurt! It is not fair!'

He raised his remaining hand to touch her face gently and forced a smile, 'It is okay, Kastani, you are safe now. They cannot hurt you.'

'No, no, no!' she wailed back, 'You cannot be dead, Terex! You cannot be! I have not finished playing games with you. You said you would be here until I am all growed up...' the last words were drowned in her high-pitched wailing and she wrapped herself over him, oblivious to the gore dousing them both.

'I am s-sorry, Kastani, I w-wanted to, to be there... I love you...'

Pounding along the corridor, scimitar slick with the blood of the flaming assassin he had just ended, Forge slid into the open doorway in time to catch Terex's last words. The screaming girl still hugging the body brought despair into his heart and he released an agonised cry of his own.

'Ahhhh! This is not right! I had them, I had them all!' he shouted angrily before spotting his own twins still cowering within the cupboard.

'It is okay, sweethearts, it is all over now,' he soothed, noting that Rebecca was still stood stock still, clearly in shock.

'It is not okay,' Kastani mumbled against Terex's chest, 'not unless you make him not dead.'

He moved over to her, holding her shoulders, and trying to ease her up, but she resisted.

'No!' she shouted, 'You have to make this better! I want him not dead!'

'I cannot do that, Kastani, it is not possible. But he died to keep you safe so we must make sure that continues to happen, so he did not die in vain. Do you see?' he tried to explain.

'You killed the other black-robes?'

'Yes, little one, they are gone now.'

'And Lennath sent them here to get us?'

'I am sorry, Kastani, but he did.'

'Then I want to go and make him dead.'

'We cannot do that. It is too dangerous, and revenge is wr…' he did not finish the sentence as a tightness suddenly gripped his organs, compressing and squeezing, driving him to his knees with agony. He raised his head to see Kastani staring at him with blazing purple eyes.

'We are going to Lennath to make him dead,' she stated again.

'Kastani, stop!' Rebecca urged, suddenly snapping out of her trance.

Straker looked at her, hoping to see some sign of the child from moments earlier but she was gone. He forced his eyes back to his own babies, terrified and pleading for him; he could not just let himself end here, abandon them to the evils all around. Perhaps he could placate her for now and convince her out of vengeance later.

'Y-y-yes,' he stammered through the pain, 'I will take you to Lustania.'

'To kill Lennath?' she questioned.

'To k-kill Lennath,' he affirmed, collapsing as the pressure throughout him abated.

'Good,' she said standing and heading for the door, 'we can leave in the morning.'

Looking out from the public address balcony was an inspiring experience, the gigantic rotunda below housing the central titular fountain that gave Mainspring its name. Seeing the thronging crowd below and the clean bright colours of the capital brought warm contentment to him; it felt as though this moment was fated from the start. He had adorned himself in ceremonial wear, a golden breast plate that would be useless in combat, the deep crimson cloak hemmed with mink fur that was reserved for coronations and, of course, his father's crown. He held a jewel-encrusted goblet in one hand, which represented bounty, but had replaced the traditional silver olive branch of peace with his own sword. The noise from below floated up to them as an incoherent drone, lacking clarity of how the populace were feeling.

The doors from the palace that opened onto the large balcony were now guarded by the King's elite, he supposed they would be his elite by the end of this proclamation, and they stood stoically at attention. Two Lustanian soldiers flanked both his father and his brother, Kendoss, both of whom had been reduced to only basic tunics and breaches. Between that small group and himself stood Mozak, dispassionately looking out over the people far below; he never seemed prepared to react but Lennath knew the Veer was primed at every moment and the safety net he represented was comforting in such an important undertaking. Stood slightly to his right was Alissa, dressed in the most beautiful and garish gown he had ever seen her adopt, she had even sat patiently while her hair was painstakingly styled with coiled plaits. He smiled at her with adoration and she noticed immediately, blushing slightly, and smiling back before curtseying to him. He felt genuine pride swell in his chest at the gesture, but this was replaced with concern when she suddenly grasped her head and doubled over in pain. Rushing to her, he caught her by the shoulders and held her tightly.

'Alissa, my love, what is it? What ails you?'

'I-I feel the pain…' she stammered before her body relaxed in his arms, 'it is passed. Pay it no mind.'

He lifted her face gently towards him, wiping away the thin trail of blood that had streamed from her nose with his gloved thumb. It left a smear of red across her cheek.

'Do not be coy with me. What has happened?'

'Promise not to be mad? Not today, not now.'

'I promise. You can tell me anything.'

'Kastani. I felt Kastani in agony.'

'What!' he exclaimed, barely able to keep his voice low, 'Is she hurt? Can you tell where she is? Please do not tell me the Veer have harmed her, I will personally…'

'You promised not to get angry,' she reminded him.

Swallowing hard, he forced a smile for her, 'Of course I did, I am not angry, simply concerned. Is your daughter in peril?'

'No, she is in despair. I cannot see why, or where, but I could feel her heart. And I think the Veer you sent for her may be dead.'

Lennath rocked back on his heels. He was certain Mozak had sent six assassins to bolster the one who had been tracking Kastani. That would mean seven altogether. Seven Veer assassins killed. It did not seem likely. Perhaps Alissa was suffering aftereffects of using the Stave so much, it had been necessary but seemed to take a heavier toll each time, mixed with the suppressed longing to be reunited with her child. He helped her straighten and then kissed her passionately, receiving a grand roar of approval from the crowd. As their lips parted he smiled and turned to face those gathered with his hand raised in a grateful wave.

'Smile and greet them, my darling, soon you will be their queen.'

Allowing a few moments for the adulation to pass, he released her hand and strode to the rail at the very front of the balcony.

'Hear me, people of The Kingdoms!' he hollered, projecting as much as possible so all gathered could heed his words, 'You have been through much these last weeks, the war may have been short but for many it was no less devastating. I know that husbands and sons have been lost, towns and livelihoods destroyed, hopes and dreams erased in an instant. It was a war born of honour but in truth it had been simmering beneath the surface for many years. The disparities and jealousies between the sister Kingdoms have created animosity instead of unity. I proclaim that this will be rectified this very day!'

Another roar of approval came from below and filled him with fresh confidence. He looked across at his kin and saw unexpected pride in his father's eyes; Kendoss remained aloof, his focus out beyond the rooftops of the city.

'For too long, you have suffered the trials of military agreements, commerce deals, boundary disputes, all between each other! We have wasted years managing borders that should not exist. Well, no longer! We will reclaim our former heritage and re-stablish a single Kingdom. Our resources will be shared, our military will be enhanced, our focus will be realigned to our outer borders. We can become stronger than ever before and return to our standing as a powerful Nation within the land!'

More cheers resounded and he felt buoyed that so many of those within Mainspring seemed heartened by his speech; he had expected more resistance.

'But there are some matters still to attend to by our own laws,' he announced, feeling his heart beating faster with nerves, 'for with one Kingdom there can be only one ruler. I decree that that ruler will be me from this day forth; King Lennath of the Kingdom!'

The clamour from below was more reserved this time and filled with uncertainty.

'Do not be confused, good people, I will explain all! Firstly, you should know that I am fully prepared for this great responsibility; the last five years I spent bringing Lustania from the edge of ruin and making her strong once again. I will do the same for us all. Many of you may be asking what allows me, the youngest of the heirs, to presume a place on the throne, which brings me to my second revelation. Over the last two months, my brothers, Gallth and Porthus, went missing and are presumed dead, I believe there has been a nefarious plot afoot and a full investigation will be conducted forthwith. My brother, Gregor, fell in battle mere weeks ago, having sided with the King and Kendoss against me.'

As he allowed the revelation to sink in, hearing the unsettled ripple of shock cascading through the throng, he considered the war he had just won; it had all been too simple. In fact, it had become so easy he had expected the whole thing to be a ruse. Not a single skirmish or battle fought had lasted longer than a few hours, and his father's sensibilities had sorely worked against him. Lennath had maintained a single fighting force, engaging his enemies wherever he found them, which had left his own Kingdom almost completely undefended. Of course, the King had wanted to preserve Lustania and avoid any unnecessary suffering to its people, so he sent wave upon wave of troops against his son's activated force. Each came and fell, Alissa's creatures securing victory every time, the mutants' losses easily replaceable in days rather than the years it took to replace a soldier. As they had advanced on Mainspring itself, the King's will had broken; perhaps he could not face the thought of the beautiful environment being sullied by war or maybe he knew Lennath would win. It made no difference, either way, surrender earned Lennath his current position and specific legal rights.

'As I have said, Kendoss chose to take a dispute of honour to the battlefield and he has lost. Tradition demands that he be executed as the conquered commander, and I cannot flaunt our very culture, thus it is with a heavy heart that this will be done here and now with all of you as witness.'

He turned back towards the two prisoners, carrying the noose that had been coiled beneath the railing with him. Looking up at his taller brother, he pasted a regretful expression to his face, 'I am sorry, Kendoss, but you have brought this upon yourself.'

'Do not toy with me, brother, we both know that you have manipulated all of this to claim the throne. You have slaughtered your own family in the name of power; you are nothing but a lowly snake!' Kendoss snarled at him.

'Nothing lowly about me now,' he retorted in a whisper, unable to hide the dark glee in his eyes. Kendoss maintained his composure, however, standing tall even as the noose was placed over his head. The two soldiers at his sides ushered him to the front of the balcony as a hush fell over the crowd.

'Lennath, please!' the King called to him in a voice tipping close to sobbing. Without his regal attire, the old man suddenly seemed very small.

'Yes, father?' he replied innocently, stepping over to him.

'You don't have to do this, son, you know that don't you? Your brothers wronged you with their accusations, but this has gone too far now! You were victorious in war and have defended your honour; if you cannot forgive Kendoss then have him imprisoned; that would still nullify his right to the throne. Do not kill your family in cold blood!'

'But father, this is the law. Who am I to place myself above the legal resolutions of our people? What message would it send to our people if I abide by different rules than I expect them to follow? Do not despair, though, for you will not suffer such a fate; as the current King you are exempt forced execution,' Lennath paused, looking into the pale watery eyes before him, 'and I could not kill you. I love you, Father.'

Tears ran free at that point, 'I love you too, Lennath, truly. I always have. But I love Kendoss just as much. Please spare him, please spare my son.'

He pulled the old man into an embrace and kissed his cheek, stroking his bearded face tenderly when he stepped back. Returning to his position by the railing, he found all eyes below watching him silently; it was very surreal.

'Citizens, hear this now! The law states that I must execute my vanquished opponent, regardless of any family bond between us. But my father has made an emotional plea, requested that I spare my brother from just process, and I am not without compassion. But the law is the law!' the last words were shouted with venom and he pushed Kendoss hard, toppling him over the rail.

A gasp of shock came from the people below, followed by an unexpected cheer when the rope snapped tight. It seemed that human bloodlust was contagious en masse. This time he waited while a cacophony of voices filled the air, unintelligible shouting, arguing and wailing echoing from the rotunda.

'So now justice is served, and I am the only remaining heir!' he proclaimed when he felt he could be heard, 'I promise you a great future as a unified Kingdom, we will be prosperous and strong, I will show compassion and parity in all I…'

'No!' came a quiet voice from below.

Lennath stopped his rehearsed speech and peered down to locate the speaker, distracted from the task by his brother's dangling corpse.

'Who spoke?' he demanded, 'Who has chosen to defy me already?'

'No defiance, Milord,' the voice came again, and he spotted a well-dressed and aged man stepping up onto the edge of the fountain to be more clearly seen, 'and no disrespect.'

'What else would you call this?' Lennath insisted, 'Who are you and why do you interrupt me in this way?'

'I am nobody, Highness, just a member of the judiciary, a scribe of laws, tenets and legal works. My name is Prius Zendar. I must raise with you a concern over your claim.'

'Concern?' Lennath almost swallowed his tongue in disbelief, 'Do you accuse me of subterfuge? Or breach of law?'

'No, Sire, no such thing!' the old man replied quickly, clearly terrified at the position he now found himself in, 'I believe that some of the laws you are adhering to may have been… misinterpreted?'

'I tire of this, Prius Zendar, explain yourself immediately.'

'Your brothers are dead, and you are rightful heir to the throne, true enough, but the crown still sits with the King.'

Animated whispering spread out from the old man like wildfire and Lennath felt a gnaw of panic in his gut.

'You are wrong, old man, the King has abdicated. My claim is right and legal.'

'But the King was your opponent in war, he cannot abdicate under duress or to an aggressor; it protects us from internal coups.'

The Prince's head swam. Could this old man be correct? How could he have missed such a thing in all his preparations? It did seem logical, in the same way the King had split the Nation between his sons to grant them rulership but no desire to his throne, perhaps he had written other such laws to ensure his safety. If this law existed alongside the myriad others, it prevented his children from killing him or terrorising him to relinquish the throne to them. Had Lennath really come this far to fail now? He looked back at his parent, sobbing openly, crushed completely by the loss of a fourth son before his eyes; he couldn't have much longer left for this world, could he? Old as he was, ill with some undefined disease and now heartbroken? Surely there was a way to spin this successfully?

'I applaud you, Prius Zendar, for having the courage to speak up righteously. I believe I once employed a member of your kin in Lustania; his work was likewise diligent. If what you say is true then I must investigate; regardless of that outcome, I will still place myself as executor and heir-apparent due to my father's ill health. At least, I will act in these functions until he recovers.'

More murmurs from the crowd and Zendar appeared momentarily in thought before looking back up at the balcony worriedly.

'That may be possible, Sire,' he began, 'but you would need…'

'Enough of this!' Alissa suddenly screamed from behind him. Turning, he watched as she sprinted across the platform like an enraged banshee. When she stretched out a hand, the two guards staggered backwards away from the King, clutching at their stomachs.

'No!' Lennath cried at her, stepping forward but finding a blinding pain in his head dropping him to one knee. He watched impotently as she closed on his terrified father. Feral as the first day he had met her, Alissa grasped the old man's beard and the front of his belt, dragging him along recklessly before throwing herself to the ground in front of the railing. Her momentum continued to drag him forward and he was launched over the low barrier, tumbling the two hundred yards to the ornamental flagstones of the rotunda. Screams of horror filled the air and Lennath felt the pain in his head abate. Climbing to his feet, he looked at the woman he loved with tears in his eyes, feeling a wave of nausea as she tossed a clump of beard over the edge after its owner. She smiled broadly at him.

'Problem solved!' she offered brightly.

He could not find words, leaning heavily on the rail and unable to see the gory sight below through the cascade of emotion pouring from him, his own sobbing filling his ears. He was vaguely aware of Alissa addressing the shocked masses below.

'People of the Kingdom! No more questions or obstructions! Lennath here is your King! You will all obey him and love him because that is what you are for! He is also my true love, Kale Stanis, and we are betrothed. You can all come to the Wedding where they will be no need to kill anyone at all! Now you can go and tell everyone that King Lennath is pleased to be ruling over you!'

He felt Mozak at his side, one strong hand gripping him under the armpit and lifting him straight.

'You should not let the people see such weakness, you are their King now,' he said, and his lack of emotion was oddly calming.

'She killed… why did you not stop her?'

'I am paid to protect you and you alone,' the Veer replied.

Lennath looked over at Alissa, still waving frantically at those in the rotunda, his heart and mind in turmoil. She was supposed to be his coerced servant, his secret weapon against all foes; how had it come to this?

A slight drizzle was starting to fall, which matched his mood perfectly, and he turned to watch rivulets of moisture cascade down Keris' defined cheekbones and along her firm jawline. She was a majestic site to behold and would have made a fine bride if their lives had been different; but their lives were not different. She must have felt his stare because she looked round at him; by that point he had returned his attention to the activity before them, however. The invaders were currently gathering their belongings together, weapons gifted back to them and food being provided from the village storehouse. He tried to control the sneer turning his lip; not only had the invaders been given free passage through their land and successfully fulfilled the ancient rite allowing them to claim the Rondure, but now they were also benefitting from their supplies?

The larger of the strangers, the one he had easily defeated in the log pull, was closest, slinging a satchel of fruits over his shoulder, and offered him a smile.

'You are very powerful, Mazt Kae-Taqar,' he said, getting the pronunciation horribly wrong, 'we would sorely benefit from your strength in the confrontation ahead of us. Any or all of you would be welcome on this venture, the threat is just as much to you as it is to us.'

'The only threat I see stands before me, and it should be extinguished,' he snarled in reply, feeling Keris place a restraining hand across his stomach, 'my People would not help you even if we could.'

'If you could?' the bearded man echoed curiously.

'We cannot leave the island,' Keris informed him levelly, 'it is why we must hope you honour your promise to return our holy item to us.'

'We will, you have our word,' the older of the women told them, cutting through their conversation, and ushering her companion to join the others as they made their way towards the beach. Many of the People were following to watch them leave and Mazt fell into line with Keris to join the procession. The indignity he felt was almost too much to bear; it was as though the prophecy had come to pass and their own Elders had sat back and allowed the worst possible outcome to happen, maybe even supported it. Why had they not just killed the interlopers on first arrival; if they had not heard that the four women were sisters, then all would now be well. How had the Guardians lost the trials? It still felt like some surreal nightmare that they had lacked the required skill or motivation to defeat the weaklings they had faced. Why had the Elders allowed the strangers to take the Rondure? Would it cause some catastrophic event if they had not honoured the ancient scripture? He checked himself before he entered blasphemous territory. It could be just as likely that the earthquakes created by the mystic orb were a warning not to break the written lore.

'We will find a way to hunt them down should they break their word,' he spoke softly to his companion.

'They will not break their word, Mazt Kae-Taqar, this is my truth,' Keris replied.

'How can you be so certain?'

'A feeling in my heart, I think, but logic also.'

'What logic? Trespassers demand our most precious artifact, and we give it to them; I see no logic that supports them returning it.'

'That is because you do not look for it. They have asked for our help, to journey with them, numerous times since they arrived. This is not a sound tactic for thieves. The story they have told is filled with tragedy and fear; their voices smack of desperation, not manipulation. They have witnessed our power and know the folly of betraying us and… this is my truth,' Keris cut herself off short.

'And what?' Mazt pressed, not missing the hesitation.

'And… I believe this is what is destined to happen. It is not in our writings, I know that, but I think they point in this direction…'

'Point in a direction? You *think* these truths may be correct? How can you mix such nonsense into a statement of logic and truth? Your head has been different since I failed to cross the Boundary, like confusion has filled you from toe to crown. I wonder if you really know what truth is any more.'

She grabbed his arm and stopped him in his tracks, forcing several villagers to dodge around them. 'I know my truth, Mazt, more surely than you. I see the fear in your eyes, know the doubt in your heart, do not condescend to me like some child! The Rondure almost destroyed the village, the Palmstones have become volatile and the desire to use them ever more irresistible; this is not chance, this is fate! Maybe this must happen, the Rondure used elsewhere expending some of its power, power that would otherwise destroy us! That is why…' her voice was a hissed whisper to avoid others overhearing but Mazt could barely contain his fury at being spoken to in this way.

'That is why what, Keris San-Zukat? What have you done?'

She met his eyes defiantly, but he could see the flame of concern there as well, 'That is why I deliberately failed in the arena.'

For a moment he couldn't find the words, his ability to think stripped from him by the simple confession. 'Traitor,' he managed finally, 'to your people, to yourself, to me!'

She grasped his hands, despite his efforts to shake her free, 'No, Mazt, look into my eyes. Tell me what you find there; deceit or truth?'

He studied her as requested and his shoulders sagged, 'I am lost in this, Keris,' he admitted, holding back deeper emotion that was welling in him, 'my truth has been stripped from me. I cannot understand all that is happening, why so much change is occurring without my ability to stop it. I am a Guardian, *we* are Guardians, it is our purpose to defend the Rondure, defend our people and defend our home, yet I am expected to allow one of those to be taken without argument? How is it that you are so certain of your decisions?'

'I just am,' she replied, 'and I wish for nothing more than the ability to share my surety with you. These strangers will stay true to their word, you will see the danger in our teachings is the very one they aim to destroy; by aiding them, we will have fulfilled our purpose.'

She smiled at him, but he could not return the expression, 'Your truth is one of convenience,' he told her, 'but I pray deeply that it is correct.'

They walked together in silence until reaching the shore, arriving just as the intruders were securing the last of their items into the long canoe they had arrived in. Even now, one gesture with the Palmstone would wipe them from existence; the idea brought Keris' recent revelations to his mind, and he balled his fists against the temptation. The High Auger was already on the golden sand, surrounded by many, if not all, of the other Elders.

'My People!' he called out, voice projecting across all those assembled, and hands raised in a gesture of openness, 'We have seen strangers come to our land in peace, not aggression. They are four joined by blood as our wise teachings have always promised. They have faced the Trials and emerged victorious, not because they are stronger, faster, or better than our own Guardians, but because it was meant to be so. They have not just enacted the right to take the Rondure, they have actually touched it!'

The crowd gasped in unison, the old holy man waiting for them to settle before continuing, 'Yes, it is true, I witnessed this miracle with my own eyes. Touched it and stand here now, unharmed. There is no doubt that all this has happened because it has to; they are not cruel, or evil or misleading, they have borne with them the weight of a threat to our land but their own as well. With our precious Rondure, they will eradicate this threat, saving themselves, true, but saving us all as well. We offer them this boon without malice and in trust, they know it must be returned to us once their quest is complete; for their sake and ours. As they leave us here this day, we must not feel fear or despair but joy and hope, for all of our teachings have heralded the day the Rondure will be released from the Shrine and that day is today! When it returns to us, we will start a new chapter in our history, carved by our very own hands. Tonight will be one of celebration and we will look to the future as one!'

Cheering filled the air and Mazt found himself smiling at last. The High Auger had placated the People with easy words but left no doubt in these strangers' mind as to the consequences of betrayal; perhaps he was not as cowed by the scriptures as he appeared to be.

'High Auger, Guardians, People,' the oldest woman announced, stepping forward to face their leader, 'I must express my most sincere gratitude to you all. Our visit here has demonstrated how much the Rondure means to you all, how strong your faith is to trust in the words of your prophecies and how noble you are to aid us without offer of reward. Know that your actions have protected all our lands from darkness, and this will not be forgotten. I, and all people, are forever in your debt; this covenant I make with you, that when the threat is defeated, your holy relic will be returned to you as a token of our future union and peace.'

There was an uncomfortable silence, but the High Auger nodded sagely at the woman, Treya, Mazt thought he recalled, before applauding her words gently, the rest of the congregation soon following suit. After a few moments, the strangers moved over to their craft and began to drag it over the sand towards the crystal waters beyond.

'I forgive you,' Mazt said aloud.

Keris cocked her head to look at him, perhaps gauging his sincerity, 'I hear your truth,' she finally replied.

He nodded and regarded the struggling invaders for a few seconds longer before striding to the rear of their large canoe and single-handedly guiding it into the sea. They scrambled aboard as he continued to push, steering them until their oars were readied and he was waist-deep in the brine. They nodded and murmured thanks in his direction but he did not respond as he gave one final shove towards the Boundary. His eyes found those of Treya, but she gave nothing away in her expression, certainly none of the positive feeling that had been indicated in her words.

Watching them row away, he considered all that had happened. The High Auger had prevented these people's deaths and allowed them the rite of Trial as per the ancient writings, but surely he had not expected them to win? Diast had let them down with his arrogance, but they had not been informed the Palmstones should not be employed; had the disqualification been planned as consolation for the strangers? Keris had deliberately failed, to try and help them succeed in taking the Rondure, but had that been a reaction of his own worries and concerns expressed to her? Regardless of all that, there had been a final Trial, one that had seemed to require the ultimate sacrifice. Diast had tried to make up for his previous failure by being the one to enter Mount Darkfire, but Mazt believed his heart had not been in it; despite all their courage, at that moment, none of the Guardians had wanted to face death. But one man had not hesitated, the one who wielded two swords, he had been willing to die to claim what was needed. That was not the heart of a villain; perhaps there was logic in Keris' truth after all.

Prophecy? Fate? Luck? It did not matter; the decisions had been made without his control and now he must abide by them. The strangers would return the Rondure to the People or suffer the consequences of betrayal; no Boundary, no will, no force in existence would prevent him from ensuring this. Finding his smile at last, he waved at the disappearing boat.

Chapter 15

Struggling with the heavy bag of linen, it was a relief when a member of the loading team scooped it from her arms with a nod and a wink.

'No need for you to carry that, Lady,' he told her amiably, 'we have been told everything that needs loading. We will get it all on, no concerns!'

'Just trying to be useful,' Rebecca replied trying to raise a smile, it had not proven easy since the Citadel, 'you have all done so much for us already.'

'This is nothing, Lady, and our pleasure. There is nary a task that can come close to repaying what the Fimarrs did for us; not just here, mind, I am talking all across Dussen. If you are keeping their company, I would recommend you keep it as long as you can!' he replied before striding off with his burden.

Placing her hands on her hips, she let out a sigh. All she really wanted was a distraction from everything, hard enough to achieve during the dark journey back along the tunnels that led to Hercatalana, and she had hoped for tasks to engage her when they reached the town. Too many people, too keen to impress with their helpfulness; she had never expected such a thing to become annoying. In many ways she was glad that this visit would be brief, an overnight stay would have meant forced civility and whole hours of solitude where her mind would replay the images of Terex's gruesome demise. But it would be far preferable if they had a choice in the matter; it was still hard to believe that they were being commanded by a five-year-old child. She cast her eyes to the front of the cart where Kastani sat at the driver's seat, sideways on, dangling her legs and staring down at her feet. She was just a little girl, helpless as any other, with simple thoughts and basic needs; or so it had appeared until…

She shook her head, not wanting to replay the traumatic events again. She had experienced several violent encounters since Frost had kidnapped her from Corinth, and even witnessed some death, but the very personal and visceral slaying of Terex was deeply unsettling. Now they were being driven into the arms of their enemy, against their will, to face who knew how many Veer assassins, terrifying mutants and Prince Lennath himself. By a child.

Kastani looked up suddenly, as if sensing the eyes upon her, and peered over at Rebecca. An angelic smile cracked her face and she waved. Rebecca could not find the strength to respond, even a forced gesture was too much, and she turned away instead, casting her eyes around for the twins. Over by the stable, the pair were with Heletha and her brother Wardin, happily playing straws; it was a simple game, a handful of straw thrown into the air and the winner was the one who caught the most strands. In their innocence the Hercatalanians had invited Kastani to join as well but she had refused, stating she had to be sure they only stayed as long as necessary.

She marvelled at the two young children, all they had recently seen and experienced, yet they held the same innocent wonder and joy in everything. How resilient children were, but it seemed the older you got, the less you could move on from; just like now. She clarified for herself that she liked Terex and had certainly been attracted to him, but they barely knew one another. Yet he had sacrificed his own life to protect her, probably mostly for Kastani, without a second thought. And she had personally slain his killer, all through luck rather than skill, but she had taken the man's life, regardless of the circumstance. She wondered if all murderers, soldiers or assassins felt as she did now about the act, if they did, then she could not comprehend how they made a career of the activity. She recognised her hands were shaking again and tucked them under her armpits.

'What are you doing?'

She looked down and saw Kastani beside her, 'Nothing, just waiting,' she replied flatly.

'I waved at you,' the little girl continued brightly, 'I suppose you must not have seen me. You still look very sad. Is it because of Terex? I am very sad about that, too.'

'Are you?' Rebecca retorted, wishing she had not, 'I do not see sadness in your actions, only anger.'

'Oh, yes, I am very angry,' she confirmed darkly, 'but still sad as well. Every time I think about a game, or something I was going to do when I get bigger, it makes me cry because Terex was always supposed to be there. It is not right that he will not be.'

Rebecca swallowed back her emotion, but a single tear broke through anyway, 'He loved you very much and he would be disappointed to see you like this. He died so you could be safe, now you are placing yourself in harm's way.'

'Terex was the best man in all the world,' Kastani stated, 'the people who took him away are the baddest, they have to be killed.'

'But Lennath is with your mother, what if she had a part to play? Do you not see there could be more to all this than you understand?'

'If mother made Terex dead, then I will have to kill her too. But I am certain she did not.'

The emotionless declaration of matricide staggered Rebecca at a new level and she felt as though she would faint. Taking unsure footsteps backwards until she could feel a wall behind her, she tried long slow breaths until her vision swam back into focus.

'What are you doing now?' Kastani demanded irritably, 'It is rude to walk away when someone is talking.'

'I-I know,' she managed, placing her hand gently on the little girl's head, 'I am sorry. I feel a little unwell, maybe tiredness? I will get some water from the tavern to clear my head. I will be back soon, do not be concerned.'

'Can I come too?' she asked hopefully.

'No!' the response was too quick and sharp, 'I mean, we need to be sure all the supplies are loaded properly. Someone needs to stay and overseer the loaders; it should be you, as this is your journey we are on.'

Kastani pouted a little but refrained from further argument, allowing Rebecca to make her way gingerly along the dusty road to the single tavern in the town. Without warning Czerna appeared, concern etched into her face.

'Rebecca? Are you well?'

'Greetings, Czerna, I am fine, thank-you for the concern. I just need some water, maybe some proper rest.'

'You are welcome to my home if you would like? I can offer water or tea and you can take whatever time you need to refresh yourself?'

'You are so generous, such a positive advocate for Hercatalana; I see why you achieved such a high position here. But I must decline; we are expected to leave as soon as the provisions are loaded,' she was about to continue on her way until basic etiquette caused her to pause, 'for which we are also incredibly grateful.'

'We are happy to assist,' Czerna replied warmly, 'but why the haste? I could not even raise a word from Straker when you arrived, he seems perturbed. Must you leave so soon?'

'Yes, we have no… I mean, it is required that we depart with all haste.'

'Before you do, I was meaning to ask about your friends? The ones who came to help when we were attacked? We had no time to properly reward them and would like the opportunity to do so.'

Rebecca took a deep breath, 'I am afraid they may be dead,' she managed, more curtly than she had hoped, 'Terex as well.'

Mixed emotion flashed across Czerna's face, but her words were well chosen, 'You have my deepest sympathies, Rebecca, I know you were close comrades.'

'Veer assassins,' she blurted out, 'they pursued us. Killed all of them. I think so, anyway, as we did not find bodies when we returned here. Scavenging animals probably dragged them off. But Terex we saw. Right in front of us…' she realised she was beginning to ramble and bit her lower lip to stop.

Czerna wrapped her arms about her holding her gently, 'I am sorry for you,' she spoke gently into her ear, 'I did not mean to press on about such upsetting matters. Please know that you have a friend in me, and in all Hercatalanians, should you ever need us, we will be there for you.'

After a moment, the embrace ended and Czerna squeezed her hand before urging her on her way and returning to her own journey. Feeling slightly recovered upon her arrival at the tavern, she pushed the swinging doors inwards and found it as sparsely attended as she would expect for this time of day. One man was stretched out on a chair with half a bottle and small glass on the table before him, looking for all intents and purposes to be asleep, another sat on a high stool beside the bar and Folt stood behind the counter, decanting something into a ceramic bottle. She was a little surprised to realise the man at the bar was Forge.

'Hail, Rebecca Pallstirrith!' Folt called, offering a broad smile that was horrific despite his pleasant intent, 'I am heartily pleased to see you this visit!'

Forge craned his neck around to glance at her sideways, but his movements were sluggish, and she wondered how much he had already imbibed. She strode over to them purposefully, standing directly behind her ally and miming a signal to Folt about how much had been served.

'He has had a bellyful already, I would say!' Folt continued loud and merrily, 'started on rum and moved on to brandy. Should be a pleasant onward journey, for him at least!' his words were followed by a raucous guffaw. Rebecca did not find him particularly amusing.

'Stop serving him now, and get us both some water,' she demanded and Folt's expression turned serious.

'I do not normally do that in 'ere,' he drawled, 'but as it is you asking…' he shuffled away to a door at the rear and disappeared.

'What is this, Straker?' she snipped at him, 'Are you a man who falls so easily into a bottle when things are difficult?'

'You do not know me, 'Becca, so do not preach to me.'

'We are in the same position here, Forge, beholden to a child more dangerous than any adult I have ever met. I would think you would find sobriety useful if we are to devise a way out of our predicament!'

'Ha! A way out? Have you spoken to her these past few days? We have no way out save for death, and I have considered that one at length. Luckily for you I could not leave my children unprotected and at her mercy. So, I think my best option is to soften the edges with some liquor.'

'Soften the edges? Where is the fighter of legend, the hero of ballads galore? That is the Straker Forge I need right now.'

'Have a seat, fair lady,' he slurred, 'I am the only Straker Forge here right now so you will have to make do! Join me and I guarantee you will feel better!'

'I am disappointed,' she sneered, 'you hide from your fear in alcohol-fuelled dullness. What would Treya think of you?'

This brought him pause and he tipped the bottle he was about to pour upright, placing it carefully on the bar before him.

'What would Treya think? What does she even know about me? Just secrets and lies, no doubt! Do you not understand? It is not fear that brings me here, I do not fear that child, nor do I fear Lennath and his Veer!'

'What then?'

'Failure,' he whispered and she felt her ire vanish.

'Failure?' she echoed, sitting on the stool he had previously offered, 'What failure do you speak of?'

'Are you so blind? Terex, I failed Terex. He is dead because of me.'

'He is dead because a Veer assassin killed him. You slayed six of their number trying to protect us; his was an honourable sacrifice and you should not sully it in this manner.'

'I could have killed them all. I would have killed them all. Terex just had to hide and wait; now he is dead.'

Instinct gripped her and she lashed out, slapping him hard across the cheek, leaving him blinking in surprise. 'His death is not your fault! Maybe you are to blame for my survival, and those children outside, but that is it! What makes you so superior that the fates of all rest on your shoulders?'

'I… that is, there are circumstances…' he looked at her and his shoulders slumped, 'You are right, of course you are right. I know it is impossible for you to understand, but I really should have saved him; if only the Veer had stayed to fight me, I would have.'

'But they did not act in the manner you hoped, sometimes that is the way with people, they act unexpectedly.'

'You mean like slapping a man across the face while he sits at a bar?' he asked, his wry smile returning at last.

She couldn't help but mirror the expression, 'Yes,' she conceded, 'just like that. Listen to me, Straker, I understand that you are shaken by his death, so am I, all I want to do is erase it from my mind, but we have no time for our sorrows. We need to find a way to dissuade Kastani from her current course.'

'Do we?' he responded, and she could find no trace of sarcasm in his voice.

'What are you saying?'

'You saw what she did to me, gods know I felt it surely enough, why should we prevent her from achieving just what she wants? We take her to Lustania, we let her kill Lennath and part of our problem is erased. I can keep us all safe while she does so.'

'She is a child, not an assassin! You cannot be serious with this idea.'

'I do not believe that she is a child. Maybe not an assassin, at least not yet, but she is definitely no child. She is dangerous, a wolf in sheep's clothing. My only real concern is what we do with her when this is all over.'

Shivers of pleasure rippled through her body as she ground her pelvis down against his, rocking back and forth in a rapid rhythm. Straddling him had proven the only way for their unions to work, any other position lacked the total control she required. Sweat covered them both as their body heat filled the small cabin and she traced her hand over his body as the sexual excitement continued to build; he was lean and smooth, a contrast to many of the men she had seduced prior to assassination. Of course, he was under no such threat; Makinson had proven a most compliant bedfellow, and sex had become more frequent the longer the voyage had lasted. Their failed encounter before the island had been forgiven, the vigorous union experienced when she had swum out to him during the Trials seemed to eradicate all negativity from his mind, and they had been together at least four times since departing with the Rondure. He made her feel desirable and worthwhile, the efforts he went to in pleasing her could not be faulted; no longer would he touch any area of her flesh that was marked from the fire, no more sweet flattery fell from his lips, and he often ended their times together without climax and without complaint. But his passion for her could never be concealed.

In the dim light she could not make out his face clearly, but she knew he would be staring at hers. His left hand grasped her buttock, almost assisting her in her movements, while his right had reached across her to massage her unmarked breast. These were allowances she made for him, neither bringing her heightened stimulation but both seemingly a fetish of his. A light groaning left him and she knew he must be close to climax, increasing her speed and pressure to ensure she would not be left disappointed. Unexpectedly, he suddenly shifted his body up, moving his left hand behind her shoulders and craning his face towards her.

'What are you doing?' she whispered, not slowing her pace.

'I want to kiss you when I finish,' he panted.

'Don't ruin this, Makinson, I am very close.'

'It will not ruin anything,' he insisted, careful not to apply any undue pressure with his hand, despite his increased excitement, 'I will read nothing into it. I think of your lips all day, every day, just once I would like to taste them.'

Rayne tried to keep her movements vigorous, despite the slightly more awkward position, hoping that an impromptu orgasm may dissuade his current thinking, but he was determined in his request. He had not attempted this before, perhaps aware that she did not feel love for him and such actions were therefore unrequired, and she wondered why it brought such anxiety to her now; she had kissed marks many times in the past. As her own climax drew closer, she conceded, already vowing that any future request would be denied. Dipping her head forward, she met his lips with her own and they kissed deeply, even as the electric jolt of orgasm shuddered through her. She could feel his own pulsing within her and allowed his kiss to become more frantic before suddenly pushing him back down onto the cot beneath them.

'Wh-what is it?' he asked breathlessly, 'Did I do something wrong?'

'No, nothing,' she said, pinning him down as she caught her breath, 'It was fine. But it was one time only. This is not a relationship, Makinson, we are just easing tension and satisfying a need.'

'I know that,' he replied, 'but it is still the greatest thrill of my life, every time.'

She climbed off him quickly and immediately began to dress.

'Are you all right?' he asked, rolling onto his side to watch her.

'Of course,' she snapped, 'I just want things clear between us. We are not some happy couple looking towards the future.'

'No, I am content to have no future. I have lived all I need to, having been with you.'

'Those are the kind of words that threaten our arrangement; I *choose* to have this release, I do not need it!' she scolded and stormed from the cabin.

She paused for a moment outside the door, leaning back against the bulkhead and taking several short breaths. Tears had formed in her eyes, but she did not let them flow. This situation was clearly unfair to Makinson, but she needed to feel wanted as much as he wanted to be with her. The kiss had been too much, however; her mind had been filled only with images of Rebecca and the toxic mix of guilt, pleasure, loneliness and climax had been overwhelming. Feeling control returning, she straightened and turned up the passage to find Treya looking at her; it almost made her jump as anyone approaching undetected was quite rare.

'Did I startle you?' her sister asked kindly, 'You seemed deep in thought.'

'I was… no, it is fine, just a moment of reminiscence. What brings you here?'

'Nothing, as it happens,' Treya continued lightly, 'this return journey feels much longer than getting to the island in the first place; I find myself with too much time.'

'It is the anticipation,' Rayne informed her, 'our voyage from Fildenmaw was one of hope, almost excitement, though I missed much of it through the poisoning! This return is full of foreboding and dark outcome; it is most likely your worry that stretches the time.'

Treya had joined her by this point and placed a hand on her forearm, squeezing reassuringly, 'You are correct, Rayne, I am filled with worry. The Rondure is a heavy burden to bear, not that I would pass it to any other, and I dread the moment of its use, not least of all because I have no idea how to do so. But there is more, I miss Straker and the children in a manner I never have before; there is a feeling I cannot shake, a feeling that I will not see them again. I wish I could have held them in my arms before I left, or felt his kiss upon my lips one more time…'

Rayne felt herself flinch at the word 'kiss' and the reaction was misconstrued by her sibling.

'I know, I am sorry, Rayne, you have no need to hear of such things; our lives have been so very different and I would change it all if I could, work harder to keep us together in spite of father's cruelty. I wish I could give you the life you deserved, Rayne, give it to all of us!'

She followed a sudden urge and drew Treya into a tight embrace, feeling the surprised tension from her oldest sister melt away at the contact. The sensation of calm safety washed through her and she wondered why she had never tried to bond in this way before. They remained locked together for long moments that felt to Rayne like hours and it was Treya who broke away first, watery eyes full of happy confusion.

'I love you, Rayne,' she blurted out, 'I always have, despite everything. I hope you know that.'

'What if this is it?' she replied, not releasing Treya's hands, fixing her with an intense stare.

'I do not understand; what if this is what?'

'What if this is the life we deserve?' Rayne pushed, 'You have a family with ties of love I could never hope to understand. Cat' is with Herc and both of you are settled and happy. I reap the rewards of my choices. What if this is all that was ever meant to happen?'

'And Alissa?' Treya countered, 'Our sweet, innocent little baby sister? Was she always supposed to lose her mind to darkness and evil? Is that why father always showed her kindness and love, always favoured her above us?'

'Maybe it was,' Rayne answered, with no hint of resentment, 'maybe he was trying to prevent it, trying to make her so inherently good that this could not befall her. Instead, he just made her weak.'

'And us strong?'

'Perhaps.'

'No, I will not believe that we are fated to our ends. All that we do is a reaction to that which has gone before. With each second that passes we make free choices; this is what directs the future, not some predetermined path.'

Rayne released her sister's hands and felt her shoulders slump, 'Which means this is all our own fault, we find ourselves here now through our own choices?'

'Yes, but it provides us the opportunity to make tomorrow better. It means that victory against Lennath is possible, that returning Alissa to us can be a reality.'

'And those things are equally improbable. You need to prepare yourself for failure, Treya, that Lennath proves too powerful or that Alissa is already too far gone to return.'

'No, I will not believe that, Rayne, if I did this quest would be folly. And I do not fear Lennath's power; he is a small man in a big body, and he will come undone. Besides, we have Silver Rain with us, and she is unstoppable!'

She smiled warmly and Rayne was transported back to her childhood, when Treya had always been their leader, their voice of reason or comfort as necessary, the one they could all rely on to lift them after a scolding from either parent. The memories were too much, and she cleared them with a blink, suppressing the sudden feeling of loss that had accompanied them.

'I wish that were true, Treya, but I vow that I will not let you down this time; I will stand with you all in victory or defeat.'

They were interrupted as Makinson emerged from Rayne's cabin into a suddenly awkward silence. For a few moments he stared at Treya with wide, concerned eyes before mumbling something incoherent and hurrying away along the corridor. The older Fimarr turned back to her sister with raised eyebrows and a pleased smile.

.

'So, you have been making good use of this time then?' she asked coyly.

Rayne felt herself flush and couldn't keep her own smile hidden, 'We are just... It is not... Do not get too excited, Treya, it is a temporary thing only. More gratitude for saving my life from the poison than anything else!'

'Of course, of course!' Treya laughed, 'No need to defend yourself! It is just odd to know that you really are human after all!'

'Very amusing, I am sure!' Rayne protested half-heartedly, 'Do not feel the need to tell anyone else about this, agreed?'

'Your secret is safe with me,' Treya promised.

'He is not a secret...' Rayne began but realised her sister was goading her. With a shake of her head, she quickly departed, walking the passages seemingly at random until she arrived at her destination and realised her subconscious had guided her. Taking a deep breath, she knocked on the cabin door.

Stepping aside as the door swung outwards, she smiled hopefully at the bleary-eyed occupant. Catalana wore only a travelling shirt, crumpled from sleep, and her red hair was unkempt, hanging unevenly about her face and shoulders. Even in her just-woken state, there was no denying how beautiful a woman she was.

'Rayne?' she asked drowsily, 'What is it? Are we arrived? Is there another attack?'

'No,' she replied reassuringly, 'to both. I just... I wondered if we might talk briefly?'

Catalana looked back over her shoulder, presumably at Herc, and Rayne spotted the imperceptible nod of her sister's head before she joined her in the passage and closed the cabin door.

'What is it?' she repeated, wrapping her arms about herself and shivering slightly, 'It is very cold, this morning.'

'It is still early,' Rayne admitted, 'my apologies for rousing you so, the timing is quite selfish.'

Cat' started to look annoyed, 'Get to the point, Rayne, what is it that could not wait to a more reasonable hour?'

'Us, Cat', I want to talk about us.'

Catalana rolled her eyes and her body language became instantly defensive, 'Look, Rayne, there really is not anything left to discuss. What has happened has happened, we cannot change it. Is this not resolution enough? Are you not content that we have been forced back together regardless of our own desires?'

'No, I am not,' Rayne replied, controlling the temper that threatened to flare, 'I ask only that you hear my words, as my sister, and as a person I have wronged. What happened at the Black Citadel…'

'When you abandoned me to die. Abandoned your sister to die,' Catalana corrected.

'Yes,' she agreed, averting her eyes to the floor, 'when my strength failed me. But know that it was not my strength of will that fled at that moment, it was my strength of heart. I was alone for so long, reliant only on myself that the love resurgent in my heart when we reunited was an alien feeling. It left me scared, vulnerable and my mind closed it down. This is neither excuse nor justification, it is only the truth. I have burned with guilt and regret since that day, suppressing it all under a cold exterior. It seems that ability has now deserted me.'

'I expect you wish you could put those barriers back in place?' she replied coldly.

'Honestly? Yes. But I fear that will never be possible again. I want you to know that I am sorry for all I have done that has hurt you, and I will spend every day forward trying to make amends. I hope that one day we will be sisters again.'

'We were sisters, Rayne,' Catalana said distantly, 'Four of us all kin, but you and I were different, closer, like sisters within sisters. I had faith in you, trusted you, knew there was nothing I could not achieve if you were there. But then you were not. I know you hated father and that he treated you the worst, but he was cruel to all of us. Did you ever think that we would have been stronger through it all if we had stayed together?'

'I did not think…' she started but her words trailed off with her thoughts.

'On the contrary, I believe you did think! You thought of all the ways in which you could benefit through running away, all the ways your life would be better.'

'You left too,' she mumbled, feeling emotion overcoming her.

'I left because you did!' Catalana yelled in frustration, 'I could not have felt more vulnerable and alone! And then you did it to me again, only the second time was worse, there was no doubt that Rask would kill me, and you left anyway! Why would you possibly think that an apology could fix that?' Rayne's eyes were drawn to the two missing fingers on her sister's hand, the digits traumatically removed because she had not been there to prevent it.

'Because I am sincere,' she mumbled, 'I do not know how to do these things, how to repair the bond between us, I can only try. And I am willing to try for the rest of our lives if you will let me. Will you give me that chance?'

There was a long pause, and she could feel her sister's penetrating stare boring into her. Finally, Catalana spoke, 'No, Rayne. I cannot. I cannot let you back into my heart with the possibility that you could leave again and break it, maybe for good next time. You will just have to live with your guilt in whatever way you can.'

She turned and swept back into her cabin. Rayne swayed on the spot, tears bursting free against her will; it felt like someone had just punched a fist into her stomach before reaching up and pulling out her heart. Her legs could no longer support her, and she collapsed to her knees, upper body slumping sideways against the bulkhead as uncontrollable sobbing overcame her.

The light buzzing drone of an insect in flight engrossed her attention, and she watched in fascination as the tiny beetle followed a zigzagging pattern down to the surface of the enormous beechwood table around which they all sat. Upon landing, the little creature tucked its wings against its back and settled two chitinous green shell halves over the delicate membranes. She marvelled at the shiny, almost metallic, effect of that protective outer layer and lay her cheek flat on the table to examine the tiny visitor more closely. Blowing gently, she smiled as it hunkered down low, seemingly gripping the wood beneath it more tightly with each of its six fragile legs. When she stopped, it immediately resumed its random skittering, almost like a dog seeking out a forgotten bone. Raising her right hand above the table, seeking amongst her skirts for the Stave with her left, she began to concentrate on shifting power from the inanimate object to her unwitting experiment. Without warning, the insect stopped, flipped onto its back, and began waving legs frantically in the air even as two chitinous growths erupted from its sides. As with all her creations, it began to gain mass rapidly and was half the size of a mouse when a sharp impact across the back of her hand distracted her from the task.

'Owww!' she exclaimed, instantly pouting, sitting upright, and looking for her attacker. All eyes had turned to her but hers fixed on the man beside her. Lennath was scowling, his mood had been sour since the death of the King and he had little reticence in reminding her of it. She cradled her hand dramatically where he had smacked it and frowned unhappily.

'Not here, not now, Alissa. Pay attention to these councils, they will guide our future,' he demanded.

'I guide my own future,' she retorted with petulance, 'so should you!'

'Fine, then they will demonstrate what obstacles may lie between us and our chosen future. The last thing I need is a six-foot beetle disrupting proceedings!'

She released a sulky sigh and crossed her arms across her chest, looking every bit the child she had once been. 'Fine. But these gatherings are boring and irrelevant, I can remove any obstacles when we find them.'

He did not respond to her again, instead motioning for the interrupted speaker to continue. Alissa looked at the tall slender man with the big white moustache and wondered how he merited a place at the table.

'As I was saying, Your Highness, there is much confusion among the dignitaries in each of the former Kingdoms. They seem content to honour all you have decreed but the mechanism of exactly how escapes them; is it your intent that trade deals are now expunged? Some areas are richer in resource than others, is it now total distribution at Crown expense? Have you made any consideration into tax relief for those businesses who specialised in cross-border trade? Where is Governance of resource distribution to sit? Centralised control is logical but how can we mitigate for historical bias in those assigned to the relevant group?'

She knew the man intended to continue but Lennath cut him off, 'Slow down, Duke Garton, please. These are such early days into my rule, yet you are digging down into details I have not had time to consider. Should this not sit with committee elsewhere? I am the King now and need capacity to focus on bigger priorities.'

'Bigger priorities?' Garton questioned, 'Forgive me, Sire, but you have just destroyed many years of trade agreement, territorial disputes and National identity in a single proclamation; failing to provide answers to these fundamental questions on new Governance will lead to anarchy!'

'Then I will appoint you as lead administrator for trade and commerce; you clearly understand these problems so you will act on my behalf to resolve them. This was always the way in Lustania.'

'I would be most honoured, Sire, and am more than happy to devote myself to just such a task,' Garton continued fawningly, 'but the directive must be your own; I mean no disrespect in saying that I fear the outcome of taking any such decision in your name without prior approval.'

The comment seemed to ruffle the new King, but he quickly composed himself and leant forward on his elbows, 'Very well. I do want total distribution, and this will be done at the expense of the receiving location, from local city coffers, at least until the five independent treasuries are unified here in Mainspring. I accept tax exemption for three months so that the aforementioned companies can alter their approach to external border trading. You will provide Governance from here and I give you leave to select your own team; my only condition is to insist that there is at least one representative from each of the former Kingdoms among their number. Does that provide you enough to at least begin with?'

'Yes, your Highness, I appreciate the vote of confidence in this endeavour. If we could also discuss...'

'No, no, not now,' Lennath interrupted again, irritation rising to the surface immediately, 'this council has much to cover and I intend to keep its duration limited. Save your question for our next assembly and you can also deliver a progress report on what I have ordered of you.'

Garton nodded cordially and resumed his seat. Alissa sighed heavily and traced her fingers across the carved table before her, what appeared to be intricated leaves entwining among one another, all growing from a central tree whose trunk was encircled by an ornate crown. She found it curious that the crown was not that worn by the king, but something rather more elaborate; at the edge of the table, the semi-transformed beetle was attempting to fly but the new protrusions now prevented its shell from opening. She felt guilty that she had disabled the little bug in such a manner and slammed her free hand down upon it, drawing everybody's attention again. Darting her eyes amongst them all, she stood and curtseyed.

'My most humble apologies to all assembled!' she pronounced with exaggerated civility, 'I had to prevent the suffering of that pathetic beast. That is what I do when I determine a thing is pathetic…' the last words were directed at Garton who shifted uneasily in his chair. A hand on her arm eased her back down to her seat and she turned her head to see Lennath smiling kindly at her. He leaned forward and kissed her forehead before standing himself.

'My consort is most humble to find a need to apologise to her underlings, do you not agree?' he asked, receiving a murmur of unconvincing agreement, 'But she has insisted that this meeting is too boring, and I fear she may be right! Come, let us finish promptly so that our next assembly provides me less questions and more solutions!'

He raised a hand to one of the younger men present, still in his forties by the look of his hairline and weathered face, 'Westan, what news of public opinion? How is word spreading of my ascendancy?'

The other man cleared his throat and then dithered a moment, not sure whether to stand or remain seated; he eventually decided on the latter, 'Yes, Highness, of course. I have good authority that all major population centres are fully aware of our change in rulership and also a good idea about the nominated union of the Kingdoms. It may be many more weeks before all outlying areas have the same detailed understanding of these changes. Reaction to unification has been overwhelmingly positive, with several support groups being quickly established to help different sectors accommodate the change; these may prove fruitful in the areas of trade highlighted by my esteemed colleague.'

'Good, good, I already knew unification was the way ahead,' Lennath hastened him, 'what of me? I want to know how my people are reacting to my position.'

Westan gulped and continued with a fearful tremor in his voice, 'Your ascendancy has been met with some surprise and… confusion? The untimely death of the former… your father has not enamoured you with the average man; he was most beloved, and the horrific manner of his death has left a smear on your throne, it seems.'

'Really?' Lennath drawled through clenched teeth, 'that is most disappointing to hear. But it feels laced with honesty and that is what I need to rectify any negative opinions. Please continue.'

Westan had gone pale but nodded obediently, ruffling through some papers before continuing, 'It seems that many are content at the manner in which you came to power and have respect that a tested warrior can now provide a realistic perspective should the need for war ever arise again. There is a general sadness at the passing of the Princes, but this seems to be born of traditional expectation rather than much in the way of strong feeling from any Kingdom. There is fear that unification indicates a desire to expand our borders further and, in light of the losses due to the civil conflict just concluded, there is little appetite for this. The revelation that you have tamed the black-beasts, this seems to be the popular name for the monsters used in your conquest, has been met with general concern and fear; I believe our people do not want to become associated with such horrors. And, finally, it is rumoured that the Lady Alissa is a practitioner of magic; as you are aware, magic has always been mistrusted within our borders.'

'Ha, ha, ha, ha, ha, ha!' Alissa suddenly burst out in laughter, 'How can you mistrust magic? It is not a person, you know, you do not invite it over for tea only for it to fail to show up on time! You people are stupid!'

'Thank-you, my dear, you raise a valid point as always,' Lennath agreed placatingly before turning back to Westan, 'I appreciate your further candour, Westan, I want you to look into a propaganda campaign, something building on the positives of unification and strength. I want focus placed on how much I care for the people, for I truly do, and how their best interests are at the forefront of my mind in all things. I quite like the term 'black-beasts' so use that, but there needs to be a sway in understanding; these are just unfortunate creatures that I have provided new purpose, they must not be feared but celebrated for the usefulness they can provide,' he addressed another man at the other side of the table, 'In fact, let's build on that idea, Allafern, look at practical employment for them; most are stronger than our current beasts of burden so can we exploit that?'

He turned back to Westan, 'As for Lady Alissa, you may express that she is volatile but shares my love for the Kingdom and all within. Her actions are only ever driven through her passion for me and, by association, every other citizen. She is no witch or sorceress, and such rumours will be considered treasonous, especially as she will soon be Queen. Is this understood?'

Westan nodded vigorously as the King opened his address to all others, 'Leave me now, I have much to consider and you all have much to do! We will reconvene in four days, so ensure matters for discussion are scriptured for me at least one day prior, I wish to be properly prepared in future. Audack? Please remain for a private consult.'

The portly General slumped back into his seat and watched as the other advisors all shuffled from the chamber in silence. Lennath leaned forward on his fists, head hanging down between his shoulders, in exhaustion or relief she was not certain.

'What do you make of that, Mozak?' he asked.

The Veer bodyguard remained in his position beside the wall and behind the throne, 'It is not my place to interfere in your politics, King Lennath, but it is interesting to observe.'

'And your thoughts?' he pressed.

'Transition of power is a difficult and confusing time. For your people, it has been thrust upon them suddenly. Patience will provide the greatest dividend; the longer a situation exists, the more it becomes accommodated.'

'How simple the detached perspective is!' Lennath scoffed, frustration edging his voice. Mozak gave no reaction to the sleight.

'Sire, if I may, I assume you have retained me to discuss further military activity?' Audack offered, 'I would request that any such direction is delayed; it will take several weeks to understand what forces are available across the former Kingdoms, let alone begin to organise them into a united army. As your bodyguard has recognised, there is no need for haste; you have succeeded.'

'Have I?' Lennath suddenly bellowed at the older man, 'And how is it that you come to this conclusion? You have somehow gained psychic ability, yes? You can read my thoughts and desires?'

Audack shrank back in his seat, hands raised defensively before him, 'I meant no disrespect, Sire!' he insisted, 'You have conquered the Five Kingdoms in mere weeks, a feat no other could ever have hoped to achieve. Your name will be legendary! I simply meant that you should enjoy this victory!'

'You are small-minded and lack ambition,' Lennath snarled, 'I have conquered these weak Nations with minimal effort, there is nothing to stop my further expansion! One Kingdom I have created in days, why would I consider stopping at that? Our neighbours are unprepared and unaware; this is the moment to strike and make the Kingdom more powerful than any could ever have dreamed! With the creatures and Alissa, I am unstoppable; all lands will be mine so what benefit do I gain from waiting?'

'Sire, I only mean that we will need time to prepare if you intend to march with a traditional army. Should you wish only to employ the crea... black-beasts, then time is no object!' Audack rambled, attempting to placate the suddenly furious King.

Lennath held the man in a withering glare for a few moments longer before suddenly rising to his full height with a smile on his face, 'I see, General, you are only thinking of how best to serve the Kingdom. And well you should, for it will not be too long before you are leading the largest and most powerful army in history! I am not so arrogant to believe that the black-beasts are unbeatable, of course they must be used in conjunction with conventional forces, I am just excited to lead us to glory! How long do you need?'

'To create a single standing army?' Audack asked nervously.

'Yes, an army that is ready to march, with defenders enough left behind to secure the borders.'

'At least three months, Sire, and even then they would be untried and untested. Six would be more realistic.'

'Understood. You have one month,' Lennath offered amicably.

Audack nodded and pushed his chair away from the table, allowing his significant paunch to be released. Without a further word, he turned and made for the door.

'So, you will set out in conquest against all lands?' Mozak questioned from his post.

'Indeed, my friend, and you and yours will benefit most greatly! Already you have received much of the payments promised, the remainder will be provided once the treasuries are combined. And I want to retain you in my employ, all of you, until my wider endeavour is complete. The Veer will be rich indeed!'

'And the limits of your ambition? Where does that lie?'

'The union between myself, Alissa and your assassins is more potent than I could have ever dreamed of. Why place limits upon it?'

'That answer is unfortunate,' Mozak replied and he suddenly became a blur of movement in the corner of Alissa's eye. Leaping forward into a diving roll, he released three small leather pouches towards the King, Lennath only just beginning to turn at the unexpected sound. Alissa slid sideways in her chair and lashed out with one foot, connecting squarely with his knee, and causing him to topple backwards. The three missiles flashed harmlessly past where he had stood but Mozak was already moving in for the kill, springing into the air to clear the throne, knife drawn and angled towards Lennath's heart. And that is where he remained, hanging impossibly in the air above the dumbfounded King.

'Traitors everywhere,' Alissa sighed, raising her hand slightly and watching the assassin shift in the air correspondingly, 'such treachery makes me feel sad. It seems that people are always trying to kill my Kale.'

'Wh-what just occurred?' Lennath asked in a fluster, 'Mozak, explain this!'

'You told me you only sought control of the Kingdoms,' the assassin growled through gritted teeth, the power with which she restrained him driving agony throughout his body, 'I cannot allow you to become despot over all things. Too soon your ambitions would target my own homeland.'

Alissa cast her gaze over to the seat where one of the pouches had impacted, the wood already dissolving away to nothing as acrid smoke rose from the decaying material, 'What magic is this?' she demanded, purple energy glowing more brightly from her eyes the longer she held Mozak in place.

'It is a unique Veer poison, an acid that breaks down the outer shell and a deadly venom that works quickly into the system. It is a searing and ugly death.'

'Now that is interesting,' Lennath mused, climbing back to his feet, 'but what do we do with you, Mozak? I had come to think of us as friends, this betrayal leaves me heartbroken. I would have been happy to spare the Veer from my control.'

'No, you would not,' Mozak corrected, 'your word has become meaningless, you are now no more than a foil for the dark one; if you were anything other than that from the start.'

'I suppose you could be lashing out because of the pain, right now?' the King mused, 'Does it hurt a lot?'

'I will never stop trying to kill you, so you cannot let me live. Just remember how much weaker you are without my protection…'

Mozak's final words were cut off as Alissa clenched her fist and the assassin's body crumpled like a sheet of paper in an explosion of blood and snapping of bones. The remaining sack of human parts dropped wetly to the stone floor, ichor pooling all about it. Releasing the Stave, Alissa rushed into Lennath's arms and buried her face in his chest.

'Oh, my love!' she gushed against him, 'I thought I was about to lose you again! I could not have survived that a second time; are you all right? Did any of that poison touch you?'

'No, Alissa, I am completely fine. You saved me. But this proves a point; we cannot be certain who is truly with us in our wider endeavours. We should be cautious, but I do not want to lose the Veer just yet. Audack!'

Alissa turned back to the door to see the quivering General had witnessed the whole encounter.

'Yes, my King?' he managed weakly.

'I need this mess disposed of quickly and quietly. Ensure none of the Veer suspect anything untoward but make sure they know Mozak has been dispatched on a personal errand for me. Make something up.'

'I could tell them he has gone to retrieve the girl? They may believe you would dispatch him from his personal protection duties for such an important task.'

'That is a grand idea, Audack!' Lennath enthused, 'I think there is definitely longevity in our relationship yet, what say you?'

'I am loyal, as I have always been, only to you, Sire.'

'Of course you are,' the King agreed.

Alissa squeezed him tighter still until he whole-heartedly returned the embrace. She waited until Audack had shuffled away to bring a cleaning party and reached up to kiss Lennath deeply. He smiled at her in a way she had not seen for many weeks.

'I will bring you all the power you desire, my love,' she whispered to him.

'I thank you, Alissa, I could do none of this without you.'

'This is true,' she confirmed, 'so in return I wish to ask something of you.'

'Anything, my darling.'

'Give me a son.'

Peering through the long telescope from the dock, he could just make out the tiny silhouette of a ship in the distance. It had the unique forward short mast, which he was certain must be completely aesthetic, that marked it as the Tabitha's Joy, but its heading left him disheartened. She was clearly not making harbour at Fildenmaw which likely meant the mutiny on board had failed, been thwarted, or never occurred. Reevus sighed heavily; of course it had failed, those cheap thugs were little more than a press gang, they would have stood no chance against Silver Rain, let alone with the rest of her travelling companions. Still, he had hoped his hirelings might get lucky and the speed with which they had returned suggested that may have been the case; if only they had been sailing to him now to collect the second half of their payment.

Dropping the scope to his side, he squinted in their direction, but the vessel was too far to be seen with the naked eye. Perhaps it was for the best that they were bypassing him altogether; if the Fimarrs still lived as he assumed, they would not prove too enamoured to see him again. He briefly wondered if they had spared Makinson, after all his presence on board had been unintentional; how could Reevus have predicted an assault by those assassins? When his son had joined them to evade the killers, he had almost considered sending a message to call off the betrayal, but the chance to claim revenge had proven too tempting. A necessary price he could argue, if the plan had succeeded, but it now felt like a fruitless sacrifice; there was little chance the woman who had permanently disfigured him would allow his son to survive.

Turning back along the wooden slats of the dock, using his crutch to support his hobbling gait, he considered his next course of action. If the Fimarrs were on some quest and had now returned from their destination, there must be something urgent awaiting them beyond this shore. It meant that any return for reprisal would be delayed for at least a few days and gave him the opportunity to disappear. It was not an appealing option as he had spent a great deal of time in recovery, building his official business and inserting himself into the black underbelly of Fildenmaw. Logically, throwing all of that away to avoid death was a simple choice but he still scoured his mind for any options that might prevent his need to flee. Approaching his own shop, he spotted Corbrag, one of the three Harbourmasters, hurrying in the opposite direction.

'Corbrag!' he called pleasantly, 'How goes it? I heard the Tabitha's Joy has changed her itinerary? Should she not be resupplying the mills and tailor upon her return?'

'Hail, Reevus,' the bulky man replied anxiously, 'I have heard no such thing, Tabitha is not due back here for another eight days by my count,' he looked nervously towards Reevus' place, 'be wary, my friend, there are strangers within, and they do not seem sea-faring types.'

Reevus nodded his thanks for the warning and watched Corbrag stride quickly away. Strangers? Surely the Fimarrs had no opportunity to send allies here whilst on their voyage? But if not them, then who might be visiting that would cause the Harbourmaster such concern? As with all questions, no answers would be forthcoming without investigation; Reevus returned to his supported limp, making his way to the front door. Entering without hesitation, he counted four men all dressed in the uniforms of the Lustanian military, gauging the relaxed postures as non-threatening while he made a meal of hanging up his overcoat and hat.

'Greetings, gentles,' he offered merrily, 'what is it this old shipwright can do for the fine men of Lustania, today?'

'Lustania?' the man nearest to the counter drawled, 'Have you not kept abreast of Royal decree? There is no Lustania, only The Kingdom.'

'Right you are, of course,' Reevus continued brightly, hobbling awkwardly behind the serving area so that he could view all four warriors within his shop, 'a lot of change to keep up with, these days. I believe congratulations are in order for you all, such swift and decisive victory over the other Kingdoms is no mean feat; did any of you see combat?'

'Of course we did!' another snapped from his left, 'Are you trying to say we are cowards or something?'

'No, no,' Reevus replied defensively, 'certainly no insult meant to you brave men, just a question, is all.'

'You do not need to know about us, cripple,' the first man continued, 'this is all about us knowing you.'

So, this was some kind of revenge for the sins of his past; it was unlikely he would be able to pinpoint any single event, but it was feasible that any of these men could well have been related to one of his victims. Now that Lustania had occupied Zendra, something like this was bound to happen; it still struck him as odd, though, because it must have taken considerable effort to track him down.

'And what is it that you know?' he asked mildly, continuing to play innocent, 'Something about my trade, perhaps? I am quite renowned for the quality of rigging I produce…'

'That's an impressive telescope,' the soldier now blocking the main door commented, 'is it of your own making?'

'This? No, I was gifted this by a transiting merchant captain. We fixed up some terrible damage to his keel in only a few days; with an urgent cargo on board, he was most grateful and presented this to me alongside my normal payment. I have never found another that sees so clearly at greater distance. It is not for sale, if that is why you ask.'

'No, I do not want to buy it, just wondering what you have been looking for. A returning ship maybe? One of significant importance?'

'Do you mean just now? While I was along on the docks?' he asked in mock confusion, licking his lips to moisten them, 'I have been there every day for the last week, looking out for my son's ship; he went voyaging recently and I fear he may not return.'

'Your son? Is that what you want us to believe?'

'What else is there to believe?'

The man closest slammed a fist on the counter, 'Stop toying with us, Reevus!' he demanded, 'We know about the Tabitha's Joy! We know you helped the Fimarr sisters leave this wretched pit and travel out to sea, helped them get exactly where they were going! You do realise they are enemies of the Crown? That aiding them is punishable by execution?'

Reevus allowed himself a relieved sigh; not avengers for his past crimes, just grunts from the new King, 'Well, of course I know *that*, good fellows, and I must tell you that I share no support for those treasonous whores! It seems that you are unaware of the true details of the 'aid' I provided; I dispatched my own son alongside a mutinous band of merchant sailors to sabotage or kill the Fimarrs. I do not wish to brag but really, I am a hero in this matter.'

'Really? You expect us to believe that?'

'Indeed, feel free to ask about the taverns, it took a whole night to raise sufficient numbers for my plot, any taverner will corroborate my tale.'

'So, when will the ship return with the bodies? We would have to provide evidence of your story to the King, you understand,' the lead soldier queried. And claim the glory for their deaths yourselves, Reevus thought.

'Alas, I am myself most perturbed, as I just this hour witnessed the Tabitha's Joy sailing past Fildenmaw, along the straits. I fear something may have gone awry.'

'Convenient that there would be no way to confirm your story if the ship does not return.'

'The least of my concerns,' Reevus faked deep worry as he continued, 'for a failure to return here indicates my son is surely dead.'

'Well, you leave us with few options, old shipwright, because this is looking like a wasted journey and it is never good to return empty-handed…'

'Empty-handed?' Reevus shot back at him in mock alarm, 'Have you heard nothing that I have said? The Tabitha has passed us already, she will round the spur in mere days! The only thing after that is the Evenflow!'

All four continued to look at him blankly and he made his gestures more agitated, 'The Evenflow! Deepest river in the Kingdoms? Sourced from Mainspring herself? As in, they could sail right up to the new King's gates if they choose to do so!'

Sudden realisation dawned upon them and the four exchanged furtive glances. After a moment, the soldier at the counter nodded to the man at the door who rapidly departed the shop, one of the remaining three replacing him at the entrance.

'Thank the gods!' Reevus beamed brightly, 'I thought I was going to have to spell it out further still! Your man is off to tell the King of this concerning turn of events, I presume? I would think that I have now played my part in preventing an unpleasant surprise for His Majesty, do you not agree? So, what reward is forthcoming? A few coins would be sufficient, the majority of my payment is the knowledge I have aided the Crown.'

A menacing smile spread across the lead soldier's face, 'Oh yes, I can guarantee you will get what you deserve, being such a loyal citizen and all.'

'Come now, my friends,' Reevus continued, conciliatingly, 'there is no need for threats or violence; perhaps I have overstated the value of the information provided. A kind word of my positive involvement would be more than adequate. Let me provide you a little refreshment before you are on your way?'

'I don't think so, cripple,' the warrior snarled, 'you have given us all that we need, and I can think of no reason to allow you to live, after all, if you are a traitor, we may not get another chance to execute you.'

Reevus eased himself slowly back from the counter, 'Be reasonable, I am, as you stated, merely a cripple. There is nowhere I can go that you could not find me if my words turn out to be false; surely the King is a regent of forgiveness and peace, not cruelty? We can avoid things getting ugly, can we not?'

'Too late for that in your case!' the soldier now by the door scoffed, his allies joining his laughter, 'Looks like we will be finishing someone else's job by killing you!'

'I implore you, one more time, do not do this!' he begged, stooping low in an act of subservience.

'Too easy killing a pathetic weakling like you! Easy but fun!' the leader replied, drawing his sword.

Reevus scooped up the harpoon that lay behind the counter with his foot, hiking it into the air, where he caught it easily. As his opponent swung forward with his heavy blade, Reevus thrust out the hooked spear, piercing the man's bicep and feeling the metal tip slide over bone in the process. The sword fell uselessly to the floor as its wielder screamed agony and stumbled back from the counter.

Both other men had drawn their weapons now and Reevus smiled towards them, 'I did implore you to avoid this,' he goaded. They charged as one, keeping enough distance from each other to trap him between them. Reaching across the counter, he grabbed the shaft of the harpoon, hauling back on it and dragging the lead soldier across to block one attacker, the barbed end doing its job and retaining the weapon within its victim. As the expected collision occurred, Reevus belied his appearance and vaulted over the serving area, lashing out a boot into the surprised face of the other onrushing man. His old injuries cried out in protest at the sudden activity, but the adrenaline was pumping, driving him on regardless. Landing awkwardly as his opponent was forced back, he allowed himself to fall to his knees; a more secure base than his feet could provide.

The uninjured soldier had untangled himself from his leader and rushed forward, stabbing down with his blade. Reevus shifted to his right, snatching up the previously dropped sword from beside him and deflecting the attack harmlessly aside. Grabbing the front of his enemy's tunic, he hauled himself to his feet, whilst dragging the man face-first into the counter. A loud bang accompanied the wet crunch of cartilage collapsing before he rebounded upwards like a spring, standing bolt upright before toppling backwards with a hand clutched to his face. The third soldier had recovered from the blow to his jaw and swept in once again with his weapon, finding it parried by the lightning reflexes of the 'cripple'. They traded blows for a few moments until movement from his left attracted Reevus' attention; dropping and rolling to one side, he avoided the waving harpoon as the lead soldier continued to flail about in pain. The wooden shaft whistled over him and slapped his opponent in the chest, generating a grunt from the impact. The distraction was perfect and Reevus thrust upwards with his sword into the man's lower abdomen, the blade vanishing up to the hilt as it tore through his soft innards.

Abandoning the blade, he defied his physical limitations and leapt up towards the ceiling, catching hold of some display netting hanging there. Dragging it with him, he entangled the thrashing leader, his limbs and the weapon jammed within him becoming completely ensnared. Reevus took a moment to catch his breath and suddenly felt all the pains throughout his body. Not ready to stop, he regarded the stunned soldier lying on the floor, nose bleeding profusely; he was groaning and would soon regain his senses, the likelihood of drowning on his own blood diminishing rapidly.

'Think of what you are doing, old man!' the lead soldier screamed at him, but aggression had been replaced with desperation, 'The reprisal for this will be terrible!'

'Old man? I am barely past forty years! But, you are absolutely right,' Reevus agreed, panting between words at his recent exertions, hobbling over to another set of display shelves and heaving a small anchor from where it lay beside the unit, 'So it would be unwise to let any of you live,' he continued, strain cracking his voice as he staggered under the considerable weight.

Watching the horrified expression on his captive's face, he made his way to the prone soldier and dropped the anchor. The man's face caved in instantly and a stomach-churning mash of blood, brains and pulverised bone sloshed out over the floorboards about him.

Leaning back against a support beam, Reevus wiped his brow and took time to control his breathing. The lead soldier continued his struggling, but he could neither release his bindings, nor tear the netting from its fastenings; he looked absurdly like a giant trout trying to escape a fisherman's net.

'You know,' Reevus said absently, 'I used to really enjoy times like these, they thrilled me like nothing else. These days I find them a little uncomfortable and very tiring; I will ache for days because of you,'

'I am sorry, whoever you are, I had no idea! You have a history that I know nothing about, and I made a mistake underestimating you. Please, just let me go and I will not return. I will make up a story about my comrades' deaths and leave your participation completely unheralded. Do not kill me!'

'When you walk into battle, you must always know that you may not walk out again,' Reevus told him sagely, 'When you understand this, you are a warrior, when you do not, you are a fool. Guess which category you now fall into?'

'No, no, this is not the end for me! I have coin, I can pay for your mercy, just…'

He was cut off as Reevus suddenly darted forward, grabbing handfuls of the net, and pulling them tight around his enemy's throat. Words were replaced by a strangled gargle and he clawed uselessly at the air, unable to raise his hands high enough to free the constriction. His face went red and then purple, eyes bulging as if they would pop from their sockets, veins distended beneath his skin. A clucking sound began to emanate from him, failed attempts to suck in air making the amusing noise, and the capillaries in one eye suddenly exploded, painting the orb red. His thrashing became slower and weaker but Reevus retained his hold, leaning forward as death gripped his victim.

'I was only ever beaten once,' he whispered, 'and it was by a far superior foe than you!'

As the soldier went limp, Reevus slowly made his way behind the counter to retrieve his crutch and leaned heavily on it. The skirmish had taken a lot out of him and he was disappointed at how exhausted he now felt. He looked at the assembled corpses and weighed up his options. He could head out now, catch up with the messenger they had dispatched, kill him, and take a warning to the King himself. Informing the ruler of the impending arrival of the Fimarrs would surely outweigh any perceived crimes and possibly even earn him a position in the despot's hierarchy. Or he could ride out to the spur, flag down the Fimarrs ship, warn them that the King knew they were on their way and hope it balanced out his attempt on their lives. There was a final option, of course; slip away quietly now, leave both parties to their respective fates, and pray any survivors never found him.

Turning towards the living quarters behind the shop, he smiled to himself; he always took option three.

Chapter 16

A warm breeze washed over her, soothing tensions and bringing an unexpected smile to her face; the rocking motion of the ship was comforting, as any venture onto water had always made her feel. The return voyage had been so uneventful, so peaceful, it was easy to forget the reason for their travel and the stakes riding on their success. Stroking some loose hairs back out of her face, she shook her head to allow the wind to cascade her long locks down her back. She seldom allowed her hair to hang free, it was not practical for fishing, hunting or combat, and she had not realised how much it had grown since last she had worn it down. Everything felt preternaturally perfect and she wondered again how her father could ever suggest that adventuring had been a miserable way of life; even the dangers and hardships they had encountered strengthened them and provided valuable learning for the future.

'Hail, Crystal,' a voice greeted from behind and she turned her head to see Bentram strolling to join her at the prow.

''Ail, Bentram, 'ow are you zis morning?'

He moved beside her and cast his gaze out over the wide river they traversed, 'I am well,' he provided, thoughtfully, 'although, perhaps a little anxious as we near the conclusion of our journey.'

'I can understand zat, I zink,' she agreed, 'zough I still cannot believe you convinced my sisters to alter zeir plan! Returning to FIldenmaw and killing ze man oo betrayed us seemed like an irresistible option to me!'

'Revenge is very satisfying, I agree,' he continued sagely, 'but it is fleeting. Whoever that shipwright is, or was, his threat is done. Dealing with him and then completing this journey on land would waste precious time; I would say we have wasted enough of that.'

'But zis plan, an audience wiz ze King? 'Ow can you be certain 'e will listen? For all we know, Lennath 'as carried out his plan wiz ze blessing of 'is fazer!'

'I will not deny that as a possibility but, like I told Treya and Catalana, I met him once, during a Royal Inspection in Lustania; he did not strike me as a conqueror. If anything, he has little interest in power; how else do you explain the creation of the Five Kingdoms?'

'I do not challenge what you say, Bentram, but I 'ave learned on zis journey zat zings are seldom as zey seem. Per'aps your anxiety is caused by zis?'

He smiled and shook his head, 'No, I think it comes from the thought of explaining to the highest power in our lands that his son is using dark magic for evil deeds! It is going to take some convincing, I think!'

'We 'ave the Rondure,' she assured him, 'surely zat is proof enough of our claims?'

'I hope so,' he answered, fixing his stare straight ahead, 'but we should be prepared... what is that?'

She peered out to where he was pointing, a dark shadow in the sky, moving against the natural flow of the clouds; a flock of birds? Straining her eyes to see more clearly, her peripheral vision detected something else amiss; far ahead in the river, a narrow channel of ripples vying against the even tidal spread that accompanied their own vessel's direction. Her father had taught her many aspects of both line and net fishing and what she saw now was something all net-men would look for as a sign of whether to haul in early or not. If ripples like those were approaching, you could be sure your nets were already full of fleeing fish; those ripples indicated a predator closing to strike.

'Get ze ozers!' she cried out to her comrade, physically pushing him back to encourage his legs to start moving, 'Tell zem we are under attack!'

As his feet pounded away across the deck, Crystal frantically scoured her immediate surroundings. Her eyes fixed on what she needed; with all her gear packed away in her own cabin, the dock line would have to do. Snatching up the coiled rope, much thinner than she preferred, she swung the small hook on the end experimentally; it was poorly balanced and very light so she would need to adapt her technique, stick to more basic movements. She spotted a member of the crew watching her curiously.

'Go and tell ze Captain zat somezing approaches! 'E must prepare for evasive manoeuvres and ready you all to defend zis ship!'

He stared at her dumbly for a moment before finding his feet and racing away. Returning to the prow, she searched the water for whatever was approaching. Above, the dark shadow was fast-moving and had begun to break into individual silhouettes, larger than standard gulls, for sure. Detecting the surface ripples once more, she noticed they were much closer and had altered to a zigzagging pattern; most predators used such a tactic to startle and confuse their prey, whatever this was, it was incredbly fast and now preparing to attack. Rushing to starboard as the trail in the water swept under the bowsprit, she threw herself to the deck as a dark creature erupted from the surface of the Evenflow, tearing through rigging as it came, and landing on board with an enraged, gargling roar.

For a moment she was paralysed with shock; the long slick body adorned with the chitinous legs of a crab along its length, one cold staring eye in its shark-like head and the blank white orb, where the other had been irreparably damaged, were all too familiar. This was the beast that had attacked their home and left her father so badly injured, the creature that had been captured rather than killed by the hunters from Lustania, the monster she had now missed two opportunities to kill. She would not miss a third. Springing to her feet, she began to spin the hooked end of the grappling line, watching as the predator took a moment to understand its surroundings before shaking itself free of the trailing ropes it had torn through upon its arrival. With the rotation up to full speed, Crystal launched her weapon forward, delighting as it took instant purchase in the soft, slick hide. The beast let out an angry snarl and turned to her, translucent lens nictating briefly over its cold back eye as it fixed her in its gaze. Lunging in with lightning speed, she was barely able to leap out of the way of the razor jaws as they snapped shut. Planning on an elegant roll beyond its reach, she had not accounted for the slaloming movement of it body and found herself partially trampled by scuttling legs. Ignoring the bruising impact, she allowed her body to go limp until the creature had passed by, getting her feet underneath her and springing to the side immediately. Teeth crashed together again in the spot she had just occupied, but the monster displayed phenomenal reactions; her dodge had been instinct and luck, and she could not maintain those for long.

Suddenly the door from below decks burst open, Herc Callid and two crewmen leaping forward, weapons at the ready. With only one working eye, the monster had to snap its whole body around to assess the newcomers, allowing Crystal to roll away to the edge of the deck. She tugged at her weapon but realised the hook still held tight and now several coils of rope were tangled about the animal's body and some of its legs; she could not release it. Looking up, she watched as the beast darted forward, slipping left as Herc brought his axe swinging down towards its head, his blow splintering the wood beneath them. Wasting no energy, the creature turned its dodge into a strike, clamping its mouth down over the head and torso of one sailor before skittering away with its kicking and screaming prize still held in its jaws. The undulation of its body allowed it to lash out with its heavy tail as it passed, the second sailor being brushed aside and Callid taking the full impact of the blow. Thrown bodily from his feet, the big woodsman disappeared back through the doorway from which he had arrived, undoubtedly tumbling down the ladders beyond.

Crystal pulled hard on the rope again, hoping to distract the beast from its current prey but it was too strong; the line grew taut before she was yanked unceremoniously from her feet. Dragged for a few yards, she turned the graceless movement into a roll and regained her stance, desperately looking about her for another weapon. The monster seemed distracted with its meal and she felt bile rise in her throat as it clashed teeth together, slicing the dangling lower body and arms clear. The human remains slid across the deck amid the wash of blood released and she had to turn away to avoid vomiting. She almost ran into the other sailor, his face ashen and his eyes transfixed on the horrific site, and she shoved him hard.

'Wake up, man!' she snapped at him, anger the easiest way to mask her own fear, 'Zat zing could kill you in seconds! Find anozer weapon but do not get too close to ze beast!'

He stared at her for a second before disappearing back through the cabin door, not exactly what she had hoped for. The creature was trying to scoop the rest of its victim from the deck but the shape of its head, designed for hunting underwater, prevented it from doing so. It screeched in frustration and turned to locate another target. Crystal had found a small sickle, probably used for descaling fish, stuck in the top of a nearby barrel and hauled it free, turning to face the massive beast with her makeshift weapon held tight. After a moment's uneasy pause, it launched itself forwards again, this time Crystal ensuring she dodged towards its blind side. Despite rolling further than previously, she found herself in the path of its rearmost legs again, lashing out with the hooked blade she held and finding it completely ineffectual against the bony appendages. The trailing rope had gathered amid the gory aftermath of its previous attack and she instinctively ran across to grab it.

Her opponent had turned quickly after missing its mark, but distraction worked in her favour again, more sailors were arriving from the side doors, accompanied by her other travelling companions. The creature darted into the nearest group, scattering men in every direction, several overboard. Rayne and Treya were within the group, the assassin leaping over the attack, catching an overhead line, and swinging herself up onto the stored longboat, while Treya lashed out with her sword, the blade finding purchase in the slick flesh between its ribs before being dragged from her grasp as she was bowled aside. Crystal dashed across the deck and slid down to the free end of rope she had spotted near the foremast; in moments she had lashed it together with the grapple line she had retrieved.

'Drop ze foresail!' she cried out to all those now above decks.

Sailors ran towards the relevant rigging even as the monster flashed back across the space, snapping up another man in its maw and barrelling others to the deck. As two men began hauling themselves up one side, she realised the other was now inaccessible due to the damage done during the beast's arrival. Without warning, it tossed the man in its mouth aside and lunged for her again. This time she jumped up and forward, keen to avoid another trampling, striking the creature's nose with her knee as she did so; sent into a wild tumble over its back, she heard the agonised roar from her unintentional blow. Like a normal shark, it must have been highly sensitive across that area, sending it into an enraged thrashing; Crystal caught hold of the ropes wrapped around its body and held on with grim determination.

'Ze restraints!' she managed amid her desperate struggle, 'Cut ze holding lines on ze foresail!'

Despite the jarring impact of being tossed around atop the monster, she could see the sailors had released one end of the yardarm and another crewman was trying to shimmy along it to the other side, but his progress was too slow. A flash of silver indicated the throwing knife, undoubtedly cast by Rayne, and it sliced cleanly through one restraint, the foresail lurching down at an angle but still not falling free. Finally, an arrow struck the yard, Catalana having taken a supported stance for improved accuracy, bisecting the remaining restraint and allowing the foresail to drop free at pace. The heavy weight dragged the clewline she had tied to her own grapple back towards the foremast, hauling the massive beast with it. Leaping clear, she crashed awkwardly into the deck, sliding painfully across the surface before two sailors arrived to help her to her feet.

'Are you okay?' one asked with concern.

'No time!' she yelled at him, 'Zat line will not 'old it for long! Kill it now!'

All on deck charged forward, lunging and slashing with blades, spears and hatchets until the creature ceased its struggles. Crystal pushed the helpful mariners away and limped over to Treya on a throbbing knee.

'Crystal, you look awful, we should get you some attention,' the older woman said as she arrived.

'Not yet,' she replied urgently, 'zis beast is not ze real zreat! Look to ze skies!' She pointed up to where the silhouettes had become more distinct shapes, giant black insect-like creatures and something that seemed to be a mix of lizard and bird. 'Scouts for ze enemy! We must stop zem!'

Already the flying troupe were ending the circling pattern they had been following and beginning to peel away upstream.

'Take them down!' Treya called out to everyone, 'However you can!'

Catalana was quickest to respond, already having her bow at the ready, and two arrows found their mark, dropping the black mutants from their graceful flight into the Evenflow far beneath them. Soon others joined her, one man even sporting a crossbow, and a flurry of missiles soared skyward; it was not enough, and Crystal felt her heart sink as three creatures were soon out of range.

'Crystal?' Treya asked, placing an arm about her shoulders, 'Let us get you to your cabin. What happened up here? Where did that thing come from?'

'It was in ze river,' she replied despondently, 'ze same creature zat attacked my 'ome in Zendra monzs ago. If I 'ad killed it zen...'

'Do not be ridiculous, this is not your fault!' Treya scolded.

'Wait, can you not see what this means?' Bentram suddenly interrupted, joining them as the rest of their party and the Tabitha's Captain gathered about them.

'My apologies if recent events have obscured the obvious,' Treya sighed, 'just say your piece and be clear about it.'

'The creature, and those from above, they all came from upstream, followed the Evenflow to find us.'

'So, it is clear Lennath knows where we are,' Catalana added, 'you are saying we should be prepared for more attacks?'

'No!' Bentram continued in frustration, 'Well, I mean, yes, we should. But that was not my point! The only settlement upstream from here is Mainspring, the centre of the Five Kingdoms and personal home of the King.'

'Which is why we agreed to take this route, to meet with him and attempt to garner his support. What is your point?' Treya asked irritably.

'My point is that this indicates only one devastating truth; Mainspring has already fallen to Lennath. Our enemy is victorious, and we are sailing right into his hands.'

'I can make shore here,' the Captain offered, 'you can disembark, make new plans as necessary, disappear into the Kingdoms if needed. I will return to Fildenmaw and insist you never returned from your investigations out at sea.'

'Many thanks, Captain, but no,' Treya said quietly, 'we have already come so far, we have secured the very item we needed and now we know exactly where our enemy resides. Any delay at this point would be futile. The last thing that arrogant cur will expect is a direct confrontation and I say we give him just that. This is our chance, our only chance, to defeat him and save Alissa. I vote that we do not waste the opportunity; what say the rest of you?'

Crystal felt her courage renewed when all hands raised as one.

He pushed the half-eaten slice of steak around the plate distractedly, lost in his own thoughts and having little appetite for the delicious food before him. The high-pitched scraping of the elaborate crystal utensil against the gold-inlay plate echoed about him, but it neither broke through his reverie nor pulled him from it. He had eaten very little over the past few days and this just added to the heavy sullenness he found himself suffering; the loss he felt over the death of his father was almost palpable and there was nobody to share his pain with. He cast an eye over at Alissa where she was wolfing down her meal and reaching for another soft bread roll; it was as if they had reversed roles since her arrival. He remembered the first few days after allowing her some freedom within the palace; she had refused to eat anything, generating concern that she would die of starvation before succumbing to his demands. Now, of course, she had a new focus and was ensuring she ate for two, though the likelihood of her falling pregnant already was slim; he was sure it took many months to conceive. And she had been obsessed with her new desire for a male child, forcing herself upon him at every opportunity. As a younger man he would have revelled in such consistent attention but now it just left him irritated and drained; it had also become impossible to talk to her about Kastani. Lennath wanted to find the girl, he missed her greatly and was worried after Alissa's outburst during the executions; if the Veer had failed to retrieve her, and with creatures summoned to the conquest of the Kingdom, then nobody was tracking her. She could be lost to them forever.

Shaking his head, he sat up in his chair, keen to lighten the darkening mood. Raising a goblet from the table, he watched a serving girl rush over to fill the cup with wine from the Kaydarellan orchards and thanked with a nod and smile. The reaction from Alissa was instant as she swung an arm around and plunged her fork into the girl's thigh. A scream erupted from the servant and she collapsed to the floor holding her punctured leg, writhing and sobbing in pain. Alissa was already on her feet, dinner knife raised high to plunge into the other woman.

'Treacherous whore!' she screamed, placing one foot on her chair to launch a leaping strike at the girl, 'He is mine! Nobody will ever touch him but me!'

Pushing off, she rose high into the air and dropped towards her terrified victim, being caught around the waist mid-flight as Lennath stood and prevented the murder.

'Enough, Alissa, she brought me wine, I have yet to decree that as a crime punishable by death.'

The woman in his arms wriggled around, slashing out with the blade and forcing him to duck his head back to avoid a cut to the face. Pulling her against himself, he freed up his left hand and wrestled the makeshift weapon from her, nodding at the serving girl to beat a hasty retreat. Her cries echoed back to them even as she was aided away along the corridors by a footman. Lennath pressed his face into Alissa's hair and shushed her softly.

'Calm, my love, be calm. There is nobody else for me except you. And even if that were not the truth, I require no defending.'

She continued to strain against him, but her efforts were half-hearted, 'It is not true, Kale, you need me to protect you! Remember last time? You died! And what if one of these witches spirits you away from me again? I could not bear it!'

He held her tight but sank back into his seat, pulling her down with him. Her delusion that he was her former lover was tiresome but had drawn a true affection and love for him which he could not deny; he would accept any reason for her to return the emotion he felt for her. At times he even wished that history had unfolded differently; if she had remained at his palace all those years ago, instead of accompanying her sisters to face Ramikain, they may still be together now, but without the madness, the murder, the conquest. It was wistful to imagine such differences, but he could not help but wonder. He suddenly noticed she was shaking fitfully in his embrace and he could hear her whimpering softly.

'It is alright, Alissa, I am not angry at you, there is no need to cry. All will be well.'

'I am not crying because of you, Kale, I am never unhappy now that you are with me. But it is gone! The special one, they have killed it!'

'The special one?' he queried but already knew the answer. One of the mutants they had located rather than created, a water-breathing abomination such as he had never seen. Alissa had taken an instant shine to it, the uniqueness of its chaotic design and the fact it was born of the ocean; he had seen no need to make more of the sea-dwellers, recognising them as hard to track and control, and his conquest having little need for sea battle. Of course, now that he had set sights on the lands beyond the Kingdom, it could become more pertinent in the future. After a scout had returned to warn them that the Fimarrs were travelling up the Evenflow by ship, she had insisted on dispatching the creature to patrol the river on their behalf. From her current reaction, it seemed clear their pet had found the enemy and been unsuccessful in their destruction.

'Shhh, my darling, it is only one of a multitude, you must not mourn them so deeply.'

'It was the only one! The only one that swam and, when I was in it, I would swim too! There is no feeling like it, can you not understand! And it is just another punishment inflicted upon me by those who call me kin!'

'I know, I know, but soon they will be no more. When they come here, we will destroy them.'

'No!' she suddenly cried shrilly, breaking free of his grasp and throwing herself back against the table edge, 'You must not let them come here! They will destroy us if you do!'

'Nonsense, Alissa! They can be no more than twelve in number, maybe adding another forty if they sell a convincing argument to the ship's crew. What chance do they stand against my soldiers, the Veer and your creatures? Even the great Silver Rain could not defeat such an array of enemies; there is nothing to fear.'

'You are wrong!' she wailed, dropping to her knees before him and grasping his hands tightly, 'Stop them before they come here, sink the ship, destroy them beyond our walls!'

'Alright, alright, my sweet lady. I will destroy them beyond the city, but I will not do it in such an inaccurate manner as crippling their boat! I want to see them die with my own eyes, want to place their bodies upon a pyre myself. They are a symbol of resistance against me and their defeat must be total, it must be public.'

Her head fell into his lap and she sniffed, wiping her face against his breeches, 'I want them dead, too, but I don't see why we cannot just do it without a spectacle.'

He took her chin in one hand and raised her head until she was looking into his eyes, 'It is very important that my people see any resistance to my rule crushed before me with ease. I ask only this one boon from you; for this confrontation, for this one time, follow my instruction when we face them? Please?'

Her tearful eyes regarded him, full of love mixed with fear, and her lip trembled as she spoke, 'I will, Kale, I promise. But not here, not inside the city?'

He leant forward and kissed her, 'Not inside the city,' he agreed. Easing her aside gently, he stood and strode towards the door, 'I want you to assemble the nearest beasts, bring them all here and they will demonstrate your power to our people.'

She nodded her assent from her position on the floor, now cross-legged and appearing so much like Kastani that he felt a pang of loss in his heart once again. Turning back towards the door, he almost ran straight into Audack who was hurrying into the dining room.

'Show more awareness, General!' he snapped, holding his ground and forcing the older man to step back, 'What is the meaning of this intrusion?'

'A thousand apologies, my liege,' Audack babbled humbly, 'I merely wanted to inform you as soon as possible! The Tabitha's Joy has been spotted less than a day's voyage from our Southern docks. It is the vessel that carries the Fimarrs! I fear they have come to confront you once more!'

'I know all this, you fool,' he replied irritably, 'do you really believe they could come so close without my awareness? I want them here; I was about to summon you to make arrangements!'

Audack looked confused and flustered, quite a common occurrence of late, 'Of course, Sire, what do you require?'

'This is to be the end of my time with the Fimarr sisters, only Alissa will remain of their ilk and their legend will vanish next to mine. We will meet them at the foot of Mainspring herself; you will prepare a personal guard of at least forty superior soldiers to escort my chariot, men of strong will as the beasts who serve us will be present in number and I want no displays of fear. In Mozak's absence, you will lead all available Veer to the battlefield as well, I will take no chances this time. Speaking of which, how have your interactions with them gone since… the incident?'

'Not well, in truth, Milord. I fear they are beginning to suspect something. Many of the kestrels they use to carry messages have now gone unanswered and uneasiness amongst their number grows.'

'It is of no matter, once our enemies are dead, we will dismiss them from our service and provide evidence that he was killed attempting to defeat the Fimarrs during their journey. That should tie the matter up neatly.'

The General looked unconvinced but nodded his understanding of the orders, 'Very well, your Highness, would you like any war machines prepared atop the walls? Or hot lead to pour down the winding road should they make it that far?'

Lennath snorted derisively, 'If they make it to the winding road, then they have defeated the defences I just mentioned! If their tiny party can achieve that, they deserve to enter the city!'

Audack shifted nervously and attempted an unconvincing smile, 'Right you are, Highness, I will assemble the guards and assassins as requested.'

'Wait, wait, there is more. I want an announcement across the city, all citizens to attend; the final destruction of those who would stand against the Kingdom will be a showcase of epic proportions and our people should be on hand to witness the fate of our foes. I want the southern-exposed stretches of the winding road filled with spectators, I want them lining the base of the wall, in fact, let them watch from the ramparts themselves! I want cheers filling the air when we wipe the last token of resistance to my rule from the surface of the land. To that end, our visitors will need to be unobstructed from the Southern docks onto Hematia Fields; once there we will offer them surrender or strike them down. Is this clear?'

'But they will be here by tomorrow morn!' Audack exclaimed, 'How can I arrange all of this…'

'I am not concerned with how,' Lennath reminded him with a dangerous tone, 'just make it happen.'

The General bowed low from the waist, 'Of course, my King!' he affirmed and backed eagerly out of the room.

'Kale?' Alissa called softly to him from her place on the floor.

'Yes, my darling?' he answered, mind still playing through the plans he had just set into motion, 'Are you feeling better now?'

'Not really,' she admitted, 'I would rather you just sent your killers to deal with them or let me use the creatures. But I am content provided they do not set foot here. But I wanted to ask something else.'

'Anything for you, my Queen.'

'Lie with me. From now until we face them?'

He sighed resignedly, 'Yes, of course. It will be my greatest pleasure.'

The sound of his own heart hammering in his chest filled his ears, dulling the environment about him. He felt like he was going to vomit, and his legs were unsteady, as though they may collapse under him at any moment. Unable to stop the trembling in his hands, he had fixed one upon the pommel of his sword and tucked the other into his belt; he now knew what it was to be a condemned man walking towards the gallows. Ahead of him the rest of their small group walked in single file, no sign of fear or trepidation amongst them, and he wished somebody had answered his unspoken question; did they even have a plan? He was drawn in by their courage, stout belief in their cause, and determination to confront their enemy, but what chance did they have? He had assumed there was a way into Mainspring that would be concealed, a secret passage or forgotten gate allowing them access to their enemy in his private quarters, unsuspecting or even sleeping. The death march he now found himself on indicated no such advantage. He could not fathom why, upon arrival at the docks, they had not decided to turn back, return to Fildenmaw or any other port, plan and prepare an alternate scheme. After all, being expressly told by a King's messenger that their enemy awaited them on the field of battle not only confirmed their lack of stealth, but indicated he was prepared to destroy them. Treya had insisted this was the way it should be, though, placing all her faith in the artifact they had brought back with them, an artifact which had done little to aid them when attacked on the Evenflow.

In front of him, Rayne turned her head and spoke to him in a low whisper, 'It is not too late. You can still leave; the Tabitha's Joy has probably not yet departed. Lennath expects only the Fimarrs, everyone else is insignificant to him.'

'Run like a coward while I watch you all walk into certain doom?' he replied, trying to keep the tremor from his voice, 'How could I call myself a man afterwards?'

'This is no time for bravado,' she scolded, 'your assessment is correct, we are likely facing our doom, and I do not believe it is a course we can now change. But you have no place here, you have no bond to us and no reason to risk your life alongside us. I am offering you the chance to live, to return to your normal life and whatever future that may bring you. I would consider it a favour.'

She turned back to the front with her last words and he thought he had seen the slightest shimmer in her eye as she did so. He strode forward until he was alongside her, taking hold of her arm as he whispered into her ear, 'I cannot leave you, Rayne. I may have meant little to you, but you have become everything to me. I will stand with you, fight with you, and die with you if that is our fate. I lo…'

She shook his hand free and silenced him with an icy stare, 'No, Makinson, you do not. If you will not leave then you will remain silent; get behind me.'

Disappointed with her reaction, he dropped back again, trudging up the earth track towards their destination. The path rose and he fixed his eyes on Mainspring, the hilltop city beautiful against the azure sky, now that they were closer, he could make out the dark shadows along the ramparts, the walls, even the road winding around the massive hill; were they soldiers? It was an impractical defence if that were the case, too many, too cramped, they would find it impossible to fight effectively without their fellows getting in the way. As he finally cleared the rise they had been climbing, the wall of sound hit him, and he almost staggered at the scene.

A sprawling field stretched out beyond them, the track winding its way through the long grasses that swayed peacefully. This was a contrast to the sound of weapons clanking or rattling together where they were readied or drawn as required by the forty-strong detachment of soldiers who stood regimentally before the King's chariot. That impressive vehicle, gold and white dazzling in the morning sun, held two people dressed in regal finery; Lennath and Alissa he assumed. Instead of horses, the chariot was hitched to four black creatures, mutated and twisted into abominations like the one killed onboard ship, each still holding recognisable semblance to the animals they had once been; a wolf, deer, hare and badger he guessed. Whatever their former natures, they were now monstrous and deadly predators, and he found it oddly reassuring that they were secured in such a manner. Several hundred yards to their right, stood a short, fat soldier with the regalia of a General or similar high-ranking officer. About him, lacking military spacing or discipline, were scattered twenty or so black-clad Veer; though no weapons were drawn, Makinson had experienced these killers first-hand and knew they represented a far greater threat than the soldiers. Spanning the field behind these two small groups was a pacing, growling impatient assembly of mutated beasts in such numbers as he could not have imagined. Such was the oily, black nature of their hides that it was almost impossible to distinguish one from another and they looked like nothing less than the writhing, churning mass of his darkest nightmares. The unholy noises emanating from them cut through him like an icy blade, shattering his very will.

In contrast to the certain death facing them across the grassland, he could now tell that those he had feared to be defenders previously, were, in fact, crowds of normal folk. Stretching along all the roads up to the city and around it, the babbling din that rose from them was not quite the cheering of support for the King he had imagined, traces of uncertainty and anxiety evident in the sound. Where the fields met the nearby treeline, even more citizens had gathered in throngs, creating human walls to this arena of death. Makinson swallowed hard as they stopped, turning alongside the others to face the forces arrayed against them. He spotted the King's messenger from the corner of his eye; now that they had been artificially positioned, undoubtedly by the King's command, the young herald was sprinting away from them. He wished he had taken Rayne's offer. He wished he had not joined them on the Tabitha. He wished Silver Rain had not spared him in Corinth all those months ago.

Waiting as the scene was set before them, Lennath smiled; it was even more perfect than he had envisaged, his enemies had made no attempt to flee or void this confrontation. He had never felt in such control. Reaching out a hand to one side, he felt Alissa squeeze it and knew that she was ready; after all she had told him of the hate she had for her family, this must be a glorious moment for her as well. He prayed she would retain some self-control. His opponents had lined up along the track they had arrived upon, maybe six hundred yards distant; seven of them stood side-by-side like something out of the ballads of old, heroes standing to face overwhelming odds... He shook his head; no, they were not heroes, heroes won such conflicts and there was no chance of that. However, he had to concede how things would appear to the audience he had forced to attend, after all, quelling rebellious minds was one thing, creating martyrs for them something else entirely. He cast his eye along their line; Treya Fimarr had led them to this point and the usual arrogance had been replaced with resolve in her face; next to her was a man he recognised from the battle in the palace but had no name for; then stood Catalana Fimarr whom he could never forget, their sordid time together flashing back to his mind even now; Herc Callid, stoic as ever, was angled slightly towards her in a protective stance; then another stranger, a woman in leather skirt and boots with sleeveless jerkin who he did not recognise at all; before his gaze fixed on Silver Rain. There was another man beyond her but he was of no consequence, Silver Rain was the only concern; certainly, she was significantly outnumbered, and he had witnessed her defeated by a single Veer, but that had been Mozak, a Grandmaster amongst their creed. She was the threat he had to manage, but not at the expense of the spectacle he had promised, after all, if things became too uncertain, Alissa could surely destroy the woman as she had the man who defeated her.

After a few moments to build the tension, he raised his hands above his head, the drone of the people fading instantly and the unnatural bellows of the monstrosities behind them following shortly after as Alissa gripped the Stave and forced them into silence.

'Welcome witnesses, Kingdom-folk, my loyal masses! Here, standing before us all, are the last insurgents against my rule! They came here with the intention of killing me, of destroying the unity of the Kingdom, to ensure that we, as a Nation, are crushed back under the boot-heel of our neighbours! They have killed many in their efforts, successfully turning us against one another, I even have evidence that points to their part in setting my brothers against me. If ever there were enemies to the crown and to the Kingdom, then they stand before you now. Many of you, I know, will demand their deaths right here and right now, but that is not the King I choose to be! I am merciful and forgiving! I offer them the chance to surrender and face a fair trial!'

His voice echoed across the scene amid a deathly silence. He had hoped for cheering support at that moment but could not ignore the uneasiness that many would be feeling; his rule was still in its infancy and none could assume his expectations; perhaps they felt that silence when he spoke was the requirement.

He was surprised when Treya answered, 'Hear my words, people of the Kingdoms!; she announced, voice full of surety, 'I am Treya Fimarr, daughter of the hero Rork Fimarr! Like my father before me, I have made a stand against evil in all its forms; I have toppled tyrants, cut down despots and slain murderers, not because I wish to, but because I have to. My father always told me that if good can stand in the face of evil, then it must, not to win, just to show evil that it has lost. Lennath is your King because of lineage, not merit, he is tyrant, despot and murderer which is why I stand here before you!'

A gentle murmur rippled through the assembled commoners and a flash of irritation spiked in him. Keeping his voice level, he responded, 'Spoken like a manipulator of words! What more could I expect from someone so keen to have me overthrown? I reserve my patience despite the recriminations and insults! Do you surrender?'

'You are masterful with lies, Lennath!' Catalana now returned, 'They are like your camouflage, hiding the predator until you strike! You offer surrender as if it will not end in our execution, you have amassed a force against us that we cannot hope to defeat. I see no mercy, just a calculated attempt to playact the beneficent leader! We will not concede to you, we may die this day but even this will set the example for all others; you are a paper-king and you will fall!'

'Not today!' he screamed back at them, rage spilling over, 'You will face justice and I will silence your treacherous mouths for good! Arrest them!'

Twenty of the guards before him broke away, striding forward in perfect step as they had been briefed prior to assembling. As he watched them cover the ground towards his foes, he flicked out a hand to Audack. Immediately, three of the Veer set off as well; their sole job would be restraining Silver Rain. It seemed highly unlikely that there would be any resistance; after all, what would it achieve? There was simply no way the seven assembled before them could defeat forty soldiers, thirty Veer, thirty-seven of the mutant creatures and Alissa herself; was there? He licked suddenly dry lips and leaned forward on the edge of the chariot. But if there was no point in fighting, why were they refusing to surrender?

He turned to Alissa, 'Make certain the beasts are ready to strike.'

The soldiers approached in perfect formation, focussed solely on maintaining their military discipline, like they were completing a parade rather than wading into battle. Of course, they had no reason to expect resistance from such a small party. Treya took a deep breath; she had never made a decision that was so likely to result in the death of her allies, but there were no other options. She needed an opportunity to get close to Alissa, to use the Rondure in whatever manner it allowed, and the element of surprise had been stripped from them on the Evenflow. Surrendering would provide the proximity she required but by then they would be restrained and most likely disarmed, nullifying the artifact from use; the only chance they had was to draw the chariot closer. They had to get Lennath frustrated enough to attack in person which was going to be harder than planned; she had anticipated an army lying in wait, but not the Veer or the monsters. At least if they could draw somebody into battle, she may have the opportunity to slip past and get to her target. As plans went, it was fragile and already on the verge of shattering. Glancing to her right, she saw Bentram was watching her and gave him a confident smile, receiving a nod of his head in response. The guards were now within fifty yards and she drew her sword, her allies following suit.

'Listen to me, men of Mainspring!' she called out, 'We have no quarrel with you. Turn away in peace while you can. We cannot allow you to stand in our way.'

'Charge!' came the only reply and the twenty men broke into a jog, swords, warhammers and pikes brought to bear. Gritting her teeth, Treya set her feet and focussed on the man most likely to reach her first.

'I'll draw the Veer away!' she heard Rayne call, seeing her sister break ranks and sprint to the right. Makinson immediately followed and Treya cursed silently, the man obviously did not understand the threat or Rayne's tactic; if she had to concern herself with him, she would be less effective against the deadly assassins. He had also left them as only five against twenty. An arrow flashed forward, striking one enemy in the joint between chest plate and shoulder, causing him to topple sideways. Treya anticipated Cat' would only get one more shot before their opponents were upon them.

Sensing, rather than seeing, her allies spring into action, Treya took two steps forward before pivoting to the left and spinning in a tight circle, allowing a pike to slide past her and slamming the hilt of her sword into the side of her attacker's face. As he staggered sideways, a second man swung an overhead blow towards her with his warhammer and she whipped her blade across to block, dropping to one knee to keep her head clear of the attack. Pushing down against her, she could feel her own weapon dropping under the weight and spotted another soldier rushing forward with a sword thrust. Angling her blade downwards, the warhammer slid down to her left, taking its owner off balance with it and allowing her the freedom to roll off to the right, the secondary sword attack slamming harmlessly into the ground behind her. Swinging round with a kick, she caught the swordsman in the ribs, dropping him to his knees and giving her the chance to spring back to her feet. Creating some distance between herself and the soldiers, she parried another warhammer and took a moment to check on her comrades.

Their small number was limiting the number of guards who could attack simultaneously, but it also prevented much breathing space as they fought. Bentram appeared to be in his element, fighting effectively with both swords, gaining an advantage when against a single foe but also capable of holding two at bay simultaneously. He was surrounded by three men currently but the blood flicking from his blades indicated he was winning. Beyond him were Herc and Catalana, four soldiers already prone about them and only one of them moving. Others had taken their place but Callid had secured a pike and swung it before him in long powerful arcs, forcing their foes back. From behind him, Catalana took cover while loading before springing out to fire rapid shots at close range, the lack of time aiming overcome by the immediate proximity; even as Treya watched, another arrow flew forward into a guard's hip, dropping him amid cries of agony. At the end of the line, she knew Crystal had been left exposed by Makinson's departure and could not see her sister now; soldiers were crowding the area with combative activity, however, so she assumed the other woman was still fighting.

The urge to go and help her new sister was powerful but quickly vanished as a pike slammed into the ground mere inches from her position. Realising how lucky she had just been, she returned her focus to her own foes, stamping down on the pike shaft, pleased when it was tugged from the soldier's grip. Taking a second step forward, she swept her sword upwards, feeling the impact against his breastplate as he was thrown backwards by the blow. The thudding impact against her midriff indicated she had left herself exposed and she bent double under the blow. Despite having the wind driven from her, she snapped her arm down over the warhammer shaft that had hit her, dragging the guard closer and hearing his cry as one of his peers cut him down with a sword-swipe meant for her. Stepping herself clear of his body, she completed another spin and launched the warhammer towards the confused swordsman. He raised his hands to deflect the weapon, allowing her to perform a low lunge, stabbing him just below his armoured breastplate. Pulling her blade free, she skipped several steps out of reach to avoid any unexpected attacks and returned to a ready stance. Appraising the two men now facing her, she smiled.

'Fleeing is still an option!' she offered with bravado, but her mind was wondering how Rayne was faring.

At full sprint, she knew she could not maintain the distance from her pursuers, her pace had been ever slower since the fire. Judging how far her enemies had been from her when she had broken from the main group, they would be within throwing distance momentarily. There was no cover ahead of her and three Veer behind, she could not remember a more hopeless situation; well, she could remember *one*. Trapped in an escape-proof room with fire raging all about her. As her breath became more ragged she corrected herself again, there was another more hopeless situation, one she had never really escaped; her life since leaving home.

The slightest distortion of air provided enough warning of a throwing knife slicing the space between her and her attackers. Luckily, the speed at which they were moving provided enough time to react and she dipped her left shoulder to allow the weapon to fly harmlessly by. The move reduced her speed still further, and she had to hope she had drawn the three men far enough from the others by now. Slamming her lead foot down hard, she forced herself into a sideways cartwheel, spotting further thrown items careening past her as she did so. With her opponents expecting her to continue in the new direction, she launched herself back the other way in a giant bunny hop, landing in a crouch before performing a high leap and backwards somersault, descending in a scissor-kick down across the face of one pursuing assassin. The man she had struck fell back into a rearward roll before vaulting back to his feet; his two peers halted their own runs and encircled her immediately. For a few moments, there was a lightning flurry of attacks from the three men, taking all her skill to deflect and parry. The curved tip of her main knife scratched across the back of one attacker's hand and he backed off for a moment, providing her a much-needed reprieve.

'You are surprisingly good, woman,' the man she had kicked offered, 'I did not see the somersault coming. You have my respect.'

'I do not want it,' she replied coldly, alert to any aggressive movement, 'I was trained by Grandmaster Mozak himself, if you cannot anticipate my movement, then you have already lost.'

'We were all trained by the Grandmaster, Silver Rain,' he reminded her, 'but we are three against your one, this contest is already over.'

'I agree!' she replied, throwing herself into a forward flip with one leg outstretched. This time he read the move, swiping her leg to the side, and flashing forward with a kick of his own, stamping down on her abdomen as she landed. Electric daggers flashed up from the impact, but she ignored it, grabbing his foot and twisting violently to the right. He followed the movement, avoiding his knee being jarred loose, twisting in the air, and breaking his fall with a shoulder roll. Flipping her legs back up over her head, she intercepted the anticipated follow-up attack from his peer, feeling the blade slice through the tip of her boot before one foot struck her foe's bicep and the other his throat, driving him back. Following the move into a flip back to standing, she knew she was too late to block the third killer. The three-pronged fighting-fork was almost in her throat when the Veer was thrown sideways unexpectedly.

Rayne watched as Makinson dragged the assassin to the ground with the force of his charge, throwing wild punches against the other man's body whilst trying to draw his own short sword. The Veer he wrestled with pushed out against him with one hand, freeing space to lash out an elbow into Makinson's temple. A glaze filled his eyes following the impact and immediately a knee rose into his chin. Rolling away, he fumbled for his weapon, but the scabbard was empty. His enemy spun his legs above himself, twirling acrobatically to his feet, Makinson's blade held in his hand. Scrambling to his knees, the warrior lashed out with a punch, the blow being met with a straight kick and Rayne heard the sickening crack of knuckles separating. The Veer flung out a shuriken, the tiny weapon glancing Makinson's shoulder as he twisted to avoid the attack, but it had only been meant as a distraction and the assassin raised the short sword above his head.

Instinct drove her forward, common sense telling her to focus on the other two attackers in favour of this one, but she was already in motion. Sliding in beneath his raised arm with her back towards him, she caught the elbow of his raised hand and slammed her head backwards into his face. Stamping onto his left foot, preventing him from the evasive moves ingrained in every Veer, she wrapped her fingers around his raised arm and pulled down with all her strength. Twisting at the last minute, she dodged the dropping blade, forcing it into her opponent's stomach, the tip punching easily out through his back. Stepping to the side, she grabbed the back of his head, intending to slam a knee into his face, but was surprised when Makinson kicked up into the hilt of the sword, pushing it into the Veer up to the hilt. Allowing her enemy to collapse into the grass, she extended a hand to her ally, hauling him to his feet.

'Idiot!' she cursed him, 'Why have you not stayed with the others?'

'You are welcome,' he answered, cradling his injured hand, 'He was about to kill you!'

'I was fine,' she insisted, turning to face the other two Veer who appeared to be in some shock over their defeated colleague, 'Prepare to defend yourself, this is far from over!'

She sprang forward, feinting towards one assassin before casting a ballet kick out towards the other. Both sprang back and she dropped low into a spinning crouch, throwing four blades as she went, one slicing across the thigh of an enemy with another caught and thrown back at her, narrowly missing her cheek. She could see Makinson struggling to pull his sword free of the fallen Veer and knew she had to keep both these men occupied. Launching herself into a charge, she leapt into a two-footed kick, knowing her adversary would block with his forearms. It created the perfect springboard and she vaulted back in the opposite direction, towards the second assassin. He ducked, as expected, but she caught his shoulders, dragging him backwards on top of her. As he landed heavily upon her, she wrapped her arms about his waist, jamming her blades into his sides to maintain the hold, and her legs around his throat. Tensing her body, she rotated the knives in his sides and pulled her legs towards the ground, attempting to throttle him. Despite being pinned and choked at the same time, the Veer was unwilling to concede and lashed out at her with his own curved blades, hacking into her thigh several times before she had to release him. Pushing him off to the side, she wrenched forward with one knife, opening up his side completely. Despite his injuries, the killer clamped an arm across his gaping wound and tried to roll to his feet; he was much slower now, though, and she rolled forward to meet him, driving a straight punch up into his genitals before slashing his throat open when he doubled over in pain.

She already knew she had taken too long and slid herself out of the waterfall of blood from her most recent enemy to locate the remaining Veer. Somehow, he had not yet killed Makinson, her comrade backing away fearfully, blade held in his weaker left hand and blood seeping from several cuts across him. Whatever the reason for his survival, she would question it later, she grabbed her remaining two throwing blades and released them as one. Even as they span ahead of her, she was already on the run, feeling the wincing agony as she pushed her ravaged thigh to its limit. Her enemy turned at the last moment, swatting one knife aside with his dagger and dodging his head back awkwardly to avoid the other. A smile curved his lips as he turned towards her, Makinson taking the opportunity to lunge forward; the assassin kicked out without looking, buckling the young man's knee backwards and leaving him screaming in a collapsed heap.

'So, the glory of your death falls to me?' he drawled with pleasure, 'So be it.'

This time she made no clever dodge, no attempt at misdirection and this seemed more unexpected than anything else she could have tried. Throwing herself against him with a flurry of precise blows from the two knives she wielded, she found him equal to every attack. She threw kicks, knees and headbutts amid each stab or slice but his speed and awareness were formidable. Finally, she angled a thrust towards his heart, certain she had found the opening required, but he turned elegantly with her lunge, catching her wrist while at full extension and forcing her into an agonising armlock.

'Your discipline fails you, Silver Rain,' he whispered against her, twisting her arm more painfully as she tried to angle her other knife towards him, 'Do you know you are famous back in our home? Your death will bring me great prestige.'

'Y-you are as arrogant as you are stupid,' she managed, dropping her knife from her free hand and reaching into a seldom used pouch on her belt.

'Really? Let us see if that is your opinion when I open your brachial artery...' he began but his blade never reached her armpit. Jerking her arm as far forward as she could, she released the silver dust she had retrieved into the air between their faces before blowing hard. The tiny particles flashed into his face, irritating his nose but slicing into the soft tissue of his eyes. Crying out in shocked pain, he stumbled back, releasing her from his vice-like grip and rubbing at his eyes which were already leaking blood.

'What have you done? I am blind, I am blind!'

'You are just another victim of Silver Rain,' she told him, walking slowly forwards, 'this was my calling card, my motif; I had thought it a thing of the past, but you have resurrected it for me. Be grateful that you are blind, for now you cannot witness your abject failure.'

Taking her cue from the man himself, she lashed out her curved blade up and into his armpit, watching the instinctive reaction as he clamped down on that side. Grabbing his free arm, she pulled it straight and stabbed up into his other armpit, relishing the jet of blood before he snapped that arm down as well.

'I am beaten!' he cried out, 'I concede to your greater skill!'

'What? You are Veer!' she hissed at him, 'You fight until death, you know no surrender!'

'Please, do not finish me, I can be of help to you in...'

She sprang forward, gripping his head in her hands and jamming her thumbs into his eyes. She felt the outer layer give way under the pressure and pushed even harder amid her victim's screams. The sticky tar-like sensation passed, and she pushed even harder, feeling muscle, cartilage and membranes pierce beneath the tips of her thumbs. Submerged up to the knuckle, she felt something spongey and realised her foe had stopped screeching or struggling. Pulling her gore-soaked digits free, she stood and allowed the adrenaline rush to pass; she had never been subsumed by such anger before.

Makinson's screams had died down to groans and she walked unsteadily over to him, collapsing to her knees beside him.

'Are you okay?' she panted.

'My-my leg,' he stammered, 'it is… I cannot do anything. It is agony!'

'It can be healed, do not dismay. But you are done here; you can play no other part than burden in this battle. Remain here and lay still.'

'Burden?' he replied in misery, 'I just wanted…'

She cut him off with a deep, lingering kiss. 'You saved my life,' she whispered into his ear, 'rest now my champion.'

Placing his short sword back into his hand, she pressed her palm softly against his cheek before setting off towards the others.

Audack paced back and forth amongst the Veer who stood about him. Things were already not going to plan; the King's proclamations had quickly devolved into maniacal desperation and he could find little salvageable from his exchange with the Fimarr women. He knew exactly what the problem was, his sovereign lacked character, willpower and direction; all traits he could reflect in himself. What he could not understand was the current situation; seven warriors facing these odds could not hope to win and he could not see such a futile sacrifice generating enough compassion to begin a rebellion. Surely there must be another plan? For watching them slaughtered in this fashion sat uncomfortably within him. Maybe his feelings would have be skewed against them more had Frost been with them, but the Veer had reported his death weeks ago. Even that had not brought the resolution he had hoped; there was something else perturbing him which he could not place his finger on.

He peered out to the most distant combat, where Silver Rain had been facing three of the elite assassins. She was now heading back to her party at a run, her foes and the man who had followed her presumably dead, yet the other Veer still with him had failed to show any reaction to her victory. He wondered what emotion, they suppressed to maintain their veneer of dispassion.

He tracked ahead of her, to the remaining five fighters and shock filled him with a sense of dread. Treya Fimarr had defeated those around her, leaning heavily on her sword in exhaustion but sporting no obvious wounds. The dual-sworded fighter had proven skilful indeed, using the blades for a series of feints and parries against his remaining foe who bore only a warhammer. Despite backing away, he could not move the heavier weapon fast enough and soon his defences were breached; a blade struck his upper arm, another sliced across his armoured chest and, finally, both rested against his neck like a pair of scissors. The two men exchanged some words and Audack prepared for the inevitable but, instead, the soldier was permitted to drop his weapon and flee from the scene. The giant, Herc Callid, had smashed foes aside with anything he could set his hands on, his paramour having felled several with her bow from the safety of his shadow. As Audack observed, a pikeman missed with a heavy blow, Callid gripping the head of the weapon and hefting the wielder up and over to crash into the ground beyond. Wasting no time, he grabbed his enemy by the tunic, hauling him up over his head and slamming him back to the ground fiercely. Which left only the woman with the rope. He had been most impressed by her, dancing and twirling her strange choice of weapon as beautifully as any ballet he had ever seen. The soldiers had not known what to make of it as she struck them from distance and at unexpected angles, disarming them with ease and confusing them beyond the ability to fight. Her final foe she had managed to lasso about the wrist, dragging him stumbling towards her before dipping down to sweep his legs. Flailing to the ground, she had been upon him in a moment, wrapping the rope about his neck until his body had gone limp. She had spent her time since then, checking on each of her fallen foes. He imagined she could be killing them, slitting their throats where they lay, but something told him this was not the case. They were doing all they could to avoid their opponents' deaths, because they were good people, because they were heroes.

Audack looked across at the King, his anger and disappointment in the scene before him evident in posture and gesticulation. Was it too much to assume if you could face the heroes, see them bearing down upon you, that perhaps you were the villain? He shook his head; he was a loyal soldier of Lustania, now the Kingdom, and he fulfilled his commission to the best of his ability. When orders were issued, it was his duty to follow them, no matter the cost, was it not?

'See here, false King!' Treya Fimarr's voice floated across the field to them, 'Your soldiers are defeated, if you want to lay claim to us, then you must do so yourself!'

'Do not mock me, woman!' Lennath roared back at her, 'None may do so and live! These men were nothing, just a whet to my appetite! If you refuse to be taken as captives, then you will be taken as corpses! Kill them!'

He waved in Audack's direction and the Veer all began to move as one. So now it would be over; three assassins had fallen to the hand of Silver Rain but surely twenty-seven more was too much. Whatever the Fimarrs had planned, it had most surely failed. The General looked down at his hands, turning them over before him; he had killed many men in his time, during many battles, warfare was no clean business, but each one had felt just. He raised his eyes to regard his King once again, meeting the gaze of his Commander-in-Chief; Lennath's eyes burned with a crazed anger that could not be concealed, if Audack was honest with himself, it had always been there. A thin trail of spittle ran down his chin from the most recent outburst; how suited he suddenly appeared for his bride-to-be. How much like the villains from the ballads. He nodded his head for Audack to join the Veer in their attack and the General turned to jog after them, waiting until he had caught up with the rearmost men before addressing them.

'Listen to me, assassins, you have been well-paid for your service and now the King demands you slay those before you. But I say to thee, hold fast and change your course!'

'What are you talking about?' the nearest killer demanded, 'Why would you defy the orders of your Regent? Does he plan to renege on payment?'

'No, he has all the funds he needs to pay you. But, know this, your Grandmaster is not in the Dussen lands, seeking the missing child, he is dead! Killed by the King!'

'Impossible,' the Veer retorted, 'no man could hope to defeat Grandmaster Mozak in battle!'

'He turned on Lennath and his witch, told them he could not permit their conquest to continue! He feared for his homeland, for all of you! But even his might could not overcome their dark magic. But you, all of you together, maybe you could achieve the victory he could not!'

'Why should we believe you?' the assassin asked with growing concern in his voice.

'What reason do I have to lie? There is no gain for me in turning traitor to my King, but there is honour in doing what is right. Here,' he held out his hand, offering the ring he had taken from Mozak's hand, 'do you really require more proof?'

Wild fury filled the eyes of the black-robed man before him and he released a strange ululating howl, 'Veer! To me! Treachery must be answered!'

The others turned to him as one, waiting for him to justify his call to arms, 'Lennath has murdered the Grandmaster and for that he must die!'

A sea of black washed past him and Audack collapsed to the ground, tears welling in his eyes and all strength sapped from him. Watching the assassins as they rushed towards his Regent, he was filled with both guilt and relief at once but there was no way to undo his actions now.

'Traitor!' he heard Lennath calling to him even as the ground before the Veer cracked open and a monstrous black worm-like creature erupted before them, crushing several with its arrival and soon being joined by several of the creatures that had stood guard behind the Royal Chariot. As an almighty battle broke out between perfect predators and perfect killers, he watched even more of the black monstrosities bounding across the grass towards the Fimarrs.

He had just betrayed all he had honoured for so long, turned on his own King and shattered his own beliefs. And it appeared it would be for nothing.

'Damn that scum to the dung-heap!' Lennath cursed, gesturing wildly with his hands, 'Can you believe such a thing? After all I have granted him? He will rue this day my love, will he not?'

Alissa tried to answer but only a guttural croak emerged, words were too much effort at that moment. She felt the Stave in her hand, a comforting warmth emanating back through her arm up to the shoulder and the regular pulsing of power like the ticking of a clock. Her eyes were open wide, but she could see nothing immediately before her, instead she processed hundreds of images simultaneously, quelling natural urges and fears and replacing them with direction and purpose. The moment Audack had stopped to speak to one of the assassins, she had known something was wrong, immediately summoning those beasts she had hidden underground to intercept their attack. Although they were outside, it felt very similar to the vision she had already seen; Mozak had still been alive and leading this charge in that foresight, however, so this could be mere coincidence. Directing more than half of her pets against the greater threat the Veer represented, she could already feel the grinding agony when one of the animals she was linked to was slain. She did not relish the thought of the second group engaging her sisters simultaneously. Trying to answer the question for a second time, she managed a loud sob.

'Alissa? What is it my darling?' she could hear his voice, but it sounded far away or separated by a wall, 'Is this too much? What can I do?'

'M-many,' she managed eventually, 'Too many.'

'What have I done my beautiful Queen?' he replied, voice thick with emotion, 'I should have listened to you, done what you asked and destroyed them before their ship reached harbour! I am sorry my darling. Just hold on for this last battle and you will be free of them.'

She knew he was caressing her cheeks gently with the back of his fingers, wiping away tears that she did not know she was crying; her skin could not feel the contact, however. She tried to tell him that she needed to focus but wracking strain gripped her muscles, and she released an agonised scream instead.

'It is too much!' he cried desperately, 'I will end this for you, now. Stay here and be safe. Worry only about controlling your beasts and nothing else. When we have claimed victory, your respite will be as long as you need.'

He lifted her from the back of the chariot, like a groom carrying his new bride across the threshold, walking her gently to a patch of softer grass and moss, and laying her tenderly upon it. The arm holding the Stave was fixed with rigor, held up to the sky despite the relaxed posture of the rest of her body. He leaned over her to place a kiss upon her lips and finally she could see him, a dark blur within a deep purple haze.

'I will destroy them for you and then we can have the future we desire,' he promised, turning away and leaping back onto the chariot. Amongst the multitude of awarenesses swarming through her brain, she felt those hitched to the war chariot suddenly urged into motion as her lover joined the charge against the Fimarrs.

'No,' she mumbled weakly, 'do not leave me! Do not let them separate us again.'

She was faintly aware of the remaining twenty soldiers forming a square about her with their own bodies, a human shield around the true weapon of war.

Like a living, moving shadow, the nightmare army surged across the fields towards them. It was all she could do to hold her nerve, already calculating the slim chance of survival for any of them; the plan suddenly seemed ill-conceived and futile. Desperate to run, she kept her feet planted and looked across at her sister. There was no flicker of concern, no tell-tale trembling or beads of sweat; Treya stood motionless, watching the horror descend upon them.

'This is it, sister!' she shouted over the cacophony of thundering hooves, bestial grunts and predatory roars, 'This is the chance you said you wanted!'

'That it is, Cat',' Treya responded calmly, 'just need to pick my path.'

'Look!' Bentram cried out from behind them, 'Lennath himself has joined the charge!'

Catalana peered through the throng of charging monsters and spotted the bright chariot amongst them, rumbling haphazardly across the rough ground in the wake of the other creatures.

'I cannot see Alissa,' she observed.

'No, he left her behind to 'manage' this battle for him,' Treya agreed, 'it could not be more perfect.'

Catalana could not imagine in what sense their predicament could ever be considered perfect, but it did mean Lennath would not be able to intervene if Treya could get to their youngest sister. With the wall of death approaching, it was a big if.

'Now?' she asked.

Treya gave the slightest of nods, 'Now,' she concurred before breaking into a sprint towards their foes.

Cat' watched her running, unable to recall any moment of greater courage she had ever witnessed. Pulling five arrows from her quiver, leaving only one until she could reclaim any from her recent victims, she jammed the missiles into the ground before her. Noting a mutant that resembled some kind of goat/fox hybrid altering its course to intercept Treya, she lifted one arrow to her bow, notching it and drawing back the string in one smooth motion. Holding the weapon at maximum tension until the perfect opportunity presented itself, she released the arrow with a loud twang. Rocketing through the air, the shaft was mere yards away from Treya herself before it flew into the gaping maw of the beast, puncturing its soft palate, straight into the brain. As the hideous creature crashed to a sliding death, Treya disappeared from view and Catalana was left to pray she had not collided with the monster and been crushed.

'There! The General!' she heard Herc cry out, turning to see he had already moved forward of her position, readying his axe to meet their enemies. Focussing on the field beside the scene of carnage where the Veer were engaging more of the mutants, she could just make out the fat General sitting with his head in his hands. He was one of Lennath's men, had been present when they fought in the Palace, was clearly the military commander of the force arrayed against them. But he had done something, said something, that turned the invincible Veer assassins away from her party and into an attempt on Lennath's life. Now a single monster, smaller than most of the others, maybe transformed from a rabbit or shrew but having grown to the size of a large dog, had slipped past the deadly assassins, and was bounding towards the unsuspecting man. It would not be an undeserving death for the atrocities he was complicit to, but she could not find it within herself to simply let him die.

Notching another arrow, she drew back and released, the shaft flying straight and true but skimming over her target by half a yard; the distance was not as far as it appeared. She took up a second, stringing it quickly and closing one eye before firing this time, removing other distractions from her aim. This time the arrow found its mark, slicing into the flank of the animal but not felling it. She could see the General finally reacting, trying to scramble to his feet and withdraw a weapon; he would be too late. Snatching up a third arrow, she dropped to one knee and took a deep breath. Lining up her shot in front of the speeding monster, she half-exhaled, blocking out all distractions around her, and released the bowstring. The arrow slammed into the eye of the creature, causing it to crumple to the ground before the old warrior and allowing him to finish it off with two blows of his warhammer.

The other beasts were almost upon them now and she reached for the slender sword at her side until she spotted Treya again. Her sister had survived and was now skirting the distracted pack of beasts as they continued their bloodthirsty charge. But she had been spotted; by Lennath. The current King was spurring his vile team forward, clearly intent on driving his chariot right over his target. Catalana pulled the last of the lodged arrows from the dirt and ran off to the side as fast as her legs would carry her.

'No Cat'!' Herc called after her in panic, 'Do not allow us to become separated!'

Hearing, but not heeding, him she slid to a halt at a point where fewer of the approaching animals were in her line of fire. Targeting a shot aimed for Lennath's head, she knew it would not prevent the chariot from continuing its course into her sister. Altering her aim further forward, she released the arrow. It caught one of the two lead creatures in the throat, the pain and surprise enough to cause it to rear and stumble. The monster behind it continued its own course, crashing into and over the one before it and soon all four animals had been dragged to the ground, the chariot crashing into their massive bodies before flipping up and over them. She thought she saw Lennath being thrown from the vehicle but could not confirm it as the charge was finally upon her.

His cry of warning had come too late, the distance between himself and Catalana may as well have been miles for all the chance he now had of getting to her. He felt his heart sink as a wall of black caused her to vanish, and turned back to the descending horrors approaching. Swinging his axe out before him, the first few beasts angled themselves clear of the weapon, darting around him as the rest of the horde pressed on from behind. One creature, perhaps twisted from a pig or boar, crashed blindly into him, driving him to the ground. Suddenly underneath a trampling chaos of feet and the occasional gnashing muzzle, he realised the monsters were not charging so much as stampeding; driven wildly forward by Alissa's power. Kicked and battered amongst the array of legs and feet, he could feel claws and nails tearing at his body and ducked his head away from snapping jaws as opportunistic bites were taken towards him. But the beasts were too close together, pushing and thrashing amongst one another, making their attacks ineffective, though the trampling was no less debilitating.

Finding space to wield his axe once more, Herc twisted it as best he could, catching the lower abdomen of an equine mutant with the honed edge, its natural kick-reaction dragging his weapon deep into its hip joint and out of his grasp. Kicked like a ball further into the angry pack, he found himself face down, stamping limbs punching at his flesh and driving the air from his lungs. Desperation to find Catalana, alongside rage at his predicament, fuelled his muscles and he pushed up with arms and legs, feeling his back impact with the belly of another monster. Righting himself with a roar of outrage, he tossed the heavy monster off himself and slammed a double-handed hammer blow onto the snout of the nearest other creature. Another threw itself at him and he dodged to the side, catching the savage beast in a headlock; spines that had sprouted around its neck like a mane jabbed into him like a pincushion, but he held on regardless. Hauling upwards, he tightened his hold and, as several other creatures turned to try and bite him, he threw himself backwards to the ground again. The awkward angle and jarring impact did the expected job, breaking his foe's neck and he tried to roll clear before anything else could pounce upon him.

He was not quick enough, and a slimy tentacle suddenly whipped about his neck. Instantly clawing at the disgusting appendage, he found he could not get purchase, even as it began to constrict about his throat. Turning to face the horror he now fought, finding it to be short and squat; a bulbous wet head with four tentacles sprouting from its neck was sat atop a six-legged insectoid body leaving him utterly clueless as to what it had been in the first place. With each breath becoming more strained, Herc dug his fingers into the suckered underside of the tentacle and tried to pull the creature within his own striking distance but it was far stronger than it looked. The more he pulled away, the tighter the grip became, and he could feel his senses numbing as circulation was cut off to his brain. As the chaos around him began to sound tinny, and black shadows filled the edges of his vision, he was aware of the massive impact in his side and the immediate sensation of flying. Something had rammed him, the flaring agony in his hip and ribs told him as much, but inadvertently saved him from the tentacled horror. Being tossed through the air felt strangely calming, like he was simply a voyeur of the carnage about him, but reality was brought painfully back to him as he crashed into a landing and tumbled across the solid earth. Fire filled his side as he tried to take steadying breaths and he assumed ribs were broken. Although cast free of the throng of black mutants, he could make out none of his comrades; there was no time to search for them as the triple-horned beast that had rammed him charged forward to continue its assault.

Spinning and twisting her body in a blur of dancing energy, Crystal kept the hook at the end of her reinforced line in constant motion, lashing it out in whichever direction enabled her to hold another beast at bay. Completely surrounded, she had been able to strike out at snouts, eyes, joints, anywhere that would cause the monsters to pull back from their attacks momentarily. She knew it was futile, holding them off was fine but her strikes had to be short and sharp, thus causing no real damage. This had kept her unharmed so far, but the creatures were likewise uninjured and getting more enraged with every strike. Breathing hard already, she knew that her current exertions could only be maintained for a few more minutes; if she tried to land a more damaging blow against one of the animals, it would most likely snag her weapon momentarily, allowing another beast to strike.

Her mind whirled back to her father's words and she began to realise he may have been right all along; the thrill of an adventure could not outweigh the mortal danger she now found herself in. Even when agreeing to Treya's plan, hearing her spell out that getting to Alissa was the only goal, that the rest of them were to be an expendable distraction, the reality had not truly entered her mind. If her focus was not completely absorbed with maintaining the constant motion of her unique weapon, it was likely she would have given in to despair already.

An image of Rayne flashed into her mind, the very image she had seen moments before the monsters had flooded over them. Sprinting across the front of the charging animals, the black-clad redhead had shown no fear, almost no interest, in the nightmare about her, intent only on getting as close to her sisters as possible before the combat began. There had been no sign of Makinson, it seemed he had already become the first casualty of the battle. Crystal had hoped that the assassin might have noticed her, perhaps returning and slaying the creatures while she kept them distracted, but that hope had vanished within moments; only Treya and the Rondure were important right now. She knew in her head that her own life was not relevant in this situation, that she had played her part already in helping them to retrieve the magical artifact they needed, but that knowledge did not quell the fear of imminent death or the regret at having left home without making amends with her father. How would he feel knowing she had died because of her own bullheadedness?

The question remained unanswered as a beast acted outside of her expectation. With her rope at full extension, striking the eyebrow of a large creature with an ovine head that had sprouted a short wide beak and curved tusks from the corners of its jaw, another animal, looking like a giant wolf, with little mutated difference other than the complete lack of hair and black scaled skin, leapt forward into the rope. Catching it within its maw, the monster began to bound away and, with the remaining coils wrapped intricately about her body, Crystal was dragged along with it. Such was the pace of her sudden travel, that other horrors were not quick enough to slash or bite her as she passed, but coarse grass and ground beneath tore at her unprotected flesh. Moving beyond the confines of the battle, the animal increased speed as it turned in a wide arc back towards the rest of the pack, causing her to roll as she was thrown wider around the same curve, all the while becoming more entangled in her own weapon, coils of rope now binding her arms to her sides.

Without warning, her painful journey ground to a halt. As her breath returned in huge, desperate gasps, she stared at the sky in confused shock for a moment. Her entire body was awash with throbbing, stinging and burning pain; she had heard tell of prisoners tied to the back of horses and dragged behind them until death, if her own experience was anything to go by, then it was a most horrific form of execution indeed. Realisation quickly dawned on her that either the rope had snapped, or her tormentor had stopped; forcing herself up onto her knees, she followed the trail of cord with her eyes, finding the beast slowly stalking towards her. Struggling against her bindings, she knew she could not break them and even climbing to her feet felt impossible against the tangled restraint. As the creature closed in for the kill, she held her breath and closed her eyes, feeling the single tear slip free at the knowledge her life was over. Its hot breath washed over her face and she began to say a silent prayer to Yanis. Then the creature licked her.

Cracking the reins hard again, the cart hurtled forward behind the straining horses, bouncing precariously along the uneven dirt road.

'Slow down!' came the cry from behind him, 'You will break her concentration!'

'We need to get her closer, give her a chance to stop them all!'

A hand fell onto his shoulder and he turned to look into Rebecca's eyes, 'No we do not,' she told him levelly, 'take a look.'

Pulling back on the reins, Forge hauled the vehicle to a stop and leapt to his feet on the driver's seat. Sure enough, the chaos of battle that had been present on the field below when they arrived over the last peak had now become eerily still. The swarms of black-beasts had stopped their aggressive onslaught and were now milling around aimlessly from what he could see. There was no sign of those they had been battling from this distance, and he prayed they had arrived in time. He could make out the hollow square of soldiers formed up close to the base of Mainspring; it seemed likely that Lennath or Alissa or both were protected within. His mind raced with what to do; somewhere down there was his true love, the mother of his children and his reason for living, he had to find her.

Behind him in the cart his twin children huddled among swathes of blankets, the only way to avoid their injuries from his frantic race in the vehicle. He offered them a smile, but it was clearly all they could do to avoid bawling their eyes out; things had been upsetting and frightening for them since Terex's death and it would take much effort to help them move on from these events. Effort that would be infinitely less if he prevented the loss of their mother this day. In the centre of the wagon, Kastani was kneeling perfectly still, eyes wide open and glowing with a sickly purple energy, power and heat palpably emanating from her. She had been motionless in the trance-like state since he had shouted back to them that the battle was raging; the creatures below had ceased their aggression seconds later and it was no mere coincidence, the little girl had somehow soothed the entire army.

Jumping down from the cart, Straker rushed to one of the team horses and began to unhitch it.

'What do you think you are doing?' Rebecca demanded, climbing down to confront him.

'I have to get down there,' he replied, continued to undo straps, 'Treya is on that field somewhere and we cannot be sure that Kastani's control will last; she needs me.'

'We need you!' Rebecca said curtly, 'What if one of those things breaks away and comes for us? What if another Veer does? Or even just a soldier? Are you willing to value your woman over your children?'

Forge paused for a moment, eyes closed, and head hung in thought, 'It is not a question of value, just practicality,' he replied, 'you are safe here, she is not. There are no creatures, Veer or soldiers anywhere nearby because they are all down there, with her. I could take you all with me but that would only be increasing the risk to you. I am left with no option but to trust that you can keep the children safe. So, can you?'

Her shoulders dropped and the indignation drained from her voice, 'Yes, of course I can. And I will, I am just... I am terrified of her, Straker, what am I supposed to do if her trance breaks?'

He thought for a moment before gripping her shoulders firmly, 'If she does anything other than keep those things docile, and certainly if she tries to turn them on Lennath, I need you to incapacitate her.'

'Incapacitate?' she repeated cautiously, 'What does that mean? We both know what she can do, how would you suggest I do that? I am no child-killer...'

'By the gods, Rebecca, you have come to think of me darkly!' he replied in exasperation, 'In spite of all else, she is still my niece and little more than a baby! I would not advocate her death under any circumstances! Here, take this cudgel, if things begin to change for the worse down there, a quick blow to the crown will knock her unconscious. Understand?'

Rebecca took the small blunt club from him and tested the weight in her hand, 'All right,' she said after a moment, 'but what if it does not work?'

He sighed at the persistent questioning, 'Just pray that it does,' he told her, 'I have to go.'

She nodded and he ignored the lack of belief in her eyes as he swung himself up onto the released horse, 'As soon as I know she is safe, that they are all safe, then I will be back, I promise.'

Kicking his heels into the flanks of his new steed, he galloped towards the confrontation below, wishing he felt more confident that he was riding towards rescue rather than vengeance.

Soft grass pressed against his face as awareness flooded back to him. Had he been unconscious or stunned, it was unclear, but the circumstances leading up to his current position suddenly returned to him. He had been urging the chariot forward, not really needing to use the whip as Alissa controlled the beasts directly, but his adrenaline had been up, and he could not resist. Then one of the front creatures had reared up for some reason, his whipping driving the one behind to continue despite the obstruction; the chariot had flipped over against the living barrier and he had been thrown clear. Pushing himself up to his knees, he turned back to find the overturned vehicle only a few yards away; he was lucky to have avoided being crushed.

Standing, he took in the wider scene to try and gauge how the battle was progressing; the chariot-bound animals were groaning and growling in pain, injured beyond the ability to be useful, but the others had also stopped in their attacks. Most were moving around in confusion, a few even running towards the safety of the trees, but none were battling their respective targets. The surviving Veer seemed intent on regrouping further towards the river, maimed and broken members of their group being aided by the less injured. He could not make out the members of the Fimarr party but if any had survived the initial onslaught, they were not being made to suffer now. None of this made sense.

Reaching for his sword, he remembered he had not brought it with him; set the wrong image amongst his people according to his advisors. Scanning the immediate area for a useful weapon, he spotted Treya Fimarr. The loathsome woman was taking full advantage of the creatures' confusion and was now racing towards the guarded zone where Alissa lay. There was no time to intercept her, so he withdrew the throwing knife he always kept hidden in one boot. He was no expert with the weapon, but he had no other options. Taking careful aim, he drew back his arm and prepared to launch the blade.

Sudden pain lanced from his bicep and the knife fell uselessly from his grip. Crying out and dragging his arm into his body, he saw the arrow that now jutted from either side, blood flowing freely from the double wound. Bending in pain, he screamed out his agony again and snapped the feathered end of the shaft, looking for the perpetrator. New ire filled him as he spotted her; Catalana Fimarr, bow still raised before her while her free hand searched the empty quiver on her hip for another missile. She had ruined his chance to stop

Treya, he would now have to hope his soldiers could last long enough for him to catch up before she got to Alissa. He flicked his eyes down to the dropped knife, but it was difficult enough to throw the weapon with his dominant right hand, it would be pointless to try with his left. But he had another option, one that did not rely on accuracy. Retrieving the small leather-bound sphere from his belt pouch, taken from the body of Mozak, he smiled darkly. Before him, Catalana had dropped the bow and scooped up a warhammer from one of the fallen soldiers before her. That had not been a fruitful option for her last time they met, and it would not be now; leaning back for maximum power, he whipped his arm forward, hurling the weapon with lethal accuracy.

Transfixed as it hurtled towards her, he did not notice the nearest creatures suddenly focussing their attention on him.

Feet pounding the uneven surface, lungs bursting under the exertion, she refused to slow down even the slightest amount, knowing now that her feeling of unease had been merited. She had been in her headlong charge since leaving Makinson, covering the gap she had created when leading the Veer away even as the mutant charge was descending upon her comrades. Instinct told her that Treya would need her, that she couldn't face their enemies alone, that Rayne was the only one who could really help her. Thus, she had taken an impromptu gauntlet, sliding under the legs of raging beasts, vaulting over their backs, dodging every claw and tooth diverted against her, loathe to allow anything to cause delay; unwilling to fail as she had on the island.

Despite the concentration required to remain alive in such a reckless scramble, she had noted Crystal surrounded by the black predators, seemingly holding her own, Herc Callid disappearing underneath the charge, undoubtedly killed under the crush, and Bentram backed between two large corpses, preventing more than one animal at a time attacking him. Now her attention was wholly on Catalana.

Her sister had shot Lennath, stopped him from hurling a knife at the retreating Treya, though Rayne doubted the man could have done any significant harm with the blade. That had been her last arrow and now she was resorting to close combat, striding purposefully towards him. It was a battle she had already lost once, and Rayne could not allow it to happen again. Lennath appeared enraged and far from concerned but, instead of taking up a weapon to face her, he had retrieved something and thrown it instead. It looked harmless enough, which is why she felt Catalana had failed to react, but Rayne had seen such weapons before and knew it to be lethal. And so it was that she demanded just a little more from her screaming muscles, one last push to ensure she got to her sister in time.

Leaping forward as she came within range, she tackled Catalana at shoulder height, dragging her unexpectedly sideways and crashing them both to the ground in a heap.

'Damn it, Rayne!' Cat' shouted at her, recovering quickly, 'What are you doing? I can take him! I want to take him!'

'I know you do,' Rayne replied, trying to catch her breath, 'but that was an acid pouch.'

'What?' Catalana continued angrily, 'What are you talking about?'

'The ball he threw at you, it is designed to break on impact. The inside is lined with a powerful lime-based alkali but, when the package splits, it releases the acid.'

'Acid? What is an acid?'

'A caustic substance that burns through most solids. It makes the Veer poisons more effective; the acid eats through armour, clothing and flesh, distributing the poison more quickly into the bloodstream.'

'Well, thank-you, then,' her sister conceded, 'as you are here, shall we kill him together?'

Rayne felt her heart leap with pride at the confident smile on her sibling's face, 'You have changed so much since we were children,' she told her.

Cat' looked slightly confused, 'Yes, I have, but this is no time to reminisce. We must act now!'

'Alas, I cannot,' Rayne admitted, 'you see I am not quite as fast as I used to be.'

Colour drained from her sister's face as Rayne rolled onto her side so she could see the arm where the pouch had struck; already the flesh was bubbling and running free in viscous lumps as the acid began to dissolve her.

'No!' Cat' sobbed, tears immediately pouring free and falling upon her sister as she knelt up beside her, 'No, this cannot happen, you are Silver Rain! What can I do? There must be something!'

'No, Catalana, there is not. Unlike on the ship, the poison cannot be sucked out because of the acid, and it is too high up an injury to tourniquet; the poison is already on the way to my heart. I am sorry, but you will have to continue alone.'

'Not for me, Rayne, please do not die for me! There is not enough time left! I have to forgive you; we have to make things right again! It was always you and me together, you were always the one to protect me, to save me. How can it be that I cannot do the same for you? Please! You are Silver Rain and you cannot die!' she was wailing uncontrollably as she begged, but her eyes continued to fall upon the affected arm, flesh burned down to the bone already and pungent smoke rising as the potent acid began eating through marrow.

'You know it is too late, Cat'' Rayne managed weakly, clasping her sister's hand with her undamaged limb, 'but you must know, while I have the strength to tell you, that I never stopped loving you. I was not there to save you after I left home, but you continued to save yourself; you are everything, you have everything, that I could ever have dreamed of. Do not throw these things away, cherish them for me? And I am Silver Rain no longer, for many years now I have been only Rayne. Rayne Fimarr. Your sister.'

Catalana's weeping became more intense and it was clear she wanted to say more but the words took time to come as she cradled Rayne in her arms, kissing her forehead and rocking her in distress, 'You are my sister, Rayne,' she managed eventually, 'and I am yours. I love you and will do so forever. You are forgiven any wrong you have ever done me, intentional or not and I am so sorry that I have ruined our last days together; if I had known…'

'You are only human, Catalana,' Rayne struggled as she felt fire bleeding into her lungs, 'you must not punish yourself for hating me, I hate me, too. I forgive you and tell you that you have been justified in your treatment of me. Just carry forward my love now, for you, for Treya, for Alissa and please tell…'

Her voice trailed away alongside the last breath she would ever take.

Picking her way forward, Treya continued to skirt around the few beasts that remained this far up the battlefield. The sudden drop in their aggressiveness was inexplicable and fortuitous, but she would take no chances in getting too close, and she doubted the soldiers up ahead would be as compliant. Closing within eighty yards, one of the armoured men saw her and dropped his pike in her direction.

'Come no closer!' he warned, attracting the attention of his peers.

'This is your chance!' she called back, 'All of you! Walk away now, leave my sister to me and you will live the rest of your lives outside of my wrath.'

'The King gave us our orders; we are loyal to our sovereign and our country.'

'Your King sits on a throne of lies and murder! Look around you, he has failed completely! His assassins turn on him, he has lost control of his beasts; even now they look to destroy him!' she pointed back with her sword where several of the creatures did look ready to make a move on him, tracking his run as he approached; she had maybe a minute to convince them to let her pass, 'And I, a daughter of Rork Fimarr, have challenged him; does this tell you nothing?'

'I will discuss this no further. If you continue your approach, we will cut you down!'

'If that is your final answer,' she continued, 'then so be…'

Here words were cut short as Alissa suddenly appeared bolt upright within the barrier the soldiers had created, Stave held at arm's length and wild purple energy crackling from her eyes, fingers and mouth. Several of the guards cowered away as she continued to rise, feet leaving the ground as the energy itself seemed to lift her.

'No,' she commanded, voice resounding with an unearthly echo, 'this is not the way! This day will not see the defeat of Alissa Fimarr and Kale Stanis, it will not see the end of Ramikain's legacy!'

The purple around her suddenly burst free from her in a shockwave, covering everything in a putrid violet haze. As it swept across their surroundings, everything it touched suddenly froze in place. Treya felt her own muscles restricted and it took all her effort to push her limbs into motion, even then finding it like moving through treacle. She instinctively knew it was the Rondure that had reduced the paralysing effect and forced her arms to obey, to reach into the satchel at her side and grasp the magical orb in one hand.

The result was instant and disorienting; all resistance in her body vanished and she stumbled forward as if she had been pushing against a door that was suddenly opened. Alissa rotated in the air towards her, surprise crossing her face for a brief instant.

'Of course it would be you!' she rasped irately, 'You, who killed my love, now hoping to finish me as well. But you have tasted my fury once, this time it will be your doom.'

'Stop this, Alissa!' Treya cried back, 'It is not too late! It will never be too late! I did not kill Kale Stanis but, even if I had, it would not change how I feel for you! I am not here to kill you, Alissa, I am here to save you.'

'Then you will die!' Alissa asserted, unleashing a crackling bolt of energy from her open palm, arcing in towards her sister's heart.

Treya shielded her eyes against the light and held up the Rondure, feeling it heat up as the energy was drawn inside. Lowering her other arm, she smiled, 'No, Alissa, see how the Rondure nullifies your power. You cannot win this day. Throw down the Stave and we will find a way to resolve all that has happened.'

'You are a fool, Treya! My hate for you burns deeper than you can ever comprehend! There is no possible resolution between us without your death!' Another bolt of energy accompanied her vehement words.

Treya felt the pain in her heart but it was emotional only, the energy again absorbed by her artifact. She had no idea how to stop Alissa but something inside her, or maybe from the Rondure itself, drove her into action. Racing forward, even as more bolts rained down around her, she leapt up onto the shoulder of a frozen guard, using his height to help her springboard up towards her sister. Alissa swung the Stave around to stop her and

Treya slammed the Rondure against it. At the moment of impact, there was a huge, fiery explosion of amber and purple light.

He had seen everything play out before him, unable to move or speak, trapped within the controlling power placed upon him. Close enough to hear the argument, he had been certain Alissa would slay Treya where she stood; would have done if not for the strange item the older Fimarr had brought with her. Even when Treya attacked, it seemed there could only be one victor. But then the items had touched, his eyes were still struggling to adjust following the blinding flash, and a powerful shockwave had blown him from his feet. Luckily, it had also startled the beasts that had been approaching, the animals now in terrified flight from the scene of the blast. It felt like he had been hit in the chest with a battering ram and he had been more than two hundred yards away.

Staggering to his feet, he blinked several times to try and clear his vision but the imprinted image of the two women clashing in mid-air remained scorched into his retinas. Rubbing his face to no avail, he tried staring, the longer his eyes were open, the more the image faded and allowed him to see his surroundings. A large crater marked the spot below the clash of artifacts, burned cadavers and body parts indicated the damage the blast had done to the soldiers in close proximity. And Alissa had been at the centre of that blast.

A lump filled his throat and he felt tears running down his cheeks; she was gone, the only woman he had ever loved and the one person who had supported him loyally throughout his conquest. His wife and Queen-to-be. Tipping his head back, he released an anguished cry of outrage until his voice suddenly cut off. Staring down at his chest, he saw the tip of a curved dagger poking out from just below his collar bone; reaching up and touching the dripping tip, he found it easily punctured a small hole in his finger. There was the slightest scratching sensation in his lower back, and he realised the blade must have been slipped into the muscle there and driven upwards because of its shape; in doing so, his lung and windpipe had also been severed, making any exhalation impossible.

'You delight in reminding people how you once penetrated me,' a voice spoke softly in his ear, 'so I thought I would return the favour.'

His lips moved wordlessly, no sound forming despite his best efforts, and he saw the tip vanish back into him before there was a twist of the weapon inside him, firing torment through his organs at the same time as removing all sensation from his legs. Collapsing in an unceremonious heap, his mouth continued to work soundlessly as he stared up into the vengeful eyes of Catalana Fimarr.

'You are nothing more than the wretched, pathetic boy I first met. You will not be mourned, you will not be remembered,' she cursed before spitting in his face. She walked away and he found he could not turn his head to watch. After a few moments, that felt like hours as he lay crippled in the grass, a larger beast moved into his vision. He was very grateful for the lack of sensation as it began to eat him.

It had been several minutes since the monsters had stopped attacking but he had not yet risen from his knees or sheathed his swords. There had never been a time in his life when his arms had ached from the strain of combat like this, or total exhaustion had made the prospect of standing a daunting one. Having witnessed only a handful of these twisted chimeras slaughter over fifteen hundred men in short order, he found it unbelievable that he was still alive. Lifting his head, he counted three slain beasts before him and wondered why such a feat was within him now when it had not been then.

Placing the tip of one sword into the ground, he used it as a crutch to clamber to his feet, swaying instantly and leaning on the larger corpse next to him. He had been extremely fortuitous during the battle, the body of one creature killed by a blow from Herc, landing next to another that had been accidentally gored by one of its own kind, creating an organic cave for him to take refuge within. It had prevented more than one animal attacking at a time, but he had still suffered several cuts and scratches throughout the combat; if he had been surrounded and exposed like the others, he would most surely be dead. Delicately replacing his swords in their scabbards, he hobbled from his seclusion like a time-weary venerate, moving towards the spot where Herc Callid was standing.

Dismay filled him at the scene he came upon, standing next to the much larger figure, and he could not find words. He stared numbly at the prone form of Rayne Fimaar, lying still, skin an ashen grey and one arm horribly mutilated, as if melted. Strangely, it was the most peaceful he had ever seen her, with none of the suppressed pain or anger etched into her face, as it had been since he met her. Having lost family himself, he had an idea of how painful this must be for the other Fimarrs until he realised they were not there. Callid seemed comfortable in the silence and they remained that way until Crystal arrived.

'Oh no!' she exclaimed with genuine emotion, 'Zis cannot be! My sister, is dead? But I 'ave only just begun to know 'er. Zis is too tragic!'

Moving forward as if to kneel beside Rayne, she visibly jumped at the sound of Catalana's sharp voice, 'No! Nobody is to touch her except me!'

'Easy, gentle lady,' Herc soothed her, placing a restraining hand on Crystal's shoulder, 'she meant no harm. And you are not the only one who will feel this loss today.'

Catalana was carrying Rayne's trademark knife and it was slick with blood, her tear-streaked face filled with anger borne of sorrow, 'Only me,' she reaffirmed, 'I want to be the one to tend to her.'

'Of course, Catalana,' Crystal assured her, 'I meant no disrespect, it is ze shock, ze loss, I do not know what to say…'

'It is fine to say nothing at all,' Herc told her, 'we deal with death differently but know that we all feel Rayne's passing to the depths of our hearts.'

Crystal looked up at him and nodded, her eyes watery and wide. Bentram wondered why he did not have any tears to shed; was he too accustomed to death? Had he not found an attachment to these women despite all they had been through? Or was he just numb to everything right now?

'You have my deepest sympathies,' he offered quietly to Catalana as she knelt beside the body and began to tidy the attire as best she could, 'she was a brave and true companion, strong and skilled; an exceptional warrior.'

'She was my sister,' Catalana stated.

'She was,' he agreed, 'in all senses of the word, I think. If you do need help, I would be honoured.'

'She died because of me, it is my duty,' she continued.

'She died because of Lennath,' Herc corrected her sternly.

'Well, he is dead,' Catalana snapped, 'so the remaining blame lies with me.'

Another silence fell and Bentram watched with heartfelt sympathy as the grief-stricken woman tore the sleeves from her own shirt to bind the barely attached arm into place. He hoped Rayne had not felt the pain of that injury before she died, it must have been excruciating.

The sound of footsteps through the grass attracted their attention as General Audack approached cautiously, weapon belt discarded somewhere along the way. He held his hands up in a gesture of peace and did not encroach too far.

'My apologies for intruding on so personal a matter,' he stammered, 'but I must parlay with you. And offer my condolences for your losses.'

'You 'ave no right 'ere! You are our enemy; why should we even allow you to live?'

'It is fine,' Catalana interrupted her half-sister, 'he turned the Veer against Lennath. In this battle, at least, he has been our ally.'

'Aye, you speak truly,' Audack replied, voice a nervous tremor, 'and you saved my life with your remarkable bowmanship, a debt I can never hope to repay.'

'Is that what you wished to parlay?' Cat' asked, not looking up from her ministrations.

'Partly, Milady, but also to inform you of your right.'

'My right? What do you mean?' she questioned irritably as all eyes turned on the portly soldier.

'Well, we are still in the aftermath of battle, so I know heads and hearts may not be clear, but the Kingdom has experienced an unprecedented event, and you are at its centre.'

'I am in no mood for this, soldier, be on your way,' she chided, losing interest in him instantly.

'Would that I could, Milady,' he continued apologetically, 'I beg a minute only.'

'Get on with it then,' Herc rumbled at him.

'Of course!' he replied quickly, 'Know that I am General Audack, Lord High protector of the Kingdom and steward of her armies…'

'Quicker than that, I think they meant,' Bentram urged him, keen to move him away from the emotional situation playing out before them.

'Yes, yes, my apologies once more. Well, the entire Royal family had died before Lennath took the throne and they, like he, were yet to sire any children. With his death today, it means the Throne lies empty. Our law provides two options; the first is to seek out the nearest blood relation, which could turn out to be anybody; the second option is to pass the mantle to the victor in battle. That means the person who killed the previous King. You, Milady.'

Bentram was completely taken aback by the revelation. What kind of society allowed a complete stranger onto the Throne? Although, thinking back to the history he had learned in the Academy, many successions had come about from a conquering force slaying the previous rulership.

'I realise this is not an ideal time, Your Highness,' Audack continued, 'but I will administrate on your behalf until you are ready to claim your rightful position. And I understand if you choose not to retain me in post upon your ascension.'

With his piece said, he bowed before turning and heading towards the winding path up to Mainspring.

'Cat', did you hear what he said?' Herc asked, 'Surely this cannot be true?'

'I heard him,' she said, 'but I have Rayne to care for now. I will consider his babbling when she sits safely with the gods.'

Galloping as fast as the horse would carry him, Straker Forge hunched low over his steed's neck, reducing the wind resistance against them to gain every extra ounce of pace available. He had seen her, watched helplessly as she confronted the magically enhanced Alissa, remained supernaturally frozen in place as the sisters had clashed and felt his world collapse at the resulting explosion which freed him from the magical restraint. Racing towards the crater left in the wake of that event, he could not see how anyone could have survived but his heart rejected the logic entirely. Reining his mount in as it began to stumble and slip over body parts, he leapt clear and pounded into the centre of the circular depression. It had to be twenty yards in radius, the earth within it was scorched black and still hot he realised as the soles of his boots began to soften. Racing back up the side of the crater, he scanned about the scene, ignoring the mangled and charred remains of the soldiers, desperate for any sign of Treya. Hoping that a miracle had avoided her being incinerated.

A weak groaning caught his attention, drifting to him over the preternatural quiet, and he rushed to follow the sound. After a hundred yards, he came upon a body, slender and frail, barely out of childhood, a young woman he recognised, Alissa. Whatever power she possessed, it had clearly protected her, as she looked intact and unharmed, save for the myriad tiny scars she had inflicted upon herself. However, all across her body, patches of melted metal from one or both of the artifacts had welded to her flesh. Reaching down, he tried to pull one free and snapped his hand back immediately; the metal was still searingly hot. The groaning became louder and he saw her eyes begin to flutter open.

'Alissa? Is that you? The real you, I mean?' he asked gently.

'Who? Wh-where am I? What happened?' she responded groggily.

'It is me, Straker!' he offered, 'There was an explosion, an evil artifact had control of your mind. You are…'

'The Stave!' she suddenly shouted, eyes flying wide, 'What have you done to it? Where is Lennath? I will kill you all if you have…'

She did not finish the sentence as Forge punched her squarely in the face, knocking her cold. He hung his head in defeat; even without the artifact, she was not cured; maybe there really was no way back for the youngest Fimarr. But if she had survived, been thrown clear of the blast…

Leaping to his feet, he turned one hundred and eighty degrees and sprinted past the crater and beyond, hoping that Alissa's survival was not pure luck. Almost exactly the same distance from the site of the explosion, he found Treya. Rushing to her, he pulled her into his arms, carefully stroking hair back out of her face, smothering her in kisses even as he tried to wake her. Slowly, she began to rouse, and he gave a silent prayer of thanks to the gods. Pulling her head close to his shoulder, he held her tightly, beginning only now to notice the burns that had been inflicted upon her, similar in pattern and regularity to the metal that had mottled Alissa.

'Wh-what happened?' she mumbled weakly.

'It is all right, my love, everything is all right,' he soothed, 'you did it. Stopped Alissa and Lennath, saved all the lands. You are every bit the hero your father was. It is over.'

'Alissa?'

'She is alive,' he managed between gritted teeth, 'we can deal with her later. You are all I care about right now. You are my hero, my love, my world. I want us to never be apart again, agreed?'

'Agreed,' she said, still not fully coherent, 'Am I really all right? All I can feel is pain and it is difficult to move.'

'You will be well, my sweet lady, I promise, we will do all we must to make you well again. Every living person owes you that at the very least,' he assured her, running his eye down to her mangled left hand, the one he assumed she had been holding the Rondure in, a burned and devastated appendage now, almost as high as her elbow. Continuing to stroke her hair, he shifted his gaze further down, noting the small burns irregularly across her, until he arrived at her right leg. Or at least the cauterised stump of her knee where the right leg would have been.

'Yes, my darling,' he said again, 'it is over, and you will be well.'

Epilogue

Climbing down from his horse, Makinson bent over and adjusted the metal hinges of the knee brace he now wore; he could lock it into place for riding, but it became too restrictive for casual walking. Idly readjusting the upper strap, a habit he had developed in the early days, he looked up at the small hill before him, the last resting place of Rayne Fimarr. He had only been here twice since the burial, such was the distance between here and Fildenmaw, and he promised himself, as he had done on both previous visits, that he would make the journey more regularly in future. Sighing deeply, he passed through the small wooden gate, placing a single copper coin in the Ballanis honesty box, and made his way slowly up to the grave he sought. It was one of three at the very top of the mound, mother, father and daughter brought together for the eternal sleep; a beautiful sentiment that filled him with sorrow. He briefly wondered if his own father already lay dead somewhere or if there was truly a reunion between families in the afterlife.

As he approached, the dark-skinned woman already at the foot of the grave turned to him and smiled.

'Makinson, is it not?' she asked in a melodic voice. He regarded her closely as he neared; she was strikingly beautiful, but her eyes were red-rimmed from crying.

'Aye, milady, Makinson of Fildenmaw. My apologies, but I do not remember you. Where is it we have met?'

'It was only once,' she replied wistfully, 'at the coronation in Mainspring. My name is Rebecca Pallstirrith. You told me of your part in the final battle against Lennath; you were a little drunk.'

He smiled in embarrassment, 'In which case, you have my apologies for any offense caused or advances made!'

'None required,' she laughed back at him, 'you were a perfect gentleman. You were also very excited about your story,' she looked down at his knee brace, 'I take it that your leg has still not recovered?'

Bending and straightening the limb gingerly, as if just reminded of the injury, he replied with resignation, 'The finest physicians in Zendra did their best work, but they told me the damage was too severe; I will need the brace for life.'

'I am sorry to hear that.'

'No need to be, I have accepted the limitation. And it was worth it,' he said the last with his eyes fixed on the fresh gravestone before them.

They stood in silence for a few minutes, lost in their own memories of the woman they had known.

'Were you close before the end?' Rebecca asked tentatively.

'I like to think so,' he replied, nodding.

'Did you love her?'

He pondered the question whilst still staring at the chiselled stone and the small bouquet of lilies lain before it, 'I did indeed. But it was not returned, alas. How about you?'

His question clearly took her by surprise, and she flushed, 'I... I suppose I did love her, but not romantically. I wish I had the chance to resolve the situation with her...'

'It was not my intention to bring further sorrow to your visit, Lady Pallstirrith. Can I repay you by escorting you back to Rennicksburg?'

'Do not worry, my sorrow is just as great whenever I come here. I would not dream of cutting your visit short, Makinson, no matter how noble your offer. Besides, I have escorts already,' she reassured him, waving a hand to the secondary gate at the side of the cemetery. Two men stood by a horse-drawn wagon, chatting idly whilst waiting for her; one was dressed in the finery of the gentry, flamboyant shirt and feathered hat amongst his ensemble, a pistol holstered at his hip and another under his right arm; the other was a shorter, more tanned individual, with pointed goatee and nape-length black hair combed back over his head, missing his left arm.

'Are they...?' he began, and she smiled again.

'Yes, bounty hunters. Chaucer and Black by name. But do not worry, there is no cost associated with their protection, they are my good friends.'

He nodded, 'Well then, my services are certainly not required! I hope you do not feel I have intruded on you here, today. It would be most pleasant if our visits coincide again.'

'No intrusion, Makinson, I was at the conclusion of my stay. Hopefully, we will meet again.'

She offered her hand and he kissed it cordially before watching her saunter back down the hill to her bodyguards. Another smile crossed his face and he looked up; was this mere chance or was Rayne still manipulating things from beyond death? Shaking his head, he placed the single iris he had brought with him on top of the lilies and knelt at the foot of the grave. As he did with every visit, he read the inscription upon the gravestone;

'Mark thee the final resting place of Rayne Fimarr; assassin, adventurer, hero, sister. She touched our hearts without ever knowing and opened her own before the end.'

The scripted words flowed easily from her tongue, this being the fifth time she had performed the ceremony in the space of a month. It had been a superb idea of Herc's to overcome the growing concerns around devout nationalist pride, and one that preserved the fledgling structure of the Kingdom. She felt it quite ironic that almost all the senior officials and councilmen had believed Lennath's dissolution of the separate kingdoms structure was actually a positive change amid his brutal power grab. After all she had heard since taking the throne, reverting to the old borders would have created misery and discontent in both population and economic senses. A smile flickered across her face unbidden; a year ago she had only needed to concern herself with ensuring her store prices were competitive, now she was learning all the intricacies of governance and politics in a very steep curve. Of course, she had Herc with her, Chief Advisor to the Crown and Lord High Protector of Mainspring were now his official titles, and they had barely been apart in the whirlwind journey that had carried them to where they were now. She wondered if he, or any member of her family, could ever have foreseen Catalana Fimarr as Queen of the Kingdom.

'Take this warhammer of gold,' she pronounced, loudly enough that the large audience within the presentation hall could hear, 'and use it to smite down all enemies of the Kingdom, both internal and foreign.'

Holding out the symbolic weapon, the metals used in its construction too soft to make it functional, the man kneeling before her took it reverently in both hands, raising it to his lips before placing it carefully in the specially made sheath at his belt.

'I will defend, with steel and heart, my region, my country and my Queen,' he answered.

'Take this blessed scroll,' she continued, this time holding out a rolled parchment tied with blue silk, 'and use it to promote peace, education and law amongst all of our people.'

He repeated the process he had performed with the warhammer, but the scroll found a home within a leather loop on the strapping that crossed his body.

'I will be fair and true, in mind and spirit, to all of the people of my region, my country and who serve my Queen,' he stated.

'Take this single kiss,' she said finally, leaning forward to place a gentle kiss upon his forehead, 'and know that you are entrusted to represent me in all matters.'

He smiled up at her, 'I am honoured above all others to be chosen for this duty. I will not be found wanting by my region, my country or my Queen.'

She returned his smile before looking out across the assemblage, 'All here witness that on this day, in the city of Mainspring, I have decreed that Bentram Galadon is

High Sheriff of the region of Lustania. This title and responsibility will remain upon him until removed by death or Royal decree!'

Enthusiastic applause burst out, filling the hall with joyous sound, and carrying beyond the huge windows. Almost immediately, the city bells began to chime, announcing the completion of the ceremony; as the last of the five Sheriffs to be formally titled, it was even more significant than the previous four, bringing final balance of governance to all five regions. It was not surprising that Lustania had been last, it was the region with the most turmoil and animosity to work through, and Bentram had been very reluctant to take the post. In that respect, it made him the perfect fit.

She placed a hand on his shoulder as he rose and faced the crowd, waving his gratitude for the vocal support. Turning to watch Herc, still finding his well-trimmed hair and beard an odd sight, she wished he would concede to a similar ceremony to mark his position. He consistently refused, however, saying that he required no recognition, and the people need not focus on him at all; his only role was to support her. Sometimes she could not understand his mind; he never made her feel anything other than safe and supported, had generated clever and appropriate ideas on how to repair the national damage done by Lennath, and followed her lead in every matter. Yet, when she had suggested they wed, even with the assurance that he would remain as Queen's consort rather than King, he still refused. He professed to loving her deeply but would not remarry after the loss of his wife, under any circumstances. She could not deny it was upsetting to be rejected, but she loved him too much to allow it to come between them.

She looked back at the assembled nobility within the hall and was amazed at how quickly the populace of the Kingdom had been to accept her as sovereign. The overwhelming pressure of that responsibility weighed on her for every second of the day but having Herc by her side made it bearable. Rebuilding physically and politically was well underway now and she had ambitious ideas for the future, not least of all generating a strong unity with Dussen, but could already feel the biggest detriment her new position had brought. She had not visited Rayne's grave since the burial and seen Treya and her family only once since their victory; it seemed family would be the price of rulership.

Wrapping the thick rope several times around the post before tying it with a bow hitch knot, he proceeded to varnish it in place with a mixture of oil and wax that would harden into a weatherproof seal. The project had been a significant feat of coordination and teamwork for everyone in the village, creation of the net believed to be an impossibility when first conceived. Now it was finally in position, a mesh of rope and leather woven for this sole purpose, becoming almost unbreakable in the water and resistant to the inevitable salt corrosion. It was over a mile and a half in length and stretched the entire distance of the bay mouth, one edge just under the surface of the water and the other weighted to reach the seafloor beneath. The idea was simple enough; prevent large predators from entering the cove and generating a safe breeding ground for the smaller fish communities. They could benefit from this through managed fishing of the bay, and the net itself allowed just enough space for a shallow-keeled boat to pass over it with rudder and centreboard raised, enabling them to hunt further afield if desired. Yes, the idea was simple, but the delivery had been far more challenging and proven to them all exactly what they were capable of.

Staring at the final fixing for a moment, Mareck placed his hands on his hips in satisfaction and released a heavy sigh; months of work were now at a successful end. He looked at the men about him and smiled broadly.

'It is done!' he exclaimed, and they burst into wild celebration, the excitement quickly spreading back into the village. Mareck made his way back to the settlement amid vigorous shaking of hands and back-slapping to congratulate him; all knew that the monumental achievement would never have come to fruition without him.

He could not deny the elation that filled him at the climax of the task, but it was still tinged with sadness; he had been driven in his work, which had kept his mind off Crystal. Of course, he knew about the defeat of Lennath at Mainspring and the part played by the Fimarrs, but no stories indicated her presence amongst their number, and he had no way to know if she even still lived. As he feared, adventuring had taken her away from real life with no promise of return.

Arriving back in the village, he promised all who asked that he would join them in the tavern for a drink later, a marquis had been set up at the rear of the establishment to ensure the entire village could celebrate together. For now, he headed back to his own home, keen to allow the mental and physical weariness to claim him for a few hours. Pushing the front door open, he kicked off the heavy boots he had preferred throughout the project and ambled through to the parlour.

''Ello, Fazer,' Crystal greeted him from her favourite chair beside the fireplace.

For a moment he stood in stunned silence, taking in her smiling face, so beautiful and unblemished, and the fine clothing she wore, completely different from the basic attire she had departed in. The moment he realised he was not hallucinating, he rushed over to her, dragging her from the seat and up into a tight embrace.

'Oh, my daughter! My Crystal! You are alive, safe, home!' he gushed, unwilling to loosen his grip in case she vanished outside of his hold, 'I feared I had lost you forever! What happened to you?'

'Fazer, Fazer,' she soothed, gently disentangling herself from him, 'I am sorry you 'ave been so worried, but all is well. I 'ave so much to tell you about but firstly I wanted to say zat I am sorry for 'ow we parted. I wish we could 'ave avoided zose arguments; but I am returned to you now and do not regret ze decision I made. I made a difference, Fazer, I took action where ozers stood still; it was fulfilling but, more importantly, it was ze right zing to do.'

Mareck ignored any implied sleight from her words, after all, he had been one of those who had stood still. Instead, he smiled warmly and nodded.

'Yes, you were born to be important, I have always known that. Is it too much to hope you have returned for good?'

She looked away, unable to meet his eyes, 'It is. Much 'as changed in zese past monzs, I 'ave not taken so long to visit you out of some desire to punish you; I 'ave new responsibilities and new goals. But I am 'ere for now and I want to 'ear all about what you 'ave been doing. Word of the grand net has reached as far as Mainspring, many there would like to 'ear of your success first 'and.'

'Mainspring? You have been there all this time?' he asked, a little deflated that the luxurious surrounds of that city may have been the sole reason for her not returning to him, 'What responsibilities could you have had there?'

'As it 'appens, I was not in Mainspring,' she admitted, 'zere is so much to tell you but I suppose I should explain why I will not be able to stay 'ere wiz you, and why I want you to consider coming wiz me instead.'

'I am sorry, Crystal, this is all a little unexpected.' he said, 'I think I am struggling to keep up with you. Go where with you?'

'To Giltenberg.'

'The capital? What for?'

'Because zat is where I live now, I 'ave been made 'Igh Sheriff of Zendra.'

He drew back the heavy bolt and pushed the large barn door open; it still irked him that they had lost the storage space because of the conversion, and they would regret it during the harvest. However, there had been few other options; there was no way he was conceding to having her in their home. Picking up the tray he had lain aside to open the doors, he made his way inside and over to the wooden staircase; it had been built to replace the more difficult climb of the ladder up to the former hayloft, handcrafted with help from a couple of the farm labourers. Balancing the tray carefully, he ascended, watching the wooden mug of water closely, keen to avoid it spilling into the chunk of bread beside it; there was nothing worse than soggy bread. At the top of the stairs, he walked to the centre of the floor and placed the meal on the small wooden table fixed to the floor.

'Lunch,' he stated, looking at the occupant of the makeshift room. Pouting, as she usually did, her blonde hair hanging messily about her face, she stared at him intently.

'It is a stew, and it is hot,' he continued, ignoring her stoicism, 'I dare say it will not taste so good when it cools.'

She shifted from her crouched position by the wall onto all fours, mimicking a cat almost perfectly. The chains that bound her rattled with every movement and the metal welded across her skin reflected the dim light in a strange kaleidoscope around the room; they had tried to convince her to wear clothes, but she tore them to shreds when forced, although it seemed she was content to cover her modesty with underwear now.

'Eat you!' she hissed at him, 'Heart, liver and lungs! Rip you apart and douse myself in your blood.'

'Really? This again?' he sighed, 'I've no time for you in this mood, Alissa, eat or do not, it makes little difference to me.'

Turning away, he was halfway down the staircase when the rattling intensified and he knew she had crawled to the table, 'Good girl!' he called without looking back. He was almost at the outer door when the bowl crashed to the ground a few yards away, spraying its contents up the wall. Shaking his head, he left and bolted the door behind him, replacing the heavy padlock to prevent the children from ill-advised curiosity.

Making his way back to the main house, he spotted the three of them playing something that looked like tag with small bean bags and waved when they noticed him. He marvelled at them, they seemed completely unaffected by the trauma they had recently lived through. Even Kastani had reverted to the little girl he had first met; there had been no sign of the power she had displayed, no mention of Lennath, Terex or her mother. It felt like all three of them had erased it from their minds; they never even asked about his regular visits to the barn or Treya's long bedridden stint.

Watching them play happily filled him with a joy he had not dared to believe would be his again, a joy he felt he had lost during the events at Mainspring. But he had not lost them, and he had not lost her; only one thing could ever threaten them now, the thing that always had threatened their stability, secrets and lies. He had confessed everything to her now, the existence of Crystal being the final oath he had given to someone else; everything except the curse. It had been the price of his arrogant youth, to be unbeatable in combat, be the very best warrior in existence but none could witness his victories, and none could be told directly. As a result, he had held that secret for eighteen years, if he ever revealed it to anyone, his mystical ability would be lost forever. He would be just a normal man again, maybe even less if the witch who cursed him was to be believed.

Rubbing his neck against the sudden stiffness he felt there, he strolled to the house and up the stairs. Entering the main bedroom, he saw Treya lying in the bed she had called home for months, writing in a journal; it was the fourth such book she had started, chronicling her experiences so she claimed. She looked up as he entered and smiled.

'Hello, love, is everything all right with 'Lissa?'

'Well, her aim is not improving!' he replied with a wry smile, 'She eats when she is hungry but remains defiant. It has been long enough now to assume that your theory is correct; the remains of the artifacts on her skin are preventing any power she has left.'

Treya's smile faltered slightly, 'And her manner?'

He moved over to the bed and wrapped an arm about her shoulders, feeling the rough burn scars on the back of her neck against his bicep, 'No change, my sweet lady, I fear that her mental state may not have been linked to the dark magic she was manipulating. Perhaps seeing you could change things?'

'No, I cannot, it is too much…'

He followed her gaze to the wooden prosthetic leg that leaned against the dressing table.

'If you use it, you will become proficient. You could see the children outside, visit Alissa, stroll the grounds with me. You do not have to be trapped in here…'

'I know!' she snapped before pressing her head into his chest, 'I am sorry, Straker. I will try, but it just feels too soon. My leg, I mean, my stump, still feels painful to touch, placing that thing on it is a prospect I cannot face yet.'

'It is fine, my darling,' he replied kissing the top of her head, 'In your own time. I will be there to help you whenever you are ready.'

'Thank-you,' she responded genuinely, 'but tell me what else troubles you? I can feel your heart beating and it reveals you are nervous.'

'Aye, that I am,' he admitted and pulled her a little closer to him, 'I love you, Treya Fimarr, with all of my being. There is nothing I would not do for you and no request I would not honour. Some time ago you asked me to hold nothing from you, no secrets, no lies. Well, I have one more confession for you. It is a tale that will take some time to tell and it will leave me forever changed…'

'No,' she interrupted him, 'I am happy as we are. If this secret is so important, then keep it; I will trust that you are keeping it for the best.'

He craned his neck down so he could kiss her lips gently.

'No, my darling, I am ready to unburden myself, to provide us the pure strength that will come from knowing everything about one another. I am going to tell you why I have never been defeated in battle…'

Warm sand slid between his toes as he stood on the shore, looking out to the horizon. Beside him, the High Auger had been silent for almost an hour, transfixed as he was himself by the vastness that was now presented to them.

'Half of the Seasons have passed now,' he stated gruffly.

'This is the truth,' the High Auger muttered distractedly, 'almost to the day since the Boundary vanished.'

'They have not returned,' Mazt pointed out.

'Another truth, one that did not require you to vocate. There has been no sign of any vessel, theirs or otherwise. It means nothing.'

'It means we are betrayed!' Mazt insisted, turning towards the old man in frustration, 'Why can you not admit that the prophecy was flawed? That giving the Rondure to those outsiders was a mistake?'

'Hold your tongue, Mazt Kae-Taqar!' the High Auger snapped back to him, 'I recognise the fear and uncertainty in you, but I will not tolerate blasphemy! The prophecy cannot be wrong, it is our truth! Have you not considered that this is merely a test of your faith? One that you are currently failing?'

Mazt dropped his eyes to the sand in shame, 'I had not, High Auger, I feel only impotency as we wait for an agreement to be honoured. It grows as anger within me.'

'We are safe here, free of this wider outside world even without the Boundary to protect us. When the Rondure is returned, all will be as it was. This is the truth, you must find a way to make it your own as well.'

'Yes, High Auger, I understand your truth now. I will remain patient. Maybe in the days ahead we can discuss sending an envoy to find the Fimarrs…'

'No, Guardian, we will not!' came the sharp reply, 'I will not risk any of our people out in the unknown wilds beyond our shores. We remain here. Who can know what foes, dangers or evils could be brought crashing down upon us if we announce ourselves?'

Mazt held his tongue from the retort he wanted to give. The High Auger's responses smacked of fear, not faith; they had already met examples of what other lands had to offer and they left much to be desired. The People had nothing to fear from the outsiders. He knew in his heart that the Fimarrs were not coming back, too much time had passed for that, which meant they had to go and retrieve the Rondure themselves. The High Auger was the only thing holding them back, and he would not live forever…

Printed in Great Britain
by Amazon

80283074R00263